# AMERICAN MOSAIC

# AMERICAN MOSAIC

The Immigrant Experience
in the Words of Those
Who Lived It

............

JOAN MORRISON and
CHARLOTTE FOX ZABUSKY

················· E. P. DUTTON • NEW YORK····················

# TO OUR PARENTS, OUR HUSBANDS, AND OUR CHILDREN

For information contact:
E.P. Dutton, 2 Park Avenue,
New York, N.Y. 10016

Library of Congress Cataloging in Publication Data
Morrison, Joan.
American mosaic.

1. United States—Emigration and immigration—
History. 2. United States—Emigration and
immigration—Biography. 3. Oral history.
I. Zabusky, Charlotte Fox, joint author. II. Title.
JV6455.M67      973'.0992 [B]       79–22950

ISBN 0–525–05368–9

Published simultaneously in Canada
by Clarke, Irwin & Company
Limited, Toronto and Vancouver

Designed by Barbara Huntley

10  9  8  7  6  5  4  3  2  1

First Edition

# Contents

PART I

**THE LAST OF THE OLD**
The Traditional Immigrants

PART II

## THE WARTIME INFLUX

Heroes, Victims, Survivors

# PART III

# IMMIGRATION
A Continuing Process

·················· **Acknowledgments** ··················

We are grateful to the Morris Museum of Arts and Sciences for
providing the original inspiration for this work and to all those who
helped us find our subjects, most especially, Louis A. Antal, president
of District 5 of the United Mine Workers of America; Robert Hender-
son, director of the Language Acquisitions Institute at the University
of Pittsburgh; Professor S. Frank Miyamoto of the University of
Washington; Rosemarie Myrdal, Bicentennial historian of Walsh
County, North Dakota; Paul Nguyen, director of the Archdiocese of
Seattle Resettlement Office; Wallace Turner of the San Francisco office
of the *New York Times*; Ellen Adolph, Miriam Fox, Mary Hall, Yoshiko
Ishii, June Shimizu, and Nancy Walker. Our heartfelt admiration and
appreciation to Beverly Kokinos, our faithful transcriber, who somehow managed to make sense out of a variety of accents without losing
her good humor. Above all, we want to thank all those we interviewed,
who gave to us so generously of their time and memories.

# Foreword

All too often we lack the means of knowing the thoughts and feelings of the people around us. We and they are inarticulate, having lost the power of expression not through lack of will or ability but through disuse.

How much more difficult it is then to recapture the ideas and emotions of strangers separated from us by time or place. Men and women of wealth or education make themselves known in words on paper through written records left behind. Those not accustomed to the pen or typewriter remain vague figures in the distance, whom we can only dimly perceive, whom we cannot recognize. Yet face to face peasants, workers, and housewives are often expressive. The worth of what they had to say early on persuaded scholars, travelers, and other observers to set down the words of such people through oral interviews or in some other permanent form. The tape recorder simply provided a more efficient means of doing so for it creates an immediate record and spares the reporter the need for taking down and transcribing notes. Like all methods of knowing others, oral history is subject to abuse, but it can also add to knowledge about the past and the present.

The very nature of the immigrant experience erects barriers to the understanding. In moving, people create cultural and linguistic gaps. Their own habits and phrases are the products of one place; arriving in another they confront habits and phrases no more comprehensible to them than theirs are to the strangers about them. The gap is wide enough between Kentuckians in Chicago or Georgians in Harlem. It is far wider for newcomers from Eastern Europe or Asia. In addition, most immigrants by social origins were people unaccustomed to contacts with the unfamiliar. Now and then a merchant or politician or priest was an exception. But the great majority were workers or farmers, attached to their villages and towns and easily bruised in the process of migration. Their records are particularly valuable.

In *American Mosaic,* men and women from every part of the world think back upon the meaning of their arrival in the United States. The reader will recognize a few famous names; but the voices are mostly those of unknowns—a homesteader, a garment worker, a barber, a wetback, or one of the boat people. Some migrated between 1905, when the gates were still open, and 1930, when they slammed shut. A second group in the next three decades were refugees from dictatorship and war. A third, the most recent, came in the aftermath of the liberalization of American immigration laws that restored the country's traditional welcome. The motives that impelled these people varied, as did experiences within the United States. The interviewers have garnered a comprehensive sampling of that immense variety.

The interviews are not records of what actually happened in the course of migration, but retrospective accounts of a deep human experience, as recalled by those who lived through it. Remembered images of the Old World countryside provide a vivid contrast with recollections of New York's East Side, of a Dakota farm, and of an iron mine in the Mesabi range. Though each story is unique, a common sense of realism informs them all. The difficulties encountered and the successes achieved mingle in these memories, as in the appraisal of one childhood—"happy though poor." The words of the artless people assembled here say a good deal about the meaning of America.

*March 27, 1980*                                                  Oscar Handlin

························ **Passage to America** ·······················

We are all immigrants or the children of immigrants. Even those "original Americans," the Indians, walked across a land bridge from Siberia some thousands of years ago. In the five centuries since the European discovery of America, an estimated fifty million men and women made the journey to this country, a mass migration without precedent in recorded history. They came in waves, reflecting events and conditions in the Old World, some driven by war, famine, or prejudice, some lured by tales of gold and free land. They came from every nation, from every class, and from every religious persuasion. We are a diverse people, but we share a common heritage: in the background of every American is a farewell to the familiar, a long voyage, and a fresh start in a strange country.

For the first one hundred years of our national life, immigration was free and unrestricted. Although the voyage was difficult, the fare was minimal—and land, work, and citizenship were available in the new country. In the beginning, as was natural, immigrants came mainly from England, the "mother country." But as the years went on, they came in increasing numbers from all the nations of northern and western Europe. The potato famine in Ireland in 1847 brought hundreds of thousands to the cities of the East Coast. The failure of the social revolution in Germany in 1848 sent us a crop of motivated intellectuals eager for a second chance at freedom. Limited land and a rising population in the Scandinavian countries led many to come to the plains of the Middle West to take advantage of the free land made available by the successive Homestead acts.

The slow evolution of a national policy of controlled immigration began in 1882, with the first federal legislation excluding certain "undesirable" categories of immigrants: lunatics, idiots, convicts, and those likely to become a public charge. The first Chinese Exclusion Act was also passed, restricting the immigration of Chinese into this country and barring them from citizenship. In subsequent years, categories of the undesirable were expanded to include anarchists, polygamists, diseased persons, illiterates, prostitutes, and criminals. Further legislation excluded other Asiatics.

But for most, the gates were still open. As the nineteenth century drew to a close, many immigrants from southern and eastern Europe began to appear on the incoming boats. Grinding poverty and war drove Italians and Greeks from their homes. Pogroms in Russia and Poland brought Jews in growing numbers. Hungarians, Czechs, and Poles fled from political oppression and military conscription. Between 1900 and 1914, a record 12,928,517 people entered this country as immigrants. No other nation had ever received so many people in such a short time.

The problems of assimilating such large numbers of immigrants, together with the fact that many of the recent arrivals seemed more "foreign" than those already established here, led to a growing pressure for restrictive laws on immigration. The nationalism associated with World War I added to this pressure, and in 1921 the first of several quota laws was passed. These laws greatly reduced the total number of immigrants allowed in and set a limit for each country based on its proportion of the United States population in 1910, later amended to 1920. It was an attempt to maintain the North European status quo in our national ethnic mix, and it effectively barred those who most wanted to come—the poor of southern and eastern Europe.

In the late 1920s and early 1930s, worldwide depression brought immigration almost to a halt. There was little money for boat fare, and would-be immigrants knew that there would be no jobs if they did manage to come. Fascism began its climb to power in Italy, and Hitler took over the reins of government in Germany. Many Jews and political opponents of these totalitarian regimes attempted to come to the United States for refuge, but the restrictive laws allowed in only a few. Between 1936 and 1939, several proposals to liberalize the quota standards on a humanitarian basis were turned down in Congress. In a particularly dramatic incident, a boatload of German refugees was chased away from the Florida coast by federal ships, and the passengers were obliged to return to Europe, where many of them eventually met their deaths. It was a sad period for those Americans who remembered the inscription on the base of the Statue of Liberty:

*Give me your tired, your poor,*
*Your huddled masses, yearning to breathe free,*
*The wretched refuse of your teeming shore.*
*Send these, the homeless, tempest tossed, to me:*
*I lift my lamp beside the golden door.*

During World War II, populations were dislocated on a large scale. In addition to the millions of Jews sent to concentration camps, hundreds of thousands of Dutch, Danish, French, and others in occupied Europe were plucked from their homes and sent to German factories as "slave" laborers. Countless others fled repeatedly to escape the war's destruction. By 1945, there were an estimated ten million displaced persons on the continent of Europe. Many were eventually repatriated; the remaining one million, who were unwilling or unable to return home, waited in DP camps in Germany, hoping for resettlement. They were mostly concentration camp survivors and those whose homelands had come under Communist domination. A worldwide effort was clearly necessary and a number of nations came forward to help.

In the United States, a combination of religious, philanthropic, and ethnic organizations pressed for emergency legislation to accommodate some of these refugees. At last, in 1948, the Displaced Persons Act was passed, making 400,000 quota places available within a four-year period. During the following years, additional special legislation was passed to permit the admission of refugees from the Hungarian uprising, the Communist takeover in Cuba, and similar one-time events.

Finally, in 1965, there was a comprehensive overhaul of all existing immigration legislation. National-origins quotas were abolished, discriminatory restrictions on the entry of Orientals were ended, and a new policy of "first come, first served" was substituted. It set an overall annual limit of 170,000 immigrants for the Eastern Hemisphere and 120,000 for the Western Hemisphere, with no more than 20,000 allowed in from any one country. The new law also established a system of preference categories, aimed at uniting families and attracting people with special skills. It made provision for displaced persons and refugees from political, religious, and racial discrimination. This law is still in effect.

Immigration is a continuing process. A recent government study reports that legal immigrants account for about 30 percent of our country's present population growth. Nearly 400,000 entered in 1976. In addition, it is estimated that there are at least an equal number of illegals coming in every year, mainly from Latin America and Asia. Because they cannot qualify as skilled workers or are hopelessly far down on the entry lists, they slip over the border at night or overstay their tourist or student visas. Some hope to marry an American and thus obtain legal resident status and eventual citizenship.

Refugees are still coming, too. Soviet Jews continue to arrive as fast as they are permitted to, seeking freedom from discrimination. Since the fall of the Saigon government in 1975, over 215,000 Vietnamese have immigrated to this country. And in 1979 we began to admit tens of thousands (14,000 a month) of the pathetic "boat people," who had fled their Southeast Asian homelands in flimsy boats, only to be turned away by one neighboring country after another. The newcomers come on jet planes now, but the desperation that drives them and the hopes that draw them are the same that brought earlier generations of immigrants.

There have been many studies of the patterns and problems of immigration, of its effects on the economy and on the political system. This book is intended to supplement those studies by giving a picture of the human side of immigration through the words of those who actually experienced it—telling why they came, how they came, and how they adapted; what they gained, what they lost, and what it all meant to them.

Over a four-year period we interviewed a wide variety of immigrants. Among our informants were representatives of all countries from which immigrants came in significant numbers and from all periods for which there were still living members. We included men and women from a variety of social and economic classes, from both rural and urban backgrounds, and from all parts of the United States. And we looked for different reasons for coming—religious, political, economic, familial—even though the numbers in some categories were not as statistically significant. Our focus was always the human story behind the figures.

Our only tool was the tape recorder, which we tried to make as unobtrusive as possible. Fortunately, it seemed to inhibit very few. We had a set of standard questions, but sometimes the stories seemed to come out by themselves, with little prodding. When that happened, we were content to sit quietly and listen, not to intrude. Each of us interviewed approximately half the informants, and we shared the job of cutting thousands of pages of transcript to the "core" included here. We share also the responsibility for the editing, which usually included taking out extraneous and repetitious material and rearranging it in order to clarify time sequences. In addition, for some immigrants the real story is in how they came, for others it is in the journey, and for still others it is in what happened after they got here, and we have focused on what is significant in each case. At no time, however, did we put words into people's mouths. In our editing and rearranging, we have stayed close to the meaning and intent of the speaker. These stories are *their* stories, not ours.

The date following the country of origin of each narrator gives the time of his arrival in the United States. For some immigrants, particularly the DP's of World War II, several years elapsed between the time they left their native country and the time they finally reached the United States. In those cases the sequence of events is made clear in the narrative.

Except for a few well-known immigrants who gave permission for their names to be used, we have changed names and identifying details to protect the privacy of those we interviewed.

Our interviews centered on three basic questions: Why did the immigrant come? How did he come? What did he find when he got here? The answers were often similar, equally often diverse. Many of our informants conformed to the patterns described in the classic studies of immigration. Anna Ohlson's family came from Norway seeking free land in the Middle West; Sylvia Bernstein fled from religious persecution in her native Austria; José Garcia came for "money, simply money." And yet there were individuals who did not fit the pattern, like Walter Lindstrom, who came for adventure, perhaps because he had read *Huckleberry Finn* as a boy, and Branwyn Davies, who came because a revolution had disrupted her plans to go to China and she was "all packed for somewhere." A flood of humanity crossed the ocean in the past three centuries, but each drop in that flood was a living, breathing, complex, unique person.

On their arrival in the New World, the immigrants typically found waiting for them backbreaking toil, crowded living conditions, loneliness, sometimes prejudice and hostility. Michael Kinney thought he was "down in hell" on his first day in the steel mill; Serge Nicholas wept alone in his rented room in San Francisco; the Gurchikov children were ridiculed at school and called "hunkies" by their classmates. And there was the immediate problem of learning a new language, new customs, new ways of earning a living.

For many there was a displacement in time as well as in space. It took Western civilization nearly one thousand years to make the journey that many of these men and women made in a month. In their native villages were the well and the church, the ox and the plow, the barn where milk was put out for the trolls. Here, they had to learn to turn on faucets, ride the subway, keep up with an assembly line. It was as if a giant time machine had taken them and shuffled them about.

The initial shock of immigration was frequently cushioned by settlement in an ethnic community. Sometimes whole families came together; or when the first of a family came alone, he worked until he could send for another and then another of his kin. Small enclaves grew up, peopled entirely by natives of a single town or region, like the one described in Albertina di Grazia's narrative. These enclaves provided the "warm nest of the familiar," as Oscar Handlin has called it, to which the individual could turn for support and reassurance while learning new ways in a strange country. A recent study of ethnicity and mental illness suggests that serious breakdowns are less common for newcomers living in such a community than for those who live apart from it.*

Yet, for all their psychological support, such enclaves do retard the complete assimilation of the immigrant into the dominant American culture. Serge Nicholas expresses this view when he remarks that he is grateful to his period of army service for "finally getting me out of the ghetto." A nation of immigrants must always be, if it is to be a nation at all, a "melting pot" of sorts. How completely the original ingredients should disappear in the process is necessarily a value judgment.

In the past, the immigrant and his family were encouraged to assimilate, to become 100 percent American. The sooner they accomplished this and the easier they found the process, the greater were their chances of sharing the riches of America. This theory was vigorously promoted by the public schools; the children, who were products of those schools, sometimes learned to be ashamed of their foreign heritage. In their eagerness to become part of the American scene, they rejected their families along with the ancestral names and the "old-country" language and customs and lifestyles. What this cost in pain for the old and guilt for the young can never be measured.

Today, the American attitude toward ethnicity has changed, and a foreign background is no longer something to be concealed. There is an emphasis on ethnic pride and the value of ethnic differences. Perhaps instead of a melting pot, we might now more accurately call America a vast mosaic, in which colorful individual pieces are fitted together to make a single picture.

In spite of their initial hardships and stresses, many immigrants did manage to achieve what they came for—they found, if not the pot of gold at the end of the rainbow, the little self-owned house, the secure

---

*Judith G. Robkin and Elmer L. Struening, *Ethnicity, Social Class and Mental Illness,* Working Papers Series, No. 17 (New York: Institute on Pluralism and Group Identity, 1976), pp. 20–21.

pension, dignity, freedom to worship, the chance at an education. Some of the images are unforgettable: Max Levy walking on the streets of Boston saying to himself, "This is it—freedom." Maria Nikitin surveying her modest apartment and saying, "The gypsy was right, I am rich." A few, like Tacwyn Morgan and Secretary of the Treasury Blumenthal, have succeeded beyond their wildest dreams. Even those who haven't fared so well recognize that the lives of their children, at least, have been enriched. In this current period of self-examination, almost self-doubt, for the United States, it is interesting to note that most of our informants consider their lives over here, however hard, a great improvement over those they had led in the countries of their birth.

It has been suggested that Americans are a better breed, winnowed out of the Old World by their own daring. Were they able to endure the long journey and the slum conditions because they had stronger minds and bodies—a sort of Darwinian "survival of the fittest" process? Perhaps. One is almost led to believe it when one considers John Daroubian's survival in the Armenian desert, Riccardo Massoni's persistence in becoming a doctor against all odds, Tania Shimiewsky's repeated feats of human endurance. These people seem almost superhuman. And yet there are no figures to compare them with those who were left behind. It would be interesting to run a cross-check on the lives of the brothers and sisters who stayed home. As of now, we can say only that those who did come had the imagination to dream of a better life, the ingenuity and perseverance to make the journey, and the strength to endure harsh conditions, to survive and adapt, sometimes to flourish.

It became apparent to us as we worked on these histories that the same aspirations and stresses that drove our forefathers to emigrate still operate today—poverty, religious and political oppression, the desire for education and a better life, sometimes simply a sense of adventure. But, of course, there is no typical immigrant. The variations in country of origin, time of coming, age, sex, health, and class are almost infinite. In addition, there is the character of the immigrant himself and the mysterious workings of chance.

Each individual story is unique. Together, they make up the mosaic that is America.

# PART I

# THE LAST OF THE OLD
## The Traditional Immigrants

*It was 1906. I was six years old and we were on a train with some other immigrants going from New York to Chicago. I had learned a little English before we left home, and I remember when people on the train spoke to me in Russian, I said, "Speak only English. I'm an Americanka now. Don't speak Russian to me. I'm an Americanka."*

*My brother and I were entered in school in Chicago right away. And my brother, who was ten, was surprised to see me on the stage of the auditorium of the school the first Friday we were there. There was a program, and different children were supposed to do different things, and I was supposed to wave the American flag. I was very proud. I waved it and waved it and waved it with all my might. I thought I was really an Americanka then.*

**Sonia Walinsky**
··················· FROM RUSSIA, 1906 ···················

# Walter Lindstrom
······················FROM SWEDEN, 1913······················

*At eighty-three, he is still tall and erect, with piercing blue eyes and work-gnarled hands. He lives with his wife in a small house on the South Side of Chicago.*

The place where my ancestors lived was on a small island off the coast of Sweden. It was a little farm surrounded by dark pinewoods.

My father often told me there were trolls in those woods, who crept out at night to do mischief to us. I had no reason to doubt him because the bowl of milk that we put out for them every night was always empty in the morning. Of course we had plenty of barn cats, too.

My family had about fifteen acres of poor soil, which did not yield much in the way of crops—a little barley and rye, root vegetables, and some fodder for our cows and horse. We lived in a small house at the edge of the fields, just four rooms around a big central stove, which gave heat in the winter and provided a place for the women of the house to do their cooking. Water came from a well and we had oil lamps to see by in the dark. At that latitude in Sweden it is dark in winter from about three in the afternoon till nine in the morning.

To acquire this piece of land surrounded by forest, my ancestors from way back in the 1700s had to become legal servants, bonded to a feudal baron for whom they were required to work a certain number of days each year without pay. This they had to do in order to become legal owners of the land they lived on. It was part of the feudal law and had to be obeyed. I remember my grandfather, and even my own father, having to go to do such work every year on the private domain where the lord of our land lived.

I was the oldest child in the family, and also a boy, so I had many chores to do. I had to chop wood, split kindling, carry hay, carry water, and take care of the farm animals. My little sister Greta, who was four years younger than I was, used to follow me about the farm as I did my work. She was chubby and very fair-haired and she would sit on a log while I chopped wood, chattering to me or to her doll or to herself. It was good company for me, because wood chopping is a lonely job.

When I was about eight years old, Greta got a high fever and it turned into meningitis. She cried all the time, day and night. I used to go into the barn to get away from hearing her. There was nothing that could be done for her, and after about a week she died. I remember how my mother and my grandmother prepared her for burial. Some branches of evergreen trees were placed on the bottom of a wooden coffin. On these branches several sheets of linen were tucked in, as on a bed. After this was done carefully, Greta's body was laid in the coffin and more linen was put over her. She looked very peaceful lying there, with her two stiff braids sticking out on either side of her face. No more crying.

After that I chopped wood alone. I had three more brothers and two more sisters in time, but I was never as close to any of them as I was to Greta.

Our usual diet consisted of potatoes, bread, salt herring, barley porridge, and milk. Meat was seldom seen. One time I remember my father and his brother came in from the fields with two big birds which they had shot while working. They were pheasants and they made delicious food for us. I can still remember how they tasted.

I caught a bird once too, a capercaillie, something like a big black grouse. I had startled it while walking in the woods and caught it in my arms as it flew up. I held it there with its heart beating against mine for a long time and then I let it go. My father scolded me later when I told him about it. But how could I have kept it, with its heart beating against mine so loudly?

In the fall, winter, and spring, I'd be going to school in the neighborhood. The first hour, at nine, was taken up with religious stories. Then there would be history or geography. The teacher would refer to cities in relation to what was manufactured in them. Brussels, for instance, was known for Brussels carpets; Bern or Zurich for Swiss watches; Smyrna for Turkish figs, and so on. The third hour would be arithmetic. Recess was from twelve to one. In the afternoon, there would be reading and writing and then gym and woodwork. This consisted of learning how to make things, such as bookcases, chairs, picture frames. At night I would go to what was called "continuation school," where more woodwork was taught. I made a beautiful table with drawers, for which I got honor marks. Did I forget to mention something? Well, perhaps. The teacher never forgot. He never forgot to pull our ears, either, when we made mistakes.

The library at our public school was a treasure house, full of books from the whole world. It had *Robinson Crusoe, Gulliver's Travels, Uncle Tom's Cabin, Huckleberry Finn,* Jack London, *Tom Sawyer, Around the World in Eighty Days.* There was no end to what we could choose from. Nor was this all. The boys in the neighborhood and I ganged up and bought paperbound books every week from a bookstore in the city on the mainland; books the school library didn't have— Sherlock Holmes, Nick Carter, Buffalo Bill. We never bothered to look at the names of the authors. It was what was inside the covers that interested us. Buffalo Bill, for instance. What a man! And what a country. America! Huckleberry Finn, Tom Sawyer, running away from conformity on a raft in the river to freedom, where they didn't have to comb their hair or take orders from the widow. You could probably say that it was because of those books that I finally came to America.

When I was fourteen I was confirmed, and then school was over for us on the island. It was time for me to earn some money if I could. Many ships, mostly freighters, came to Sundsvall, the industrial port on the mainland near us, to take on cargoes of lumber, pulp, cellulose, mine props, to go to foreign countries. Sometimes I got a chance to help load the cargo. I would be hired by the longshore contractor for low pay because I was only a boy. The money I turned over to my parents, who, in turn, gave me more work which had piled up while I was away working. There was always the everlasting wood to be cut in the forest, hauled home, sawed, and chopped to fit the cookstove in our kitchen. And there was no more Greta to sit and watch me in the woodshed.

Then in the summer the fields had to be plowed, potatoes planted, harvest to be gathered in the fall, barley to be threshed. I beat it with a flail until the grain separated from the straws. Work, work, all the time. No end. No compensation. Only an existence.

I kept on pressing my father that I wanted to go. Somewhere, someplace. Anyplace. Maybe on a ship. Maybe to America. I always remembered the alluring tales of the Wild West—Indians, buffaloes, everything.

And what tales the immigrants had to tell when they returned from America, the promised land! Nuggets of gold hanging on Christmas trees, diamonds on the waysides, sparkling pearls in crystal water begging to be held by human hands. And how good those homecomers looked—fur coats, cuffs on well-creased trousers, and money! Sure, big American bills. Not small like Swedish bills.

A friend of my father's by the name of Fritz had just returned from

America and he said he had money like grass. He told father that he would go back to America in a short time—maybe three months. I kept asking father to let me go with him. Finally, father gave in. And so preparation for my voyage began.

A tailor made me a suit with cuffs on the pants, just like Fritz's. Mother sewed shirts for me, with collars attached. Ticket for the ocean voyage, plus other railroad tickets, were bought and paid for at a steamship agency in Sundsvall. Father also gave me the twenty-five dollars required at the port of entry in the new land, so that one wouldn't starve to death while looking for gold and diamonds. I was also given ten dollars in case something would happen. Everything was all set. Then, in the last minute, Fritz changed his mind. He wasn't going. His mother was sick, he explained. He didn't want to leave her. So father gave me a choice as to whether I would go or stay home. Sure I'd go. I was seventeen years old. Strong. Weighed a hundred and fifty pounds. A bargain in the labor market of the New World. Besides, I had an uncle in Minnesota. He'd fix it for me. Everything would be as easy as pie.

I remember the day I left home. Mother had prepared some home-baked beans and salt pork. She was very quiet when I left. Maybe she cried later. Father went with me to the railroad station. He looked pretty sad and I saw tears in his eyes as he wished me well.

After two days, I arrived in Gothenburg. There I stayed in a dark room the steamship company had rented for me. I had to wait one day for the transatlantic ship to come. It was raining and I just sat there in the room. Just sat watching heavy raindrops falling on the window.

Finally the big ship came and I walked on board. I had a suitcase and a trunk in the hold and I also had the tickets, besides thirty-five dollars. By and by the ship lifted anchor, and we left—left the harbor of Gothenburg, heading out west on a stormy sea. I was on my way to a faraway country, to strange people who spoke a language I did not know. I stood on the steerage deck, silently looking back at the coast of my native land. . . .

When I arrived in Minnesota, I stayed with my uncle for a while until I learned a few words of the language. Then he got me a job as a farmhand on a farm on the Plains. I had to chop wood, haul hay, take care of cows and horses, and help with all the farm work. I spent the whole winter there. It was just like the work at home, only I wasn't with my own family and I couldn't speak the language very well. But I studied and I learned and I practiced with a boy who lived on the farm. And, after a while, I began to be able to speak English.

In the spring I was paid off—seventy-five dollars minus five dollars the farmer deducted because I had broken a pitchfork while I was working. I took that money and I went to St. Paul to look for another job. I was sitting in a park there, looking at the Mississippi River and wondering where to begin, when out of nowhere a man came up to me. He asked if I wanted to work on the *Fury*, a paddle wheeler hauling barges on the river. I went with the man, who turned out to be the mate on the *Fury*. I worked on that boat for a whole summer. Forty-five dollars a month, plus board and a bunk to sleep in. The paddle wheeler was a government boat. The work consisted of hauling gravel barges from a dredge, which scooped gravel from shallow parts of the river. When the barges were loaded, the paddle wheeler hauled them down to deep spots a few miles south and dumped them. My job was to tie the barge to the boat, then, when we got to where the river was deep, open the latch and let the load drop out, then go back for a new load. There were two crews: four hours on, four hours off.

I was on the river I had read about in *Huckleberry Finn*, but it didn't seem the same somehow. . . .

When fall came the paddle wheeler *Fury* was tied up for the winter and everyone was laid off. With some money in my pocket I went to Chicago to see what I could do there.

I got a job as an orderly in a big city hospital. It was an ideal job for a young immigrant. I had my room and board and a small salary, and after my day's work was done I was free to go to night school.

I took courses in English, then in English literature, and later in history and philosophy. I was beginning to think of going to college when I met a young woman who appealed to me. A few months later we were married and I gave up thoughts of college. Married people didn't go to college in those days. However, I kept on with my reading—I always had a book in my hand. I read Dreiser, H. G. Wells, Huxley, Sinclair Lewis, Upton Sinclair, Hemingway. I'm still reading. Right now I'm on the works of George Orwell.

The hospital work wasn't suitable for a married man, so I got a job with the Baltimore and Ohio Railroad—first as a coal passer and later as a fireman. I worked at that job until 1938, when I was laid off because of automation. I determined then that I would never be dependent on a company for my work again. So I started out as an independent contractor, doing small cement jobs—laying sidewalks, putting floors in basements, and making walls. I always worked with my own hands, although I sometimes had four or five men working under me.

Now that I'm retired I often go to the public lectures or plays at the university. Last week I went to a lecture given there by a famous astronomer from Harvard. He told about a new theory they have now; that a tiny particle of antimatter—something very dense but very small—passed right through the earth in 1908. It left a big circle of wreckage in Siberia and it came out somewhere in the South Atlantic.

There was a flash of light seen over northern Europe at the time that it was supposed to have hit. As he was talking, I remembered seeing such a flash, sitting in my farmyard in Sweden when I was a boy. It was so bright it took the color out of everything, even though it was daytime when I saw it.

After the lecture, I raised my hand and told the astronomer I had seen that light. He became very excited and asked me where I was when I saw it and what year it was. I was able to date it pretty exactly, because it happened at about the time of the death of a cousin of mine. The astronomer wrote down my name and the place I lived in Sweden. Then he told me I was very lucky, because I was probably the only person in the room to have seen that flash. In fact, I was the only person he had ever met who had seen it. Most of the other people in the lecture room were young students, and the astronomer himself was only about forty years old.

Just think. I had seen that flash from my farmyard in Sweden when I was a boy, and I had to wait till I was eighty-three years old to learn what it was. Isn't life strange?


# Pauline Newman

···················FROM LITHUANIA, 1901··················

*The calamitous Triangle Shirtwaist Factory fire of 1911, in which 146 women and girls lost their lives, was a landmark in American labor history. It galvanized public opinion behind the movement to improve conditions, hours, and wages in the sweatshops. Pauline Newman went to work in the Triangle Shirtwaist Factory at the age of eight, shortly after coming to the Lower East Side of New York City. Many of her friends lost their lives in the fire. She went on to become an organizer and later an executive of the newly formed International Ladies Garment Workers' Union, of which she is now, at the age of eighty-six, educational director.*

The village I came from was very small. One department store, one synagogue, and one church. There was a little square where the peasants would bring their produce, you know, for sale. And there was one teahouse where you could have a glass of tea for a penny and sit all day long and play checkers if you wanted.

In the winter we would skate down the hilltop toward the lake, and in the summer we'd walk to the woods and get mushrooms, raspberries. The peasants lived on one side of the lake, and the Jewish people on the other, in little square, thatched-roofed houses. In order to go to school you had to own land and we didn't own land, of course. Very few Jews did. But we were allowed to go to Sunday School and I never missed going to Sunday School. They would sing Russian folk songs and recite poetry. I liked it very much. It was a narrow life, but you didn't miss anything because you didn't know what you were missing.

That was the time, you see, when America was known to foreigners as the land where you'd get rich. There's gold on the sidewalk—all you have to do is pick it up. So people left that little village and went to America. My brother first and then he sent for one sister, and after that, a few years after that, my father died and they sent for my mother and my other two sisters and me. I was seven or eight at the time. I'm not sure exactly how old, because the village I came from had no registration of birth, and we lost the family Bible on the ship and that was where the records were.

Of course we came steerage. That's the bottom of the ship and three layers of bunks. One, two, three, one above the other. If you were lucky, you got the first bunk. Of course you can understand that it wasn't all that pleasant when the people on the second bunk or the third bunk were ill. You had to suffer and endure not only your own misery, but the misery from the people above you.

My mother baked rolls and things like that for us to take along, because all you got on the boat was water, boiled water. If you had tea, you could make tea, but otherwise you just had the hot water. Sometimes they gave you a watery soup, more like a mud puddle than soup. It was stormy, cold, uncomfortable. I wasn't sick, but the other members of my family were.

When we landed at Ellis Island our luggage was lost. We inquired for it and they said, "Come another time. Come another time. You'll find it. We haven't got time now." So we left and we never saw our luggage again. We had bedding, linen, beautiful copper utensils, that sort of thing.

From Ellis Island we went by wagon to my brother's apartment on Hester Street. Hester Street and Essex on the Lower East Side. We were all bewildered to see so many people. Remember we were from a little village. And here you had people coming and going and shouting. Peddlers, people on the streets. Everything was new, you know.

At first we stayed in a tiny apartment with my brother and then, finally, we got one of our own. Two rooms. The bedroom had no windows. The toilets were in the yard. Just a coal stove for heat. The rent was ten dollars a month.

A cousin of mine worked for the Triangle Shirtwaist Company and she got me on there in October of 1901. It was probably the largest shirtwaist factory in the city of New York then. They had more than two hundred operators, cutters, examiners, finishers. Altogether more than four hundred people on two floors. The fire took place on one floor, the floor where we worked. You've probably heard about that. But that was years later.

We started work at seven-thirty in the morning, and during the busy season we worked until nine in the evening. They didn't pay you any overtime and they didn't give you anything for supper money. Sometimes they'd give you a little apple pie if you had to work very late. That was all. Very generous.

What I had to do was not really very difficult. It was just monotonous. When the shirtwaists were finished at the machine there were some threads that were left, and all the youngsters—we had a corner on the floor that resembled a kindergarten—we were given little scissors to cut the threads off. It wasn't heavy work, but it was monotonous, because you did the same thing from seven-thirty in the morning till nine at night.

*What about the child labor laws?*

Well, of course, there were laws on the books, but no one bothered to enforce them. The employers were always tipped off if there was going to be an inspection. "Quick," they'd say, "into the boxes!" And we children would climb into the big boxes the finished shirts were stored in. Then some shirts were piled on top of us, and when the inspector came—no children. The factory always got an okay from the inspector, and I suppose someone at City Hall got a little something, too.

The employers didn't recognize anyone working for them as a human being. You were not allowed to sing. Operators would have liked to have sung, because they, too, had the same thing to do and weren't allowed to sing. We weren't allowed to talk to each other. Oh, no, they would sneak up behind if you were found talking to your next colleague. You were admonished: "If you keep on you'll be fired." If you went to the toilet and you were there longer than the floor lady thought you should be, you would be laid off for half a day and sent home. And, of course, that meant no pay. You were not allowed to have your lunch on the fire escape in the summertime. The door was locked to keep us in. That's why so many people were trapped when the fire broke out.

My pay was $1.50 a week no matter how many hours I worked. My sisters made $6.00 a week; and the cutters, they were the skilled workers, they might get as much as $12.00. The employers had a sign in the elevator that said: "If you don't come in on Sunday, don't come in on Monday." You were expected to work every day if they needed you and the pay was the same whether you worked extra or not. You had to be there at seven-thirty, so you got up at five-thirty, took the horse car, then the electric trolley to Greene Street, to be there on time.

At first I tried to get somebody who could teach me English in the evening, but that didn't work out because I don't think he was a very good teacher, and, anyhow, the overtime interfered with private lessons. But I mingled with people. I joined the Socialist Literary Society. Young as I was and not very able to express myself, I decided that it wouldn't hurt if I listened. There was a Dr. Newman, no relation of mine, who was teaching in City College. He would come down to the Literary Society twice a week and teach us literature, English literature. He was very helpful. He gave me a list of books to read, and, as I said, if there is a will you can learn. We read Dickens, George Eliot, the poets. I remember when we first heard Thomas Hood's "Song of the Shirt." I figured that it was written for us. You know, because it told the long hours of "stitch, stitch, stitch." I remember one of the girls said, "He didn't know us, did he?" And I said, "No, he didn't." But it had an impact on us. Later on, of course, we got to know Shelley. Shelley's known for his lyrics, but very few people know his poem dealing with slavery, called "The Masque of Anarchy." It appealed to us, too, because it was a time when we were ready to rise and that helped us a great deal. [*Recites:* "Rise like Lions after slumber."]

I regretted that I couldn't go even to evening school, let alone going to day school; but it didn't prevent me from trying to learn and it doesn't have to prevent anybody who wants to. I was then and still am an avid reader. Even if I didn't go to school I think I can hold my own with anyone, as far as literature is concerned.

Conditions were dreadful in those days. We didn't have anything. If the season was over, we were told, "You're laid off. Shift for yourself." How did you live? After all, you didn't earn enough to save any money. Well, the butcher trusted you. He knew you'd pay him when you started work again. Your landlord, he couldn't do anything but wait, you know. Sometimes relatives helped out. There was no welfare, no pension, no unemployment insurance. There was nothing. We were much worse off than the poor are today because we had nothing to lean on; nothing to hope for except to hope that the shop would open again and that we'd have work.

But despite that, we had good times. In the summer we'd go to Central Park and stay out and watch the moon arise; go to the Palisades and spend the day. We went to meetings, too, of course. We had friends and we enjoyed what we were doing. We had picnics. And, remember, in that time you could go and hear Caruso for twenty-five cents. We heard all the giants of the artistic world—Kreisler, Pavlova. We only had to pay twenty-five cents. Of course, we went upstairs, but we heard the greatest soloists, all for a quarter, and we enjoyed it immensely. We loved it. We'd go Saturday night and stand in line no matter what the weather. In the winter we'd bring blankets along. Just imagine, the greatest artists in the world, from here and abroad, available to you for twenty-five cents. The first English play I went to was *Peer Gynt*. The actor's name was Mansfield. I remember it very well. So, in spite of everything, we had fun and we enjoyed what we learned and what we saw and what we heard.

I stopped working at the Triangle Factory during the strike in 1909 and I didn't go back. The union sent me out to raise money for the strikers. I apparently was able to articulate my feelings and opinions about the criminal conditions, and they didn't have anyone else who could do better, so they assigned me. And I was successful getting money. After my first speech before the Central Trade and Labor Council I got front-page publicity, including my picture. I was only about fifteen then. Everybody saw it. Wealthy women were curious and they asked me if I would speak to them in their homes. I said I would if they would contribute to the strike, and they agreed. So I spent my time from November to the end of March upstate in New York, speaking to the ladies of the Four Hundred [the elite of New York's society] and sending money back.

Those ladies were very kind and generous. I had never seen or dreamed of such wealth. One Sunday, after I had spoken, one of the women asked me to come to dinner. And we were sitting in the living room in front of a fireplace; remember it was winter. A beautiful library and comfort that I'd never seen before and I'm sure the likes of me had never seen anything like it either. And the butler announced that dinner was ready and we went into the dining room and for the first time I saw the silver and the crystal and the china and the beautiful tablecloth and vases—beautiful vases, you know. At that moment I didn't know what the hell I was doing there. The butler had probably never seen anything like me before. After the day was over, a beautiful limousine took me back to the YWCA where I stayed.

In Buffalo, in Rochester, it was the same thing. The wealthy ladies all asked me to speak, and they would invite me into their homes and contribute money to the strike. I told them what the conditions were that made us get up: the living conditions, the wages, the shop conditions. They'd probably never heard anything like this. I didn't exaggerate. I didn't have to. I remember one time in Syracuse a young woman sitting in front of me wept.

We didn't gain very much at the end of the strike. I think the hours were reduced to fifty-six a week or something like that. We got a 10 percent increase in wages. I think that the best thing that the strike did was to lay a foundation on which to build a union. There was so much feeling against unions then. The judge, when one of our girls came before him, said to her: "You're not striking against your employer, you know, young lady. You're striking against God," and sentenced her to two weeks on Blackwell's Island, which is now Welfare Island. And a lot of them got a taste of the club.

I can look back and find that there were some members of the union who might very well be compared to the unknown soldier. I'll never forget one member in the Philadelphia union. She was an immigrant, a beautiful young woman from Russia, and she was very devoted to the local union. And one Friday we were going to distribute leaflets to a shop that was not organized. They had refused to sign any agreement and we tried to work it that way to get the girls to join. But that particular day—God, I'll never forget the weather. Hail, snow, rain, cold. It was no weather for any human being to be out in, but she came into my office. I'd decided not to go home because of the weather and I'd stayed in the office. She came in and I said, "You're not going out tonight. I wouldn't send a dog out in weather like this." And I went to the window and I said, "Look." And while my back was turned, she grabbed a batch of leaflets and left the office. And she went out. And the next thing I heard was that she had pneumonia and she went to the hospital and in four days she was gone. I can't ever forget her. Of course, perhaps it was a bit unrealistic on her part, but on the other hand, I can't do anything but think of her with admiration. She had the faith and the will to help build the organization and, as I often tell other people, she was really one of the unknown soldiers.

After the 1909 strike I worked with the union, organizing in Philadelphia and Cleveland and other places, so I wasn't at the Triangle Shirtwaist Factory when the fire broke out, but a lot of my friends were. I was in Philadelphia for the union and, of course, someone from here called me immediately and I came back. It's very difficult to describe the feeling because I knew the place and I knew so many of the girls. The thing that bothered me was the employers got a lawyer. How anyone could have *defended* them!—because I'm quite sure that the fire was planned for insurance purposes. And no one is going to convince me otherwise. And when they testified that the door to the fire escape was open, it was a lie! It was never open. Locked all the time. One hundred and forty-six people were sacrificed, and the judge fined Blank and Harris seventy-five dollars!

Conditions were dreadful in those days. But there was something that is lacking today and I think it was the devotion and the belief. We *believed* in what we were doing. We fought and we bled and we died. Today they don't have to.

You sit down at the table, you negotiate with the employers, you ask for 20 percent, they say 15, but the girls are working. People are working. They're not disturbed, and when the negotiations are over they get the increases. They don't really have to fight. Of course, they'll belong to the union and they'll go on strike if you tell them to, but it's the inner faith that people had in those days that I don't see today. It was a terrible time, but it was interesting. I'm glad I lived then.

Even when things were terrible, I always had that faith. . . . Only now, I'm a little discouraged sometimes when I see the workers spending their free hours watching television—trash. We fought so hard for those hours and they waste them. We used to read Tolstoy, Dickens, Shelley, by candlelight, and they watch the "Hollywood Squares." Well, they're free to do what they want. That's what we fought for.

# Anna Ohlson

···················FROM NORWAY, 1906 ·······················

*The little house stands in a grove of poplars surrounded by level Dakota prairie. There is a woodshed, an outhouse, a barn, a pond with a few ducks. Inside the snug kitchen, Anna Ohlson and her husband share a pot of coffee with a visitor. They are both in their late eighties, and she is somewhat palsied, but he still chops the wood for the cookstove and she still bakes bread twice a week. On the wall over the table is a fading photograph of the first log house built on this land. Six small boys, a beribboned girl, and a handsome blond couple in their thirties gaze solemnly at the traveling photographer. The little girl in the picture is Anna Ohlson.*

I came over from Norway with my mother and father when I was a little girl. I don't remember too much about the trip, except that it was long; but I remember looking out of the train window when we got near here and thinking how flat it was. We were used to mountains in Norway, and here it was all prairie wherever you looked. In the old country, you know, the farmers live in one circle. There's quite a few houses together. And here you'd see all that empty land and then one little house and then another stretch of land and another house. It looked very lonely to me.

When we came here we moved into a homestead that my father had taken out. It was all woods that he had to clear. But after he cleared it, there was good land. It was a pretty spot. I went to school two miles up the road. I was the only girl with six brothers and we all had chores to do. I milked the cows and separated and carried the milk out again to feed the cows, washed the dishes, and helped wash the clothes. We all had to do what we could, you know. I had to pump water out of the well and carry it into the house and then heat it to wash the clothes and then go carry some more. With that big family, it took a lot of water. My mother made soap. I'm not sure how she did it—with lard and a can of lye and an awful lot of stirring, I know. And of course she made bread. She baked about twice a week. We all had to work. And then, during harvest time, when I was old enough, I'd take lunches out to the field to the men. We had the thrashing team there. They'd go out at seven and they'd be out all day. My mother would bake about sixteen loaves at a time then and churn butter and cook big meals. It was a lot of work.

My mother was always talking about the mountains and the fjords. She was homesick, I guess, at first; but she had a lot of work to do, and more children were born here on the farm and it became home. You know, she always had time for a little fun, even with all her work. I used to have playhouses out here in the fields. I'd go out and put some stones in a circle around and I'd say it was my house and I'd stay there with my dolls. She'd come out to me with my lunch and she'd say, "Oh? Is this where you're living now?" And she'd give me my lunch right there and sometimes I'd move my house and she'd have to look for me and she'd laugh when she found me and say, "Oh? You've moved again." We had fun then, with all there was to do.

And Christmas, we always had a good time at Christmas, even if we didn't have much. One year my father couldn't get a fir tree for us—there aren't any around here, you know. So he cut down a little poplar and we put colored candy and paper chains and candles on it and it looked real pretty. And we'd have a pork roast and rice—that's a must at Christmas. And we used to go *Yulebekking* during Christmas. That's a Norwegian custom. We'd put on masks and different, funny clothes, dress up crazy; and then we'd go from one place to another, all the neighbors' houses. And we'd stay dressed up till they guessed who we were. And then they'd serve us something to eat, you know. We'd do that from Christmas till the sixth of January.

And other times we'd go visiting, you know, the whole family, and the kids would play tag, drop the handkerchief, all those games; I can't remember all of them. I remember when we got a bicycle, there were six boys and I, and we got one bicycle. We all took turns using it. And when the boys were small, they'd take the tines from the rake and put a little wheel at the end and go and push them along. They'd run and see who could go the fastest, you know, while pushing that wheel. They had more fun than anyone would think of. And Fourth of July we'd have picnics. They'd set up stands in the town and have lemonade and homemade cake and a few fireworks.

Sometimes we were snowed in. The snow would come up so high you couldn't see where the fences were. My father had to take a rope when he went out to the barn to take care of the horses and cows. The rope was so he could get back to the house through the snow when he was through. We were cut off one time for two weeks. Finally, my father went into town to get coffee and salt and hear the news. We really needed the coffee. My mother couldn't stand it without coffee. He went in and it was two days before he came back, because while he was in town another blizzard came up. But we got along all right. We had plenty of wood and we stayed warm and we did the work that had to be done.

We were luckier than one family that lived to the south of us. They came to settle in a new place and made a dugout in the side of the hill to live in while they built their house. It was just a young couple, a man and a woman. And I guess they didn't know how quickly winter came, because pretty soon the snow came and they still didn't have their house built, just the dugout with a blanket hanging for their door. They saw that they were going to have to spend the winter there, and the man decided to go into town to get the things they would need: flour and salt and coffee. And I guess they figured they'd spend the winter in the dugout. The woman was expecting a child, so she didn't go with him. Well, a blizzard came while he was gone and he couldn't get back for eight days. When he finally was able to get back, he went into the dugout. The wind was blowing in through the blanket and his wife was dead on the floor. Cold. But the new baby was there—crying. It had been born while he was gone. He covered his wife, though she was dead and cold already, and picked up the baby and wrapped it up. And then he went through the snow—it was still snowing—about three miles to the next farm, where there was a woman, and he gave the baby to her. And, you know, that woman nursed the baby and they say, though I don't know it's true, myself, they say she got milk in her breasts when she held the baby in her arms. Anyhow, she raised that baby up and she grew up to be one of the prettiest young women in the county. I've seen her myself.

But we never had any trouble like that. We had a good house and plenty of wood.

When I got to be about sixteen I went away to work on a cook car. You go around with the thrashing team and cook food for them as they go from farm to farm. The thrashing crew chief hires you. There's lots of fun in that, you know. Lots of work, but lots of fun. There's young boys, men, from all different countries there. French Canadians, Norwegians, Americans. One woman and I did all the work. We'd get up in the morning before it was light and start the stove up and give them breakfast. We had to give them a meat-and-potatoes breakfast. Of course, we had something we could warm up, otherwise we'd be up all night. We had a table and chairs, benches, and we'd set about sixteen at the table. Then about ten o'clock we'd carry lunches out to the field to them—sandwiches and doughnuts and coffee. And then, of course, the big meal at noon. And then another lunch about three—sandwiches and coffee and cake, maybe. And then another big meal at night. And in-between times we'd wash the dishes and do the cooking. We were busy. But, you know, it was fun. They'd help us in the evening with the dishes and there were a lot of young people, so there was a lot of laughing and joking. And the thrashing crew moved from farm to farm, so we got to see different places. It was mostly in this area we went, around Grafton. We worked August and September and if there was a lot of rain, sometimes into October. The cooks were paid the same as the men—four dollars a day—but there were two of us, so we had to divide it. We made more money than we would with housework. That was the only other work women could do then.

There was lots of fun in those days. Dancing. Somebody would bring a fiddle and we'd have dancing in the house—here in this house we'd sometimes have thirty people dancing and singing and drinking coffee. That's how I met my husband. He came in one time and I was drying the dishes and he came up and helped me.

It was hard work then, but there was more time, too. If someone was sick, the neighbors would always do his planting or thrashing for him. And when a woman had a baby, the other women came in. If a farmer was going to town past here, he'd always stop and ask if we wanted something and pass the time of day. Now, they go right by in their cars. And the men, I think they work harder now, because they have the machines and they can keep going. The animals made you rest. They had to have their rest at midday, and so you took a rest, too, then.

After I was married, my father died and my husband and I took over the farm. My brothers were all farming around here and I guess we'll all die right where we grew up. That's my brother Arne's farm over there. [Points to the north.] We had some hard times, all of us. When the dust storms came and the grasshoppers—those were terrible years. My little girl asked, "What is rain?" Just think, she had never seen it. But we kept going. No money, but we had milk from the cows and some eggs and root vegetables. You couldn't sell wheat for anything, but we had enough to eat. We were lucky. Plenty of people lost their farms around here, but we didn't owe anyone and we hung on.

Of course, there was a lot of work to do. I had seven children to raise and I baked twice a week and kept my chickens. And every year I canned two hundred quarts of fruits and vegetables. We used to go berry picking in the fall. All of us, the children, even my husband, we'd go out along the river and bring back big pailfuls: juneberries, blueberries, cranberries, sometimes blackberries. The fields were full of them. The children would help; they loved to help. . . . I wish I could have those days back.

# John Daroubian

·····················FROM ARMENIA, 1919·····················

*American children who failed to clean their plates used to be told: "Think of the starving Armenians." John Daroubian is one of those legendary sufferers. He was driven into the desert; he ate wild grasses; he watched his small brother die crying for a crust of bread. At seventy-six, Mr. Daroubian still works, earning a comfortable living for himself and his wife with a small import business in New York City. He has warm, dark eyes and a skin like old parchment.*

I was born in Cholmolka, a small village but a beautiful one, because we are in the bottom of one of the highest mountains. The weather was just magnificent. Beautiful spot. It was a town of about three hundred families. Among us there were only about eight families of Turks. The rest were all Armenian. It was very peaceful—not progressive—only a village, you know. Over there you can't expect much. Everyone knew what to do. Summer come or spring come, they went to the fields. And the local Turks and the local Armenians, they were very friendly. They never had a fight. There was always fear of Turkish massacres because we always used to hear, "There were massacres in 1896." And that was quite fresh in our people's minds. And there was always that animosity—not with our local people but with the higher-ups, the authorities. But with our local people we were all right.

Around 1910, already we were feeling that things were not going right with the Armenian people and the Turkish people. We could feel that it was coming.

So in 1915 it finally did come, when the war started. Then, of course, the Turks had a very good opportunity to get rid of the Armenians without getting the attention of the world. You may say, "Why did the Turks want to get rid of the Armenians?" You see, Turkey used to be Armenia first. They planned that all Armenians would be wiped out so that there will not be any claims anymore. They planned to eliminate the Armenian element completely. Whenever they could, they massacred them. But they couldn't do that to all of them everyplace because of European people. They are always scared of European opinion. We were lucky in 1915. We were one of the first groups that were deported. At that time people weren't used to killing and robbing. They always feel there is law and order. Later on, ordinary people found out that they could do anything they wanted in Armenia. There is no such thing as law and order. Once they knew that we were unprotected, they began to kill, rob, beat, anything, everything. . . .

One morning in April, our little village was surrounded by gendarmes—policemen. Must have been about five or six in the morning. They were knocking at our doors. "Get up!" They gave us an hour and a half. What can you take in an hour and a half? There were nine in the family. I was ten years old. I had a year-old brother, a three-year-old brother, a nine-year-old brother, two sisters, my parents, and an old grandmama. We took whatever we could. Everybody had to carry something, like a blanket or if there was something to eat. How much can you carry? By ten the whole town was emptied out. The gendarmes are leading us. Anybody left behind, they beat him up. If he was a little bit slow, he got a good beating. In fact, they beat up my father just because he was begging them, "Will you give me another half hour? Just let me get a few things."

So we started. They never told us where we are going. None of us knew. In fact, they told us, "Oh, you may be back. Leave everything here and very likely within a month, within weeks, you may come back again. Leave everything here. Lock it up." So this is the way we left.

We went toward Arabia. In the Arabian Desert you can't get anything to eat. It's all dry. Sheer desert. There's nothing you can grow. We can't work. We can't do anything. They didn't want to kill us, massacre us. But this way they thought we would die on our own. We went toward Aleppo. We had one donkey, but how much can a donkey carry? My Grandmama was old and the baby couldn't walk yet.

It took us forty days and forty nights to get to Aleppo. Of course, we rested at night. But in the open. The gendarmes were with us all the time. We had a little money and we could go round the little villages and buy. But the only thing that you can buy is bread. They didn't have much. They were poor people anyway. Only thing we could get was the yogurt that is famous over there. We could get yogurt and bread and cheese. At first we could get those things. Then we began to eat greens, certain grasses that are eatable. You cook and you boil and you put in some breadcrust or a little rice if you had it, or a little wheat if you had it, and just boiled it and ate it. That's all you could get.

Of course, the elderly people couldn't keep up. So the gendarmes beat them. "If you can't keep up, we'll just leave you here," they said. If someone died, they didn't even let us dig a grave so that we could bury them. If a baby died, they'd say, "Fine. Just drop it there. If you want to carry it, go ahead and carry it. It's up to you."

When we reached Aleppo, they said, "From here on, you go by train." Just like cattle they filled us up in the trains. No sitting space. You could hardly stand up. They just packed us in like cattle. Of course, we couldn't take our donkey. "Just drop it. Leave it there," they said.

From Aleppo we went to Amman. Now, it takes maybe only a day. It took us six days by train then, because they didn't have coal or electric systems. They used to use wood. Very poor wood and they have to feed all the time the train. You know, "puff-puff-puff, puff-puff-puff." Any time there was a little hill the train was slower than a man can walk. And to go through the desert that way—it took us six days. Everybody was sick. Before at least you were getting open air. You were able to go out and eat grass if necessary, and you could get some water if you wanted that. But this way, whatever you had you just ate. If not, you were hungry. That's all there was to it. And, of course, dirty clothes. People began to get lice. Those trains had been busy transferring soldiers back and forth before, and they were full of bugs.

When we got to Amman, they didn't let us in the city. They didn't want us to be seen. They didn't want the big-city people to give us any help. They wanted to let starvation do their killing, rather than they, themselves. There was an old fort there, near a mountain. Cherbok. It used to be a center for Arabic invasion five hundred years ago. They took us there. There were no people in the fort. There were caves where the soldiers used to stay or to keep their animals. They were shelter; not a home, just a cave built within the hill. So they said, "Here it is. This is the place you're going to." Who's asking? This is it. They left us. They said, "Here you are. Go on and do whatever you want."

People came and looked at us. They heard that we were Christians and some of these natives were very backward, so they hurried to look at us. What did we look like? Pigs or something else? They thought, "Let's see what the Christians do look like." They were Arab people but good people. I can't say anything bad about them because they did not hurt us. They did not kill us. They couldn't help us because they don't have much of their own, either. But at least they left us alone and we were grateful for that.

People started dying. Five or ten a day. Five or ten a day. We were three thousand at the start, let's say, and at the end we were only about five hundred. I lost my grandmother there and my baby brother. My parents said, "God took them away. How lucky they are. They don't suffer anymore." We were all sick. We were in a little cave about as big as a small room. My father was sick in one spot. My mother was sick next to him. We were nine people and we had nine feet of room, and everyone just slept there on the floor. On the other side of the cave was my uncle's family. Evey inch of space was taken. My mother and father were talking together one morning and my mother said, "I had a dream. We were in our house and one wall fell down." She said to my father, "Either you will die or I will die. The wall fell down." They took it seriously. But what can they do?

My other little brother, Michael, was about three then. One night toward dawn, it was still dark, he began to cry and ask for bread. He kept calling me. He was saying, "Brother John, brother John, please give me a morsel of bread." But there was none. I said, "Please. The morning is coming. I will go out and try to get bread." But morning came and he was gone. [*Breaks down.*]

After that my father died. So what is left now? I was the head of the family. I had two sisters older than me, but we didn't dare to send girls out for work. They were fifteen, sixteen years old. Beautiful girls. And the Arabs around us, they didn't do killing or anything like that, but if they did see a pretty woman. . . . So we couldn't send the girls out to work with the other people. I was about eleven at the time and my brother was about ten. So we used to go out to the fields and gather wood for fireplaces for the Arab people, and they would give us a handful of grain—either wheat or flour—and we would bring that back. In the meantime, the girls would go nearby to see if there was grass, wild grass that's eatable, wild spinach. There were half-a-dozen names of different kinds they knew that was all right to eat. And we used to bring the grain and at night my mother would cook the food and we began to live.

So we began to learn the language a little bit and we learned their ways. And the Arabs around us began to like us a little bit. Except, again, our only trouble was taking care of our women so that they would not be taken away. But that didn't last more than a year and a half. Then the Turks began to retreat from the lower end of Arabia. British soldiers began to come in when Lawrence of Arabia started to take over. The Turks didn't want us to live as British subjects. Now they send us back again. All of a sudden, they say, "You have to go back. Leave everything here." By this time we were used to it. The five hundred or so people that were left had begun to get along with whatever we were making. So the Turks started again: "You've got to go back." This time, again, they filled us in the trains just like cattle, again. Like before.

We got to Damascus. It was funny when we got to Damascus. Remember we were kids. We thought we'd try and see a little bit of the town, you know. We went only about two hundred feet. There was a nice bridge. The river is going underneath. You know in Arabia you don't see no river. There is no water. If you get a little bit of water, a little spring, that's a miracle. A miracle. We didn't get water. But Damascus is a huge, big city, and they have a huge, big river and a lot of gardens. It's really very pretty. So we wanted to take a look at it. The gendarmes came. They took us in. They took us to the police station and then later back to the train station.

From Damascus, this time, they took us to Hamar between Damascus and Aleppo. Well, they took us over there and, again, they left us. "Go ahead. You're in Hamar now. Do anything. Do anything you want. Go ahead," they said. What can you do? You got no money, no home—just go. There were caves outside the city. We went into them and this is it. We can't go into the city, because they won't accept you there. So, again, we had to start all over again. No home. This time we were worse off because we had already used up whatever we had. We knew the language a little better. That was a help. My brother and I began to go to town. It was only a mile or so away from the caves, but still it was away. We started right away doing hard work. We carried things, carried packages, other heavy things from one place to another. Rugs or anything. Anything. Wheat. Bags of wheat and so on. They don't have automobiles or trucks or things like that over there. It has to be a donkey or a man.

More people began to die now. We lost, I think, about a hundred people there. We were lucky. We were lucky. In my uncle's family there were ten or twelve and only one was left. Only one. My other uncle, there had been five in his family. There was only one left. But we still had my mother and my brother and I and my two sisters.

We're always hoping we'll go back to our old hometown, our beautiful Cholmolka. So we started off on foot. We went toward Aleppo. It took six days to get there. On the way we were robbed twice. And what are they robbing anyway? I mean, there is nothing left. We had about two handfuls of raisins and a couple loaves of bread—two or three days eating. In the meantime, we used to get grass during the day. As we walked we used to get it, if there was any. We would spread around and walk to gather the grass that's eatable. We would bring it together at night and cook it, if possible. If not, wash it and eat it like salad. As I say, a couple of times we were robbed. What are you going to do? No court. No nothing. All those people knew we were not protected and they could do anything they want.

Finally we reached Aleppo. We went straight to the Armenian church. There was already a big line before us. They are coming from all around. The survivors. They are all coming. Where can they go? They open the gate and there was a big yard full of people. All they could give us was a little soup. That was the most they could give. We stayed there about five or six days and then they had a sort of a place where they used to produce wool. They would spin wool to make socks and sweaters and so on. And most of the women they put in there. Let them work there. But the boys were left out. Sometimes my brother and I would dress up like girls to get in there and work and get some food. We managed like that in Aleppo for quite a long time—about a month or so.

There was an orphanage there and finally my brother and I got into the orphanage. It was supported by England, America, and other European countries. I was a little stronger, so the minute I got in the orphanage I began to work. If you had work, then they treat you a little better because you're producing. You're working. So if the others used to get one slice of bread, you used to get two slices, maybe. Or a bit more soup than the others. And I began to work and I got a little bit more than the others. And that helps. And a month later, one of my sisters came. And then the other sister. And my mother. But we were producing. Lots of others couldn't. I don't know. Evidently we had a little bit more energy or something. Whatever assignment they gave us we did better than the others. They let my mother come in, because, you see, all these children that came in, they were all sick. They needed mothering; they needed nursing. So my mother did that.

They were dying in the orphanage like nothing, because we didn't have doctors. We didn't have prescriptions. No medicine. We had shelter, one slice of bread, maybe soup, the least that life can survive on. Every day, two or three young would die. Every day we used to see them. There was two men, that's all they did. They used to come with a bag and just put the bodies in the bag and take it to the cemetery.

One day, two brothers came from our hometown. We had been next-door playboys. They were really, really sick. They could hardly talk. They could hardly stand up. Their bodies were off shape. This kind of sickness is funny. A good-looking boy turned out to be just so—so ugly. I could hardly tell them, but they knew me. They could tell who I am. They were crying when they saw me. They began to cry more and then they began to feel a little better; as if they were someplace and not worrying anymore what's going to happen. . . .

Then 1918 came. The war was over. We were dreaming of America. We had some of our relatives here. Our cousins were here. One of our cousins wrote a letter—a distant cousin. He wanted to marry my older sister. He knew her from the old country anyway. What do you say? What can you say in a time like that? We knew the man and he suggested that I come with her, too. What other arrangement can be better than this? We figured this is just fine. So we wrote them back and started preparing our papers. The rule was, you couldn't bring your fiancée in, but you could bring a close relative. So my cousin said, "This is my brother and my sister." So that is the way we got our passport.

We came by ship. We came to Ellis Island. What are they going to do to us on Ellis Island? Many, many of our people were sent back. Some people were sent back because they couldn't speak right; some because they were sick. There was always something. I'm worrying, "Will this thing work? What are we going to do? Will I get in? Will I get a job? Can I work?" By this time I must have been about sixteen. We got to Ellis Island and, thank God, we didn't encounter any trouble. We stayed there two or three days. Then they sent us to Hoffman Island for quarantine. Evidently there was sickness on the ship. We were checked and checked again. Doctors came and examined us and so on. Then finally we got in. Our relatives came and got us.

After that begins the New York life. It was funny. As I say, I arrived Friday and the first thing I asked my cousins was, "Where is the school?" These people couldn't understand. "What is this?" they said. They are in this country for ten years and they haven't seen where the school is. They didn't think of it. They were hard workers, hard laborers; they have no education. My cousin was a shoemaker and he was making four dollars and five dollars, or, at the most, six dollars or seven dollars in those days. And that was big money for that time—because he didn't have any good education and he didn't have a good trade, and whatever he had saved, he had given us. In the old days, Armenians came with the intention of going back again. Before 1910, they came to make a little money and go back again, with the hope that someday there would be an Armenia. So they didn't think of schooling. But all that was over now. The first thing I said is, "School. If not tomorrow, Saturday. If not Sunday, I must be in school by Monday." And that Monday I did go and I registered myself in the public school on Forty-second Street. Evening school.

Well, I had a bit of a hard time getting a job because there was a depression after World War I. There was a depression, 1920. So there wasn't any job. My cousin helped me. I would get a job for a day and then for two or three days. Finally, one of my cousins, who worked in Roosevelt Hospital as a kitchen helper, said, "If you want to come, come. You can work with me." I would go to school at night and work with him during the day. I used to make ten dollars a week. We both worked hard. And after that there were openings on one job or another, and, in the meantime, I was continuing my school. I had a little English that I had learned in the orphanage. In two years I finished the public school and then I entered the high school. I studied there three years and then I went to Columbia University, working all the time in the daytime in the hospital. And then I got a job with an Oriental rug man. I started working with him and I learned the Oriental rug business. I worked with him for three or four years and I started on my own. I started with hardly any money—whatever little I had saved.

A year later, another Armenian cousin, a distant cousin again, wanted my other sister to marry. They knew the ropes by this time. And now I was in America. It was not as hard a problem anymore. So a year later, my brother, my sister, my mother, they all came. We all lived together with my brother-in-law and later we rented our own house.

In 1931, when it came that I had to get married, I went back to the old country—actually to Beirut, where my wife and her mother had gone from Turkey. I went back for her. I knew her, but I don't think she knew me, because she was much younger than I was. I knew her when she was two, three, or four years old. But we would write. I married her and brought her back to this country.

Her father was one of those whom the Turks massacred; one of the first that the Turks took to kill. There are other Armenians in this country who saw their whole families massacred—shot, stabbed, clubbed to death. When I tell my story, comparing with theirs, mine is hardly anything. Because ours was a slow death. They say we were the lucky ones. Theirs was immediate. I don't know whose is better. One is just as good as another. . . .

# Peter Kekonnen
·····················FROM FINLAND, 1905······················

*When Peter Kekonnen came out to northern Minnesota at the age of sixteen, there was still virgin land to be had. He made a home for himself and his family in the wilderness. Now close to ninety, his eyesight dimmed and his strength failing, he lives with his oldest daughter. His granddaughter and his new great-grandson, also named Peter, were visiting at the time of the interview, and for a moment the baby was put into the old man's arms. Time seemed to melt away as the two Peters, with identical turned-up noses, broad cheekbones, and slant-set blue eyes, clasped one another.*

I was born in Finland in 1889. When I was sixteen, I came on an immigrant ship to the United States. I landed in New York and went on an immigrant train with many others from the Scandinavian countries to the state of Minnesota. I wanted to have a farm, and it was possible to get land then, but I needed money for farm animals and tools and to keep me going until I got a crop.

So I went to work in an iron mine—the Mesabi iron range, the biggest in the world. Maybe you've heard of it. I got two dollars a day for my work and I paid fifteen dollars a month to an old Finnish woman who ran a boarding house, so that I was able to save a little. But the work was hard and it was dangerous. We went down in a shaft. Nowadays that iron mine is all open pit, but then we went down in a shaft. There were no electric lights in the mine then, not even any carbide lamps. We had candles. The air was bad because there was only one shaft, so there was no movement. We were coughing all the time, all of us. And the iron dust got in our lungs. Plenty of young men I knew died of silicosis from that mine in later years. Even the candles wouldn't burn well in that air. For some reason, one candle wouldn't burn alone; if you had two candles close together, they would burn. One alone was no good. So that's the way we always used them—two together.

Conditions in the mine were bad in other ways, too. The roof was not propped up right, so there were many rockfalls. One time I was working with two friends in a deep section of the mine and there was a rockfall. All the top seemed to come down on us. The candles went out and everything was black. After a long time, some men came to us from the other part of the mine, and when it was light I saw that my two friends were dead.

There was a strike in the mine in 1907 and we were out of work for two months. The miners wanted a second shaft dug and also some other improvements in the working conditions. But we lost the strike and I had to use up some of my savings to live on.

When I was seventeen I met Solveig, the daughter of some Finnish people who lived on a farm near the mine. She was fifteen then. It wasn't easy to visit her. I had to hire a horse and wagon to go out to her farm, so I didn't see her very often. But we decided to marry when I had enough money for us to have a farm.

Finally after two years we had saved enough. So we were married and I got a homestead in the woods near the border of Canada. It was eight miles from the railroad, and that first day we had to walk, leading our horse and two cows. We couldn't use a wagon because there was no road, just thick woods. But we had some belongings on the horse, and I carried some and so did Solveig.

It was all woods that we had, with a lake nearby where I could get fish and waterfowl. The first thing I did was to dig a well. Then I cleared some land and built us a log cabin. When the summer was over, it was all ready—two rooms and a place for the cows and the horse. I had to work hard to get the land ready to plant. There were trees to be cut down, stumps to be pulled out, and rocks to be moved. But the soil was good—thick and black. No need for any fertilizer. It was very different from the thin sandy ground of my father's farm in Finland. There we worked and worked and still could hardly grow anything.

Here it was almost like magic. I planted potatoes, beets, cabbages, carrots—everything grew. And Solveig gathered wild cranberries and blueberries and boiled them and put them in bottles for the winter.

The next year our first child was born—Nellie, a girl. And then we had Peter, then Carl, then Christian. I built another room onto our house and cleared more of the woods, so that I could plant more crops. As time went on other Finnish families settled near us. We had Lutheran services in one of the homes and sometimes a party at harvest time or at Christmas. A school was built.

Sometimes the Indians would come to visit us. They were friendly, although there had been trouble with them years before. They would come out of the woods, two or three of them, and we would spread out some food on the table and eat together. A funny thing—you know we Scandinavians like to put a lot on the table for guests? Well, we learned not to put out more for the Indians than they could eat. Because whatever was left, they would put it in their pouches to take with them. I guess they thought if we offered it, they could take it. They were always hungry. That was why they did that. They had a hard life in the woods.

It was hard going into town at first because we had to carry everything with us. But after a few years the county built a road, and we could go with the horse and sleigh in the winter. In the summer the road was muddy, not easy for a wagon, so we walked then, maybe once a month to get the things we needed—coffee, salt, flour, cloth. The rest we grew for ourselves.

I became an American citizen in 1907. The first vote I ever cast was for Teddy Roosevelt. We didn't have any radio, of course, or newspapers then, so we walked to the railroad and waited at the depot for the news to come over the telegraph. We really felt like Americans then, electing a president.

In February 1918 there was a terrible flu epidemic that went all over the world. Maybe you've heard of it? One evening I came in from the barn and we all had supper together as usual and went to bed. In the morning none of us could get up—Solveig, the children, and I. We were all very sick. It was a high fever, very high. We were very weak and it was hard to breathe. The neighbors heard our cows mooing and came over in the late afternoon and found us. Solveig was the worst of us all. She was out of her head with the fever. Next morning the neighbors took her on the sleigh to the depot eight miles away; and then on the train to the town where there was a hospital.

The children and I stayed in the cabin. We were sick, but not as sick as Solveig. The neighbors took care of our animals and chickens and brought us a pot of soup and some bread every afternoon. They were afraid to come in because of the sickness, but they would open the door and put the food inside and then go. One day the man came with the soup and the bread, and, after putting it down, he stood inside the door for a while, not talking. Finally he said, "I have to tell you Solveig is dead. She died in the hospital in the town. . . ." They buried her with the other flu victims in a graveyard near the hospital. She was twenty-seven years old. . . .

In a few weeks I was stronger and began doing the work of the farm again. I had the four children to take care of now. The oldest was nine, and Christian, who was the youngest, was only three. The neighbor woman brought bread for us still, but after a while I thought, "This isn't right. They have to take care of themselves and I have to take care of us." So one morning I made the bread myself. I had seen Solveig do it often enough, and my mother too, in the old country. I did the farmwork and chopped the wood and fed the children and cooked and washed the clothes. And in the fall I gathered the cranberries and blueberries and put them in bottles—and some of the vegetables, too. I did everything myself until Nellie was old enough to help me. And, as the boys grew, they helped, too.

We stayed on the farm until the children were grown. The three oldest got married and left for the town. And when Christian was seventeen, he went away to the University of Minnesota. I sold the land then and made my living as a carpenter in the town. I didn't want to farm anymore. One alone is no good. . . .

I went back last year and saw the place. It's all cleared now. The woods are gone and the farmer there has tractors and machines and electricity—even to milk the cows. He doesn't have to touch them. And they have a big car and can go to town in ten minutes. The lake is still there and the well. But everything looks different. It's easier now, but I don't think they are as happy as we were when I first cleared the land.

# Albertina di Grazia

·······················FROM ITALY, 1913·······················

*Albertina di Grazia is plump, black-haired, fashionably dressed. She and her husband, a prosperous New Jersey builder, live in an impressive, modern house, equipped with climate control, room-to-room intercom, and a central stereo system. But she remembers the little mountain town of Montazzoli in the Abruzzi region of Italy, a world that was virtually unchanged since the Middle Ages.*

Over there we worked for a baron and hardly saw money from one end of the year to the next. All the people in the village would go down the mountain and work on the baron's land. They were given a little piece of land that they could have for their own garden, but basically they were working under the old feudal system. In the school, whenever they needed you to work, they just pulled you out. That's why nobody learned anything. My father couldn't read or write. He had to sign his name with an X when he came to this country.

My father came over first, not long after he and my mother were married. He had to borrow money to come, from several people. That's how hard it was. He worked here for a few years while my mother and I stayed with her parents in Montazzoli, just a little mountain town with a church and a well and a market.

I was five when he sent for us. There was a carriage that picked us up and took us to Naples where the boat was. The only thing that I remember was that I was hugging my grandfather around the neck and I was screaming that I didn't want to go. Then there was a long boat trip; that was an ordeal. And in New York when we arrived there, we had to stay on the boat for a while. There was some complication, I don't remember what; and I could see my father and he could see us and he had some oranges with him and he threw them up to me on deck. [*Chuckles.*] I can remember that.

The next day he took us to Scotch Plains where he had bought a house, an old house. The town had been mostly settled by Scotch and English a long time ago. They were what you might call the old families. Some of them took an interest in the Italians and gave them work, because Italians are good workers, you know. We found other people there that we knew from Montazzoli. That was how we had heard about the place. So it wasn't lonely, as if you're the only family. . . . Before long, my mother had twelve boarders, Italians who had come over without their families and were working to save money. They worked in the woods for a lumber concern, cutting down the trees, sawing them apart, and taking them to the train; and whenever they had any spare time, they worked on the land. My father planted a field of potatoes, a field of corn, tomatoes, everything. We had a pig and a goat and we canned everything that we could.

It was sixty-six years ago, but it seems like, oh, two hundred years ago. Oh, life was so different. There were woods around us and the women would go out for wood and carry it in on their heads and they'd use that wood in the outside oven. The men had built a big oven in the backyard where my mother would bake six or seven loaves of bread. We made our own pasta and we made our own soap. We had a goat for milk and my mother made cheese. It was so good. And my father made wine, too. They'd learned how to do that in Italy, so that's how they knew how to make it. He had those Concord grapes that grow around here. They're not as good as the California grapes, but he made wine with them. They mashed up the grapes and put them in barrels, and then it fermented for about two or three days. And then they would take the wine from the bottom and put it in another barrel. They would get a pair of high rubber boots and wash them clean, you know, and then stamp on the sack with grapes in it while it was in the barrel.

Every year we'd kill the pig that we raised. All the families around here, Italian families, raised pigs. We all got together and helped each other, like in the pioneer days. Our cousins would kill their pig and they would invite us over, and for that day we'd have dinner with them and we'd help them cut it up and everything, and they'd make sausage. And then the next week, when we killed our pig, they would come and help us. We'd boil down the fat, melt it down, and we'd make sausage. It was almost like a festival then.

Before we had our own cow, I used to have a little pail and go to the farm only a couple of blocks away, and this woman would fill the pail with milk. It was such good milk. There were all cornfields here, then. We had cornhusk mattresses, you know. They'd plant fields of corn for the animals to eat and they'd feed the corn to the animals, and then we'd get together at night, the men and the women, in harvest time. They'd take turns. They'd say, "Tonight we'll make your mattress and tomorrow night we'll make ours," and they'd take the better husks and put them away in the mattresses.

It was really a very happy childhood, even though we were poor. We had everything to eat because we raised our own animals, you know, and everything. And there was an Italian club on the street where I lived and they'd have a dance every weekend, and people would go there and some of them knew how to play music and they danced. At home in our living room, we had no furniture, just chairs. No rugs. But we had a Victrola and I always remember how we danced around on the bare floor. And we were always so friendly with our relatives, you know—always being together. I thought it was kind of happy. We'd celebrate Saint Nicholas Day, because that was something special in Montazzoli. We'd have potato-sack races and fireworks and an Italian marching band and food stands with all those Italian things—candies and sausages and pepper—and a parade and special clothing. People would run out from the curbs when the parade went by and pin money on the banner, and the money would go to the Saint Nicholas Society. They were saving money for the church because we didn't have any church here, then. We had to walk to the church in the next town.

When we finally got our church, they sent an Irish priest to us called

Father Mulligan. He was a wonderful man. He went around to every house in the town, in the parish, and visited us and talked to us, and he said, "Well, I've got to see this Montazzoli you all talk about." And when he had a chance, he went to Italy and he visited Montazzoli. He went to the old church there and—do you know what—he got so interested in the town, he came back and told us about it. How things were there, now. And the people here decided—we were all doing better then—decided to start a fund. And now we send money over there every year for a day nursery for the women who have to work in the fields or the factory while they have little children. And the people from that town were so grateful that they sent us the bell from their church. So it's as if we're still part of Montazzoli, in a way, and they're still part of us. They're still coming over from there. Last year we had a second cousin from Montazzoli, a young man staying at our house. He's an immigrant to the United States. So they're still coming. It's still hard to get work over there, so they're still coming.

My mother had eight children, but she never went to the hospital to have her babies. There was a woman that helped all the ladies have their children. And then, you know, everyone would come in and help the new mother. Like, one person would come in one day and another one would come in another day. They'd all take care of her for a week and do everything for the family—cook and wash and take care of the children.

I had my children at home, too. I had a doctor that was just starting out and he came for all my children, except the last one. By then he'd become a surgeon and he wouldn't come, you know. So I had to get another doctor in Fanwood, and he said he wouldn't come to the house to have a baby. He said, "You have to go to the hospital," and I said, "Well, I don't want to go to the hospital. I have four other children. I can tell them what to do from the bed." They were big children then. I hated to leave them for a week. And he saw that I wouldn't go, so he said, "Well, if you get a nurse to help me, I'll come to the house, being you've never gone to the hospital." So he came to the house with a nurse, and later on he said to me, "No wonder you didn't want to go to the hospital. You were just like a queen in that bed." I had embroidered sheets and I was sitting up there giving orders and the women came in to help. He was right. I felt like queen then.

My husband came from Montazzoli, too. I was seventeen and he was only a little older than I was when we married. He was very ambitious and he didn't want to work in the woods like his father. He said, "I'm going to learn to be a mason." He was the oldest in his family and he told one brother, "You become a carpenter and I'll become a mason and Joe will become a plumber. Then we can build houses together." And they each worked and learned their trade, and by the time they were twenty-five, they had built their first house, and they're still building houses. They've built houses all over this county.

We've done very well, but we've worked hard for everything we have. My husband built our first house himself, with his own hands. Now we've got things easy. We've got a beautiful house. We own property all over the town. We've built developments all around here. My husband's retired and can take it easy. And our children: One son's a lawyer, a state assemblyman, the other is carrying on my husband's business, and our daughters are schoolteachers. We could never have done this in the old country. We came over here with nothing but our bare hands. We were dirt poor. This country gave us a chance to work and to get something out of our work and we worked hard for our children. And now they've got what we worked for. We're satisfied.

# Taro Murata

···················· FROM JAPAN, 1907 ·····················

*Tiny, slender, delicately boned, he has a wispy white forked beard and a shiny yellow pate, like a figure on a Japanese screen. His high-pitched voice is just barely audible. His even tinier wife serves Japanese tea and wafer-thin, almost flavorless cookies to the interviewer. Outside the living room of their Seattle house is a cherry tree, beneath the branches of which the old couple often sit to write their daily haiku poem.*

I came over at the age of nineteen on an immigrant boat from Japan, the *Saramara*. We had to pay sixty dollars for the fare. I had heard that the United States was a nice place to make money.

When I came over, Japan was very, very poor. People traveled around to beg for something to eat. Not on my farm where my parents lived, but around us. We ate all right, but we had no money.

The first job I got was on the railroad in the State of Washington. There were about two thousand Japanese working there at that time. Young boys, most of us. We called it a "gang," you know; a group of boys working on the railroad, building the road or laying the tracks or spreading the stones. Since I knew a little English, I interpreted between the foreman of the railroad company and the Japanese boys, to tell them what to do. I didn't speak too well, but I could understand a little bit. I worked for three years doing that. I worked nine hours a day—hard work—and I would earn about $1.25. After two years I got $90.00 a month from the railroad. We lived in a little car right on the railroad track and we cooked our own food—rice, vegetables, sometimes some meat. We paid one of the boys to cook it after a while, while the rest of us worked.

It was mostly immigrants, you know, working for the railroad—Japanese, Italian, and some other Europeans, Irish. Sometimes they agreed very good, but sometimes they fight, you know. We each like to live with our own people, because we could understand them better. Even in the camp or in the freight car that the railroad gave us, we stayed together most of the time.

I didn't spend much money and I saved. And after about three years I went back to Japan to marry. I didn't know my wife, but she was from the same town I was from, and my parents and her parents arranged it. When I brought my wife over I didn't want to work on the railroad anymore, so I got a job in Seattle with an export-import company—the Oriental Trading Company. It sold goods from Japan to suppliers in the United States. And I worked first as a stock boy, loading, unloading things, and later in the office. I saved my money and then, after three or four years, I decided to set up my own business—a dry cleaning business. We had two children by then and I thought it was better to have my own business. I worked long hours on that cleaning business and sometimes the fumes from the chemicals made me sick, but I liked having my own business. And my wife helped me and we made enough money to buy a little house and to educate our children. They both went to the university here.

I became what the government called a "leader in the Japanese community," because I arranged for a deal with the Teamsters Union for the Japanese stores and businesses in Seattle. You know Dave Beck? I don't know if you've heard of him, but he was head of the Teamsters here, a very powerful union. Nobody could drive a truck in Seattle if they weren't a member of the Teamsters Union. But we Japanese wanted to drive our own trucks for our little businesses, not hire someone else from outside. And so I worked out a deal with the Teamsters Union. Not with Dave Beck himself, but with his assistant, so that the Japanese could drive their own trucks, even though they weren't really members of the Teamsters Union, because they didn't let any Japanese into that union in those days. Because of the deal I worked out, I became well known in the community with all the businessmen, and the government knew my name, too. I thought that was good, but later on I had some bad luck because of it.

My daughter took a nursing degree and went to work in the hospital near here. But my son, he wasn't so lucky. He got a degree from the University of Washington in engineering, aeronautical engineering, and the year he got through, 1937, there were sixteen graduates in aeronautical engineering at the university. There was a tour arranged for them to go around the Boeing plant—that's a big plant, building aircraft here. It was big then, too. And the other fifteen all got hired by Boeing, but my son, he couldn't get hired because he was a Japanese. Even though he was born in America they wouldn't hire him to build aircraft, because there was a lot of suspicion of Japan in those days. This was shortly before World War II. My boy was very disappointed. All that study and he couldn't get a job. He didn't know what to do. His professor got him on for a while as an assistant at the university. But that wasn't permanent.

At that time the Japanese consul here knew there were a lot of Japanese boys all over America that couldn't get jobs, so he invited him and the other boys to go back to Japan and get a job. They paid their fare, everything. And they all went back to Japan. My son wasn't born there, of course, but he went back to my country where I was born and he got a job. He didn't want to go, but he couldn't help it; he needed a job. He got a job with a company that makes all kinds of airplanes over there. I didn't get any letters from him all through the war. I just knew he was working for the aircraft company and then that he was in the army, and that was all I knew. All those years.

You know about Japan and the United States and World War II. Pearl Harbor Day came. I could hardly believe it. I was shocked, deeply shocked. More than that—I thought, "They're crazy! Crazy!" You know, I couldn't believe it about Pearl Harbor. I was angry for the Japanese government to do this. Later that day, on December 7, the FBI came and picked me up. Right away I was picked up because I was one of the Japanese leaders of the community. They must have had our names on a list somewhere, and they picked us all up on the seventh of December. I couldn't even communicate with my wife for a while. We went to an internment camp. It's different from a relocation camp. Internment camp was for those who were under suspicion, like the leaders of the Japanese community, some Italians and Germans who were in this country, and other people who had relatives who were in countries that were at war with us. There were two things against me. One was my son in Japan, and the other was I was a leader of the community.

I couldn't go out. I couldn't go anywhere. There was barbed wire and they were watching with guns. Otherwise it was all right. They treated us all right. The Germans and Italians who were there were those living in the country who hadn't applied to be citizens. But, of course, at that time Japanese couldn't apply to be citizens. If you were born in Japan, you could never be naturalized. That's how it was in those days.

I finally got in touch with my wife and she went about trying to sell the business. It wasn't easy. She finally got so behind in the rent, she gave the real estate people the whole place for the back rent. It wasn't like when you sell a business and you get something for your customers and your good will. We just dropped it, left it. We lost the business. We lost the business. It was a little business; I don't say it was very good, but we lost that little bit that we had.

*Did you feel angry at the American government for this?*

No. Angry at the Japanese government for starting the war.

Later my wife had to go to a relocation camp and then later she could join me. We stayed in the camp until 1946, and then they began to let people go away.

While I was in camp I had plenty of food and plenty of time. I just couldn't step outside the barbed wire. I worked in a cleaning shop for the people inside the camp—about four hours a day. I had plenty of time. If I wanted to study, I could do it. I studied a lot of philosophy and all about the Japanese religion, too. And I started going to the Japanese Buddhist church. And I started writing haiku poetry.

When I came back after the war, I borrowed some money from some friends and started up the business again. I worked here until I retired.

After the war we brought my son back. I paid a lawyer and he got permission to come over to see us. We wanted him to stay, but he couldn't do it. He can't come back anymore, since he went over there and fought on the other side. That's what the lawyer said. So he stayed there and works for the same company. We have grandchildren over there and he has a Japanese wife. [*Sighs.*] They're very far away.

Two things I wanted to do when I first came: one was to study, because I didn't have enough money to study in Japan, and the other was to make money. When I came here I had to work, so I never went to the university, and I don't like to tell you, but I didn't make much money either. Just a little for myself and my wife to live on. Nothing extra, but we got no worry or anything.

Every morning my wife and I sit there [*points to cherry tree outside window*] and write haiku poetry together. I learned to do that in the internment camp.

One of Taro Murata's haiku poems:

*In the night snow falls*
*Upon the chrysanthemums.*
*Waking, I feel cold.*

# Gunnar Johanson
·························FROM ICELAND, 1905·······················

*Gray-eyed, deeply tanned, over ninety years old, he still works his*
*North Dakota farm.*

I was almost eighteen when I came here on June 14, 1905. I came from a little fishing village in Iceland, and there was nothing to do there but work on the sea and unload the ships. Most of the boys there wanted to go out on the ocean and fish, but my mother said no. She was afraid for me, you see, because my father and two brothers had been lost on the sea, and, well, she didn't think that was the kind of life she wanted me to go into. She was absolutely against me going to sea. Well, one thing added to another and she finally consented that I should go to this country. I didn't want to stay home. I wanted to go out and see the world.

I came alone, but there was another boy from Iceland that left when I did. We went to Liverpool first and had to wait for a few days for the ship to Quebec. That was how people came from Iceland in those days. I was all right when I got on the boat in Liverpool, but the trip over was rough and by the time we got to Quebec I was very sick. I had a fever of 102 degrees. Later I found out it was scarlet fever, but I didn't know that then. I must have caught it while I was in Liverpool, because it takes about ten days for the sickness to show. I didn't want to let them know at the port in Quebec that I was sick, because I was afraid they wouldn't let me land, so I walked past the Immigration man and tried to stop myself from shaking. We had to go to a hotel there overnight until the train was ready to leave, and when we went out to catch the train we found it had gone two hours before. So we had to wait in the station and it was cold there and wet. We had to wait all afternoon for the train. When we got on I hardly knew what I was doing. I went and layed down on the berth, and for two days, three days, I couldn't eat and hardly drink. The boy who came from Iceland with me gave me a little water. That was all I wanted.

We got to Winnipeg and went to stay one night with a woman my mother had known, a woman from the old country. And the next day we had to get the train to go to the United States. It had been raining for days and we had to walk knee-high through the water. I was shivering and shaking, so I hardly knew what I was doing. We got on the train and came down here and got off in Grand Forks, North Dakota.

My mother had written to a family we knew from the old country, and I was to go to be a hired man on their farm. It was a homestead they had taken out years before. The farmer met me at the station and took me to his house, but I was so sick by then I went right to sleep. His family and his children nursed me. They were good people. The daughter of the house, who was twelve then, took special care of me. I didn't notice her much then because I was sick and so young, but that's the girl I married when we both were older. They got a doctor out, Dr. Lax. He wasn't a real doctor; he was an Icelander who knew about medicines and things like that, and he gave me some pills and by and by I got better. All the children of the family came down with the sickness about ten days after I arrived there. Only the mother and father were well. They all got better in a few weeks.

I really was too weak to work on the farm that summer, but I helped a little, and in the fall I began to do a man's work—taking care of the horses, getting the hay. I helped build a barn there, too. I worked as a hired man for that farm for three years. He had three other men—boys, really—working on the place, and we all had to sleep in one bed. We slept crosswise with our feet sticking out. I was tall, so I used to put a chair by the bed to rest my feet on. When you worked as a hired man, the farmer furnished the room and board and washed clothes and everything. You lived there. I didn't need to worry about living or anything. The wages wasn't high, but I thought it was okay.

They treated the hired men like one of the family then. Nowadays they won't even feed the hired man! Now a hired man got to go into town and eat. Pretty near everyplace that's true. They just give them the money and tell them to go into town. And they don't even want them to sleep at night. Now they got to go down to the hotel. That's why you got to pay such an awful price for a man these days—three or four dollars an hour, you know. . . . Well, it was different then.

I had to get used to things on the farm, like working with a plow. Of course, I hadn't worked on a farm in Iceland, and there we had just had little patches anyhow and you just used a hoe, you didn't have a plow. And I didn't know how to milk cows, but I learned. The farmer showed me. It was a lot of work. We'd be walking, probably walk behind the plow all day. Twenty or twenty-two miles a day walking behind a plow. And we had to cut wood, of course.

It's kind of tough when you're young and you don't know the language. But it's lucky they were all Norwegians and Icelanders around here. There was hardly anything else in Grand Forks. There were Yankees. There were quite a few of them and they thought they were something, believe me, because they could talk English and we couldn't. They kind of ran the town, you know. But around here we're all Icelanders or Norwegians. It's like a little Scandinavian town. I didn't even have to talk English the first few years I was here. Not till I started working in the lumber camps.

After a while I thought I'd like more money, more cash to spend. I wanted to save up to get a farm of my own. So I decided to go lumbering. I worked in the woods for thirteen winters, cutting down trees and logging and chipping and all that. There's some hundred men working in the camps. You work all day, hard work. It's a rough life, you know, in the camps. You work all day and play cards every night until nine. Then the lights went out. First it was hot around the stove, then the stove would go out. Before morning you were pretty near frozen stiff, because there was nobody firing the stove. We had just a couple of boards to sleep on with some hay on them.

We didn't get to see women in those logging camps, not for four months; and they sure looked good when you got out of there. [Chuckles.] Yeah, we'd go to Minneapolis and the wages didn't last long there. Two or three days and you were broke and you had to go out again. You'd throw your money away. That's what you'd do, just throw it away. Have a drink, free drinks; you'd treat another guy, he'd treat you; pretty soon your money would be gone. Yeah, it's lots of fun, but you suffer afterwards, too.

I didn't save the money I thought I'd save. Year after year I'd spend it. I'd make it and spend it. But when I was thirty-six years old I'd had my fun and came back here and married this girl that had nursed me when I was a boy. We rented a farm then—two quarters of good land, good flat land. There was an old log house there; I fixed it up and right after we moved in we got a snowstorm for three days. The snow blew right in the room. We had one of them small wood stoves, you know, and we built a fire and we were warm. It was nothing because we were young, you know.

After we rented a few years, the family we rented from wanted the farm back, and we had a little money so we bought this place and I'm still farming it.

I work about five hours a day in the summer and spring, and I help with the harvesting, too. My son has the next farm and he helps me. He does the harrowing and the plowing and I work the cultivator. It's not much. You get up on the cultivator. You turn a lever, turn the wheel. The only problem is getting up on it, it's so high [indicates with his hands about five feet high] to the first step. But once I'm up on it, I'm all right. I have a mirror so I can see behind me. It's a little hard to turn around now for me. And I keep going. I do two hundred acres and do each one five times, so that's a thousand acres I cultivate. You see that pile of stones out there? I'm still getting stones out of the field. I put those on top this summer. It's easier to grow stones than it is to grow potatoes out here. [Laughs.]

We had five children out here and had some good times and some bad times. Lots of fun, lots of hard work. One year it snowed so high there were ten-foot drifts in the yard. You could walk straight into the loft over the snow. You couldn't see the barn door at all. And our last baby was born on Christmas Eve. The doctor came out and he said, "Well, you got a nice Christmas present," and that's my youngest boy, Fred. He's the one that lives on the next farm.

My wife died two years ago. She was in a rest home, a nursing home, for five years before that. I went on the bus to see her every day. Yeah [sighs], after all them years. Yes, she's dead now. I keep house for myself, make my coffee, keep the cookstove going. They say the first hundred years is the hardest. I've only got a little bit to go.

# Bridget Fitzgerald
···················· FROM IRELAND, 1921 ·····················

*Tiny, with tip-tilted nose and curly gray hair, she speaks in a breathless, high-spirited brogue, pounding the table frequently for emphasis. Widowed years ago and retired recently at seventy-five, she lives on Long Island with her only child, a married daughter. She spends her days looking after her grandson and "keeping everything spotless."*

My mother would've had about fourteen children, or fifteen, sixteen, maybe. There was ten that lived. Over there they have a flock of children, and the older one watches the next one, the next one watches the next one, and the next one watches the next one; that's how they do it. If the mother would have to wait on every one, well, what would it be like? The parents don't worry about one child. My mother used to take an old wooden tub—we didn't have a bathroom, you know—and she'd fill it up full of water and she'd throw three kids in it all at once and one washed the other. And that's how we washed. And then the next three kids would do it.

When we were children you got your own food; you went looking for it. If you didn't have it in the house, you went out on the farm and you got it. You had turnips, you had parsnips, you had parsley, you had scallions, you had lettuce. So we'd eat the turnips, get a trout with a pin and a piece of thread, build a fire, get a potato, roast potatoes, cook a fish, eat raw turnips, and anything we'd eat came out of the ground. There was no canned goods.

We had our own sheep. We'd clip the sheep and take the wool off them, you know, and then we'd card it and roll it and we'd spin it. You learned from your mother and the people around you. We learned to card and spin. The older people, they knew all about the dyes, and we'd go and gather the crottles [a kind of moss used for dying woolens]. I don't know what you call them here. They were round and you'd scrape them off a rock or stone. And you'd get them different colors and boil them down. You'd boil them down in pots. We used water from the river. Then we'd put in the shanks of wool and tie them and dip this one brown and the other one green and whatever colors we wanted. If we wanted to leave it the natural color, we would leave it that way. We'd send it to the weaver and she'd make blankets out of it.

My mother baked all the bread. She cooked over a fireplace, open hearth, in a big pot with a crane on it. Burned turf. We took to the bogs and dug it up. You'd dig with a two-cornered spade and you put it down on the ground and you throw it up. And you let it dry a little bit, and then, when it's been about two weeks laying there, you go and turn it over. When you turn it over and you dry it some more, then you stack it. It makes a beautiful fire, beautiful. [*Deep soft whisper.*] Beautiful. It smells wonderful.

We used to pull flax. You pull it out of the ground and you tie it in bundles. And they have a place where you soak it till it gets good and rotten in water, and you weight it down with stone. Then pull it up on the riverbank and dry it. And the kids all go out and gather it up and bundle it. And they ship it to England and England doesn't give you anything for it.

Yeah, England didn't do anything for Ireland. They took everything away from the Irish and give the Irish nothing. If you were a Roman Catholic you didn't stand a chance in Ireland. There were no Catholic schools, but they had Protestant schools and good teachers and seven or eight children going to school and two teachers. That's how it was. I think the British were afraid to educate the Irish.

It was up to the Catholics themselves to get an education. What could they do? I went to school three years and that's about it. Some education. I didn't realize it then, but now I know. I didn't have the mind to think about those things when I was young. If I had, God knows what I would be today. I'd be a rebel of some kind.

I remember the troubles in Ireland. The Black and Tan come into every house and tore the beds apart and pulled the kids out of bed and ripped up everything looking for guns and ammunition. We had plenty of guns and ammunition, plenty of it. Well, my father was a hunter. He needed those guns for food, you know. They would've taken everything. They didn't get them, though. They didn't get anything. We hid them under the big, long kitchen table. Underneath, it was double boarded. Some was there. The rest was sunk, buried in the garden. Those Black and Tans, they were English, out of the slums of London. All jailbirds. And the English turned them loose on the Irish.

We lived with my grandfather and he had a farm, and while he was living that was fine. We had plenty of everything. But once he went, everything went. The government seized part of our farm for back taxes then. And a woman bought up the rest of it, and it left us in a hole. We all went to work. I was nine. I hired out on a farm, herding cows, doing that kind of work. I had to live with the family.

*How was it? Were you lonely?*

Yeah. Don't make me think of that. [*Heavy silence.*] . . . There was nothing in Ireland. Thanks be to God I got away from it. There's nothing there. My mother's biggest mistake was that she never came over here. It was the biggest mistake she made in her life.

When I was eighteen, going on nineteen, I came over here. It was something everybody was doing. I wasn't the only one. There was hundreds and hundreds of people coming here. You know what you needed then, mostly? I'll tell you. Strong and healthy, that you won't become a public charge, because then, I mean, you go right back.

As soon as I landed, I went to an agency where they had special jobs. You get in with the people that had all the money and pay you better money, pay you better salary. They sent me to this job—it was a big estate out in the country and it was all for one woman. It was one of the great families. I shouldn't say the name. She had fifty people working for her—parlor maids, chefs, cooks, personal maids, two chauffeurs, two footmen in the pantry. There were so many of them. The laundress was Irish. The rest were everything else; everything, from all over the world. Lots of English. The butler was English. The footmen were English, but the housekeeper was Irish like me.

I was a "useful girl." You work one day a week in each department—with the butler, the parlor maid, the chamber maid, the personal maid, the footman, and you learn everything. It's good for you. You watch, you use your head. You pick it up—how to set a table, how to arrange fruit, how to arrange flowers, how to polish fruit, how to set a banquet table. Everything's got to be just so. You have to know how to set your wine glasses, your water glasses, different kinds of glasses. If you're going to serve fish, you got to know where your fish fork goes, where your salad fork goes, where your butter plate goes, your bread plate goes, your napkin goes. You have to make beds their way and dust their way. Lay out clothes, fix stockings. You never had to polish silver or anything like that. You didn't have to; they had buffers, machines. It was all done by machinery. My God Almighty, these two rooms wouldn't hold the silver service. They had buffing machines for all that.

I had my own bedroom, servants' quarters—a bathroom to each two girls. They'd give you a clean uniform every day. At night there were men who took your uniform and the next day you had a clean one. They worked nights doing the heavy laundry. They had pressers, steam pressers. You took your buttons off, little brass buttons, and you put them on the next day. I wore a plain white uniform, all white—no cap. The parlor maid wore a cap, but I had my hair cut straight, bangs and straight; that was the style.

There were three cooks for the servants. Servants all ate together in a large dining room. The food was out of this world. You'd get roast beef, chicken, fish, fresh corn. It was a long table with chairs and everybody helped themselves. And you cleaned your plate off and put it back on the side, and they had help that took those plates away and washed them. You didn't do it, you know.

I'd have off from two to five and then I'd go back to work. And a half-day off in the whole week. That's all anybody got. You could go out between two and five, if you wanted to go out, but it was in the country. You could do whatever you wanted to at that time—go to bed, go to church. There was a chauffeur to drive you to church if you wanted to. They supplied cars for you. You'd be surprised how nice those people can be to you. You would never know that they had money. They treat you like a human being. Never look down on you as though you're beneath them.

Once a year they threw a party for the help. It was a servants' ball. They hired an outside hall. They didn't take it into the house. More than a hundred people would come. The help from different estates all came. You'd dance, you'd eat, you'd sing. It's just like a party for young people and old people. It was beautiful.

In the winter we'd go to the house in New York on the East Side. Then, on my day off, I used to go to the park and walk around. Sometimes we'd meet friends, go to a dance, go to Coney Island, go to Rockaway. That's how I met my husband, at a party. . . .

I was left a widow when my daughter was five years and nine months old. I made it, though. I went to work in a hotel as a linen-room repairer; you know, repairing draperies and slipcovers and stuff like that. It was hard, working all day and coming home and doing everything. I'd sit up till two in the morning, sewing, making my daughter's clothes. I didn't think anything of it. What the hell? It's a living and you have some self-respect and pride. You know what? Let's face it. Some people don't want to work. They're plain lazy. It's no shame to be poor, you know, but it's a shame to be lazy. That's why I say a lot of these women in New York, they sit around, they say they can't have a job. They're big, strong, healthy. They don't want to work. But I was never out of work a day in my life. My God, there's plenty of cleaning jobs at night in office buildings that they could do. You know what I would do with the home reliefers or welfare clients that are in New York, if I would have anything to do with it? I'd gather them all up and I'd go down and get a thousand brooms and hand each one a broom and say, "Go out and brush the streets. You get off your fanny." That's what I'd do.

I've worked all my life. I'm still working. I like to work. I like to work around the house. I don't like to sit around. That's what's troubling me now. My daughter's going to do the oven. She won't let me do it. She won't let me do this, she won't let me do that. If I do the bathroom, she yells, "No, you're not going to do it. You're not going to do it. People'll think we treat you bad."

# Elizabeth Dolan

*She came to the United States at the age of sixteen and went to work as a nursemaid.*

I lived with the family, with a doctor in the Back Bay, an old Boston family. They used to have a lot of help at that time. There was a cook and a chambermaid and a waitress and chauffeur. There were two children, and I just had to feed them, you know, see that they eat, and take them out walking and in the carriage, the little one. I think I must be there about two years, and then I took up cooking. I wanted to know how to cook, so's I could be able to cook for the children. Sometimes you have to, you know. I went to night school special, and I liked it very much. I learned a lot. So then I used to cook for the children, and if the other cook be gone, out for the day, I'd take over. Yeah, I did. I liked it very much.

Then I got a better job. I went to work for the Worthinghams, one of the ten oldest Yankee Brahmin families in Boston. I remember when Mrs. Worthingham died, there was two columns in the *Globe*. She was a millionairess. She was on Commonwealth Avenue. It was directly across from the Ritz Carlton. She had a cook, which was me. She had a kitchen maid; she had a parlor maid; a butler, which was English right from England; a chambermaid; a lady's maid that used to travel with her on her trips; a laundress; and Stanley, the chauffeur. And she had three Rolls Royces.

We always went in the back door. You didn't think you were going up to that big iron front door, did you? Mercy on us! I remember one time I had two operations, and I wasn't allowed to come out, by doctor's orders, to do any cooking for a certain number of weeks. And Mrs. Worthingham, wealthy as she was, came up to me one day and told me, "Well, now, you should be well enough to be able to work." I resented it, because I wasn't.

And I also resented the fact that Mrs. Worthingham came to me and said, "I do not want you to buy"—I did the ordering—"to buy any roast beef for the help. They don't need roast beef. You can buy other things, but not roast beef." And I said, "The people today have to have roast beef. It's a must, at least once a week, for the blood." Mrs. Worthingham and me had quite some words over it, but, you know, I won out, and I ordered that roast beef once a week for the help. If it was good enough for her, it should be good enough for the help that was doing the work for her.

# Katherine O'Hara

*Small, vivacious, with bright eyes, she lives alone in a small New England town and cares for her tiny home and garden by herself. She still goes out to clean houses several days a week.*

I wanted my mother to be happy. I used to say to her as a little girl, "You don't have to worry now, because when I grow big, I'm going to America and I'm going to make plenty of money and I'm going to send it home to you. You're going to have everything, mamma." It seems so strange that it came to pass.

It was during the time that there was all those bills coming in, due to the fact of my mother's illness; because there was so much to be done—hospitals and taking care of her. She was ill a long time, and it was very, very sad. You'd see the automobile come rushing down the street, and you'd see that it was the sheriff in there. I knew what was coming. The sheriff was coming to the house, and the bailiffs was coming all the time, and he would have to be telling the boys to go and get whatever remaining cattle was on the farm, because they would seize them for the money that was owed. And we needed those. We needed to eat. I think it more or less left me scared to death, seeing it, you know. And I'd always think, "I'm really going to go to America and I'm going to make a lot of money and I'm going to send it home."

Then we had a foot-and-mouth disease and all the stock died. We had a lot of land and we had a lot of horses and a lot of sheep, and I used to go horseback riding to count them. And one day I went over and they were all dead, the cattle. I can still see them. They were lying down, and they had gotten near the brook, and as soon as they tasted the water, they had died. It was a very severe loss. My mother was living at the time. It was a big blow to us. Hard luck came in more ways than one.

There were seven of us, and we were all home when my mother passed away in 1926 at the age of thirty-nine. She left all of us very young. My sister was very young, I was young. I had one brother older than me. I was very, very sad, because I was crazy about my mother.

She was so young and she was so good. I mean I idolized her, and I just couldn't take it. I used to pray every day for her to live and not to die. To this day I miss my mother. I always claimed I never wanted my daughter to be as close to me as I was to her. I prayed when I was carrying my daughter that she would never have the feeling for me that I had for my mother. I'd never let myself get that close to my daughter, and I never was. It hurt—don't think it didn't. But when I'm gone, I don't want her to feel the way I did about my mother. [*Cries.*]

My father really should have been a priest. He wasn't happy with a family and a farm or a business. He wasn't meant for that type of life. He never adjusted, being a farmer. He had been a well-educated man. He was educated for nine years in the seminary. He was about to become a priest, and the last six months there was a change of mind. He never told anyone why. That was a secret he carried to his grave. And then he started business after that. He had a grocery store and a liquor store combined. That's where he married my mother, and then after that they moved out to the country, to the farm. He had a farm, a nice estate, but he was a man that was never cut out for farming. He struggled along as best he could, and then he got into a lot of debt when we had a depression, and everything went down. And then there was my mother's illness. When she passed away, I was around fifteen.

Then, when I was eighteen, my father decided I'd have to come to America—I had an aunt out here—to work, help out with money that was owed, so he wouldn't lose the home. I was thrilled. I didn't want any more of the sheriffs.

I arrived in Boston on May 8, 1930. My aunt was not at the pier to meet me. The immigration authorities took over. They were very kind. They asked me how much money I had to pay for a taxi, and I told them—I had learned the money on board the ship coming over. They took me to Commonwealth Avenue, where my aunt worked as a cook for a millionaire family. When we got there, the caretaker said that my aunt had moved on to the summer residence, but she had arranged for me to stay in a rooming house.

The next week I went into an employment agency, by the name of Mrs. Benson, on Berkeley Street in Boston, and I got a job with a society lady in Brookline. There was nine on the staff, and I was a parlor maid. I waited on table. It was a very nice job and a lovely lady. She gave me twelve dollars a week, but it wasn't enough for the demands my father had put on me. In September I left. When I was leaving her, she gave me a five-dollar gold piece for good luck.

I went back to Mrs. Benson's office. A lady by the name of Mrs. Elliot had interviewed four girls for a position, and I saw the lady and I liked her from the start. Mrs. Elliot and I sat down, we discussed everything, and she hired me right there for sixteen dollars a week. She had a big house in Westwood and she had a cook. And there was another girl there, a laundress. I took care of the children. I bathed them, gave them their breakfast, got them ready for the school, and the lady took them to school—drove them by car. It was the time of the Lindbergh kidnapping, you may remember.

In my own heart, I didn't like being a servant, but I never showed it. As far as working, as far as wages, everything was what I expected. But as far as my own life and my own feeling, no. I resented the fact that I had to work the way I did under somebody else. I always felt the jobs I had was inferior to what I had home. But I expected to be able to pay off all my father's debts. That was all I was interested in. As far as myself was concerned, I didn't care.

For two solid years I sent money home. I never bought a stitch of clothes. I used what I had when I came over. I bought nothing.

My father wrote to me when I was five years in America. He told me that now everything was paid and everything was fine and I was to return home. He had a man over there, and he would like me to settle down and get married. I refused to go. I said I was not going home. I had no desire to go back. My mother was gone, and I certainly wasn't going to go to my father to pick out someone for me. I had common sense enough for that. He never wrote to me for two years, my father. After a couple of years, he softened up and he wrote to me.

Then I met my husband. He was French-Canadian—very tall, dark, handsome—and I fell in love with him, or thought I did. Well, he was an unfortunate man. His parents, his family, always liked liquor, and he was trying so hard to keep away from it. It didn't work. I stayed married to him for eleven years, and I got very ill over it. We were living in Boston proper. I did everything to keep that marriage, but when my little girl was six years old, I went to the German church, to Father Kugler, and he told me to go ahead and get a divorce. He says there was only one drawback: If I ever met someone, I might want to remarry again, I could not be married in the Catholic Church, which I understood. So I went ahead and got the divorce. There was no alternative.

I didn't have any problems with the Church. I went to Mass, I received Communion, although I was divorced, because I was not remarried. But then after that I met a very nice man and I remarried. Then I did not go to church, and I did not receive Communion. I only went Christmas or something. I missed my church. I always knew I would, but even though I missed it, I always knew I wasn't doing anyone harm. My daughter was brought up a Catholic. And then I went back to the Church. When my second husband died, I went back. . . .

I went back to Ireland three years ago, for the first time. I went down to County Wicklow, where the old homestead was. That was a sad entrance for me. I found it very severe to go in there. That's where my mother died. My brother is still living there. I felt sorry to see my brother on the farm. I thought it was severe, cold, hard work. It was not an easy life. They don't feel that same way, but I was writing a letter to my niece the other day, and I was saying, "I'm so glad because one of my brother's children is going on to be accepted in Dublin for some kind of a good position." I said to her, "I'm so happy, because I feel the farm is so severe." I don't know why.

# Michael Kinney

···················· FROM IRELAND, 1930 ·····················

*He retired three years ago, after working thirty-five years in the same steel mill. Now he's happy with his free-pass trip on the bus and says proudly, "I can get on the bus at nine and ride till four in the day, and it don't cost me nothing." He spends his time "playing around in the yard and going down and get a beer and a shot and come home." He has a daughter who is a schoolteacher and a son who went into electronics. Both have left Pittsburgh.*

I was raised on a farm in County Kerry. Well, you were never finished. There was no such a thing as six hours or seven hours or eight hours. You got up in the morning, you start working, you kept working until it got dark, I guess. You had to milk the cows, feed the pigs, feed the chickens, the hogs. We worked every day there—Saturday, Sunday, Monday, Tuesday, Wednesday. . . .

They were making better here than there, so I come out in 1930. That was the time of the Depression, too. It was hard to get a job. I come by boat, and I come right here to Pittsburgh, because that's where my brother and sister were, and I had aunts and uncles here. Stayed with my aunt. And if I had the money at the time, after a couple of weeks, I'd go back home again. I was very lonesome. I was all right until the evening come, and oh, my God, I used to long for that home. I used to cry, I may as well tell you. We used to dance at the crossroads at home and go out every night and have a good time. And it's a whole year to get to know anybody here. Yeah, I was very lonely for a whole year, but then I settled down.

Everything surprised me. Everything was different. Different food— well, it's not the food alone. Back there we never used to ride, we always walked. We never went to ride a bus—we were lucky we had a bicycle. And I had to get used to the electric lights. I was always trying to blow that light out when I came here. And no gas and no water on the farm. You went outside and brought water in. The fire was there and everything was cooking. We used to cook a big pot of potatoes, you know. We used to eat five or six potatoes at home. And I seen my aunt here cooking a couple of little potatoes, and I thought to myself, "Why is she cooking them couple of potatoes? That's all they eat here, one or two potatoes?" But I got more to eat here than I got back there, you know.

I said that the first year I come out here, if I had enough money to go back, I would go back. I guess because I was very lonesome. Work was very bad at that time. I worked for six months and then I got laid off again. And then I was getting one day a week, and I was getting two days maybe one week, and another week I wouldn't get no day at all. Sometimes maybe I didn't make enough money to pay my board, but I was staying with my aunt. Maybe sometimes I would be hungry if nobody belonged to me in this country. I seen the bread line down at Father Cox's.

The first job I got was warehouse work. Remember when P. H. Butler stores were here? There was a warehouse down at Seventeenth and Penn, by St. Patrick's Church. That's the first job I had, unloading cars and loading trucks. I went down there, and there was a lot of people down there looking for work at that time. That was '30. And the boss had come out and he said, "No, nothing doing." I went down there for a whole week. "Nothing doing. Nothing doing." And this morning when he come out and said the same thing, he did like that to me [*beckons*] and he called me over and he says, "You've got an old country suit."

I says, "Yes, I do, and that's the only one I have."

"When did you come over?"

"Two weeks ago."

"Well," he said, "don't spend no more carfare coming down here. You'll be the first man to get a job here, if there's an opening. Give me your telephone number."

And two days after, I got the job. He was an Irishman himself.

So I worked there till '36. I got laid off, and then I worked out on Second Avenue. I worked eleven months in that strip mill down there, they were building at that time, 1936. Went to work at seven in the evening and worked till seven in the morning, and I got forty-five cents an hour. Laborer, drilling and concrete work, digging ditches and everything. And then they finished and I got laid off and I went over to Homestead [another steel mill] and I got a job there and I stayed there until I went on pension.

I done all right. I never got fired on any job and I never had no trouble with no boss ever. I put in thirty-five years; I was never laid off at Homestead. Sometimes the place I worked used to shut down, but I used to get moved around. Used to have a labor pool, and I worked general labor, brick gang, different places. I done a lot of different ones. Started out as a laborer, went third-helping, went second-helping, part-time first-helper, and on down.

Well, when I started at first—the first day I started in the mill—they put me down the hot flues, you know, underneath the furnace. Cleaning the flue dust out of the furnaces. They got trenches about this wide, and you crawl back in them. I had to get a pair of safety shoes and a pair of gloves. They put me down underneath the furnace, and I was ready to die down there. Thought I'd never come up out of there. It was like being in hell. [*Chuckles.*] Well, I went to the labor shanty. I wanted my money, I wanted to quit. He said, "I'll give you a nice job tomorrow." So he put me on the outside working, and I stayed there. I was unloading cars—manganese, silicon, aluminum, all that stuff. . . .

I was only married about a year, and they wanted to put me to the war at that time. I was working one day, and the boss told me to go on such a job, and I told him, "No, because I'm going to the army next week." So he says to me, "Are you married?" and I said, "Yes." He said, "You got a kid?" and I said, "Yeah, I got one kid." So he asked me what board I belonged to and he didn't say any more, just, "Go on the job, and I'll see you later on."

I was downtown at the post office for my examination and everybody was called, their name, they had a roll call. Everybody was called, and I'm sitting there, and he said, "What are you waiting for?" I said, "I'm waiting." He said, "I got nothing for you." I showed him the letter, and he said, "Oh, you got to be examined, too." They finally asked me what board I belonged to, and I told them I belonged to Number 10 out in Morningside, and they called up and they said I had a deferment. My boss put me in another job. This job he put me in, that called for a deferment at that time. He went up to the draft board and he got me deferred. The mill had claimed the deferment, but nobody told me. So he said, "Did you claim a deferment?" I said, "I didn't claim nothing." He said, "You got one; go on home." So the next day I went to work and they asked me how did I make out. I said, "I don't know. They told me to go home."

Then I got up to third-helping in the furnace. Third-helping ain't bad. You help in the furnace where they make the steel. They called us *slaggers.* The heat is coming out of the furnace, throwing stuff into it. Hot! Anything you do on the open hearth is hot. Third-helper—whatever is supposed to go into the steel after they tap it out, you have to throw it in there. They put aluminum in, they put silicon in. Fifty pounds, most of them are. You have to stand from here to there and throw it in.

Then I got a job second-helping. Second-helping gets everything up for the heat, and the first-helping—well, the first-helper, he runs the furnace. Second-helper's pretty rough, hot. He has to dig them heats out, open up them topping holes, and go back there and let that steel out of that furnace. Goes back and opens up that hole, digs it out with a big mask, big asbestos coat, pants up to there, gloves up to here. The second-helper puts the dynamite in, then another foreman shoots it. They didn't have that one time. You had to burn them out with oxidant. They used to have oxidant in pipes, and you had to stick a pipe and burn it out. Sometimes they blow out and blow you off the platform. A lot of people got burned. Oh, I had lots—on my back—but not any bad ones. No, I never had no bad ones.

Off and on I was first-helping. Sometimes I used to get bumped back and some of the furnaces shut down, and then you got bumped back again, and then you go back up again. Everybody has his own furnace, second-helping and first-helping. The third-helper, you helped them all. You go from furnace to furnace. But the first-helper and the second-helper, they stay at their own furnace at all times. No matter how big the furnace is, there's only three men in it.

We worked hard. We had hard days and we had easy days. We worked hard. And some nights we went to work and we slept. It depends on how the work was coming in. Depends on how the furnaces were tapping, and this and that. Sometimes you might get five or six heats; and sometimes you get two, you were finished. Well, maybe you get five or six furnaces, you be busy all night. There's three or four hundred ton of steel in a heat.

What about when they used to tear a furnace down? You had to go in there, and a mask over your head and hand leathers and burlap sacks and wooden shoes. You'd go in and catch two or three hot chips and throw them out, and you run out. Hot! [*Chuckles.*] You could only stay in there three minutes and run out. They used to pass out and they used to take them to the hospital with the heat. Salt tablets, and they tell you not to drink too much water.

And I seen a lot of people getting hurt in the mill. A lot of people getting killed in the mill, too. I seen an explosion. A couple of pits blow up. And there was a bulldozer, and I seen a man blowed out of it and his foot taken off. A crane man, and the crane blowed up on him one day.

That don't happen now. At that time, they used to put water in them pits, you know. You ain't allowed to use no water now. You see, when that water gets in that slag and that water stays underneath that slag and you touch that slag, that thing blows up. Everybody be round the day after and making safety rules, this and that. But they done away with the water, and that saved a lot.

Everything has changed at the mill since. A lot they were doing by hand at that time is done by machinery now, you know that. They don't work as hard now as they did at that time. Everything was shovel; they have machines for doing it now. They bank the doors of the furnaces now by machine. At that time we banked them by hand with a shovel, bank the back wall up by hand. Now they have a machine shoots that stuff back on the back wall. Yeah, a lot of improvements. It's a lot easier, but still there's a lot of pressure. I guess they're going faster—hurry up, hurry up, hurry up! There's more hurry up now, I guess, than there used to be when I worked there. Hurry, hurry, hurry, hurry. I guess they want to break a record.

If you do your work, they don't bother you. But there's some people, you can't ever please them. Some people joined the union; they thought they wouldn't have to work at all then, because the union was in back of them. Grievance, grievance, grievance. Well, you got to do your work regardless whether you are in the union or not, you know. I went through a lot of strikes. We went a hundred and some days one time. In 1959, a hundred and sixteen days. We were on strike in 1946—remember the winter of '46? In '49 they were on strike and in '64. Yeah, I was in a lot of strikes there.

The first strike I went out on picket, but after that I didn't go picketing anymore. There was no need of doing it. There was nobody going to work anyway. They kept some of the bosses in there, supervisors looking after the mill, that's all. Nobody wanted to go in anyway. So I went around trying to get another job, that's what I did. In 1956 Dave took us all out, just so we would know how to go out. David MacDonald did that, just so the men could get the feeling of it and know what it was to go on strike. During the Korean War, in 1952, we were in and out a couple of times, when Harry Truman took over the mills. In and out. You were in one week and out the next week, and there was a Supreme Court decision. I was glad anybody tell me to go back to work; because if I had a vote in it, I wouldn't vote at any time to go on strike. I don't think I would. I think what the company offer you, you just as well take it, as you go back in the end with almost the same thing anyway. What's the use going on strike? It's like seventeen cents an hour more and you wanted eighteen and a half, so you were out for six weeks and then you end up getting the eighteen and a half.

I finished up on the night shift. You had one daylight, one afternoon, and one night—no matter if you stayed till it be a hundred years—every third week, a week at a time. So I finished up, and I was even on nighttime when I finished up, too. I only worked four hours that night. They told me to go down the washroom and sleep.

Everybody in the mill says, "I'll see that my kids won't work here." But they're all going in there, though. They're glad to get the job. Well, I thought it was as good as any other place. I had no other trade, and I don't think I could make it better any other place. I got something.

They paid me. They paid me what was coming to me. They didn't cheat me out of nothing that I know of. I ain't sorry for staying there. I guess I done as good as any other place, that's what I say.

# Sophie Zurowski
······················ FROM POLAND, 1895 ······················

*A widow, 109 years old, she lives in a nursing home in Gary, Indiana.*

My husband worked in the steel mill all his life. Hard work. He was working hard. None of my boys ever went to work in the steel mill. The one that got to be a druggist, when he was going to college he went to work over there to make a little money, and he said, "Daddy, I don't know how you could stand that place!" My husband said, "Well, I could stand it. If you want to make a living, you have to stand it."

# Steve Madich
······················ FROM YUGOSLAVIA, 1910 ······················

*He was still working underground, loading coal, when he retired at sixty. Now eighty-six, still tall and straight, he lives alone in a small mining town in western Pennsylvania, in an immaculate apartment, which he cares for himself. Once a year, on the last Friday in July, he attends the Serbian Day picnic in a nearby city, where he participates in the games, eats barbecued lamb, and talks to relatives and old friends he hasn't seen since the last Serbian Day celebration.*

That time, 1910, there was talk about America—making big money and things like that. So I thought maybe I'm going like the other guys to make some money. But they never tell the truth—what they had to do to make a few dollars, how they had to suffer to make a dollar here.

I was seventeen years old when I left. There was about four, five different men from same village. We went in a group. Well, I come in New York and first thing they took us on that island to examine whether we got enough money to come, where we want to go, and things like that. They give us a package for food, to come from New York to Duquesne, Pennsylvania. That goes with the ticket. Everything was included, right up to Pennsylvania.

My first thing was to try find a job and work. That was a mining town, and the people from my village was working in the mine. So they come and they took me and I went to work in the mine. For a while, I didn't make very much. I was loading ton of coal for fifty cents. That's all I did. I load the coal in the mine, I load it in the car, and it's got my check on it. That means that they know who load it, see. The car takes it outside, and they dump it on a two-inch screen. What goes through the screen, goes for nothing. That was for the company. And what's left on the screen, I get paid for. For a while I didn't load very much coal. I been making maybe around three dollar in ten hours a day.

First I work with a man that was work in the mines before. A greenhorn works only ten days with a man, and he learn how to work. Then after that they don't bother me. I don't have no boss. I begin to learn English. I learn with the guy that I work with—sometimes Polish or Slovak—everything was Chinese to me at the first. But I learn. I was young man and I learn.

At that time, 1910 or 1911, was a strike in Westmoreland County. I noticed that they been picketing, so I left, because I didn't want to interfere with nobody. I went in South Bend, Indiana, and got a job for Studebaker. I work in the shipping department, loading them buggies and wagons—they was the brewery wagons, you know—in the boxcars. I was there one year, and then the strike was over. I come back in coal mine, but I didn't come back in the same place. They never got the union; they lost. So I come in union mine in Ohio.

I was in Ohio a long time. I was in West Virginia, too. Well, there's always some reason to change job—either better money or better union. Here is a local union better, and there is a not so good one, you know. Depends on the people. I come back in Pennsylvania again, because the union was going all over.

I became a good miner. I used to load ten ton on the average. It was hard work, all right. After that I learned to fix the place up with the timber. They used to call me "timber man." I had the timber-man job for a long time in the coal mine. It was a better job, but it was real dangerous. I have to go where nobody else goes. I have to be the first one to go in, because I have to fix the place for the other people. I didn't worry about the danger, because I learn to know what's going on. I know what I look for. I know what I'm doing. It was dangerous, but you have to be careful. You have to know what you're doing so you don't get hurt.

Well, you have to watch. If you're not watching, you'll get hurt. To tell you the truth, I wasn't so greedy. You know, you load the coal and you want to load that car regardless what's up there. The drivers come with the mules to pull the car out. If you load it with a full load, they pull it out. If you don't load it, they miss you. So certain people they got slag loose up above, but they want to load that car. That means they are greedy. They want to make more money. Well, me, I was never like that. When I see the loose slag up there, I pull it down whether I lose car or not. After I clean that up, then I load.

Only one time I lost one week work. I used a pick and I hit something on the bottom—one of them sulfur spots—and the sparks come up in my eye. That was after 1913, when the compensation pay comes in. Before you wouldn't get it.

I happen to participate in that fight. I went to march in Washington to pass that law. United Mine Workers, they had to send the people, so that's what I was representing. I was not just a follower, I was instigator, too—very active. I had the leading position in the local and things like that. In the National Miners Union, I was sort of a board member, but I never had no salary from union. I participate in every strike we had since 1914 to 1933.

The coal operator was so strong. They had the government in their favor, and they tried to break union. They did break it in western Pennsylvania. Yeah, we was broken—little by little, one by one, in 1927 and 1928. I had twenty-two months on strike. That's the time we lost. I was blacklisted, too. Well, I'd been a bad boy, I guess. Yeah, that was terrible. But we never slowed down. If we lost, we fight harder.

Until 1933, when Roosevelt got elected and Senator Wagner passed a bill to have a right to organize; and even after 1933, after Roosevelt was elected, we still have to go on a strike and give up National Miners Union and join Beck's United Mine Workers. And we fight on three front. We fighting the government and we fighting coal operators and we fighting our union administration. We was inside, but we was fighting John L. Lewis and his clique. The union wasn't improving. Every time they make a contract, they make a contract that don't satisfy us. They selling us out—all the big fellows. They don't like me, because I fight them.

Well, I was anxious to fight for anything, for something better. That was my idea. I dedicated my life to that purpose, to fight for something better—for everybody, not just for myself. I don't regret; because after I retire now I get paid for it. Right now I'm getting over six hundred dollars a month. Well, I got union pension, then I got Social Security pension, then I got the black lung benefit. I fight for all them things.

# George Palochek

*He has been retired for eighteen years and now spends his time gardening and making end tables with elaborately carved designs. His work shed in the back yard includes a soft armchair, a sink, and a small refrigerator filled with soft drinks. The walls are covered with family photographs. Through the open door can be seen a fence hung with strings of garlic and the twelve hundred Bermuda onions he has planted this year.*

I was getting on to start sixteen years old, and then you can't get no passport to United States, because Franz Joseph [Czechoslovakia was then part of the Austro-Hungarian Empire] taked you in the army. I wrote to my sister in Pennsylvania and she send me hundred dollars American money. My mother, she sew them in the pants. And me and my brother-in-law, we start. We start walking—from Hungarian country to Hamburg, Germany—one month. We walk till we got tired, sit down little bit, and walk again. It's a long way. A lot of people, they knew where we going, they said, "Come on," and they give us break, milk. We had lots of cooties and itching and everything. [*Laughs.*]

I came in February 1912 and I start work in the mine, and in March I was seventeen years old. I helped the track man, laying tracks for the wagons. Then I worked on the cutting machine, drill machine. I worked any kind of job except bossing. I wasn't bossing.

Yeah, $2.15 for ten hours, and they take seven cents off for lamp. You have to buy your own tools, too. I left house five o'clock, I come home five o'clock. Them days you had to walk where you going to start to work. You had to start six o'clock work and work ten hours. And two hours on the road—one going in, one coming out. And a lot of them working on Sunday. You get no double time or overtime, you don't get time-a-half, nothing. They didn't know nothing about that. You just get the same thing. Well, I work lots of Sundays. Those two dollars, big dollar bills, so. . . .

There was no kind of safety in the mine them days. You kidding? A cave-in—after they take the coal out, you have to pull the posts out. You have to know whenever it's "boom, boom" you hear, that's a fall going to come. Them posts start cracking, you go. Oh, yes, you get warning. But I see them take out lots of good guys—young fellows died. If you kill a mule, you got fired. But if you kill a man, nothing. Because they had to buy a mule. They don't have to buy a man. They bring the body in the house and don't pay you nothing; never even buy flowers. What the heck, I was lucky I got a job, and that's it.

I worked five years in the mine, and then I was twenty-two, I enlisted in the army. War broke out April the seventh, so I enlist in May. I said, "I live in this country, I'm going in the army." Two years I was in the army, and I was a corporal. War was over 1918, and they want me reenlist. "No," I said, "I think I go back in the coal mine."

When I come from army, in the mine was $7.50 instead of $2.15. No union yet. Union didn't start till, I think, after '22, around there. I become good miner. I began to monkey with the machines. I run a chain machine, and I have to drill holes. I have to fix the track for cars coming in and load the coal. All that I have to do. Well, it was hard work all right.

I was twenty-four; I had one friend I know from the old country, and he said, "How about getting married? I know a good girl." I never seen her before, never know her before. She look okay—young kid, seventeen years old. I went and got the license and everything. Then we went to priest, sign everything, then wait three weeks. When we got married, I said, "Let's go home, because tomorrow work." I don't want to miss work for a woman! It worked out all right, I guess. Oh, heck, fifty-eight years since she hooked me!

I was working under Black Rock Coal Company and there was a strike—1927, '28. They want to break the union, and they hire maybe twenty cops from Philadelphia, you know, to watch. You couldn't say nothing about the union. I know a good many of them; they was scabbing here. I seen *this* guy come in a boxcar, *that* guy come in a boxcar. They said, "Come on over here." I said, "I'll starve and the whole family before I'll go scabbing." I wouldn't go. No, I don't want to get killed. I waited—I'll bet one year that I didn't work. I went to haul moonshine, sell it. My kids was never on relief—no.

Union come anyhow. Oh, with union it's different. Million times better. Better money and hours and everything. And when I know they got the union, I came here, to Renton mine, and I stayed here. That's where all my teeth are at, all my teeth.

Thirty teeth I got knocked out here, with the machine. I was working on a drill machine and it kick back—and clear through in my mouth and nose, a hole. I ain't got no bones in my nose. [*Pushes nose with hand.*] Lucky I didn't lose my eye. I was in a hospital, but I wasn't home for very long before I went back to work.

My sons went in the mine, too, but they quit. All my boys were in World War II, and when they came back, they didn't want it no more. They saw how hard I worked.

I bought this property because it was only ten minutes from the mine. I can see the mine right from the front, and we hear the noise sometimes, you know; pulling cars or—not machinery, but like a railroad noise and stuff. And sometime the whistle blowing.

When I was sixty-five, I went to work. Yeah, I went to work on my birthday. And they wouldn't give me no lamp. They said, "George, that's all. When you're sixty-five, that's finish." And I stood up on my head. That was on television, clear to California—sixty-five-year-old standing on his head. [*Laughs.*] Well, that's it, that's the law. No lamp. My shovel over there, it's itching. It wants to go digging.

# Vera Gurchikov

·················· FROM HUNGARY, 1911 ··················

*A tiny, wrinkled old woman wearing a babushka, over eighty years old, her blue eyes still sparkle. She lives in a small, neat house in a quiet, lower-middle-class town that was once a thriving iron-ore mining community. Her kitchen is filled with pictures of her sons in uniform. Mother of six, grandmother of four times that number, and now even a great-grandmother, "Baba" centers her life around the little Russian Orthodox church in a nearby city.*

We are Carpathian-Russian people, from the Carpathian Mountains in Austria-Hungary—a little village, a couple houses, small—and everybody had a little place to plant. People did all kinds of jobs. My father, he made shingles for the roof. Some children went to school; not me—never. I was far away from school—no school in our village. I talked only Russian. Lots of people talked Hungarian, too, in my town, but I didn't go to school and I didn't learn. Summertime I went to work on a farm—you know, picking fruit. Wintertime I stayed home—made cotton thread, made clothes—no machines.

Over there was rough. No doctors, no nothing. You get sick, you use a plant, something like that. No stores, only a little one to sell salt. No meat in the old country, not like here. We ate potatoes, cabbage, beans. It was bad over there. We lived in a little house, the roof made out of straw, one room. Summertime we planted food in the garden, ate it in wintertime. We had cows, pigs. There was no work over there—only summertime, work for the farmers. We came here, we wanted to make some money and go back better. But we found out it was different here. It was good, you know. It was better than over there.

My brother worked in the mine here. He sent me money. It was 1911, I think. I was young girl, sixteen. I went by train to Fiume [now

Rijeka, Yugoslavia], then ship for two weeks. Oh, it was rough! Oy, oy, I was scared! I wanted to go back, but I never went back. I was scared for the water.

I stayed with my brother, and I cried. I was far away from home, you know. Then he took me to New York to work for a lady. I lived in the house, did housework, cleaned the house. No cooking—only watching the kids, laundry. It was nice. I stayed for two years, and after, I went to work for a restaurant. I washed dishes there. I stayed in New York altogether three years.

Then my brother and my sister-in-law, they said it was time to marry. They found a man from the other side, from another town about two, three miles away from my village. He came here before me and worked in the mine. He told me stories about when he was a young man, single. After work, he went with friends to the saloon in the next town. They walked by the railroad tracks. Gangs of American boys were hanging around, watching for them. They called them "greenhorns," and they beat them up; they took their money. It was bad.

We married and he worked in the mine all his life. He worked ten hours a day, six days a week. And no money. He worked in the mine and we lived in a company house. It was right here, up the road about a mile. The mine gave a house, a company house. It cost $6.00 a month. But my husband made only $1.50 a day. There was a company store—only a company store, no other stores. We bought all our food  and everything from the company store. Payday came, everything came out of the pay. They kept us right down, you know. We couldn't move, couldn't go anywhere. Only a little train to go to Wharton, to do a little shopping. We had it rough here. The bosses had a hand on us in the mine, in the company house, all the time. There was no place to go, just stay here.

There was a man here, a Russian; he worked for the mine, like a boss, a supervisor in the mine. He had a good job. The mine wanted men, he told everybody. They wrote letters to the other side, and they sent more men; because the mine was killing men. Work in the mine was dangerous, very dangerous. The bosses knew it, but there was no other way in them days. It was the only way they could get work done. That's why they got young boys from the other side. They kept pushing them in the mine, pushing them in. A lot of young men, young boys, came over, and they be killed off in the mine, just like that. They had a cemetery, right next to the mine. They keeped sending back to the other side for more boys.

We lived in this little place, where everybody was the same. All the neighbors came from my same village. We know everybody. The mine gave a little land, we made gardens, had cows, pigs, chickens. I didn't go no place; I stayed home. We lived almost the same here like over there. Of course, the kids went to school. American kids went to the school, too, but our kids stayed alone. They called our boys names all the time. They called them "hunkies." They made fun of them. My oldest son—when he was a little boy, he was ashamed that I wear babushka. You know, it's not American.

In 1932 the mine shut down—Depression. We had nothing—just welfare. Nothing to eat in the house. My son, the oldest boy, was in high school. But he went only two years. He had to quit. And he went to CCC [Civilian Conservation Corps]. They took care of him; he worked in the woods, cutting trees, like that. They sent home twenty-five dollars a week for him.

He got out in 1937; he was seventeen years old. The mine opened up again and he went to work in the mine. My husband worked there again, too, until twenty years ago. My husband worked underground all his life. My sons followed the father into the mine. I had five sons—two work underground, three work outside.

This town was all Russians. Only a few American families. They worked in the mine, too. But they could read and write. They were supervisors, bosses, electricians. My husband and other Russian people was just labor class. The superintendent of the mine—when he went by in a car, you waved to him. We told our sons, too. First they were afraid. But they grew up, educated, then no more afraid—they were Americans, just like the boss. My sons are American born, they have a little education, they want better conditions. The Americans called us Communists. But it's not true—we are Americans. After 1939, it was better, because boys like my son, educated, a couple years of high school, they started the union. Now they work eight hours a day, forty hours a week. No more company store.

Then World War II came and lots of boys quit, went to work in the arsenal, went to the service. Three sons got drafted. I lost two sons—one nineteen, one twenty-one—in Germany, both of them. [Shows pictures.] One was killed October 1943, the other one was killed December. I brought them back; I brought both home in 1948.

We saved some money and we build a house. I live here in this house thirty years. All my kids are near, all married, big families. It was sometimes good, sometimes not so good. I forget many things. Only my two boys I remember.

# Casimir Kopek
········ FROM POLAND, 1910 ·······················

*He arrived in Chicago before World War I and worked in the
stockyards for fifty years. Now retired, he lives with his wife in a
South Side apartment building, which he owns. But his neighborhood
is changing and he is angry.*

I was in hospital in Chicago and fellow in bed next to me was a nigger.
  "You kept my people in slavery!" he says to me.
  "I never keep anybody in slavery," I say, "I *was* slave!"
You see in them days just like niggers was slave here, Polacks was
slave to Russian czar. Polack barons sell them for taxes to go in
Russian army. That's what they used to do. Have to stay in army
twenty-five years. That's slave! Like what Americans do niggers. But I
never slave anybody. They going to take me in Russian army and I run
away to America. I no slave anybody. Why they mad at me?

# Matthew Murray
························ FROM IRELAND, 1914 ·······················

*He lives on the top floor of a three-decker tenement in a Dorchester
neighborhood once wholly Irish, now partly black. Like many Irish in
Boston, he worked for the Metropolitan Transit Authority until his
retirement.*

I arrived here a week before Christmas, 1914. You really want to know
why? I wanted to get away from the war, England. That's why. I went
right into it here, right in it. I was in the army, in the big war, the first
war. I was in England, France, Belgium, Germany.
  I was just a farmer in Ireland, County Galway—planting and reaping
potatoes, corn, cabbage, turnips, onions. 'Twas hard work, real hard
work. Well, my brother and some sisters brought me out here, sent me
a ticket. I was tickled to death to stay away from that hard work. I
knew you could pick money off the street here. That's what I thought.
[*Laughs.*]
  They were in Dorchester, and I stayed with them for a while. Then I

went to a boarding house, at 274 Dudley Street. There was about fifty there—all men, all Irish. I worked for the MTA [Metropolitan Transit Authority] for forty-two years. I worked mostly with Irish. It was a beautiful job. I worked on wires. You know the wires that the trolley runs on? Well, that's them. I take care of them. And putting the wires up. Kind of dangerous, oh, yes. Got a few shocks out of that, I have, indeed.

But I had a good time. For forty-two years I had a good time. The work was nice. I used to go out on calls, to see if a fire was happening—on the emergency. It was beautiful. I liked that. I retired in 1959. I had to, you know. I couldn't do the work anymore. Too weak. Since then I've been doing nothing—not a thing. Fighting with the wife, that's most of it.

Most of my friends are Irish. . . . Oh, I got all kinds of friends—colored and everything else. At that time they was easy to get along with. I used to go down Broadway there and the best friend I had was a colored guy, Clark. His name is Clark, and he's colored. I get along with them all right. I don't like to see them getting so close, though. They all go around here now, you know.

# Grace Calabrese

······················FROM ITALY, 1924······················

*A widow with two married children and a comfortable life, she has spent most of her life working in New York City's garment trade. Now retired, she is active in a senior citizens organization, helping to sew for various charitable projects.*

I came in 1924. I was going to be fifteen years old. My father was in the U.S.A. since 1921, and three years later, when he had his citizenship papers, there was a law that he was entitled to come back to Europe and pick up his family, so he did that. Our ship was supposed to land in New York City, but something went wrong and we landed in Providence. So from there they paid the way on the train, and that was such an experience to me. We were traveling at night, and all the lights when we crossed the bridge—oh, I went wild!

We stayed one week in my cousin's house. She had three rooms. My father finally found an apartment with steam and all, you know. We didn't have no money, very little, but my mother says, "Whatever I have is okay." So we get this nice little apartment in the Bronx, and my mother got some used furniture; but she says, "The bed I want new, I don't want nobody's."

My father, he always wanted to give us a start. He always wanted to live in a better section, as poor as we were. He said he had three boys, he wanted to bring them in a nice section in the Bronx. It was a Jewish section there. They were like the better homes. He thought the people were refined and he wanted his family to be that way, you know. That was the best thing he did, because he raised the family always nice.

We were here only about a week and my father says to me, "Come on, you have to start traveling with me. I have to show you all the trains. You have to get to work." He needed help. I wasn't supposed to go to work, not even fifteen, but I was the oldest girl. He needed help so bad, I went to work. He took me to New York eight days later after we arrived here. "Now," he said, "you have to learn to travel by yourself." Oh, I was so excited! He put me on the subway and he made me go back and forth two or three times to teach me. I was a little bit afraid, yeah. But, you know, then the next day I went the same way. I didn't even move an inch. And I started to learn a little bit the trains.

I find a job in New York. They used to make keys, locks. I worked about a couple of months. That was one of my first jobs. There was all American people. There was no Italians at all. I didn't know one word English. First experience I learned to speak English among those people. I know as much as I know today. I didn't learn another word anymore. That was the end of me, and I was mad a little bit with my father, because I asked him, "Pop, I know you need help and I'm the oldest girl in the house. I'll go to work, but let me go to an evening school for a couple of hours." They were afraid to send me. They think somebody was going to grab me, things like that. So I never went to school here, and until today I am mad at my parents; they didn't make me go to school a little bit.

My grandmother was a dressmaker in Italy, and somehow was in me sewing. I used to love that. I wanted to sew all the time and to get a job that I loved. So then I find, about a couple of months later, there was an ad in the paper, in the Italian, the *Progresso* paper, and I said to my girlfriends, "How about if we try this job?" They telling in the paper, "No experience required, will teach you." In the garment industry in New York, about Thirty-seventh Street I think it was. So we got to New York, the three of us; and being that I used to sew so much, I was pretty good with the electric machine, and in half a day I learned how to run that machine. Two days later they didn't like it, my two friends. I kept going on, and then after one week they thought I was pretty bright and they gave me something else to do. I was making the whole garment. I stayed there about two months, and after that I moved on, to the better shops where they made a better garment, like suits and things like that.

. The conditions wasn't bad. I came from Europe—I thought it was fine. We had dressing room, bathrooms. For me it was good. Then we had trouble, when the NRA* came in, you know, because there was no union then when I first start, see. Two, three years later the NRA came in, and the union started to come in. I was there—I even went to work on a Sunday, you know, because we wanted to work—we needed the money so bad. I didn't understand then, but afterward we realize that the union was good, because we got a lot of good out of it, you know. We got holidays paid. But before we didn't care. We didn't know any better; let's put it that way. We came from plain people, we didn't know. We just wanted to work and make a few dollars and that was it.

One Sunday I almost got in trouble. We were working. There was a cousin of mine who was the presser and a couple of girls—we were working, and all of a sudden we heard banging on the door. The union. They *knew* some shops were working, see? So we went through the back doors. They came in one door and we ran through not to get caught, because then they beat you up! I knew people who got beat up. There was a lot of problem then. But then at the end, when we was organized, I think it was the best thing that happened—was wonderful. The pay was better, the conditions were better, and everything. We had our holidays, and we worked five days then. Before the union, if the boss needed you on a Sunday, you went on a Sunday, too. . . .

From the first day I arrived over here, I really enjoyed this country. I loved it and I said I'd never go back; for a visit, yes, but not to stay there anymore. I forgot everything about Italy. I didn't want to know anything else about that. I was so interested over here. It was my home. I really loved it.

Everything was so big to me over here, and I felt why go back over there. I don't know, maybe because I came from a small village. The homes, the running water, which we didn't have there. We didn't have no running water. The thing was the well, when you washed the clothes. The food was different: for instance, drinking only black coffee, demitasse—that's all we drank in Italy. And when we first came over here they came out with the brown coffee, you know. Ooooh, that was awful! Yeah, but now you try to get me to drink that black coffee in the morning when I get up! I think that's crazy, and I did it all the time. See? You change. This was it for me. For me, was a new world, and I loved it, and I made the best of it, and everyone I met was my friend. . . .

---

*National Recovery Act. New Deal legislation to increase production, protect labor, and reduce unemployment.

We were a group all from our town that we came together. This uncle of mine, my mother's brother, he brought his whole family over here, too. We lived close, about four blocks away; and on a Sunday, visit one another. One Sunday you spend two hours by me, have a cup of coffee, and so on. You see, whoever we met over here, they group together, you know. And when they heard, like, say, "Mrs. Baretta came from Italy and she's got a daughter. How about if we match her up with our son? You know, they're from the same town and we know one another." And that's how it worked in those days. In fact, my mother—when I had to get married, she wouldn't *allow* me to marry anybody else from a different town. It's got to be from the same town. [*Laughs.*]

You know, in those days, the family come to propose, not the boy. Yes, the family come. You know, "My son wants to marry your daughter." "Okay." And it was no problem for us, because we thought that's the way it was supposed to be. They used to match them up, sort of. Of course, if I liked the guy—because a couple of them I says—my mother says, "Grace, he's fun, he's nice, he's got money." I says, "Ma, I don't like him. *You're* not going to marry him; *I* am. You want him? *You* marry him." I wouldn't marry anybody if I didn't like him.

But I liked my husband. He was poor, he had nothing. I liked him, that's all. So you make the best of it, when there's love in between. We struggled and we got somewhere. It was hard—which I could have had easy with somebody else. But that wasn't for me, that's all. I think I like what I went through in my life. I mean working and with my husband, you know. I was like a little independent girl. I wanted to do something for my family all the time. When I first got married I wanted to—you know—work together with your husband, make something out of yourself.

I'm happy what I did. We struggled. We struggled. We worked very hard, and, you know, today I'm happy with what I did. I don't want to go back and be better than what I was. I really enjoyed my life. It was such a clean life we had, so nice.

# Joseph Baccardo
·························· FROM ITALY, 1898 ·····················

*The old-fashioned striped barber pole turns slowly outside the little wooden barbershop in a small town near Philadelphia. Joseph Baccardo sits on the porch in the sunshine, waiting for one of his regular customers to show up. He's been in business in the same place since 1902.*

My father was born in 1843, and when he got to be a young man, he had to go into the army. There was a war on then between Italy and Austria. After the war, he went back to Sicily and got married there, but there wasn't much work, you know. So finally he decided to come over to the United States to try to better his condition. But he never had any luck. When he arrived here it was during Cleveland's last term, and there was a money panic and everything shut down in this country.

He suffered over here and we suffered over there, because he wasn't able to send us very much. We had to do the best we could. I had a brother who was five or six years older than I was, and then there was myself and a little girl, Maria, and a baby brother. Maria loved my dad very much and she missed him. She was in the habit of waiting for him when he came home from work in the evening, on a certain corner not very far from our home. When he came to this country, she couldn't understand why dad was gone. I always say she died of a broken heart. Anyway, she passed away and then the baby passed away, and then there was just my mother and my brother and me. . . .

Finally my father came back to bring us to this country. He brought a little money with him, and we all came back the cheapest way—steerage. By then I was about nine or ten years old. Of course, we'd never been out of our own town. We went to Palermo and there we got a ship and came to New York. At that time passage was very slow. It took a couple of weeks. My mother was sick most of the time. Finally we came to Ellis Island, and then to New York to visit some friends, and then out here to Pennsylvania, where a friend of my dad's was working. Dad had been boarding with him while he was here.

We rented two rooms in an old house and bought some furniture from a young couple who were moving out. They sold us a little stove and four chairs and a table and a few pots and pans and a bed for my mother and dad. First my brother and I slept on the floor, and then they bought a couple of little folding cots for us. We slept in the kitchen and mother and father in the other room. That's all we had for about ten years.

Pop was doing manual work, you know; that's all he knew. He was working with a gang building the county road out to Chester. It was a gravel road then. He used to get up at 2:00 in the morning on Monday and walk to the job. That was about ten miles. That first summer I got a job there, too, as a waterboy. I carried water to the men working on the road. We stayed in a shanty during the week, and then Saturday night we walked back home. I was getting 40 cents a day for ten hours, and dad was getting $1.10 a day. We tried to live off my 40 cents, so that we could bring $6.00 back home. We lived as cheap as possible—beans, macaroni—and we'd cook it ourselves in the shanty. We laid out stones in a circle and then we'd cut a lot of young trees and put them around like a tepee, and we'd cook our food that way. . . .

I hear people talk about the good old days. Well, look how many people suffered. All those bridges, all those roads, all those railroads— they were all built by people who worked hard to build them. It took a long time, and time and effort and sweat and blood. My father had to work his heart out to get anywhere. And yet, no matter how hard he worked, there was never enough money. My dad and my mother pretty near died in the clothes they got married in. They had to economize. Today you don't see people with patches on their britches anymore— unless they put them on just for show. . . .

When it was time for me to go to school, I didn't have anyone to take me over to introduce me to the sister. I had to go on my own. There was a Catholic schoolhouse, so I went over there and I mixed with the boys, and when they saw me—well! I had a little round cap, like Chico Marx wears, you know. I don't know whether it was homemade or bought. So they started to have some fun with me—took my hat and got me bawling—and I came home and then that was the last of that school for me. I wouldn't go back anymore.

Later on I went to the public school. The teacher saw me hanging around in the yard and took me upstairs to see if I knew anything or not; gave me some tests. They put me in the first grade, and I was ten or eleven years old and the other children were six, so that made everything more difficult. They kept advancing me from grade to grade every year, but I wasn't learning anything. I just wasn't picking the language up. And every year in the spring I had to quit school to go and work on the roadgang with my father. Finally, when I was in the fourth grade, I quit school altogether.

I already had an after-school job with a barber here in town, sweeping and carrying water and all that. So when I was fourteen and he asked me if I wanted to learn the business, I said, "I'll ask dad." And dad didn't care as long as I was making money. So that's how I got into the barber business.

I started at fifty cents a week [laughs], and I got up to six dollars after two or three years. In those days, you'd open the shop at seven in the morning, and nine at night was closing. And Saturday was eleven o'clock closing. You'd be there all the time. I had one pair of trousers and I used to iron them so I'd look all right, but I didn't know how to use a cloth, you know, and my trousers were pretty shiny.

When I was nineteen the boss died, and I opened up the place on my own the next week. The same shop I'm in now—just one chair—that was all there ever was.

It was a cold place. There was only three-quarters of an inch of wood partition between me and the outside and nothing but boards underneath. When the wind blew, I got chilled. During the bad winter of 1909–10, the cold went right through my hands and my feet so I could hardly move them. I used to have to soak my feet after work, it was so cold in there. It was terrible. Later, when I'd saved some money, I had a concrete floor put down. Then I had plumbing put in—little by little; I didn't do it all at one time. I lived in the back. That was cheap, so that was good.

I can still remember when my wife and I were married and we moved a little stove into the kitchen in back and we had candlelight at night. We had a little farm, too; it was all open around here then. We had tomatoes, peppers, cabbage. I used to get up two or three hours early in the morning and go down there and turn it all over by hand and plant it and weed it. We canned everything.

I did pretty well for myself and my wife helped me. She's from an American family, so she does the reading and the paperwork for me and fills out the government forms and all that. We have a little car, and on Sundays we like to go for a ride in the country or to visit my brother. I'm eighty-nine now, but I'm still cutting hair for my old customers and I still feel pretty good. Only I got varicose veins—that's an occupational disease of barbers, you know.

## Zosia Kaminsky
······················ FROM POLAND, 1924 ······················

I'll never forget that moment when I had to leave and the train went away. My family, everybody was there. My mother, my father, sisters, brothers, little nephews, some friends. And I remember my mother made me a little pillow, so I'll be able to lay down in the train on the bench.

Of course I was very anxious to go, to see the world. My husband's taking me to see America and to see the whole world. Everybody was crying. I couldn't understand why they're crying. When the train started moving, then I was crying, too. My mother, my father, my sisters and brothers, all crying. [Bursts into tears.]

## Julia Goniprow
····················· FROM LITHUANIA, 1899 ·····················

The day I left home, my mother came with me to the railroad station. When we said good-bye, she said it was just like seeing me go into my casket. I never saw her again.

# Ludwig Hofmeister

······················FROM GERMANY, 1925······················

*At seventy, he still spends two or three days a week at his store in Buffalo, now working at a new skill—setting diamonds.*

I come from the Black Forest, where they make the cuckoo clocks. My father was a clockmaker, and when I got to be fourteen I got out of school and then I was an apprentice, first for watchmaking, and then for clockmaking. I didn't want to do that at all. I wanted to be a forest ranger, but that was out of the question. I had to do the same thing like my father, you see.

When World War I broke out, I was five years old. First of all, my brother had to go to war. He came out of the army in 1918 and he was never really happy anymore. I don't know whether you know the history of World War I. Germany collapsed completely. It was disastrous. There was no food. It was a horrible time. And then, two or three years later, the inflation started. This was madness! We had millions in our pockets and couldn't buy anything for it, you see. And this was the time when my brother thought of leaving the country.

Well, he got in contact with an uncle in upstate New York. It's rather a small town, and at that time it was a farm town. There was nothing but farmers around. My uncle was a farmer. He signed the papers for my brother, but he also told him right away that his town will not be for him—my brother was a watchmaker, too, see—but maybe he can find some work in Buffalo, which was about eighty or ninety miles away. So he came with his wife. Then my older sister decided to go to the United States. She worked as a housemaid at a doctor's house, and she did rather well. She liked it. She joined the Lutheran Church, and at that time they even had German service in that church. She was rather happy.

My mother was the kind of woman who wanted to get the family together. And besides that, things got worse in Germany. My father wasn't the kind of man that wanted to leave, because he was already in the late forties. When I think about it today—that a man of forty-eight leaves the country and don't speak the language—that's quite something, let me tell you. So my mother was the driving power that we should get together with the family again, and it worked out that way. We finally made up our minds to leave—my other sister, myself, and my father and mother. We were lucky. We had a house, our own house, that we could sell, and we could pay our own fare. We sold *everything*.

When I look back at when we left, that was a sad day, I'll tell you. [*Breaks down.*] I'll tell you why it was sad. My father, when he said good-bye to his brother, he said, "I'm not going to see you anymore." That sort of struck me funny that he would say that, but at forty-eight he probably thought this is impossible that he can make a trip back. He never did get back.

Oh, the trip was something, too. We took a dog along! [*Laughs.*] When I think about it, I think we must have been out of our minds. We liked the dog, but, really, you need everything but a dog! We had to go on a train, but we had to change trains about an hour later, and we had to take the dog on the train. I was the caretaker, and it wasn't a very pleasant thing, I'll tell you that. If you ever could see a movie of this, I don't know what you would say.

We were stationed in Hamburg in a tremendous big place. It was sort of an assembly building, where you get processed, you see. There was an exodus from Europe at that time, and they had all races in this place. You could see people from Russia, Poland, Lithuania, you name it. I can't describe the way I felt—it was part fear, it was part exciting. It's something I'll never forget. We were there about three days. We had to go through examinations in this place. It was well organized, I must say that. Everything was more or less taken care of. From there they got you on a train, and you didn't leave that train till you got to the boat.

But I'll tell you a story. This is a strange story that I never could understand. I was there another eight days by myself. After we were examined, my father got a call: The doctor said that I had a heart murmur and I will never go through Ellis Island. They would reject me. Now why this was, I can't understand, because I was examined before. Otherwise, I would have never come to Hamburg in the first place. But, anyway, this was the story. Then they told my father. "There is a way out of this." If I wait another week, there will be a boat leaving and I can go first class. In first class you don't have to go through Ellis Island. Well, it was a shock, of course. This cost, naturally, extra—first class. Now whether this was a racket or what, I cannot tell you. I was always wondering, because that heart murmur couldn't be that bad, because I was playing soccer in this country for years.

So I was there another eight days myself, and then I went on the boat. First class was, of course, beautiful. We had showers, we had everything that was just wonderful, we had the finest food that you can think of. The food was excellent. I never saw so many oranges in my life. And there were people that I just had to look at, because they were dressed well. You know, they were tourists—people that went to Germany back and forth, people who were there for pleasure. I had a good time. And you know the excitement when you see the Statue of Liberty!

Nobody went to Ellis Island from this boat, because it was only a one-class boat, only first class. All they did—I just went past, and the doctor says, "Are you sick?" In German, of course, he said it. "No, I feel very good." And that was it. [Claps hands.]

My brother came and picked me up. We had to go on the subway, and I saw the first black people. I did see black people in Germany, but you know where they were? In a circus. They were circus performers from Africa.

My mother was very happy. And she was even happier when she could go to the markets and see all those vegetables and oranges and apples and potatoes and bread! I was home for quite some time, until my brother got me a job in a jewelry store. This man had a big clock business, and I was good already in clocks. I could fix clocks and watches, and whatever I didn't know he showed me. He spoke German. I worked there until 1929 or 1930. That's when things really got bad, and then he couldn't keep me any longer. He didn't want to let me go; but on the other hand, I got a little bit older then, too, and I felt maybe it was good for me to go somewhere else. It was a very hard time, but we were always willing to work. Somehow it seems like foreign people that came in those days were always willing to work, to take any job. I found a job with a man that worked for the trade, for other jewelers. I advanced always a little bit. I learned from one place into another. I knew more and more how to be a finished watchmaker, you see.

When the Depression came, that was really bad for watchmaking— for the jewelry stores and for watch repairs. People couldn't pay the prices. It was impossible. I tell you what happened. People working for the trade, for jewelers, didn't have enough work anymore. They were starving. So they figured, "Well, why don't we go out on the street and give the same price that we worked for the trade and give it to the people?" Then they opened up a cut-rate watch company. You probably never heard of this. This was a very unusual thing. They repaired watches for a dollar and a half! That was including mainsprings and I don't know what else. It wasn't exactly the greatest job anymore. You had to work fast and things like that. But in the meantime, they did business. The Depression helped them. I worked there for quite some time. It wasn't exactly what I liked but was better than nothing. I had to change a great deal, but I adapted myself somehow. It wasn't that hard on me.

Then I got the idea, why don't I do this on my own? Why should I work here and slave away like crazy? Why don't I do this out on my own and work for the trade or open up a place? My brother came in and we did it. This was in 1937. I rented an office downtown, and I went out to different towns and picked up work, and we made a living. In the beginning we didn't do so well, but eventually it worked out pretty good. Then we went down on the street and had a store on the street; on the ground floor, like a retail store. We did very well there, too. I mean we made a living—you know what I mean? We made as much as we made when we were working for somebody else, and that was good enough for us.

We worked there till about 1939, 1940, and then, of course, the World War II started and I was at the age for draft. I had to register right away, because I wasn't married. June 1941 I was drafted and went to Fort Dix, and my brother took over the business. Of course, his wife helped him, too. I mean this was all hard work. He had to take over nothing but work, believe me. But before I left, I put some money into the business so that we could get some watches. Bulova watches was a big thing in those days. So we got the Bulova agency just before I left, and that sort of started us into the retail business. And that's how I left my brother.

I was in the army, and I forgot about everything else. I can honestly say I was very happy. I was sort of tired of sitting on the bench, and this exercise in the army did me good. I felt very good. I mean, the army didn't do me any harm. People ask me, "Did it ever come to you as a German to have to fight Germans?" Well, this feeling certainly is there. You can't deny it. But somehow I had so many things to be happy about in this country. I liked this country, and I owed certain things—because at twenty-one I had my own car already. Would I ever have a car in Germany? Never. I've been thinking about this in the later years, and I don't know, I think I figured, "Well, look, maybe I don't have to come face to face with one of those guys and shoot him down." I don't know what I would have done if I ever would have faced a German. I think my impulse would have been to say something in German. I don't know.

I went to school in Providence, Rhode Island, to the Brown University, for interpreter. This was in 1942. When we went overseas, my job was interpreter of prisoners of war. After the invasion in 1944, I had to be an interpreter in Germany, in the Rhineland, and I only had to deal with civilians. The people came with all kinds of problems. They didn't have enough heat, they didn't have enough coal. It came to such a point that the commanding officer said, "Look, you can solve these problems better than I can. Tell them they should do this, they should see the *Bürgermeister*, or something like that. 'We can't give them anything like that.' " In the meantime we had a good time in Germany. They had the best wine in that area.

At one time I had to go out with a captain. See, all these people that had some kind of a function as a Nazi, they had to get them down to headquarters for interrogation. They wanted to know just what they are. And my job was to get these people. Now, I didn't use an approach like an enemy soldier. I went to these people, like: "Look, I want you to understand that you have to come down. They want to hear what you have to say, and there is nothing wrong." I built it up so, because this was sometimes pitiful, let me tell you. I went up in the country, and here was the man working the field; I had to go up to this man and I had to tell him, "Please get ready. I have to take you down." The woman was crying, and I said to the woman, "Don't cry, because he'll be back in a few hours. All they want to know is what his job was with the Nazis." His wife said to him, "I always told you you should stay away from these jobs." She was arguing with him yet. And this was genuine. This was not fake, you know; these were country people, farmers. So he went along, and the whole family was standing there and crying when I took him away. This is one of the jobs I had to do.

There was one big Nazi, and it was a pleasure for me to arrest him. He must have been one of them guys that made himself rich, because he was living very, very, very luxurious. I had no pity on him, because he was a big fat guy, and I didn't like him.

But I never had any trouble and I never had any fear either. You know, sometimes when I think back, many times I went into these houses alone. The captain, he didn't even want to go in. He said, "Well, you go in and get them out." They could have been—I don't know what—but somehow I never had that feeling. I always had that confidence: "Well, look, these people are not altogether as bad as you think they are." I think I did a good job. I did a good job for one reason: I was not an enemy to these people, somehow. That's the only way I can explain it.

Then Hiroshima took place, so that ended the war. In another two months I was out of the army. All around, I was very lucky.

Our business was doing very well. My brother built it up. He had help from his sons. They came in after school and they were learning, working on watches. When I came back, we got very busy. We built our own store, a much bigger place, not too far away from the old one. We got to have a regular jewelry store then, and with the years we built up a reputation.

In those days I was in a soccer club, a German club. There were American girls, too, from German-born parents. And there were other German girls that were from the other side yet. I wouldn't say that I was looking for a German-born girl exactly, but it seemed to me the connection would have been so much easier at that time, that we had more or less something in common. To bring a girl home to our parents that wouldn't speak any German—this would have been a real handicap. Not that it would make my parents unhappy, but it would be so embarrassing. I don't know how you would communicate, unless you would move away from home and then come back as a married man later on. So that was, I think, one of the reasons that I wanted to bring home at least a girl that could speak German.

I had a friend, a very good friend, and he fixed me up with a date, a blind date.

MRS. HOFMEISTER: It was in the Olympic Tavern, and they were playing a German waltz. He came in, and I said, "That's my man!" just as sure as I'm sitting here. And that's how it went.

LUDWIG HOFMEISTER: She came over from Germany when she was fifteen, almost the age I was, so we had that much in common, although she was probably more Americanized than I was. And then we got married. We moved out here, and we were very happy. We have two children, a son and a daughter. They didn't come into the business, and I didn't push it. But it definitely is in the family, with my nephews and their children. The son is in clock repairing, and the daughter is interested in the business, too. She's very clever and very artistic. She can do a lot of fine things. She was even sitting down fixing watches, already. Seems to be in the blood, I guess.


# Demetrius Paleologas

······················FROM GREECE, 1915 ······················

*A millionaire businessman, he is now eighty-four and retired from a very active and successful career as a restaurateur. He was a founder and past president of the state restaurant association and a member of the advisory board of the Office of Price Administration during World War II. As president of a local Greek-American society, he raised a hundred thousand dollars to build a church and a school in his native village. He is proud of his family, of his achievements, and of both his countries.*

There are some festivals in the country, where they sell animals, and one day my father went to Tripolis and bought a horse for 275 drachmas. That horse was a little horse, and it was scared. After we put him to work, he got sick. Then we don't know what to do with our horse, it was so bad. My father says, "Put him somewhere and let him run himself, kill himself somehow." But I said, "I'll tell you what I'm going to do. I'm going to take this horse and sell it to the festival." But the last festival was six hours away, and they said, "For God's sake, you won't be able to sell it."

Nevertheless, I went down there, and it was about eight in the evening, and a fellow came in to me and he says, "How much you want?" I says, "I want 350 drachmas." He says, "That's too much money," and he left, and I went to sleep. In the morning another fellow come in, and another fellow, and nobody wants to pay the money that I ask. Eventually, the first fellow came in and says, "Why you want to sell your horse?" I says, "We have not much food up there, and we're up in the mountains, and I'm an orphan, and I'm going to the United States, so that's why." He said, "I'll tell you, I'm going to give you 225." "No, 325." "Well, 325 . . ." Another fellow come in—he knew me—and he said, "Hey, why don't you divide it up? Come down 25." And then he give me 300. When I come back home, my father told my mother, "This boy, my son, he's going to succeed. I'm going to send him to America."

I was nineteen. I came to St. Louis, to my father's friend. He says, "I'll take you in." If I tell you the condition we were—lice—oh, you have no idea. So he took me to a clothing store and he bought me underwears, socks, shoes, whole suit of clothes, shirt, and everything. And he took me to his place of business—he had a little restaurant— and they had a shower downstairs. He said, "Take all your clothes, throw them down there, wash yourself good, and put the new clothes on."

This man was very nice and he give me a job in his restaurant—wash dishes. We used to live with three, five, six beds in one room, over the restaurant. Then immediately I thought that I should learn how to speak and how to write, learn the language. Not only that, but I says, "Where am I going to go now? Remain a dishwasher all the time? That's no good. I don't like to remain a dishwasher." And after I was doing the dishes, I was looking at the cooks, and I tried to help the cooks. And in the evening—seven o'clock in the evening—I walk about a mile and a half, walk like the dickens, to go down to the Lincoln Avenue School and start learning the English language.

In six months, I became a third cook, then I became a second cook. Inside a year, one of the chef happen to be sick and I took over as a chef, too. But I said to myself, "I'm going to become a cook, how much I'm going to make?" So I ask the floor boss, "I want to come into the dining room to help—you know, the busboys and like that. Could you give me a job?" So he give me a job.

In 1920—almost five years—I decide to go into business for myself. I had six hundred dollars; that's all I had saved. I and another fellow go in business together. A candy shop and sandwich shop, right across from Cleveland High School. I had a partner; he was a lemon. He was no good. He didn't do nothing, and I worked like a dickens, and then I decided I can't go on. I sold my interest to him for fifty dollars, and then I had to look for some job.

Then a friend of mine—he knew I was a good worker—he says, "Why don't you look for a place?" I says, "I ain't got no money!" He said, "I'll help you." He was very great for me. Then I found a place and I start a business at the Greenwood Restaurant, and I made a success. . . .

When my son graduate from high school, I ask him, "Jim, what do you want to take up now? You going to college?" He said, "Daddy, I want to take business." "Why? You have personality, you have good qualities. You have something that I didn't have, because I come illiterate from the old country. Why don't you become an attorney? How about a doctor? How about an engineer?" And he told me this: "As long as free enterprise system prevail in our country, if I'm a good businessman, I'll have business. I'd like to take hotel, restaurant management." I took him over to Ithaca, New York, where they have a school, you know, to learn the restaurant industry. Then when he come back, I said, "Jim, I'll give you half the business as a partner." I don't have anything now, except a few shares in the restaurant.

My daughter, she's a wonderful girl. When she graduate from high school, I gave her a party at the church—had about 375 people. The principal came to the party, and she introduced him to the people. He said, "Olympia, I want to congratulate you, but I want to see your father and mother get up." We got up. He said, "Mr. Paleologas and Mrs. Paleologas, I want to congratulate you for the wonderful children you have. Your daughter, Olympia, and James, they are the ambassadors of the Greek race in our school."

# Nick Pappas

···················· FROM GREECE, 1922 ·····················

I went all over the world and I never went back to my village. See, I can't go there as a tourist, because they think I'm the Lord here. They write to me and say, "We hear that you are a multimillionaire. We hear that you control the government of the United States." These are the illusions, you see, when you are successful a little bit.

# Arthur Wong

·················· FROM CHINA, 1930 ······················

*He arrived in New York's Chinatown at the age of seventeen. Now sixty-six, he is the owner of a laundry in a small seaside town in New Jersey, where he has built a respected place for himself and his family.*

In Chinatown there are family associations—the people that come from the same village, same surroundings, and so forth. They help one another, and they help me find jobs. As you know, the Chinese people in this country are very well known in laundry and restaurant trade. I was here no more than two weeks, and my relatives, friends, and the family association, they would say, "Well, why don't you go to such and such person's laundry and learn the trade? And there are other people in the restaurant; why don't you go learn as a waiter?" They say, "Waiter makes a better salary; besides, he makes tips. But in the laundry, you work eighteen to twenty hours a day and you're not getting too much. It's hard work and all. . . ." All sort of advice. But in a restaurant as a waiter, you have to know the language.

So one of the fellows in the family association, he says, "Why don't you come to the restaurant, and I show you how to wait on tables? Meanwhile, you take a menu and just learn the different dishes, and I show you how to set the tables and so forth." So this is what I did. I went to the restaurant and learned as a waiter. I know a few words in English at that time, but that job didn't come through very well, because the people talk to me, I can't answer them. All I know is how to set the table and "You want chow mein or you want chop suey?" It's not enough. After about a month or two, one of the relative find me a job in a laundry, and so that's where I ended up, in a laundry.

I guess the biggest adjustment would be the separation of the family. You feel homesick and it's really a hardship. Although I say I have step into a family association, the people is like acquaintances. Nobody's intimate. The adjustment is when you feel sick, when you have sickness and you are all alone.

At that point, I have no contact with American—none whatsoever. I landed in the ghetto. When I begin to understand English and I begin to step a little further from Chinatown, then I begin to notice things are different—outside Chinatown.

I want to work in a restaurant so bad and I don't know the language. When I came over on the boat, I have five shipmates—they were all young men—and every one of those shipmates, they go to school. I'm the only one that didn't have a chance. I see them every so often and they talk English among themselves, because they went to school. And I put this thing through my mind, and I said, "They speak English and I came over with them to have all the opportunity. I have none."

And then I wanted a job so bad as a waiter in a restaurant. So how am I going to learn the English? I don't have a chance to go to school. Well, I talk with these fellows. They say, "Why don't you go get a dictionary?" and suggest that I should go to Sunday School classes and go join a church. The only purpose was to learn English, not as a religious person. I went for six weeks; I slept most of the time [*chuckles*] in the church. I don't know what they're talking about, but I gave up afterward, because I work six days—six and a half days—in the laundry. Six and a half days, from Monday to Saturday, and then Sunday morning from eight to twelve or one. Then you got a half a day off. And each day is eighteen to twenty hours a day, and it is about ten dollars a week. [*Laughs.*] Great life! We don't know any better, see. What you don't know, it doesn't hurt. So we work.

Well, I took the advice of these young fellows and I got myself a dictionary. I think I carried that dictionary for about three to four years, in the back of my pocket, just like a pack of cigarettes. Good thing I have good eyes in those days; otherwise I wouldn't be able to read it, it's so tiny. I walk on the street and I see a word and I bring out my dictionary and I find out what that word means. So when I learn one word and two and three, in time I build my own sentences; and I learn my own language that way. If you accumulate words like the way you put money in the bank, two words in your notebook a day, 365 days a year, you will learn over seven hundred words in one year. From seven hundred words, that's all you need to get around; and from seven hundred words you can build thousands of sentences. And this is how I did it.

After a few years in New York, working as a laundry worker until I master a few English, I went to work as a waiter, a part-time waiter. And I work seven days! I work five and a half days in the laundry and work the whole weekend in the restaurant. And then came the war, and defense work open up; and some of my friends went to work in a defense plant, and they recommended that I should apply for defense work. So I went to work for Curtiss-Wright, making airplanes. I started out as an assembler, as a riveter. By the time I left for the army, I was an assistant to the foreman. I had twenty-eight people working for me at that plant, after only a year and a half. I had a good job. I got a deferment from the armed services until the situation got critical, and then I got drafted by Uncle Sam—said, "Come here, son!" Well, actually, in those days you felt privileged to handle a gun to defend your country in World War II.

When I got back, I went back to the laundry. [*Laughs.*] One day I hear there's a laundry shop for sale, and through friendship and grapevine I find this little laundry in New Jersey. And we looked at it and we bought it and we started our really long, successful journey till today. We work at it for twenty-seven years, and I think we did pretty well.

Practically most our dreams has been fulfilled, up to this point. I came here to do what I like to do and hope to do, and I've been fortunate. With a little luck, we have accomplished. I got a family and started out, big long struggle, and own my own home, raised the children, educated them. They are all coming along. First-born was a boy, now twenty-eight years old. He's already got two degrees in his pocket. He's now an American diplomat in the foreign service. My daughter is doing social work, as a hospital consultant for patients. And the youngest one, twenty-two years old, he just graduated from college and was awarded a full fellowship to study marine biology.

Now I'm retiring from my long struggle. Certainly I don't think there's any other place in the world we could do what we did, with what I have. All I have is ten fingers. I have no money, no education. But I know I have one thing—an opportunity to prove what a man could do.

# Ho Yang

···················· FROM CHINA, 1920 ·······················

*He is an officer of one of the family associations that handle much of the cultural and social life of San Francisco's Chinatown, arranging funerals, festivals, and religious ceremonies. In his seventies, he is short, vigorous, affable.*

My village in Kwantung Province was very small, only about a hundred people, and it was really poor. Most of the people had only a rice field about as big as this room. [*Indicates an area about twenty by thirty feet.*] And if you were lucky, you had two or three like that. We used cows for plows, you know, because buffaloes were expensive. A whole life would depend on the cow. In fact, when a cow died there, I think the family wept more than when their relatives died.

The people in my village, if they heard of some friend or relative, even a distant relative, going to Canton, they'd say, "Oh, how good that is. I wish I could go. He's going to have good food and clothes." It was really enviable, you see. And America was the dream. My father went to Canton and worked there, and after a while, he saved up enough money and he came to the United States. And when I was thirteen, he came back to China and got me. He couldn't bring my mother for some legal reason, and my sister wanted to stay with her, so I was the only one he brought back.

In China I was educated in the old-fashioned school. All they teach there is just literature, Chinese literature. They never teach geography or mathematics or anything like that. So it was hard for me in the American school. But I caught on after a while and I graduated from grammar school, high school, and junior college right here in San Francisco.

Later, I went back to China to get married. I had a friend over here who said, "You want to get married? Maybe I'll write a letter to my niece in China." And I said, "Well, all right, you can try. It won't hurt." And it turned out to be all right with her, and we got married over there, and we've been together more than forty years now. She didn't come from the same village I was from but not too far away, two or three miles away. She doesn't speak too much English—just enough to say hello, good-bye, and a few things.

There's really two reasons people like to live in Chinatown. One is the language. Some Chinese have been here thirty years and they've never been out of Chinatown and they can't speak English. The other reason is the work here. People own little shops. There must be over two hundred shops in Chinatown. Little butcher shop, little curio shop, noodle shop, all those kind of shops. It's usually just a husband and wife, and the kids work in there. And the small restaurants are family style. Everybody helps: washing dishes, waiters and waitresses, and all that. The money isn't too good, but it's all in the family.

Many of the Chinese ladies, they go to the garment factory—a sewing shop, you know, right here in Chinatown. My wife did that. There are a lot of these shops here, and the main reason the ladies go in them is this: If you don't understand English, you can't go to work in an American place. Also, Americans pay you by the hour for so many hours, and, of course, you cannot be too slow. Too slow and they fire you, you know. But in Chinatown they go by piecework—so much a dozen. If you're fast you can earn just as much and even more than in an American place, but some of our people are slow, you know. Old ladies, they go slow. And ladies with children, it's good for them, too, because they can bring their little kids with them and can run around there. And if the ladies have to leave, they're free to go to take their kids to school, if they've got kids in school; because by the piece, the less time you spend there, the less money you get. Sometimes they call those companies sweatshops, because the pay is still low, but they're better now than they were before.

*Do they make Chinese clothing in these shops?*

Oh, no, American-style clothing. They make dresses, formal gowns, dungarees, T-shirts, all those things.

There's still a whole lot of Chinese life in Chinatown. Of course, we have the weddings with dragon gowns and firecrackers and a lot of relatives. And when a baby is born, we have to have the party, you know. It's traditional for the new mother, after they birth the baby; the first month they're not supposed to go outside the home, you know. And they drink a lot of black vinegar, made from black beans. It's supposed to help the mother clear up all the unwanted blood. I don't know if it's true or not—that's a job for the doctor. But the tradition goes on. And they use pig feet and ginger. It's pretty tasty. We have a lot of those parties. The two things you have to have are a red egg [for happiness] and pickled ginger [to give the new mother and baby long life]. Then there's the burial and the ancestor ceremony. It's traditional when a Chinese dies that they bury all his things with him. Like my father had a special teapot that he liked; we buried that with him. And all his clothes that he liked, we buried those, too. For ladies, we put jewelry in, jewels and bracelets; even gold bracelets and jade we put in.

Every year we go out to the cemetery to worship the dead three time—once in March and once in July and once in October. March is the biggest one. It's similar to Memorial Day here. We go out to the cemetery and we have a big feast, firecrackers, and a whole roast pig. We put it on a big cement table and put out three pairs of chopsticks, three teacups filled with tea, three small cups filled with wine—that they pour on the tombstone. I don't know why everything is three, but it's got to be three. And everybody bows and then they say to the dead people, "Come and eat it," you know. After it's over, they take the pig back home and eat it. It's a very big thing here.

Once a year, of course, we have the Chinese New Year celebration and a parade with floats and a big dragon—very colorful. People come from far away just to see that dragon.

Probably the most important thing the association does is to run the Chinese schools. It's to teach the Chinese culture and literature and that sort of thing. The trouble is the majority of the children don't want to go. We got the school going up to twelfth grade, but the most of them only go just through sixth grade. Even my own three kids, they don't like to go to the Chinese school. They say, "Oh, Pop, what's the use of learning Chinese? We're in this country now."

# Ibrahim Hassan

···················· FROM PALESTINE, 1922 ·······················

*He is a large man, dressed in a business suit and tie, in the office of his flourishing Oriental rug store in Lincoln, Nebraska. At seventy-three, he still attends to business daily, though his son is the real manager of the store now. A Christian Arab, he is active in church affairs.*

In 1913, or just about that time, the sparks of war started to fly—the First World War—and the Ottoman Empire, under which we were subjects, started to make its move and conscript young men in the army. A good many of these boys can afford to run away, and my father was one of those. He migrated to the United States. He couldn't bring me and my mother with him, because he was running away and he wasn't able financially.

Well, my father was a struggling immigrant, but he started a restaurant in Lincoln, Nebraska, and he succeeded in saving a few dollars. After World War I was over, in 1920, he went back. I was anxious to see a father, because I didn't remember my father very well. And when he came back again, I was happy. He stayed two years and then brought me with my mother here. You see, after you drink the water of this country, honey does not taste good in the wells of Jacob.

I had the emotional feeling, the sad feelings, departing away from my home and my town and my relatives. I think that I never see them again, going across the seven seas. That was a very sad, very sad affair. And I wasn't looking forward to what I'm going to see, because I don't know what was ahead of me. But I know what I was leaving behind.

We landed near the Bowery. It was not like I used to imagine it. Well, you magnify the United States in your mind, you see. If you happen to land in a good area, all right, your dreams are fulfilled. If you happen to land in a bum area, like the Bowery, you have that disappointment, till you wade through it. Until I was taken, after a few days, out in the upper part of Manhattan—then I changed my illusions about this being a dump city and bad and so forth.

After being in New York for two weeks, we came here to Lincoln to live. I was intense; I was very studious all my life. I wanted to study and become somebody. The law was foremost in my mind. There was this man had this dry-goods business, and also he imports from the old country. He said, "What are you going to do with the boy?" My father says, "The boy's going to school." "Oh, what do you want to do that for?" he said. "Now, if you send him to school and he wants to be a lawyer, he has to go through school ten years—college, specialty, and so forth. And during the course of this time, if you put him to work he'll earn two thousand dollars a year at least." I heard that and I hated the man. It sounded logical to my father. So he wanted me to work. What the hell could I do? I couldn't do anything. I was a kid.

I got hold of a map of the United States and I drew with a pencil around from Lincoln a circle like this—not knowing the geography of the country and the means of transportation and so forth. I picked up some small Oriental rugs and some of these fine, handmade linens that were made in Italy. They're expensive—you have to sell them to the rich. And then I traveled.

This is the first adventure, and I was successful. I had the advantage from several standpoints, you see. Coming from the Holy Land, for one thing, they thought I was holy. And then my youth. I learned how to find the rich people's homes. I learned to ride the taxi in the town and tell him to take me to rich people's street. And I look at this house—looks nice, looks very rich. I put the number down and the name of the street, and I'd go back to the hotel and I called these people up. All I needed is one, and then the other one will send me to the other.

I came back here in 1931 and I took a store. I displayed those linens in there, plus Oriental rugs. But you didn't do well in there just from the first day. You had it good and you had it bad; but by perseverance— if you give up, you don't succeed, and I wasn't the kind to give up. And it worked.

In 1933 I was married—a girl of Arabic origin.

*Would you have considered marrying an American girl?*

Well, at that point it was not very advisable. The boy of Asiatic extract, he had to be obedient to his parents, you know. He could not exercise his own thoughts or have his own choosing—unless he became a bad man, a renegade. So the tendency was to marry your own religion and your own nationality, and you lived happier. . . .

My two daughters say to me, "I'm American." Yes, it's wonderful, you are an American. But you have an origin and you should be proud of your origin and the contribution that your origin brought to this United States. This tree, this almond tree—the roots were almond. Yours was apple, and others were orange roots. Now we have these three, four trees in this garden. Each one is different. Each one is useful.

Each one is delicious. And that's the way I feel about the United States. It's a beautiful garden composed of so many wonderful and delicious fruit trees.

# Branwyn Davies
······················· FROM WALES, 1923 ·······················

I was born in a little town in South Wales and was orphaned at a very early age. I lived with a sister and brother-in-law, and in 1923 my brother-in-law was offered a post in Shanghai, China, and I, naturally, as part of the family, was going there with them. The house was sold and the furniture was sold and we had the tickets. Then we got word there were uprisings in Shanghai [against the British] and the whole thing was canceled. The house was gone and the furniture was gone and we were all packed for somewhere. So the family got together and decided, "Well, let's change these tickets and go to America."

# Sylvia Bernstein
······················· FROM AUSTRIA, 1914 ·······················

*Tiny, spry, she talks animatedly and laughs often. She is active in Jewish affairs. Years ago she founded Hadassah in her upstate New York town and, more recently, a senior citizens club at her temple.*

Austria, you must understand, was a very anti-Semitic country. When I was a little girl my father had a butcher shop, and next door was a pork store. Naturally, that man wasn't Jewish. He was a very nice man, but when he got very drunk, he would come to my father and say, "Mr. Bernstein, that little one I'll take away from you." So my father ran home to tell my mother not to let me out. Because he could take me—there was no laws for us!

I used to see, when Czar Nikolai had a pogrom, the Jews would flee across the border to our town. My mother, on Friday she says to me, "You have to go and take soup to those poor refugees." So I came into that big room—like where the horses and the wagons stay—with a kettle with soup tied up in a sling, and there was a woman with breasts cut off—flat! You should never see that!

At the time I went to school, was like a Catholic school. A priest came and taught them their religion. I came in one day late to school and the teacher says to me, "You know, you're late. You must kneel in front of the Madonna"—you know, the statue. I looked up at that statue—I was little, as you see I am today [*chuckles*]—and I says, "Oh, no. If you kill me, I wouldn't." So he says, "If that's the case, you'll have to take your punishment. Put your hand out." I put my hand out and he hit it with the ruler.

A soldier spit on me because I give him a drink of cold water. I couldn't stand the—what would you call it in English?—the oppression, the anti-Semitism. I said to my mother, "Mamma, I'm going to America." She says, "I will not let you go to America. First of all, you're so young. And second of all, what are you going to do in America? You don't have a trade." I come from a family of ten children, and between all the ten children was only two girls, the oldest and the youngest, and that was me. I says, "Mamma, if you won't let me go to America, I'll run away. I can't take what you and my brothers and sister take. It's against me. I'm a human being."

I had a brother that came here in 1911. He was a tailor in New York. So I wrote to my brother, he should send me money, a ticket, I'll be glad to pay him back. I was fourteen years old. But you must remember, at fourteen they wouldn't leave you in without parents. You have to be sixteen. I says, "I'll try to pass for sixteen."

The trip . . . I'll tell you. My mother was afraid, a girl alone. My mother said to me, "Don't talk to men, because if you talk to men, you become pregnant." That's the sex life I grew up with. [*Laughs.*] They sent me with an English boat—was more modern in those years. We are watched when we come. An agent takes over the refugee. Oh, I came here like baggage. I went to Hamburg with the train, and from Hamburg to Liverpool in a small boat. Every time, the agent waited, and he put another mark on my clothes, the next agent should know who I am.

So I come on the boat, and I can't speak English. It's sad—you don't understand what they say, only by the faces. There was a Russian from America, so I could talk to him a little. He says, "You want a cup of tea? There is the chef. Go over and ask him for a cup of tea." I says, "How do you ask in English?" He says, "Say to the chef, 'Give me a kiss.'" And I didn't know. I went over to the chef and I says, "Give me a kiss." He was an elderly man and the English are very polite, understanding. He looked at me and I looked at him, and I knew something was wrong. . . .

In Ellis Island it was very exciting. There you can talk Jewish and you can talk Polish and you can talk everything. I came on a Friday. They go into a big room, and they feed you and they watch you. They give you a room with another girl—after all, it wasn't a hotel, darling!

But it was of comfort. You're constantly watched. They watch you. If you go out, there's a woman go after you. "Where do you want to go?" You should excuse me, you have to go to the bathroom, and you don't know. . . . You're primitive, according that. I come from a very small town. So they show you—and they were very nice.

But they're very strict; because that time was white slavery. An agent came over to me and says, "How old are you?"

I says, "I'm sixteen." And I had a big head of hair, so I made braids I should look taller.

He says, "You're sixteen? Where is your sixteen years? You're so little. You're going to a brother?"

"Yes, I'm going to a brother."

"How long you didn't see your brother?"

I says, "Two years."

"Would you recognize your brother, if you'd see him?"

"Yes."

They bring in a man, they say, "Is this your brother?"

"No."

They know who my brother was—they did this more or less to see. They were *very* careful and very cautious, very nice.

Sunday my brother picked me up, Monday I got a job, and Tuesday I went to work in a dry-goods store, a haberdashery. I was here three months, the boss said, "I have to go out and the telephone in the back room is out of order." He says to me, "That telephone man comes, tell him it doesn't ring." So when the man came and he says, "What's wrong with the telephone?" I says, "No ding-a-ling!"

*How did you learn English?*

I begin to learn on my own. People come in the store and I have to ask them what they want and I read constantly the funny papers—the Katzenjammer Kids. From their motions I learn. . . . I never saw the inside of a school. How could I? I had to make a living.

I stayed with that boss for seven years, and then I got married. My husband worked in a factory where they make uniforms. During the First World War the tailors made an awful lot of money, because they sold uniforms. So we saved up a little money and we moved to upstate New York. My mother-in-law said to my husband, "What are you taking her away to a small town? She's a Yankee?" By her, if I wanted better, I was a Yankee. He didn't listen, and we came here in 1920. My husband set up a tailoring business—cleaning and dyeing. We lived on top of the store. I had to get up six to cook, because when they opened the store they needed the gas for cleaning and pressing.

My husband did very well. We were wealthy. . . . You know when I went to school? When my daughter was going to college. I says, "Now is the time that I go and learn how to spell, so I can write her nice letters."

Quite a few years ago we bought a home on Fairview Drive, on the hill—a beautiful home. I'll tell you an incident. A neighbor came in to welcome me to my home. She was Irish. I talked to her and talked to her, and she looks and looks, and I talk to her—like I would talk to the wall. And she kept on looking—overly bright she wasn't—and I got very disturbed. I says, "Where are you looking? You heard so much of the dirty Jews? Are you looking for the dirt?" The first move was to tell her that I know what she has in mind. Till this very day—and it's many, many years after—they are my best friends, my husband's and mine.

# Vladimir Zworykin

·················· FROM RUSSIA, 1919 ······················

*Known as the "father of television," this well-known inventor was vice-president of RCA Laboratories, has received twenty-seven major awards, including the National Medal of Science, is a member of the National Inventors Hall of Fame, and holds more than 120 patents.*

I came to New York and I took a room in some house. It was Fourth of July and nobody told me anything. In the morning I heard "Bang! Bang! Bong!" I ran out; I grabbed something and ran through the back door and met the proprietor of this building. She said, "What are you doing?"

I said, "Get out, they are shooting guns here."

"Who's shooting?"

"I don't know who's shooting, but you don't want to be shot."

She said, "Come on out. It's the Fourth of July."

I said, "So what?" [*Laughs.*]

# Lydia Orloff

···················· FROM RUSSIA, 1934 ·······················

*She is eighty-seven years old and frail. Her face resembles a skull—almost fleshless, dark shadows everywhere, thin lips; yet her sunken eyes sparkle, her sparse hair is rolled on curlers and neatly covered with a bright print scarf, her voice is strong and vibrant, her movements agile. She talks with gusto, with humor, and with total recall of all the tiny details of her early life as a member of an aristocratic family. Now she is housebound and relies on the priest's wife for her meals. Her tiny rented room in Brooklyn is cluttered with souvenirs of her past—hundreds of photographs (her husband in dress uniform, herself in a ball gown, her estate in Volosova), visiting cards of her family and friends, a blanket made from the hide of her favorite horse, even the key to her St. Petersburg apartment.*

My grandmother was lady-in-waiting for two czars—Alexander III and Nicholas II. And she wanted I should be, too. I was presented to the czarina before I finished school. My grandmother insisted. I was only thinking not to do something wrong. The room was very big. The czarina was sitting up high on a sofa. The butler opened the door, then I had to do such and such steps and then stay and wait. After I made two reverences, she said, "Sit down, please." I sit down. Then she asked me what school I finished and then she said, "Probably you have fiancé?"

"No. I don't like young men. They annoy me only."

"What do you think to do?"

I said, "I think to learn history."

"Your father allow you?"

"I think so. Why not?"

Then she asked about my brother and then she said to me, "I hope to see you again."

I had to go backward. Where is the door? My grandmother was waiting. She asked me, "Tell me, please, you didn't do nothing foolish?"

I didn't want to be lady-in-waiting, because when you are in the court, you have to be liar. If you tell what you think, it is not good. I finished school and I married. I was very young, only sixteen, and my husband was twenty-five. He was officer in the czar's regiment.

He came from Volosova, and after our wedding we came there to spend some weeks in his house. When we came, all the station was in flowers. "What is this?"

My husband was laughing. He said, "This is for me, because I am born there and the people are so eager to see what wife I have." They had come with flowers in the house; the rooms were full of flowers—and it was winter. There is not a flower to buy there in winter. It was people all around and everybody wished us happiness.

But I was too young and too stupid to be a wife. When he said to me to undress, I said no.

And he said, "But we have to go to bed."

"Yes. You go out and I go to bed."

He asked me, "You don't know nothing?"

"What I have to know? What I have to do with you? Go and sleep in your room."

And in the morning, the housekeeper—she was very old, she was housekeeper to his father—she came to us with the coffee and I am alone in bed. She said, "Where is your husband?"

I said, "There, in his study." And so it was one day, second day, third day.

Then my husband was thinking it is better to go to Helsinki, to a hotel. We came there at six and he said, "Now, today it is our day. First we go to the theater and then we go to a restaurant and I show you how it is to eat supper in a restaurant." I never been in a restaurant! Oh, no, never! So I put on a good dress—I had a lot of dresses—and we went to theater and then to the restaurant. At home I had champagne maybe at New Year's, but there my husband gives me champagne and I drink and I drink and I drink. Then he said to me, "I think it is enough." And we came to our room.

I said, "I have to have a maid," because at this time the dresses have not the zipper, but hook, and I cannot hook myself. He said not to disturb the maid. So it was him—he help to open my dress.

So, it is all going on. . . . I remember only I was in bed, and he said, "Be quiet, it is all normal. Tomorrow you can stay in bed. Don't brood. Go to sleep." And so we stayed there one week or so, and then we came back to St. Petersburg.

When we came back to St. Petersburg, I have to do visits. It means you have to meet the people who know your husband. It was Sunday, because they use only Sunday for such a visit. I had a gray dress, all gray, and hat and gloves. I remember I come home—I was not quite dying—exhausted! Sometimes you go to third floor, sometimes to sixth floor. In one day, four, five, six, seven. You take off your coat, you stay ten or twenty minutes, then you dress and go away. When they are not home, you leave the card. If nobody is there, from one side you are happy; on the other side, you are sorry for your feet. Then, if I came to visit them, they come to me with the visit card, too. Everyone has a day. I have Friday. Friday I was home and everybody came for tea, or a cup of wine, if you wish, till seven.

We had a small house in St. Petersburg, seven rooms only. I had a maid, a cook, my old butler, and two coachmen. My husband had military porters, only to run, to clean things for my husband, but not to wait on the table, not in our rooms. I had only one responsibility—to do good things. In Russia, each lady who had a little bit money was doing something for the orphans or the old people—something good. I had my orphanage, together with a friend of mine. Not orphans, but children not from married people. We had only twelve children—not in our home, but we gave them education. We had nurses and a doctor there. We came, we spend time with them. We came sometimes after the ball, at one o'clock or two o'clock, to see how it is there. Then we see if they can finish the high school, or if they are better for something like electrician, or we give them other possibilities. For the girls, maybe seamstress or make hats. We were like mothers. When we came to them, they run to us: "Mamma! Mamma!"

Sometimes there were balls. I remember a big ball St. Petersburg nobility gave to czar when it was two hundredth year of Romanovs. I think it was 1913. I was present. The dress that I wore, it was like a Roman toga, lavender or lilac; very simple, but the back of the dress was long—because ball dresses are long—long and with sable. I don't like jewelry, but my husband and my grandmother said, "This time you have to have everything." And I had two diamond necklaces. And I had on the head a feather with emeralds mounted in silver. You can imagine how brilliant this was!

It was in a big, big room with a balcony, one great balcony all around. People were sitting on the balcony. When somebody wanted to dance, he came up the steps, invited the lady, and they came down and danced. The czarina was sitting in the room where we are dancing, but there is a special box for her. Only her son and Olga were there with her, because Tatiana was in this time sick—measles or something. . . .

The czar's regiment was never fighting, but in First World War all regiments fight. Everybody are thinking my husband is dead, and then I have a letter from Germany: "Your husband is wounded and he is prisoner in Germany."

I left St. Petersburg when the Revolution came. I didn't want to believe it. I was thinking it is only temporary. First they say all the servants have to go. My cook, my butler, they don't want to go. And I received a letter that I don't permit my butler and the cook to go. I said to them, "Please, go. . . ."

The butler said, "I can't complain. Everything is good. I live very good with my lady."

The cook said, "I choose my lady and I stay."

Then the commissar came and said to me that everything I have belong to the people, the Russian people, and not to me. We are only robbers.

I said, "No. My father was hard worker, and my husband is officer."

He said, "We know these officers—drunk all day."

"My husband is never drunk!"

"Shut your mouth! I give you twenty-four hours. Tomorrow you go out. The house is ours."

My Julian, the butler, he said, "It is better you go, because it is something mad going on. I do everything." He and my cook, together, all night they packed and packed and packed. At the morning, Julian said to me, "Here is the ticket. Go to Novocherkassk, to the house of my sister." He had five or six great barrels with my things.

But when I came to the door, the soldiers said, "What is this?"

Julian said, "It is mine, all mine. I stay in this place long time, and now is revolution, and I can take what I want."

The soldier said, "Good. Go, old man." And Julian took me to the train, and I had everything what I needed.

In Novocherkassk, Julian's sister was like a second mother for me. She help me, but I have to cook. That was a comedy! Something like spaghetti, I put in the cold water—I don't know how many. And after it was ready, it was a lump! Not eatable. [Laughs.]

One day at eight in the morning, I was alone in the house. Somebody knocks on the door. Somebody was going to break the door in pieces—the door and the doorbell together. I looked from the second floor and I see only the hat, officer cap. I run the steps and I open the door, and my husband stands there! I was together laughing and crying. I said, "My goodness! How you came here?" He asked, "May I get my belongings?" I said, "Why?" Such a question! It was three years and somebody had told him his wife is married a second time. Now he was so happy to find me waiting for him.

Then he go with the White Army, and I go with him. We are with the army all the time—forwards, then backwards, then forwards. And finally we retreated, and with the army we came to Constantinople. In Constantinople we are sitting and planning where to go. Most people went to France, but we are thinking so: Too many people go to France. It is difficult to get a job. Better we go to Italy.

In Italy, my husband was first a teacher for English and French. Then he was painter, then in balalaika concert. Yes, he did everything. I tried this and that, but it is not so good.

Now here is a story. You know, many years ago in St. Petersburg, when I was a child, I had had ballet lessons—from ten years till I married. Then, in Italy, somebody tell me there is a troupe who needs a ballerina and it is very good paid. It was a Russian troupe, but entrepreneur is Italian—Turelli. I was thinking maybe I go and try it. But first, I try at home. Umph! It is going hard, because I haven't made exercise all these years. But I tried. I came there to the troupe and I had a big success. I was not a star, but starlet, then I was prima donna. We danced everywhere—Rome, Venice, Milan, Florence. I danced in *Nutcracker*, then Bluebird in *Sleeping Beauty*, then *Scheherazade*, *Faust*, everything.

But then my husband said to me, "You know, Lydia, I lost my name because of you. Now I am not Orloff, I am Nadicheff"—the name I took as ballerina—"because people call me Mr. Nadicheff. It is not right. I love you, but I know how great success you have. I know it is your career and probably you be something. Choose what you wish."

I was thinking, thinking. It is very nice, applause and everything. But when you are old, you have nothing. And I said, "I stay with you." He was so happy.

We decided to go to America, and we went to Milwaukee, because we heard Russian people was there. In Milwaukee there was a big, big department store—Schuster's. My husband came there and he found job. He was the chief of all the cleaners. I give, meantime, Russian lessons. We have very nice, small apartment, only two rooms—one big room, one smaller, and bathroom and kitchenette. We stayed there until my husband passed away.

I was all alone. I knew no people there, I didn't talk English. I wanted to poison myself with gas. I opened the gas and I wanted to die. But in a moment I was thinking the door is not tight, other people could die, too. I opened the window and then I ran. I ran around Milwaukee and I came to lake. And I was thinking, "No, I can't. . . . Better I go away." I had a friend in New York, old friend from Russia, and so I came there.

First I stayed with my friend, but she died. Then I looked for place like a nurse-companion lady. And I found. Sometime it was temporary, and then I had a rest. I was living in a boardinghouse on Seventy-eighth Street, but then I have—I call it "spell." Such a dizziness, I don't see nothing, I don't feel nothing. When I have such a spell, I have to have somebody. So I came to live in Brooklyn, with family of our priest.

I didn't know what Brooklyn is. Nobody told me. If I knew, I never came to Brooklyn. We live in two-family house. One day, it was the day when I had my Security check, I buyed what I need and I come back. The first door, I didn't shut it, because I want to enter in the lobby and open our door. In this moment, two black men come, one on this side and the other one on the other side. I wanted to call somebody, but I have not voice. They wanted my bags, one with money and the other with everything I had. They took everything from me. . . .

I have mind to leave New York, but I have nobody. What will happen to me?

# Max Levy

*Now retired, he ran a successful accounting business in Boston. He was seventeen, a student in Odessa, when the Bolshevik Revolution broke out in 1917.*

Reeshelievskaya Street was a well-lighted street in the evenings, with expensive apartment buildings, large stores of every description, richly decorated store windows with all kinds of merchandise, ice cream parlors, watermelon lounges, and restaurants, all ready to serve the evening crowd of students. The street was wide, with trees on both sides, wide sidewalks with wooden benches for accommodation of the strollers. This was where all the students used to congregate in the evenings, to chat, to exchange views, discuss various cultural subjects, and, by all means, to meet with girl students. Our lives were full, satisfying, interesting, and we enjoyed every minute of this paradise. It seemed that we students belonged to one family, with education restricted only to the few, with intelligence and education blended together into a high standard at our school systems. We students maintained among ourselves an environment of the highest quality. Our attractive school uniforms added considerably to the beauty of such evenings. The girl students in their white starched pinafores over their green dresses, with their brown, wide-brimmed straw hats, completed the enchanting atmosphere of those evenings. . . .

The last time the Czar Nicholas visited Odessa, in the summer of 1916, he came unexpectedly, without any guards. at 6:00 P.M. on May 9, 1916, I was on my way to Reeshelievskaya Street, when I saw huge crowds running towards Pushkinskaya Street, which runs from the bank of the Black Sea to the railroad station, where the czar and his family stayed. I heard people shouting, "The czar is coming!" and then the cortege reached the part of the street where I was standing.

First came the police chief of Odessa in his big automobile, followed by another big automobile with the mayor of the city. Then, a few minutes later, the "hurrahs" reached a deafening uproar, and the automobiles of the czar's family appeared. In the first very big automobile was sitting the Czar Nicholas II, and next to him his wife, Czarina Alexandra Feodorovna, both smiling those artificial, picture-taking smiles, and nodding their heads. In the second row of the same automobile was sitting the Grand Duchess Tatiana Nikolaevna, waving her hands. Next to her the Czarevitch Alexei Nikolaevitch was standing up in the automobile, in a soldier's war uniform, his hand touching the visor of his cap, saluting. In the second big automobile was sitting Princess Olga Nikolaevna and next to her Princess Xenia Nikolaevna, both smiling those hard smiles without any feelings and slowly waving their hands. In the second row of this same automobile was sitting Princess Anastasia Nikolaevna, by herself, wholeheartedly smiling and waving both her hands.

I was much impressed with Anastasia's sweet smile and general attitude. She seemed really natural, expressing goodness and humane feelings, in contrast to her sisters. Although the cortege was moving slowly, it took only a few seconds for the automobile with the Princess Anastasia to disappear from my view. Within these few seconds I observed a great deal about Anastasia. I noticed the few freckles on her face and an attractive dimple in her left cheek. I was standing in front of the other people on the sidewalk, and I directed my waves to Princess Anastasia, shouting her name. In all that thundering shouting by so many people, it seemed that she heard her name mentioned and followed my voice until our eyes met. She turned slightly in her seat, waved her hand toward me, smiling pleasantly, until she completely disappeared from my view. Dreams of a young boy—it seemed to me that she was singling me out of all the thousands standing there with me. Little me, an obscure individual, getting the attention of a princess! I knew it was my imagination, but just the thought of it made me happy. Even today, sixty years later, I still remember distinctly her sweet smile and beautiful face with the dimple. . . .

The Revolution began with the time that Rasputin was killed. I remember distinctly when it was in the papers about him being killed, the students celebrated in the classrooms. They made caricatures of him on the blackboards, and this was in December 1916.

There was no established government in Odessa at that time, and living conditions were very bad. Everything was a shortage. There was not enough fuel, wasn't enough bread, there were lines always at the stores. Many stores were closed—they didn't have any merchandise to sell. It reached the point where students lost the ambition to study. The schools were cold, the home where you lived was cold, there wasn't enough food, there wasn't enough clothing. There was no police; there was no government at all; so it was chaos, actually. At night we were afraid even to go out. Many people stole uniforms. They used to just walk up to you and say, "Why don't you take off your clothes?" They took off my school uniform jacket one night that way.

Then, in 1918, General Denikin occupied Odessa. He fought for the monarchy, and he closed the city. He didn't let anybody out. Trains didn't run out or in to Odessa. We just had to stay there. Finally, in the spring, a few of us students somehow stole out of the city. We bought some knapsacks and we took a few belongings, and we started to walk. The only way was to walk—there were no trains. We walked along the railroad tracks, until we got to some city where the trains were running, and we got home, to Zaslav.

The Germans occupied the Ukraine, where I lived. But the Germans behaved very badly in Ukrainia. They stole from the farmers, they killed farmers. They were very, very bad. This brought the people of the Ukraine against them, and the peasants revolted. The Germans fled, and then the Bolsheviks attacked the Ukraine. The Polish government attacked the Bolsheviks. Everybody wanted the Ukraine, the richness of the land.

When the Polish government came into our town, the door opened up to western Europe, and life was changed for the better. People started to travel, and I went to Warsaw to see if there's any possibility of going to America and to get documents, like a visa. I didn't completely decide to go. I still hoped that things would normalize in Russia and I'd get a good education and be able to get myself established. It was a very difficult decision for me to make. You take twenty years and throw it away. Twenty years of your life! In my student days I never thought about coming to this country. I never intended to come. If it weren't for the Revolution, I wouldn't be here.

You see, the condition of the Russian Jews was in such a state. Of course the Russian Jews were persecuted. But a certain sector of the Jews didn't notice it, didn't feel that much. Now American people go and see *Fiddler on the Roof*, and they think that was the condition of the Russian Jew. But it wasn't so. Some Russian Jews had homes, they had businesses, some were rich, educated their children. There were some substantial Jews but not very many. Now for those type of Jews, America was no place to go. Mostly people who came here were the poor people. They came here to improve their financial conditions— mostly working people, and most of them were ignorant people, too. I mean they had no education. So I never thought about coming here, because I was in school and I was going to graduate and go to the University of Kharkov and be settled somewhere. . . .

While I was in Warsaw, the Bolsheviks attacked the Poles and kicked them back, and on my way back home from Warsaw I met all kinds of people fleeing our territory, because the Communists were attacking my town. I came to Tarnopol. Tarnopol was the boundary line between

Austria and Russia; now it was Poland. The war was going on. There were no passenger trains, but there was a military train going to my town from Tarnopol. I approached a military Polish man, and I says, "I want to go to Zaslav." He says, "It's a military train." Finally I convinced him, and I went on the train.

About twenty miles out of our city, the train went off the track. Then they were coming, the Bolsheviks, from the other side. We noticed them attacking the train, see, some with those long pikes—the Cossacks used to carry them. So everybody jumped out of the trains and went on the other side. But I, on the contrary, jumped on this side, and two Cossacks were running against me with those pikes, you know. So I stood up and waved a white handkerchief, and they came and they undressed me, took over all my clothes. And they gave me a pair of dirty pants that one soldier was wearing. They caught the other ones and they took us, leading us away, to some prison or somewhere. And we traveled.

They brought us to Kiev. They have there what they call a *krepis*—it's a fort—and they kept us there. The walls were *that* thick. In fact, on the window sills people slept. And you were lucky if you got a window sill, because we slept on the floor. To accommodate so many people in one room, they can't give you cots. We slept on the floor. If you got some straw, you were a lucky man.

They used to give us a Russian bread for ten people. We weren't allowed to have any knives in our room, so somehow somebody got hold of a piece of tin, and they cut the bread in ten pieces. Now you can't tell which one is smaller, so one man stood against the wall with his back to us, and one man cut the bread, and each piece he said, "*Komu?*" *Komu* means "Who for?" So the man against the wall said, for instance, "for Levy." That means that piece of bread belongs to me, whether it was small or large. And that piece of bread—you were so hungry that you were afraid you're going to eat it now, you'll be hungry for the next twenty-four hours. So you used to take a piece at a time, a piece at a time, but the temptation was great. . . .

I became friendly with one of the guards, a soldier who participated in the killing of the czar's family. It was unbelievable to me, so I questioned him, and he described to me Anastasia's features, her dimple and freckles, and I remembered that evening in Odessa when I saw the czar and his family. Then I was convinced that he was telling the truth. . . .

So who did I meet in this prison? The head doctor was my school chum's mother. She was ordered to be a doctor there, against her will—she had to. I told her I had to get away. So she said, "Look, I have a right to give out permits. I can give you a document for three days that you're a *sanitar* [male nurse], and then you're on your own." And I went to Kiev.

When I was in Kiev, running around without a passport and without food, begging to sleep somewhere and being afraid of being arrested and put back in prison, I definitely decided that if I get back to my home, I will definitely try and go back to either Europe or America. That was my decision at that time.

Finally, I got back home, and there was a complete exodus of people, because they were afraid. The rumors were that the town was going to fall into Bolshevik hands. I couldn't remain there because I was an escapee. And my fiancée and her mother had sold their house and were ready to leave. We decided to leave together. We packed up a big bag—a special packer was for that. He packs and he knows how to pack—a samovar and the pillows and bedding.

We went by wagon, you know—you hire a wagon with a peasant—to Tarnopol. That's where the train began to go to Warsaw. Going there, to Tarnopol, we had so much abuse and insults from Polish soldiers and from Ukrainians, too. It wasn't funny. When we got to a little town before Tarnopol and it got dark, toward night, the *khotins*, the Ukrainians in Austria, tried to tell the driver not to go on at night. They wanted us to stay there. We wouldn't be alive today. But that peasant himself kind of got scared. He said, "No, I'll go." And when we came into the town of Tarnopol, the Jewish committees—they organized committees to meet all those refugees from the Ukraine—and they met us, they gave us a place to stay.

Of course, passports—we didn't have any passports. You had to acquire passports in Poland, Polish passports; but the Polish government wouldn't give you a passport unless you have proof of what nationality you are. So the Ukrainians, they formed a government in Warsaw, in exile, and you went to them, and for money they gave you a Ukrainian passport. If you had a Ukrainian passport, you got a Polish passport. So we lived in Warsaw I think about a year, and in the meantime we got married. In one room, my wife slept, her mother, a girl we took with us from Zaslav slept with us, and another boy from the same town, and I—in one little room.

So finally, after waiting and waiting—they had a HIAS [Hebrew Immigrant Aid Society] there, and people used to stay—those refugees—in the thousands, every day, looking at the lists if they see somebody's looking for them from the United States. . . . And one day I come over there and look and I see, good enough, my wife's name was there. See, her father was already in the U.S., and he bought tickets for us with a Jewish agency. So then we went to the ticket office, the boat ticket office, the Cunard Line, and they had the tickets, they had money, everything waiting for us. [*Laughs.*] So then we got the visa and we left.

I remember there was a full train, mostly Jews. We took the train from Warsaw, Poland, till the German border. Then we changed into a German train. We came to Berlin in the evening, the railroad station; and there, too, like anywhere else, there was the Jewish elite from Berlin. They came and they gave us sandwiches and talked to us.

And from there, of course, we traveled—it took us quite some time. We went from Rotterdam across the Channel to England with a small ferry. And then in England they had to bring us to the port, whatever it was. They put us in those flat platforms, with horses, and we had to stand up, and everybody looked like cattle. You were just like cattle. And they brought us to a place which belongs to the Cunard Line, and we stayed there for about two weeks. It was dirty, filthy, but we had to wait for the ship. When I think about it now, it's really heartbreaking. I mean, we were not human beings—in the trains, in the ship, just like cattle. All the way to America!

We traveled by ship about six days. Then we came to New York. We had to go through Ellis Island. They examined you whether you can read or not. They don't let you in here without—not in my time, anyway. You could sign your name, is all right. You write your name. My mother-in-law wrote her name in Yiddish, was good enough. A very young girl from Hungary, a beautiful girl, she just couldn't read or write—no language, nothing. She hired me to teach her. So I gave her the lessons there, and I taught that girl how to sign her name and how to read it. That's all. To go through Ellis Island.

Then we came to New York. We went to the train. I didn't speak English, but I had everything written down, so I say "Boston." [*Laughs.*] We went to the house that my father-in-law rented. Of course, the life was a poor life; but in comparison to the economy of Russia, especially in the last few years of the war, it was paradise. We still had gaslight in our apartment, but while we lived in it, they installed electricity. And of course we had a dark toilet and a little bath. And there was a little window going out into a skylight, and the next building, the next apartment—his window also came out to the same skylight.

When I came here, the first thing I did is I went to a bookstore—all the Jewish intellectuals used to gather there—and I bought a Russian-English textbook [*laughs*], and I started to study right away. The first thing I did. Then I had to look for a job. So they got me a job somewhere in a factory where they made bags. My job was to pack them in with newspapers to keep them in shape when they sell them. I got eight dollars a week. Then a friend of ours worked in a factory where they made ladies' handbags. He said, "I'll get you a *good* job, ten dollars a week.'' But ten dollars a week was money in those years, you know. So I worked there. Then it didn't suit me either, so I found a job in a shoe factory. I came there and told the man that I wanted to cut shoes, I'm a shoe cutter. He put me there, and I saw him standing and watching me, whether I can do it. So I pretended. I pulled the leather this way and the other way, and I looked at it, to cut the shoes. I worked there for quite a few years. They were good to me. When I needed money for school, I told him, one of the sons. He always gave me a check; he took off from my pay, every week so much.

I wanted to go to school, so I went to Northeastern University—at that time it was actually a prep school. I went nights there and tried to study English. I was working and going to school, and I didn't mix much with the American people actually, but just with foreigners. Like for instance the prep school; I met people who came the same time with me from Russia and who also were going to school there. We were the Russian intellectuals, and we chummed together. I remember we couldn't speak English, but we wanted to get the experience; and they used to have a theater in Boston, a stock company, St. James Theater on Huntington Avenue. We used to go there every Monday. We could hardly understand it, but just to get the swing of the English language we used to go there. So I had no knowledge until the time I went to the university. Otherwise I had no knowledge of the difference, of the democracy of this country at all.

I knew it was a poor life. People work in the sweatshops, and they live in those cheap apartment houses. In those years it wasn't so easy to accomplish things, as people do the last thirty, forty years. For an illustration: When I came here, I wanted to go to M.I.T. I wanted to be an engineer. I had a background for it, too. But then I realized that if I go to M.I.T.—a friend of mine and my wife's cousin, too, graduated M.I.T., and they couldn't even get a job. All those scientific corporations were conducted by non-Jews and very anti-Semitic. If you are a Jew, you couldn't get a job in those places. This man I knew, he came out of M.I.T. with flying honors. He had to become an insurance man. So even in education, you had to select something when you came here that you'd be able to make a living.

What impressed me most, first, is when I went to Boston University. I had my documents from Russia; I had them translated by a translator I found in the West End. And I went to the Boston University College of Business Administration. It was on Boylston Street, right where now is a mutual insurance company today. I went in there, and the dean of the Business School was Dean Lord. He was a very fine man, very interesting man, and a very good man. I went into his office—and you had no difficulty going into his office—just walked in the door and walked in. To a dean! I looked—maybe there is some soldier there, outside, or somebody watching—nobody. I walked in and I walked to his desk and I plunked that paper on his desk. I couldn't speak English well; I was going to prep school. And I walked away a few steps and I stood at attention. That's what I was used to. And I start talking to him and I was kind of afraid. I was shivering a little. He immediately read my mind. He was a good mind reader, or he understood things. He got up, he walked over to me and put his arm around me, and he said to me, "My friend, don't be afraid. You're not in Russia; you're in the United States. We are a free country. It's a democracy here. You are just as good as anybody else. Come on, sit down."

So I sat near him and we talked, and I had to consult my dictionary. I had a little pocket dictionary, so I took it out and looked there, you see. I had a very nice discussion with him. Half I didn't understand, half *he* didn't, I suppose. He was my friend till he died.

When I walked out of his office, I walked around and I said, "My God, I'm really in a free country." Mind you, a dean! I couldn't conceive such a thing. A dean! Talking to you that way and asking you to sit down and talk like, as he said, "to my own son." And that's the time that I really felt the democracy. Then I started going to school and I see the way boys call the professor "Prof" when they talk to the professors. You know, the old country wasn't like that. You couldn't just talk to them. I felt democracy, you see. I just felt it. That is the time when I actually realized and appreciated the value of living in a free and democratic country.

Well, it was a struggle. It wasn't easy to go to school and I had my difficulties. I had family problems. I had personal problems. I had money problems. But there's one thing that I had, is that I wanted to get somewhere, and that kept me alive and gave me the courage. And I still think, as my Dean Lord told me when I talked to him—he died a few years ago; he lived to about ninety, I guess—he said to me, "Max, I expected from you more than what you accomplished." *He expected* because he knew my ambitions, what I wanted to do. But, of course, not everybody can reach just what you intend to. And I'm glad I reached what I *have* reached. That's all there is to it. . . .

## Ida Levy

·······················FROM RUSSIA, 1921·······················

*After her divorce from Max Levy over forty years ago, she went to work as a cleaning woman. With some help from her ex-husband, she managed to support herself and her three children and to send them all to college. Now she lives in a nursing home in a Boston suburb.*

When I was a little girl my life was very dull, like all the rest of the people in Russia—poorness, no time to invest in pleasure. I lived in Zaslav. It was supposed to be a big city, but you can cover it in an hour—the four corners of the city. No trains, no streetcars, no other communication. You go on foot or with two horses and a wagon. There was a hospital, there was a bank, but not much to speak of. It was just like *Fiddler on the Roof.* Everybody didn't have anything to eat, didn't have any clothes, didn't have a lot of things. There was no school. A teacher came in, and he used to teach me Hebrew and Russian. I had one cousin that went to *gymnasium,* and I had another friend that went. But you need money for school. We had very nice people living next door to us, and they had six children and nobody went to school. One learned from the other to read a little. Others didn't even know how to sign their name.

In our village were Polish and Jews and Russians. We used to buy milk from the Russian peasants. They milk the cow and bring it to market and sell chicken and eggs. I liked them. Some Russian people I liked very much. I could speak with the Russian people, and I had a lot of friends.

We lived in somebody else's house. My mother and myself occupied a room, because my father was in the United States. When he was a boy he served in the Russian army, and he had enough of it. And when the [Russo-Japanese] war broke out, he ran away to be able to exist without being in the service. Somebody lent him the money and he came here in a ship that has no luxuries—a freighter. He must have been away about five years, and then he came back, to try out whether he can take it. There wasn't too much luxuries here [U.S.] neither, but it wasn't as bad as Russia. So he came back and he stayed with us five years. Then he went back to America again for good.

While he was home, we bought a little house, four-room house, made of clay, with a tile roof. The house inside wasn't bad. We had floors—other houses didn't have any floors, they just had open earth. It was four rooms: dining room, living room, kitchen, and bathroom.

I had a boyfriend. He was a student in Odessa, but he came from my city and he used to come home for vacations. We met like a lot of young people do. He had a friend who was a neighbor of ours, who says, "I'll introduce you to a girl, a friend of mine. She's very pretty. You're going to love her." [*Chuckles.*] And he claimed he loved me. I don't know whether he meant it or not, but he said it. He used to send me letters. And when he came, he was practically living in my house.

He lived in our town, but I was from across the tracks. [*Laughs.*] My father was a tailor and his father and his brother had a city job. They took care of the citizens—birth certificates and burying certificates and things like that. He had a very lovely sister. She graduated *gymnasium* and she used to teach people. And they were better off; they had a beautiful house. . . .

During the First World War, we had French soldiers in our town. We had a clean little house, my mother and myself—there was nobody else in the house. When the soldiers came in to invade the house, they saw it was fit for officers better. So they just left it for the officers and they remained someplace else. Three officers stayed in the house. Then they got off to the front, you know, for the invasions, and somebody else, another group, came in. We stayed in the house, too, and they used to help us. They used to bring butter, sometimes bread, sometimes cheese.

During the Revolution, the Bolsheviks came. We were afraid to be home, so we went into the neighbor's house, because he was a man. He had six children, three big boys, so we stayed there. Through the window we can see the Bolsheviks come over with bayonets and open up the lock and take out anything they wanted.

They left, and we went back. Then more soldiers came in and they were mad and they pulled out drawers—you know, where you prepare things for Passover—that must have been April—and throw them just at your face, at your head. My mother wore a fur jacket, and they took it right off of her. They took everything—letters and pictures and everything. They didn't take them because they loved them—they destroyed them. I had beautiful pictures from friends, you know, and they tore them up. And then they left—to invade other cities or villages or whatever. After the invasion, after they came in, the people from the villages had a chance to come and take whatever they liked from the Jewish houses—furniture, curtains, anything—and I told you there wasn't too much. Still, it was a house that was livable. We were afraid, because the Bolsheviks were killers!

My father used to send us money. On account of the Revolution, the mail didn't get into the cities, and it was stopped in Poland—Warsaw. My father sent boat tickets to go to America and three hundred dollars in cash money, and *somehow* we got the message.

So we packed up whatever we had—anything that was possible to take, like underwear, a tablecloth, something like that. And we left the house, everything else. We didn't sell it. There was nobody to sell it to.

My husband [Max Levy, page 93], who was my boyfriend then, came home from Odessa. There was no school at that time, because of the Revolution. So he came home and he was hiding. He couldn't go out on the street, because he was young and he was supposed to be in the service. He decided to leave his family and come with us. He thought it would be good for him. We hired a horse and a team and we ran. . . .

So we came to Warsaw and the refugee committees were looking up the banks for our money, for our ship tickets. And they couldn't find them. We didn't know where the money was, because the communication wasn't so wonderful. So whatever we had, we had to sell it in Poland to be able to eat. We were living with so many people in the same apartment—no privacy, nothing. So you're just miserable. It took us about seven or eight months, and then a telegram came and said that this and this bank has got the money.

We wrote to my father that such and such a boy—they had a nice name in the city, and the boy claims he's in love with the daughter, and we want to take him along; because he had to have a visa. A lot of people took other girls or boys with. My father was a good man and he was willing. He sent him a ticket and he sent him money. Then we had to sign papers that we're taking my boyfriend as a future husband of mine.

The thing is, when it came close to get ready to leave, we were afraid. They said that a lot of people were stopped by the American consul. They are stopped if they took people with. So it was a chance, unless I would be married. I didn't want it, didn't want to get married. I wanted to be free. I was nineteen years old. I had a boyfriend—I didn't mind that. I could have taken my time, but we were afraid. What is he going to do when we leave? And if they stop him coming, what is he going to do? He had no profession, nobody needs him. We were afraid that he'll live a hard life; so to save him, we got married. We went to a rabbi and we had a wedding performed. It was just a week before we sailed. If I had known then, I wouldn't have bothered.

So we went by train to Rotterdam, I think. I don't remember. Then to Liverpool. And then we went by a big ship, a beautiful ship. Third class, but it was very beautiful. We had a downstairs cabin, just my mother and myself, because they separate the men—a cabin with bunk beds and nice spreads.

We came into New York six o'clock in the evening, and it was havoc—the rushing people, the trains, people running to the trains. And the buildings—I couldn't look up to the top of them. In my city, I never saw an extra person, I never saw a train, never saw. . . .

We had to go by train to Boston. In the station, Grand Central Station, I wanted to have a drink. I had fifty cents in my palm and I put it on the counter and I [*makes motion of drinking*]. Then a woman came along—must be Good Will people—she brought us a basket with pears and apples and things like that. We were hungry and that woman saved our lives, I think. Then the train came. There were people that helped you. What do you call them—like Travelers Aid? They used to come and say, "Where are you going? Where are you coming from?" And they used to place you in the train. So it was easy.

We came to South Station and nobody was there, so we knew that there was going to be trouble. But then somebody came along. "Are you coming in from New York? Do you belong to this or that family?" they used to ask. And imagine what a thrill after so many years, somebody said to my mother, "Your husband was just here." We missed him coming to the train—maybe he came to a different entrance, you know. But we had his address in Boston and they took us to the apartment, and finally he came along.

We came in, and the house was furnished, new furniture. There was a kitchen, two bedrooms. It was wonderful. The stove—imagine, no coal! You just turn the valve and there's fire. It was something beautiful. We sat and looked and were surprised. I wouldn't look twice at it now—it was nothing to look at—but it was nice then.

And my father went into the stores and bought us beautiful stuff: fish, smoked fish, and rolls and coffee and everything. We didn't see it for years in Russia already. Then we started going out for a walk and looking in the stores and seeing all the beautiful things that there were.

When I was in Russia I didn't have to want anything. There wasn't anything to want. I had a pair of shoes, a dress—that's all you needed. You didn't have to buy theater tickets or things like that. There wasn't even a movie in the city. So how could I want anything? Here, I loved it. It was very interesting and very beautiful, until we got acquainted, and then we wanted everything that other people had.

My father was an old-fashioned guy. He loved my mother. To him, she was the queen of the house, and that was to the end, till they died. He told me he invested the money on me and on my husband to come here, and I have to stay with her. There wasn't any other children but me, so I have to stay with them—stay with my mother especially, to help her go shopping and things like that. So I did. I used to sneak out in the afternoon to the movies for seventeen cents, so my mother shouldn't know. She wouldn't like it. She used to tell my father that I left her all alone, and he didn't like it. Then I would have to be punished. So I did it on my own. I "went shopping" and I went into the movies instead.

In a few weeks my husband got a job in a factory, and then he started going to school. But I became pregnant. I didn't work and I didn't come in contact with any people. I didn't have any neighbors to learn from. I didn't have any family to learn from. I envied the people that were here from before. I thought they were so smart, with the language, speaking. I used to look at everybody's face, not knowing what they mean. I was always envious of the people in the schools.

Then I had a baby and I had to take care of bigger things. I didn't do anything with my life by being here. I wanted to go driving and go to movies and go to theaters and things like that. I was disappointed in my married life, so I didn't do anything at all. But I don't blame the country for it.

There is one satisfaction in my life. I didn't have a good married life, but I had three beautiful children, one son and two daughters—very well educated, very nicely mannered. They are wonderful, and I look up to them, and I think that's enough for a poor woman.

# Gregory Leontyeff

························ FROM RUSSIA, 1923 ························

*One of the last of the Cossacks, he is now churchwarden of a Russian Orthodox church in northern Indiana. His calendar is the church calendar. He lives in a small apartment on the church grounds, so that he can be available for regular services, holiday celebrations, births and deaths and marriages. Bent with age, he bows stiffly and kisses the hand of the interviewer before settling down to reminisce.*

Cossack—that's the society that in whole Russian history, they protect the country. My father Cossack, my grandfather Cossack—maybe two, three hundred years, people from my family belong to Cossack society. All person of my family, all my relatives, was officers in the Russian Cossack army. I like to be the same way. We have eleven Cossack sections—Don, Kuban, Siberian—eleven different Cossack areas. The biggest one is Don Cossack. I am Don Cossack.

When I was nine, I was in a military school. I live there and I go home just on vacation—Christmas, Easter, and summertime. When I finish the middle military school, like high school, I go in the military academy in Petrograd for two years. In 1912 I graduate and go in Poland, my first officer duty, about nineteen miles from Austria border.

We have a small Cossack soldier school, right in the regiment. We teach the regular Cossack to be sergeant. You know, sometimes he just can't write his name, but he good Cossack and we have to train him. What we do in the military academy, all Cossacks have to learn that. So I teach the Cossacks how to ride on the horse. You know, something way down on ground, and full speed I have to lean off my horse and take that from the ground. Then I come up and touch ground on the other side, stand up on horse, and so. Then we have to teach our horses to lay down when we need it, in case we fight. Then I have to teach how to take the wounded man sometime—somebody wounded, we don't like to leave them. Then I have to watch how the Cossack keeps the horse, how he clean it.

That was just small town, about nine thousand person, mostly Jewish people. The officers have nothing to do, but the commander all the time he make something for the officers to do. But, anyway, the time when we are free from the duty, the officers drink, because nothing to do. No theater, no family, nothing—just officers we meet every day. Same face today, same face tomorrow. But sometimes, we walking in evening time in small garden, the orchestra play and we try to have a better time. This commander, he don't like the young officers be friendly with the young ladies. He have daughter, and a couple times I see her with her friend in that garden. One time the soldiers started singing loud, and she jump a little bit—unexpected. Well, that give me chance to start speaking to her, and from this evening—well, you understand. Every day more and more. But then the First War started and during the wartime the Revolution started, and not until five years later we marry. . . .

The first day war was declared, we was in the fight and we have Cossack officers killed. We move about twenty miles in our Russian territory, and I was on the duty that time. My company have to be ready to fight if something happens—by the saddle, all horses ready just to tie up. And early in the morning, just started light, about sixteen Austrian soldier, cavalry, come in the village, just about one hundred feet from yard where we was, and started shooting. They don't hit nobody, but I right away give command "To the horse!" and we start to chase the Austrian soldiers. We catch them maybe a mile and a half, and then that Austrian officer turn his horse back to meet my attack. But was too late. We was already shooting. And . . . I very sorry . . . they were all taken care of. [Breaks down and cries.] Sixty years, but I can't forget. I had to kill officer by hitting him on head with end of my gun. I can feel that in my body. He was young man, my age, maybe he have fiancée waiting for him. . . .

During the war, all the time the cavalry in the first part, where the front fighting. We take that line first and keep it before the infantry come. All the time we was in the fight. But then we start to hear stories—dirty story about czarina—that the czarina a German spy, Rasputin a German spy, that the czarina have to be put down from the throne and send her in a monastery, and so and so like that. Then started Bolshevik propaganda, a newspaper, not a real newspaper, but small. It said, "Put your arms down and meet your enemy and kiss them. Go home, because the people who have lots of land, they make big money and you're going to be hungry," and so and so.

Then, in 1917, March 1, we have a telegram from the main headquarters—because the czar was at that time the head of the army.

Czar say he going down from throne and he ask all soldiers to be honest
to new government. Then they ask all our men to make promise to
new government, and we do that—except maybe a few person. One big
general, he declared that he make oaths to czar and he don't do that for
nobody else, and they take him right away from the front, no matter
that he was already big general and a very good commandant. But we
fighting in the same way like we do in the czar's regiments. We feel
very bad, but we have to serve our side. Czar order us to listen and be
honest to new government and we do that—up to the end of August
1917, when government in Petrograd was under influence of Bolshevik.

The first thing, the new government say the soldier don't have to
listen to the order of his officer. You understand what that means?
During the wartime, that mean that officer is commander, but he can't
send his soldier in a fight. He has to ask first special committee,
representative of the soldier, if this committee say okay. Such
condition in a very, very short time destroyed all army. At that time
we started fighting against the government.

[Eventually, he and his regiment were sent to Petrograd, to help in
the fighting there. After two days they were surrounded. They started
negotiations with the Bolsheviks.]

I was the head of committee, like a president of delegation to talk
with the Bolsheviks. We go to Smolny Institute, the head of Bolshevik
at that time. I ask them when I find Lenin, I'd like to speak with Lenin.
First time they don't give me chance, but later they bring me in
another room. Lenin was alone. I know that he is very wise, but still
only a man, that you can speak right to him like a man. I say, "If you
don't like to make peace, okay, we start to fight again, and you don't
know what will be the end of this fight." He said, "We need another
conversation. We speak again to make a little peace between your side
and our side."

[Shortly after this meeting the battle lines shifted, and Gregory
Leontyeff and his regiment were able to move south and rejoin other
White Army units.]

I come back from the front, end of May 1918, and I was appointed
administrator of officer school in Novocherkassk. I was lieutenant
colonel then.

My fiancée—she was not my fiancée yet, only Miss Olga—was in
Novocherkassk, too, with her father, and I see her again there. We
married in October. Two months later, I leave Novocherkassk and I
take my wife with me. I say this is our honeymoon. We was in the fight
all the time, but she was with me; sometime in tent, in very poor
condition, sometime not bad condition. I was adjutant and I always
have office, and sometime we sleep on a table in this office. Poor
condition, but we together. For just two months after our marriage we

live in one place, and after that we have honeymoon . . . to 1970, when she die. All the time was our honeymoon, in the whole world. . . .

[With the White Army, the couple retreated to the Crimea and from there went to Constantinople, where the refugees lived until they could make arrangements to go to other countries.]

We hear from people who travel to United States before us. We have letter that very easy to find job over here, and, like a proof, we have a letter that some people who lived in Constantinople only five, six months ago, over here in United States have own car already! For us, for the European, you know, the man who have own car, that means he rich man! So we get visa, and American Red Cross, in connection with Russian organization over here in the United States, they pay our ticket.

My friend who was with me in officer school and in Constantinople, he come in the United States one month earlier than I did. He don't stay in New York, he go to Indiana, and we go to him. He speak with his boss and he give me job in celluloid company. Don't ask me—slave labor!

Well, first everybody say we going back. Then I was all hopes for come back and save Russia. But after a few years, I don't believe it—especially when I find that President Roosevelt recognized Soviet Union, and they do everything to help to make stronger Bolshevik. Then I became citizen.

In Depression time, people don't work, can't pay rent. I find job making new roads, but that my last job. After that I can't find nothing. Well, then I bought farm, with my friend. He recommended to me, "Gregory, you don't need too much money. When you buy baby chicks, you need couple hundred dollars. Then you raise the roosters, and money that you have from the roosters give you chance to raise a lot chicken." So, we buy chicken farm. We built first chicken coop—no house, nothing. [Chuckles.] This first chicken coop for living, for my family. We have bathroom, we have water, good condition, just no electric. But when I build fourth chicken coop and when I take first baby chicks, at that time we started build house. Well, I don't make money in the farm; but I have a big piece of land, and we started sell eggs, sell garden stuff, like tomatoes, everything except potatoes. Was bad time during the thirties, but when the war started in the forties things better. I put three girls through college. . . .

Only one thing that's important to me, I am very sorry that it not happen. I teach my children that they have to speak Russian. They speak, but my grandchildren no. Well, I don't blame them. Honestly, I don't blame them. I understand the social condition.

But I am happy. In all way, I am happy. I am happy that I am in

United States. [*Breaks down and cries.*] Many people say that so and so bad, so and so bad, but I never feel that. I always thankful for this country. Hard time, good time, bad time; but anyway, I feel free. I feel myself right here born American. No matter that I don't speak good English. I am American anyway.

## Ivor Davies
·····················FROM WALES, 1923 ·····················

I was always grateful for the chance to become something more than I would have in the crowded valleys of Wales, where they was almost waiting for dead man's shoes, you know.

## Thomas Neil
··················· FROM SCOTLAND, 1929·····················

There was no work in Glasgow—seven shipyards and they was all shut down. I said I'm going to America where a man can make a living. I came out on the *Skandia*, and I went through Ellis Island and the immigration man says, "Where you from?" and I says, "Glasgow," and he says, "What state is that in?" and I answered, "It's in a hell of a state," and he let me in.

## Andrew Fraser
····················· FROM SCOTLAND, 1930 ·····················

*His early years in the Highlands left him with a passionate interest in classical bagpipe music—"not the usual drums and pipe bands"—and he has established a school in this country to train pipers in the traditional mode.*

The choice in Scotland was either to be a farmer or gamekeeper or such. Or, if you are mechanically inclined, you must go to the shipyard. That's all there was. I had an uncle was a gamekeeper, and every year when I had my summer holidays, I used to go and stay with him and my aunt, and I just loved it. The glen where my uncle lived was Glen Esque, and Glen Esque was a little glen with a loch or a lake up at the head of it, and the main road just went up by the lake until you had to turn around and come back. There was no way over the hills. You could go by foot or by pony, but you couldn't go by anything else.

A gamekeeper is sort of lonely, but it's beautiful country. You wear the kilt and you walk in the heather, and, you know, you're close to wildlife—the deer, the roe deer, the grouse. And then on August 12, the big shoot used to start. The gentlemen came, and we were the gillies—we drove the grouse. We were the servants for the people with money. There were some Americans—Pierpont Morgan, J. P. Morgan—I remember he came. It was a very enjoyable life.

As I said, if you were mechanically inclined, the only place is the shipyard. All the big vessels—the *Queen Mary*, all the *Queens*—really were built in the Clydebank. And no matter where you go in the world, you'll find a Scots engineer in some capacity. And when I was fourteen I went to serve an apprenticeship in John Brown's shipyard in Glasgow, to be a marine engineer. I put in four years learning the trade and I enjoyed it.

But then the Great Depression was on. I'd served my apprenticeship, and there were very, very few jobs around. I had in mind going to Australia. But just about the time I had completed my apprenticeship, an uncle of mine came home from Oregon, and he had a real good story. He said, "Never mind Australia. America is the place for a young man. Why don't you come to the States? You can stay with me, and if you don't like it you can always go back. It's as simple as that." I really got fascinated with the idea. Well, I'll try America, and if I like it I'll stay, and if I don't I'll still go to Australia.

It had been for years difficult, extremely difficult, to get a visa to come to the United States. It was about five years as a rule. However, with the Depression and many people coming back from America, my visa came through within just a short time.

I came over on a boat, third class, twelve or fourteen young fellows in one room. Then Travelers Aid met me in New York and put me on a train to the West Coast. What amazed me was it was so hot—it was August. I felt like I was going to smother. And I never saw so many colored people. I couldn't believe it. I only saw one before in my whole life, in Glasgow. The trip took the better part of a week—to Chicago, then the Rockies, and then on to Portland, and finally my uncle's place.

He had a great big dairy farm. It was a commercial farm, with so many cows. We milked about a hundred and fifty cows every morning and every night. My aunt and my uncle and my cousins and everybody milked cows. So I learned for the first time in my life how to milk cows. You, see, over in Scotland the women milked the cows, not the men.

My aunt was Indian—pure American Indian. She was a wonderful woman. I didn't even know she was Indian, until one day I saw real Indians, and I was so excited, and she realized that I didn't know and told me.

Well, the first winter I stayed with my uncle, and I did very low-priced work, like slashing brush. I wasn't too happy about that. I went to Portland several times looking for a machinist job, but jobs were scarce, and nobody believed that at my age I'd served five years.

The next spring I got a job as what is known as a "packer" on a sheep ranch. They give you a saddle horse and about three mules, and they teach you how to put a diamond hitch on and put food on horse- and muleback. They had three big bands of sheep and they used to take them out on the desert in the wintertime, and in the springtime they put them up on the high mountains to feed as the grass came out. That was in the Cascade Mountains—beautiful country.

They hauled those sheep in great big trucks and took them off in bands. Then the herder with his dogs would look after them. They just went along and camped as they went. The owners rented a barn and cached all this food. And my job was to pack the mules with what the herders would need, and then I'd haul the food into the camp with the mules.

Usually it took me about two days to get to the herd, and that night, when the herder came home, I'd have his meal cooked. I'd stop overnight with him, and then I'd start back again the next day for the cache, and then I'd go to the other herd.

I felt I was a cowboy. I had a gun and I had a saddle horse. I just rode all day, and when I'd stop for the night I would hobble my mules—you know, tie the legs so they couldn't go too far. And then I would just have a camp and sleep under the stars. It was wonderful!

Well, I had this season's job all through the spring, summer, and fall. I felt that I needed more technical education. You know, I'd served my apprenticeship mostly with my hands. And if I was going to really go anyplace, I felt I needed more math. So I went back to school for four years. When I finished this schooling, I went out on the regular merchant ships as an engineer. And I sailed intercoastal for five years—East Coast to West Cost through the Canal. I sailed to Japan and China, the Philippines. Oh, it was wonderful. I loved that life.

During the war I was the youngest chief engineer in the American Merchant Marine. All my helpers were older than I was. I was very happy, because I really had what I wanted. I was at the top and I was young.

After the war, I went ashore with a private survey firm, until I finally just hung out my own shingle, as they say, in the fifties. I'm in a very specialized field. I advise the insurance adjusters on how accidents occur, and I do a lot of ship appraisals for insurance, for litigation, for whatever. . . .

If I hadn't left Scotland, I would probably have gone to sea. I'd served my apprenticeship, but there would never have been the opportunity like there is here to come ashore and expand yourself. Never. There's no doubt about it.

# Hiroshi Yamada

···················· FROM JAPAN, 1901 ························

*Semiretired at eighty-nine, he lives on a quiet street in Seattle on the income from three apartment buildings that he owns. He still drives a car up and down the steep hills and tends a vegetable garden in the rear of his house. He spends much of his time going over and rearranging his extensive collection of documents and photographs of life in the relocation camp. Prominently displayed on the mantelpiece is a photograph of himself and the American camp commandant taken during World War II.*

After I came here I worked in a hotel and I saved my money for years. Finally I had enough to get married, and my wife and I started our own business, a beverage bottling plant. She and I, and later on our children, all worked in it and we had it going pretty well. It was a success, you might say. But when everything was established and things were going well, the war broke out—World War II. Pearl Harbor.

I couldn't believe it at first. I couldn't believe it at all. It was a Sunday. I was in church with my children, you see, and this news came to me. My God! I thought. It couldn't be true! I just couldn't realize that it actually happened. There was a feeling of mixed emotion. That's the truth.

Then we had to be evacuated. Sent to the relocation camps. There was another beverage company and they said, "Mr. Yamada, we're going to lease your place." I had to do that. I had to accept it. Then, when I came back, the business was gone. Once you lose your customers, it's all gone. If I started again I'd have to start from the bottom, you see. Unless you have a big capital you can't compete with an established business.

A few days after Pearl Harbor a couple of men came and they showed they were FBI men and they said, "Would you go with me?" So I packed up and went to the relocation camp and heard them say, "You got to stay here for so many years." I couldn't go home—for so many years I couldn't go home. I stayed for about three weeks in the immigration station and then I was shipped to North Dakota, a relocation camp there. My wife stayed home to sell the business and take care of the young children, and then, pretty soon, she had to come to the camp, too.

There were some Germans also interned with us. They were sailors from a German ship that happened to be here when the war broke out. And they wanted to go back to Germany. There were also some who were picked up in this country who were immigrants—but hadn't been naturalized. The soldiers and the officer from the boat, they thought these immigrants were second-class citizens. They shouldn't be here; they should be back home in Germany in the war. There was strong feeling between them. But the Japanese, of course, we couldn't be naturalized. If we were born in Japan, at that time we couldn't be naturalized here. So we were forced, more or less, into the relocation center. It was the American government's fault, you see. That was the difference from the German situation.

*How did you feel when this happened? Were you resentful?*

Well, you don't have much feeling. I feel this is war; you can't help that. That's what I felt. In ordinary times you might be mad about it, but this is a special time and it can't be helped. These were the conditions. Some people had strong feelings against it, but it's all a matter of how you take it, I guess. That's all. I tried not to upset myself.

In the camp I thought I'd take it easy, more or less. It's a good time for me to rest, you know, so I didn't report to the unemployment office. But then they sent me a notice: "Here's a job. You have to take it." And so they gave me the job of adjusting the housing. You have to distribute evenly. Here's only one room, small room, and there's about four or five people. You have to assign them to make it fair and study what's available and who wants to be together and settle the arguments so that friends can be together and families.

We organized a self-government. We had popular vote, you know. We had to deal with all the problems that were going on, like health needs and labor disputes in the pickling plant—the government had set up a pickling plant where the people worked right on the relocation-camp grounds. We had a mediation committee and a judge.

We had a camp newspaper and a community council. We took up all sorts of items on our community council: putting partitions in the laundry room, creating a beauty parlor, a barber shop, a fish market, a confection shop. We had to estimate the number of square feet for each of these and approve each one. Everything had to be figured out and settled, even complaints about dogs in the camp destroying people's lawns. We tried to do everything democratically.

One time, we had a lot of trouble about dogs. This was brought up to the community control committee. I have one of the papers here about it. I'll read it to you: "Something must be done in regard to dogs in this project. There are three or four cases of biting reported every week and strict regulations are desired by residents before any unfortunate incidents occur. Dogs are a nuisance, unsafe, and immoral. With the garden works about to begin, the dogs lead to break up the harmony of the Good Neighbors Policy by destroying the neighbors' gardens." We had to settle that, too. The dogs had to be tied up or penned.

Every problem had to be referred to the council, and we had discussions about everything. One of our projects was a Red Cross fund drive. And we had to set the quota for the war fund, which we set at two thousand dollars for the year from one block. You see, we made money with the pickling plant, and so the people had money to invest. The council encouraged them to invest it in the Red Cross and the war fund drive.

*Did you take care of crimes, too?*

Crime? There wasn't much crime. I didn't see any crimes. Exceptional cases, the police would come and take them out from the camp. In general we didn't have any trouble at all. A very law-abiding community. We're all family people, you know, we Japanese. We put pressure on our people not to commit a crime. There's not much crime in the Japanese community, and that's how it was in the camps, too.

I feel it's because of the moral education we had. Your conscience always stops you from doing anything wrong. In Japan when you're raised, or in this country raised in a Japanese community, it's a small community and you all know each other. If you do anything wrong, you're an outcast. So naturally you don't do anything wrong. Your conscience won't allow it. That's why I think we carry the same feeling where we go and are very law-abiding, honest, tell the truth. No stealing. We can't afford it. Everybody watches you and you'd be an outcast.

Then we started the co-ops for buying the merchandise; because you see we were not allowed to go out of the camp, so we would order things. And we said, "Well, why don't the camps get together? Each camp put up five thousand dollars. There are nine camps—that's enough money to use as cash." So we'd order the goods in quantity and ship them to those places that needed them. Sort of like Sears Roebuck, you know. Each family in the camp put in twenty dollars, and we raised five thousand dollars for our camp and five thousand dollars for the other camps. The government sent food to the camps, you know, but this was for clothing and other things—everything except food. We had no trouble. And the government even arranged it so that we had a meeting of representatives from all the camps, at the Morrison Hotel in Chicago. They gave us permits to go out and to arrange things. I've kept all the records.

Many soldiers went from our camp to fight for the American army, and fifty-six of them were killed in action. I encouraged them to go. And when they were killed, I told the mothers and the families about it because I felt I had to. After the war we had a memorial service and a monument. [*Shows picture.*] Of course, there was an element that thought we shouldn't fight against the Japanese. There was that element in the camp, too. But mostly we all worked together and tried to settle the disputes.

Most of the American officers of the camp were people that were students of sociology and they understood human relations and so forth. That's a help. We didn't have too much difficulty because people tried to understand. Actually, a few years ago, in 1969, I had a reunion with the head of the camp administration, the American head. He came this way with his wife and he notified me and we had a special get-together. I was happy to meet him, too. We worked very well together.

*How did you feel when you heard about the bomb being dropped on Hiroshima?*

It was a horrible shock, a terrible shock. We all thought there was no more Hiroshima, you see. That it was all burnt down. And it must be 50 percent of the people in this area, the Japanese in this area, come from Hiroshima. It was burned, you know. I was lucky, myself. My sister, she lived there but she was safe. My sister's son, he was killed. He got off the train and was walking toward the house of a friend and he was killed instantly. Well . . . we were very surprised. We couldn't do anything about it.

After the war there was some hard feeling against the Japanese people among some of the local people here. You know, if they were fighting the Japanese and they had sons or relatives killed in action. . . . Well, they resented us for this reason. We have nothing to do with it, but . . . we were Japanese.

Well . . . we managed to make it anyway. I think people are more understanding now. And then, of course, when we put the monument up and they knew how many Japanese had died fighting for the United States, I think some of them thought again about it and felt kinder toward us.

# George Kistiakowsky

*He is a prominent scientist, professor emeritus at Harvard University, and a former presidential adviser. Born in Moscow into a family of the Russian intelligentsia, he fled Russia after the Revolution and made his way to Berlin, where he studied chemistry at the university. He received his Ph.D. in 1925 and was looking forward to an academic career.*

What frightened me was, basically, that I was a person without a country. I had a so-called League of Nations passport, which meant nothing. To get a visa anywhere was exceedingly difficult. No country wanted Russian émigrés, and I was, for good reasons then, not confident of myself as a scientist.

When I got my degree, Professor Bodenstein asked me what did I want to do with myself, and I said, "Well, I would like to go into an academic career." He said to me that he could get me a junior job without any problem but that the anti-Russian feeling in Germany then was so strong—generally antiforeigner—that I would certainly not get a professorship and why don't I try a more open country—obviously I couldn't return to the Soviet Union—and go to America. I decided to try to do it, even though I knew nothing about what the United States was like. Professor Bodenstein recommended me to the so-called International Education Board, financed by the Rockefeller Foundation then, and they gave me a fellowship.

I came to Princeton on a student visa. Within months I knew that this was the land I wanted to stay in. I had never liked it in Germany, because I felt myself a foreigner, was made to feel a foreigner. Here, it was an extremely warm and friendly atmosphere. There were little things. I mean, Professor Bodenstein in Berlin liked me, obviously. But to the very end, he was to me "Herr Professor." I was never invited to his house as a student. After I got my degree and did work for him for six months as a postdoctoral assistant, I was once or twice invited to his house. But he was still to me "Herr Professor," and I was to him "Herr Doktor." I go to Princeton, and within a month or two my boss,

Hugh Taylor, began calling me George and told me to call him Hugh. I was on a first-name basis with many other students and junior faculty members.

I was also on first-name basis with the mechanic at the local garage. It didn't disturb me, perhaps because of my family background, perhaps because of my reaction to the formality of the Germans. I felt many times, at least in those days, pre–World War II, the United States reminded me of prerevolutionary Russia.

I have no recollections of any particular difficulties. I had some irritations because of my difficult name. I was offered an otherwise very attractive industrial job at the DuPont Company, through Professor Taylor, who was a consultant there. "But," said Hugh to me, "they insist that you change your name, because they are afraid that their bookkeepers will have difficulty with *Kistiakowsky*." I thought it was so offensive, I said, "To hell with them!" I also remember being slightly hurt when I got an invitation to a garden party from the provost of Princeton University, which was addressed to "Dr. and Mrs. Kiftikafty."

I did a great deal of research, published very quickly, was quite successful that way in Princeton, where I stayed until the summer of 1930. Then I was offered a job at Harvard. I went there and I've been there ever since. . . .

I got into public life gradually. I suppose my almost inbred concern about civil rights got me involved, emotionally, in anti-Hitlerism, anti-Fascism, and I participated in various activities in the late thirties. I went enthusiastically into war work in World War II, because I was very anti-Nazi, anti-Fascist. I was convinced this country would be involved, and, although not very consciously, I had a feeling of gratitude to this country and therefore I felt that was part of my job. It was only fair that I would give some of my time to it. So I joined the National Defense Research Committee in Washington, as soon as it was organized in the summer of 1940. And I enjoyed the work, because although here and at Princeton I had been a pure scientist, never asking myself if what I am doing has any practical application—in Washington, I've always defended the importance of basic research—I have also liked applied work.

One thing and another led me to the appointment as head of the Explosives Division at Los Alamos Laboratory, which put me into a key role in developing the atom bomb. Well, with that background, it's not surprising that I was asked to participate in various advisory military roles in Washington after the war. That, in turn, led to my selection as a member of the President's Science Advisory Committee, which was formed in the fall of '57, sort of Eisenhower's response to Sputnik and American alarm about advances of the Soviet Union.

Eisenhower liked me, and so when Dr. Killian, the first science adviser, retired, he selected me as his successor, and I was that the last year and a half of the Eisenhower administration.

I think I enjoyed public life. In the beginning, when you haven't done it before, it sort of thrills you to hobnob with the big generals and that sort of thing. And, of course, the White House atmosphere—in the beginning I was terribly scared and awed by it all, but gradually I realized that Eisenhower developed a considerable degree of trust in me and my judgment, and I got to like him very much and admire him in some ways. So, toward the end, it was a very pleasant experience. I was confident of what I was saying.

Also, talking to Eisenhower actually influenced me very much to ask myself the questions whether our military policies were right or not, because he was by then very much concerned about what he called the "military-industrial complex" and its impact on American democracy. He stimulated my thinking in that respect, and then, the end of it was the Vietnam war, in which I was involved very much in antigovernment efforts, obviously unsuccessfully.

I had really swallowed line, hook, and sinker the cold-war position of the United States: It was all the fault of the Soviet Union, the threat of destruction of the United States by the Soviet Union, and so forth. I think I've learned much better since. I know perfectly well that the cold war is a fifty-fifty proposition, that United States actions have been as provocative as those of the Soviet Union. Having learned how really dishonest much of our public representation of military activities has been, I've gradually moved from a position of being a technician, carrying out the militaristic policies of my betters, to an individual who challenges these policies. That's all I am doing now—talking about the need to stop the nuclear-arms race, and I'm writing on the subject. I've published this one paper that caught public imagination, the "Paranoia Paper," and there is one other coming out that is even more explosive, on why we should not deploy the neutron bomb.

More and more I have moved into what I jokingly call a "do-gooder" position. Another way I describe it is by analogy with the Middle Ages, when men used to sin profusely in their earlier life and then toward the end went into a monastery and started praying furiously, and that way got to heaven. That's what I'm doing now—praying, I mean. [Chuckles.]

# Agnes Martin
···················· FROM CANADA, 1931 ·····················

*On a dusty street on the outskirts of Albuquerque, New Mexico, artist Agnes Martin lives and works in a Spartan storefront loft. Most of the single huge room is a studio, where she works on the stark, rectilinear paintings for which she has become known. A tiny space is reserved for living—a cot, two wooden rocking chairs, two dressers—vintage 1920s—a hot plate and a coffeemaker, a refrigerator (almost empty except for a wooden box of peaches, a carton of yogurt, and a bottle of milk). There is no phone. Ms. Martin herself is as Spartan in appearance as her surroundings. Her gray hair is cropped close to the head, her skin is tanned and lined, her eyes are a sharp blue. She wears oversized carpenter's overalls with a gray, man's sweatshirt, a wool stocking cap, and heavy hiking boots. This is no pose. In spite of paintings that sell for forty thousand dollars each, exhibitions at the Whitney Museum and the Museum of Modern Art, honorary degrees from universities, and speaking invitations from all over, she believes that worldly success, money, and material comforts distract and ultimately destroy the true artist. Like her person and her home, her story is spare—brief and to the point. When she said what she had wanted to say, she stopped. No amount of prodding could induce her to add another word.*

My sister, who is just a little older than I, married an American and went to the United States. And after she had her first child she was quite ill, and I went down to help her. When I met her friends, who were just a little older than I was myself—this was in 1931 and I was nineteen years of age—I was so surprised. They seemed so free and easygoing and generous—as against earnest and determined and darkly aggressive or competitive, which I expected. They also had all been to either colleges or a university, and they told me how easy it was to attend these institutions and how there was student employment and how low the fees were, and I became determined to attend university in the United States and to become an American citizen. I went home and came back on a student visa and attended the little college in the town where my sister was in residence.

I can't possibly tell you what a marvelous experience it is to be a student on an American campus. On the American college campus, the reason it is such a wonderful experience is because of the students, because the atmosphere is altogether one of good will and optimism and mutual respect. Students withhold judgment. They are more than merciful. And American students are generous. As the whole world knows, the most outstanding characteristic of Americans is generosity. And the students are also responsive. I still go to universities sometimes and talk to the students, because I know that if I present them with positive things that they will respond.

After I had worked a few years—after I had graduated and worked a few years, I went to New York to go to university. And there I had the marvelous experience of being in this capital, the greatest capital of commerce in the world. Besides, I got to go to all the museums, and I decided that I wanted to become a painter.

All the time I was at the university, and I attended universities for eight years, I worked at the same time at many different jobs. And when I was graduated, I continued in a pattern of working one or two years and taking a year off to paint. And in this way I lived in almost half the states, and I traveled in all of the states. And I have worked at every occupation that I can think of. For instance, I have worked for a logging and mining company, and I've worked with the Indians and with the colored people and with criminals and delinquents and misfits, and I have worked washing dishes and waiting tables and as a janitor. I've worked at child care, nursery schools, and ordinary schools, high school, colleges, and universities. I want it to be understood that I've done the lowest and the highest, I guess, and all kinds of work in between.

All the time that I worked at all these different jobs—most of the time they were what is considered low-class employment—I want to say that I never felt that I was not respected or that I was looked down on in any position that I held. Can't you see the freedom in America? That it's not just political? Can't you see American liberty? Can't you see self-reliance and self-expression? That is the American atmosphere. And I want you to know that in other countries it is not that way. There is not a bourgeois class in America. A bourgeois is a person who thinks only status, and in a status society, acceptance has a very narrow range. People think that they can only associate with others who are "their sort." You can see that not in any corner of this nation is the status atmosphere really maintained.

I kept up on this working at everything, and painting, for thirty years, and then I was able to show my paintings in a gallery in New York, and since then, for the last twenty years I have just painted.

In America you can do anything you want, live anywhere you want, and, finally, do what it is that you most want to do very easily—perhaps not without what you might consider to be sacrifices, but they're not really sacrifices. The truth is: It's a breeze in America.

# Isabella Mendoza

···················FROM MEXICO, 1915·····················

*Plump, toothless, and well into her sixties, she has flashing black eyes
and an air of amused vitality. Her remarks are frequently punctuated
with a throaty chuckle. Settled at last after a lifetime of migrant
labor, she lives near Santa Cruz, California, in a dilapidated frame
house that her children have bought for her. Although she rarely steps
out of the door, she is not alone, for her world comes to her. While the
interview was going on, two of her daughters drank coffee at her
dining room table, a son-in-law packed mangoes on the kitchen floor,
and five grandchildren watched the color television set in the living
room. Other relatives wandered in from time to time to bring a bit of
news or borrow a cup of sugar.*

I was born in Mexico in 1913, and when I was four months old, my
father took off for the United States. At first he sent money for us and
then he got lost. I don't know; he got lost in the United States. He lost
himself somewhere. And my mother said, "I'm going up there to look
for him. I'm going to find him." She got a little money together—sold
things in the market—and she came up here with me and her sister;
that's my aunt. We went to the border and came across. We didn't have
no papers, no nothing . . . but in those days it wasn't so hard. My aunt
knew someone who knew a guard at the bridge, and she went up and
started to talk to the guard, and she gave him eight dollars. And while
they were talking, my mother took me on her shoulders and waded
through the river on the other side. It wasn't so deep then; the water
just came up to her shoulders. And when we got up on the other side,
my aunt stopped talking to the guard and he let her go across because
she'd paid him the eight dollars.

We went first to El Paso, Texas, and waited at the station till a train
came, and we went on the train to Kansas because that was where we
heard somebody had seen my father. And my mother said, "I'm going
to find him. I'm going to find him." When we got there we met a friend,
and he said to my mother, "Your husband just left to Chicago," and we
took a train and we went to Chicago. But when we got there, my father
wasn't there no more either. Later we heard that he died in the flu
epidemic. I don't know if you heard about those people that was in the
flu epidemic. Yeah, a lot of people died in that time. Well, he was one of

them. But, of course, we didn't know because nobody wrote us. Anyhow, if they did write us, my mother couldn't read. But we didn't find out about that till later, of course.

All my mother's money was gone by then, so she started working with a rich lady—sweeping, cleaning house, cooking, all that kind of thing. And after a while my mother got together with another man and she told me that was my father, and I said, "No, that not my father," but, well, I started calling him my father because he raised me. And when I was about eleven or twelve, we all came to California and started to work in the cannery. I worked in the cannery, too, and in the fields picking apples and prunes and that sort of thing; made a little money.

I never learned how to read or write, just to speak English. I went to school a little. Not a real school, but a big room with a table and chairs. And I learned English; but the teacher, she didn't know no Spanish, so she couldn't teach me so good. There were no lot of Mexicans here in those days, so I only went to school three or four months, and I can't read nothing to this day.

Then I met up with my husband and we started having kids. I was fifteen when I had the first one. And we worked in the fields—cut apricots, peaches, pears; went to Fresno—picking grapes. My children worked in the fields, too, picking apples. They started before they went to school. My two boys were four and five and they helped us fill the baskets. I used to work till it was time to leave to make something to eat, and then I'd come home and cook for my family, for my husband and the boys. And then I have the baby, a little girl.

You know what I'd do when she was small? I had a tomato box, and my older boy and my other boy, they make a little wagon with the wheel and I'd put the baby and the pillow in that tomato box. And I put her in there and I go out and pick apples from the ground and I pulled her along in the wagon. She was about a year, less than a year old then. And when she started walking, I had a little dog, and the baby would go walking down in the middle of the apple orchard and the dog would follow her; and when she would stop, the dog would stop, too. He was a baby-watcher for me. The only thing is, when we were working and she was small and she start hollering, "Mamma! Mamma!" "What do you want?" I'd say. "Mamma, I want some chichi." That means she wanted to feed from the breast, you know, milk. And my husband would say, "Go on, feed that kid over there." So I'd leave the can or the basket when we were picking apples or olives; I'd leave the can there and go feed her, give her some milk, and then come back and help him fill the basket.

It was kind of hard because we was always going from one place to another, back and forth, back and forth—apple orchards, lettuce fields, the grapes. Sometimes you'd sleep in the car—you'd be worried about getting killed on the road. Or you'd camp in the dark, and nobody wants you on their land anyhow. We'd be in Riverside and the orange season would end over there, and we'd go to Fresno for the grape season. We'd travel day and night to get to Fresno. And then tomatoes up at Tracy, so there you'd go. And then plums over here toward Santa Clara; that's where there's a lot of plum orchards. I know this whole country like a book: all the vegetable, all the fruit. I like to stay in one place, because when the children are small it's hard to move all the time.

And some places, they didn't like the Mexicans to go in there, you know. Like once we was in this town, Portersville, and they chased us out of the restaurant. My husband was going to buy us some hamburgers to eat, and they chased us out. "Get out of here!" they said. . . . But now things are better. Everything is friendly. I got a lot of friends now—Mexicans, Anglos, all kinds.

The thing is, traveling around like that, you don't get ahead. The money looks good, but the money would creep away: gas for the car, or you'd break down, you have to get parts for it, see. Then you got to eat, so you'd go to the restaurant with a whole bunch of kids—and all of them were small—it cost money for food in a restaurant and milk and everything. So you don't make nothing much. So, finally, we settle here near Watsonville. There's a cannery here. My husband work with the cannery, and the children would help with the picking in the brussel sprouts and the other fields around here.

Of course, there's stores here, too, that will cheat Mexicans if they see that they don't know too much. They go into the store just in their work clothes, you know, kind of dirty, and the store owner says, "Aha! We have a dumb one here," and, say, the Levis cost eight dollars a pair, they'll sell them for fifteen dollars. Well, boots—they don't have the right size—they'll say. "Oh, well, give him a size larger." They cheat them because they think they don't know any better. But still it's better here than moving around all the time.

My husband died a few years ago, three years ago, and the children are all grown up now. My daughters bought me this house. Two of them live here with me with their kids. Their husbands are away. And the others live around here.

I had two sons in the service. One is still in; he's a career officer. He's a captain in the army. He was in Vietnam, Korea. Got wounded three times. One day he came home and he said, "Mamma, you got to be a citizen. I want you to be a citizen."

"No, I can't get papers because I came over the river."

And he said, "Yes, we're going down to the Immigration. I'm going to talk to them."

So he went down with me and the Immigration says, "Come in, was you born here?"

And I say, "No."

They get out my fingerprints and check on them and look up my name. They're supposed to put me in jail for a couple of hours for passing illegal . . . but my son was with me and the officer said, "What do you remember? Do you remember the name of the school you went to when you was little?"

And I said, "No. There was a little house and they had benches and tables; that's all I remember."

He said, "How much did you pay to come to the United States?"

"Well, I don't remember. We just came across; that's all I know."

Then he went in the office and he got the record on my son in the service and the other one that was in the service and he said, "All right. You get the papers. Pay twenty-five dollars." That was the fee, you know. So I went down to the office and they stamped my fingerprints on a card and said okay.

So finally I got my papers—after forty years. Forty years illegal, and they never caught me.

# Alistair Cooke

·····················FROM ENGLAND, 1932·····················

*For over forty years, writer and broadcaster Alistair Cooke has interpreted the United States to his native England. His "Letter from America" is still broadcast weekly all over the Commonwealth, and his books on America have been consistent best sellers. In recent years, as host of educational television's "Masterpiece Theater," he has also been interpreting England to American audiences. Silver-haired, urbane, relaxed, he looks back on his life thoughtfully in the study of the spacious apartment on Fifth Avenue, where he lives with his American wife.*

I was born in Manchester, England, the capital of smog. When people—much later—did statistical studies on disease, they found that Manchester had the worst lung-cancer rate of anyplace in the world. It was the center of the cotton industry, and there were smoking factories, grayness, and brown air, a layer of mud on the sidewalks all through the winter. The more prosperous it was, the worse it was. But the word *smog* had not yet been invented then, so the Mancunians assumed that that was life—just like babies: Whatever happens to a baby is life.

We lived there till I was seven. But my mother had chronic bronchitis and the doctor in Manchester finally said, "There are two places you can go. You can go to Egypt or you can go to Blackpool." Well, Blackpool was fifty-two miles away, and going to Egypt in the middle of the war was hardly "on." So we went to Blackpool, and I was brought up there.

To me, as a small boy, Blackpool was like an early entrance into paradise, because it had always been a holiday place. It was the place where all the Lancashire cotton workers came for their holidays—the Atlantic City of the northwest coast. The cotton towns in Lancashire used to close down in sequence, so that, for instance, Burnley would have a week and then Blackburn and then Oswaldtwistle. These were known as *wakes*, which is an inland Lancashire pronunciation of *weeks*. So you had the Burnley wakes and the Blackburn wakes and the Oswaldtwistle wakes, and so on. A whole factory town would close down for a week, and everybody took off, thirty-five or forty miles or whatever—a tremendous distance—to come to Blackpool with their families. The place had more boardinghouses than any place in Europe, I suppose; so the population, which in those days was maybe a hundred and some thousand people, would in August get to be over a million people there on the sands. There were three promenades and three piers and a twenty-mile stretch of sand. There's something about the attraction to a little boy of Blackpool that was reproduced later on as the attraction of America to an undergraduate. In other words, it was a "pleasure beach," as they call it.

I went to what was then known as the secondary school in Blackpool, which was subsequently called the grammar school—a very, very good school. Then I got a scholarship to Cambridge. I went there from 1927 to 1932. And was lucky enough to get a first-class honors degree in English. In those days a first-class degree was regarded as a passport to some kind of good job. If you'd been president of the Union, which was the debating society, or you'd edited the university magazine, that was a further passport. After I graduated, I stayed on for two years to teach in the English School and also to run the university magazine, *The Granta*, named after a branch of the river there. I also started a university dramatic society, called The Mummers. It was the first mixed dramatic society. We got a license from the vice-chancellor, who said he would permit it, though he thought that having men and women act together was "unnatural." Before that, in the two existing societies, the ADC and the Marlowe, all parts were played by men, you see; and that, I guess, in the Cambridge of the late twenties, was normal.

In 1932 I ran into a man who had what he told me was called a Commonwealth Fellowship: twenty-five fellowships a year for advanced study in American universities, given to students from the United Kingdom, from the empire and the Commonwealth.

*Sort of a reverse Rhodes Scholarship, was it?*

Yes, except that we were normally two years older than the Rhodes Scholarship people, because we had to have done two years research after we graduated. This fellow said, "Oh, you'll have a marvelous time. You're well paid for two years, and at the end of the first year, they almost require you to buy a car and drive around as many of the forty-eight states as you can, and then you do your second year, usually at the same place." Well, this sounded like what we used to call "money for jam." The idea of being paid to spend two years in America, or almost anywhere, was very exciting to an impecunious undergraduate.

I was a child, after all, of the twentieth century, and one of the great things that hit us was the movies. And out of the movies we had all developed a picture of America. I hate to tell you, it was not a picture of slogging pioneers and people taming the prairie. As far as I was concerned, it was a series of cocktail parties, and Douglas Fairbanks and Joan Crawford in *Dancing Daughters*, and that sort of thing. It was, you know, the prospect of high jinks and pretty girls, a sort of passport to Babylon. It was going to be a prolonged party. So when this man told me about the Commonwealth Fellowships and said, "It's a picnic—it's subsidized," I decided to apply for the thing.

There was no examination or anything. You simply put down all your credentials and then you were interviewed. The final choice was made on the basis of the interview. Most of the people who applied, of course, were academics. They were going to be physicists, historians, whatever. The most bizarre applicant in my day was a man who was going to Pacific Grove, California, to learn about oysters, because the oyster beds in the English Channel had been very badly devastated by mines from the First World War, and he was going there to learn how to rehabilitate the oyster beds. But next to him, even more exotic and more suspect, was my specialty: theater! I had applied for work in theater direction. The Committee of Choice was made up mostly of academics, with an occasional statesman—Lord Halifax, I recall, was the chairman—and when I appeared before them they were very much of two minds. They said, "Theater direction? What sort of thing is that?"

In the summer of 1931, I'd been to Germany and worked with the *Volksbühne*, which was the National Folk Theater. I was a fervent disciple at that time of the more extreme directors of Germany and Russia. It was a time when the theater was being taken out of the hands of the actors and the playwrights. *They* didn't matter. The great thing was the gymnastic manipulation of actors on a stage, and the director was a sort of dictator, you see. I was really sold on this theory of being a theater dictator, and I was taking a very snobby view of the London commercial theater and so forth.

I didn't have enough sense as a young man to play this down. I remember Lord Halifax, who, you remember, subsequently became British foreign secretary, saying to me, "So you intend, then, when you come back here, to revolutionize the English theater?" And I said, "That's right." [*Laughs.*]

Apparently my gall worked, and my credentials were pretty good, and they said, "Well, he seems a likely young fellow." So I got a fellowship.

The Commonwealth Fund sent us what they call *literature* telling us how to get along in America. I'll never forget one absolutely baffling little pamphlet they sent. It told us, of course, how to handle money and how banks worked and this and that, but there were two warnings that I'll always remember. One was about the "buffalo moth." They warned you that when you left for your summer trip, you should put all your clothes in mothbags or mothballs or whatever it was at the time. They said, "This is a special kind of moth," and that, "it will eat your clothes up." This was fascinating—the buffalo moth. It sounded very big, like most things American.

The other thing that they warned you about was something called the "badger game." This had happened to one of the Commonwealth Fellows and he'd lost his entire summer allowance. It's a gone word now, but I think everyone in America over fifty knows what the badger game is: If you meet a girl somewhere in your travels, and you're foolishly invited to her room, shall we say, you have to be very careful, because there might be a knock on the door and her "husband" would appear and stick you up and take your money. Well, this, of course, suggested fascinating possibilities.

They also sent you a book on the national parks. We really didn't know much about the landscape of America, except that it was huge. There were skyscrapers and there was the prairie and there was the Mississippi and then there was San Francisco. That was my rather tenuous information.

Then the head of the Fund came over to England—a nice man named Edward Bliss Reed, from Yale. He gave a little dinner at Cambridge, and he warned the Commonwealth Fellows that there might be a revolution while we were in America. You see, this was really the absolute pit of the Depression; it was the summer of 1932. It was the worst and it got worse and worse. Well, I hate to tell you that, frankly, that too seemed exciting. You see, I was a totally nonpolitical character at the time, and revolution was something that you directed on a stage or that they put on in the movies, you know.

The Fund also sent each of us $600 for an equipment allowance, which, in the depth of the Depression, was something. That was to buy clothes and so on. They told us that it would be rather colder here, so you ought to have a warm topcoat. And I remember going off and buying an enormous coat, made from a gnu—the antelope, that is. It's very, very light and very, very warm. And they told us that people dressed very lightly indoors, because of this extraordinary thing called "steam heat."

On September 16, 1932, I took the train from London to Liverpool. Our ship was called the *Laconia* and it took ten days to cross the Atlantic. Aboard were about five other Fellows of the Commonwealth Fund, and that was the beginning of this great jaunt. We were really paid at an extraordinary rate. I mean, they paid your first-class passage over, and they gave you $50 for tips—in the Depression and to a young twenty-three-year-old! And when we arrived in New York at the end of September, they paid our September allowance of $150. We were paid $150 a month, sort of as a maintenance allowance, in addition to our university fees and rooms. Well, I've never been richer in my life. It was ludicrous, but, oh, very acceptable. In addition, they took care of all our medical and dental expenses and so on.

When we arrived in New York, they took us round to Radio City Music Hall, which was a big new thing then, and then to a play, *Of Thee I Sing.* I remember walking through Times Square and there was an enormous queue, a great line. At first I thought it was for the movie at the Astor. It wasn't. It was a bread line, a soup line. And sometimes you got stopped on the streets by men, well-dressed men, who wanted a quarter or a dime. This was the first shock. But, as I say, you're young, you're callow, especially if you're being subsidized.

After our little party in New York we were dispersed to our universities—Berkeley or UCLA or Chicago. I was to go to Yale. We took the train up to New Haven, and what amazed me was the boxes of the houses. They were all wood. You know, I'd never seen a wooden house that I could remember, unless it was a woodshed. And the fall colors, of course, were a shock, very exciting.

When I arrived at Yale I was aghast at what a friend of mine called "girder Gothic." It didn't seem to me like America at all. Of course, there was Colonial architecture in New Haven, too, which I eventually learned to recognize.

There were three other Commonwealth Fellows at Yale that year, and we sort of stayed close together at first. We'd go out for tea and we discovered it wasn't an institution in America. They brought us these ridiculous things called "tea bags." Of course, they're rife everywhere in England today, but then we'd never seen them. We thought it was outrageous. I suppose we reacted in a normal, somewhat snooty, way.

I was enrolled in the Yale School of Drama, but I found it was hopeless from my point of view. What I wanted to do was to get practice in direction. I'd directed several plays in Cambridge, and I'd been watching these boys with the *Volksbühne* in Germany. Well, the first thing they said at Yale was, "We can't provide for people doing research in theater direction or dramatic criticism. You'll just have to sign on in the usual way." So I went to a lecture with—h'm, well, I won't mention his name—but he sort of said, "Take out your notebooks. Now we're taking up the Greek dramatists." And he put down "Sophocles" on the board. He spelled it out. He said, "Sophocles was a soldier." And I thought, "Oh, my God," because I'd been tutoring people in the tragedy paper for the honors degree at Cambridge, which was pretty damned advanced stuff, and I thought, "This is awful. I'm six years back."

I put my case before the head of the Yale School of Drama, and he wasn't very sympathetic. I can understand. He probably thought, "Here's this brash Englishman who thinks he can direct plays and he's supposed to be coming here to learn." Then I went to the Commonwealth Fund and told them, and they said, "Well, just skip it. Work in the stacks and do a lot of reading," and so forth and so on. So I did a lot of reading in the library. The Commonwealth Fund even sent me a commutation ticket so I could go to New York to see plays. The whole thing was a picnic!

At the end of that first year, we made plans for the summer tour. I had a friend, a Scotsman, who was a parson, though not a practitioner, and we agreed to go together. And there was another Commonwealth Fellow in Chicago. So we flew out there to join him, bought a car there, and took off. We had a Sears Roebuck tent and a Primus stove and all the equipment for camping out. We were really going to rough it. We didn't know there were any cities until you hit San Francisco.

We drove from Chicago to Yellowstone and then up to Banff and Lake Louise in Canada and then right down the coast to San Francisco. The first night we camped out in the Wisconsin Dells, and then we discovered there were things called "motor courts." They were early primitive motels with a tiny space between the cabins, and they were so cheap that it did seem ridiculous to start bedding down every night. So we put the tent in the trunk and forgot it. We never tented again.

Incidentally, I still have the little notebook with our expenses, which says, "ten gallons of gas—fifty-seven cents," and "lunch for two—thirty cents," and so on. In fact, in San Francisco, we went into

Jack's, which is still there—it was a restaurant we were told you must go to—and you knocked on the door and you got liquor inside and, you know, some wine. And I have a note there in my notebook which says, "dinner for two—$1.40!" One dollar and forty cents with an exclamation point. That was just outrageous. We took things a little easy after that big splurge.

We were typical Britons, and my voice was much more British in those days. Americans were always razzing us with lines like, "Jolly good, old chap!" But we were struck by their friendliness and directness. People always wanted to know what you were doing: "What are you *in*?" you know. That was not very good manners in England. You might be in a room for five hours with a man in England and not have the slightest idea whether he was a plumber or an archeologist, but here there was curiosity and friendliness, too.

The summer tour was decisive in my life. It was all being seeded in the bed of the unconscious. I discovered things about America which most Englishmen didn't know, and I found this very exciting. The whole trip, and what I saw and what happened on it, made the landscape and the people to me so much more dramatic than Broadway.

That first year, '33, was the great year of Roosevelt, and the country's spirits were so uplifted; even though there were eleven or twelve million unemployed, the striking thing was the hope and optimism everywhere. It was an exhilarating time. The NRA had started, and Roosevelt was just about as benevolent a dictator as Frederick the Great, whose pictures I'd seen all over Silesia. You didn't make cracks about Roosevelt. Everywhere around the country were these pictures, in saloons and bars and restaurants, everywhere. He was the great god Franklin. . . .

From San Francisco we went on to Hollywood. Hollywood was the thing! That was my aim; because, of course, I was a great movie buff.

At that point we all went our separate ways. I'd undertaken to write six pieces for the *London Observer* on Hollywood. It was to be called "Hollywood Prospect," and I'd written to Chaplin and Lubitsch and C. Aubrey Smith and several others. So I stayed in Hollywood and did these interviews. That's where I ran into Chaplin and I spent nearly all the summer with him. It was marvelous.*

I came back east rather late, by train, and I stopped off at Amarillo, Texas. I got off the train, and it must have been about noon or early afternoon, and I went into a hotel and the clerk said, "Yes?" And I said, "I want a room." And he said, "How 'bout the seventh floor, uh?" And

*For a fuller account of his association with Chaplin, see the book *Six Men* by Alistair Cooke.

I said, "Fine." I knew the seventh floor was above the sixth floor, but I didn't know it was the code for something else. [Chuckles.] I got up there and I unloaded my little typewriter, because I was writing these "Hollywood Prospect" pieces, and—knock—he came in and said, "Anything you'd like?" I said, "Well, I'd like some ice water." He seemed to be running the whole place. He said, "Fine. Sure, I'll bring some ice water up."

And then he said to me, "All those girls downstairs," he said, "they got an eyeful of you, yes, sir!" I said, "Oh, really?" I didn't know what he was talking about. Off he went. About five minutes later, there came a knock at the door, what we used to call "shave and a haircut, two bits." I went to the door and there was this flaming brunette. When I say flaming, I mean she had more rouge than you could see through. A real tootsie! She came right into the room and said, "Are you busy?" and she sort of bounced on the bed. I said, "Er—yes, I am." I was petrified. Right away I thought it was the badger game. I was at this little typewriter—I must say I think it put her off, because she came and looked at what I was working on. It said, "Hollywood Prospect, No. 2" and "Form and Content in the Cinema." Oh, boy. So she said, "Well, maybe I better come back a little later," and I said, "Yes, do that." Then she said, "You know, I'll come back, say about nine." Gulp! I said, "Fine," and she left.

Well, I'll tell you, I locked that door and banged out my article, and I went out on the town to eat. I wondered what to do. It was about 6:00, and I saw a movie theater which said, "Sneak Hollywood Preview— Two Big Features Starting at Midnight." [Chuckles.] I was a glutton for punishment in those days, so I saw the regular feature, and then I stayed on and saw these two. They used to give you cards for the previews, and then they sent them back to Hollywood and reshot the movies or cut them or recut them. I stayed on in that movie theater until about 2:30 in the morning, and then I went back to the hotel. My train was leaving at 6:15, I think, so I just left a call, slept, packed, and beat it. [Laughs.]

The second year, I went to Harvard. A friend of mine had told me they had the Hasty Pudding Club and the Harvard Dramatic Club, and I realized I'd be much better off up there. I directed everything in sight. I directed the Hasty Pudding in a musical; I directed a couple of plays for the Harvard Dramatic Club; I formed my own theater group and we did Auden, and Shakespeare in modern dress, and all kinds of things. That was my busy year. I'd never done a musical before, and that was great fun, because you made a lot of buddies and we went on tour. In those days they performed in Cambridge, Richmond, Washington, Providence, and Boston. Then came the Easter vacation, and I was beginning to think, as all the Fellows were, "Now I've got to get back to a job." Very unpleasant prospect. You see, I'd been subsidized; I was what they now call a "foundation bum."

Then came a real fluke. I wouldn't be here if it hadn't happened. I wouldn't be here today. I was walking up Washington Street, in Boston. And on the newsstand I saw this Boston paper, and there was a big headline which said: BBC FIRES PM'S SON—the prime minister's son. "Well," I thought, "Whoosh! What's this?" And I looked at the thing, and it said that Oliver Baldwin, son of Stanley Baldwin, the prime minister, had got into some sort of hassle with the BBC, and they fired him. He'd been the BBC's film critic. So many things turn on a fluke. You know, if Oliver Baldwin had not been the prime minister's son, there would have been no news for Americans in the fact that the BBC had fired their film critic. It wouldn't have made page eighty-seven. But he was a rather explosive character, a Socialist who had reacted ferociously against his Tory father, so it was a newsy thing. The last sentence of the news report said: "So the BBC is looking for a new film critic." And I said, "Aha!" With all the arrogance of youth. I thought, "That's the job for me." There, you see—*chutzpah*, I guess is the word, must have been a big factor in my life.

I went at once into a telephone booth and phoned the head of the Commonwealth Fund. They had sent out a little paper to all the Fellows, saying, "If you can be considered on a short list for a job in England, we will send you over for an interview." Well, that's pretty lavish. They'd send you over and back. The "short list" was a phrase that applied to diplomatic posts, where there are two thousand applicants, and they instantly make, on the basis of your credentials, a short list and then there's an interview. I didn't know whether they did that for the BBC, but I called the Commonwealth Fund, and this fellow, Edward Bliss Reed, in New York, said, "Oh, yes. Absolutely splendid. Great, Alistair!" So I went to the Western Union counter and I wrote out a cable to the director of talks of the British Broadcasting Corporation. I didn't know who he was, or if they even had a title "director of talks." I wrote: "The Commonwealth Fund, of which I am a Fellow, will send me to Britain for an interview if I may be considered on the short list for the post of BBC film critic."

Now, I was totally unknown as a journalist, but there *had* been these six pieces on the movies in the *Observer*. When the telegram arrived at the director of talks, by the grace of God he was in his room with a famous English literary critic of the day, Desmond McCarthy, and the director said, "Alistair Cooke? Alistair Cooke? I've heard that name somewhere." Desmond McCarthy said, "Oh, that is the man who wrote that series in the *Observer* during the summer." They rustled up the *Observer* and read a couple of pieces and said, "Oh, well, he could possibly be considered." So they sent back a cable, which I always like to think of as a typical BBC cable. All I can remember of it was that it said "without obligation on our part . . ." Well, that was enough for me. You know, this was another free trip across the Atlantic, so I picked the date, which was sometime in April 1934, and I went over on the *Aquitania*.

It arrived late, as ships do, and I had arranged the interview for that afternoon. I got to the BBC an hour or so late, and there was a very down-the-nose executive, who was the assistant director of talks. He greeted me, not very warmly, and said, "Well, you're frightfully late. You see, anybody expected for this post is going to be asked to write a talk and then broadcast it internally, and this takes time." I said, "Well, have you got a typewriter? I'll do it right now. If you'll give me a room, I'll bang out the last movie I saw." He said, "Really?" [*Chuckles.*] This was not quite the pace they worked at there. So they got me a typewriter and a room and I said, "Give me fifteen minutes," and I banged out this piece.

I came back and he was beginning to look more cheerful. I said, "I'm ready any time," and they put me in room 3D. I still broadcast from there, in Broadcasting House. They said, "When the light goes on, you start to talk." I will never forget the movie, to which I am eternally grateful. It was called *Blonde Bombshell*, with Jean Harlow and Franchot Tone and Lee Tracy and C. Aubrey Smith, and it was a rather hilarious satire on the movies. I wrote this up and broadcast it, and the minute I finished, this fellow came bounding in, a transformed character now, grinning all over, and said, "The DT"—that's the director of talks—"would like to see you." I was whisked off to this rather forbidding-looking man in a big office with a lot of telephones. He asked me about myself, when I'd be back and so on, and he told the other fellow, "You know there are two hundred and sixty applicants for this job, but dismiss them all. This young man's got the job."

Well, of course, I was on cloud nineteen. I came back with the job in my pocket, and, after another summer in Hollywood with Charlie Chaplin, working on a film script on Napoleon, I went back to England and became film critic of the BBC.

I'd already begun to notice, reading newspapers and everything else, even among my own friends, that the general impression of America seemed to be fairly abysmal. There was not much foreign correspondence from America. After all, Europe was the seat of power. Over the winter I began to think about this, and I thought, "There is need of a program about America. People know nothing about it. They don't know about the country, its extent, the people or their habits," and so on.

I put this to my great friend, now my close buddy, the director of talks. I said, "You know, there should be something on radio about

America." He agreed; so I devised a program which I wrote and directed, called "The American Half-Hour." I did two programs on New York—one about a race riot in Harlem, and another one about La Guardia—and I did a program on New England, another on the West, another on education in America, on American humor, on Mark Twain—thirteen in all. In the spring of '37, there were tremendous floods on the Mississippi and I did a program called "River, Stay Away from My Door."

They were a very successful series. I became known then not only as a film critic but as someone who would do things on America. What I had to offer, I think, was a strong contrast between what people thought it was like and what it was. Well, I could see a whole lifetime opening up. I think it was probably a very good decision. I made it instinctively, and I've never regretted it.

Through all the time back in England—over two years—the urge to go back to America became stronger and stronger. America became more and more glamorous, as any country does when you're away from it—greener pastures and all that. I used to play my home movies of Santa Barbara in the middle of the gray London winter. Finally I decided, "I'm going to go back." I applied for an immigrant visa. There was no question of just coming over for a visit. I'd decided to make the move and to stay. I wanted to be back at the party.

Later that summer—1937, and back in New York—I started doing a weekly talk for NBC. And then the war came along, and I started doing talks for BBC and almost became their correspondent here. They asked me if I would alternate with Raymond Gram Swing, who was the great, great name in those days as a commentator. He was broadcasting to England once a week—a Sunday talk, called "American Commentary," and they asked me if I would alternate with him, which I did. And that's how I started. That was the big switch for me, because that was a political commentary. I was doing news things all the time, but that's how I really got into politics and political reporting.

When the war was over, the man who was head of BBC Radio said to me, "Now the war's over. People are fed up with political commentary. What we'd like you to do is to talk about the things you used to talk to me about. You know, about American children, and the fall coloring, and the history of ice cream, and all the things that interest you about the country and the people." So we set up this program, which later was called "Letter from America." It was the broad canvas, and I've been working away on it ever since. . . . I hope I've made some sort of breakthrough, because there'd always been hard news, you know, and maybe a profile of a politician or an author of great fame. But I was more interested in the land and the character of the people, and the mores, what they once called "human interest" and now call "color."

# THE WARTIME INFLUX
## Heroes, Victims, Survivors

*I saw it—the way they picked the Jews up and put them on a pickup truck. No matter what age they was, they pushed them on there. It was terrible. You were standing and you couldn't say anything, because then they grab you, too. I had a girlfriend and her grandmother was a Jew. She was picked up and not even her own daughter and grandchild could help.*

## Emmi Hofmann
····················· FROM GERMANY, 1956 ·····················

*There were stars on the houses that the Jews lived in, and we knew that they came and took them away, but we didn't know where. We thought maybe they went to some safe place or they were putting them somewhere in another part of the country.*

## Klara Zwicker
····················· FROM GERMANY, 1957 ·····················

# Elise Radell

*She has fresh coloring, crisp graying hair, and a casual, matter-of-fact manner—no accent at all. After working as a dietician for several years, she now teaches consumer economics at a community college. She and her husband, a highly successful real-estate man, live with their two sons in a spacious house on a hill, overlooking two ponds and a golf course.*

I was born in 1931 and Hitler came to power in 1933. As a little girl I never noticed anything. We were much integrated into the society. We had friends that were Jewish, that were non-Jewish. There never seemed to be any difference. But by 1937 or 1938, the Brown Shirts came along. All of a sudden, we became very much aware that we were Jews. We didn't know quite what to do with it. I remember going to school one day and somebody said to me, "You're Jewish," and threw a rock at me. I came home and I said to my mom and dad, "What is this being Jewish? Other people are Catholic. There are a lot of Lutherans and there are all kinds of churches, and why are they throwing stones at me?" And my parents said, "Well, that's the way it is." And then they took me out of regular public school and they took a private tutor for me—a young man who used to come to our house every day. I remember sitting in the dining room with him and we studied. I didn't study very well because I liked him more as a friend than as a teacher. I was about seven or eight then.

My grandfather owned a very large apartment house, where we lived. In fact, it was the first apartment house in Ludwigshafen, where I was born, that had glass doors that opened and an elevator. It was on the main street, and I remember the Nazis, on the days when there were parades for the Nazis, coming onto our dining room balcony; because our dining room balcony faced the main street in Ludwigshafen and it had to have a flagpole holder. And they came in every time there was a parade and put up the swastika flag. I didn't like that. I didn't like them and I didn't like that.

Then came the famous *Kristallnacht*.\* I don't remember the exact date. That morning, Mina, the maid, and I were going to get milk from the milk store. As we opened the door, the SS was there. They pushed us aside and came into the house. *"Guten Morgen,"* they said, *"Guten Morgen,"* I remember. They were very polite and then they went about this utter destruction with axes. They knew exactly how to do it. We had a breakfront in the dining room and it was one piece of teakwood, maybe seven feet long, and they knew just how to wreck it with one ax. Zzaszhh! Just ruined the whole thing. And the china closet was knocked all over and the pictures on the wall, with just one rip in each, and the furniture all just went. They were scientific about it. They had been told exactly how to go about it with the least amount of work. The pillows were ripped and the feathers—at that time there were feathers, you know—they just flew all over the house, and it was total destruction. Just ruined everything. My grandmother locked herself in the bathroom. The rest of us just stood and watched this destruction. Everyone was in shock. There was no fighting back. We were just stunned. Afterward, they took all the Jewish men, put them in jail, and then transported them to Dachau.

My father had been out of town on business and didn't come home until the next day. And then, out of some strange, unbelievable loyalty or honor or whatever the Germans were brought up to believe, when he came home and saw that all the Jewish men were gone, he went to the police station and gave himself up.

Now, I, as a Jew, can't quite understand how the German Jews did this; how my father could come back and turn himself in. But, being raised his whole life as an honorable citizen, to him this was the height of being honorable. And it's very hard for me to accept. I can understand intellectually; I don't understand it emotionally. . . .

After this, all the German Jewish women and children began to live together. I remember a cousin, a neighbor, another neighbor; we all lived in our apartment. We had the largest apartment. The train from Dachau to Ludwigshafen came at 2:10 every morning, and everybody

\*November 9, 1938. On this date, SS men broke into Jewish houses all over Germany, destroying furniture, pictures, and valuables. At the same time, over thirty thousand Jewish men were arrested and taken to concentration camps. The event became known as *Kristallnacht* (crystal night) because of the smashed glassware that littered the floors of the houses after the raids.

woke up at 2:10 A.M., because you never knew who would come home. We had a distant aunt and her daughter living with us, and one night her husband came home and it was my Uncle Julius. I loved him dearly before that. And he walked into our house and I wouldn't look at him and I said, "How come you didn't bring my daddy?" I just couldn't understand how he came home without my daddy.

Later, much later, eventually my daddy came home. My father was six-foot-one then, and tall and handsome, as a daughter sees her daddy—an eight-year-old daughter. And he had all his hair shaved off and he was down to ninety pounds. He came home and he never spoke about it again. Never mentioned it. It must have been so unbelievably terrible. But he came home. All I remember is his shaven head and that he was very skinny. But he hugged me and he kissed me and he said hello. *"Guten Tag*, Lisel. Everything's all right."

Those who could got boat tickets then to America, to Shanghai, wherever they could go. You couldn't get a visa to America unless you had relatives there. I think Roosevelt could have tried to open the quota a little bit. Maybe he did try; I don't know. But we had an aunt who had come to the U.S. in 1936, and she did everything she could for us. We had to go to Stuttgart, which was the center where all the visas and passports were given. My mother always took me along because I didn't look Jewish. I had blue eyes and blond hair at the time. We had to go by train, I remember. We finally managed to get the visas and everything, and we got on a boat and landed here in August 1939. The last trip over.

We begged my grandparents to come with us, but my grandfather was a great German nationalist. Not a religious man. He just didn't believe in God, and, therefore, what sense did temple make or religion make? He was an atheist. He was a German. And he said, "No. Nothing will happen to me." He wouldn't go. But now I think back—I have a feeling my grandfather knew my grandmother wouldn't make it through the physical. She was a very sick woman then. So he stayed with her. First they were deported to France, and then they were on one of those trains. The last we ever heard. In fact, we have a picture of them going on one of those trains—stepping up to the car that was going to go to Poland or wherever they went to be gassed. A friend of a friend saw them and took a picture. I have the picture now. I never look at it. . . . Right to the bitter end they were properly dressed. My grandfather had on a tie and a white shirt, and my grandmother had a dress on and a brooch and whatever shoes she had. And they got into that train! That's what I say about the German Jews. Down to the bitter end they had a false dignity. That's what they knew and that's what they were told to do, and they did it in the most elegant and dignified way they knew how. Right down to the gas chamber. And I'm sure that they walked into that gas chamber with their heads held high and that was it. . . . [*Breaks down.*]

I say, "Why didn't they fight? Why didn't we all fight back?" But if you're raised in a certain milieu, you cannot change. And besides, the fight would have been hopeless. That's something we know. The Poles' fight was hopeless, too, but at least they did it. You know, I'm torn. I always knew, after I got my senses back and was settled, I said, "I never could marry a German Jew," because I don't quite believe in going into the death chamber with your head held high, without somehow, somewhere, fighting back. It might be a terrible thing for me to say. In a way, I feel like a traitor when I think that, and, in another way, I feel, "Well, I'm an individual. I'm a free soul. I can begin to believe the way I would believe—and choose what I would choose." I don't blame my parents, because there were too many who did it the same way. But I don't think I could do it. . . .

We landed in Hoboken. We sat on our suitcases on the docks there, waiting for my uncle and aunt to come and pick us up. And they did and they took us to Seymour Avenue in Newark. They had an apartment and we moved in with them. My aunt and my uncle and my cousin, who was three years older than I was. That night I remember waking up. I had a terrible stomachache, and my aunt and uncle had taken my mother and father out for their first American ice cream cone. There were no ice cream cones in Germany, you know. I woke up with this terrible stomachache, and my cousin came over and said, "What's the matter?" And I couldn't speak English and I said, "My stomach hurts," in German. And he said, "Wait a little bit. I'll look out the window." And he looked out the window and the ice cream parlor was just down the street and he called and they came home. And my parents came in, and my aunt and uncle too, and they saw I was really sick. The family doctor came over at two in the morning and he said, "Uh, oh, Elise has appendicitis." The very first night. I had had it on the boat, but the boat doctors kept saying, "She's seasick. Yes, she's seasick." Anyhow, I was rushed over to the hospital and they operated on me and took out the appendix, and I had a little peritonitis afterward. It was all free of charge, because we couldn't pay.

In the hospital, I couldn't speak English. I didn't know anything. I couldn't even ask for a bedpan. It was dreadful. Short visiting hours; parents could only come once a day. And the girls in the room with me were Margo, Margaret, Marsha, Mildred—all the *M's.* And I couldn't tell one from the other. It was awful. The first thing I learned in English was: "Please, may I have a bedpan?" And the second was: "What time is it, please?" so I could know when my parents could come. The other children were all American. If they spoke, I couldn't understand them. They served corn on the cob one night, and in Germany, corn on the cob only went for the pigs. Nobody ever served corn on the cob, and I didn't know what to do with it and I started to cut it with a knife and fork and they all laughed and I was mortified and humiliated. I remember it was a terrible time. But I came home finally and I was all right.

And then it was time to start school. I was eight and a half by then. They put me in kindergarten. I was the big girl and I couldn't understand one word and I was put in with all these little ones. I never opened my mouth. Once the teacher asked me to get something from the back of the room. She wanted the scissors and I brought the crayons, because I didn't understand. And the whole class laughed and I was mortified and I said, "I'm not going to school anymore." But I went again—September, October, November. In December I opened my mouth and I started to speak the way I do now. I never practiced. I was just determined not to have an accent, and I wasn't going to be laughed at and I wasn't going to be left out. And when I knew I could speak, I opened my mouth and spoke. Then I got moved up right away. I went to first grade. I could pass that. Arithmetic is arithmetic, you know. And then I went up to second grade and then third grade and, then, right up to fourth grade. They skipped me.

My father got a job in a fabric store as a stockboy. He had owned a large textile firm in Ludwigshafen. Now he earned eleven dollars a week. And my mother was working as a seamstress in a dress shop and she was earning seven dollars a week. Finally we earned enough money, and we moved out from my aunt and uncle's house and got a one-room apartment of our own, which was nicer.

I finished grade school and high school and then had to pick out a college that was very inexpensive and where I could live at home, because we still had no money. I really had no right to go to college, but my parents' pride was to have braces on Elise's teeth and to send her to college. So we managed. I had braces on my teeth and I commuted every day from Newark to Pratt Institute in Brooklyn. I never knew it was dreadful, because I always had companions who commuted too. We got up at six in the morning. We were there for an eight-thirty class. And I did four years at Pratt Institute and I graduated with honors. I was going to go on to graduate school, but my father got sick: ulcers. I had been accepted at NYU Graduate School, but my mother and I were standing on the sundeck at Beth Israel Hospital and my mother said, "Elise. Poppa's sick. We got no more money. You can't go to graduate school." And I said, "Okay. You know what? I'm going to go downstairs to the dietician and I'm going to ask her if she needs a therapeutic dietician." And I was hired at once. Right there. I had my

training. I was qualified. I could get to the hospital by bus. I had my
degree and I went to work. And I worked until I met Ray and we got
married.

My husband's an East European Jew. I had always said I couldn't
marry a German Jew. But we're both Americans. To us, Judaism is a
religion, not a patriotic thing. We're both Americans.

We send our children to a cultural Jewish school because we don't
belong to a temple. We don't know if there is a God or not. I hate to say
I'm an atheist; maybe "an agnostic" is better. I don't know. And yet, I
feel the children need something, somehow, somewhere, for our
Jewishness. So there is this cultural Jewish school, an offshoot of the
Workmen's Circles in New York. Eastern Jews, garment workers, who
were not religious, started those schools. They've been carried on and
there's one here now. That's where my sons learned about the
Holocaust. I've never mentioned it and my parents never mentioned it,
and until a year ago, when they studied it in Sunday School, my own
children didn't even know that their grandpa was in Dachau. . . .

Last year my husband had a heart attack. I knew what the dangers
were. We decided it wasn't going to destroy our family or us. That was
the time I looked back and I said, "If my parents could have gone
through all the Holocaust in Europe and all that danger, I can go
through this." And Ray made it, and he's well now, knock wood. . . .

I remember when all this first started with the Jews in Germany.
There was a chance that you could send your children to England on
children's transports. My mother wrote a letter to my father in Dachau
in some kind of jabberwocky so that the censors would not understand. You should excuse me, the German censors are not the
brightest. Anyway, she quoted from Goethe and, somehow, she coded
it, asking whether she should send me with the child transport to
England, where the English will take the children into their homes;
not quite as their children, but as their companions, maids, helpers.
And my father wrote back, again quoting from Goethe. I don't know
the exact translation, but it means: "When I return I want to find you
all there." And that ended it. In other words, he was saying, "Do not do
that. If we're going to go under, we're going to go under all together.
We're not going to do this."

I have my children. I have my husband. We enjoy each day whatever
we do. And the children, we always take the children with us when we
go. We enjoy having them. We see things that we wouldn't see without
them—look up at the clouds. I don't walk around looking up at the
clouds, but my children tell me to and I do. . . . I understand now why
my father sent my mother that message from Dachau.

# Enid Armstrong
·················· FROM SCOTLAND, 1941 ··················

*In the early days of World War II, thousands of children were sent from Great Britain to the United States to escape the blitz. By the end of the war, five years later, for many of them this country had become home. Enid Armstrong was one of these "blitz kids" who eventually settled here. She is now happily married, for a second time, to an American oil executive with whom she travels extensively. Her three children, by her first marriage, live with their father.*

When I was about twelve years old, it looked very bad in the British Isles. We thought the Germans were on the verge of invading, and everyone was alerted that the church bells would ring and all kinds of signals would go off when the Germans actually landed. Since I was an only child and my mother was of a nervous temperament, she decided she'd like to send me out of the country. So she wrote to my father's brother and his wife, who lived in New York and had no children. She asked if they would take me temporarily until this crisis was over.

They wrote back and said, naturally, they'd be more than happy to take me. So I was shipped out on the Caledonian Line, along with a number of other young girls my age being sent to visit with relatives in the United States and Canada. We went in convoy and we could see the destroyers ahead and behind us as we went. We had to wear life belts the whole time we were on board, and we couldn't go up on deck after dark, and we had to be very careful with lights and so forth. Everything had to be kept very dark. I wasn't really alarmed about the possibility of being torpedoed; I was more concerned about being seasick, and I was curious about what it would be like in the United States.

When we arrived we sailed up the Narrows, and I saw my first sight of the Statue of Liberty. That was very, very thrilling. I had done a lot of reading before I left Scotland and, unfortunately, the encyclopedia that I had access to was written a long time ago, so that I got a totally different impression of New York from what I was going to see. At the time my encyclopedia was written, the Flatiron Building on 23rd Street was the tallest structure in New York, so when my aunt and uncle picked me up at the dock and drove me up Riverside Drive, I kept asking them, "Where is the Flatiron Building? Where is the Flatiron Building?" I'd never heard of the Empire State Building.

That first night we ate out at Schrafft's. I've never forgotten it. In those days, Schrafft's was a really quite pleasant, attractive restaurant. They had seven-layer cakes and things that I had not been exposed to. I thought it was really quite nice.

My aunt and uncle lived in a very small apartment, a one-bedroom apartment with a little dinette off the kitchen, and they turned that dinette into a little room for me, with a folding bed. Actually, I didn't get a folding bed right away. I slept on the sofa in the living room for almost a year before they decided it was going to be a longer stay than they'd planned and that it was worth getting a bed. [Laughs.] By that time we had got rather tired of folding up sheets and putting them on every night and taking them off in the morning.

As soon as I arrived I had a little set-to with my aunt. I wasn't exactly flexible at the age of twelve. In Edinburgh, I'd gone to a private school and, of course, they wore uniforms there. Now, I had brought all my school clothes from this private school and all the undergarments involved. You know, with the cold weather in Scotland, there were vests and bodices and bloomers and liners to the bloomers and black stockings and little tabs that you used to button on the bloomers, little bone buttons, all that sort of thing. My aunt decided this wasn't really appropriate garb for the Bronx, and she felt I had to get some new things—at least some new stockings and not wear the black ones to school. As I subsequently learned, only orphans from an orphanage wore black stockings over here. She was mortified that I would walk down the street in these black stockings, but I said these were my school stockings and my school clothes and I was going to wear them.

So I wore them for the first day to school and I quickly learned that this is *not* what you wear to school, and I came back the next day and said, "Yes, I would appreciate it if we could go and buy some stockings."

I remember when I first undressed for gym. We all lined up—in those days they didn't have locker rooms, you just lined up against the walls of the gym and changed into your gym suit—and I began taking off all these bloomers and bloomer liners and stockings and undoing all the little tabs and everything. And the girls were just lined up, watching me. I finally had to give in and let my aunt buy me some proper underwear. She still talks about it to everyone who will listen, about how determined I was. I wasn't going to let anybody change me all that much, but I changed by the next day. Of course, I wasn't thinking in terms of becoming an American. I was only there on a visit.

There was another emotional thing that happened to me in school. They had assembly in the public schools then. This was on a Friday afternoon and you had to wear a middy blouse with a blue scarf for that assembly program. As we were lined up outside the auditorium, one of the little girls asked me if we salute the flag in our country, and I said,

"What do you mean, salute the flag?" And she said, "Well, we put our hands over our hearts and we say this little pledge." I got absolutely terrified, because I had been brought up as a Scotch Presbyterian, and the one thing I knew was that you never bow down before idols. [*Laughs.*] I got into a state of panic about having to go through this little ritual with a flag. Finally, I learned to recite this little piece, but I'll never forget how I felt that day. I didn't know what I was being led into.

And then, the first thing in that assembly period, after we'd said the pledge, we had to sing—oh, dear, what is the name of that song? "Of Thee I Sing"? Oh, it's "America," isn't it? Which is the same tune as "God Save the King." I knew these were different words and that got me all choked up. The principal turned to me in front of the whole auditorium and asked me what did this remind me of. And I couldn't tell him because that was a tender moment for me.

Actually, the children were very nice there, very welcoming. I was something of a novelty, I guess, for most people. They had not encountered anyone fresh off the boat from Scotland before. That part of the Bronx, I think, was heavily Jewish then, and this was also new for me, because I'd heard about Jews. I'd read about them in books, you know, Shylock in *The Merchant of Venice* and that sort of thing [*chuckles*], and knew that they were, you know, very crafty in business and stuff, but I had never actually met any until just then.

They were so kind. They just took me to their hearts. I was overwhelmed by their hospitality. They would take me home to show to their mothers and fathers, you know, and this sort of thing. Most of these were people who had come over to the United States. Their parents were mostly first-generation immigrants; either the parents or the grandparents were from the old country, and these were the first generation who were going through school. They were really out to get an education. All the time I lived in the Bronx was a very interesting time, educationally, because there were high standards and they were really out to learn, and it was very stimulating.

It took me about a year, I think, to adjust to my uncle's and aunt's way of doing things. They'd never had children. It was difficult for them to sort of cope with somebody like me. And I missed my mother's way of doing things for a while—you know, like the way scrambled eggs are fixed. My mother always cooked them dry and my aunt cooked them wet. I had to learn to eat new food and I was a very picky eater. I used to have a terrible time with liver. I used to bury it in the mashed potatoes and swallow it whole. I hated spinach, too. But my aunt liked to serve a well-balanced meal and I had to eat a little bit of everything.

I never actually thought of myself as becoming an American. I always made the assumption that I would go back to my parents when the war was over. Well, several years went by, and I was in my last year of high school before V-J Day came. That was 1945. It was decided that I should not go home immediately, because I was in my last year of high school and it seemed it would be prudent to let me graduate first. I never thought about staying. I just thought that I'd go home and pick up where I left off. But I did, on my aunt's advice, fortunately, apply to a junior college in Brooklyn before I left—just in case. I think my aunt had more of an inkling of the problems that were going to come up than I did. I was just doing what I was told to do. I was sent over there and now I was going to be sent back.

I arrived back in Britain. Immediately I got into difficulty with my parents. My mother had this mental image of this little girl she had seen last at twelve years of age, and I was, obviously, not what she was anticipating. I was already, you know, a young woman, and I had a set of attitudes and she wasn't happy about them. They were awfully petty things, but they made a difference. The first minute I got off the boat, I saw her and it was all I could do just to go up and say hello. And when I did, you know, she gave me a look from head to foot and said I wasn't wearing much makeup. How come, you know, I wasn't wearing the last word in makeup. Well, this was a battle my aunt and I had fought all through my teen-age years. She was afraid my mother wouldn't approve of my wearing any makeup, so she wouldn't allow me to wear any, even Tangee natural lipstick, until I was sixteen years old. And certainly nothing else. And yet my mother was expecting me to be made up like a movie star. She was very disappointed about that.

There were other things, of course. She didn't like my shoes and we had to rush out and buy a good, stout pair of British shoes, which gave me blisters on both heels inside of a couple of hours. There were all kinds of battles. How was I going to decorate my room? Well, *she* was going to do it, you know. I was going to have nothing to say. Pictures that I'd had up on the walls in the apartment in New York I couldn't put up, because she wasn't having any nails in *her* walls. We really didn't get off on the right foot at all. She was determined to make me over in the image she had in mind. She could see that I was extremely attached to my aunt and she got upset that I wasn't resuming my relationship with her.

Things in Britain were still very, very bad. Life there was much harder. They were actually worse off after the war than they were during it, as far as food supplies were concerned. It was really amazing. I lost weight the first few months I was there, because the diet was so sparse. We couldn't even get Spam anymore—we were living on sardines. And it was so cold. That was a very cold winter there. I remember going to work on a temporary job and wearing my overcoat all day as I put ration books in file cabinets. It was just so cold. It was the food and the cold and the family situation.

And then, there was the problem with education. My mother quickly found out that my U.S. high-school education was not going to get me into a university in Great Britain. She had a dream, you know, that I would graduate from Edinburgh University, and when I went to talk to the Scottish Board of Education, they laughed. They said, "You couldn't possibly get into a university here. You'd have to have private tutoring for two years just to sit for the examinations." And in any case only a very small percentage of civilians were going to be allowed into the university, because the men were all coming home from the war and they were going to get first choice. I probably couldn't have gotten into civil service for the same reason.

My mother could only see me becoming a shopgirl, and she'd sooner die than have me do that, you know. That's definitely lower class. There's still a great deal of class consciousness in Great Britain. And my parents had really scrimped to put me into a private school, so that I would have a better opportunity. At that point I realized that my future did not rest in Britain for all these reasons: personal reasons, educational reasons, the difficulties of living. I wrote to my aunt an anguished letter, saying, "Please, can I come back? I'll eat all the spinach and liver you want me to."

I came back, but I didn't become a citizen until I married. It was my first husband who insisted that I get my citizenship, because he was not going to be married to an alien. [Laughs.]

I didn't go back to Britain for many years, because I married and had children, and my first husband was never interested in going to see the land of my birth or my children's heritage or anything of that sort. He'd been in the Battle of the Bulge in the Second World War as an infantryman and slogged across Europe, and he wasn't interested in seeing any of it again, under any circumstances.

But with my second husband I've been back many times—he's enchanted by Scotland and England, anyway. We had a wonderful family reunion in Scotland a couple of years ago. My Uncle Angus, who was eighty, decided he'd like to get his whole family together for afternoon tea. A son who lived in Canada and his wife went over, and my second husband and I. It was a charter flight, a very inexpensive charter flight, only a hundred dollars or so round trip. And we thought it would be a lark to go over for the Memorial Day Weekend and have the reunion. And I said to my husband, "Look, it's that cheap, why don't we take my aunt and uncle?" So we took Aunt Emily and Uncle Dick, the ones who had taken me in when I came to this country. They hadn't been back to Scotland since they were married, and that was almost fifty years ago. So we took them back, and it turned out to be a marvelous get-together.

There were two or three generations there, and I think it was the first time all the McKays have been under one roof in I don't know how many years, because some of them were not talking to others, you know this sort of thing, but they all decided to bury the hatchet for this one occasion. It was very touching, because Uncle Angus was the one in the family that everyone was terrified of. He'd been to Russia several times and thought that was a great country. He was a Labourite, and everyone else was Conservative in the family. He was sort of a black sheep, politically, in the family. They didn't bring that up at the reunion, of course. Uncle Angus died about six months after the reunion. I'm glad we were able to do that, to get everyone together for the last time.

# Hilda Gerhart

···················FROM GERMANY, 1946·····················

*She was left with grandparents in a small Bavarian town in Germany at the age of three, while her parents came out to the United States to establish themselves in New York. The war intervened and she wasn't able to join them again until she was seventeen, by which time they were divorced.*

When we started school, we had to go "Heil Hitler," and even now, when I try to tell which hand is left and which is right, I always have to go "Heil Hitler" to myself to know which is the right hand. [*Laughs.*] It seems so natural, you know. You had to do that. And yet, in the small town where we lived, we weren't too aware of the Nazi connection. My grandfather worked in the mayor's office, and he had to belong to the party, the Nazi party, but it wasn't anything much. It was just that you had to pay your dues, more or less.

My grandfather had a radio, and the people upstairs from us, they could hear what station we had on. And then one day Hitler made a speech, you know, and my grandfather, he'd listened to it once already someplace else. Once was enough, so he turned it off. And the people upstairs, they reported it. They reported my grandfather and he got questioned. He got called in: "Why did you turn Hitler off?" He said, "Well, I heard that speech already. I didn't think I had to listen to it twice." The next day he got that radio out of the house, and we never had a radio again until the American soldiers came. But he got all the information. There was another woman in town, her husband had died, and she had a radio; so he used to go to her place every night after dinner just to hear the news from six to seven. He listened to the Swiss stations. It was illegal, but we got to know everything that way. I mean, I did know there were concentration camps but only because my grandfather listened to that. My grandfather would come home and discuss everything, and I never repeated a word outside my grandfather's kitchen.

There were no Jews in our town, but in the next town there were Jewish people. In 1938, Hitler had that thing* when he arrested all the Jews. They rounded them all up. They took all the men. The women were left behind, but everything was destroyed. My aunt worked in that town. She went to work the next day and she had to come back home in the morning because it was so sickening. They had destroyed everything. Some of the schools in that town had Nazi teachers, and they instigated the kids and let them off from school, and the kids went to those Jewish people's homes and the women were still there. My aunt said that as she was passing, kids came, and this one woman grabbed just a little box and one kid went up to her and grabbed the box from her. I guess it was jewelry or something she was holding on to. And the kid spat at her and beat her up because she didn't want to give up the box. Three days later they found her. She'd committed suicide. They found her in the river. . . . There were only five or six families living in that town that were Jewish. You knew them by name, so I knew who the woman was, but I'd never really spoken to her. I think it must have been on a Thursday or a Friday night. I went to see the houses on Sunday, and they were all smashed up—the furniture, everything. A lot of people went to see how it looked.

When I think about the war, even one little bit, I still get terrified. I remember when all the planes flew over our town, we stood there, looked up, and said, "I wonder where they're going now." Because there were planes and planes and planes. You know they're going someplace. You know they have a target and you know they're going to hit something. On New Year's Eve they killed like a hundred thousand citizens in Nuremberg—mostly women and children. They have a memorial there, and I'll tell you, if you see that memorial, you'll feel bad to be an American.

Before the Americans came, the day before, there were orders to blow up all the bridges around here. And we had this one little bridge, one small bridge what held four tons, you know. Tanks couldn't even go on it. It was like a little railroad bridge. This German soldier blew it

*Kristallnacht. See page 138 (Elise Radell).

up, and everyone was telling him, "Don't blow it up. Everything is gone. It's too late now. You're not going to hold them back or nothing." But this guy was still doing his duty and he blew the thing up. And he had so much explosive on that little bridge that four houses in our area got completely demolished. I went home and was hysterical. And it was such a little bridge, you know. The tanks couldn't have gone over it anyway, it was so tiny. One little German soldier, and he went from town to town; he blew up all the bridges. That was the real end of the war, you know.

The town that I come from, there's a lot of people in America, a lot of sons and daughters emigrated here. A really large percentage of our town came. When the war was over and the American soldiers came into town, we had this one guy who was a businessman and he spoke a little English; he got a basket with a bottle of wine and the bread and the cheese, and he went to the end of the town where they came marching in with the tanks and he greeted the American major. He made the major come right over, and told him, "You can come right through our town. There's nobody going to resist or anything." He told him, "A lot of our sons and daughters are in America." And the soldiers came marching right through, but there was not one shot. . . .

The war was over and they had trials for everybody who was in the party or who had a position. A lot of the townspeople worked to make baskets for the munitions. They worked Saturdays, Sundays, too. And my grandfather in his little trial, he said, "You never saw me work on Sunday for Hitler." His sentence was he had to repair all the church windows. So you know he wasn't a Nazi.

Germany was really in a bad state, and my grandfather said to me, "You're never going to have anything good over here. Why don't you go over there to your mother; you'll have it a lot better." He wanted me to have the best. It broke his heart, you know. It broke his heart to send me away, but I think he really thought it was going to be better for me. My grandmother was, well, you know, anything my grandfather said was okay with her. You know how it is, you're a teen-ager and you think, "Oh, America! That's appealing," right? And I went to the consulate and made arrangements, and off I went. Because my mother was in this country it was faster for me, of course.

My mother had remarried, and she had three girls and another one on the way when I got here. My mother was like a stranger to me. I could never get close to her. It was the strangest feeling. I finally called her "mom," but it didn't make any difference. And to this day. . . .

They lived on the East Side and, of course, they were immigrants. And they weren't too far ahead yet. They lived in a railroad flat, and it was really a sight when I walked in there. Oooh! It was just like a dungeon. It was dark; they had to have the lights on all day. And they didn't have much furniture. They didn't have much at all.

You see, I really did have it good in Germany. I think I had it better over there than I would've had it here. Since my grandfather was in the mayor's office, he had all these little things going. He had the milk route and the place where they collected the eggs. My grandmother went once a week and collected the butter from the farmers and brought it to the stores. She always wound up with a half a pound of butter. That's how we got through, and I didn't feel any hunger or anything. We really had no problems with money or food. You never felt if you needed something you couldn't go out and buy it. There was no thing such as got to wait until next week, until you get a couple pennies together, you know. So it was a big change for me when I got here. We'd heard that this was the land of milk and honey; well, I got some impression of that milk and honey. Achh!!

I wanted to get out on my own, and I got into a marriage a little too quick and that's why it turned out bad. I had a daughter. I started working again when I knew I was going to leave my husband. I did sewing at home. Got a little nest egg so my daughter and I could get out. And I got my own place. I couldn't ask anybody for help. I wanted to do everything on my own. And then I started teaching sewing, and that's how I kept myself going. . . .

A friend of mine had a little girl, and she wanted to send her little girl to relatives in Germany. The same thing as happened to me. The little girl was three years old, the same age. And she said, "I'm sending my Putzi over to Germany, because I have to work and we want to buy a bakery, and I'll have to leave her." Well, when I heard that I became almost hysterical. I said, "Don't do that. Don't do that, because I know what it's like when you're left behind with someone strange. Don't do that to a child." She sent the child and I didn't speak to her for quite some time afterward.


# Lieselotte Mueller

···················· FROM GERMANY, 1951 ·····················

*She came from Hamburg in 1951 and settled on Long Island. Now she is a busy housewife and mother, taking an active part in the PTA and other school activities.*

Once in a while I noticed it—I must have been thirteen or fourteen. There was just another customer like me in a little store, telling a political joke, and then I heard somebody of the other customers say,

"You'd better shut up or you land in a concentration camp." That was the very first time I heard the name *concentration camp*. I thought—I mean, just thinking back now—it's probably just a little bit tougher than a jail. I never even wasted a thought on it, or I didn't even ask anybody, either. You know, you are so brainwashed, you don't give it a thought.

My father belonged to the Nazi party from 1928. I think people who joined then were really idealists. From the time that the war started, he was with the police department—not with the SS but with the police. He was like a jail warden but in a little higher position. He would have a camp in Norway or in Poland. He had always different camps with political prisoners, also Jews. When he was in Poland, he became very disillusioned. He objected violently when he saw how they were treated and what they got to eat. So then he was deprived of all these jobs, and then he just had to be a guard in the prison—not a concentration camp.

When you were ten years old, the whole class had to attend these group activities automatically—there was no way out. And whenever you went anyplace, you always had to raise your arm and say "Heil Hitler!" Also, in the morning, we first all said "Heil Hitler!" And we had pictures of Hitler all over the classrooms. It was in a way a little brainwashing.

Then they had—well, they called it *Kinderverschickung*—sending children to the country. This was to get children out of dangerous bombing areas—evacuation, I think you could call it. They were all organized by the Hitler Youth, and it was all paid for by the state. We were mostly in hotels in the country. Like the Hamburg children would be sent to Bavaria, where it was safe, where there were no bombings and alarms. We had regular classes every day in those camps.

Besides the teachers, some of the Hitler Youth leaders went along, and on Sunday morning, instead of church, we had these Hitler Youth services for hours, learning songs and the history about every Nazi in the country. We also went on camping trips and outings, and at that time, I must say, I found it just as interesting as many girls here with Girl Scouts and Brownies.

In 1943, we had these big air raids on Hamburg, and from then on there was no more school until the war ended. Most schools were bombed out, and it was impossible. They wanted to make you join one of those camps out in Bavaria or someplace like that. I had been during the war to many different places such as these, but after the very bad air raids, my brother and I just didn't feel like going again—not knowing whether you will see your family again. After all, we were only ten and twelve years old at that time.

During the next two years, besides running into bunkers I kept very busy with the Hitler Youth. This unit had a whole building, a complete complex, and I went every day. I started to do office work and things like that—without pay, a few hours a day, enjoying doing it.

I remember one of the other girls in my class who did not come. The leaders would come to the house and talk to the mother and father and tell them it's their obligation to send their daughter. But they would excuse themselves—illness, and she had to help. You did find ways around it. I was embarrassed that *my own brother* didn't want to go. Inasmuch as I was rather active, they were after me, like the devil after a poor soul, to get my brother to come before he gets into trouble. He said, "You can go alone. I don't enjoy it." I really thought Hitler was the greatest and Germany the greatest and that we would win the war and everything would be fantastic.

When the war was over, I still didn't think that the Germans were as bad as we were told by the Allies. We were then forced to see these terrible movies—you know, about concentration camps. And even then I still did not believe it. I thought that this was, in a way, all propaganda. It took me quite a few years before I really saw the light and could see that the Nazi regime would have never worked out well.

Right after the war it was pretty difficult, because a lot of black market was going on and everything was rationed and not enough to eat. Then, in 1948, we got this money exchange. No matter how much money you had, you all just got sixty marks until next payday. I was rather depressed at the time the money changed, because I had just saved three or four hundred marks to go on a trip; and now all I had was my sixty marks, so I couldn't go. If anybody would have said, "Would you like to go to the U.S.?" I would have jumped at the opportunity— just to get out of the country.

A few years later I met my husband, and he mentioned that he was going to emigrate. He wanted to come because of better chances and opportunities. At that time we thought that America was the greatest, and in a way it is.

We came to this country in December 1951. We were here only a few days and we both had a job. There was this Swiss company, and one day I just walked in and asked if they couldn't use a bookkeeper, and they were just looking for one. So I got $50, and I worked for that company for about five years. My husband started with a machine-tool company for about $1.30 an hour.

Once, when I was working, opposite me was a Jewish girl sitting, and I didn't know this for the longest time. We only spoke English together. Then somebody one day said to me that Maria—or whatever her name is—is German. "Why don't you talk German to her?" I first thought, that's terrible—she knows how bad my English is and she doesn't even attempt to speak German with me. So then I just said to her, "Why don't you try to talk German with me?" and she explained to me that she had lost her family, her child and husband, in concentration camps, and she just couldn't cope with it. I think she probably hated me. In those days I was rather hurt, but now I understand.

When I had children and started to help in the school library, and I saw all these books about the World War, I was thinking, "Well, as soon as my children start to learn history—these wars and Hitler—that will probably be very embarrassing to them." Eva [oldest daughter, eighteen years old], for instance, and I have discussed World War II, and she said, "Was it really that bad?" I said, "Yes, these things happened. But you cannot make the whole nation responsible for it now, because we didn't know it." Then, of course, I reminded her that Americans in Vietnam haven't done so hot either.

# Tanya Shimiewsky

···················· FROM POLAND, 1950 ····················

*Wearing the traditional wig of Orthodox Jewish women, she sits and talks quietly and unemotionally in the large living room of the rooming house she and her husband operate in Chicago. The neighborhood is changing, and as blacks move into the area, the Orthodox Jews, afraid, move out. Tanya and her husband are trying to sell their house.*

When the Germans came to our town, we were scared in our own houses. Then they made the ghetto. In my town! They moved all the Jews from the whole town together, just in a few streets. And they brought in Polish people from someplace else and they put them in the houses where the Jews used to live.

We had to wear the Jewish star. It is still always in my subconscious. When I get dressed, I always look whether I have it on. It never leaves me. It was a yellow star and black—a yellow patch and the Star of David on it, and *Jew* written there. We had to wear it on all clothes, whenever you went out. If you were caught without it, they put you in jail.

This was in '39. It was very bad. They used to take the men to work. They took them to clean and to do other things. They established sewing shops to make for the military, and my husband had to go to work. But he didn't want to go, because he had to work on Saturday. But they said that it is going to be safer to work, then they're not going to send us out from town.

One time my husband came home, and they beat him so much at work that he was spitting up blood. When this happened, I said, "Well, let's run away." He said, "As long as I have my bed, I don't want to move. I'm staying right here."

And one Saturday I heard that they took people, whole groups of people, and they send them out to Germany. And I saw that my husband doesn't come home from work. I didn't know what happened to him. I went out and someone told me she saw that they took them out. "I might as well tell you. They took Karl in there with the whole bunch." And they sent him away someplace. They were working putting rails for trains. And then he was in other concentration camps, in Auschwitz, and—I forgot already what concentration camps— Buchenwald, Dachau. He came out, he was like this, forty kilo, eighty pounds—this big man.

I stayed on with my mother and my child—she was then five years old. To be safe that they shouldn't send me out, I got a job, too. I started to sew men's pants. And one day we heard that they're going to send out the rest of us, the whole town. It was on a Saturday again—it was always on a Saturday—we had to come for a medical examination. We were allowed to take a little knapsack and a little food. I put one dress on top of another, and another on top of the other, and a coat. The Polacks were standing inside, just looking. We had a janitor with a daughter, and she was always saying, "This house is going to be mine." And now we could see how it was true. They were just standing on the side and laughing. When we left our house, my mother said, "I will never come here again."

We had to strip, take off all the clothes. There were men and women we knew, and we had to stay in one line, nude. And the doctors marked the people who were able to go to work *A*, and the other people *B*. Here—on them. I had *A* and my mother had *B*, and I knew right away that we're not going to be together.

They took us to a big marketplace and they were selecting, saying *A* should go one side and *B* another side. And I left my little girl with my mother, and she was crying. She was very close to me; she didn't want to stay with my mother. I said, "You're going to be with your grandma. Stay here. Mamma's going to come back right away." I still have guilty conscience that I left her. I always say to myself, maybe I should have stayed with my baby and my mother. And the other mothers with little infants, they ripped out the little children from them and threw them over fences. . . . You are crying and I not cry. . . . Maybe we skip this part?

*No, please go on.*

It was pouring rain, pouring rain, and we were standing all night in this big rain—everybody. And then in the morning they took us to Lodz, and my mother stayed with my daughter and I never saw them again. They told us that they sent the children and the old people someplace else to help in the fields, pick spinach and do little things. But a few people stayed on to help them, to manage with the people that were left, and a few days later they came in to the Lodz ghetto. These people told us that the Germans open graves, and alive they put them in there and shot them there.

In Lodz this was a closed ghetto. There was barbed wire around. They give out rations and there was so little food that when I came in and I saw people looking out from the windows, I thought they were corpses. They didn't look like people anymore. This was in '42. I had a little food with me—it happened that I took it, not my mother—preserves I used to make and cookies. And when they saw these things, the Lodzer people, they just couldn't believe that we still had food.

My husband had a sister in Lodz, and I stayed with her and her husband. But he was so hungry that he ate up all my food. I used to go out in the morning, and she went to work in the afternoon. She left for me food on the stove, but when I came home there was nothing. He had eaten up everything. Then she hid it under the bedcover, so he shouldn't know where the food is. She said, "He's going to eat you up. You're going to starve with nothing to eat." She took my piece of luggage and she put in my ration, my bread and everything, and she locked it up in the closet. But he broke the lock and he took it out and ate it. . . .

In my shop we made slippers, house shoes. We took old dresses and ripped it for little strips and braided it, and then sewed it up on the machine and put on soles and made slippers. We didn't get paid for it; we just got our ration of food.

When I finished this job, I was sent to another place at the end of the town, near the cemetery. There they made mattresses from straw. We had to go ourselves and fetch, even in the snow, the biggest frost. We had to fetch our straw ourselves and fill it in the sacks and carry it in the house. And then we had to sew in the ends and make the puffs and make the border—the whole thing.

In the meantime, there were selections. The Germans were coming, and all of a sudden they locked up streets and they took out people. One day they took out all the old people. Another day was a day of children—all the children had to be ready. Did you hear the poem about Korczak, Janusz Korczak? This was in the Lodzer ghetto. He was taking care of a house for children who don't have parents; and one day the Germans came and they said, "We're going to send away all the children." He and his wife stood in the head of the line, and he said, "I'm going with them." And he went to the ovens with them.

I was—I don't know—lucky or not lucky. I stayed on till the end. In '44 most of the Jews were sent out already, and we were all concentrated on one street. We used to go out and clean away. We were emptying out the houses and making bundles, and this went to Germany—all the feather beds and everything.

The Jews were managing the jobs. They were our leaders, they represented us, but they were more for the Germans than for the Jews. This Jewish leader from the ghetto, Rumkowski, was in cahoots with the Germans. When he came then to Auschwitz, the Jews killed him right away. All these Jews who were managing, who were in contact with the Germans, lived like on the outskirts of town. One man and his wife, they had a boy, and they wanted me to come to their house and take care of the boy. They had luxury still—beautiful surroundings with trees, flowers, like an orchard, a maid who baked every day the best things. And we, the plain people, had to starve. For a while I worked in his garden, and the maid brought us out food, so the lady shouldn't see—food for the girls who worked in the garden.

After the holidays, after Rosh Hashanah, they sent us all out. The women and children were sent to Ravensbruck. From this camp some children are still alive—this is the only camp where they kept children alive. There they took us out, they stripped us, they took away all our clothes, and they were searching us in and out. They took us for showers, and who didn't have clean hair, they cut it off till the bone. There were gas chambers, too. We lived in shacks, no heat. The beds were like bunk beds, three levels. They gave us so little food—a piece of bread and soup like water two times a day. And there were the gypsies. Gypsies were sent to the concentration camps, and German girls who were stealing or committing crimes. But they were younger, and there was homosexuality—lesbians that you couldn't recognize that this was not a man. One young woman, my friend, one time she got sick and they took her to First Aid, like a little hospital, and they used her as a lesbian. They kept her there the whole time.

We young women—of course, I was still young—were sent out to Wittenberg, and there we used to work in factories. We were making airplanes. I was put to make airplane wings, to solder and to put in the nails. When we went out in the morning, on the march to Wittenberg, we had to sing songs when we went through the town, so the German people wouldn't know. We were wearing like army outfits, pants and jackets like khaki material—just a group of people.

In the evening we went back, and we didn't have hot water. We had just a little stove and we had to wash our clothes in cold water and then hang it up by the stove. Once a week they took us for showers. And we had calls—everybody got together and they took us out for hours, standing in the frost—to count us. I have a friend and she always reminds me, "Tanya, remember what you said? 'Think they are making a movie, we are hired to make a movie. Take a look—the sun, the beautiful sky—it's just the same for us, like for them.' Anything not to give up."

And that's our life. I was there till the end of the war, till April 28—and the Germans left. There were a lot of airplanes, and we knew that the war is close. And all of a sudden they walked out. One day we went out and we saw there were no Germans around. We didn't know what to do. There was still bombing going on, so we thought it's safer to stay in the camp. We went in the kitchen, their kitchen, and we got our food. We were happy. It was over. It was over.

I don't remember how long we stayed there. The Russians came to the camp, and they said, "Girls, why are you sitting here? Come out. You're free." So we went out to the town. The German women with the children, they run away, because they were afraid of the Russians. And the Russians found us an apartment, a German apartment, with food, and they gave us clothes.

Some German women stayed, and you should see their cellars— *speck*, meat, fruit preserves. They had cellars stacked with food, and they gave us willingly, because they were afraid of the Russians. A lot of people died during this period, because they got so much food and they ate this fat stuff after so much time they didn't have anything. . . .

Would you believe it? We *walked* back to Poland, a group of maybe eight or ten girls. We got hold of a wagon, a little wagon on four wheels, wooden, with a hold-on like a cross, to hold on to and pull on. Daytime we walked. At night we went into a German town, to the mayor, and they gave us money and food and lodging for the night. And we would stay just a night. But sometimes some girls rubbed their feet, they couldn't walk anymore, and we had to stay a while longer.

Once we heard that from this town a train is going to go, supervised by the Russians already. It wasn't a train for persons, just for cattle. We went on the train. When we came to Poland, the Polacks said, "So many of you survived?" We were glad we came to our native country after Germany, and this is how they welcomed us. This broke our hearts more than anything else. But there was a committee of Jews already who helped the incoming people. They gave us money, and I looked around for somebody from my family. There was no one.

Then we went to Lodz. They had organized already a kibbutz with young people, and they took us in. It was a house in the town, a beautiful house. I was maybe the oldest one. I made a beautiful table for Friday night, I lit the candles, and I kept it in a traditional way.

There was another house where they had just the young children—ten, twelve, fifteen years old maybe. These children were taken out of churches—they were hiding Jewish children during the war. These children had nobody. They didn't want to live, they didn't have the will power to go on. And the committee asked me, "Tanya, would you want to go and live with these children? Because you're more mature than anybody else here." I wanted to be a mother to these children, because I thought that maybe somebody else is taking care of my little girl. I still didn't believe that my daughter's not alive. We gave them clean clothes and we washed them. They had unclean heads and they had skin disease. There was a salve to rub in, but they said they don't want to do it. They just gave up. I sat down for hours—I don't know how I had this courage to do what I did—and I rubbed them and I comforted them. I went out to the market with the boys and we bought chicken and vegetables and fruit. I saw to it they should prepare the food, and I supervised how they should cook. I taught them everything. We got on very nice, like a family life. It took a while until they got to themselves. They recovered later on, but. . . .

There was a book with all the names of the people who had arrived, and when. But when I looked under my town's name, I couldn't find my husband's name; I couldn't find anybody. Nobody's alive. Nobody. I had three brothers and three sisters and one sister-in-law. And my oldest brother had three children, two girls and a boy. Alexander was the boy, and there was Rachel and Anastasia. And then my brother who died at the ghetto—blond beautiful curls and dark eyes. And then my sister had three children, and then was another brother with two children, and I had one child. That's all the whole family, and nobody survived. Just me.

One day I asked one of my friends to go with me to my hometown, to see how everything is. I was afraid to go by myself. I went back to our house, and it was occupied. In one apartment lived a girl who was our maid before the war. And in another apartment lived a worker. So I went and sat in the park, and a Polish woman came up to me and she said, "I know you. You're Mrs. Shimiewsky." I remembered, when we knew that we were going to be sent out, we started to sell our furniture, and she came to buy my kitchen cabinets. When she saw my little girl, she said, "Mrs. Shimiewsky, give me the girl. I'm going to hide her for you. When you come back, I'll give her back to you." This was the woman who wanted to take my girl. She said, "Why didn't you give her to me? She was such a beautiful girl. . . ." I'm just wondering how I can sit and tell this story. I'm not going to sleep tonight. . . .

Our kibbutz started to send people out to Israel. They had a way of sending illegally, because the Poles didn't let us go out. The kibbutz had people, smugglers like, and they paid the smugglers to get together a group of people and take them over to Austria or Germany. Eventually, some of these children I was taking care of came on the *Exodus* ship. I helped send a lot of people out, but in my heart always, I wanted to go to Israel, too. Even if it was dangerous, there was the war there, it was a big honor when we were able to go.

And then one day, somebody who worked with a big committee, who took care of people who came back, came to me and said, "Do you know that your husband is alive in Germany?" He was working for a DP camp, on the American side, driving a truck to Munich to pick up flour and sugar. He didn't know that I'm alive. I said, "My place is with my husband. I have to go to him."

There were some other friends who wanted to go to Germany, too, so we went together. We had to pretend we weren't Polish, that we were displaced by the war and going back to Italy. The Polacks looked in our baggage, and I had a pair of skates. I found a pair of skates, and I always wanted to go skating before the war, so I took them with me. And they said in Polish, "A beautiful girl—what does she need skates in Italy?" And they took them away from me. I had to pretend I didn't understand. I couldn't protest, I couldn't say anything.

Finally we came to Germany, and I went to the DP camp. My husband lived in a room full of men—again bunk beds! And I had to sleep in bed with him with a whole full house of just men. I saw I can't stay there. I said, "I want to go to Israel." He said, "Let's stay a little while and see." But I went back to Munich and found a big apartment. My husband came, and we started family life together.

It was '45 or '46. We didn't have to pay rent, and we got some food rations from the Americans, some money from the HIAS [Hebrew Immigrant Aid Society]. We worked and we went out, too. We wanted to catch all the operas and the operettas, or whatever. I started to bake, and we invited people for the Friday and Saturday meals. Then I was celebrating my eleventh anniversary. My tenth anniversary I was in concentration camp, and this was eleven years after we got married. But how could I celebrate? All these people had lost their wives and husbands, and I am celebrating. But they were happy that we're together, that at least somebody survived who can celebrate.

My husband and I, we became partners with another man in a kosher restaurant in Munich. We took over after a German, so the rabbi came in and he made kosher all the stoves and everything, and then we started. The first day we opened the restaurant, they broke out the doors, so many people were pushing in. They were all from concentration camps, of course, in business already. But they wanted a little

Yiddish, Jewish food. It was such a success! We kept it for a long time, till we left.

In the meantime we had a baby, my daughter Sarah, and later a son, Daniel. We were doing well; we had luxury. But we knew Germany was not the country to stay. We decided we were going to emigrate. We had all the papers, all the pictures, all the tests, to go to Israel. We had a little money saved up. But then there was the devaluation of the mark, and we lost everything in one night.

I had relatives here in America, and in the meantime they wrote to us that if we come here, we have a possibility to work. Then we decided. We were ashamed, because everybody went to Israel. But we decided and we made papers to go to America. It was 1950. My little girl was three years old and my son was a baby.

I've been here twenty-five years, and I still have dreams. When my grandson was born, I reminded myself about when they took the babies. The memories start coming back, and all these things are just alive again. Would you believe that a person can take so much? I still say I'm going to go back to Poland and look for my daughter. I still see her as a little girl; I don't remember that she would be old now.

I never told my children all these things, never told them what I went through, because I didn't want to hurt them. Now I think I was wrong. Maybe they would understand life better. This is for them.

# Wojtek Pobog

·················· FROM POLAND, 1949 ······················

*He is a gentle man, soft-spoken, and he looks at his blonde wife often as if for confirmation of what he says. He was a child in Warsaw when World War II began.*

We were in church and the church was packed, and we could hear the Germans marching on the streets and this rhythm of their boots on the street. And, all of a sudden, the priest started singing one of the most beautiful songs in Polish. It's sort of a Catholic hymn, "God Who Saved Our Poland." I remember everybody in the whole church started crying. And that's how I remember: looking back in an open door, in a brick church, and there the soldiers are turning around in the square and marching up the main street.

During the German occupation, I remember standing in lines waiting for—not for bread—the only thing we could get was rice and cinnamon. For kids at my age it was a big adventure. The German Stukas, these German diving planes, would dive and shoot right across the people waiting in lines. But for us, for me and my brother, it was sort of exciting, because every time the line would disperse, we would be in the front of the line, and we could get the rice much sooner. We didn't realize the danger.

We knew that it would be very hard to live in Warsaw, so my father decided, well, we might as well go back to his uncle in another town on the other side of the Vistula River. My uncle had a restaurant over there, and my father thought maybe he could find some work. The Jewish people in this town knew that they would sooner or later be evicted from their homes anyway, and they wanted to save as much of their belongings as they could. So my father started taking belongings of the Jewish people, and taking them on the boat across to Warsaw. He was helping the Jewish people, and they were paying him. Well, the guy who was working with him got drunk one day and started mouthing off and spilled out about my father. The Germans caught my father and they started working on him—for about three days and three nights. At night, they kept him in a pigsty. I used to go at night and hand him food on a long stick, because he couldn't straighten up. They were beating him for three days, and after three days they let him go. This was right after Christmas.

We were staying in my uncle's attic. The Germans were having a New Year's Eve party in his restaurant, and the guy in charge asked my father to come down, because he wants to forgive him for everything. He wants the whole family to come down, because they want to drink a toast for a good year. So we had to come down to his table. The German says, "Here is a toast to you. Everything else forgotten. Heil Hitler!" And my father—as beat up as he was, with black eyes and everything else—he took the glass and just poured it out and threw the glass down. They didn't say anything at all.

The following day, the two Gestapo men came in and gave us half an hour to get together with all the Jews from the town to start walking to Warsaw. We couldn't take anything with us. They just kicked us out from this town, said, "You're not welcome here. You just go."

All the time they were bringing more and more and more Jewish people from all around Poland, sending them into Warsaw. They were manipulating the people back and forth for about a year and a half. The way I recall, first they wanted the Jewish people to move to a certain part of town. Like, say, if you take New York, they want all the Jewish people to live in Brooklyn, for instance. And if you were a Pole, you had to move out of Brooklyn and go to Manhattan.

When they sent so many of them to Warsaw, then they started another story, a panic story, that I remember as a kid in Poland—that the Jews are spreading disease. I remember that we, as a school, had to walk to a certain place where they were showing us movies how to protect yourself against the Jews spreading lice and spreading typhus. They were showing us pictures, movies, and you could see under magnifying glass how the lice look. And then, "Beware of the Jew."

Then they say, "Well, you have to seal this block, not to spread the disease." That's how they started this, you see. It was a very slow process. And then they started isolating the sections by saying that this is a typhus epidemic, and they put barbed wire. But the Jewish people could leave and go to work; then at night they had to go back to the ghetto.

At that time there was no wall around the Jewish ghetto. The ghetto was tremendous, like thirty or forty blocks, maybe. Then another part of the town—there would be typhoid scare. Then they said that because of all these typhoid scares, they have to build a wall around. The walls they built were, I would say, twelve or maybe more feet high, right in the middle of the streets. One of my friends lived right next to the ghetto. Half of the street had the big wall, and he lived on one side and the ghetto was on the other side of the street. We used to watch how they used to chase the poor Jewish people around there.

My father was always involved in politics, and he had some friends in the underground. I don't know how much he was involved in it, because it was a great secret. However, I kept my secrets from him just as much as he kept from me. My teacher asked three of us fellows once if we would stay after school. She inquired if we would be interested in learning how to ride a motorcycle. Well, for a fellow thirteen years old to ride a motorcycle was like going to the moon. We went after school on the outskirts of the city, and there was nobody around there. We would just go maybe for an hour, once a week for about three or four months. We had classes how to take the bike apart and how to put it back together and everything else. Then they gave us a little emblem resembling motorcycle goggles, and that meant that I was a runner for the Polish underground!

My father used to bring Polish papers, with the news from the British BBC. My father told me where to go, and I used to distribute these among the people. They were very tightly written. I used to carry these newspapers or pamphlets in my glove, and whenever I saw that the German patrol was coming and stopping people on the street, I would take the glove and throw it in the sewer and just walk right through them.

Then the insurrection started on August 1, 1944. I was visiting my friends on the other side of Warsaw. All of a sudden it was very quiet. Something was funny, because all of a sudden there was nothing moving—no streetcars, everything was stopped. The Germans were all over the street with guns drawn. So I started running home, and wherever I saw a German, I ducked into a door or somewhere. It was after eight hours I finally made it home.

For the first three days we were building barricades. Everybody—the whole population—was on the street, bringing the chairs from home and everything that they could think of. They were building barricades in each intersection. And that's the time when I got so mad, that I can't do anything because I was only fifteen, that I joined the scouts. And showing them that I have this emblem that I am a runner, they immediately told me, "Fine, if you are a runner, you are in. You can walk between the sections delivering army communications from one place to another." That's how we got into communication—not by radio but by little kids who are running from one place to another. We didn't even realize what was going on, because we were so brave, we thought we are on top of the world.

The Germans used to bomb systematically. You could set your clock. For instance, today they would be shooting on the other side of the street. At seven o'clock in the morning they would start, and they would first finish the corner house. Fifteen minutes later they would finish the next one, then the next one, then the next one. At ten o'clock, they had half an hour for coffee, and for half an hour you didn't have to worry. You could go on the street, you could walk around. Then you had to run like mad into your own basement and hide, because they would continue until they finished the whole entire block, with heavy artillery. Then they would switch and start shooting on this side of the street, and all the population would go into the ruins of the other side, because they would never shoot to the ruined side. Eventually, when we were leaving Warsaw, you could stand on one side of Warsaw and you could see the other end. There was hardly anything left.

When the insurrection was over, all the population had to leave Warsaw. All the able-bodied men and women had to go to compulsory work in Germany. They were taking us by streets. On the sixth of October this section of the city was leaving; the next day the next section of the city was leaving. We were allowed to leave with whatever we were standing with. We were walking through the streets, with all these Gestapo guys standing on both sides of the street with submachine guns, looking at you. Everybody had to leave—one and a half million people. We had to empty the whole Warsaw. We were marching in long columns, maybe six hours. We went to a little camp outside of Warsaw, and we stayed in this camp for two days. They were looking at you like cattle and say, "You, you, you, and you." If you objected, you just got a kick in the behind or in the face, or wherever they felt like it. They took me and my brother and they kicked us on one side. My mother looked young, so she went with us. My father looked old, and they were forcing him to go on the other side, to stay in Poland. He begged them to go with us, and they let him.

*Did anyone try to stay behind?*

Why would you stay behind if you have nothing to eat? You ate all the pigeons, you ate all the dogs, you ate all the cats. There was nothing else left to eat. There was nothing.

There were long, long trains—cattle cars—and they loaded us on the cattle cars, put the bars on, and we stayed there maybe a day and a half before the train started moving. And two days later we were in Germany.

We got off the train at night—all the women on one side of the railroad track, all the men on the other side. Dark as the dickens. We said, "Let's follow the first man," and we started going. We were holding hand by hand, and you could hear the machine guns going, bursts of machine-gun fire. Scary as heck!

They took us to a little tiny town, and we worked. It was almost the end of the war and Germany needed people to work, because all the able-bodied Germans were at the front lines. We had to wear a *P* for Pole, like the Jews were wearing the Star of David. We used to get up at four o'clock in the morning, have a bowl of soup, get on the train, go three hours to the place of work—on the railroad. We had to change the burnt-out ties and broken rails.

Then the Germans stopped pushing us to work and they brought more guards and we couldn't get out from the building. We saw the Russian planes flying over more and more. They kept us in because they were sending the entire Auschwitz across through our village. Even the German population was not allowed from their homes, because, you see, German population was not supposed to know what was going on. But you could see from the windows what was going on. It was something terrible. It was so awful that you could never imagine. They were like walking skeletons. I remember the Jewish women were pulling their sick people like the Indians years ago—two sticks connected with some kind of cloth or something. Two of them would be laying on there. These poor people were so exhausted that twenty of them—or maybe more—were pulling these two dying women on these cots. Unbelievable sights.

Then one day, they put us on three railroad cars going west, and for three weeks we were on the railroad cars, with all the Germans fleeing the Russians. This was really a sight to see: Every train was going in one direction. Like if you have three rails, where trains might be going in both directions, all the trains would be going in one direction. Nothing would be coming back.

So we were sitting in these railroad cars, but somehow we survived. We went through four bombings. One was the famous one that you must have heard of, where they wiped out the whole Dresden. We were seven kilometers from Dresden and we stopped in a little woods. The whole sky was red. Everything was exploding day and night. It seemed like this was the end of the world!

From there they moved us to the northern part of Germany. This was the end of February of 1945. We were working outside of Schweinfurt—building a tunnel. It was a private company that took us over, not the German government. They gave us hardly nothing to eat, and everybody got dysentery, because we started eating all kind of garbage that we could find in the fields, drinking water from the river. At that time the guards were regular old army slobs, over sixty years old. They were no good for anything else. Some of them were really crippled—one arm or maybe one hand missing, and here he was, guarding you with a revolver.

One day all our guards left; everybody took off. We were so happy that we could be free now, that we started running around the town like idiots. You could see the Germans did the same thing. They all put white flags in their windows. They started giving us bread and food. Next day the Gestapo start coming in and arresting the Germans that had the white flags in the windows and they start kicking us around. Back to work.

The war was coming closer and closer and closer. At night we used to hear the heavy artillery. We were counting the days. Then the guards ran away and they hid in their homes, because they were actually living in this town. After three days of this unknown situation, we decided that at night we're going to take off and start walking toward the American lines.

On the third day we finally saw the American tanks. They came in such a great force, they were going on this road for about four or five hours. Finally, we had enough courage to run toward the Americans and tell them that we are Polish. There were some Pennsylvania Poles among them, so that's how we were freed.

They needed somebody to dig holes where the Germans were blowing the communication lines. They gave us some old American uniforms, and we were working for the Americans for about three months. And later, when we finished there, we worked as orderlies in the hotel for the American lieutenants and captains in Bad Kissingen. Afterwards, they started moving back to the United States, and we moved from one camp to another in Germany until 1949.

First my parents—especially my father—wanted to go back to Poland. However, we learned there was no use going back. So we were waiting and waiting. We couldn't emigrate so easily. My father was fifty-nine years old; nobody really wanted him.

You could emigrate to Canada. Canada was lumber work. You got two people, a team of horses, and you go for two years out of civilization. And once every six months, they would fly you over to town for a big bash, and then they fly you back. And all this time, you could save—the government would save your money for you and they pay you all the money after two years. You're cutting the trees and, with the team of horses, you would take them to the nearest river. Many young people, hundreds of young people went there. And they did well. However, they were not taking families and they didn't want any families.

Belgium opened the door, but Belgium opened the door to coal mines. Many people went, and they were trying to come back because they couldn't take it; and then the Belgian police were hauling them back to jails. The Belgian mines, you're working on your belly because they are so small, the veins are so narrow that you have to work on your side to work this way, and they couldn't take it. They were trying to come back, but once you signed for three years, they consider that you were escaping a contract or something. So you were not supposed to do that.

All the time we were writing to American organizations, asking if we could find a sponsor. Finally, we put our picture in *New World*, a Polish newspaper, and some farmer in Minnesota picked it up. He never wrote to us. We just got a notification through the American Embassy in Frankfurt, that such-and-such a name is sponsoring us to Minnesota.

We came on an army troop ship from Bremerhaven to the United States, and we arrived here on the nineteenth of June, 1949. That's a date I'll never forget. They gave us ten dollars per person and a ticket to Minnesota. I remember we were so surprised that in Chicago and in Detroit so many people on the railroad station spoke Polish. We arrived in the afternoon in St. Cloud, Minnesota, and this was the funniest—I wish I would have had a camera at that time. You can imagine: a family of four immigrants, everybody dressed up to kill, because we wanted to make an impression. We had one suit per person, made by a German tailor by paying American cigarettes. And my mother had a dress made out of a curtain from a window. And we got off in the middle of nowhere! There's nothing. The train stopped, they put this little step, and they said, "Get out." The train left, and we're standing there, and—nobody! We said, "Where are we? No, it can't be here."

At the very end, there is an old guy standing, in a straw hat, overalls, and a beard all the way down to his waist—completely white! He's standing there and watching us, and we're standing here and watching him. Finally, my father went to the old man, and it was him!

We were glad to get out and to be somewhere, but to be honest with you, it was a shock. It was a real shock! First, he didn't have work for all of us, only for my mother and my father. They were working on the farm, cleaning the sties and digging. It wasn't good work. And because they were old, he considered that they cannot do too much, and he was paying them fifty cents a day.

Somebody in the village nearby needed my brother. And I was lucky enough that his nephew needed me on the farm right next to them. It was very hard work. Besides working from four-thirty in the morning till seven-thirty in the evening, I was expected to be a nanny to five children—the youngest was a year old, the oldest was seven. I struck very well with the kids. Kids understand people that don't speak English. They don't laugh at you, and somehow I picked more from them than from anybody else.

I was working there only two months, and the doctor that I worked for in the camp in Germany came to Ossining, New York, and he got us jobs in the hospital there—me and my brother. It's a big Polish community, and through the Polish priest my parents found a position in a nursing home.

And *then* . . . the Korean War started and they started looking for boys. I was the first one out. In a way, when I look back now, it was a blessing in disguise. That was the best break in my life, as far as learning English and getting on my feet in this country. At the beginning, I was a little bit kicked around, because somebody tells me, "Throw the butt out," and if you don't know the slang, how do you know what *butt* means? So everybody threw the cigarette away, while I was standing smoking. For this I used to go on latrine duty and clean till midnight. But after two or three such incidents, I was on my toes. I was watching everybody. I was living only with Americans, and it finally drove me insane, to the point where I finally couldn't take it any longer. One day I just got so frustrated that I started cussing in English. And everybody says, "Now you're one of our own."

They put me in the Signal Corps and sent me to France. But in the meantime I met my wife. I had an American girlfriend, but I was looking for a Polish girlfriend. It's something with the background. There is no common ground to discuss with somebody who didn't go through it. It would be like boasting to somebody for the rest of my life. Helena just happened to fill the bill. She was here not quite a year ahead of me, and we had an awful lot in common. She was very attractive. She was only seventeen, and I was twenty-two. We decided that we would get married. That money that the government pays the allotment to the wife we can put in the bank, and when I get out we could start something somehow. And that's what we did. We got married on my furlough. We had twelve days of our honeymoon that we spent together, and then for twenty-one months I went to France.

After I was discharged from the army in '53, I wanted to go on the GI training. I tried three different companies. I went to a company where they make chain saws, because I wanted to get GI training on the job as a tool and die maker, and they sort of pulled my leg. They said that I cannot get this until I will work for several months, and they put me on the assembly line. I sprained my back after four days only. The foreman told me to lift something, like a 125-pound generator, and I sprained my back so badly I couldn't straighten up. I was such a hothead that I just walked out from the company. I said, "I don't want you, I don't want anything."

I tried to join the electrical union in White Plains, and I couldn't get into it. They told me you have to have somebody from the family in the union in order to get in. If you were not Italian, you couldn't get into the electrical union. Maybe somewhere else you have to be Polish to get in. But they were strictly an Italian community.

I noticed that it was very hard for any Polish person to become of any importance. He could only be the fellow on the line. The Italians were in between the foreman and the rest—they were like the lead men. The foreman had to be either English or Irish or a Scotsman. The Poles were the ones who were sweeping the floors and washing the windows and doing the most menial jobs. You couldn't break the barrier, and this was one of the main reasons to move out from this community.

So we rented a little apartment in Connecticut, and I started working for this company—it will be twenty-four years ago this year. I started as a chemical operator. It was a very filthy and dangerous work. I was following a process—the foreman told me what to do. I realized that I never get anywhere until I get a degree. I didn't really feel like going too much to school, because I was eleven years out of school at that time and my English wasn't that good. But I jumped into it. And eleven years later, with my wife's patience, going nights—three nights a week and Saturday—I got a degree in chemistry. Now I am head of a laboratory in pharmaceutical development, four people working for me, and I really enjoy my work. . . .

I've been to Poland. It was the year I graduated. When I saw Warsaw again, no matter that they are Communists or not, to me this was the land I was born. I walked through the streets, and I knew every street and every corner, and I knew everywhere I was going. The streets that I walking on and the church that I was going to—it survived somehow—still has the marks from all the shells. They left it the way it was. You walk through the streets of Warsaw, they've left the places where they were executing people. Every day, people still bring fresh flowers in these holes where they were shooting people. It brought many memories.

I have to admit, when we went back, for a while I had the same resentment as we had during the war toward the Germans. Now, I'm a Christian. I cannot hate somebody forever. When I went over there, I had big discussions with my cousin, who is an architect, and he can't forgive me for not hating the Germans. He says "You should hate them all the way down to your fingernails. You order machine, for instance, from East Germany. It comes in a crate and on the crate is written by the German worker, 'Deliver to the Polish swines.'" They open this thing and in the gears somebody threw sand. There is this hate which is still there. I don't resent German people, but it gives me goose pimples.

I feel more American than I feel Polish. I subscribe to *Time* and to *U.S. News* and read everything from the first page to the last pages. What upsets me when I discuss politics with native-born Americans— and I am very avid politician—that they take me as a foreigner, usurping some of their duty. I can feel in many instances the dislike of my criticism of certain bills that are being passed through Congress or something like this. They don't realize that I am criticizing this not as a Pole—I am criticizing as an American. They're taking me always as a Pole, and I resent this.

Most likely to some people we are clannish, but this is for convenience sake. My father is eighty-seven years old and he never learned English. He never really adjusted to this country at all. If I have to take care of my parents, I might as well live next door to them. My brother—he married Helena's sister—lives across the street. If I go on vacation, he can look after my parents. Our girls think that we are very, very ethnic. But I noticed that they are just as ethnic as we are. I mean, they admit right away that they are Polish. Like Christina, the younger one, she doesn't even want, in school, anybody call her Christina. She wants to be called Krysia. Catherine, our older daughter, all of a sudden shocked everybody. She took Polish in university!

I would say that at times we tend to discriminate and criticize other nationalities, like I'm sure they must discriminate against us. It's only human. When we get together sometimes, around some family birthday party or Christmas party, and everybody has a few drinks, we say a few jokes about the Germans and the Jewish people, about the Irish and about the Italians. Well, I'm sure they're doing the same thing in their own house, so what the heck!

Maybe this is sad to talk about, but yesterday my folks decided they would like to be buried in Doylestown, Pennsylvania. There's a Polish shrine to Our Lady of Czestochowa there. They say they want to lie among their own people.

# Grete Rasmussen
···················· FROM DENMARK, 1950 ····················

*Tiny, blond, and blue-eyed, she is now a nurse in a Southern California hospital. She and her husband have no children. They spend much of their spare time organizing the local chapter of People to People, a program that promotes international good will by placing foreign visitors in private homes.*

I grew up in a home where my parents had a tremendous compassion for people. Many times we really couldn't afford to buy certain meat—even if my father had a farm. I had only two dresses: one for church and one for school. But anyone who was in trouble, they came to our place. Another thing about us as little children—there were widows in the town, and old people, and my father and mother sent us kids. We started the fire for them. I was trained all the time to just do for other people.

I always wanted to be a nurse, and I wanted to go into a big university hospital. So I went from my home, a little town near Esbjerg on the west coast of Denmark, to Copenhagen.

I was a student nurse during World War II. It was a gruesome time, and that's the reason I am a pacifist. I was in the school, down in a big gymnasium, when they just came in, the Germans. It looked like a scene from a movie. It was a scary experience.

We had to give up the army. Our king said, "There's a better way of fighting," and right away the young people started going underground. First of all, we heard about Norway being invaded. We knew that the Norwegians was fighting in the mountains and everywhere else. We were concerned about the Norwegians. The talk was in the university, "How can we help them? We must do *our* part." That's when they started blowing up the railroads. I was not in the underground right away. I didn't feel like I could be in it, being a nurse.

When Hitler said all the Jewish people had to wear the star, the next day, who's the first one to show up with the star but the king. And then everybody did that, and the Germans said, "What can we do with people like that?"

Then Hitler told us that we had to give the names of Jews. That

Sunday—I'll never forget—when he said that all the Danish people were to give up the names of Jewish people, all the church bells started ringing at eleven o'clock. I remember going to church. The minister went up to the pulpit and he said, "We are Danish people. We will never give up our brothers and sisters. We are going to be behind them and help them. Every Dane is going to." That was in every church in Denmark. And the Germans couldn't do anything, because it was too unified. They couldn't shoot everybody.

I was almost seventeen and I was working nights sometimes to earn extra money, in a little pension place, where old people had a home. There was such an old, sweet lady, I just adored her. I remember the night the Nazi Gestapo came in and they asked for her. When I saw them take her, I think something happened to me. I opened that window and looked out and saw them take her and throw her in the big truck. And that was the day I said, "Now I'm ready to go in the underground. I'm going to help anywhere I can. I'll help get the Jews off to Sweden."

Many times we had them hide in the hospital. It was one or two on a floor. The doctors put them in traction, or we put oxygen on them; we'd do all kinds of things. We sure had to do a lot of work to write up charts on so many people. Sometimes there was a raid in the hospital, when we were held up with guns, and they went through the charts.

At night we took them with an ambulance to Helsingør. That's where we put them on the boats for Sweden. We gave the children a lot of narcotics so they wouldn't scream. It was really dangerous. I don't know how we did it, but at that time we had the strength for it. It was awful, though, let me tell you that. Sometimes at night, if you finally go to bed and you hear something walking up the step, you *jump* up, because if somebody had been caught of your group, you live under fear night and day. Is he strong enough to hold out and not give our names? You never knew what torture the Germans did.

When Hitler sent his last troops up, they wasn't soldiers anymore. They were little fifteen-, sixteen-year-old boys. They were scared, and they shoot everywhere. They started shooting all over the place, these kids. I mean the young soldiers. They just shot like wild, because now they felt, "We have nothing to lose." Many people were killed. You had to be careful not to hate.

It was hard not to hate. Very, very hard. I had a time where I really struggled with this. I remember coming home once. There was no train running, and I had to bicycle home. And every time I saw a German, it was just that hate came over me. I said to myself, "You're making yourself sick." And when I was home, my mother said, "You know, I don't care if he's your enemy. You must not hate for your own sake—because they are human, God's children." I said, "I don't care.

Spit on them!" Until one day a little German soldier came in with a big gun he almost couldn't carry. He didn't look more than fifteen or sixteen. He looked white and he said, "Could I just buy a little milk? I haven't had food, and I can't walk another step." My mother looked at me and she said that was her salvation, because I not only gave him milk and egg and bread, I gave him a whole bagful of food. From that day I couldn't hate anymore.

When peace came to Denmark, I remember going in the nurse's uniform to the king's palace, screaming that we want to see the king. The church bells started ringing. We threw the curtains down off the windows. There was light in *every* window in all Denmark that night.

But then the bad time came. People started coming from these camps down there in Germany. They were supposed to go to Sweden, and we had to go down to the harbor to feed them and get them sorted on the boats. The sights was awful. I had heard about it, but I was shocked. They were just like skeletons with skin on it. It was shocking. Some of them were half dead. We couldn't even put them on the boats. We just took them in ambulances up to our hospital. . . .

After the war, when I finished training, I thought to myself, "Well, it'd be very nice to see a little of the world." I took one of the highest examinations you could take, and then the Danish Nurses Association said, "Would you like to go on a trip to United States as exchange nurse?" I was to learn what they have here and go home and teach in our country what we had here. I had an uncle in California, so I went.

My father had died, and my mother was very upset that I would nurse gangsters and Indians and cowboys. She wasn't very happy about that. I found out it was a different picture when I came here. It's a shame we get the wrong impressions. And I'm always so afraid that we give the wrong impressions to other people, too. When I came, people asked me if I would speak about Denmark, and I went around on speaking tours. I worked very much for the American Scandinavian Foundation, promoting exchange.

The first thing that was kind of shocking here—I came on a ward, and they were all Negroes. For me it was surprising, because it's the first time I was working with black people. We always learned about your Negroes, but we had never seen them. I had seen one in school. I had to pay twenty-five cents for seeing him. He was singing for us, and we all took our little handkerchiefs and wet them, and we had to rub to see if he was really black. In Denmark we always learned the horrible things about the poorest Negroes—how you treat them, you know—so my heart went all over to them, until I found out they really were treated as nice as everybody else in the hospital.

I was here a year, and then I went back to my job at the hospital in Copenhagen. The hospital in California kept on writing, "Please come back to us, because we need you here." Well, I didn't really know, but I thought they probably needed more nurses over here. Because in Denmark they're better paid and better trained, so they really have nurses enough. So, kind of the missionary in me, I said, "Well, I'll go back to the United States."

In the meantime, I started going steady with my boyfriend in Copenhagen—yes, the same one I'm married to twenty years this year. So I said to my boyfriend, "Well, I'm going back. Why don't you try to come out and see how you like it over there?" I went over here and he came right after me.

I love the hospital out here in Pasadena, and they've given me a nice position. I'm a supervisor. I'm supposed to go home about three-thirty, but I never get home before five or six. You see, if I see a person lying, dying by himself, nobody there, I just can't leave him. No, I can't. I was trained like that as a student nurse. This could be your father, mother, sister. How would you feel if there wasn't someone with them, holding their hands? So I stay . . . and then at night, I start thinking, "Oh, I hope they've turned that patient." So I call. . . . I learned during the war that life is very precious and you have to do your little bit to make it better. . . .

# Riccardo Massoni
···················· FROM ITALY, 1939 ·······················

*A strong-featured, vigorous-looking man of sixty, Dr. Massoni is a surgeon at a medium-sized hospital on the East Coast.*

My father was a well-known anti-Fascist lawyer in Italy before the war. When I was a young boy, about six or seven years old, I remember him coming home once, all beaten up, with black and blue marks all over his head. The local Black Shirts, they knew my father. At that time, Leghorn was only maybe a city of a hundred and twenty thousand people. In a city of that size, a lawyer with an excellent reputation was a prime target, and particularly with competition among lawyers as there was. So it was one way to eliminate competition very readily, and when a guy doesn't join the Fascist party, he becomes a prime target. Most of the lawyers on Saturdays would go out on the march with the Black Shirts, and my father wouldn't. That was enough to put him in the limelight. He was walking home and they called, *"Avvocato Massoni."* That means Lawyer Massoni. And he turned around, and as he turned around, they had long sticks just like our policemen carry, and they kept on banging him on the head, and he just put his head down trying to save his face. And he was beaten very badly. Another time they made him drink castor oil in the town square. That was their way of torturing and humiliating people.

You had to be very much afraid at that time. Say, if you were on a train and somebody started making sly remarks about the way the trains are running under fascism or the way the people are starving, you minded your *p*'s and *q*'s, because you knew that that person could very well be an *agent provocateur*. You had to be afraid of your neighbors, you had to be afraid of your maids; you never talked in front of anyone. And every time there was an attempt, for instance, on the life of Mussolini, the Black Shirts would roam Leghorn and search for the dissidents. And they would just beat them to a pulp. It was not a very pleasant way to live, but in retrospect now, I think it had its fascination. Those were glorious days because there was a true struggle of ideals, you know?

I remember the whole family listening to a radio broadcast from Paris—around the radio at night, keeping it low so that nobody else would hear. It was during the war in Spain, and Italy had some troops there to help Franco, and so did Germany. But there were also some Italians belonging to the so-called Garibaldi Brigade who were helping the established government—the one that fell. And the official Italian broadcasting was always—the Fascist would always win, you know. I remember as if it were now hearing on the Paris radio that the Garibaldi Brigade beat the Fascist to a pulp, and it was the first time that Italians fought against Italians on foreign soil. That was the famous battle of Guadalajara. And the Garibaldi Brigade gave them a real beating, which is always the case when someone of his own free will goes and fights against somebody who couldn't care less what is going to happen. Someone that doesn't have an ideal to fight for, they are bound to lose.

With very few exceptions, Italians were Fascists on the surface only. To give you an example: When the Germans came in, they had to put concentration camps. Some of the political, a few religious, prisoners were kept there. But the doors were left open. And when the Germans weren't around, they let the prisoners go home at night. They stayed with their wives at night and came back in the morning, just to report for reveille. They would never get maltreated, nothing. They would go home and eat. I know of instances in which the prisoners brought back to camp some food for the guards—*home cooked*, you know. So that it was a different breed. You see, the Germans were trained—they loved it, they were fanatics.

When he knew the war was going to break out, my father took the whole family to Paris. I was walking on the Champs Elysées the day war was declared. That's when the idea crystallized in my father: that the two young male members of our family—I was nineteen and my cousin was seventeen—would come to the United States. We were both medical students, and we would continue medical school. We were of age to serve in the army and we would have been put in the Italian army. And dad said, "No, if you have to fight, you might as well fight where you believe in and go on the winning side and fight for the side that you want to fight for. And if you can continue your studies, fine. And if you can't, then you can serve wherever you are expected to." So we came.

You know, those were tragic times. It was very difficult to get passage. Poland had already been taken, and the Germans were pretty close to Holland. They were expected momentarily to move into Holland. There were an awful lot of Germans in Rotterdam, where we went to get the boat. German Jews particularly. Passages on the boat were very difficult to obtain. We had two tickets, and we were with two other young men who also had tickets, and at the last minute, as we were ready to board, there was a family who really—if they had been caught by the Germans, they would have been exterminated. They were German Jews. So we gave them our tickets because we were young men. We felt, "Well, we can always make a go of it." But here was a father, a mother, a daughter, another kid. We gave them our tickets. The boat pulled out and hit a mine in the harbor and sank while we were watching. We could see it. You never know how things will come out. They had thanked us and we had felt generous. . . .

We took the next boat and it turned out to be the last boat to leave Rotterdam. That boat was like a Grand Hotel. There were refugees from all over Europe: American citizens getting home, Cubans going back to Cuba, Jewish refugees from Germany, and political refugees, young and old, all mixed together. There was the Russian Ballet of Monte Carlo who performed at the Met many times and a band from Cuba that was leaving Europe. Everybody else was older, so they sort of adopted us, and we used to eat with the Cuban band and had it nice. We had good times on that boat. And when we got into New York City everyone was going. Everyone had a place to go. Everybody knew where to go except us. The Cuban boys were getting their instruments, and the Russian Ballet was getting ready to perform at the Metropolitan, and all of a sudden I realized that that was *it*. My last contact with Europe was over. I felt afraid.

We had a little cash and some things we planned to sell—gold cigarette lighters, a fine leather briefcase, that sort of thing. I remember going into a telephone booth and trying to figure out how to dial a hotel and find out if they had a vacancy, in broken English. I said to myself, "This is really going to be rough." We took a cab, and immediately you change your way of thinking. What in Paris cost a few francs, here it looked very little, but then you translate it into francs and Italian lire and you say, "You mean to tell me I've already spent this much just to take a cab? I'm not going to last a week."

The hotel was on Eighty-eighth Street, right off Broadway. It was a real rathole. We unpacked enough to change, and I said, "Okay, let's go take a look now. Get the first glimpse of New York." We went down to the street and we looked up and saw the sign *Broadway*. I said, "Don't tell me this is Broadway, what we have heard so much in songs." Remember we were at Eighty-eighth Street. It wasn't uptown. We were flabbergasted by the poor taste of the shops. We were fresh from Paris, from the Rue de la Paix. I remember there was a window and a shop full of junk. Dust and dirt all over. It was unbelievable, you know, and I said, "My God! Where on earth did we come?" If we had been off Park Avenue or Fifth Avenue or Madison Avenue, the impression would have been different, but that first taste was absolutely terrible. That first impression. And I said, "Oh, if I was only walking down the Champs Elysées instead of this place. Or the Via Veneto in Rome. What are we doing here?"

We had to get used to eating very little. The food was so different and, of course, we didn't have much money. You'd go into a cafeteria for instance and you'd ask for a sandwich and they'd say, "Rye or white?" and you don't know what they're talking about. What is that? A sandwich is a sandwich. There is no such thing in Italy as rye bread or white bread or whole-wheat bread; it's bread. Bread is bread. Now what is he asking me about the bread? And they say it so fast. I couldn't understand a word. I would just mumble anything. Imitate the first word that he said and if he didn't come back at me with another thing, otherwise I would say anything, you know? Because I just didn't know. And, of course, things that I knew, like spaghetti or macaroni, they were so terrible. But then little by little I learned.

We moved out to Brooklyn, and I remember the delight I used to have in going to delicatessens somewhere there and really loving those hot pastrami sandwiches as if there was no tomorrow. In those days that particular part of Brooklyn was nice. It was cheaper and we liked it. I remember there were small little homes, one after another, and clean streets. Very orderly. The people that rented us a room in their house, they were nice people of Russian origin. Very cordial, really nice. It was like a little bit of the country. And then little by little we began to realize that all the world is alike, you know. We saw some nice people, we saw people that we didn't like as much, but by and large they were friendly.

We found out that people here were terribly ignorant of what was going on in Europe. And so were the newspapers. They seemed to have no idea what Nazis were, or Mussolini. The only one that was making any sense was FDR; the others just had no idea. They didn't know what was going on in Europe. People thought it was a war that didn't concern them.

We used to say, "How can't you see it? Poland first, next Czechoslovakia, France. Do you think Hitler's going to be satisfied? What's the matter with you? England will be next, you know." But somehow it didn't register. You see, it was the usual thing. "Well, you don't know America," they'd say. I remember there was one senator that used to say, "We don't have to worry about Hitler. We can survive. We don't need to arm ourselves." I was very young and I wasn't used to this country, and I had a definite idea that that guy was on Hitler's payroll. I was used to the fifth column, and I said, "That guy couldn't possibly not be on Hitler's payroll."

At that time I didn't know the tremendous industrial potential of this country. I couldn't realize that there would be a time in which this country could produce one Liberty Ship a day. I had no idea this could be done. I didn't know that they could build three thousand planes a month. But I was certain that the worst thing we could have done was not to get ready for it, because we would have been next for sure, one way or another. I tried to communicate. It wasn't just a matter of the languages. There was no question of not understanding what I was saying; it was just a question of the others not having the slightest idea of what was going on in Europe.

My cousin and I decided to start seriously approaching our problems. First the language. We used to go to Forty-second Street movies for a quarter. We'd watch the same movie three, four, or five times. It was the only way. We would grasp first the ideas of the movie and then concentrate on certain parts to learn the words and meaning. Not with a dictionary, just to get the ear accustomed and then look at it again, and then it would come back a little bit more. By the third or fourth time we would grasp certain expressions. At first it was just a jumble—"Brrrrrr," it sounded like this. Then a little more. We could distinguish a few words here and there, and then little by little from a common sound we could distinguish a few words until they made sense. I had had a couple of years in school of English, but everything was different. It was hard for me to understand the spoken word, and when you don't understand it feels like a jumble. So that was difficult.

I was looking for a medical school then, but I didn't know how to apply. I had no idea. Then, finally, I said, "Well, there must be some way in which I'm going to find out how to get in medical school." I asked people, "How do you apply to medical school?" First you get it from the wrong people: "We got plenty of medical school. You know what? I know a medical school here—Cornell." And I, like a jerk, go there and say, "Can I have the application?" As a matter of fact, I didn't even know what an application was. I thought it was a matter of fact that you did it like you do at the University of Pisa, just sign up and go. In Italy, if you pass your Classic Maturity [examination at the end of secondary school] you are *in*, period. Or you were at that time. I had no ideas that schools were private. I didn't know how the system worked. Finally, I said, "Well, this is ridiculous. Let's go to a doctor and find out." I saw a sign, *M.D.*, and I just went in. I said, "How do you go about it in this country? I understand that it isn't automatic." He said, "Well, it's a little bit different here." At first I was disbelieving. This guy can't know what he's talking about.

Then I went to a place called International Student Service. I thought, "Geez, they should know." But they didn't help me. The man there said, "Well, I can tell you one thing. It is going to be a lot easier for you to be a millionaire in five years than to get into medical school." He didn't even tell me how to go about it. I walked out, and as soon as I got downstairs I said to myself, "This guy has got to be wrong. I'm going to show him. Someday I'm going to walk up there and show him I did it in *less* than five years."

But little by little I learned this: First of all I had to take an exam for foreigners in the English language; second, it wasn't automatic to get in a medical school; third, I needed a lot more science courses than I had; and fourth, it would take a lot of money. But my father always said, "To every problem there is a solution." So I worked on the language and I kept applying to medical schools. I applied to seventy-five medical schools. I even applied to the University of Hawaii. And they all turned me down. But I said, "I'm going to be a doctor. I don't care how hard it is or where, but I'm going to be." I was confident that this would take place and I think this confidence was not entirely justified. I found out later, because I know that there are people that are very bright and they belong in medical school and they never made it. So maybe it's good I had this confidence—that this confidence was exaggerated—because then I didn't know any better. I just didn't know any better. Dad had said, "To every problem there's a solution," so it's got to be so because my father couldn't be wrong.

I kept applying and I was fortunate. Harvard accepted me into the Graduate School of Arts and Sciences. They gave me an oral interview and I could hardly speak English. All we talked about was fascism, and I tried to straighten them out, really. They were very attentive. Every time I couldn't find a word during that oral exam, I would say it in English, in Latin, or in Greek—anything, if I could express myself. I thought it would be a handicap, and instead it turned out to be an asset, because they admitted me right there on the spot.

Now I began studying with a dictionary and taking science courses. I took histology, neuropathology, chemistry. I did well in those because language wasn't a factor there. I got an honor grade in neuropathology; so I said, "Well, now it's time." And I went to see my professor. He had an office in the Massachusetts General Hospital. He said, "Well, what can I do for you?"

"I want to go to medical school, because that's what I really want to do."

He said, "Well, I'll be glad to give you a letter of recommendation."

"No, that's not going to help me. There are an awful lot of people with very, very high marks who don't bring credentials from Italy, from a *gymnasium*—with Greek and Latin and history of art and philosophy, but little in the way of science. I won't stand a chance. There's only one way. It's for you to pick up the phone and say, 'Hey, Joe, I got somebody. You want to take a chance? He doesn't know the language, but he did well in my course and I think he'll work hard. Will you take him?' "

So my professor said, "Okay. Wait outside." I was praying hard and fast. It was a beautiful crisp morning in Boston. Really beautiful. I remember it as if it was now. Finally he called me in and he said, "Do you have fifty dollars?"

"Sure, I got fifty dollars," which I didn't have.

He said, "Do you know Tufts Medical School? It will take you starting July 1."

So I rushed home, sold the last of my things from Italy for that fifty dollars, and I went in to see the dean of Tufts Medical School. He said, "Do you have the means to support yourself?"

"Oh, money is no object," I said—because I didn't have any, so it couldn't be any object, you know. Once I got that acceptance, that's all I needed, I thought. The rest will come.

All the time I was in medical school I worked. I had dozens of jobs. I had three and four jobs at a time. I was a busboy and dog walker. I broadcasted a couple of hours a week for the Office of War Information. I made beds in the university dorm and I washed dishes. Any kind of job, it didn't make any difference to me. It was a step forward and I did it and I never felt degraded by any kind of work.

I was lonely, but I didn't have time to feel lonely because I was so busy working. Everybody would go home for holidays and I would still be there. I had a hot dog at the Wursthaus on Thanksgiving Day because I couldn't afford turkey. I used to feel depressed, but then I used to say, "Don't feel so sorry for yourself. Remember maybe this is your chance. They're going to play and instead you're going to work, and by the time they come back, you'll be that far ahead. And you're handicapped by the language, so you have to make it up by working extra."

Saturday night everybody would go out on a date, and that was the night for me in which I could really study, because I could study all night long, and at five in the morning I would get up and make my rounds with the *New York Times*. I delivered it every Sunday morning. I remember that winter. Boston is cold. The snow would be high. I wasn't used to it either. Remember, I was coming from Italy. I used to say to myself, "Oh, if only the *Times* wasn't so heavy on Sunday."

My daughter's at Radcliffe now. Before she went, she said, "I'm going to miss the *New York Times*." So I got on the phone and ordered it, and it's thrown on her doorstep. I called up and I said, "I want my daughter to get the paper. I want you to deliver it to my daughter, room such-and-such, the *New York Times*, including Sunday. How much should I make the check for?"

My daughter doesn't realize how much it means to me to be able to do that for her. Or when she tells me, "Dad, my tuition is due," to be able to say, "Okay. I've deposited it in your account. Just go to your bank and transfer it." She complains I talk too much about money. She doesn't know what it means to me. When I had to do it, I had to go and give blood transfusions and sell my suitcase and sweaters and shirts and ties in order to pay the tuition. She doesn't realize the pleasure that I have. She gets mad now because I'm talking money to her.

# Alexandra Danilova

·················· FROM RUSSIA, 1939 ··················

*In orange leotard, pink tights, and worn ballet slippers, visibly tired after teaching a class of aspiring ballerinas, Madame Danilova relaxed briefly in a tiny lounge at the School of the American Ballet Theater in New York City. It was her lunch break and she had scheduled two interviews between her morning and afternoon teaching schedules. She yawned occasionally, stretching her arms in a graceful arc and closing her eyes, the long, false lashes curling against her cheek. One long leg was crossed lightly over the other, the foot pointed naturally, automatically, toward the floor. Over seventy, she is still a respected member of the American dance community and has recently come to popular attention for her role in the film* The Turning Point.

I am orphan. I lost my parents when I was two years old, and I was brought up first by my grandmother. One day, I was trying to wake her and she didn't awake, didn't awake. So I start to cry—I must have been about four—and a neighbor came and they found out that she had died in her sleep. It sounds more awful than it was, because I didn't understand anything about it. I was thinking she was asleep. And then I was taken to my godmother. She had a friend who married a five-star general and who had just lost a little girl. She took me in instead of her little daughter, and that's how I came to St. Petersburg.

I had the normal life of a little girl. . . . In school we had a Christmas performance. I was supposed to be a butterfly and fly in the garden— you know, sing and hop around. It seems that I did that very gracefully, because everybody told me I must be the next Pavlova. It turned my head and I drove everybody absolutely crazy, because I stayed opposite the mirror doing all kinds of movements. Once I went on my toes—without ever seeing the ballet! So my aunt—I called her *aunt*—said, "Oh, how wonderful! Would you like to be a ballerina?" I said, "Yes," and so she switched me to a theatrical school. I was eight and a half and I started in theatrical school.

First, we went through a certain examination—physical examination and "looking" examination, to see that you have no bow legs, that you are not cross-eyed, that you are not ugly, and that you look attractive. Yes. Then they ask us to run or to skip. There were, I think, 360 girls and they took 17 from that. After that, after one year, they dropped to 8. Because, you know, it's so special that you have to be dedicated, serious. We had only 48 girls and 28 boys in the whole school. It was a boarding school, run on private money of the imperial family.

Well, during that school we had the war and then, after that, of course, the Revolution came in 1916. I was lucky that I finished my theatrical school, because the Bolsheviks wanted to close it, thinking it was too bourgeois, dancing. But somebody talked them into it, and everything was saved. We continued our lessons, but suddenly we had nothing to eat and finally hunger came. There was no heat and no food and it was difficult to dance. Everything was sort of slowly decaying. It was gruesome, and I was thinking this would be my life, and you live only *once*. I felt if I don't leave this country, I'll just die. I just made up my mind, regardless of what it will cost me, I have to get out of there, because it was cold, dirt, and hunger. I didn't think about dancing. I was thinking as a human being. It was a kind of terror in a way, you know—petrified of being arrested suddenly for your thoughts or a wrong word at the wrong time. Everything started to demoralize, slowly but surely. There was no future. No.

Everybody who finished the school went on the stage of the Maryinsky Theater, and I became a dancer of the Maryinsky Theater. Mr. Balanchine* was a dancer, too, and we decided that we had to go

*George Balanchine, choreographer and now artistic director of the New York City Ballet.

and see what abroad is. He organized a little concert group and we went to Germany. It was a very little group—two pair of dancers and one singer and one pianist. First we went to Berlin. I loved it, because there were so many trees. It was very clean and everything was on time. It was run so perfectly. And then, of course, they have all this *Schlagsahne,* [whipped cream] and I became like a barrel. I gained so much weight.

I didn't plan to migrate forever. I just wanted to see it. But then Mr. Diaghilev heard about us. He was then a great man who had the Ballet Russe de Monte Carlo. He invited us to his company. And when we went to that beautiful Monte Carlo, we saw real art and we stayed with him. We went around—Vienna, Berlin, Paris, Brussels, all over Europe. I didn't think about going back. I just danced and enjoyed. Then I started to receive telegrams from Russia—it's time for me to go back. But, you know, I thought, "No, I'm not going. I'm staying here forever, because I like it." It was 1925. It didn't matter where I was, really. I was like a turtle, carrying my home, living in my trunks—because we stayed like two weeks maybe in Paris, or in London we stayed three months. Monte Carlo was headquarters, and we stayed there five months. Well, sometime I missed Leningrad—such a beautiful city— the white nights. The garden of the Winter Palace was open and people could sit all night, sort of romantic—walk where Pushkin wrote *The Queen of Spades.* Everything was historical. I did miss it very much at the beginning.

I came here [to the United States] many times with the ballet. I'm sorry to say I remember everything seemed to me gray and very dirty. You had this elevated railroad. I thought that was dreadful. And there was not so much beauty, like gardens and monuments and rivers. Here it was very factoryish. People push, and they don't say "excuse me"—no manners. That was a shock, yes; because Russians are very polite. It's always "please" and "thank you very much." I thought not everybody cares about you. Here you felt that you are very much on your own. I didn't think the audience understood us. Even the critics said, "We don't know what to think about it."

When the war started we were in South America, and we came back here and were stuck here. Well, who wants to go back where there will be shooting? A tour was made up by Mr. Hurok. And I think because we are artists, dancers, having had success, they appreciated us. Say that you are from the Ballet Russe, then you are really somebody!

But, you know, living in hotels here, residential hotels—a woman has to do so much work. In Europe the maid always used to wash your underwear. You just ask her and give her a dollar, and every week the maid used to bring your nightgown, beautifully done! Here, I said, "Would you do my laundry?" and they just looked at me. And here you have to cook! When I lived in Paris, I had a cook. I could afford it. But here it is impossible.

But I started to get the habit of staying here, and then I liked it. This time I didn't find it as dirty. . . . I decided that I will become a citizen. I love America very much. I think it's a wonderful country. I really do. People grumble, but I say, "Well, America is like a young child. It has to have mumps and it has to have scarlet fever." And that's how it goes. It's just two hundred years, you know. They try this president, that president. They try to do this, they try to do that, until they try everything. I feel absolutely American. Yes, I am like a converted Catholic. [Chuckles.]

# Victor Machinko

···················· FROM THE USSR, 1954 ·····················

*A Ukrainian who left the USSR during the chaos of World War II, he works now as a skilled mechanic in Cleveland.*

I feel more than average American. I see how some people behave at work. They are never happy. They pay the taxes, which are probably the smallest taxes in any countries I know of, and they complain about it. They would like things given to them. And some of them are lazy, too. Some of them like to stay on unemployment. We know a couple that are collecting unemployment, and they say, "Gee, I like it. Now they are going to call me back to work. I don't want to go, because I can do whatever I always wanted and never had the time." They don't want to go back to work.

I get involved in arguments with them sometimes. I haven't met any Americans as really patriotic as I am, because they don't realize what they have, and I do. They don't appreciate it. You've got some Communists even, you know. I'm working with one. They don't know what it is like.

You have everything here. People don't realize, but you have everything here if you're willing to work and save money. You can live a comfortable life and there's plenty of everything. The comfort people have—always a couple of cars in the driveway—and the way they spend the weekends here: go to the shore, to the lake. You can't compare the life over there and here. You just can't beat America. I've been in about fifteen, sixteen countries for a short time or longer time, and lived in a few of them, and you just can't beat America.

# Serge Nicholas

*He was born in Manchuria of Russian parents. Now fifty-eight, he heads the Department of Physical Education at a northern California college. Sailing is his avocation, and he served as an official judge for the Olympics in 1968. He has been a Fulbright scholar twice, is on the screening committee for future Fulbright selections, has headed various professional organizations, is a Rotarian, and is chairman of his local Red Cross organization. He also has the West Coast franchise for a large fiberglass sailboat corporation.*

My family was originally born and raised in Russia and settled in China during the Russo-Japanese war of 1905. When a change of government took place during the Revolution they stayed on. My father being an engineer and my mother a doctor, both professionals, they were very wealthy people out there. I'm embarrassed to say that every time my nose was wet there was a governess to help me blow into a handkerchief, and I was never allowed to cross the street by myself.

Then in 1938 Manchuria was occupied by the Japanese government. They came in and closed our school. There were atrocities. Educational opportunities were nil. They started taking a lot of youth, Russians that were living there, and sending them out as cannon fodder for the Japanese army. I managed to escape from Japanese-occupied China to Tiensin to Shanghai to Hawaii, and from Hawaii to San Francisco. It was difficult to get out. I think, if not for my parents' wealth and connections, it would have been very difficult—bribery of Japanese high officials and people on the border and on the train and everywhere else. In Hawaii I managed to buy on the black market two American dollars; cost me forty dollars Chinese, almost all I had left.

I was looking forward to coming to America and I had an impression, possibly from Hollywood pictures, that this is a country where, if it rains, gold pours out of the skies and fills your pockets. Everybody drives cars. I really believed that everybody lived this way. I expected a brass band to meet us at the San Francisco pier. And there was nobody there. I put my foot down on the soil and saw the gruesomeness of the embarkation area and the slums and the filth and dirt of the port. Not everybody had it as we saw it in the movies. It was disillusioning.

I wound up in a Russian ghetto. People aboard the boat knew

someone that had a room and a restaurant. Every day I had to go on foot about three miles each way—couldn't afford a streetcar—to clean up the toilets and wash the floors and so on. Not for money, but in exchange for the room and a bowl of soup or something that was too old to serve the customers.

I knew very, very little English, not enough to communicate. I worked at simple things, delivering packages. Then I went to the employment agency and got my first real job, for which I was paid six dollars. That was my first week's wages—six dollars a week, ten hours a day. My pay was ten cents an hour. Of course they were taking advantage of us greenhorns, but I was very proud to be able to make some money, some spending money. And it was possible to live then on very little. Accommodations were cheap; food was available at the place of work, another restaurant.

Then a big event happened in my life—somebody helped me get into the Hotel and Restaurant Workers' Union—and I started making twenty-five dollars a week! And I couldn't even wash the windows! One time I did that, and the union representative got to the restaurant and raised holy toledo and gave my boss hell. I am supposed to do just what I am supposed to do—prepare Coney Island hot dogs and hamburgers.

After I started getting twenty-five dollars a week I went to Brooks Brothers to buy a suit. I asked the man for a two-breasted suit, and one guy called the other guy and said, "Hey, listen to this!" [Laughs.] And I paid something like five dollars down and so much a week. That was another thing that was different, the credit system. At home, even for big items, we had to pay cash on the line.

I went to school, studying English at night. There were nice, dedicated teachers who took their time, helped and guided me. They helped me into high school. Even though I was beyond the age of nineteen, I went to a high school here just to be with American children and to be in an environment where I will learn rapidly. It was a good school but we look different; we wear different clothes, we look like foreigners, you know? It was not easy for me. You come home tired out and *homesick*, play a few Russian records, and cry yourself to sleep. This really happened.

I wasn't satisfied to be always washing dishes or making hot dogs, even though it offered me an opportunity to get some spending money and live it up a little. There's one thing my parents had drummed into me—get an education. If you're a professional, have a skill, that's the biggest investment one can have. The government can take your personal possessions away, and you might be forced to go somewhere else—but if you have a skill or you're a professional person you can always start fresh on the basis of the investment you put in before. . . .

After about eight months my English improved; I went to the community college; I made friends. I got a job as a soda jerk at the college and I could communicate with other students and my social circle started to expand.

I even got a job teaching ice-skating. In my school days in China I was a champion ice-skater. I was skating at the Winter Palace on December 7, 1941, when news of Pearl Harbor broke out. A whole group of us went immediately to Selective Service to volunteer. We went to the navy, the marine corps—they wouldn't have us because we were not citizens. We went to the army. The army wouldn't have us. The only way we could do it was to get first papers, then with the first papers go to Selective Service to be inducted. So we volunteered to Selective Service, and in January 1942 we were in service.

That first day they give you the army intelligence test. At five in the morning they give you the IBM tests with the pencils, and the sergeant comes out with the stopwatch and gives you instructions and you start. You read the first question, translate from English to Russian, from Russian to English; by the time you put down one response he says stop. You had to answer fifty questions and you only answered one, possibly wrong. I guess I scored as a very low moron. So I went all the way through the service as a buck private, without even making Pfc. I was driving tanks and I was wounded in Leipzig exactly one week before the end of the war.

My experiences in the army were not exactly happy, but they were the making of me. The army was a University of Life for me. It was an environment where from early morning till late at night, I had to speak the language and take orders in English. I *had* to communicate. I had been living in the Russian ghetto, and if it hadn't been for the war I might not ever have had any reason to leave. It's so easy for the immigrant to become part of that community. This is a big obstacle. You pick up a Russian newspaper or your neighbor speaks the same language—so you don't advance. You are just in the past and the whole world goes by at a very rapid rate. It becomes too comfortable. It takes a force, a push, an unusual event, to get you out of it. The army did it for me.

When I came back, the GI Bill gave me a chance to go to college. I think that this is one of the few countries in the world that gives the GI's so many benefits—education, rehabilitation, mustering-out pay, etc. If not for this, I really don't think I would have had an opportunity to get an education. I also had fringe benefits for being disabled at the time. I had to swim a lot because of my wound and to be physically active, and I thought, "Well, look at the coaches; those guys seem to be healthy and enjoy a lot of respect from young people." And I always loved sports, so I went into physical education and I'm glad I did.

I got married . . . Irene was working and I was going to school at the time. We lived in special housing for the GI's, a barracks that was subdivided into tiny little apartments. We had a rented table and two rented chairs and a rented bed. And we made our furniture out of orange crates that we covered with *New Yorkers*. There was the satisfaction of working together.

Finally I graduated from the university. Now comes the time to get a job. This is the one time in my life that made me unhappy—1947 to 1948, the days of McCarthy, McCarthyism. Superintendents looking for a person with my skills, interviewing me: "You are a Russian?"

"Yes."

"Are you a Communist?"

"No."

"What do you think of Joe Stalin?"

. . . Things of that sort, just egging me on. It was so stupid, especially for educated people, superintendents, to ask such questions. I mean, if I was a Communist and in need of bread and butter, would I tell him about this?

I had pride. Here I finally achieve something. I am an American citizen. I put in time voluntarily in the service. I have become a man. I have a college degree. I'm ready to go into the world. And not one place, but *everywhere* you go, "Oh, Russian." And, Goddamn it, I am not Russian, I am an *American*, and proudly so. That was a very difficult period.

But finally I got a job. I went to the university nights and summers and I got my master's degree, then I worked for the doctorate. And pushed all the way up till I got very, very successful in my field and gradually went into administration. Along the way came the Fulbright fellowship and the opportunity to be a judge at the Olympics, the high point of my career. I have no regrets, I've been successful, I've worked hard. And even now, I'm still pushing . . . driving!

# Edward Teller

*Some historians of science claim that science in the United States blossomed only after the influx of refugees from Europe before and during World War II. There is no doubt that American science was significantly influenced, and its character dramatically changed, as a result of the contributions of brilliant men like Hans Bethe, Eugene Wigner, Stanislaw Ulam, Leo Szilard, Enrico Fermi, and scores of others. One of these men was Edward Teller, popularly known as "the father of the H-bomb." He spent the war years at Los Alamos, working on thermonuclear bombs, and was later instrumental in establishing the Lawrence Livermore Radiation Laboratory. Since his retirement in 1975, he has been a senior research fellow at the Hoover Institution on War, Revolution, and Peace in Palo Alto, California, where he devotes his time to energy issues. His outspoken opinions on public affairs have often made him a center of controversy.*

My coming to the United States is the fault of my wife. I am, not in my mind, but in my heart, a Goddamned conservative. But I am surrounded by radicals of all kinds—for instance, my wife. She says "move," and then the irresistible force moves the *almost* unmovable object. First my father said, "Move out of Hungary." Then Hitler said, "Move out of Germany." Then my wife said, "Go to the United States." So I moved! Of course, the three individuals mentioned I am by no means putting in the same class!

I grew up in a disturbed time. The First World War started when I was six years old, and after the First World War came the brief Communist regime in Hungary. After that, anti-Semitism was a painful and continuing influence on my life. It was a very disturbing thing in my school years.

While in high school, I seem to have been aware of the difference all the time. And that, perhaps together with some clumsiness on my part, made it an experience that was not dreadful, but unpleasant. The only other thing I need to say is that I seemed to have a very early and spontaneous interest in mathematics; and that because of that same anti-Semitism, it was made clear to me by my father that I'd better leave Hungary as soon as I can.

I did not like the necessity to leave my home and my surroundings. And after I left, for years I had the desire to go back. I left—and I was not yet quite eighteen years old—to study in Germany. For the next ten years I went home for extensive visits, but my last visit was in 1936, and from that time I did not go back to Budapest, nor do I expect ever to go. Now that Hungary is solidly behind the iron curtain, I have no desire to see what is left of the society in which I grew up.

I first went to Germany in 1926. I went very definitely with the idea that science would be my spiritual home. Germany in those years was the center of science. And in '26, of course, Hitler, for somebody not deeply interested in politics—and I certainly was not, science took all my time—Hitler was hardly a cloud on the horizon. Yes, Germany looked good from the point of view of science. That was an exciting time—the beginning of quantum mechanics. What I found there, what I learned there, in science, is to my mind the most inspiring portion of my life. I cannot sufficiently emphasize the intellectual accomplishment in which I took part. In the end, for me to leave Germany and this scientific atmosphere was as great a shock as to have to leave Hungary. And, of course, the reason was the same, anti-Semitism, although in a more virulent form—a form which then led to the Second World War and made it most unhappily, most forcefully clear to me that what I'd like to do—be interested only in science—has, to put it mildly, some disadvantages.

There was a wonderful movement in England to rescue scientists from Germany, and I was one of those rescued. England brought out many more scientists than they could offer permanent positions to. And it was made clear to us, in a very pleasant way, that we are welcome to stay as long as we like—for instance, forever—but if we get a good invitation from elsewhere, we should not turn it down out of a sense of obligation to England. I got two invitations from the United States, and the invitations were attractive. Even so, I probably would have refused, because wherever I am, there I want to stay. But my wife, to whom I was then married for a little over a year, had studied in the United States for a year on a fellowship, and she very much wanted to come. So I told Mici, "All right, you want to go to the United States, go to the embassy and get our visas. I won't lift a finger." You see, I was not interested in coming.

She left our passports and we forgot about it. When she went back to pick up our visa three weeks before our departure, she was told, "No visa." She came home practically in tears, and I wickedly smiled and I said, "Well, okay, we stay here." That's what I wanted all along. But she had a friend, a Hungarian, Thomas Balogh—now Lord Balogh—who was financial adviser to a government minister. He knew everybody. So Mici went to him, and in two days he was back with the following amusing information: "A nonquota visa can be issued only if you exercised your profession for which you are invited for two years prior to the invitation." I was invited to a university; I've got to be a teacher. Now, in Germany I was working at the university and I was comparable to an assistant professor, and that was all right. But then for a year I had a Rockefeller fellowship, and that was not teaching. So I could not get a nonquota visa.

However, there was no trouble, because American embassies were so scrupulous not to let in the wrong individuals that the regular Hungarian quota was not filled, so all I had to do was apply for a quota visa. And that was what we got!

In America I found little to surprise me. You see, when I was eight years old, we had a governess who was a Hungarian girl who had emigrated to the United States, grew up in the United States, lost her parents, and when she was eighteen years old, came back to Hungary.

She stayed with us for six years. A very wonderful woman. I would say that to some extent I was Americanized between the ages of eight and fourteen by that young girl, who was very American. I learned my English from her.

Well, you know, having had to move from Hungary to Germany to England to the United States, the one thing that was constant in all this time was my scientific association. America in '36 was really an underdeveloped country, as far as pure science was concerned. Of course, in technology America was the leader and had been for a long time. But in pure science, America used to be a little backward. And the scientific community here welcomed the people who came over from Germany and Europe with open arms. I was a little distrustful. After all, I had had a shock in Germany. And the British—well, they were very nice, really wonderful, but they were a little bit standoffish. In America, there was *complete* acceptance from the word *go*.

Because in some respects I was better educated than my American colleagues, I could be useful—and I was happy to be useful. I had no ambitions, except to be a good scientist, which I enjoyed. My years at George Washington University, from '35 to '41, were, I think, really productive. It was a remarkably good time in every respect, except, of course, for the worry of increasing trouble in Europe.

Well, you know, came '39, the discovery of fission. Some of my friends—among them Eugene Wigner, Leo Szilard, Enrico Fermi—got interested in that. They said, "We have to develop it." And, in the course of time, I was invited to join the group at Columbia, not in my capacity of scientist—although I was a scientist and was recognized—but in my capacity of an *un*controversial person, because, unfortunately, the two great men, Fermi and Szilard, didn't get along with each other, and I was a friend of both. I had to come and join them to help along. Then later I was taken up in the Manhattan Project.*

And, later, I worked on the hydrogen bomb and got into a fight about it, and I want to explain to you, in very few words, my position in that fight. First of all, I was deeply convinced that if there is a scientific technical objective—in this case, deriving energy from fusion rather than fission—one should explore it. And here were a number of people—it turned out to be a majority opinion among the scientists—who were opposed to that on moral grounds. Well, you know, these moral grounds looked to me exceedingly shaky. As a scientist, I felt that I ought to do what I can to find out what can be done. And how it should be *used* is up to everybody. To take a different point of view is really a bad case of elitism. This produced a conflict within the scientific community, where I was in the minority, and I lost very

*Secret project to develop the atomic bomb during World War II.

many friends. Now let me say I feel justified in what I did. However, to lose a great majority of my friends was a very heavy blow. Most of the people who received me with open arms in '35 were now no longer friends. I survived in the end by finding new friends and by helping to organize a whole new laboratory in Livermore.

But let me add one more thing. When I came to this country, I thought technology was overemphasized. After the Second World War, the climate in the United States changed abruptly, from protechnology to antitechnology, from indifference to science to putting science—pure science—on a high pedestal. First I thought there was too little science. Today I know that there is too little attention to applications.

# Eugene Wigner

·················FROM HUNGARY, 1934 ·····················

*Soft-spoken and self-effacing, Nobel Prize winner Eugene Wigner is now professor emeritus at Princeton. In his spacious office in Jadwin Hall, he is surrounded by photographs of old friends, colleagues, and teachers. When he mentions a name from the past, he jumps up to locate the picture and looks at it lovingly. Like his friend and colleague Edward Teller, he was born in Budapest.*

When I was seventeen, my father asked me, "Well, son, when you grow up, what would you like to become?" And I said, "Well, father, if I am honest, I would like to be a scientist and, if possible, a physicist." My father said, "How many jobs for physicists are there in the country?" And I said, "Four." And he said, "Do you think you'll get one of those jobs?" I said, "Perhaps not." And so we decided that I study chemical engineering.

I studied that for one year in Budapest at the Institute of Technology but then decided to try the Institute of Technology in Berlin. I got my doctor's degree, Doctor of Engineering, there in 1925. Then I returned to Hungary and worked in a leather tannery as a chemical engineer. But I continued to like physics, subscribed to a German physics journal, and, in fact, my interest grew in the subject. Soon thereafter I received an offer from the Technische Hochschule in Berlin to be an assistant. I decided to accept that. Well, I had become interested in quantum mechanics, and Berlin was a wonderful place for that. We had Schrödinger, Planck, Einstein, von Laue there. You have heard of these people.

Quantum mechanics was essentially unknown here in America, and

Ehrenfest, the Dutch physicist, advised Princeton University to invite two people interested in it. He suggested that two friends be invited so that they don't feel so lonesome.

Well, one day in 1929 I received a cable from the United States, something of this sort: "Princeton University invites you for the spring term," at a salary which was fantastic—three thousand dollars! I first thought this was an error in the transmission of the cable, but my friend Johnnie von Neumann, who was at the University of Berlin at that time, received the same cable, so that we decided it must be true. We both accepted the offer. He got married before he came here. I did not. At the end of the spring term in Princeton we both received an offer of a half-time appointment for five years, and so we spent one term here in Princeton and one term back in Germany.

People were very nice to me, but just the same, in the early days in Princeton, I never felt at home. I was unmarried, I had no very close friend, except Johnnie. There were official invitations, and the dean invited us for coffee every Thursday. But it was sort of formalistic. I could not speak very good English, and, you know, Princeton was a bit of an ivory tower and I was not part of it. I don't know how to explain it. In Berlin, I would go to a dance and dance all night, and I'd get acquainted with a lady; I'd take her out for dinner or we'd go to the theater together, and we'd have a good conversation. But here . . . a part of it may have been that my English was poor, but I don't think that was all.

There was a significant difference between science in Princeton and science in Berlin, and I must say that the Germans had many good points. They had a colloquium, a Thursday colloquium, which was wonderful. They kept abreast of the development of physics. About four papers were reviewed at each session by four different people. There was an audience of about forty people, and some volunteered to review the papers which they thought were interesting. There was nothing like that here, which was a great loss. The other difference was based on the fact that the high schools in Europe were much better, I am sorry to say, than the high schools here. The first four years of college here compared to a great extent with the last few years of high school there. Perhaps I am a little biased.

*How did you think that American physicists and mathematicians compared with the European scientists?*

Well, it is difficult to compare with Einstein, Planck, Schrödinger, Heisenberg. Physicists like them we did not have here. We did have excellent experimental scientists, but only few at Princeton. But the country as a whole was truly outstanding in that field. After all, Michelson and Morley were the ones who were largely responsible for the experimental basis of relativity theory. There was Compton. But Michelson and Morley were in one place in California and Compton was somewhere else. And as far as theory is concerned, no university had the qualifications of either Göttingen or Berlin in those days. American physics was more experimental. You see, the two great theoretical innovations of the century—relativity theory and quantum mechanics—were created in Europe.

Well, soon enough, Hitler came to power and I received a letter: "Your connection with the Institute of Technology has ceased." I was fully expecting it. My mother was Jewish and that was enough. If one of your grandparents was Jewish, you were dismissed. That was in '33 or perhaps '34.

I then became a visiting professor in Princeton, but they sort of advised me to look for another job. They felt that I was not really good. I thought maybe they were right, and, luckily, I received an offer from the University of Wisconsin.

This was a blessing in disguise, because in Wisconsin I felt at home from the second day on. They were different people. They were down-to-earth people. They knew how to plant potatoes, even [chuckles] if they did not plant potatoes. The atmosphere was entirely different from that of Princeton. There was camaraderie. People were closer to each other, they worked together. We were friends—not only colleagues, but friends. We went to the theater together, we went on excursions together. I soon wanted to be American, and I got naturalized in '37. I fell in love with a young lady in Wisconsin, and we married. She was an American. It was a tragic thing. She had cancer, and she went to heaven after eight months. Well, excuse me, this has nothing to do with. . . .

A year later I received an offer to return to Princeton. This was a job with tremendous reputation—the Thomas D. Jones Professorship—and perhaps the most respected theoretical physics professorship in Princeton. Well, by now I was Americanized, and Princeton, also, had changed. And, of course, having such a wonderful position, people did not look down on me anymore. And, further, Princeton had changed enormously in the course of the years—it became much less of an ivory tower than before. Perhaps I also changed—my interest which was, before, heavily concentrated on the students who collaborated with me, grew and extended to all students—and the interest of my colleagues was extended to me.

The only area in which we disagreed was a somewhat political one. I was afraid of Hitler. I feared that he might succeed in extending his power over the whole earth. This seemed absurd to most of my colleagues, and my desire to contribute to the defense of the country was unpopular at first. One of my very close friends, Robert Wilson—now director of the Fermi Lab—when I vigorously advocated our participation in a defense project, told me: "You are pleasantly disagreeable." But as this indicates, our relations were, on the whole, very friendly and cordial. With the Pearl Harbor attack, all this changed and they were as anxious to contribute to the defense of our country and of freedom as I was.

I participated in the uranium project during the war, then returned to Princeton to continue my teaching and research activities. I derived a great deal of pleasure also from my association with students—several of them became leaders in our field. This provided me, and continues to provide me, with a great deal of satisfaction.

*And you've been very successful.* [Professor Wigner received the Nobel Prize for physics in 1963 for fundamental research on the structure of the atomic nucleus.]

You know, there is a German proverb: *Der Dummer hat's Glück.* This is how I feel. I was lucky, unbelievably lucky. . . . As to success, one achieves it best if one does not strive for it too vigorously, has a good deal of luck, does one's duty, follows his inclinations, tries to be understanding and useful. It sounds sanctimonious, and perhaps even boastful, but it is true nevertheless, that being considerate, mindful of the sensitivities of others, gives one more peace of mind, more satisfaction, than success or anything else.

# Ursula Ritter
························FROM GERMANY, 1946 ·····················

*She is blond and fine-featured, a housewife in a prosperous seaside town. Currently she is taking courses toward a master's degree in physics.*

During World War II my father was a scientist specializing in underwater research for the German government. He worked in a camouflaged laboratory by a deep lake in the Alps. My mother and sister and I lived with him there in a farmhouse in the village. I was totally unaware of the war until early in 1945 when the French captured the village. I was six years old then. Two tanks came in, only two tanks, that's how small the village was, and we were very afraid when we saw them coming. My mother and the farm women wanted to hide in the haystack, but my father thought the soldiers might shoot into it, so he sent us to the basement to pray. He wasn't a religious man, but he thought it would keep us out of the way and could do no harm.

There was no shooting and the soldiers left in a short time. The next day, delegations began to arrive of scientists employed by the Allied forces. My father had thought his work was secret, but the Allies must have had him on a list. They all wanted him to work for them.

The French came first, but one of them was rude to my sister and we didn't like them. I don't remember much about the British, but when the Americans came, it was in a big limousine that could hardly fit into our narrow road. It was driven by a big black soldier who gave my sister and me an orange, the first we had ever seen. My sister and I liked the Americans best, and my father must have too, because he agreed to go with them. I don't know how free he was to say no. We later learned the Russians were taking scientists from their sectors, too.

My father packed up his papers and went to Washington with some other scientists. He continued his work there.

For the next year my mother and my sister and I received money and extra rations from the American government. Margarine, chocolate, meat, and milk powder. We got tobacco, too. Although none of us smoked, it was useful to trade for other things. In 1946 my father was able to send for us, and we moved to the United States. Only my mother ever looked back. . . .

# Friedrich von Dietze

························ FROM GERMANY, 1947 ······················

*His manner is commanding, his speech precise, and his posture erect. He holds a management position in a major American corporation. With his wife and six children, he lives in a comfortable house with a swimming pool and spacious grounds in an affluent suburban community near Washington, D.C.*

At the time when I was invited to immigrate into the United States, I was thirty-two years old and the year was 1947. The situation at the time was that Germany had lost World War II and most of us were out of work—at least out of the work that we were trained to do. A scouting team was sent out from the United States to find German specialists with unusual knowledge and skills and invite them to immigrate into the United States. The operation was known as

Operation Paperclip, presumably because a fair amount of red tape went with it.

I had, during the war, done research and development work for the German navy. That work had been successful, and I was in a somewhat important position during the war and had done what at the time was rather advanced research and development. I sort of expected that they would get in touch with me, because I had somewhat of a key position in the development of torpedo direction, which was of great interest to the Americans; and so I was not too surprised when I was invited to go to the United States.

I had worked at a torpedo research station on the Baltic. During the last four or five months of the war, this research station was overrun by the Russians and we were evacuated to a more western experimental station. This is where I was when the war ended and for a few months after the end of the war. A small group was asked by the British armed forces to write down our experiences for the British navy. This ended in November of 1945 and I moved to the southern part of Germany, where I had a small cottage in Berchtesgaden.

I had no other place to go. My whole family—that is, my wife and my child—had been killed during the last phases of the war through military action by the Russians. I moved to my cottage—you might call it a chalet—and I was looking for work. That wasn't very easy, because the German economy was simply not functioning very well at the time, and there was an inflation of sorts going on. The famous cigarette money was in effect, where, in essence, the value of everything was measured in terms of cigarettes. Food was very scarce, and if one felt that one didn't get enough, one would have to go to the black market to get it, which involved either very considerable amounts of money or having some merchandise to trade—mostly cigarettes or precious things like cameras or things of that nature.

I found some employment here and there. I repaired some radios and dug some ditches, and for periods of time I did nothing. I had no financial problems since I had a little money and I had some objects of value, which I sold. I remember selling some stamps from a stamp collection at one time that brought some money. I also sold a camera. I wouldn't say that I lived very comfortably, but I can't say there was any great hardship. I can't say that I felt very depressed or anything. Berchtesgaden is a beautiful spot, and I had friends that I visited and I traveled somewhat and I invited friends to join me. Also, just the business of staying alive was very complicated. Whether one worked or not, one had to spend considerable time finding food, finding wood to burn in the stove, and just keeping alive, so to speak.

I didn't find it particularly demoralizing. It was clear that things were eventually going to get better, and one just felt that there was a period of a number of years where the scars of war had to heal somewhat and normal relations would return.

The winter of '47 was probably the low point. One morning in the middle of that bitter-cold winter, I was approached by an American soldier who identified himself as a member of the military police and asked me to accompany him to Munich. I had heard of the program and I was not considerably concerned, so I went with him to Munich. A job offer and emigration offer was made to me, which I accepted. I had given this matter some thought before I was ever asked and felt that I would go if asked, simply because in the United States, in my profession, which is that of an electrical and communications engineer, there were tremendous opportunities. It was well known to me that America was leading in this field and that I would have opportunities to work in that field again—probably better opportunities than in Germany.

The Americans had the well-oiled machinery. They collected German specialists in a town in Bavaria and kept them there for a while, until the papers were in order and the FBI check had been made. Then they were shipped to the United States with military transport vessels. So I left Germany in May of 1947 and found myself in Washington, D.C., working for the Department of the Navy, in the technical field similar to that I had worked on during the war. The whole idea was to build on the knowledge that I had developed during the war.

During the first three years I was under navy custody. I had no status—meaning I could not leave navy employment, among other things. The first six months I lived in navy barracks with some modest supervision, which was never explained to me, but, as I found out by trial and error, in essence consisted in us being home at night; and if we wanted to travel, we had to clear that with our liaison officers. During the first six months all my letters were censored. Whether the letters coming back were censored I don't know, but I know that my letters were censored. Otherwise we were completely free to do what we wanted to do. It was as comfortable as a navy barracks would be at the time.

I found the Americans, including the military, surprisingly friendly and helpful. Two things impressed me. They are very small things, but nevertheless they were typical. The first one is that at the entrance to the Navy Department in Washington there were two huge piles of newspapers, where everybody took his paper and threw a nickel on the pile. There was always money lying and nobody ever touched it! The second thing that impressed me—how neatly everybody lined up and queued up to wait for the bus. This is something I hadn't seen in Germany, either. So, by and large, the United States at the time presented a very friendly, neighborly-type picture, and I cannot say that at any time I was made to feel that I really was the former enemy. I never had particularly any hostility toward the United States. I found it deplorable there is war between the two countries, which, after all, are over three thousand miles apart. But I cannot say that I felt any great hostility.

The most significant difference, of course, was that at the time that I left, there was very little food in Germany, whereas there was no shortage of food in the United States. One of our main occupations was to pack huge food packages and send them to Germany to support whatever was left of our families or relatives or friends. Both I and all my colleagues in the same program—there were others from the same program in Washington, D.C.—exchanged notes on how to and where to get the best bargains and pack the biggest packages to be sent to our friends. It was a rather complicated operation, but we could send what we wanted to.

The naval-barracks situation stopped very abruptly after six months, and we were told that we could live wherever we wanted to; and also our pay base changed. We came from a *per diem* allowance to a monthly paycheck and had simply to take care of ourselves as everybody else. I looked for a place to live in Washington, D.C., and I found a furnished apartment in a very pleasant neighborhood which was within my means. Also I got married again, late in 1947. I went back to Germany to marry, and the navy brought my wife back on one of the transport ships. It was a complicated procedure. She adapted rather quickly. Her English improved very quickly and she enjoyed herself quite a bit. We moved from a furnished apartment to an unfurnished apartment after a while, and then after two more years or so we bought a small house in a suburb of Washington, where we lived for the duration of my work in Washington. Life was very pleasant.

The navy custody ended about three years, I believe, after I came to the United States. At the time it was not possible to get an immigration visa within the country. I had to go outside the country to the nearest American consulate, and for Washington, D.C., that was determined to be Niagara Falls, Ontario. So the navy transported me there—I believe it was in 1950—and arranged for the necessary papers—and there were lots of them—and I was granted an immigration visa and immigrated officially as an immigrant alien. After that I was just another immigrant.

# Karl Reinhardt

*Once scientific director of a large chemical corporation in East Germany, he was entitled to special privileges for food, tobacco, clothing, and housing. He was even offered a high governmental office. But prestige and material rewards seemed empty.*

When Hitler came to power in Germany I was twelve years old. Why shouldn't I join the youth movement? What I saw was what Boy Scouts are doing here—going out camping and finding their ways according to the stars, and it was a type of those activities which, of course, would appeal to a youngster of my age. So why should I understand my father when he said no? He didn't want us to have anything to do with this. And yet, at school I'd be asked, "Well, why don't you join?" And they were smart enough to have programs that looked good to young people. Young people can be easily impressed. The social welfare for the aged. All those programs were certainly well-organized, and a youngster doesn't ask, "Where does the money come from? How do they do this?" You just see that things are being done and you think they are the right things.

All those things which happened in concentration camps, those details one didn't know at the time. It's always difficult to tell this to someone. The general public didn't know. Yes, they know that there were people put into concentration camps, and then we'd ask the teacher, "Well, what about this?" They'd say, "They are people who are opposed to us. They don't want to be loyal to the government. They had the choice to be loyal and that is why they were taken away." And, of course, the foreign radio station reported other things; but there, again, it was quite dangerous to listen to them and, on the other hand, there was very effective propaganda within Germany.

Sometimes we meet Jews in this country who lived in Germany before the war, and we say, "Oh? When did you leave Germany?" And they say, "1938, 1939." Then it's as if a curtain descends. There's a feeling of constraint. We think, "Oh, yes, that's why they left," and we feel they are thinking, "They were there. They were Germans before the war and during the war. They were there." I don't think I'm one of those Germans who have what they call "the German guilt complex." I know I wasn't responsible for what happened, and I was a child when Hitler took power. And yet, when I meet Jews from Germany, inside I want to say, "I'm sorry. I'm sorry," even though I know I wasn't responsible.

As I say, I wanted to participate in the youth movement, and when the time came I couldn't wait to be a soldier so that I would have a chance to fight for my country. I was drafted in '41 as a paratrooper and went to Russia. I was wounded there—got a shot in my elbow and my arm is stiff as a result. Because of this injury I was sent to an infantry unit back in Germany.

It was during this time that the plot was organized for the attempt on Hitler's life. Some of the people with my unit were involved in that plot, and I became involved in it in a minor way.

The world looked quite different in 1944 than the way it did in 1941, when I became a soldier. I had been in Russia, had seen many things and heard many things and had met people from completely different quarters, learned about things which I had not known before—the concentration camps, other things. It was really devastating to think that as a child you thought, "Well, this is good," and then afterwards. . . .

Well, of course, the plot failed and nothing developed.

In 1945 the war ended and I was able to continue my studies. I graduated as a chemical engineer and then continued at the university for a doctorate in chemistry. We were in the part of Germany that had been taken over by the Russians, and when I finished my studies in '52 I was immediately employed by the Agfa firm in a very good position—not because I was extremely good, but it was simply that so many chemists and engineers had left, and there were positions and nobody to fill them. It was a position that people sometimes have to work almost their whole lives in order to get. I was put in charge of a laboratory and was immediately part of a privileged group in East Germany, as a member of the *intelligentsia*, as they call it. I had special privileges to buy things ordinary people could not buy: tobacco, food, clothing. My wife and I had at our disposal a new house. And the money which I earned was good. Whatever we couldn't buy, we could go to Berlin, West Berlin, and buy things there. It was relatively easy at that time. One had to pass some unpleasant inspections and questioning when one wanted to go then, but one could go there; so we didn't really have any serious economical, financial problems.

I was even approached to become a member of the *Volksrat*. That would be the equivalent to a congressman in this country. But I didn't want to have anything to do with it.

We had hoped that things would change, the situation would normalize, probably that the division of Germany would end. But we came to the conclusion that it would not change in our lifetime. The Russians had taken over the company. Everything that was produced was sent to Russia and the Russians determined the price. They had a man in the plant who watched over political things and reported everything we said. It made us a little bit nervous.

The main thing was you couldn't trust anybody, and that was a very bad thing. This was one of our main motivating factors for leaving. I was married by then and had two little girls. You don't want your children to grow up in such an atmosphere. See, you couldn't even talk to them about how things were. Of course, at that time they were young, but as they grow up, how can you influence them and give them your views? Our older daughter was going to school at that time, and we knew what the influence of school could be. We had both grown up under the Hitler regime in Germany. School was much stronger than what the parents could present.

Were we willing to make concessions? Of course, one cannot live there without unconsciously making one compromise after another. It's not a matter of making a very drastic decision. One rushes from day to day, and one has to live there, and one knows that there's not much one can do about things one doesn't like.

For example, we listened to the West German radio station. One should not do that. It was a crime. And our daughter was young then, five years old at the time, and loved to listen to the West German good-night song, a lullaby. And she knew very well the name of that station and where it was on the radio dial. Now, at school the teacher might ask children, "What stations do you listen to?" The teachers did that. They often did.

And how can you tell such a small child? "You may listen to that station, but you must not tell your teacher." Then you have to instill in them that you must lie, that you cannot tell the truth to everyone. These are the conflicts that make you decide there's no end to it. It's just one thing after another, and you have to say to yourself, "All right. Stop objecting to everything and give in, or leave." We decided to leave.

We knew we could not take much with us and we had some old furniture which we sold. Two days later I was approached at the plant. "You sold furniture. Are you planning to leave?" It was the local man who was the representative of the Communist party. I said, "It's old furniture. We want to buy something new." From this moment there was a watchman standing outside of our house watching us, watching the apartment. It made us a little nervous. We had some things which we wanted to save—some books which were handed down from my wife's family, very old editions, which we really didn't want to lose. So we had to send them in small parcels, which was legal, to West Germany to friends.

About the third or fourth time we went to the post office, the man at the window that took the parcel looked at the name and said, "Well, you know something? I think you are planning to leave."

"How can you say that? We have so many friends over there. These are birthday presents."

"I have sent off enough people. I know. If you have something to sell, let me know. My daughter could use a new stove." This was the postman, a nice elderly man. He probably was good, but if he talked so freely to me, he might talk to the next person. So we went to all the post offices in the neighboring cities and mailed our parcels from there.

And when the day came, we decided that my wife and children should leave early in the morning, go to the railroad station, and take a train, with just the things which one would take for a weekend trip. I worked until noon on Saturdays and I went to work as normally and made arrangements with someone to drive me to another city at noon. There was no problem about that. With my position I often made such arrangements, and I didn't have to explain why I was going. I left with just my briefcase. I took the train from a neighboring city and, as it happened, when I walked on, the train was full, so I went to the dining car and the only place that was available was at a table where the director of our purchasing department was already sitting. We talked casually. My story was that I was visiting someone in the Berlin area. I don't think he was suspicious. I didn't look like someone who was about to go away.

Everything went all right and I arrived in West Berlin that evening.

MRS. REINHARDT: The whole experience wasn't funny to me a bit. I was constantly afraid that they might see or recognize what I was doing. Although I didn't have anything with me except for the stroller with the little girl in it, I did have pillows. It was forbidden to take feather pillows to the West, but I said to myself, "I'm going to take these pillows," and I put them in the stroller, along with the little girl. When the police came and checked the ID cards, nothing happened; but the policeman came back and stood in front of our door of the little compartment, with his red band and shield, and I thought, "Oh, my God, he's waiting for me!" I thought he would say, finally, "You have to come with me." And then, when the train stopped in West Berlin, I got out and the man didn't pay any attention to us. It was just a coincidence, but I was so afraid. I had imagined so many things that would happen and what I was going to do. When I left the railroad station in West Berlin, I remember there was a huge square, and I had several large purses and the little stroller and the other little girl in my hand, and I didn't know how to manage to go across the street. There was a lot of traffic and a policeman came toward me, and I said, "Now!

That's the one who's going to get me!" And, of course, he wasn't, because it was in West Berlin, and all he said was, "Ma'am, may I help you get across?" And for a few years after that, somehow, seeing a policeman I would always have a tiny little shock. "Is something wrong? Do I have a clear conscience? What can he do?"

KARL REINHARDT: I worked in West Germany as a chemist for a while, and then, sometime in 1955, I was visited by some people who introduced themselves as representatives of the United States government, and they asked me if I would like to work in the States. They were part of the Operation Paperclip. So I said, "Why not?" And I filled out the questionnaires and got a Secret clearance and eventually flew with my family to Wright-Patterson Air Base in Dayton, Ohio.

When we moved to Dayton, we thought, "How big is it? About a half a million people? That's not so bad. Something like Frankfurt." Frankfurt has a theater, a symphony orchestra. It has the flavor of a big city. And when we came to Dayton we found it was sort of a provincial little town. But it was a very nice area, it was clean, and the people were open and tried to help. We have always been impressed by the Americans we met.

There were some little incidents that made a big impression on us. For instance, one of the first things we had to buy was a car. Of course, living in the States without a car is impossible. My wife didn't know how to drive and I didn't know any better at the time, so I said, "Well, I can teach you how to drive." So we were driving in an area near the air force base, and during one of those driving lessons we somehow got the car stalled. Probably we had flooded the carburetor, and we couldn't start it again. A car came and stopped; a man in a red hunting cap asked if he could help. And he worked on the car for about fifteen minutes and finally pulled us out. I thought that was very friendly of this man, and then, two weeks later, I met him at a reception—he was a second-star general! And I could not picture the same situation in the Germany I knew. It would be much more formal. People here are open and friendly.

We've never had second thoughts about our decision. I can be more myself here. I think I can live here without concern as to what the reaction of other people might be. And here there's the possibility of change. Here the system works. Look at this business of the Nixon-Watergate and all. If he'd been allowed to continue his course, I would have been quite concerned about some future aspects in this country. But here the system worked.

# Klara Zwicker

*She was born shortly before World War II in a small industrial town in the Ruhr Valley. Now married to a long-distance bus driver, she is the mother of two small boys and is an avid gardener and home dressmaker. The family lives in a neat, green-and-white cottage in Providence, Rhode Island.*

It's foolish to hate other people just because of their nationality. Like the Jews. I was shopping at the mall with my friend last year and, you know how it's crowded at Christmastime? We sat at a table in a lunchroom with two other ladies and we began talking, and when they learned we were German, they got up and left. They were Jews and they didn't like us because we were German. But we didn't have anything to do with that. I was a little girl then and Germany was a dictatorship. And, anyhow, none of us knew. They didn't put it in the papers. We didn't know. We knew that they took the Jews away, yes. There were stars on the houses that the Jews lived in, and we knew that they came and took them away, but we didn't know where. We thought maybe they went to some safe place or they were putting them somewhere else in another part of the country. We didn't know. And, besides, if we did know, it was a dictatorship and we were mostly women and children. The men were all away in the war, and my father was killed and my mother and I were all alone. And most of the other people around us were women and children and old men. And we didn't know what was happening and we couldn't choose our government. And Hitler—he was not mentally ill—he really was crazy.

My mother, she never disliked the Jews. There was a store in our town, Bamberger's, a Jewish store, and my mother always said that after World War I, when she would go there with her family to shop, if she didn't have enough money the people in the store would always give them credit or maybe let them have something for nothing. They were kind and my mother always said that; even when Hitler was talking about the Jews, she said that. But I guess he was against them because they owned everything.

My father died in the war when I was five. He was a soldier and he was in the German army. He died down in Italy and then my mother was a widow and the two of us were alone. Everything got bombed. I slept with my clothes on constantly. I was always sleeping with my clothes on, and in the middle of the night when the siren goes, my mother would drag me out to the bunker. We'd be sitting the whole night long until the alarm went off, and then the planes would come down and shoot all these people. I remember seeing all these people laying on the street, dead. They couldn't make it, so they were running to the bunker and they got shot. And the houses flew up in the air. Oh, I remember that. Yes, I remember it very well.

People got separated. My mother took care of a baby for a year, which was lost. No one knew who the baby belonged to, and she got stuck with it until the parents finally came and picked him up. They got separated during the bombing, and someone took the baby and put it in a different bunker, and then nobody knew what happened to it and they didn't know what to do with the baby. You know, the Red Cross was overloaded with all the injured people, and the baby was crying, so my mother said, "Here. I'll take him home and take care of him." And we took him home. And then, after a year, the parents finally came and they were so happy and so grateful to my mother.

The worst time was after the war. We had nothing to eat. The money was worth nothing. No food around. Everything was flat. We had no coal to burn, no heat in the house. We had to go out and steal. We were holding up the trains and we took this coal from the locomotive. I did it myself. We put up the sign for stop, all of us. Only children, because the adults would get arrested. Children they didn't arrest. When the train stopped, then all of us kids were climbing over the locomotive and throwing all the coal down. You know, we are standing there with big sacks, gobbling them up and hiding them in the bushes.

My mother remarried, but it wasn't very nice for me because my stepfather was not good. After my sister was born, my half-sister, he rejected me completely. That was the reason I wanted to get away. I couldn't take it anymore. My mother didn't let me move out until I was twenty-one, and I thought, "Well, I might as well go over to America. What can I lose?"

Well, I really like it here. It's nice. It's worked out well. I'm married. My children are Americans.

I like to go home to Germany. I get all excited, and after a while, then I've got to come back. Got to see everybody, you know, and see what's going on. And then when I'm there I feel like I should come back here. It's always such an in-between, you know. I like to go home, and yet when you're there you're somehow disappointed, because you always figure when you left everything's going to stay like that—but it doesn't. And I feel like an outsider. I'm not in there anymore.

I've been back to Germany to visit three times, but everything is so crowded. The apartments are so small and my mother lives in a very old place and they don't even have a bathroom. And when you come there with your two kids, you know, no bathroom; you go to wash yourself in the kitchen and everything is so tiny. Ah, I just get so tied up, I can't breathe there. I lived for a while with my sister there, because her apartment was bigger and they have a bathroom. So when I was visiting my mother, I always went to my sister to take a bath. What trouble! I couldn't live that way anymore, I just couldn't. No, no. And you have the car here and you can go when you want to and it's really nice.

Sometimes when we're joking, when I'm visiting my family, we say: "If Hitler hadn't fought against Russia, maybe we'd be the big country now and everything would be different." He really got crazy as the war went on. He was crazy to fight Russia. In the winter, that Russian winter. Yes, if we hadn't fought against Russia, we might have won the war. We'd be owning everything now. And Germany would be rich.

# Lore Steiner
·················· FROM GERMANY, 1938 ·····················

*A Jew, she left Germany to escape Hitler.*

I have not knowingly passed on any traditions from Germany. You are formed by your home and upbringing, so I have probably passed on things that I take for granted. But knowingly, I don't think so. I would rather not carry on anything from Germany.

# Willi and Ilse Kienzle
················· FROM GERMANY, 1955 ·····················

*They are both tall and thin, a well-matched couple. He is gregarious, likes to tell jokes, teases his wife good-naturedly. She is quiet, serious, intense. Their house is unmistakably German. The furniture, the draperies, the china, the pots and pans, even the radio console have been imported from Frankfurt.*

WILLI: Before the war I was in the merchant marine. I worked on a German liner, the Hamburg-American Line. I was a chef, because that's my trade. The war broke out and we were in the Channel at that time, with two thousand passengers for New York, but we couldn't make it. We had to turn around. They put the passengers on trains and sent them to Holland, and they put them on a Holland-American Line and sent them to New York, because the people were all right. There were no reason to keep them. They had us [the crew] on board for six or eight weeks. They hoped that it get straightened out, but it didn't, you know, so then they let us go. I was drafted and I was put in the navy—cooking. [Laughs.] I mean, them guys got to be fed, you know.

First we were in the North Sea. When the army moved into France, we moved on sea and took the ports, one after the other: Boulogne, Cherbourg, Le Havre, Brest. We stayed then all the time in the British Channel. We had our home port there in St. Malo, a little tiny town, real old-fashioned, beautiful. I would like to go back there and see what it looks like.

There were battles constantly. I had my battle station, too. It's not just that I'm a passenger. No, just cook in between, you know. But if the whistle blows I have to go out, too. I had rockets to operate and I had machine guns. Oh, yeah, you have to do something. You got your job. If there's no alarm, then you go back to your work; but if there are alarm, then you pull off the soup and take everything down and go out.

You get used to it. It's not frightening, because you got all your friends, all young people on board—nobody is older than twenty-eight. It's not a picnic. There's always danger, but you don't realize in that age. I mean, you are hoping nothing happen, but you got your buddies there. How many times do you sit together with them in the evening, drink a case of beer, and he tells a story about his parents, where he came from, what he did. And so we knew each other in and out, like a family.

When General Patton broke through with his tanks, we were going in and out like a shadow, and we took our wounded soldiers back, because there was no connection on land no more—the Americans, you know. It was all controlled by the planes, the railroads were bombed. . . .

When the Americans landed there in Normandy in 1945, we had to pull back. We had to pull out of our port, St. Malo, and we went to Jersey—the Channel Island, Jersey. This is British territory, and they were occupied by us. We were in a mansion or a hotel—it was like a castle—right on the beach. We had to defend that strip of beach in case of emergency. There were gun towers there and some bunkers, with guns, and we were spread out.

From there we did a landing, to the French coast. What we had in mind was to pull out some loaded American coal ships and sneak them away. We were short on coal there at that time, and we needed coal for electricity, for our hospital, for the generators to operate. The landing was, I think, March 1945. We went in there with four tugboats and pulled them out—the whole ship, with the crew and everything. Well, we went in there and we couldn't get out no more, because we were going on to the sand. It was too low, the water, and we run aground. We had to jump ship and go back on the other boats.

And then, on May 8, the British came and took us over. There was the capitulation and the war was over. They took us to England. We were officially POW's.

First they put us in a big camp of about twenty-five thousand people in Southampton, and there we were tested by the secret service. You had to come in that room there and they asked you questions. They want to find out what your political feelings are, and according to that they group you and put you in different camps in the country. You had camps with more security or less security. We didn't have almost no security at all. We were called the "good guys." The "bad guys" they locked up. It was a small camp, only a thousand men, way out in the country. I don't know what town it was. It was between Coventry and Rugby—in the Midlands someplace. We had about twenty-five British soldiers, but they were carrying no weapons, no rifles, no nothing. The gates were open.

I never had it so good! I was cook. [*Laughs.*] See, food is very important. I was cooking for the British officers and men in the British cookhouse. Not for the POW's—they had their own cookhouse inside the camp. I lived outside the camp, outside the gates, the barbed wire. But it didn't make no difference because the gates were open anyway, so you could walk in and out any time. We could go for a walk after duty hours. We could go out seven miles. We were practically free, except you can't go home.

We couldn't fraternize with the British. We were not allowed to talk to them at the beginning, but we talked anyway. They were waving at us, especially the girls. They knocked on the window when we went through the little villages and say, "Hey, German boy, come on in and have a cup of tea." We had a cup of tea in the back of the bars and they give us a schnapps, too. Oh, yeah, there are always friendly people in the world, no matter how times are. They said, "I was a farmer before the war and I am a farmer now and I didn't make no money on this." The big men make the money on war, you know. That's like it is all over. The little guy is the one who suffers, not the big one. There was no bad feelings. They realized—they're intelligent people—they say, "There was a war. What can you do? You had to go." Everybody's doing his thing for his country, you know.

Sometimes we had to go on working groups, we had to go out and help the farmers bring the harvest in. You have to do something in camp. They don't just lock you up and let you sit there. You have to work. And you get money for it, but you don't get it in cash. They put it in the bank for you. It piles up in there. And when you are released and you go home, then they give it to you. If you got no clothing, they give you clothing, and you don't have to run around like a hillbilly. We had camp money, too—maybe five dollars a week. And for this you could buy in the canteen some cigarettes, writing paper, or shaving cream. Like in a penitentiary. [*Laughs.*]

I was there two years. They sent the Italians home first. Then they started with the Germans, after a lot of articles in the papers. The people say, "Why you keep them Germans here?" They were worried. Their own soldiers came back from Europe, and we pitched in and worked for them, and it was like we took their jobs away. So they started to repatriate.

I came back to Berlin in 1947. It looked pretty bad. Everything was bombed out. There was still some restaurants left, so I applied: "All right, we need somebody." So I was cooking. We didn't have much to cook—no pork chops or anything like that. Just lots of vegetables cooked in water, and that's it. But I was cooking and that was enough for me. If the times getting rough and nobody got anything to eat, then there's always enough to lick your fingers, and you pull through.

ILSE: Now what about me?

WILLI: Oh, that's another thing. In wartime it started to be the custom that the girls write unknown soldiers to keep them happy out there. We reversed it and wrote to unknown girls back home. We picked big companies or factories in the hometown, so I picked Siemens. We wrote a letter, me and a buddy; we wrote a letter together. We offered two lonely sailors looking for two lonely girls back home, and we are suffering so much and this and that. So that's how she got the letter from me, and we start writing. Then I came on furlough—that was way before, 1943 or so—and we met. She lived in Berlin, too. And we kept writing as long as we could, as the mail went through. When I was in England, I wrote her when I came I'd visit her. And we got married when I came back.

Then I went back to the hotel work. I like it better. I like the fancy cooking. It's more generous. You don't have to count the eggs when you put them in a pan. If you want to make a chicken soup, you get the chicken. In the other place you get chicken base, and they *call* it chicken soup.

But they switch me around in the hotel. I had to replace the other chefs on their days off, and I had two different shifts, and there's nothing I could do. I was the youngest chef at that time, and they said,

"You got to do it." And we still worked six days. In our business I always had to work Sunday. That was a handicap. We had friends and they say, "Why don't you come over on Sunday?" I say, " Sorry, I have to work on Sunday. I'm off Monday." Yeah, on Monday everybody else is working!

I had an uncle and an aunt living in the United States, and they wanted somebody from the family. They said, "You want to come over? We have the five-days week here." And I thought that sounds pretty good. And I liked foreign countries. I liked people and I want to see how they live. My uncle had to send in the affidavit, and it went pretty fast.

I came over by myself first, to see what it looks like. If it didn't work out . . . . But I found a job the next day. They needed cooks here—trained cooks. I got it from a New York agency. They sent me out to the Tavern Restaurant in Newark.

It was harder than I was used to. And hot—much hotter than in Germany. The cooking is different. They do everything much faster and not so particular and not so fancy. Just as long as the order gets out, no matter how. In Germany you do more artistically, arrange colors and everything more—it's got to look like something. But here they just slap it on the plate and out it goes. What we did here with four cooks behind the range, we did that with thirty in a big hotel. Thirty cooks, yeah. Because you do much more fancier work. Everything made to order more or less, better arranged, neat and all that.

I adjusted to that, but it was hard. What bothered me was long hours. I had to work a nine-hour day, and I feel they didn't pay me enough, and so I wasn't satisfied with the job. They took advantage of the language barrier; they didn't pay as much. You know, when you come over, they call you "greenhorn" and they say you're a dummy. So I had to start lower than the others, and in a few weeks you find out what the others make and you say, "My goodness, I work as hard as he does and they give me fifty dollars less. Why?"

Then I talked to some kitchen steward we had there, and he felt sorry for me and said, "I know a company, they have industrial feeding. They run the cafeterias for the companies. In plants, it's Monday to Friday, five days." I said, "That's what I'm looking for." So he gave me application for the company, and I'm still there—twenty years. At least I live like a human being. I go home on Friday afternoon and say, "See you Monday."

After seven months I sent my wife the ticket for the boat.

ILSE: I didn't want to come. Why should I go there? Why should I go to a country who bombed our whole city for nothing?

WILLI: No. I thought everybody was doing his job. He's doing his job for his side and I do my job for my side, and it just happened. We bombed London and they bombed Berlin. Why should I hate that pilot? He gets his orders to drop them, you know. He don't know what's down here.

ILSE: Honest to God, it was hate—plain hate. I hated everybody what was not German, because we had too much bombing, too much shooting.

And we worked so hard for everything. We worked so hard for the little bit that we had over there. And then you have to leave it? I thought you ripped my heart out when I left.

WILLI: Everything went through fast. I found an apartment in a hurry, but it was not the right place. She was disappointed when she came and saw it. It was downtown in Jersey City, and that's not the best neighborhood, you know.

ILSE: That was, I would say, a disaster. When I arrived in New York with my little girl, I couldn't speak one word English—not one word. And when I saw New York, right away how dirty it is on the docks there—oh, it was terrible. His uncle and my husband, they picked us up and first we drove to the Bronx, and on the way, what I saw I didn't like. So New York didn't say anything to me. The best thing was the Statue of Liberty. When we came in, I liked that.

The same night we came to Jersey City, where he had the apartment—with nothing in. One bed and three people. Can you imagine an empty apartment? His uncle offered to take Christa for one night, but he made it very clear only for one night. The next day we did go out and we wanted to buy a couch, and he had only twenty dollars. [Laughs.] Anyway, we bought a couch and we picked up our daughter, and then we was home and he went back to work and I was sitting in a empty apartment with my daughter, crying, and she was crying. . . .

I was against everything. In Jersey City the street was so dirty. And then the way they brought the kids up, I couldn't get used to that. You know, how easygoing they was with the kids. They could be fresh to you. That's quite a difference when you come from a. . . . I hope I don't embarrass you, because it's really not nice to talk that way.

There was one German woman—she was married to an American guy—and she translated everything for me. Then she said, "Why don't you bring Christa up to my house to play?" I only went up once, because she told me I have to come up the steps and bring the newspaper and make noises so the rats go away! These things we don't know in Germany.

Christa was seven years old, and everybody said she has to go to school. That was very difficult because she couldn't talk English. Nobody was there to talk German, and so I had to bring her to school every day. When she got here to school and she find out how easy it is according to Germany—well, that did it right away. And she was a big attraction there. The teacher, everybody, said, "Oh, Christa . . . " She was in the middle; she was different. Of course, she really liked that.

Christa started after four weeks talking already, but I tell you I was very stubborn. I didn't want to learn English. I tried to find every German store I could. And I just went to the supermarket and picked up what I needed. When somebody talked to me, I just went by. I didn't want to talk. I wasn't happy at all.

Then we moved in another apartment in West New York. That was almost a German neighborhood. There was a German church, there was a German butcher, there was a German furniture store, and there was a bakery where they talked German. So I didn't need English.

And then we bought the television, because Christa said, "Everybody has a television. I want a television." So I started to watch one show—"As the World Turns." And that show I watched every day at the same time, and I remembered the names just from hearing. Oh, that's Penny, and that's grandfather, and that's this one, that's the other one. And then I could imagine what they was doing and what they was talking. I still didn't try very hard. Then, in the evening, they watched television—Christa and Willi—and they always kept translating. And one day they translated it wrong, and I corrected them, and that did it. [*Laughs.*] From that time on there was no translation in the house anymore.

We have friends—their own kids are not speaking German! That's terrible. That was one thing I was always after Christa. Even if she really wanted to speak English, I just ignored it. She tried to, but I was stubborn, too. She'd say, "Mother, today you got to speak English to me." I said, "I don't understand you. You got to speak German." So she talked English, and I pretended I didn't hear it. . . .

I was unhappy. Honestly, I wanted to leave him. I wanted to go back, but I couldn't save the money fast enough. Everybody told him, "Send her back and then you will see she is healed." But it was just the opposite. When I came back to Germany, I thought I never make it here again. I felt at home there, just like I was never away. I knew when I came back here, I wouldn't be happy anymore. And that was when I started to look for a job. Because when I came back, I said right away, "I'm learning to drive. Going out to work. I'm saving money so I can go back." By that time, my daughter was a half-American.

I'm still unhappy. That still hasn't changed. I have too many memories over there. On a clear day, I feel fine. When it is so humid, I could take my suitcase and go. And there are so many, many other things. I mean, you try inside a house to make it the way you like it. Well, our whole living over there is completely different. You know, the furniture and—I don't know how to explain it. Our quality is better over there, too. When you go out here and buy something good and spend a lot of money, it still doesn't satisfy me because it's still not the way I really wanted. It's very, very hard to explain. We tried, but you never get it the same way.

Well, I don't feel unhappy all the time, but . . . on holidays, you get homesick. We take everything more serious over there. Here you make a big carnival out of it. I tell you the truth, I'd rather spend Christmas Eve here alone than going to my daughter. It's not her husband, but it's the family. It's more American people, and she is right in the middle. She has a lot of German in herself and she wants to make it the German way, but then they make fun. They don't realize that for us it's more serious.

WILLI: It would be nicer if Christa married a German. I only would prefer it because of the language. I knew people—friends of ours—their daughters and sons are married to Germans. It's a completely different relationship when they are together. Because they got more in common. They can talk about more. They can even sing a song together. He got different songs than I got. And if we drink a couple beers and he says, "Let's have a song," then he sings something different than we do. I don't know his lyric, and he don't know my lyric. It's a kind of invisible wall in between.

Our friends are mostly German, people that we met here; because you have the same ideas, you have the same background more or less, the same schooling. You get more contact with people that think more alike than other people. And because you can talk your language, you can express it exactly the way you wanted to. You don't have to look for the right words and put it very carefully. This way, you can talk and he knows what you mean, and it goes faster.

ILSE: Well, now with Christa expecting a baby, I guess that really ties me down here now. I have to concentrate on that. It's terrible. You're not home here and you're not home there. You have actually a split personality. I mean, this is where I live, and that over there is my home.

But there is one wish I have. I never want to be buried here. That's what I keep telling him. I say, "Send me over." If I know I'm dying, I would go over. I'd rather die over there than here.

# Tacwyn Morgan

· · · · · · · · · · · · · · · · · · · · · · FROM WALES, 1946 · · · · · · · · · · · · · · · · · · · · · · ·

*Tall and thin, with sandy hair and an easy smile, he's a specialist in computer technology. He and his wife share a love for music and for*

*long walks in the woods near their Michigan house. His hobby is
fixing things, using his hands, but he still has to be pushed by his wife
to buy the tools he needs, "because that's the way I grew up." He says,
"The amount of my disposable income always embarrasses me."*

I was born in a little village called the Hole in the Wall. I'm quite
serious—except that the name was Adwy'r Clawdd in Welsh. The wall
was built by a king, to separate Wales and England, and they had this
gate in the wall, where they would trade when peacetime was in
existence. That's in North Wales, and the nearest large town is
Wrexham. It was a mining area. In fact, most of my relatives were coal
miners—North Wales coal miners. My mother made sure we avoided
it. She said, "Once you start in the coal mines, you can never get out of
it."

My father was a farmer. I never remember him. He died when I was
ten months old, of flu, in 1918, the worldwide epidemic. My mother
never married again. She kept the farm right through the Depression. It
was rather grim. It was quite a small farm, five acres or so. We had dairy
cows, and we'd sell the milk around the village.

'Twas an old farm we'd rented. Most of the small farms—well, I
suppose you call them sharecroppers over here. We didn't have running
water. We had to carry water from a well, probably about three hundred
yards down the valley. And of course if you don't have water, you don't
have flush toilets. My mother thought flush toilets was a very, very
unhealthy thing to have in the house. Oh, she thought that was
terrible. [*Laughs.*] We didn't even have electricity on the farm; did most
of my homework by kerosene lights. I remember electricity coming
into the village, in about 1929. I thought the streetlights were really
something.

We went on welfare. We moved out of the farm, into a nearby village.
You see, with my mother being the wife of a farmer, she did not qualify
for the widow's pension. We had no pension. My two oldest sisters,
they went into maid service. One sister went to work in the post office
in one of the nearby villages, and my other sister went to work in one
of the more well-to-do families in Wrexham. And then my brother quit
school when he was thirteen and went to work for the local grocery
store as an errand boy. And if I remember correctly, his salary was
three shillings a week and whatever he could eat.

It was quite difficult, but then we had nothing to compare it to. We
felt, well, it was life, and we didn't realize that we were practically
destitute. I went to local schools. I'll never forget H. Ellis Hughes—
marvelous guy. He was the principal of the grade school I went to. He
was proud of the fact that he was Welsh, and he had a magnificent choir
with the kids. If you went to his school, you went one of two

paths. You either took a scholarship class, which meant you went to high school, or you went in the choir. There was no in-between. And, since only a few of the kids were able to go through the scholarship class—for instance, the scholarship class where I sat was probably about twelve kids out of a school of about five hundred—it'll give you an idea of the size of the choir. [Laughs.]

The high school was in Wrexham. I was the only one of the four kids who went to high school, because we couldn't afford to send the other three. When they started working, then I could be sent. I graduated from high school when I was sixteen—this is in 1934—and I answered an advertisement and went to work for the telephone company in England. Things changed remarkably then. They sure did. I was bringing in a steady salary, nineteen shillings a week, about three and a half dollars a week. From then on, I was on the way up. Of course, my mother was the one that noticed the difference, because all of a sudden she had two incomes coming in. My two sisters were married by this time, and my brother and I looked after my mother.

I was a telephone man. I climbed poles, I'd dig holes, I installed telephones, I put in telephone exchanges. I enjoyed working with electrical things, and I certainly enjoyed telephone work, so I guess I got a little bit of a reputation.

I remember when war was declared. We were expecting the bombs to drop any minute, you know, and I spent that first night under the kitchen table, waiting for the bombs to come. They did bomb, but it wasn't until much, much later on. About twelve months later, they started to bomb on a regular basis. Here's this little village in the depths of Wales. Nobody's ever going to bomb that. Except that they constructed a model of a city on the top of the mountain, and they'd have little lights flashing to make it look like it was a big city, so that when the bombers would come in—the poor Germans—they just bombed. They killed about twenty sheep, and there's craters all over that mountain—nothing else but craters.

They did bomb Liverpool, and the route to Liverpool was directly overhead of our little village, so we'd hear the bombers going in night after night after night. We had to have blackout, because if we didn't have blackout then the navigators in the German airplanes would take fixes, you see. Living in a blackout is quite something. You grope your way around. I mean no flashlights. You had to feel your way around and go into buildings and grope your way in. And, of course, being a telephone man, you'd go off on emergency. So you'd have to drive out at night, and you had these special headlights—things that are just little slits, and you could hardly see with them. You had masks over the headlights and little slits in the front and little hoods over the slits. You could see somebody coming, but there was no light at all. All cars and motorcycles, they all had these little hoods on the headlights.

At the time of Dunkirk, they were looking for people that had experience in radio so that they could form small groups to locate any enemy spy stations that might start up, because they were expecting if there was an invasion of England a lot of spy stations to start up. The notice came around to the post office requesting the nomination of anyone who had radio background. I don't mean programming; technical radio background, the use of radio equipment. My boss contacted me and asked if I would be interested, and I said yes.

I went to Nottingham, about seventy miles from home. In England that's a long way. You go more than a hundred miles either way, you fall in the water, you know. I trained there for about four months. Special training, learning Morse code, direction finding, how to handle a gun—because we expected if we had any trouble we'd have to use a gun. [Chuckles.] We were a civilian outfit attached to the War Office, a sort of paramilitary group for antispy work, you see. It did sound exotic, only nothing ever happened, because they never invaded. Finally, about twelve months later, the group was disbanded and I went back to the telephone company.

I was transferred down to Cardiff, in South Wales, about one hundred miles in the other direction. I had an important job there. I was the electrical supervisor in charge of the head post office, which included about eighty people, telephone exchanges, toll exchanges, teletype operators, the repeater station, and all the electrical stuff in the post office—I had to keep them all working. I loved that; I'm a fixer. I was pretty young at that time. Let's see, it was in 1941; I was just twenty-three years old.

The war had been on for two years, and all this time I'd been trying to get into the RAF. Oh, my gosh, yes, I wanted to fly. But I was in a protected industry, and if you left a protected industry to go in the service, they'd drive you back again. They told you when you could go. A lot of telephone people had already gone into the army, see, and they were hanging on to supervisors that had the heavier technical background. I had to run this post office in Cardiff with—pardon the expression—women! Which was a novelty then. Now I don't mean operators. I mean actually doing the wiring and maintaining the equipment. So I had young women, boys too young for service, and men too old for service.

Well, all this time I applied—oh, I guess it must be four times—to be allowed to join the RAF. Finally, in 1942, when they began to get ready for the invasion of North Africa, all the training schools were looking for more and more people, and finally I was given permission to join.

I joined the RAF in 1942 as a navigator. I wanted to be a pilot, but they said, "Ooh, you got all this electrical background, and you know

mathematics, and you can handle a radio—h'mm, you're a navigator."
So I was a navigator. Oh, a big disappointment. Well, after going
through boot camp and the early training courses, I found myself on
the *Queen Elizabeth* coming across the Atlantic to Canada to train. No
warning at all. You couldn't train too much in England. You'd likely be
attacked by German airplanes. So the training was done in Canada or
in the States or in Rhodesia. I came over just before Christmas, '42, and
I left about September, I guess—about nine months. I trained in
Canada in an airfield on Lake Huron, Ontario. Oh, land of milk and
honey! You see, Ontario is such a big agricultural land, and there was
so much food. I think that's another one of the reasons why they
trained in Canada, just so that they could build the guys up physically.

So, for the New Year, 1942 to 1943, I went to Detroit, to see what a
big city looked like. That was my first sight of the U.S. Oh, my God,
what an impression that made! Overwhelming—absolutely overwhelming! You know, having been in England, blacked out for three
years, and coming down and seeing Detroit—automobiles and Christmas lights, all the life and the activity.

That's where I met Louise. I'm a war bridegroom, you see. We met at
a USO dance at a YMCA in Detroit. There was I in uniform, and Louise
was a hostess there; and we got talking and found out we both loved
music, and before you know it, I was engaged. The second time I saw
her I proposed to her. I didn't want to propose to her the first time,
because I thought it was a little bit fresh. I got down every other week.
Eight hours on the bus. I had to do my courting fast, because when you
have a forty-eight-hour leave and sixteen hours of travel time . . . . I
saw her six times. After I left Ontario, I didn't see Louise for three
years.

I went back to England on the *Queen Mary*, and I continued my
training in England for four more months. Then I went out to North
Africa, to Cairo—late '43. We went on missions from Benghazi, flying
up in the Mediterranean, because by that time the Germans were out
of Africa; they were in Italy. But they were still attacking the British
shipping, so we were protecting the British ships against the German
attacks, submarine and air attacks. And February the twenty-second,
Washington's Birthday, 1944, I was shot down, north of Crete on the
Aegean Sea.

The Germans were still in Crete, and they were having a very tough
time trying to keep them supplied because we were attacking them.
We were flying out of Tobruk. They were trying to get this convoy
through, and we were given the job of attacking this convoy. We sank
the supply ship, but my plane was shot down. The pilot was killed
when we hit the water. There were three planes shot down, and I was
the only one that came out of three planes. We were only about fifty

feet off the water when the plane caught fire, and we just went straight in the water. Didn't have a chance to parachute or anything. I didn't have much time to think. I didn't say any prayers, didn't have my life flash in front of me or anything like that. It was just a couple of seconds.

When I came to, I was in a plastic bubble. I had to release my escape chute, open the escape hatch, and get out. When I came up, there were no planes in sight. The supply ship was sinking. The two German destroyers were still there, just about half a mile away, and I was hoping they couldn't spot me, because Crete was only about three miles away, and if I could wait till darkness, I could easily make it. Then I could get in touch with the Greek underground and be out of there. But a German plane came around to look at the wreckage and he spotted me in the water and the destroyer came over and picked me up.

A bunch of nice guys in that destroyer. This was an Italian destroyer with a German crew, and the only place that had a lock on it was the captain's shower. So that's where they locked me—in the captain's shower. The engineering officer came down and asked me if I was comfortable and took my clothes and took them down in the engine room and had them dried for me and gave me a pair of socks. He was quite friendly, a nice guy.

The next day they had me up on deck, asking questions. I was prize exhibit number one. They wanted to know all kinds of things. "Ask him this, ask him that." They wanted to know who won the soccer final, and who was it who kicked the goals, and how are things in England, do you have enough to eat. And I thought if things in prison camp are going to be like this, it's not going to be too bad.

So that was it, and I went up to Stalag Luft One, up on the Baltic coast, and I was there for fifteen months. Prison camp, as I experienced it, wasn't as bad as it has been painted. They put you behind barbed wire, and they give you food and Red Cross parcels and clothes, and say, "Look, if you don't give us trouble, we won't give you trouble." It was confining, it was cold, it was miserable, but it was endurable. Not enough to do. That's the boredom more than anything else. But I was lucky, really, because a group of us—Canadians, English, there were no Americans in that group—we got together and we said, "Look, why don't we stick together?" So we were all put in the same room, fourteen of us, and we stuck together. We said, "Why don't we pool our Red Cross parcels?" We would pool the food and somebody was appointed for a cook for this week and somebody'd be the KP for this week, and we'd take it in turns, and we ate well. We didn't really starve until later on in the war, when the Red Cross parcels didn't come through and we had to live on German food, which wasn't so good.

There was almost a college there, with collections of books. You could find anybody that could teach you almost anything you wanted to know. Sanskrit? There would be a guy that'd teach you Sanskrit. There was a course there on how to organize trade unions. There was a course there on automobile racing. There were excellent courses.

There were well over a hundred tunnels dug in our camp. The problem with a tunnel is getting rid of the dirt, you see. The Germans would see fresh dirt all over, and, "Where did the dirt come from?" We flushed dirt down the toilet, we stuffed dirt in the hollow walls, we stuffed dirt in the roof. We had all kinds of ways to get rid of dirt. But nobody ever got out through a tunnel, because the Germans had microphones in the ground and they knew how far you got. And when you got so far that you're likely to break out, they would run a tractor backwards and forwards and all the stuff would fall back down again.

There was some escapes from the camp. There was one guy who was an Olympic hurdles champ. He decided to try to escape from there.

They built a dummy fence in the camp itself and this guy would practice. It just looked like a guy who was practicing his Olympic games, but actually it was a model of a fence. And he kept on practicing faster and faster, until he got it down to go over that fence in two and a half seconds or something like that. On this one day, he had somebody pick a fight over there and somebody started to play a game over here, and the guards were watching the game or watching the fight. And he went over that fence and they didn't see him. They picked him up about a week later, and the German officer who was interrogating him asked him how he got out of camp. He said, "I jumped over the fence." The German officer wouldn't believe him. He says, "It's impossible for you to jump over that fence, in daylight, with the guards around." He said, "Well, I went over that fence in two and a half seconds." And the guard said, "Well, if you can go back at the same speed, you won't be punished." So he went back over the fence in the same two and a half or three seconds, and the German officer said, "Hmph, go on. Stay in and don't bother us anymore."

We had a radio of our own that we put together ourselves. Do you watch "Hogan's Heroes"? Well, it was just like "Hogan's Heroes." The only parts that we had to bribe the Germans for were the vacuum tubes. Remember the old vacuum tubes? We couldn't make vacuum tubes. We bribed German guards to give us those. All the rest—the tuner and the condenser, the coil, the wiring—everything was made from things we'd picked up around the camp—barbed wire, clothesline, and bottle necks. And it was made so it could be taken apart, and every day it was put together in a different barrack. Two guys would run this radio. They'd pick up the BBC from London, and they'd take the message down in shorthand. Newsboys would take the news all the way around the camp and read it in every room.

Then toward the end of April, the Russians were getting awfully close to Berlin. We could hear the Russian artillery hitting Berlin. And then one night, I think it was about May the first, the Germans walked out—just disappeared. It was about two in the morning, and immediately our spies—we had lookouts watching and waiting for this—they came and dragged me out of bed, because I was to have a job in the office telephone exchange. So I had to go down at two in the morning, walking across the prison camp. My God, was that eerie! Walk over to the barbed wire, into the areas where the Germans lived, and you had never been there. "There's a switchboard. Make it work." I had to figure out how this German switchboard worked and get the batteries going and get it working.

There was one day after the Germans had gone and the Russians hadn't arrived yet. And then the next day the Russians came in and took over the area. We were there for three weeks with the Russians. Then American bombers came to take us out. It took them two and a half days to fly us all out, twelve thousand Allied flyers.

I rejoined my family and immediately sent a telegram off to Louise, saying, "I'm coming." And it took me nine months to come. You see, after the war was over there was no way for an Englishman or a Frenchman or an Italian to get over here, because all the passages were booked by Americans—soldiers coming home with their war brides. It took me nine months before I finally found the right guy in the Air Ministry in London who controlled the boat passages coming over to Canada. I asked him what it's worth to him, and he said, "Forty pounds. And as far as the records are concerned, you're married to a Canadian girl and you're a Canadian war bridegroom." So I came over on the *Aquitania* with about ten thousand Canadian war brides—not bridegrooms, brides.

And then I had a problem getting across the border from Canada. The customs guy said, "It's too late now. Come back tomorrow."

I said, "Can't I fill in these papers now?"

"Oh, okay, come on back to the office." He was a big, big guy, and he's filling in the application: "What's your name?"

"Tacwyn Morgan."

"How do you spell that?"

Well, I told him "T-a-c-w . . ."

He said, "That's an interesting name. It reminds me of a book I just read."

"Do you mean *How Green Was My Valley?*" And he was so delighted, he just made out a visitor's permit for me right then.

Louise was waiting for me. She'd been waiting all day. Well, it was quite a shock when we saw each other, quite a shock. You know, memories change, and her image of me and my image of her were quite different from what we really expected. You see, the person who writes letters—I mean there's no accent in the letters. And the person that wrote the letters and the person that you knew—it was very hard to get the two of them to merge, to be the same person again. Took us about three or four days or so. And all of a sudden we realized we were the same people. We looked at each other and decided, "Yes." So we were married. Having been a prisoner of war, I had the right to ask to be released any time I wanted to, and I wrote back to the RAF and said I would like to be demobilized.

At first I was very shy here and I wouldn't go to the store to buy anything. I'd go in and ask for a loaf of bread. They'd say, "What'd you say?" 'Twas the accent, you see. So I wouldn't go shopping, I was just so shy. So I took a Dale Carnegie course—at Louise's instigation. We were making about fifty dollars a week and really couldn't afford it, but she said, "That's what you need." I took the Dale Carnegie course, and *wow!* did that ever. . . .

I was just a high-school graduate, so I realized that a degree—just the possession of a sheepskin—carries some weight. We were going past the University of Detroit one night, and I happened to say, "Gee, I wish I could go to night school." Louise took me in there and we signed up. I got my degree over seven years of night school, in mathematics.

I went to work for the Michigan telephone company back in 1946. I'm still with the same corporation, different departments. I transferred to a special computer project in the marketing department, and I became rather knowledgeable in computers. I built up a reputation of being the guy that can—give him a piece of chalk and a blackboard and he would explain any technical thing. I was assigned to head up the computer portion of the executive training course. So here I was—this shy Welsh boy in big heavy farm boots—talking to hundreds of the top executives of the Bell system.

It's a pretty wonderful life—everything. I can't put my finger on it—not anything in particular. How easy it was to get an automobile. How easy it was to buy a house. To be able to scrounge enough money together to put a down payment. All the years my brother was there in England, he never got on to buying a house. And he'd been working then for twenty years for the post office.

You know, you can get a radial-arm saw in Sears and Roebuck. You couldn't get that in England. You'd have to save up twelve months to get a radial-arm saw, and there'd be so many other things . . . . You don't have so much disposable income. In England your income is to live with.

I've never regretted it. No, my home is here. I like America. I like Americans. I like their freedom. It might be a little bit of this feeling that in England I was a Welshman. Back there when I went to work for the telephone company, I was a "Welsh kid from the hills." That's how I was known. It put you in your place, you know. In America, you don't have that feeling.

And I like the booming and the surging and the drive. Look what they've done with computers! Computers have been my life for the last twenty years. Even if I say so myself, I think I've been to some extent instrumental in getting computers used in the Bell system. I was the first one to recommend that they use a computer for handling all service-order systems. We put this in Detroit *against* the wishes of the head office. We fought tooth and nail to get this in. The support I got and the feeling of adventure in doing something that nobody'd ever done before—you could do this in America. I could never do it in England.

I've had a very rich life since I've come over here. The fabric of life has been very, very rich. Very, very rewarding. I can't imagine my getting that same kind of reward anywhere else. In Canada or in England, no, I wouldn't get the same. Of course it's all Louise's and my relationship. The relationship—that's the core of how much it developed. And it's difficult for me to separate the United States from Louise. It's Louise to me.

# Frieda Ross

······················FROM GERMANY, 1948······················

*An attractive blonde in her early fifties, she works as a laboratory technician in a large cosmetics firm in Connecticut. She and her husband and four poodles live in a neat, split-level house, furnished with European flavor. She is a talented needleworker and an excellent cook and pastry chef. Every weekend, holiday, and vacation afternoon, she serves coffee and homemade cake with whipped cream, remembering her favorite Bavarian custom.*

It sort of was an odd feeling, I guess, if you lose a war. I don't know—the youth couldn't see the faults of it all, actually. I mean Hitler; to me, I didn't know what he did, but he was almost like an idol for the youth, you know. The youth all liked him. They didn't see what he'd done wrong, really. Hitler Youth and all that—they had uniforms like the Boy Scouts here. They were really big in sports, swimming, running, any kind of gymnastics. The little ones, from ten to fourteen years old. I belonged to it. Well, you had to, from school. You weren't really asked. If you went to school, you had to go there. But I didn't belong to the *Bund der Deutsche Mädchen* [League of German Girls], the ones from fourteen to eighteen.

Since I was only a teen-ager, the war didn't bother me that much. I didn't know any different, really. I went to school, we went out skating, and in summer we went swimming. There was nothing open, like cafés or dancing. Usually in Germany the girls looked for boys three, four, or five years older. I don't know why. But that group was gone during the war. That's why, when the war was over, we went with the American GI's.

When they came in and took Munich—actually, you know, it was no fighting. Munich gave up within an hour. I think they raised the white flag and gave up. And then the first ones were the Seventh Army. Then more or less for a month there was disorder. That was the worst time. The government was no more, and the Americans didn't have a government yet. All the jails were opened. All the prisoners got out; all the prisoners of war got out. We weren't afraid of the Americans, but we were afraid of all the other prisoners who got out. They started to shoot at the Germans. I don't know what they'd done to them, if they'd done anything to them or what, but they were actually—some of them were volunteers, and they came from camps in Poland or somewhere, and they'd worked for the Germans. How they got there, I don't know. But those were the ones who were then all turned loose. There was a curfew. You had to stand in line for bread; I think for about a month, maybe, until the Americans really took over.

Not too far away from us was a prison camp for English and French soldiers; and, well, I was a young girl, and when I went by there they always waved. But you weren't supposed to talk to them. And then when they got out, we started to talk to them, and they gave us some food. Well, they were very nice.

Then the GI's got friendly. At first you met them just riding around. They just stopped with the jeep and asked you this and that. I met a couple of them through friends, when people started to work for them. Well, when you met one and you went out, then you met friends of the guy. "You have a girlfriend?" "*Ja.*" "All right." Then they went out together. At the very beginning, when we went out with them, the army even had these small trucks or buses, and they even took the girls home. The Germans—once you started going out with the GI's—were very nasty. They resented that! I know girls that had their hair cut. Yeah, they were very resentful, the Germans. And those were the son of a guns who weren't in the war! My mother didn't like it, either. Not because they were the enemy—I don't know, maybe because they were men not speaking the language, maybe. I brought them home, too. They brought us food. They brought my mother coffee and things like that—what we didn't get for a long time.

We went out in a group. We never went out singly. It was quite a group. There was Ingrid, Helga, Gisela. They had those NCO clubs, Red Cross clubs, dancing. Oh, you could go many places where the Germans couldn't go. Only a GI could take you in. They were sponsored by the army, but they were originally German clubs, cafés. They just took them over, I think—something to do for the soldiers while they were there. In Garmisch they had a couple of big hotels where the GI's could go on vacation. Being in Munich, we went to Garmisch a lot. Well, the GI's had cars, so you went in for a show or something. It was a lot of fun. Oh, yeah, it was fun. We had a good time.

Jim was one of the first or second boyfriends I had. I had a couple I went out with, but I sort of stuck a little bit with him. I went with him for three or four years over there, and we wanted to get married. But—no marriages. One of the women's organizations over here was behind all that—trying to stop the war brides filtering into the States, I think. Of course, a lot of illegitimate children got left there because of that, too.

I think it would have been much nicer if we could've gotten married first and stayed there. I mean, first of all, living with the guy would have made it easier to get to know him, I think. But coming over here and *then*. . . . You meet these people in the army, they are GI's, away from home, not civilians, and when they come out, they are different people. It's kind of a shock. A new country, a new life, and a new guy. That was hard, yes.

Jim was shipped home in March, and I came in November. I had to wait until my papers came. My parents were sort of disappointed that I met somebody and left. He could have been French, English; it didn't matter. My mother never admitted it, but maybe, deep down, she did blame the Third Reich that she had to give up her daughter. She was a little bitter because of that. She didn't even say good-bye. She didn't even go to the airport.

When I came here, I was ready to go back; but then I was too proud. Well, it was a big difference from Germany. I was lucky, because I came out here to Middletown. If I had met somebody from New York, I wouldn't be here. [*Chuckles.*] Well, that airport out there was sort of a shock. It was very small then, you know, compared to the European airports. Idlewild, they called it then. That was a terrible thing. It was only wooden barracks. I mean Munich was there with a *brick building!* And then you drove through New York and saw all these—I always thought they were balconies, and they were fire escapes. And those buildings! Those brick buildings with no stucco on them! I thought they didn't finish them. We don't have them over there. When I looked at all those different sections they had there, I would never have stayed, no. I think I would have worked and went back home again. So it was really disappointing, until you came out in the suburbs.

I came in November, and I didn't get married until February. But then I got married on "Bride and Groom," on television. I was staying with Jim's family, and I used to watch that program, and they must have said something about writing in, and we did write in. They took us right away, because we met in Europe and he was sent home first. So we went in for an interview, and they liked our story. It was a different story to tell on TV, rather than the normal, you know. They put us on—I remember it was a Monday. It was George Washington's Birthday, and they figured probably they have even more people watching.

My husband's parents hated it. His father was the vice-president of a bank, and they were very well-to-do, and they wanted a big wedding. I thought it was quite interesting. It didn't bother me at all. I had no family here, so I couldn't care less, really. To me, I must really say honestly and truly, it was more of a show. I really didn't take it that serious that I even was married. It was really a show. They did everything—the wedding gown, makeup, everybody dancing around you, and what have you. They gave all that they advertised—bedroom set, vacuum cleaner, ice chest, wool blankets, silver, whatever. They gave all that they announced.

Well, we lived with my in-laws for a while. My mother-in-law knew all the elite in town. One was the vice-president of the electric company, and another one owned a store. They sort of had their circle. What are they playing? Bridge, maybe. I sort of went along with them, you know. But I missed the cafés—which are nice and cozy to sit in. The coffee in the afternoon, and the cake.

I wanted to do something. I got tired of sitting home, and I went downtown and got a job. I started out in a department store, in the budget dresses, and then I moved around in other departments and I thought it was quite nice. And I guess they must have liked me. They asked me to stay and be a buyer there. I didn't realize what that was. And going to New York sort of frightened me a little bit, I think. Well, I saw an ad in the paper that they were looking for somebody in a laboratory, and because I was a pharmacy assistant in Germany, I trotted up there and I met Dr. Sawyer. He was quite impressed, and he assured me it would be a much better job; they paid more. Oh, I loved it. I really loved it. I loved the lab work.

Jim went to engineering school, but he never finished. That was one of the reasons, I think, why we didn't get along. He didn't have an education. My disillusionment came soon, but I stuck it out for six and a half years. Jim must have been odd. He was odd. He was really odd—even toward me. One thing that would really bug me. In the army, he was always a nice, neat dresser. Well, he had to be, in the army, right? And as a civilian he couldn't care less, and I think that's one of the things which I really didn't care for. But then other things, too. We drifted apart. I met a lot of German people, and I sort of palled with them, and he didn't feel like going. I think just being obstinate—he was just funny. Yet he was a nice guy. He wasn't a rotten son of a gun. I still wouldn't say that. I think he made a nice husband for somebody, but he wasn't my type at all. I would have never picked him as a civilian. That's why I say it was a completely different person. Actually, I almost knew before I got married, and yet I didn't want to go home. I didn't have any money and didn't know anybody who I could turn to, you know. Had I had friends or somebody here, then maybe I wouldn't have got married. I was all by myself. I came just to him and was more or less depending on him and the family.

A lot of German girls made that mistake. I think those guys who maybe stayed in the army wasn't so bad off. A lot of them made it a career, and I often think those probably didn't make so bad, because those guys never changed. But I think a lot of the girls said the same thing I did—that they changed.

I drifted with the German group and Jim sort of drifted, too. After a while I saw that this was no man for me to continue the rest of my life, if there was a way out—a decent way out. Well, I got divorced, and then I met Mike and got married all over again.

I go back to Germany almost every year, and I keep an apartment there, but I don't think of going back to live. The first time I went for a visit was in 1955 and I liked it there. I was glad to see my parents again, and Ingrid was there and we went out. I guess I sort of thought, "Gee, it's nice here, too." But not nice enough for me to stay. Things there got better and better after that, and I used to think, "Well, you could have stayed there, too." But as you get older and older, you don't want to go back. You know, if you live that long so far away, your friends drift, too. I know a lot of people, but I have no one anymore—no close friends anymore. And now since I don't have my mother anymore, it's different maybe. But I still keep the apartment, just in case anything happens to Mike.

# Tanaka Simpson

*She was one of the first Japanese girls to marry an American soldier.*

My parents were against it and so was my grandmother, but at the last minute they agreed. Of course, they preferred me to stay over there, but they accepted it. We had to marry twice. In the embassy, that's just the paper. The real thing was the Shinto ceremony in my parents' place. A traditional marriage, with the wigs and the whole thing. My husband had to take his shoes off and wear a kimono. You know, they bought the largest kimono, but it was still too small. I think he weighed about two hundred pounds at the time. He was very, very big, and I weighed only ninety-five pounds. But this was my grandmother's request. She insisted that we get married in Shinto.

# Keiko Grant

*Tiny, pretty, dressed in a bright silk kimono, she pours tea as we sit on the floor at a low table in her contemporary living room. A wall of windows overlooks a carefully tended rock garden. Her teen-aged daughter, almond-eyed, dressed in a bulky cheerleader sweater, is having a peanut butter sandwich in the modern kitchen, where a Japanese samurai doll sits next to the Mixmaster.*

I wanted to be stage actress, and I went to acting school two years. After that, movie company wanted me, and I joined the movie company in Japan. I was in so many movies, but I was just a new face. Hard to find me in the movie. My family said, "Where's Keiko?" One movie was *Rice*. This movie was very great movie, shown at the Cannes movie festival. Oh, I enjoyed that.

Once, I went at the location, near Mount Fuji. We finished that job, and I took the train—only myself—to come back to Tokyo. Five or six American boys on same train—soldiers. I had to carry suitcase, and they just came to me, then put the stuff on. So I said, "Thank you very much. You are very kind for me." But I didn't like sit with them, because I was scared for those people. But they came with me! All five or six men were very nice. The train arrived at Tokyo and each one gave me the card. They said, "Please give me your phone number." I said, "No, I'm sorry. I don't have any telephone. And I'm busy, I don't have any time to go out." So, anyway, I had six or seven card in my hand, but I didn't remember which one was which. [*Laughs.*]

I went back to the company and worked. One of the young boys, he graduated American school. I showed him that card, and he said, "Oh, that's quite interesting. If you want to meet one man, I'm going with you and interpret for you." We called up the man—I didn't know which one he chose. But he was very nice and handsome.

I never thought that I'd marry him. Japanese people—if I was going with American, everybody looked at me funny. You know, Japanese girl marry that American GI—they were disappointed, didn't like that. But I didn't care. He was very nice. Finally I liked him, and then, you know, I loved him. I wanted to marry him.

First thing, I wrote my parents a letter. They answered, "Please, stop going with American man, because we don't know him and we don't know his background." I wrote again that I want to marry him. My father wrote again, "I want you happy for life. That's why I'm against your marry him. But if you decide that's your situation, then we agree with you. But before you marry, you must bring this man to my house." So John went to my place and he was surprised.

Well, it was very huge home. We were quite wealthy. My father was insurance company man, branch manager. He was the big boss, and under him two hundred people worked for him. Japanese style—everybody came at one time, morning, then my father lectured, then they went. When John saw that, he was surprised.

My father hired the interpreter, but he tried to speak something, too. He wrote the Japanese characters in English, only the pronunciation. He told John, "Please, sit down. Please, eat." Then my father said that he's a very nice man, sincere man. But one thing my mother worried about, because if I marry, I'm going oversea. But she wanted that I'm happy.

After that, I think four months, we married and we lived in Tokyo. Later, we moved to Hawaii and had a baby girl. First I stayed home. But very, very lonesome and frustration, because I wanted to talk to someone. That's when I wanted to go to work—any kind. I heard that someone was wanted at the Japanese radio station, so I applied for the job and they hired me.

I was announcer and director and even patched up the machines. I had three hours, morning. One hour was disc jockey—Japanese folk song and Japanese popular song—and one was interview, and then I introduced Japanese cook or. . . . I interviewed many Japanese people that came to Hawaii, the most famous people—top businessmen, movie actors, government people, the prime minister, emperor's second son. And there was big benefit, too. I went in a beauty shop, that was free. I was going to market—free. Even I was going to a movie—free. They said they don't take my money. "Oh, that's all right. I'm glad you come to my place." Everybody knew my name. That was a gorgeous life.

During this time we got divorced. Then I was by myself with Lily. I worried about her, because every night—even midnight—I was going out. VIP came, I was going to the airport. They didn't have time, so I just went whenever they can, I just interviewed. Every night a party, party, party—every night. Every night I felt bad, I worried.

I hired a baby-sitter, but Lily didn't want her. She said, "Oh, mother, that's a waste of money. I can take care myself. Don't worry, mother. Go. You just go." She was not grumbly, she was not crying.

At that time, so many people wanted to marry me. Well, I liked my job. But after five or six years, I thought that's enough for me. Now I must be thinking about Lily.

Then one day my girlfriend came from Japan to visit me, and I took her to Hawaiian Village—some kind of garden, they had beautiful Hawaiian music. We enjoyed the dance, the coffee. All the young American boys came to me and asked me to dance, and I said, "Oh, no."

One boy came to the table and he sat by me. "Please dance with me, please." Everybody looked at me.

I said, "No. Please go away."

He asked, "Please, please dance with me."

I told my girlfriend, "Oh, I'm going to dance with him to get rid of him, then I go home."

When I came back from dance, two older men came and one said, "Never mind that boy. Dance with me." So I danced with him. They sat at my table, and we talked. They said they're from New York, and I thought that's interesting city, New York. They gave me the card. Bill said, "May I see you tomorrow night?"

"No, I'm busy, so I cannot."

"Could you write to me?"

I said, "Yes, sure," and I didn't intend to give my address to him. I never wrote, no. Because I did not like him. Just a dance, that was it. I completely forgot.

Then one month later, a man called me. He said, "I'm Mr. Grant. I met you at the Hawaiian Village. You remember me? Do you want to know how I got your phone number?" I had said that I'm going back to Japan and one month later I'm coming back, then maybe I work at the radio station. So he came three days before and he went to the airport. Every airplane from Japan he checked, he watched. Three days he did that, but he couldn't find me at the airport. So, finally, he checked all radio stations. We had two Japanese stations, and he called the other one. But he knew just my first name, Keiko; he didn't know my last name.

The girl said, "Oh, yes, I know that Keiko. She's in a different radio station." Then she gave him the phone number of the other radio station; that was my radio station. He explained how he came here, looking for me. So my radio station gave to him my name. . . .

I thought he came with business, but he said no, he's looking for me—from New York, just to look for me! So I went to dinner with him. He rented a car, and I saw three beautiful leis in the back seat. He said, "That's yours." Every day he brought a new lei. Then he told me that he wanted to marry me.

I said, "That's crazy. You don't know about me."

"I don't care, I just want to marry you."

Still I liked the job, but he pushed, pushed, pushed. He went back and every weekend he called me. Then he sent me ticket—me and Lily—round ticket from New York to Hawaii—and spending money, too. That was the time he wanted to buy ring, and I said, "No, no." So he bought for me beautiful wristwatch—quite expensive. I was a little bit guilty.

So I asked my girlfriend, because I had other boyfriends, too. She told me, "That man is a very sincere, honest man. *Lily* loves him. You choose that for *Lily*."

I liked my job, but I thought that was enough. I decided to marry him. I must be thinking about *Lily*. I left Hawaii, came here to New York, to this house. . . .

*Was it difficult to adjust to being a housewife
after the life you'd been living?*

No, not difficult. But one thing is that I didn't know anybody. I didn't know even neighbor. But every time I was out—clean the yard or something—we said, "Hello, hello." Then she said, "I make for you arrangement for tea." Yes, she introduced all neighbors. I was very, very happy. Then another neighbor told me about bowling group. Oh, my groups. I have bowling group, theater group, golf. Yes, I have lots of friends, very nice friends.

And some organizations call me to fashion model kimono, to talk about Japan. I'm happy that people invite me, that they want to know about Japan. Because some people is thinking about Japan in different way, old-fashioned way. I like to tell the people about my country, about Japanese life.

When I go back to visit Japan, they are interested in me. They invite me to the radio station and they interview me. They ask what I'm doing every day—my life, you know. I talk about American women, what they do, American life.

I'm so happy with that—interpreting for Japanese and for American.

# Colette Montgomery
···················· FROM FRANCE, 1946 ·······················

*She was eighteen in April 1945, when American soldiers liberated Paris. To her, they seemed "like gods—handsome, rich, healthy, victorious." Within two months she was married to one of them. That marriage broke up after a few years, but her second, to an official in Washington, D.C., has been very happy. Now in her fifties, she is a beautiful woman with classic features and bright blue eyes that dim with tears as she recalls her long-ago self.*

I was very unhappy with my family, and I just sort of said to myself, "Nothing can be any worse than this. I'm going to start a new life." So I married and I came to the United States. I didn't speak any English and my husband turned out to be an alcoholic. The marriage was a disaster, a total disaster. I had a brand-new baby and I was totally alone. His family didn't like me, either. I was living in Brooklyn with a baby, an alcoholic husband, and some hostile in-laws. I had a terribly hard time.

First of all, I had to learn English. I remember picking out books. The first book I ever read, I read it five times before I could understand it. It was a struggle, but it was terribly important to me to understand and to read. And then I became fascinated by the country, which I knew very little about. The kind of education that the French used to give to their children was very sketchy, very provincial—mostly French history and literature. Outside of Shakespeare, they don't know much about other cultures. I discovered a whole new world, so to speak, and I discovered that this is what I really wanted. This is where I was comfortable.

But my marriage was very bad. I was terrified. I was not trained to do anything, and I was surrounded by strangers. Finally, when my child was two years old, I took her and left with five dollars, one suitcase, and a single change of clothes. I only had two dresses. I found a place to live and a job in a store within the next two days. Things were not easy for me, and many times after that they were not easy, but I could do this here. Somehow, I think it works better here. In France, I don't think I would have been able to. The French are rather inflexible.

When I'm back in France and we talk about politics, I don't like to hear anything against the United States. They say, "Well, you're not French. You're an American." And when I'm over here, they say, "Well, of course, you are not an American, you are French. How can you speak?"

It's not easy to be a newcomer to this country. You're between two cultures. You have to have a very strong identity to know who you are. I've been here over thirty years, but no one ever says, "This is Colette." They introduce me and say, "This is Colette. She's French." They still do. Even my friends, who know me, call me French.

I got very interested in the American political campaign of 1956. Actually, that's why I became an American citizen, because I wanted to vote for Stevenson. The year before, I had already sent for the papers and I'd started filling them out, and then I would find very objectionable things in the questionnaires. Like: "Have you ever been a prostitute? Are you a Communist?" Things that were nobody's business. There was this very self-serving, sort of holier-than-thou attitude then. I would resent it terribly. And I would send the papers back—can you believe it?—with notes on them, saying, "I desperately want to be a citizen, but I find some of the questions very offensive. I cannot go through with it." But in 1956, I wanted so badly to vote for Stevenson, I thought, "Well, no matter what happens, I'm just going to go through with it." Meantime, my friends said to me, "Oh, you're never going to become a citizen. You and your big mouth and all this letter writing. You're never going to get your papers." But, somehow, I sat and did the whole thing, and in spite of all these notes, it went through. I became an American citizen on the fourteenth of July! That was my last Bastille Day as a French citizen. I was happy, but at the same time I was very nostalgic. I felt very peculiar.

Years later, after I was married again, there was a party at the State Department and Stevenson was there. At that time he was ambassador to the United Nations. My husband said, "I'm going to tell him about you." And he went over to Stevenson and they talked, and Stevenson said, "Please bring her over, I'd like to meet her." I think he sort of got a big kick out of my getting my citizenship in time to vote for him. He was very gracious. I was absolutely speechless, but he just bowed and said, "Madam, I wish there had been more Frenchwomen like you in that election."

# Enzo Berardi

*Elegant and courtly, he is a captain on a passenger ship based in Miami.*

I came up during the Fascist regime. I had to belong to the party, to the youth movement, the Young People's Fascist Movement; otherwise, I couldn't go to school. We used to have the uniforms—black shirts and short gray pants and little caps and blue scarf. And I remember that we had to go on Saturdays and Sundays to meetings and drills. You know, put your uniforms on and marching and. . . . I liked it. Well, who wouldn't? Kids, flags, drums, singing, getting together—all kinds of activities for boys of that age. You built up a sense of comradeship between boys.

We did have military training at that time, too, through the school—knowledge of small arms, rifles, pistols, and machine guns, and so forth. Well, again, it was appealing. I mean, it's something fascinating about guns. And these were real; they weren't toys. Well, we weren't small children—I was already ten years old.

I didn't come in contact with any German troops until 1934, and then they officially took over the government of the city. We were still going to school. We started having German instructors. I didn't have any dislike for them. They were excellent instructors—disciplined, very strict, and they didn't put up with any nonsense. We changed from Italian small arms to German small arms. Now they were already looking at us as young soldiers—more than just a youth movement. I'm talking about, say, thirteen years old.

At the end of 1944, the beginning of 1945, I was already seventeen years old and going to a nautical high school—a special high school just for the nautical arts—navigation and astronomy and whatnot. I wanted to be a merchant marine officer. The official cease-fire came to effect on May 1. And I graduated at the end of '45.

It took me four months to get my first assignment. One of the main reasons was because there was no merchant marine. Most of them had been sunk during the war. But I was assigned as the cadet officer of one of the remaining passenger ships. It belonged to the Italian Line. It was run by the Italian crew and officers and unlicensed personnel, but it was still under the Allied government. They were carrying a lot of troops back—American troops from the Continent back to the United

States. And also they carried war brides, American war brides, back to the U.S. We had the Mediterranean run, and we went from Southampton to Le Havre, through the Strait of Gibraltar to Marseilles, then Genoa, Naples, Palermo, Haifa, Beirut, and Alexandria, Algeria, Casablanca. And in each port—but especially Southampton, Le Havre, Genoa, and Naples—we picked up war brides. We were carrying twelve hundred war brides every trip from, let's say, age sixteen up to fifty. And quite a few had babies.

Part of the complement of the ship was a unit of nurses and doctors. These were army personnel, American army personnel, and they were assigned to the vessel to assist in any way possible: medical assistance to the American war brides coming from Europe to the United States.

That's where I met my wife. She was a nurse in the army corps. We had a very beautiful courtship aboard the ship. Oh, yes, very nice! We were together practically a year, and that's when we fell in love and decided to get married. I got married before getting off the ship. I was not quite twenty-one. I remember I had to have permission from my mother to get married.

I was sure that once my future wife could be discharged from the army, she would come to live in Italy. That's what I had in mind, but she didn't share the same idea. It was either she comes over with me and she's out of her own environment, or I have to give up mine to stay with her. I liked her, so I decided that I will try. I didn't have any choice. But if I wouldn't have been married, I wouldn't have stayed. Definitely not. What for? First of all, I could not join the American merchant marine right away. I had to go through a lot of red tape in obtaining papers, in order to be able to work on an American ship. I was a little disappointed that it couldn't go any faster, but I had to go by the rules and regulations. In my line of work you had to.

In the meantime, my wife was discharged from the army and was working as a nurse in New York. I worked ashore. I recalled that there was an Italian family in Brooklyn who ran a catering service. I had met them as passengers on my ship, and they told me that if I ever decided to stay here, they would be very glad to help me. I went to them and, sure enough, they gave me a job right away. I was making sandwiches, preparing food. [*Laughs.*] That was funny. . . . It wasn't so funny then. As a matter of fact, I was very humiliated. Here I was supposed to be a naval officer, and I was making sandwiches!

Finally I got my papers and I left that job. But I couldn't sail as an officer. After the hostilities [World War II], an alien was not allowed to be an officer in the merchant marine. I had to go as an able-bodied seaman—physical labor, handling of the ship's gears, maintenance, watch-standing; that was all I could do then. I went to a seafaring union and became a member. Then I went to a hiring hall. I'm sure you've heard of that. The shipping companies call in their needs, and the union gives out the jobs to the men standing by and waiting.

I went through all this and was assigned to my first American ship—a freighter. I stayed on that ship about six months. At that time, there were no vacations. If you wanted to spend time at home you just had to quit. Well, I wanted to come home and see my wife, so I quit.

I decided to stay ashore for a while, but I just couldn't make it. I didn't like to be enclosed every day. The sea was my life. My wife saw that I was becoming nervous and irritable, and she advised me to go back to sea. And I did. The next day I was lucky enough to get a steady job on a tanker.

This was a little better. I stayed at sea six months and then I had two weeks vacation. And being on a tanker, I was going into port quite often. Whenever my wife had a chance, whenever I was within traveling distance from New York, she came to meet me. So we were seeing each other—oh, I would say about two or three times a month—but only for one day at a time. I had explained it to my wife and she accepted it and that was it. But it really wasn't good.

I became an American citizen at the end of 1952, and immediately after that I left the tanker and I went to school and I received my third-officer's license. Then I applied to a passenger line as an officer and I've been there ever since.

After I had some more sea time, I went to school again. I took another exam and I raised my license. I became second, and then chief executive, and finally skipper. Now I run a cruise ship out of Miami. I like it! Once you leave the dock, you're in command of this vessel and you have no one to tell you what to do. It's strictly up to your own judgment. I get a big satisfaction out of running a vessel. . . .

But my wife just couldn't get used to my being away so much. She began to get lonely. There was a deterioration. . . .

[In 1959 they were divorced.] I could have gone back to Italy then, but by that time I had adjusted myself to the customs and the way of life in this country, and as I matured, as I became older, I saw that there was quite a bit of security here. I felt safe. . . . I don't think that I would have felt the same way somewhere else. You can see it, read it in the papers today—in many parts of the world, governments are coming and going and changing, whereas over here you have some kind of stability that's very hard to find anywhere else. And I am—I am *proud* to belong to this society.

# Denise Levertov

*She is a distinguished poet, critically acclaimed in England and the United States. An activist as well as a writer, she gives freely of her time to a number of liberal causes and has participated in antiwar and antinuclear demonstrations. Sipping white wine and sitting tailor-fashion on the couch in her living room, she tells her story with warmth and enthusiasm.*

Because I didn't really belong in the place that I grew up in—nor did my parents—I have always felt somewhat like an air plant. I could exist just about anywhere. I love certain kinds of landscape and I prefer some company to others, but given some pleasant company and some books, I can exist just about anywhere.

I had a strong feeling for the English countryside, for British literature. I felt very closely related to both, but I wasn't actually English. In Wales, I was half Welsh, but I didn't speak Welsh and hadn't grown up in the Welsh cultural and social traditions, so I wasn't really Welsh. I was brought up to be very proud of being Jewish; but I was not Jewish, I was a Christian. Among gentile Christians I was the freaky product of a Jewish convert father. Among Russians I wasn't really *echt* Russian, because I was Jewish. Whatever it was, I wasn't it. I wasn't quite.

My father had come to England to live, not long before I was born. He was a Jew, a Russian Jew. He graduated from an important Jewish theological seminary, and then his father sent him to the university at Königsberg for a general Western education. While he was there, he read the New Testament and became convinced that Jesus was the Messiah. He rushed home to the south of Russia to give them the good news, literally the gospel, you know, and they thought he was a *meshugganer*, and they locked him in his room. He escaped through the window and went back to Königsberg and finished his studies. Then he traveled about what was then the Austro-Hungarian Empire, and he also went to what was then Palestine. He was a scholar and he gave lectures and talked about his beliefs.

My mother was the daughter of a doctor, who practiced in a mining village in the south of Wales. Her mother died when she was two, and her father died when she was eleven or twelve, so then she was completely orphaned. She went to live with relatives in the extreme north of Wales. She very much wanted to have a career and be an independent person, not a poor relation. And, of course, to be a schoolteacher was one of the few ways out at that period. Her uncle didn't permit her to take a job in Paris, because he thought Paris was too sinful, but he knew nothing about Constantinople—which was really much more sinful—and so he let her take a job in a Scottish church school there. She went out there on the Orient Express. And she met my father and was back within the year, to get married.

My father was offered a job as a professor at an institute of biblical studies attached to the University of Leipzig. His specialty was the Jewish origins of Christianity and Old Testament themes in the New Testament. He was still a Russian citizen, and my mother was a British subject, and so in World War I they were interned—not in a camp—they were under house arrest. As soon as the war was over they left. My mother was very concerned about her family in Wales, and he loved England, and they were eager to get out of Germany where they had by this time encountered a lot of hostility. They were enemy aliens, you know.

They got to England, and my father was ordained an Anglican clergyman, and he was appointed to a church in the East End of London, because they thought, "Well, he's Jewish; he should be in a Jewish neighborhood."

I was born in Ilford, which is a London suburb. My parents were somewhat exotic in their environment. They didn't think much of the local schools. I didn't go to school at all. My sister went away to a boarding school for about a year, and they said it made her stupider, so they withdrew her and she really had no formal education either. I was given lessons at home and I was a big reader. We didn't have a very concerted plan about it, but from year to year I seemed to be doing a lot of reading. My mother had a passion for history—history and geography. But after I was twelve I didn't do lessons anymore, really. I still can't do arithmetic, and I literally can't balance my own checkbook. I used to go to museums a lot, and I used to enjoy hanging around the Victoria and Albert Museum and other places like that.

When I was about twelve I started to study ballet. It was a school where you went every day. I did that until I was seventeen. I'd always written, and I'd painted, too. I knew I was a writer, I thought I was a painter, and I had the *chutzpah* to suppose that I was going to be a painter-writer-ballerina. But I went to some auditions and I fell flat on my face from nerves [*laughs*], so I did not feel I could make my way in the theatrical world. I was much too terrified of the whole scene. I made a big tragic scene out of it at the time, and I wouldn't listen to any ballet music for a long time; and I sort of went in a completely opposite direction and I became a Land Girl. Didn't they have them in

America during the war [World War II]? You did agricultural work while many of the farmhands were in the army.

And after that I became a nurse. I didn't go into it expecting to become a nurse, really. When I reached working age it was wartime, and you had to do something. Nursing was an exempted occupation, and I went into it originally to dodge the draft. It was a wartime thing where they gave you a kind of basic training and then put you to work. Then I stayed in it because it interested me. I began to think I might as well be training—get something out of it, advance in the profession, you know—since I liked so many aspects of it.

In 1947 I was working in the British Hospital in Paris, and I was fired for insubordination. I objected to forming part of a guard for the British ambassador, who was coming to unveil a memorial plaque. It was in my off-duty time, and I objected. So I got fired, and I was suddenly released into blessed freedom. I took off with a friend, hitchhiking through Europe. I met an American in Geneva in September, and we got married in December.

He had the GI Bill, so we remained in Europe for about a year, and I began to meet some Americans for virtually the first time. It's very hard to sort out my first impressions of Americans, as such, from my impressions of being newly attached to an American. I was adventurous, and it was just part of the adventure. And I began to read American literature, because when I first met Mitch, his rucksack was loaded with books—Sherwood Anderson, Faulkner, Frost. I had very little knowledge of American literature. I had been sort of incurious for some reason about it. In fact, like many English people, I had always thought of Henry James and T. S. Eliot as essentially British authors!

I was living with Mitch, partly in France and Italy and partly in England. The departure for America took place from England, from my parents' house. That was a traumatic event, because I did not know how long it would be before I would see them again. Although I hadn't actually been living permanently at home for some years, my room, all my childhood drawing books, and all sorts of things like that were still there. Well, I'd lived in that house all my life, you know. And I remember going through my desk and drawers and systematically throwing out all sorts of things—in a sort of ritual way, because it was really quite unnecessary. It was a kind of ritual, like closing up a house.

I was a GI bride, technically speaking. We came over on the *Queen Mary*. I had a wonderful first view of New York in the dawn, with these skyscrapers sticking up out of a rose-tinted mist. It was sort of Venetian looking, because there were kinds of palaces coming up out of the water. It was incredible! I never saw it like that again. I was somewhat queasy, because I was pregnant. And it took *forever* to get through customs. God, it was slow! I was absolutely exhausted by the time we got off that boat.

Mitch's brother was there, and he was going to drive us to their parents' house in Brooklyn. They're sitting in the front talking to one another, and I'm sitting in the back gazing around me. I was sort of in a daze by this time—fatigue and queasiness. Now for some reason I still thought that New York, because it was new by European standards, was going to be clean, like Switzerland. Well, the first thing I knew, we're driving through the Bowery, and there are bodies just lying on the streets. It's not what I'm expecting at all. It looked sort of dreamlike to me—just weird, totally weird. I'd never seen a neighborhood like that—wastepaper and bottles and bums flat out on the sidewalk. Then I saw a big electric sign that said *Kinsey*, over on the Brooklyn shore, and I thought it was an ad for the *Kinsey Report*, which had just come out. "Wow, they advertise books with big neon signs in America," I thought.

My next first impression was the following day. Mitch and I walked down from his parents' apartment to the shopping street, Kings Highway. It's a bourgeois Jewish section, very clean residential neighborhood. We were walking along the street, and I see some women with fantastic hairdos, very full, long skirts—it was the after-the-war fashion—lots of makeup. I say to Mitch—sociological observation, you know—"Well, how interesting. In England or in France, anywhere in Europe, a neighborhood like this wouldn't have tarts on the street, and they certainly wouldn't be walking around in broad daylight!" He said, "They're high-school girls." You see, the English high-school girl wore a gym tunic, a pudding hat, had uncurled hair, and usually had pimples—no makeup. I couldn't believe it. [*Laughs.*] These were just girls dressed up for Saturday evening, to go to the movies or something, perfectly respectable.

I think I had a severe case of culture shock, but I don't think that I acknowledged that I was suffering from anything. I kept discovering America in the shape of how to run your house, how to be a housekeeper. It's a little hard for me to separate social change from national change. My first experience of really having to count pennies was in America. We lived in a walk-up in the Village, and it was *very* tiny. The toilet was out in the hall and it had no bathroom. It had a washtub in the kitchen, with a shower rigged up over it. You'd climb on a chair, climb into the washtub, and take a shower. And the shower curtain would come and wrap itself clammily around you. And then these things came out of the wall, and I didn't know what they were. We put one in a matchbox and we went to the exterminator and we said, "Could you tell us what this is?" He said, "It's a *bed*bug! A *big* one." So that was a new experience.

We turned out to have some terrible neighbors—anti-Semitic and baby-hating they were. They spat in the baby carriage. They screamed at us. The baby would wake up in the middle of the night—what baby doesn't?—and *after* we'd gotten back to sleep, then the phone would ring and this woman would scream, "Why don't you shut up that damn Jew brat!" Oh, boy! But you see, those things could have happened to me in London, but they hadn't, and so I don't know which were *American* experiences. . . .

I had always written, and wherever I was I wrote. I had my first book published in England, but I really developed as a poet in America and I am considered to be an American poet. In coming to America, I had to deal with different speech rhythms, and if I was going to survive here and grow, I probably had to fall overboard for them the way I did. So that there are things that stick out of some of my early American-life poems. They probably stick out like sore thumbs, where I was earnestly and eagerly being American. My diction is sort of mid-Atlantic in many ways.

I have a very strong poetic drive, and I can't imagine not writing. So I think that even if I had stayed in England, something would have happened to me, but it's impossible to say what. I certainly wouldn't have evolved in the same way, because what was happening in American poetry in the fifties was very different from what was happening in England. England was not having a very good period. It was not a very stimulating period in poetry. America was kind of bursting out all over. In fact, twentieth-century poetry in English is dominated by American poets. You've got William Carlos Williams and Stevens and Pound and H. D. and Marianne Moore and Robert Frost and Cummings and Robinson Jeffers and Carl Sandburg. You've got a whole generation of very important poets, very influential poets. You don't have anything comparable in England. And so America was where it was really happening.

I taught at Vassar and at City College, at Berkeley and at M.I.T., and now I teach at Tufts. I came here as a visiting professor originally, and they asked me if I would like to stay. I'm a full professor here. In England, because I haven't gone through the academic mill and I got into teaching sort of through the upstairs window—well, I'd have to get a lot more famous than I am to be able to support myself in England.

I feel very involved with American life, and I have an obligation to follow through on that involvement. I'm now active in the antinuclear movement, and I was politically active against the war in Vietnam. During that war, every time I went to Europe I'd feel so embarrassed. I must confess that once or twice, since I had an English accent anyway, I would say, "I'm English."

My feeling for England and for Wales, Britain generally, has reasserted itself very strongly in recent years. Oh, I used to get a pang sometimes, thinking of primroses and a hedge, but I didn't go back to England for many, many years. Then I decided I *must* go back. I went in the summer of 1970, and I had this extraordinary experience of homecoming. As the plane flew over England, it began to happen. And then the train in from the airport passes these little back yards full of roses—absolutely undistinguished, but utterly English. I began to get this *feeling*, and when I finally stepped out actually on English soil, I understood why people kneeled down and kissed the soil. I felt just like that.

I went out for a walk that evening. It wasn't a neighborhood that I was familiar with—these were streets that I'd never walked on before in my life—but they had these features which were of the most astonishing familiarity, and that familiarity was astonishingly moving to me. I would get glimpses of people in their houses, sitting around their tables. Everything seemed to spell *England*. I thought to myself, "All these years I was homesick and never knew it."

# Joseph Bergman

···················FROM POLAND, 1963 ······················

*He is short and slight, balding, and speaks English with a heavy accent. He and his family live in a large, well-furnished ranch house on Staten Island. His two daughters appear to be typical young American women, fashionably dressed, interested in clothes, hairdos, and dates.*

First I have to mention that my father was very religious. He was an Orthodox religious Jew. Me, on the other hand, somehow I was more leaning to the Christian than to the Jewish beliefs, especially what was going on was the discrimination. Usually, let's say when the holy days came, they'd throw stones or pour water on us. I would call it religious discrimination. I didn't want to be discriminated, so I was trying to behave like the non-Jewish people. I was going to a primary school, mostly with non-Jewish, because in this little town where I lived most of them were Christian. There were three Jewish families only, there in the school. So mostly, I would say, my friends were Catholics, Polish, not Jewish friends. I grew up with them.

Until the Second World War, until 1939, nothing special happened in my life. I was just at that time twelve years of age. We lived in a little town, and there it wasn't bad. We stayed in our house until 1942, but when Eichmann issued the law that every Jew has to come and stay in ghettos, from there on the hell began. At the same time, he also issued a law that anybody that helps a Jew will be killed like a Jew. So anybody that gave you a piece of bread was risking his life.

We left our house and we were hiding ourself for about a few weeks only. This was still summer, so we slept in the field. We didn't have enough food. Everything what we got to eat, it was just from the neighbors only.

After three weeks they caught my mother. They knew that we are coming around—somebody told them. We know even who it was, yes. There was one Pole—a collaborator—he was waiting just to get our house and our one acre of field. So my mother was caught and they killed her right on the spot. At that time I slept in a neighbor's barn, and I heard the shot. I didn't realize what it was, but later on I learned what it was.

From then on everybody dispersed. Well, let me mention about my family. We were eight in our house, four sisters and four brothers. One brother and sister went to Israel in 1934. Another three sisters were staying in Lvov, eastern part of Poland, which is right now Russia. They were there when the Russians came. When mother was killed, the other two brothers went someplace to the villages. There were many Catholic priests help Jewish people, give them papers that they are Catholics. And based on this paper, they could get a job. Otherwise nobody would hire you—they were afraid because of the Germans.

I am the youngest one, I was fourteen already, and me and my father, we stayed still in the same place, in this town. From then on we are completely beggars only. We would only eat whatever we could get from the neighbors, and if there was a chance to help in the fields, we would work. But sometimes they even didn't want, because somebody might see us. We are sleeping in the barn or in the stable, and that's how we survived that one winter from 1942 to 1943.

Then, in 1943, in springtime, some of the neighbors finally told where my father is sleeping. They did it for the purpose only that they were afraid if the Gestapo will catch us and torture us, we'll say everything—where we slept, who gave us food, and so on. So they just told the Polish police, the collaborators. The same night, the police came to the barn, and with bayonets they were looking in the hay if I am there. But somehow—I don't know, intuition, whatever—I just got deeper alongside the wall, between the hay and wall, got very, very deep, almost to the bottom, so they couldn't reach me with the bayonet. I heard them walking and talking, and finally they went. And next day, when I walked out from the barn, a fellow told me, "What are you doing still here? Your father was killed last night. They were looking for you."

So I went on to another village, about fifteen miles away. I told them that I am from east Poland, because at that time in east Poland the Ukrainians were killing all the Polish people. So I just lied that I am from east Poland, where my father and parents were killed by the Ukrainian people. This was about two hundred miles away, and nobody will go there and check out. I was too weak to work on the farm, and I got a job as a shepherd. It was a widow that hired me, and I was staying with her. Yes, I was with her from 1943 to 1944, but then somehow she realized—she must have taken a look when I was sleeping—that I am circumcised, and she told me she was afraid and I have to leave.

So I went to another village and I say the same lie and I got a job, working in a field. He was a Communist, this fellow. He was waking me during the night, asking me a hundred times the same question—where I am from and so on—and I was always telling him the same story. But he didn't make me go. He was a Communist and he kept me. At that time the Germans were already backing off from the Russian front. When the Russians came, I was so happy that finally I am free. Free, but still I was afraid to go home. Because what happened—an underground was formed in Poland. These were the ones that were against the Communists. All these collaborators with Nazis and so on, they went underground and they were killing all the Jews that survived and returned back. Not only Jew—Polish, too. All Polish people what was Communist, they killed them. Anyway, I stayed with that farmer until 1946. Two years wasted time working on the farm, because I was still afraid to go home.

When I came in 1946 to my native town, to find out where is everybody, the neighbors told me that the two brothers and one sister came right away with the Russians in 1944. They right away came, they sold the house, they sold this one little acre field there. They sold it and they went west. [Chuckles.] West! Well, they didn't know where they went west. West Poland, Austria. Where I'm going to look? But it somehow happened that one of my cousins—he survived also—he came there to this little town to sell his house, and he learned that I am there. He tells me, "Listen, your brothers and your sister survived and they went to Austria, waiting there to emigrate to Israel. I will take you also to Austria." And he took me to a Jewish kibbutz there.

Well, the impression was very, very bad. All the kibbutzim were where the concentration camps were. All the displaced persons were living there. And everything was still surrounded with barbed wire. You could see even blood there on some walls. I didn't see that much of bloodshed like I saw in this concentration camp. Everyplace you went, they had special place where they executed people, shot them, and there you could see all of this blood—wasn't even washed off. So this made a very bad impression on me.

And it was a very religious kibbutz. I have to pray every day and I hate it. I hated it when I was with my father at home. So I escaped from this kibbutz. Well, they wouldn't let me go if they would know that I am going to a Polish camp to live with Polish people. You know how very religious people are: to grab a soul, to save it. It's not just to save a human being; it's just to save a once-Jewish soul. So I escaped from them, and I went to the Polish DP camp.

It wasn't that simple. They wouldn't accept you, knowing that you were a Jew. How come you are a Jew coming to live with us? So I got converted. It was very simple at that time. I came to them and I said, "I am a Jew and I would like to be converted." And you know how religious people are—the same like the Jews. If somebody will tell, "I want to be converted," they will take even a devil with the horns. It's the same thing with the Catholics. They grab anybody they can, just to convert him. I thought of converting during the war. During the wartime, seeing all this discrimination, I figured I don't want to be discriminated anymore; I will convert. I didn't do it during the war, because it wouldn't help me anyway, since Hitler was killing to the third generation anyway. It wouldn't help me, so I didn't do it.

But now I converted, and they made me a false displaced-person card. I was there for one year, but I couldn't stay there, because the Americans found out that I came after the war. Well, it was Polish administration, but all the rules were given from the Americans. Everybody that came after the war the Americans wouldn't accept— only those that were brought there by the Germans. So they kicked me out from this Polish camp.

They didn't tell me, "You have to go back to Poland," but they threw me out to a camp where all kinds of different people were. It was a camp for the people that didn't have a right to stay, the right papers; they kept them there. And the collaborators, they were there— Latvians, Lithuanians, Russians, Polish. There were a lot of collaborators. They were in this special camp, and they threw me there. One night, a Russian fellow was trying to brag how he was brave, and I realize he must have been killing also Jews! Well, in heart I was a Jew. I mean—you cannot change your nationality with religion. Once you are born a Jew, forget it, you are a Jew. I wasn't afraid of him, but I realized, "What I'm doing here between these people?"

I wanted to register myself for immigration to Canada. They told me I have to wait three, four years, and they want to send me someplace north to chop down the woods. I can build myself a house there and live together with the bears. I figured with my size and my muscles, I am not exactly the person to chop down the woods. That's not for me. So I was sitting doing nothing and waiting. Eating only the corn bread and what else they were giving—pea soup, I guess. This was our daily dish.

I realized I am wasting here my time. I knew that in Poland, schools are free. I can go to school, I can get some profession. So, in 1947, I went to Polish Repatriation Mission, and I released myself to return back to Poland. I went back in 1947. They gave me right away a little room there, and I started to work in a factory where they are making wagons and bridges. And there they sent me for a course as a locksmith. I wasn't satisfied with this. I said, "I have to be something more than a locksmith." So I started to take an evening course, bookkeeping course. I finished this one-year bookkeeping course, and I got a job in an office.

I still wasn't satisfied, so I went at evening to a high school, and this was very hard to work and go for four years at evening to a high school. Then they had special courses for college at that time, because they were short of higher-education people. They give you food, they give you everything free. So I pass the examination and I enter to college, and I was studying accounting from 1952 till 1957. I had everything free, plus stipendium—room and boarding, plus pocket money. I was living in a boardinghouse, since to get an apartment in Poland at that time is just like finding here a million dollars on the street.

After I finished college, I got married. And I got a job in an ammonia plant. Actually, we wasn't in bad situation. Once you are graduated, you got a good profession, they give you right away apartment. I got two-bedroom apartment, modern apartment with central heating, with everything. She was working and I was working, so we could save a lot of money. On Polish standard of life, we were not bad. And about personal freedom I cannot complain. I could go anyplace I wanted.

There was a Jewish girl there in the plant. Everybody knew about her. Nobody knew that I am a Jew. I still didn't say to anybody I am Jew. She was telling that she's going to Israel. At that time I went to her and told her that I am a Jew also. I asked her to find my family in Israel. She went, and she found my brother, and he wrote me a letter. Everybody thought that I am dead already. It's unbelievable! Resurrected youngest! The correspondence started that way, and finally in 1959 I decided to go to Israel. My wife had a mixed feeling, since she isn't Jewish, but she didn't live very close with her family, so she agreed. She said, "It's a sunny country. Even if it will be not good, sunshine gives you happiness." We decided that we'll emigrate to Israel.

I wanted to meet my family, this was one thing. At that time, also, I was already in contact with the cousin from the United States. So I figure out: What I have to lose? If I won't like there, I will go to America. So I left Poland with the thought that if I won't like it in Israel, I will try to get to the United States.

Israel didn't want to give me regular visa like Jew. They didn't trust me that I am a Jew. I wasn't registered as a Jew. I have to have proof I have brothers and get special visa. And my wife is not Jewish. They warned her that she might have some problem because of this. I was waiting one year to get the visa, and then the Polish government took away our Polish citizenship. That was the only condition to get us out.

I guess that if I would have stayed in Poland, probably my feeling about Judaism would have disappeared completely. I regained that feeling, being a Jew, when I came to Israel. The conversion didn't matter at all. No, it didn't take. . . .

The emigration to Israel wasn't that easy, either, you know. At that time they had a lot of immigrants, and they couldn't give you whatever you were expecting to get. So I was a little bit disappointed. I mean, I left Poland where I was already settled. I had everything—a nice apartment, furniture. I didn't have to worry about future—everything free, pension plan, social security, everything. You know how Communistic country is—I didn't have to worry. And all of a sudden, I am coming there as a new immigrant, and they are putting everybody into an asbestos shanty. If you came rich you could buy yourself a house, like Americans that do it. Well, I came from Poland. I didn't have a dollar, so this was the first step for all immigrants. It wasn't a city, it was just a colony of immigrants, near Nahariya.

I was sitting there for, I guess, about two months, and I was trying to get a job. Finally, I got a job as a bookkeeper. I was working for two and a half years as a bookkeeper. I was trying to get a job as an accountant, but it wasn't that easy. You have to know somebody. If you didn't have a push, forget it. We were just second class, if it comes to job position, because they knew that I cannot go anymore back to Poland, because Poland would never take me. When some immigrant came from England or Western Hemisphere, if they didn't like it they will go back. So they had to get the better jobs. They had better apartments, better sections, better city, everything better. Right away different standard. There was this discrimination from the very beginning. So I was a little bit disappointed.

Maybe I could get better conditions if I would sign and go to the Negev. I even applied, but this so-called security office didn't take me because they were afraid of my wife; that she is not Jewish, that I might babble out some secret. I said, "Here I am again. I am a Jew, but I am not a Jew, because I came with a non-Jew here."

Family wasn't enough. I will tell you how it was with the family, okay? Everybody has own life. One sister lives in Haifa. The others live in Petakh Tikvah. And I was here in Nahariya someplace. I was seeing them on holidays only. Or sometimes once in a month I would go. I didn't live together with them, because I couldn't. To live with them I would have to get a job there, and there was no jobs.

So I started to dislike it. One, that I couldn't get a good position. Two, the climate. The sun does make you happy, that's true. It's a different mood you get when it's that blue sky and sun and so on. But after a while it's starting to pound on your head, this sun. We had it too much with the sunshine. [*Chuckles.*] I was so happy when I came here to the United States and saw a little cloud over my head.

I realized I didn't have anything to lose. In Israel I'm discriminated jobwise. I cannot get what I want. As I had promised myself at the very beginning, if I won't succeed there, I will try to get to the United States. Well, it's the five-year quota, Polish quota, because quota is by birthplace. What am I going to do? I will register myself and wait five years? It's a waste of time. I was already thirty-six. So I figured out, let me go as a tourist and find here a job and try to get first-preference quota. It was legal at that time. If you could find a sponsor who would give you a job, he would apply for you that he needs you.

So that's what I did. I came here by myself, and it was supposed to be about seven or eight months till we'll see each other. Well, it wasn't that easy. I was looking for a job. There was a question here of discrimination, if I remember. Don't worry, Americans are discriminating also. Why should you be different?

After Israel I did not expect too much. This was my first lesson—that when you emigrate to a different country, where you don't know the language, you will be discriminated. You will be discriminated against because this is not your native country and you are not born here, you don't speak the native language, and so on. Just be satisfied with whatever you can get. Don't count on miracles.

I went from employment agency to employment agency for about two months. I showed them my diploma and I overheard one of them said, "Well, listen, he has a master's degree. Maybe this is equivalent to our B.S., maybe not." I realized that they are discriminating against the eastern Communist countries' education.

Then, finally, after two months, when I already wore off my shoes that I brought from Israel, I got a job. The owner of a drugstore gave me a job and he applied for my visa. He paid me $70 a week. He figured out, "Well, you need a favor. I need also a favor. I need cheap labor. Okay?" So he got me for $70. I stayed with him one year and I got the green card,* and I asked him for a raise. I said, "My family is coming. I

*Permanent resident card, which makes an immigrant eligible for legal employment and eventual citizenship.

cannot support my wife and two children with this." It was too much for him. So I said, "Well, listen, in that case I don't feel sorry leaving you. I appreciate you very much. You did me a favor. You applied for my papers. But I cannot stay here working for $70, because I cannot make a living." So I left him and I got right away a job for $140, in a department store.

I got right away an apartment, too. That was a big contrast again. In Poland you have to have either a very good job or go someplace to a rural position to get an apartment. Same thing in Israel. You have to have money to buy. Here, I came and I see everybody getting an apartment with a Frigidaire, with a gas range, with central heating. This is the least problem here. Get only the job and money. That's very easy. That's what I found out.

Although I was making so little at that time, I realized that after a few years, when I learn and I will master the language, I will get what I'm looking for. I have seen the standard of life. It right away makes up for everything.

I could never achieve this in Israel, what I have achieved here. After all, we moved into this house in 1969, four years after she came here. In four years we bought a house already.

And I realized later on that if you want to live in your own culture, you can find Polish clubs here, or Jewish clubs, or Ukrainian clubs, and you can go there and live your culture if you want. It's not that isolated. It's important to us to have friends that speak Polish. No matter how well you speak English, there is slightly a different mentality. You cannot erase the whole background of thirty or forty years where you were brought up. Let's face it, no matter how much I feel myself right now American, still, when it comes to friendship, I look more or less for what has the same background I have.

You know what? I didn't feel well to have mixed marriage in Poland. It's accepted, but some people say to my wife, "Oh, you married a Jew!" Because a Jew was considered for them like something lower, you know. In Israel, the same. People tell me, "You brought here a goy?" It wasn't good in Israel, either. But in mixed marriage, you feel perfect here. . . .

When I left Poland, I thought maybe I will bring my children some history or something about Poland. But I find out is not necessary, because I never want to go back. I think if my children live in this country, they have to be American. Why mix? See, I was in three countries. You can be either one, but if you mix it, you never feel well. Why you have to create in children nationality, something different? They have to feel what they are here. They live here. They have to feel here. Why they have to feel different?

# Leida Sorro and her
# daughter Maiu Espinosa

···················· FROM ESTONIA, 1951·····················

*Scene: a starkly modern house on a hillside in a northeastern state. It is a late afternoon in February and snow is falling outside. Maiu Espinosa, the wife of a surgeon, has just come in with her mother, who is here on a visit from Oklahoma. Both women are tall and blond, with ice blue eyes. They move regally, like goddesses in a Northern legend, and their story, too, has an epic quality.*

MRS. SORRO: When we left Tartu, the town was burning. There was no way to go back. The country had changed hands four times: first the Germans came, then the Russians, and then the Germans came back, and then the Russians came back a second time. The last time was in 1944. There was a lot of fighting and bombing. We decided to leave. My husband bought a small boat for Sweden, and some of our friends decided to go there, but I didn't want to. It was a very, very dangerous trip, and I told them that I would take the chance if I would be alone, but I don't want to take the chance with children. If something happens with them, then it would be my responsibility. I felt that going to Germany I would have less trouble.

We argued about it. So I said, "If you don't go. . . ." I had such a strong feeling that I had to save my children. They were very young then. Maiu was four, Evie three, and my other daughter only one. At the very last minute, I got on a boat, a freighter, with the children. Later, my husband got another ship and followed us.

MAIU: We stood on the deck, watching as we left our city. All we could see was flames. I wasn't frightened, because I was with mother. She made us feel that we're leaving because we have to now, but we'll come back. It wasn't a bad feeling. She gave us this inner security of feeling safe, no matter what the physical things were. If you don't have that, nothing can replace it—the confidence. Mother, you are an amazing woman.

MRS. SORRO: I didn't know. Only I hear now. You make me very happy, Maiu. [*Weeps and kisses her.*]

When we arrived in Danzig, there were already many ships there. We were almost the last one to arrive. There was bombing around the ship and very little chance to survive, but we made it. I had a little wagon, with my children in it, and we went from one city to another, because the Russians were advancing. Finally, we got to a railroad station. It was night, and we had to wait until we had a chance to go to some other city, because the trains were so full. People were hanging on outside, you know. They wanted to get away from the Russians. All the trains were going one way.

Finally, we got to some small town, and the farmers came to hire people to work for them. And we were standing there—standing and standing, and nobody wanted us. My children were so small—three little girls—and I was kind of sad and I thought, "My goodness, what's going to happen?" The girls had those Estonian caps on, colorful caps that I had made, and they were pretty, really. A boy saw us and ran home and said, "Mother! Mother! There's a girl who's beautiful. Come here, mother, look." And the mother, who was a lady who had a big grocery store there, came smiling, and she said to me, "Come. Come with me." So we went there, and she gave us a room to stay, small room for all of us. We stayed there and I worked. That was the first time I saw a wash machine. We didn't have them in Estonia.

When the Americans came in, the people we stayed with were afraid and left us alone in the house. But the Americans were friendly and talked to us and gave chocolates to the children. They weren't ugly at all. Pretty soon we were put in a camp and reunited with my husband. We were there for five years. My little son Jack was born while we were in that camp. It was a military barracks. We had one room for our family.

MAIU: Whenever the big Americans came to check the camps to make sure that the displaced persons were not treated too badly, they would always bring them to our mother's place, because it looked the neatest. It was a showplace.

MRS. SORRO: In the camp, lots of people were really unhappy. They talked constantly about what they have lost. Constantly. And I tried to tell them how important it is that we are here, alive, and our families together. I was called Sunshine. The camp leader said, "She's the artist of life."

MAIU: My mother always gave us the idea that we should look for good things, no matter where we were. In some places there were not too many good things to see, and so it just gave us something more to do. I think it really got through to us, for it's much easier to adjust if you are able to see the good things, than to look only for the bad—or to be realistic, see things as they really are. You have to see everything anyhow, but it's easier from that angle, rather than from the negative.

MRS. SORRO: Actually, I have the feeling that I'm a better person since I've been through so much; that it has made me better. I've learned all this from my experiences. But if the war had never happened and if I had stayed in Estonia, it's possible my strength might never have come out, because my childhood was very comfortable.

I lost my husband in 1950. We were still in the camp. Maiu was then eleven, Evie ten, my other daughter eight, and my son was only five. It was hard, because we had more chances to have a sponsor when my husband was alive. We had a chance to go to Sweden, but I kept waiting for America. I had such a picture of it as a wonderland, and I wanted to see it. The Lutheran Church had been going to help us get out, but after my husband died they said it was impossible. You can imagine how hard it was to take that message. But somebody told me that the Methodist Church was for hard cases, so I went to the camp and told my kids to wait, and I visited the lady who was in charge of the Methodist office. I knew so little English that I had to use sign language, but I had a good feeling about her. She said, "I would like to see your family." So I ran to the camp again and put ribbons on the children's hats and made the children just so and came back with them. The lady looked at them. She had a beautiful smile. She said, "Of course we can help you. Now, what can you do?"

I said, "I can do anything. Ask me and I do."

"Well, that's wonderful, but let's just kind of point out what kind of work you can do."

And I said, "I can learn fast. Whatever is possible, I will do it."

Then the papers started coming. We had to go through the processing, and one child got sick, and then another; and they were all in quarantine, and it took a little time to get out, but finally we came. My husband had passed away in January, and we got to the United States in June. We were to go to Oklahoma.

From Ellis Island we took a train through the Middle West. I remember being on that train and seeing these kids, a few seats in front of us, playing with play money. We didn't know it was play money. I'll never forget that scene. There's all this money falling around, and all we had for the five of us to eat with on the train for three days was twenty dollars. Finally, Evie picked up a piece of the play money and we looked—twenty dollars! We thought it was real. And here were these children, playing with all that money. We thought, "My God! It really is true; Americans really are rich."

When we stepped out of the train in Oklahoma, I heard people saying, "Mrs. Sorro. Mrs. Sorro," and I thought, "Now, I've finally lost my mind. Who knows me here?" But there was a preacher and a couple of church members, and they took us to one of their homes and gave us a week's free stay there. They were very, very nice. And then church

members started to find me a job and an old house where we could live.
I decorated it, and in two weeks I started working.

My first job was in a candy factory packing orange slices. A sweet
job! [*Chuckles.*] In the factory, I tried to work as fast as possible. I was
soon on piecework, because I work fast with my hands. And a certain
kind of chocolates, they wanted you to put in metal foil, colored foil.
You had to pierce the foil, take the candy, put on the foil, and then
wrap it. It was too slow for me. I took a piece of the foil, put the candy
in, and twisted it—fast, fast. And the little man who was in charge
looked and looked and watched me and came closer. "How do you do
that?" "Simple! Like that," I showed him. "H'mm. Now we know how
to make it faster," he said. Later he said, "You invented something.
Thank you for that." [*Chuckles.*] I was so happy that I could do
something. I tried to do my best. I heard remarks from the other
workers: "What are you trying to do, get Brownie points?" But I didn't
know what they meant. I just wanted to do everything to show my
appreciation and to work as hard as I could.

I started to sing in the Methodist church choir. I was a Lutheran, but
the Methodists had brought me over, and, really, I think all churches
are the same to God. I couldn't say the words when I sang, but all I got
was smiles; nobody laughed at me. Or, if they did, I didn't see. I had to
go to work on the bus every day, and I managed. If people said
something about me, laughed at me, I didn't know it, because I
couldn't understand very much. I had a dictionary and I studied it. I
didn't go to school in the evening, because I worked at a second job,
too, in a ladies ready-to-wear store. I would work at the candy factory
till four-thirty, change my clothes, and walk to the store and work
there till eight-thirty, and then take the bus home. Sometimes when I
got home, there was a message that I could baby-sit for a couple of
hours for people who wanted to go to a show. A few hours sleep was
enough for me then. I was young. It's amazing how much you can do
when you really want to and have to.

My children helped me very much. Everyone had told me before I
came here, "It's impossible for you, because you have young children,
and you'll have to have a baby-sitter if you go to work." But I never had
a baby-sitter for my children, for even one day. Maiu was the one who
took the responsibility. She was eleven. They all went to school, and
she got them on the school bus. Of course, I put their clothes ready.

MAIU: Mother would usually cook soup. You know, a large pot for the
whole week. Then we would have something to eat, because usually
she came home after dark. . . . Mainly, I remember the friendliness
and acceptance in Oklahoma. We had really thought it would be quite
different. My sister and I had said to each other, "Well, no matter what

anybody does, we'll stick together. We'll be friends," because we really expected everybody to throw stones at us and stuff. We didn't expect them to be so nice to us, but they were. Only one bad thing happened. Jack didn't want to wear shorts to school. They wore jeans here, mainly, and in Germany, in the camp, almost every little boy wore shorts. He begged me not to put the shorts on him every day, and finally he told me why. He said that some of the boys were beating him up because he was in shorts. But, in the main, people were friendly.

MRS. SORRO: The years went by and the girls finished school and went to college. My son Jack inherited his father's weak stomach and ulcers, and he died while he was still a boy. Maiu and Evie stayed in Oklahoma until they grew up. Then Maiu married a doctor and went to live in the East; and Evie got a job in New York. She wanted me to move there, where there were other Estonians, but I said, "No. I'm happy here. I don't have anything against my children finding something somewhere else, but there should be one place where I can stay." So I stayed. My youngest daughter lives nearby, in Tulsa, and my son is buried in Oklahoma.

After I got my citizenship, I sponsored two Estonian immigrant families. And a few years ago, I married a man from one of those families. So I have a new life. I feel that I have been blessed, really. This country has given me many things: a home, friendship, a chance to live again.

MAIU: One of my friends says that he feels that Estonia is like his mother, and he will always love his mother; but America is like his wife, and he wants to take care of her and dedicate himself and his energies to her. That's how I feel about my country, my homeland. What it has given me is like what my mother has given me.

Until I went to the Grand Canyon, four or five years ago, I felt like I was not here. I felt that my umbilical cord was tied to Estonia. Always something of me was not here. It was very strange, but I was used to it. I never felt like I belonged. But in Grand Canyon, something happened. The majesty of the mountains, something about the eternity of them; somehow it meant that it was right for me to belong here, now. It was one of those peak experiences of life. Since then, the umbilical cord is no longer there, though I have a gratefulness and good feeling about my heritage. I think the important thing about immigration is to remain the same inside, while you adapt enough to get along on the outside—to fit in and still stay *you*.

# Felix Kucynski

·················· FROM POLAND, 1950 ··················

*During World War II, he served in the Polish unit of the British army.*
*He lives now in Allentown, Pennsylvania.*

We were paid by the British government when I was in the Polish
forces. We had very low pay, and you could see the Americans—
youngsters—who had always a lot of money; drunk, jeeps, noisy. It was
a disgrace. Not all of them, but the bad ones you always see first, you
know. You couldn't talk to them. Always drunk, fighting. At night
going in a jeep through a town, with buckets or cans behind it,
dragging—drunk, you know. You just get a bad impression. I had a free
passage to any country, and I didn't accept America because of that. I
said, "No, I'm not going to America." I had the forms, I remember, but
I threw them out. I just decided to stay in England after the war.

I was happy in England, except that there were some restrictions on
employment of foreigners. It's not like here. It's a government-
operated employment office, and one is for foreigners and one is for
British. For the foreigners, it doesn't matter what you are—doctor,
lawyer—you still got a choice of three jobs: kitchen helper, railroad
cleaner, and road construction. Friends of mine, they all had degrees,
and they all had very low jobs. Nobody could work in his profession.
There was an architect and a doctor, and they were just cleaning
carriages in the railroad station.

I had got my college degree in Poland in chemistry and I wanted to
work in chemistry; so I went to the BCI, British Chemical Industries,
and I said to them, "Look, I have a degree in Poland in chemistry." And
they wouldn't recognize it. My wife was English and she went and she
said, "He's an intelligent man. He's got all these courses. Why can't
you pay some attention?" And they said, "Not if he isn't English." I
spent three years in the army, the British Eighth Army—in a Polish
unit, but it was the British army—and I was considered a foreigner.

So when my wife's aunt and uncle came to visit from America, they
told me right away, they said, "Your Polish degree will be recognized in
the United States. You'll be able to get a job in chemistry." That's
really why I came. And three days after I arrived, I got a job in the
control lab at Baxter Chemical Company.

# Narin Petrow

*A bachelor in his late thirties, his slanted eyes and high cheekbones reveal his Mongol ancestry. He works for a municipal recreation department, leading sports programs for local youngsters, most of Kalmuck background. His large record collection includes much Kalmuck music, along with rock-and-roll and jazz.*

The Kalmucks were originally from western Mongolia. They went into Russia with Genghis Khan and settled in the Volga region—between the Volga River and the Caspian Sea—as the emissaries of Genghis Khan, when he conquered Russia in 1400 or so. The word *Kalmuck* originated, I would say, sometime in the 1500s. During the Russian uprising against the Mongols, many of them fled during the wintertime, when the Volga River was frozen. But a certain segment—about two hundred and fifty thousand of them—said, "We'll wait until a little later on, when it gets warmer." They waited and waited, and when they wanted to go back, they found that the Volga River had thawed and they couldn't go across. From this time on, this word *Kalmuck* became attached to these people. It is a Turkish word, I think, meaning *left behind.*

During World War II, when the Russian counterattack started in Germany, the spearhead that Stalin called for was composed of cavalry units made up of minority people of Russia, and Kalmucks composed a part of that spearhead. Many of them, rather than fighting for the Russians, fought against them by giving up to the Germans and picking up the guns the Germans gave them and fighting back against the Russians.

My family just went along with the Germans, I guess. I had at that time two brothers, but then we had another one. He was born in Poland, on the way west.

Immediately after the war, we were all taken to a new development which was created for displaced persons. It must have been originally about one hundred families, and slowly, every several months, a family would move out, and you asked them where they're going: "America." Next family would move out, same thing. So America was on the lips of everybody. Yet there was no understanding as to what America was really like, but it seemed like people were going there, and they were going willingly, and there was something positive about that. So everybody seemed to look forward to the time when they would go.

The procedure was first to get a sponsorship here in America—a person that could more or less guarantee a job for you, a home, a place to stay, school for the kids, if need be. The way it worked in our case was that my uncle came here earlier. He had gotten a business going and he was our sponsor.

Eventually we got the visas as a group. There were a thousand people, and there was a close-knit nature. It's as if they had a small world. My parents have their own relatives, friends to go to whenever they had to get something. They have Russian friends, Kalmuck friends, but they feel somewhat strange meeting Americans. They have no association with them. If they want to go into the city, if they want to go to a big shopping center, they bring one of us along to interpret. My parents don't speak English. They speak our language. They feel as though this is their security blanket.

My parents preach the old traditions and customs. They want me to marry a Kalmuck girl. It's brought up everywhere I go, in fact. Not my parents alone—other parents and other people, they constantly throw this on me. This is the first question they ask. There were a couple of fixed marriages. We had one, two, three, I believe, fixed marriages within the past five years. One was fixed when the kids got out of high school. I think the boy was about twenty-one years old and the girl was about nineteen. They have four kids—two girls and two boys. The guy is working as a chief architect in a very established firm outside of Philadelphia. He's got a nice house. He's got everything and he's very happy, seemingly. Whether they are fooling themselves, fooling us, I don't know, but they seem on the outside to accept it. Other than that, fixed marriages—it's a conversation piece. It's very horrifying.

One friend, he was going to American University in Washington, D.C., and he married a girl there, an American girl. His mother, on the first day that he brought her home, she said, "You come in, but your wife can't come in." But he did bring her in anyway, and his mother wouldn't talk to her. It's a custom anytime you have guest come in, you sit down and eat something, and when she prepared this she prepared just for her son, and the wife was ignored.

I wanted to get married right after college—to a Jewish girl. But then I came home and heard all this flak. So this conflict was within my mind. I say to myself, "I come from over there, but there is a modern view. What should I do?" It's difficult to divide yourself into such little pieces. I've been to school, met many people, many different ideas. I've been halfway around the world and back, become exposed to many lifestyles, and when I come back, it's as if the world I left is still the same. It hasn't changed a bit. My ambition is to move forward, and to come back would be to take one step backwards. I never lived at home for more than two or three months at a time since I went away to college.

But they're getting the message; slowly my parents are getting the message. Because I tried to explain to my parents, and many other friends of mine have tried to explain to their parents, that their theories on life and practices have remained constant since they left Russia, while the youth have been exposed to different approaches to life, different answers to various questions.

Gradually, it seems like there is a departure from the Kalmuck traditions—the language, the church, the food, the customs. Many of the younger people right now seem to be very much assimilated— Americans in every sense of the word.

I've lived like an American, according to the American ideals. I've served two years in the service and did everything that was expected of me—went to school, met Americans. But I wish I could be able to probe a person's mind while they were associating with me. It seems that many times when you meet people, you can just feel a certain unfavorable association. I haven't really felt prejudice or discrimination on the surface. But no matter how American you are inside, on the surface, if you go walking side by side with an American, there will be one difference—physically. When I went to Taiwan—totally Oriental—it was as if I was home. [*Chuckles.*] I didn't stand out.

# Paul Maracek

·················FROM CZECHOSLOVAKIA, 1949·················

*A graduate of Yale and M.I.T., he works as a research scientist for a large American company. He and his wife and four small children like to go camping on their vacations. His conversation and dress are informal and he looks very "American."*

One morning late in February we woke up and heard on the radio that the government of Czechoslovakia had been toppled and that the president was under house arrest and that the Communists have taken over. It happened very suddenly—without any advance warning, without an uprising—with just—. You wake up in the morning and it's different. It turned out that the army was under Communist control. It turned out that, in many places, the police happened to have been under Communist control. Before, the government in Czechoslovakia was a democracy. There were three major parties. One of them was the

Communist party. It was of significant strength—maybe twenty-five percent of the vote—but by no means was it the ruling party. But it had enough strength that once the Communists took over the government . . . it was difficult to fight it. Particularly since there were rumors all around, which later turned out to be true, that Russian divisions were on the border of East Germany and Poland; and had a rebellion started—so the rumor went—they would come in and crush it. And, indeed, if one looks at 1967, that is indeed what happened in Czechoslovakia when the Russians came in. And they did that in Hungary and they did this in East Germany, too.

So, anyway, one morning here we were, and the government was overthrown. Jan Masaryk [the president of Czechoslovakia] was thrown out of the window in an apparent suicide. Well, at first no one knew what it meant, but very rapidly signs became evident. People who were anti-Communist were suddenly either put into jail or removed from positions. One of those people who was removed from his position was my father, who was a lawyer in a small town—population of about ten thousand, the county seat.

He was told several days after the coup to surrender his keys to the law office and that he was no longer welcome to practice law in the town. He asked them, then, why, and was really given no particular reason that I remember; but just that he could do anything else except be a lawyer in that town. He then started to look for jobs elsewhere. It turned out that what you had to do is—when you received a job, you had to go back to your town and get permission from your town council, essentially, for that particular job. Well, soon he found himself a job—I believe as a judge—in another town. When he came back and applied for permission to do that, he was told that he can't. But any other job, he could. He then found himself a job as an administrative officer someplace else—I believe in Prague, in the Ministry of Justice. Again—no permission. Then he found a job as a clerk in the Ministry of Justice. Again—no permission. Finally, after several attempts like this, he found a job at a factory as a laborer. And he indeed was given permission.

So the picture became clear that they really don't want him to do anything except menial work, and that his career was at an end. Coincidentally, the apartment we lived in was in a building that was owned by an insurance company that wanted to expand, and so everybody in the building was given notice. We found ourselves a nice apartment down the street and began to apply for permission in order to get the apartment. We were told that we cannot have that apartment. So, to test the town council, we tried to get an apartment in the basement of another building . . . with windows just barely peeking up above the sidewalk. And we were given permission that we could move in there. Well, the picture became clear that any reasonable life was really at an end and freedom of choice was at an end. And what was coming was a fear and repression, and what was also in the foreground of my parents' mind was that their children, my sister and I, would not be allowed to continue to go to school. I was about eleven at the time. My sister was about thirteen. And we were both going to the *gymnasium*, which was the academic path, and it was clear that we would probably have to go to the vocational school, so that any kind of a professional career would be out. We had to be laborers or mechanics, which was not something that we particularly wanted to do.

It was very hard to tell what was going on. It was hard to tell who was your friend and who wasn't, who you could trust and who you couldn't; because twenty-five percent or so of the people were Communists. There were enough of them around that you just didn't know . . . what you could say, whom you could really trust. And so you trusted only those who were very close with . . . your very close friends and your relatives, mainly relatives. You *knew* you could trust them.

It was sometime around that point that my parents decided to escape; that it really didn't make any sense to continue. And the way my father put it is that it is clear that he is going to suffer—suffer financially, suffer economically, suffer politically; and, in a way, he is almost enslaved.

So we had a plan to escape—hopefully to go to the United States, where my mother's sister had been living since the early thirties. Well, this was in, say, March or April, and our plan was to escape later that spring or early summer.

You have to be very careful. Many people were trying to escape. You didn't know who to trust, and you had to make sure the plans could be carried out. The fact that my father had lost the job and we had lost the apartment made it somewhat easier. We had to move, and so we made preparations to move to Prague, where my father would be working. As I remember, the apartment we were to move into was not quite ready, so we had to spend a week or two living at my aunt's house before moving into the apartment. And this was all in the plan—because this gave us a chance to move into a private residence, where one doesn't have to register and one is not as easy to notice. Whereas, you move into a new house . . . the landlord would have to register us and know where we were. So moving into the apartment of my aunt would give us a few more days where our comings and goings would not be observed as well.

But you can't escape alone. You need help. It turned out there was a border guard that we somehow were told about, who was willing to help us. And he did this, not for money, not for anything, except that he just thought it was right—knowing all along that if he ever got caught he'd be shot. We had to make contact with him.

Our plan was to cross the border into the Russian zone of Austria. The reason we picked the Russian zone is that all the borders were being protected. But the one into the Russian zone of Austria was least protected at that point; and so that improvements, such as mine fields and dogs and fences in areas around the border, weren't made yet.

To make contact with this border patrolman, my father and I bought a ticket to go and visit his brother, my uncle. And the train happened to be going right by the border. As soon as we got to the border town, we both got off the train. My father met him with a password and I observed that this indeed happened, and then I got back on the train and continued going to my uncle's house. My reason for going to my uncle's house was to pick up a diamond brooch, which was an inheritance from my father's mother, because the only valuables that would be worth anything to cross the border would be jewelry. So I picked that up and got back on the train, and at the same border town my father reboarded the train and we continued.

Well, then everything seemed set. Our plan was to take the train out to the border, with our knapsacks. The border at that point was full of lakes and mountains and hills, and it was popular with tourists. We would make believe we were tourists and get lost on a hike.

The time of our escape was to be between twelve and twelve-thirty, and that time was picked because it's least noticeable, first of all. Second of all, everybody is off guard, and the guards are changing and they're having lunch, and things seemed to be a little bit safer. And this was on the advice of the border-patrol contact.

My father, my mother, my sister, and I took the train to the border and took our knapsacks and started hiking toward the border. Our valuables, a couple of diamonds from rings and brooches, were baked into muffins, and they were packed in a little tin in our knapsack. Normally you don't go on a hike with diamonds. So that if they had found diamonds, they would have known that we were trying to escape, and we would have to go back and have some dire consequences. The plan was that if we saw a border patrol we would stop and have a picnic lunch. My sister and I were told to eat the muffins with the diamonds in them and to offer the others to the border patrol. We were told to chew carefully.

We took the path toward the border and we were getting relatively close and suddenly up ahead we see a border patrol. Our hearts sank, and we decided to sit down for lunch, and we spread out a picnic cloth and took out the muffins and our lunch and sat down and waited for the border patrol to appear. As he got closer we recognized it was the one border patrolman that we knew. He told us to pack up our lunch.

"The coast is clear. You have to go just a little way. Make haste." He pointed the way to us. So we packed up our lunch and quickly walked to the border.

We crossed into the Russian zone of Austria. There were hills, but there was no line. It seemed very uneventful, almost. We walked for about fifteen or twenty minutes—half an hour—and we suddenly were surprised by a uniformed guard, who asked for our identification papers. We only had Czech identification papers. So he proceeded to direct us back into Czechoslovakia. We insisted—our story was that we were lost and that we would find our way, thank you very much. But he was insistent that he would escort us back. Finally it became clear that we were not going back, and he was not going to just let us walk away. So he took us to his guard post, and there ensued a long interrogation by his sergeant or supervisor. And we were trying to talk him into just letting us go, but they were really unwilling to do that.

The plan that we were trying to follow was that my mother's sister and brother would meet us in Austria. They were residents of Austria since 1945. They had a car and they would meet us at a particular place at one o'clock and would then drive us on. Well, we couldn't get to this village where we were to meet. My mother tried to talk the border patrol into letting her go—to at least talk to her brother. And eventually, after a long, long time, she was allowed to walk to this village.

It was a James Bond–type story, where one can't . . . first of all, for instance, a car is suspicious. A car standing in a small town is suspicious. No one knows who to trust. So what my uncle did was, he pulled up in front of a church and went in to talk to the pastor, as a fairly safe place to be. What they talked about, I don't know. My mother walked up there and gave a signal to make sure that she's noticed, and then he came out of the church and they drove back. What followed was some more hours . . . a long time of negotiation with the border patrol. Money may have been passed at this time, I don't know. But finally, after a long, long time, the guard allowed us to go.

Well, our plan was getting difficult, because we were planning to leave at one o'clock and had a many-hour drive to my uncle's residence, which was in the Russian zone. We wanted to do the trip during daylight hours. During night hours, any car is suspicious. And at night in particular, there were Russian checkpoints on the roads, stopping cars and asking for identification papers. Well, this made it more risky, but we proceeded anyway, because you can't stop in a motel or hotel . . . because in order to check in, you need to show your identification papers, and we didn't have them and we couldn't trust the people . . . that they would let us in without notifying the police.

So we drove for hours, it seemed, and around one o'clock we arrived at my uncle's house—slept there for a few hours and the next day we proceeded to go into the American zone.

The plan there was to go into the city of Linz. Linz was right on the border between the American and the Russian zone and was cut in half by the Danube. This is where the two zones met. Since half of the city was on one side of the Danube and half on the other, there was a lot of traffic across the bridge—particularly at noon, since there is a two-hour lunch hour when everybody goes home for lunch. From about twelve to about twelve-twenty there is a massive traffic jam. And most of the people take a streetcar. The streetcar goes across the bridge, gets to the middle of the bridge, and everybody gets out of the streetcar, walks out of it through a little guard shack where one's passport is checked. The streetcar, in the meantime, drives ahead to the other side of the guard shack, and everybody gets back in the streetcar and continues.

The plan was for us to go through with passports—or identification papers—from friends of my uncle. They weren't faked; they were papers belonging to real people that had some physical resemblance to us in age, sex, maybe appearance to some extent. They had lent the papers to my uncle. I'm very grateful to those people, because they took a risk for us and they didn't even know us.

To be sure that we do it right, my uncle was taking us one at a time. It was a bit scary to walk right by the Russian guard and casually flash the identification papers and keep going, but that seemed to go actually very smoothly. Except for the last one. My father was the last one to cross, and my uncle came back to the other side and he couldn't find my father anywhere. I don't know exactly what happened. My uncle claims that my father was so fascinated by some of the foods and items in the store window across the street or around the corner, that he went there to look at it. My father claims that he was exactly where he was supposed to be, but that, for some reason, my uncle got confused. At any rate, they did find each other finally—did cross—and we made it into Austria.

This was in early summer or late spring of '48, and Austria was flooded with refugees. There wasn't much work, and the typical thing that happened with refugees was that you went to a refugee camp, where they were assigned a bunk in a large room and given meals, subsistence meals—until they were able to arrange for immigration to another country.

We were lucky. My father found work and we were, with that money, able to get a room—a single room for the four of us—where we lived. My father first worked as a sandblaster and then in a quarry and then back to a sandblaster again. It was a very different job from a lawyer. My mother helped, too. The room was in an inn of sorts, and she helped clean the rooms and the bathrooms and that. It was difficult for all of us, particularly my parents.

My sister and I went to school and that, actually, wasn't as hard; even though it was German, we knew German, so there was no particular significant problem. It took about a year and a half to get all the papers signed and everything processed. And, finally, after a year and a half, we were able to start our journey to the United States.

At first we had to go to various collection points. We spent a night in a very primitive camp and then boarded trains to another collection area in Salzburg. There the quarters consisted of a large gymnasium-like room—bigger than a normal gym—with three-decker bunks from wall to wall. There must have been five hundred people in one room. For privacy what you could do was hang blankets from the edge of your bed. It was, again, rather primitive. We spent about a week there, while—I'm not sure what happened, but papers got shuffled and things were signed. And then we boarded another train for the ride into Germany and to the harbor of Bremerhaven.

We arrived there after several days on the train—were brought to a very clean-looking army camp of brick buildings, relatively nice in that the rooms had only six to ten people in them. It was run by the Americans and the food was good there, too. I remember that every morning we would watch the flag being raised, and reveille was sounded and it was quite an emotional sight to see the flag, which we knew would be our own. We were supposed to be there only a few days, but some clerk somewhere made a mistake on my sister's form and—it was a minor thing; the initial was wrong, or the date of birth was wrong by a month—something trivial like that. Nevertheless, that was sufficient that we could not proceed and that the papers had to be sent back for correction. So we spent about three or four weeks in that camp waiting for that to happen. Finally, the papers got corrected and we were assigned a ship.

A strange thing happened that, as we were assigned the ship, a *Reader's Digest* had just come out, and in it was an article about the new antiseasickness pill called Dramamine—which had just been tested by the U.S. Navy. The test was done a few years earlier, and the doctors reported that they'd picked one of the rockiest boats that the navy had to test the drug—the troop transport called *General Ballou*. That, indeed, was exactly the boat we were assigned to go on. So we knew we would have a rocky voyage.

The boat was equipped the way the troop transport was. Nothing had been changed, which means triple-decker bunks, large rooms. But it was going in the right direction, so we agreed not to complain. I was fascinated by the ice cream we were served. Even though I was seasick all the time, I enjoyed the ice cream.

So after ten days on that, we arrived in Boston and took the train to Detroit, where an aunt lived. I remember being terribly disappointed when we took the ride by bus from the harbor to the railroad station. I had somehow built up the technological advances in the United States and expected a supermodern, supersmooth bus to take us there. And the bus seemed neither particularly modern nor particularly smooth. It was a real letdown. But we were on our way.

My mother and my father both had been guaranteed work. That was the prerequisite for getting to the United States. My mother's was real, in that she had been a laboratory technician in pathology and she was actually able to get such a job. My father's promised job was more of a formality. It really did not exist, but it was necessary, to have him come to the United States. So when he arrived, he started looking for various jobs. He looked for anything he could find.

This was November of 1949. Jobs were not that easy to find—and particularly with the language problem. He thought of going back to school, but to get a law degree would take not only four years of law school, but college. Even though he was a Doctor of Law, that was not recognized and even would not be equivalent to a bachelor's degree. So that would mean possibly seven years of college, which was just out of the question when you have nothing to live on. He tried getting a job, first as a dishwasher, and then he got a job at a Ford assembly plant; but it was clear that all of those were really dead ends—that there would be no way out once you make a start in that. So, while looking for other jobs, he was selling door-to-door, items for a company that made lotions and creams and brushes and brooms. He worked in the Polish and Czech sections of Detroit. But sales were not very good, so that didn't really bring in much money. Finally, he got a job at a company that was an accounting-type firm for various sporting events. And that seemed to be closer to what he had been doing before. So he stayed there for a number of years, and then he got a job in one of the larger banks in the clerical-type department. After years, he had a successful second career in that field and retired in his late sixties. I think he made a good, successful second start, but it took him about three or four years before he could really find himself something that was reasonably close to his capability. So it was hard. It was hardest for them; hardest for my father, because he left his native country and his profession, his friends, and everything he had.

My sister and I had it easier. We knew a little English and we learned more fast. The children were friendly. We had come to an area of the city that was full of refugees and foreigners, so we weren't strange. It wasn't like coming to a small town when you're the first foreigner in ten years. After a year in school, we were as American as everyone else.

*Did you ever think, or did your family ever think about
what would have happened if you hadn't left Czechoslovakia?
What would your life have been like?*

Yes. We can look back at our relatives that stayed behind. Most of them did stay behind. They had to. Two things could have happened. There were two paths one could go. Those who were professionals, and I guess most of our relatives were, had a pretty hard time. Some of them wound up in jail for very minor-type things: criticism of the government, or talking to someone and saying, "Boy, if we only didn't have the Communists," or something like that. That was—if the person he told it to, told it to the police, it was certain to follow that you'd be convicted of, uh, not espionage, but some related law. And one cousin of my father's spent twelve years in jail for an offense similar to that. He was finally freed in the early sixties, when there was a general reprieve or a change of political power. People were jailed for very small reasons, and the appeals were very difficult, really nonexistent. So that was one real possibility.

You could also just give in and not criticize and just grin and bear it. And make sure that you don't make waves. In that case you might have a reasonable career. But that seems like a low way to live. . . .

# Rudy Cracovik

·················FROM YUGOSLAVIA, 1954·····················

*Rudy Cracovik felt that his middle-class background limited educational and career opportunities for him in Communist Yugoslavia. He determined to escape.*

The first time I went with a friend. We were a little silly, I think now. We were just playing, like a schoolboy's idea. We didn't plan it. We were young, you know. We figured, "If we make it, we make it. If they spot us, they will shoot us." We had a few sandwiches and that kind of stuff, and we walked the roads, about twenty miles, twenty-five miles—to the border of Italy. And we walked on the road and when nobody was around we sneaked through the woods.

Our one aim was just to escape. We didn't know the terrain. We got lost. We started walking all day. It was just like a jungle, up and down. We were tired and the rain started. It rained all night. We couldn't sleep. Everything was wet. Morning came; we couldn't build a fire, so we exercised. We kept going until afternoon. We made about another two or three miles, not halfway, even, between the border and our destination. We were sitting under a tree a little bit, resting, and some farmers called and then there came a policeman. They yelled at us. Sent us home.

About five or six weeks later, the special police, the MKG came. They said, "You have to come down to the station and we'll ask you some questions." We went down and we never left that jail for thirteen months. They were suspicious of us. They kept questioning us. It was important that they show an example to the others. I felt I hadn't done anything wrong, only that I wanted to escape. I didn't like that rotten jail. They kept me in a small room, six-by-six, can't stretch out all the way. There was a wooden bunk and a small window, about a square foot, and it was cold and poor food and there was a time for questioning. You wait and wait, you never know. You never know when you have to go and they'd bump on the door asking something; that's when it is.

Well, finally I was released and went back to work, but I became more and more bitter and I decided to escape again. I pretended I went to look for a job closer and closer to the border. I didn't have any arms or anything, but I thought, "If anybody does something to me, I'll do it to him." I went through the woods, studied the map; it was dangerous because if they caught me again I didn't know what they'd do. In the night I crawled along the border. They have grapevines, lots of rocks, and blackberries with thorns. In the night I got in the bushes. I was all bloody. I was crawling. I told myself there was no other way. Whatever happens, there's no way back. I had to make it, so I made it.

When I reached Trieste, I was scared. I saw people walking around, nothing unusual. I thought the police would come right away and say, "What are you doing here?" Because, well, what could I say? I had blood all over and scratches. Someone came up to me and spoke Yugoslavian. One of those small traders. They all live over there. They know all languages, lots of other languages. "Are you Yugoslavian?" he said.

I said, "Yes." I was pretty scared.

He said, "I know. You just got over."

"Yeah, yeah, but don't. . . ."

"No, no. Don't worry. You're free here. Come with me." So he got me a nice warm meal, a good meal, and was friendly. I told him I wanted to report myself to the police so that I'd get some kind of papers or something like that. "Don't worry. Right after you eat, first thing." He went out in the street and he said, "There's a policeman. Just go over and tell him." He was looking at me and laughing.

I was curious. I went to the policeman and told him, and he said, "I don't have time. I'm directing traffic. You're just another one. Please, back over there." He didn't care. He said, "I don't care about it." That was the first shock for me. I was free.

Finally, another policeman put me in a car and took me to the Red Cross center. They have room and board. It's international, but, actually, more American. So they kept me there for forty-five days. Good food, good place to eat, good clothes; but that wasn't enough for me. I wanted to work. I decided to go to France, where I knew I could get work. I took a train because I didn't have a passport, and the first time, the French gendarmes caught me and sent me back to Trieste. They were nice to me—gave me good food, kept me in a police station, talked with me; but they sent me back to Trieste.

It was the same thing again; nothing to do and no work. I don't like to live in a fancy hotel at someone else's expense. I'm a man of action. So a few weeks later I went again on a train through Italy all the way to the border. I used the last money I had—the train costs a lot—I didn't have much, but I had enough to buy a big bouquet of flowers. Big yellow roses. I read someplace that when you go and visit you bring flowers. I thought that this was a good investment. My idea was that with the flowers no one could turn me back. They were my passport. I look like I live there. Like I'm going to visit somebody. I combed my hair Italian fashion. So I passed the Italians on the border, they say nothing; then I pass the French ones. They were not interested. I was neat, shoes clean, and the flowers. So there is nothing suspicious. I look like I live there.

I went to the train station and I bought a ticket to Paris. And I pretended to sleep—all the way on the train I slept. I left my ticket visible. The French conductors—they're really polite and so they saw me sleeping, with flowers, and they're soft on flowers—they just checked my ticket and punched it. So I slept all the way to Paris, sixteen or eighteen hours. That's a long way. I slept and pretended to sleep and slept and kept the flowers all the time in my arm. And when I walked out on the street in Paris, I still had the flowers.

I worked in Paris for a while, but I really wanted to go to United States. I finally managed to come. A Catholic organization arranged it, although I'm not Catholic. To me it was important to be free, to be free . . . that's the first thing. After that everything is all right.

# Stefan Juranic

·················· FROM YUGOSLAVIA, 1949 ·····················

*After many years as a stockbroker in Boston, he retired to the large estate in New Hampshire that he inherited from his aunt and uncle.*

It was our own people who were the really brutal ones, the ones that did the torturing and the destruction of people's property and the confiscation in a wanton kind of a way—much more strongly than is necessary. Because the people who were in charge—what's called the puppet government—and their administrators and enforcers were for the most part people who had been on the seamy side of society before the war and now had risen to the top. They were exercising their power in as brutal a way as they could—for the Germans, but primarily for themselves.

The Germans we found, for the most part—considering that it was an occupation army, of course—to be quite understanding and not at all inhumane the way they had been in other parts of Europe. Now they did clean out the Jews, but. . . . To give you an example: My father was arrested five times under the occupation and twice afterwards, under the Communists. Once he was arrested under the occupation because he was caught trying to get into Switzerland with one of his friends in the trunk of his car, and his friend happened to be Jewish. But, you see, he was just arrested. He was in for a while and then he was let out. The Germans still put up a very good front of doing due process and doing it the legal way. The fifth time, under the occupation, he was picked up on a warrant by the Croatian government, not by the Gestapo, and he went off to a concentration camp; and the only reason he got out was because the partisans advanced at the end of the war and they let the prisoners out. After that, he was arrested primarily because of having been of a politically prominent family before the war. My grandfather had been in the royal Yugoslav government toward the end of his political career, as minister of agriculture. And they picked up everybody like that.

These arrests had the biggest effect on my mother—in an extremely positive way. When my mother got married, she couldn't cook, couldn't boil water. My parents lived in an apartment on top of one of the many hills of Zagreb, and my mother's grandmother lived at the bottom of the hill. And three times a day, the butler would carry a tray up the hill to feed the newlyweds. And then, slowly, my great-grandmother would leave out the final step of preparing something and attach instructions, and this is how my mother learned to cook. But came the war, and here is this girl who was—really, I suppose her biggest positive contribution to society was that she was a good tennis player—my mother found that, with my father in jail, somebody had to take over and provide, keep the family together. So she did. And the first thing that she established was a new language for discussing food, to protect the channels of supply. Then my mother raised a pig in a spare bathroom of the apartment, and when the pig was full grown, she took it downstairs into the basement and butchered it all by herself—made sausages, everything with her own little hands; raised chickens on the kitchen balcony. I remember sitting in the kitchen stuffing cornmeal down the throat of a live duck or a goose.

Well, the end of war was a disappointment in that, having stayed and waited for the liberation, to find that once the liberation forces came in, nothing had really changed. For example, when my father was arrested the first time by the Communists—two months after the liberation—he was put into the same cell in which he was before, with the same guard. Same guard, different uniform. Nothing had really changed, except that the people at the very bottom had risen to the very top, and the people at the very top had fallen to the very bottom.

We had expected things to go back to where they were, but they didn't. The decision was made by my parents to try to get out. With forged passes, we went to Trieste, and my mother went to the American military headquarters—she was the only one of us who spoke English at the time—and convinced them to let her make a collect transoceanic call through the secret Allied headquarters to my uncle in Washington, to tell him that, "Hey, we're here. What do we do now?" [Laughs.] My father's oldest brother had been chief of protocol in the [Yugoslav] government. He went into exile in London and from there to Washington, where he'd been stationed before. He had married an American from a very wealthy family, and he spent the latter part of the war in Washington, as the number two man at the royal Yugoslav Embassy. So, at that point, he just started moving mountains, and we got passes—we were the first civilians to go through occupied Italy on non-Red Cross and nonmilitary passes.

Let's see, we got to Trieste on November 15 of '45, and we left Trieste by bus for Venice on the thirty-first of December of that year. There wasn't any room available in Venice, because it was one of the big spots for the military on leave. My father and mother had done a lot of traveling through Europe before the war and knew a lot of people, and it happened that the general manager of the Grand Hotel in Venice was the same guy that they knew from before, and they opened the royal suite for us. [Laughs.] We spent New Year's Eve in the royal suite of the Grand Hotel in Venice—which hadn't been dusted in, maybe, three years. It was a frightening experience—huge rooms, a lot of noise outside, a lot of drunken military outside; and no lights, just candles, one of these great portraits of Venetian ancestors staring down at you. And the bathroom being way over there and the bedroom being over here, that was a memorable night.

It was in Italy my father decided that one of the first experiences one must have, if one is going to America, is to try Coca-Cola. And he took my sister and me someplace where we had a glass of Coca-Cola. It was awful, but because it was American it was such a big deal. We drank it down and said it was marvelous.

And then we started looking for a way to get into the U.S. We only got into Italy, away from the Yugoslav border. We were not considered displaced persons, so we couldn't get on the DP quota list for immigration visas into the U.S.

We bummed around a lot through Europe, and my strongest memory of that is that I had this terrible fear whenever I was left alone—when my parents went out to dinner or off shopping or something, throughout the treks in Europe—I had this terrible fear that they would find out that the visas had come through and that they would leave and forget about me and the luggage. I was really scared that I would be left in some little hotel someplace in Europe, because of the excitement of getting the visas. Finally, we went to Madrid, because in Madrid was the last remaining royal Yugoslav ambassador. He was maintaining a royal Yugoslav presence at his own expense and providing passports to Yugoslavs who had to leave without papers. So we went there to get passports and to get, for example, birth certificates. I've got a birth certificate that was issued in Madrid in Serbo-Croatian with the royal stamp. We were in Madrid about a year, I guess, and then we managed to get visitors' visas for the U.S. The theory was that we would come here, and then my father would try to get us temporary visas to go someplace in the Northern Hemisphere to wait for the immigration visas—preferably a place like Canada.

On Christmas Eve of '47, we got on a Pan American clipper and came to America by way of Goose Bay and Gander and Boston and then New York. My uncle and his wife had bought a house in New Hampshire, a huge house big enough to get all the family together. That was their hope. So on Christmas Day, we went by train to Concord and then by taxicab from Concord. We found a taxi driver who charged fifteen dollars and went the long way around the lake, so it took three hours instead of an hour and a half, but it was a marvelous trip, because we had never seen anything like American Christmas, with the lights on the houses. Heavy snow, and all these houses along the road lit up with colored lights—that was pretty impressive. The next biggest impression of America was that when we finally did get to the house and we had dinner, dessert was ice cream. We had never had ice cream in the winter before.

So we got here and we looked for a place to go. We wanted to go to Canada, because everybody felt that would be closest to America in culture, and, consequently, it would be a good place for the kids to start. Well, the Canadians didn't want us. The official reply back from Ottawa to the embassy in Washington was, quote: "Canada is not a waiting room for future American citizens."

So my father started going around to the other embassies, and he decided that we were going to Haiti because he was personally met by the ambassador, who offered him a glass of rum, and it was delicious. So we went to Haiti and we spent thirteen months there. Marvelous place. I was ten and a few months. My sister and I went to school everywhere that we stopped for more than a week. We were starting to learn English. I remember integrating a school. I was the only white kid in a school up on top of a mountain. . . .

The number came up and we got the visas, so off we came to the United States. New Hampshire was going to be our home, because my aunt and uncle were there. But my mother couldn't stand it out in the country, five miles away from a town with a population of three thousand. So, about two months after we got there, my parents left for New York City to make their fortunes.

They got an apartment on 120th Street, in a building that was full of Yugoslav immigrants. There were a lot of exiled Yugoslav politicians in New York; there were a number of people who had been in various concentration camps with my father; and these people were constantly trying to draw him back into this sort of thing. He just wouldn't have any. All these people were living in the past. My father used to sit there and just shake his head and say, "They're all sitting there assigning cabinet posts to each other as though they were ever going to go back."

My father got a job as a cashier at a Horn & Hardart. He also started going to Columbia at night, and he didn't really feel that he could go through law school, because his English was very, very bad. So he got a master's degree in business administration and then went into various business ventures.

My mother got a job somewhere sewing in the garment district. In due course, she went into business for herself. First, she started off working for Lily Daché and for a number of fashion designers, starting as a seamstress and then working her way up. Then she made an arrangement with one of the Italian fashion houses to be their U.S. representative, and she operated something out of the Plaza Hotel for about fifteen years. At the age of about sixty-two or so, she took a three-month vacation, went to Italy, got a face-lift, came back, and got a job at Bloomingdale's, where she still is, having an absolute ball.

My sister and I stayed up in New Hampshire to go to school. We would come down during vacations a little bit, but we spent our time up there. It was absolutely delightful. I don't know whether it would have been anywhere nearly as nice in a bigger town, but here I was the only foreigner around. My uncle and aunt were considered foreign dignitaries of some kind. They drove at that time a twelve-cylinder Packard coupe with a rumble seat. And they would come down from the top of the mountain, where their house was at the end of the road, in this huge Packard to drop us off for school. My sister and I were rumored to be of royal blood. That was a lot of fun. Those were rumors that we took a long time dispelling, because we didn't try very hard. People were just delightful.

It was a very soft life. They had a live-in cook and butler, so one didn't have to lift one's finger very much. My uncle had been able to take some money out with him when he left, and my aunt had been left a substantial trust fund by her father, and there was quite a bit of money there, so that they did nothing to earn money. They lived on dividends and lived very well on them. They never wanted to talk about money. One could never talk about what something cost. The important thing was, was it necessary? And if it was necessary, then the money would be there. They spent huge amounts of money to get us out of the country, to get the rest of the family out of the country, to get us educated. Without that, things would have been completely different. I was very, very lucky. . . .

There was a little bit of friction between my parents and my uncle and aunt. In fact, there was a great deal of friction, because my parents weren't bringing up their own children. To my aunt and uncle, we were considered their family.

My sister went to the local high school. It was felt that it was more important for the boy to have a different kind of an education. I don't think my parents had really much question about it. They thought that an education was extremely important. My aunt supported the education; since it was economically viable to go to the best school, why not go to Exeter rather than somewhere else? My father and mother spent a lot of time going over *Lovejoy's Prep School Guide*, just to make sure that Exeter was the best. By the time college came along for me, there had really never been any question in anybody's mind but that Harvard was the college that one goes to, and I didn't apply to any other colleges, and eventually I went to Harvard. . . .

I feel that I'm an American who happened to have spent a lot of time in his childhood in other countries. I've gone through so many cultural environments. And I think that there is an economic thing here, too, more than a nationalistic thing. I think that the more money that you have lived with, the less nationalistic you tend to be; because wealth, money, permits you to collect around you things of different cultures, and consequently you are not as culturally narrow when you have the wherewithal to travel, to collect, to go to schools. . . .

# Ilona Bertok

*Tiny, slim, with enormous dark eyes and glossy black hair, she speaks softly but with great intensity. Her grandfather was a well-known Hungarian playwright, who dealt wittily with the subject of adultery and intrigue. In prewar Budapest, her parents lived as though they were characters in one of his plays—fighting, loving, betraying each other over and over again. Doors were slammed, plates were thrown, imprecations were shouted. There were frequent separations and reconciliations. Throughout the turmoil, Ilona, the "Puritan in the household," controlled herself, bit her nails, and watched silently from the corners of the room.*

*Today she is a poet, but like many other poets in America, she teaches for her bread and butter. After a loveless marriage of twenty years, she has recently left her husband. Her two daughters are away at college.*

*Why do you think you were so different from the rest of your family?*

Well, I think it probably has a lot to do with the fact that I modeled myself to be the opposite of my mother, because I perceived my father as denigrating my mother and not valuing her. I perceived that very clearly. And so I modeled myself into some antithesis of her. She is a passionate woman. Through all her faults, the one virtue she has is that she always knows what she wants and she knows that on a gut level, and she goes about to get it. She loved my father, and she married my father for love, and after all the humiliation she still loved him. She loved him dearly. So what was I to do? Passionate love was something that I threw aside and devalued. Selfishness was not to be tolerated. My mother would cry at the table if the servants didn't give her the best piece of chicken, and she was the mother of a family, remember. I tried to be just the opposite. I suppose someone could, at the right point, have turned me around, but I don't know to what extent this was possible.

In Hungary, we lived on a scale that is almost impossible to imagine today. Everything was elegant: Oriental rugs, a large house, silver, a stable with trotting horses. We had many servants, and I remember the unease with which I handled the servant-master relationship. From a very early age I was a democrat in a society that was a feudal society, essentially. I had read the Hungarian poets of 1848, that revolutionary period. They had spoken about the equality of man, and I took this to be a dream that could come true. I had an idea of America, that it was a land of freedom and that it, somehow, coincided with this idealistic dream that I had.

At the end of World War II, I was thirteen years old. As the Russian influence in my country grew, my feelings of unease and of not belonging intensified. I saw that what was happening in Hungary did not represent the freedom that I'd dreamed of. I felt so passionate about it that I begged my father on my knees to leave. At that time, he was well regarded by the people who were in power. There was still a front of freedom in the government; and because of his association with the trotting horses, the authorities often sent him to buy horses in Kentucky, to replenish the horse supply, which had been almost completely decimated by the Germans. And so he made a number of trips to this country to buy horses. On one of these trips, he simply brought my brother out, put him in a boarding school in Connecticut, set aside some money in New York, and asked my uncle, who had been in this country for years, to oversee his education. Then, you see, he had only to get my mother and me out. He was afraid to apply for a visa for all of us, so it was agreed that he would get only two visas, for himself and me, and later my mother would follow us to Paris.

The departure was quite dramatic. We came with very little so as not to arouse suspicion—just personal belongings. I brought only a book of poetry, a medallion of my grandfather's, a few pieces of personal jewelry. We got on the train and waved good-bye to all those people that we knew. Someone was holding my cat, which I loved dearly, and I think that cat was the creature I cried most about.

I went off with my father quite happily. I really felt good about leaving my mother behind. I remember taking a needle and thread and thinking that I was going to darn my father's socks I'd learned very well to darn socks, and, well, I was at that age when mothers and daughters are best parted, as far as the daughter was concerned. So I went off with my father, thinking that he was a strong man and that I was really a better woman for him than my mother. We were the pair and I was going to be his helpmate. The little girl's dream come true.

The first inkling I had of my father's weakness was at the border when, in the middle of the night, the border patrol came into our cabin on the train. I was sleeping on the upper berth, and they stomped about, and my father was very nervous. I could tell that he handled things very poorly. If I had been the border patrol, I would have been very curious about what was going on, he was so nervous. I was terrified after that, but I was a child of great self-control and I played my role very well.

Somehow we arrived in Paris, and things were reestablished. My father and I went to restaurants and he was able to show me all around. He was a man of great style and charm. And again I had the old sense of my father. I didn't realize how tenuous our financial situation was, because he didn't let me feel it at that point. We didn't live in expensive hotels, but, you know, eating out in those days wasn't expensive, and I had the sense that everything was all right.

Then in about six weeks time, my mother arrived in Paris and joined us in this hotel. And I was aware of some terrible things going on—tension between my mother and father. It was unspeakable. I had been used to my father's and mother's quarrels and outbursts. After all, in my family, shouting was not considered to be unusual or a bad thing. But this was even worse.

I later learned that what had happened was that my father and mother had had some napoleons and gold pieces that they had buried before the German invasion, under a mulberry tree in our garden back home, in a metal box. In addition to the napoleons and the gold pieces, there was some American money—very large denominations. All of this was wrapped up carefully. And, apparently, my poor mother, who had absolutely no practical sense at all, was entrusted with digging this up and bringing it out. And she delivered what she thought was the entire cache to my father in Paris, and she felt so proud of herself—like a little kid, because in relationship to my father she was like a child, abused, humiliated by his affairs throughout the years. She was like a kid who had never grown up. So she had given him these gifts, you know, the gold pieces. It turned out, however, that in her fear, when she had taken this box into the house, she had flushed the paper money down the toilet with the wrappings.

So all of this absolute misery that I experienced in that Paris hotel, which completely undermined my sense of confidence, had to do with money. But they had the habit of not telling me. It wasn't the kind of household where people thought out what they did in relationship to children. Everybody did what felt good, what felt spontaneous. They just didn't think in psychological terms. They were just, you know, they were *they*. And so I was terrified.

We lived from day to day for a while. My father was keeping up a brave front, but I could see that he was progressively more and more crushed. Finally, we were able to book passage on a small boat. I was to come to the United States with my father. My mother had lived in Paris as a young girl for two years, and she knew French beautifully and she was a painter, so she was going to stay there. In effect, they were separating. My father and I got a visitor's visa, and that was a lie because we were planning to stay.

I spoke some English by this time. I had had Swiss governesses and an English governess before the war, so that I spoke British English, with an English accent. On the boat I was the interpreter for my father, and, again, I was very conscious of his weakness, his vulnerability—because I was the one who had to translate for him.

Then, after a trip with miserable seasickness, we arrived at the point where the boat stops and the Immigration boards in New York. This was in February of '49. And they boarded and they called us into rooms where people came in groups, family groups, to have a hearing.

My father had heard from my uncle that everything was all right with the American officials, but that if once he was caught lying, that would be the end. So he decided to tell the truth. And remember, my father came from this personal culture where you always spoke personally to officials. You talked in a certain way and you made certain faces, and maybe you slipped people some money; there was nobody you couldn't talk to personally. And, of course, his father had written all these plays about these ideal characters who were just like that: Everyone is human underneath. So during the hearing with the Immigration, my father suddenly decided he was going to tell the truth about our intention.

I guess the most painful part of my memory of coming was that scene in front of the Immigration officials. I was torn by my absolute conviction that what my father wanted to say was a mistake, and his insistence on my speaking what he wanted me to. The conflict was terrible, and my father's rage was terrible. First he shouted, then he pleaded with me. We had conversations between us in Hungarian in front of the Immigration officials. Finally, I had to say what my father wanted me to say, which was the truth.

The Immigration official said, "You came with a visitor's visa, and you're giving us contrary information. We cannot let you disembark."

We ended up on Ellis Island. I remember it as a terrifying place. There was a huge hall and there were benches and there was a stone floor, as I recall, and high windows. And people were sitting on the benches, and children were playing and crying and talking, and everything reverberated. And then there were kind of balconies up above, where the sleeping quarters were.

It was a miserable time. The men and women slept separately. I was separated from my father. We were given bedding, a piece of soap. I don't even know how many people I slept with in a room. It must have been very traumatic, because my recall of it is so sketchy, so painful. What frightened me most there was a Yugoslavian who had a kind of cigarette stand; and he had been there on Ellis Island for *two and a half years*. I had visions of us staying there two and a half years. After all these dreams of freedom and seeing the Statue of Liberty from the boat and watching people disembark, I had to remain.

Finally, my uncle intervened and guaranteed that if we became dependent, he would support us. My uncle was a *bon vivant*. He wrote a food column for *Esquire* and a number of books about food and things like that, and he knew how to live. So he guaranteed that we would not become dependent on the state.

After we landed, we went to live in a hotel on Fifty-seventh Street. In a few weeks we moved to another hotel and then another. We moved quite frequently. Most of the time I ate in the Automat, either with my father or without him. My father was trying to get settled and was attempting to do what had to be done to change his immigration status. And he hunted up some lawyer. There were many lawyers floating about at this time who would help you to become a displaced person, and I think he paid a thousand dollars, eventually, to someone. And, finally, we became displaced persons.

For a while I wasn't going to school, but then that became a problem. What to do about me? Through some friends I was referred to the Professional Children's School. They thought that would be a good place for me to fit in, because, you know, I was kind of in the middle of nowhere. And that school was used to unusual arrangements and people who didn't really fit in; so I started going there.

Nobody noticed, but it should have been a signal that something was wrong with me, because I had a great deal of trouble learning. We were reading *Westward Ho!* and I couldn't understand what I was reading. You have to realize that I was really quite fluent in reading English, so something was wrong. I remember doing math problems and getting my papers back because I had crossed my sevens. Any problem in which I crossed my sevens, the teacher automatically counted wrong, no matter how I'd done the calculations. And I did the dividing differently, you know, and multiplying in a different way. After all, there are Hungarian mathematicians, you know. So I was getting everything wrong. School wasn't satisfying at all to me.

During that whole year I don't remember a single one of my classmates. I don't remember a single one of my teachers' names. I do not remember where that Professional Children's School is located. I do not remember what it looks like. I don't remember how you walk into it, what the rooms were like. I could not tell you one thing about it. It's hard to tell you something about that experience. I knew no children other than these children, who were not really children, and who had lives of their own. My brother we never saw because he was in this elegant boarding school in Connecticut.

For entertainment, I used to go to Broadway and, for a quarter, I would buy time to play Ping-Pong. It was safe then, to do that. And I would just pay my quarter and take whatever partner I could get. I used to spend a lot of time in the movies, too. I'd go by myself and I'd just sit. And sometimes I would sit through two shows and then I'd go home. I suppose I did homework. I was a very conscientious student so I must have done homework, but I don't remember. I was almost in limbo, but functioning, externally functioning. No one could even see anything was wrong.

Then the school year was over, and some rich relative of my mother's, who lived on Park Avenue, went to his country home on Long Island and allowed us to live in his apartment for the summer. Most of the apartment was shut off and it had white shrouds on all the furniture. One huge room was left open for us, and the kitchen, which was usually peopled by servants, but now was empty. I was to be the housekeeper. My brother came home from his boarding school, and all three of us slept in this huge shrouded room. There was no air conditioning, and because all the other rooms were closed off, even the one fan wouldn't do anything for us. I remember being miserably hot.

I started keeping house, and I'd never cooked before, although I'd spent a great deal of time with our servants in the kitchen in Hungary. I used to go down to Third Avenue and carry things home. Of course, the whole business of kilograms versus pounds and what to shop for and not knowing the names of the vegetables and everything was hard. Even though I spoke English, I didn't speak the appropriate English. All that was painful. My bags would break on the way home, and I had a miserable time. I looked so inappropriate for that Park Avenue apartment that often the doorman would make me take the service elevator. Most of the people there shopped at Gristede's, you know, and had things sent up.

My brother used to make my life miserable in various ways that brothers have. And my father was getting depressed. It was a very unhealthy family circle.

I remember doing a lot of crying in those days. I had no friends—I'm crying now. Often I would go to St. Patrick's Cathedral and sit in the back and I'd just cry. No one was ever aware. That's the thing that's so amazing to me, you know. I couldn't even say I hated being there, because I had made my father come, and I knew my father was miserable, too. And I knew we couldn't go back.

It wasn't really that I couldn't stand this country. There were things that I liked; just the idea that I could walk down the street without worrying about who overheard what I said. But my fear wasn't completely gone, because there was always the constant shadow of the Immigration hanging over our heads—deportation and all these things that might happen if we didn't get it fixed. So, at this point, I do not think that I felt any of the liberation of being in this country. I was very unhappy. That was all.

After some months of this, I remember several times I attempted to use my father's razor blades to cut my wrists. But I didn't dare to do anything dramatic. I would scratch and then it would hurt, and I would stop. No one noticed that I had those scratches. The crying continued. No one noticed. No one. So one day I just took my father's sleeping pills, and I took a large overdose of them. And my poor brother came and found me.

In a way, that was my liberation, because then I was taken off to a private psychiatric hospital in Long Island. There must have been an awful lot of scurrying around with my uncle and our rich relatives. At that hospital there was a very wise woman in charge, who didn't let them give me any shock treatments or anything. She just talked to me. And being away from home interrupted this downward spiral I had been in. The most important thing, the doctor thought, was to separate me from my family. She had a friend from medical school, an old maid, who was going to take a job in Oak Ridge, Tennessee, as an industrial physician. And this friend said, "Why doesn't Ilona come and live with me?" So I went to live with her.

In Tennessee, I really began to shine. It wasn't that I was an all-A student, but I started writing in English. I gave little speeches around Oak Ridge. I was their little Hungarian. This was before the '56 Revolution and Hungarians were a unique commodity in those days, you know. I gave talks and I wrote papers for school and I was able to study history. I lived among people there, who, for the most part, were less sophisticated, less used to using language, less analytical of themselves.

I think my love for the English language, the sense of liberation that it gave me, had to do with that regained sense of control, of self-respect, of feeling free to express myself, and so on. The English language, you know, is so different from the Hungarian language. In Hungarian, one wants to use the beautiful phrase, not exactly flowery but eloquent, poetic. And English seemed so precise, so unemotional. It appealed to me. I fell in love with the English language there.

I began writing, too. I guess the thing that made me start writing was that I couldn't transcend the isolation any other way. I tried to capture the feeling of belonging, of reality, with language and poetry, particularly poetry. I've always felt that was the thing that spoke to me most, poetry.

The doctor who had taken me in was a very difficult person to live with. After the first year down there, she couldn't stand the job and they couldn't stand her. She left.

Her brother, who was working in the Oak Ridge plant, said, "Okay, we'll take Ilona." So he and his wife took me into their family. They had three children, and I was in this position of having to be grateful. So I baby-sat. I helped clean the house. I did everything and no one had to tell me. I was there first when something had to be done. I was the ideal teen-age child, and I did a lot of baby-sitting on the side, too. But it was all, you know, a matter of gratitude. I went through none of the teen-age *Sturm und Drang*. I had nothing to rebel about. They weren't my own mother and father. They had none of my values. They were benevolent, but there was no feeling. I was totally alone. I knew I had to make my own way and that they were making it possible for me. But they were not my family.

It was in college that I first began to feel comfortable. I think that it was, perhaps, the fact that I was achieving and was recognized as achieving. My last year I was Phi Beta Kappa, and I thought of applying for a Fulbright. I had a professor, who was really the first person who helped me to believe that I was good, but the trouble was that it became a personal relationship, and, even as he made me believe that I was good, I began to doubt that he had the objectivity to view me correctly.

He urged me to apply for the Fulbright, and I kept putting it off in that classical way. You know, the fear of success sort of thing? Finally, I did, and I got the Fulbright to go to the University of London and I didn't go.

*Why not?*

It was very complicated. First of all, this professor was a married man and he had four children, and he was in love with me, and I couldn't handle that at my age. He was going to take a sabbatical, come to London, and spend the year with me. I could not see this. I was a very moralistic person. I was afraid to accept the responsibility. You see, there was all this baggage that I had carried around from Hungary, about nice girls and what they do. I had had such a miserable family life. To me, the breaking up of a family was just not something I could live with, or do.

There was this other man, also a professor, who kept after me. He was fourteen years older than I was. Underneath, I was really quite young and inexperienced in many ways, but I knew I wasn't in love with him. I was pretty sure he wasn't in love with me either, but he was a lonely person. Finally I did go to bed with him, and then I felt I had to get married, because I was a bad girl. I had been to bed with somebody, and you don't do that. It was all mixed up with my fears and my sense of obligation. It never occurred to me that the pain that I would have caused him then would have been much less than the pain that I would cause a person whom I married and didn't love.

Again, I talked to nobody. I had nobody to talk with. That has been a pattern of my life. Whenever anything critical has happened, I had no one to talk with. So I got married and I knew it was a mistake, and I was married for twenty years. . . .

Everywhere I was a changeling. I didn't fit into my family. I didn't fit into my New York life. I didn't fit into my Tennessee life. The man I loved was married. The man I married I didn't love. I hope sometime I can find a place where I belong.

# Maria Nikitin

···················FROM LATVIA, 1950······················

*She was born in 1920 on a small farm in Latvia. After a lifetime of hard labor, she still works at two jobs: as a factory worker and as a cleaning woman. She lives alone in Morristown, New Jersey, in a comfortable new apartment furnished with brocaded chairs and sofa, custom-made draperies, cut-glass ornaments, pecanwood tables, and an entire mirrored wall.*

I be thirteen, almost fourteen year old, and my mother die. I have three brothers and father, and I have to take over my mother job—cleaning, wash clothes by hand. I get up early in morning—five o'clock—and I milk my cows—my father have ten cows and a lot of pigs and chickens. And I send all the milk on the farm to dairy and I bring skim milk back. I feed pigs with skim milk and I make cottage cheese. And I have to go in the field and work, too.

Then started the war, 1939. The Russians came in Latvia. They counted everything what people have: how many dresses, how many pans, how many cows. If you have something and working hard, they call you capitalist. They took piece of ground and your cows away and your horses away, pigs, and even clothes and shoes. They took everything away from you and gave to poorer ones, because you are a capitalist and somebody else no having nothing. And the Russians took one brother to army.

The Germans chased the Russians out in 1942. I like the Germans better because they no touch nothing. But they take all the young fellows in the army. My two other brothers went in German army. And they took me to Germany to work in factory.

I stayed in factory three years. We all lived in one big building; about fifty people in one big room, in beds, one, two, three high. I sleeped on top—I no want the dust coming in my eyes. Food was very poor—two slices bread with margarine, coffee, soup with potatoes, maybe once in a while a piece of horse meat. For three years I didn't have glass of milk, egg, butter. No enough food, but you can't die even.

Then 1943 I had letter from middle brother in the German army. He lost both legs and was in German hospital. I asked my boss permission to go to Neufchatel to see him. And I saw him and I talked to him. But he died.

My brother in Russian army ran away and he joined German army, and my boyfriend, too. And the Russians finded them and they shoot them and 120 people like that. And my other brother in German army got dead, too, in Stalingrad. Last letter I having from father, all the brothers killed.

In March 1945 we having air raids all the time, lots of bombing. Daytime have to work, nighttime can't sleep because all the bombs coming in—and once in a while we can't even go in the bunker; we lay down right in the potato patch. [Laughs.] In the morning early, you go out and see bodies laying like flies, but you have to go through them. Is terrible looking: some of them people without any heads, without any hands, some of them so squashed. Small kids, big kids, old people, any kind of people. Can't see nurse or Red Cross ambulance, the bodies laying there all week, nobody picking up. But you have to go on.

The Russians came in, and I was hiding in a house and I ran to attic and hided with blanket over my head. Russian came up and put hand on blanket and said, "Who is this?" and I said, "Me." [Laughs.] And he said, "Where you born? Why you not going to Latvia?" And he said I have to get registration. I no like Russians altogether, so next day I disappeared completely. A lot of people helped me. I finded passport from German lady and I learned her story, where she born and so forth. Then I made hair like that [pulls hair back] and put on babushka like German women wear them. And I went in train with Germany refugees. So then came in a Russian to check up, and I sprechen Deutsch very good then. And then a German came in to check up, and I was thinking now I be bad off. He started looking at passports and everything, looking so close, and I was thinking, "Well, I no having no more choice." Train was going very, very slow—going near border from English zone. And I just pulled at the door, and I jumped out and I rolled down. It was nighttime, raining, and so forth, and there was standing Russian soldier with hood on the head. He say, "Stoi!" But I'm running and he can't shoot me, because I'm already crossed. The English put me in the jail. They wanted to check up my paper and so forth. I told them, "You can shoot me dead, but I'm no going to Russia." So they put me in a DP camp in Lübeck. That was 1946, March.

I stayed in DP camp four years. Countries, like Brazil, Argentina, England, New Zealand, they were taking a lot of people from camp, giving jobs. But I was always waiting for United States, because my father and my mother used to talk that United States very good country and rich and so forth. So came in one day lady from New Jersey. She married a German fellow and came to visit mother-in-law. She came to camp and was looking over the girls. She picked out maybe six girls; she wanted to see which one better worker for housework. I wanted to go. She asked me, "You like children?"

"Ooh, I like!"

She asked me, "You can cook?"

"Ooh, I cook good."

"And you iron?"

"Oh, yeah, look my dress ironed."

So she picked me and she said she sending me papers.

Meantime I started signing through the church, Lutheran Church, because meantime I was thinking maybe I'll get in anyway. They were taking people to work in Virginia or Chicago or New Jersey. I never got the paper from my lady, but I wrote her when I'm leaving for America, what ship I'm going on. And then she came in to New York and she finded my face [laughs], and she said, "Come, come, come."

So, anyway, I came in to New Jersey, 27 March; April 6 I went in hospital. I was feeling sick, and I told my lady, and she took me to doctor. He put me right in the hospital. One nurse talked little bit Polish, and she said to me that I have tuberculosis in the kidney and I have to take it out. And then I'm terrible disappointed and was crying a lot.

After the operation I was better and I started right away work. They having big house—ten room. They having two children and dog. I have to wash clothes and iron; I have to keep whole house clean. And then come May month and I have to cut all the grass. I having pay only $10 a week.

One day I thought to myself, "What I'm supposed to do? How I pay hospital bills?" I have to pay doctor $300 for operation and I have to pay operation room $25 and then hospital—altogether about $1,075. And I sat down and figured out I better go looking for a job.

I had a little German book and then I had newspaper in English. I studied about three, four hours, and I put together from ad in newspaper. So next morning I got up and I walked to Morristown [about ten miles]. I was twenty-nine, thirty years old, strong—you can shoot me and I no die! And I got the job, sewing in the Maidenform Bra Company.

So I was living with the same lady, working in the house every night and every weekend, and I finded Hungarian man with store on next street. His son was driving to Morristown every day, so he gave me ride. In Maidenform I started seventy-five cents an hour. Then I worked piecework—sixty pieces, you get thirty-three cents. I picked it up and I was very good speed, and once in a while I was bringing about fifty and sixty dollars a week. But then lady said to me, "Now you pay for room and board." So I left her and went to Hungarian man and wife. I lived in his house, and I was working Saturday and Sunday and evening for just room and board. I was working eight years in Maidenform and I made pretty good; and I paid all of my hospital bills, and everything got cleared up.

Then I said to myself, "Now is enough for me. Now I go live in Morristown." And then I was looking for cheapest room. I finded one room for twenty-five dollars a month. I was very glad. I cleaned it up, but it was so small. I had an iron board and I had a chair and a little tiny table. When I was going to bed, I moved my things from bed to iron board or to chair. When I needed a chair to sit down, then I moved again to bed. And so I was just moving and moving. I was living fourteen years like that.

Meantime, I was thinking I'll go and do little bit housework and get a little bit saved for my old age. I finded at Maidenform one lady, and I went her house Saturday and I working like a horse. She gave me four dollars. Then she gave me a lot of people and then I had a lot of work. I was happy with people. They helped me and I did work and they no pushed me. I can have supper with them, I can sit down and I can talk with them. I was working in Maidenform daytime, and every night I working somebody's house, and Saturday and Sunday, too. And then I paid my room and I paid my food, and meantime I was saving money for my old age little bit so I no have to ask United States to support me. I'm very glad I'm here and I'm thinking I'm glad to support myself for whole life.

Then my Maidenform close and I finded job in Livingston, making hinges for eyeglasses. Then again I had to travel. And then I was thinking, "Now, if I pass all my life so hard, I'm going to learn to drive car." So I learned and they gave to me driver license. I was having couple of hundred so I bought secondhand car. Still I saved and I saved and I saved.

I was thinking someday I'll get better place. I want to die in a better place, like a person. Because I was living for whole of my life very tough. I wanted to go in apartment, but I worried maybe I get sick and I can't keep my apartment. And then, after I got a little bit money more, and I had a little bit in the bank and the interest helped me pay rent, then I finded me nice little apartment. Then I had to buy furniture. But all my ladies were very nice, they all gave me blankets and dishes and pictures and television.

Everybody gave me presents, so I figured out, "Now I have to be sport." I invited everybody—all the people I working for—you know, I working for same people fifteen, twenty years—some girlfriends from the factory. One of my ladies, she helped me cook and bake. I had twenty-eight people, plenty of food—potato pancakes, chicken, noodle pudding, ravioli, cakes. And everybody's so happy I have a good place. . . .

You know, when I be a little girl, maybe ten, twelve, a gypsy walked into our house and she said to my mother, "I'm laying out cards for you."

My mother no wanted it and she hollered and she said, "No!"

But the gypsy said, "All right, I'm just laying for the little girl here sitting." Then she looked at cards and she said to me and to my mother, "She's a girl be having a very, very hard life and she be someday very, very rich woman."

My mother said to her, "You crazy."

And the gypsy said, "She's going far away, cross the ocean; she no be in this country." My mother not believe it, but I opened my ears. And the gypsy said again, "Well, this girl someday be very rich."

I remember always, and once in a while I'm sitting and I'm thinking about that, what she said to me. Right now I'm looking around my apartment, I'm looking at myself. I'm not dressy, not fancy, but I'm having a couple dollar. I have a nice apartment, I have clothes, and I have food. And I'm thinking, my mother was hard-working woman on a farm. She having food, but she not have so nice things like I having right now. And I'm thinking that I am rich right now. . . .

# W. Michael Blumenthal

···················· FROM GERMANY, 1947 ····················

*At the time of the interview, he had been secretary of the treasury of the United States for almost two years. He sat in his gilt and marble office overlooking the White House and reflected on the events that led him to occupy one of the most powerful positions in the world. He recalled the day in 1938 when he saw the Nazi storm troopers smash up his parents' small shop in Berlin and take his father away to a concentration camp. When his father came back a few months later, "a shrunken man," the family determined to flee Germany.*

. . . But no one wanted us. It was impossible to get visas to any country. The immigration laws of the United States at that time involved a long waiting list before quota numbers would be available under which we could come in.

So we went to China, because Shanghai at that point was an international city and required no visa of any kind. I was thirteen years old when we arrived in China, and I went to a school, a British school, from the age of thirteen until the age of sixteen. At that time, Pearl Harbor took place and Shanghai was occupied by the Japanese, and I had to leave school. All the refugees were moved to a ghetto in Shanghai, and we had to live there from '42 to '45.

There was really very little work that involved any kind of income on which we could live in Shanghai. My mother and my father engaged in various small jobs, selling clothing and so forth, in order to make a very meager living. And I did any number of things. I worked as a bottle washer in a chemical factory, I delivered bread to people in the district, I delivered sausages, I did various odd jobs. Most of the time there wasn't really anything to do. We existed to some extent on the proceeds of money that was sent in by charity organizations—Jewish, Christian, and others who were sending money in through the Red Cross, to Sweden and Switzerland, to keep us going.

In 1945, the Japanese of course left, and the American army and the air force and navy came into Shanghai. I was one of the first people, actually, to get a job with the American air force, and I worked with them for two years. It was my first experience with Americans, and I made many friends among the GI's. They would tell me about the United States. "Oh, it's a great country," they'd say, and they'd tell me many stories. They were really from all parts of the United States, so I got a pretty good picture of what the country was like by talking to the fellows from Georgia and Tennessee and New York and Kansas and California, wherever they were from.

They seemed different from other people I knew—healthier, athletic, cleaner, more hygienic. They seemed more fun-loving, more joyful. And richer, they seemed richer, obviously. Even the privates had what appeared to be a lot of money. They also seemed more comradely with each other. Coming from Germany, I had had visions of soldiers being very hierarchical, with a lot of saluting and clicking of heels. And in Germany, certainly, that's the way it was. But the Americans seemed to me to have an innate sense of equality about each other, particularly in that postwar period. The average GI really exhibited the sense that, while he might be a corporal and someone else was a lieutenant or a captain, he was as good as that person, even though one had a higher rank or a different category. That impressed me greatly.

And those soldiers seemed to me, most of them, quite optimistic. There were very few pessimists in the group. Most of them were optimistic about what they intended to do when they came back and about their chances of doing it. Many of them talked about going to school, getting an education, using the GI Bill. They talked about buying a farm or doing something. Most of them felt they had something going for them, and most of them felt that they could do what they wanted to do.

I was nineteen years old, energetic, full of ambition, and optimistic, as one tends to be at that age, and I had lived in an environment, ever since I was old enough to realize what was going on, in which there were many, many restrictions placed on my ability to do the things I wanted to do. Those restrictions seemed to me to be irrational, arbitrary, and unfair, because they were restrictions that had nothing to do with me or with what I could do or what I was capable of doing or willing to do. They had more to do with what my surname was, who my parents were, whether or not I had the right kind of passport, whether or not I was accepted in the right kind of school or the right kind of club, or whether I belonged to this group or that. It was more who I belonged to and who my origins were than what I could do. This was a very frustrating thing, because I felt as I looked at these people, the Americans, I wanted to be like them. And I felt I could compete and do as well as they could.

The thought of going to the United States and of making a new life there dominated the thinking of not only myself, but virtually all the refugees and displaced persons who had been kicked out of their countries and traveled halfway around the world to come to this strange place. It dominated our whole lives. We knew the names and the details, the personal details, of the three or four vice-consuls working in the American consulate general in Shanghai. We knew more about them than they realized.

The whole topic of conversation in the refugee circles was what the chances were of getting your visa to the United States. You had to do several things. You had to pass a medical test, because they wouldn't let people in with a communicable disease. It was the first time I learned about the power of psychosomatic illnesses and the power of mind over body. People developed symptoms. They were so afraid they might be turned down on medical grounds that, when they'd get a letter saying "Your number has come up," they'd develop all those symptoms—chills, fever, sweating—just worrying that they would be turned down. I was part of this general environment in which it was the sole and major topic of conversation. Would I be given a visa? Would I pass the tests? Or would I have to go back to the ghetto? It was probably the most single important thing on our minds.

*Can you remember when you found out about the visa?*

Oh, yes. Yes, I remember very well when I got it. Of course, I had no passport. I just had an UNRAA piece of paper that said, "This certifies that this person claims to be Werner Michael Blumenthal, born in Berlin," etc. And the visa was stamped on the back of that. I still have that little piece of paper that I got in Shanghai from the United Nations, with my visa stamped on the back of it and the signature of the United States consul. I got it in July and I finished my job at the air force base, and, together with my sister, I left in September of '47 on a converted troop ship. I remember collecting my last pay and changing the Chinese dollars into American dollars. Altogether I had sixty American dollars to take with me.

The troop ship was very crowded. There were 36 women with my sister in one cabin, and in mine there were maybe 120 men and boys in the hold. We had five beds in a row, one on top of another, all around the hold. I made a beeline for the top bunk, because I thought I would get claustrophobia on the bottom, but it wasn't that much better, because if I raised my head just a tiny bit I'd hit the ceiling. The air was a little better on the top than it was on the bottom, that's all. In fact, the air in the accommodations was so bad that I discovered there was a better way to live on the ship. A few friends of mine found the old gun emplacements had a little shield around them. The guns had been taken out, but the shield made a little compartment on the deck, and we took our blankets and pillows and slept up there because it was pleasant in the air. So most of the time on that trip across to the United States I slept the way a lot of the old immigrants did, on the deck under the stars.

We landed first in Honolulu, which was United States territory but not yet one of the United States. I was absolutely overwhelmed by the smell, the flowers, the cleanliness. China had been a very, very dirty place. Here you could open the tap and drink the water! And I remember going into the Royal Hawaiian Hotel at Waikiki Beach and being absolutely overwhelmed by the fact that there was a fountain in the lobby, just like a water fountain. You could press on it and drink, free of charge, pineapple juice. A country where you can drink free pineapple juice! It was truly the land of milk and honey to me. And the climate was so beautiful, the sky was so nice. I was ready to stay right there. I said, "How could any place in the United States be more beautiful than this?" But my sister was with me and she prevailed on me, and I, too, kind of felt I really wanted to go to the United States proper. So we went on.

On the twenty-fourth of September in 1947, we landed in San

Francisco. A lot of people who came to the dock to meet us had come from Germany in the late thirties. They could hardly speak German anymore and they lorded it over us. They were now very Americanized, and they said, "Well, you're new people. This is what we do in the United States." Some of them spoke German with an American accent, and they acted so superior to us that we began calling them the "Mayflower refugees." They had been here maybe six, seven, eight years, and they already had jobs and wore good clothes and had a car. They had all the outward manifestations of Americans, and it was very impressive.

My sister and I were put up in a hotel by the relief organizations, and we kind of wandered around for a few days and tried to orient ourselves. On Sunday we pored over a paper and marked out the places to go to apply for a job. And on Monday, five days after we got here, we went out to look for jobs. We met for lunch that day, my sister and I, and we both had jobs. She had a job as a secretary and I had a job as a billing clerk for the National Biscuit Company. I got paid forty dollars a week and I believe she got paid forty-five dollars a week. She got paid more because her job was more skilled than mine.

*What did you do as a billing clerk?*

I sat in a big room, and all around the room were tables where there were something like forty billing clerks. They were mainly young people. They got the bills that had been filled out by the warehousemen as they were putting stuff into the trucks for delivery to each of the customers who were buying cookies. And the bill would say, for instance, "forty-seven Animal Crackers," or "twelve Fig Newtons," or "three dozen Lorna Doones—eleven cents each," so you'd have to multiply three dozen times eleven, thirty-six times eleven. We didn't even have an adding machine. We just sat all day and figured the stuff up. After a while I could do it in my head.

We did that eight hours a day, with a coffee break in the afternoon and a coffee break in the morning and a half-hour out for lunch. On one side of the room, on a slightly raised platform, sat the office manager, Mr. Duff, and every time you'd stop to chat or gossip or do your sums, Mr. Duff, who was a stern-looking gentleman much older than us, would look over his rimless glasses at you and go, "Harumph." And there he was, looking at you like Scrooge. You'd look up and then you'd quickly go back, because you're afraid you'd get fired if you took too much time doing your sums.

Within a very short period of time, I realized that progress from billing clerk to senior billing clerk to clerk to superclerk, and on up the ladder, would be very slow indeed. I had left school at the age of sixteen in China, but I had done a lot of reading. I'd read a lot of the great books; literature in French, German, English. Thomas Mann, Goethe, Schiller, Dumas; and then, since I'd gone to a British school, I'd done a lot of reading in English. People had records and we listened to music. And I picked up things from people there, but I'd had no formal education beyond sixteen.

I was really very interested in educating myself more. It was a combination of thirst for knowledge, a desire to develop a professional skill, and then all these guys were going back to study. This was just after the war and the GI Bill was very prominent. Everybody was going back to college. But I had no money. My wages, $34.10 after taxes, were not enough to go to college with. And then I couldn't get into a college, because I wasn't a high-school graduate. I felt very old. I was twenty-one, but I felt very old. I felt life had passed me by. Here are kids graduating from high school at eighteen and from college at twenty-one, and I was twenty-one. I didn't want to go back to the eleventh grade or something and graduate from high school at twenty-three; that was out of the question. I tried the University of California and they wouldn't take me, and no other four-year college would either.

But then a friend of mine explained to me that there was a way. The thing to do was to go to a city junior college. "They'll take anybody," he said. "I mean kids who have gone to high school but who didn't graduate, or kids who graduated but didn't have a good enough average. You could go there. They have general college and semiprofessional and university parallel." In the university-parallel courses, they used the same texts and had the same syllabus and curriculum as the freshman and sophomore years in Berkeley, at the University of California. And they'd worked out an arrangement that, if you had a B average or better in the city junior college, you could transfer to the University of California at the end of two years, even though you didn't originally satisfy the regular entrance requirements. So I went to San Francisco Junior College. It's now called San Francisco City College. And they gave me a test to see where I'd fit in, and I guess I did well. It showed that I had educated myself enough that I would be able to go there. Then I had to figure out how to eat. There was no tuition, but I had to buy books and take care of myself while I was going to school.

The National Biscuit Company job was a regular nine-to-five job, so I decided to find an evening job so that I could go to school during the day. There were no evening classes then. I answered a job for checkroom attendant and elevator operator at the Saint Francis Hospital and got the job. I'd work from two to ten every day. Unfortunately, they paid only the minimum wage, which was eighty cents an hour then. So I went to Mr. Duff and said, "I'm going back to school," and for a while he let me work part-time as a billing clerk while I worked at the hospital in the afternoon and evenings. I ran the elevator, ran the checkroom, carried flowers up, delivered candy, and, in fact, worked from morning until night, which allowed me to save a little money for when the semester began. Then when school started, I regretfully had to lower my income and just stayed with the hospital job. . . . During the summer I did lots of other things. I drove a truck, washed dishes, worked as a Brinks guard, worked in a wax factory, worked as a janitor. At Christmastime I carried mailbags for the post office.

Eventually, having received decent grades at San Francisco Junior College, I transferred to Berkeley and spent two more years as an undergraduate there. I graduated with honors and Phi Beta Kappa; got a scholarship to Princeton; got married and went to Princeton. I majored in international economics and I went to the Woodrow Wilson School of Public and International Affairs there, to continue studying international affairs. I thought I would work either in business or in government in the international economic area. I always had an interest in public service in some way or another. Maybe I wanted to be like that vice-consul who gave me the visa. That probably was in the back of my mind, because he was highly legitimized, and I had been very illegitimate, and this was a way of being in a profession to legitimize my status. Maybe that's the psychological explanation. But also, I was interested in government and interested in international affairs, because I had been a victim of the mismanagement of international affairs, and I thought I would like to work in an area where I could try to make a contribution to the better management of such affairs.

I wound up with a doctorate in economics from Princeton, as well as with a master's degree from the Woodrow Wilson School. And when that was finished, I was offered an opportunity to stay at Princeton and to teach there. I stayed there for three years, teaching; by that time I was thirty-one. The pay of a young professor was pretty low, and we had two children and a third one was on the way. We were still living in a housing project at the university. We'd never been able to accumulate any savings, because the children had been coming along. Also, I was not totally satisfied with the university environment, because I am more oriented toward active, participatory type of activities rather than just teaching others.

During that period, while I was doing some research, I met a man who was the president of a medium-sized company called the Crown Cork International Corporation. It was a holding company for some foreign plants in ten different countries. He and I used to play chess together, and we used to talk, and eventually he offered me a job. I felt it was a good opportunity to get into business, so I resigned from Princeton and went to work for him as his assistant. In another year or two, I became vice-president of this little company. It wasn't a big company, but it was a good job and a good opportunity, and I made a lot more money than I did at Princeton. And then in November 1960, Kennedy was elected to office, and one of his assistants called me and said, "Look, we're looking for some people who have some business experience and some international economic background, who are reasonably intelligent and who are Democrats. How would you like to work for the government?"

I said, "Absolutely. I want to go to work because of Kennedy and I want to be a New Frontiersman." So I came down to Washington and they interviewed me, and I got a job at the State Department as a deputy assistant secretary, because I had the Ph.D. and was vice-president of the company.

And the first thing that I did on my job in the State Department was to look up the name of the foreign service officer who had given me my visa. He had been a demigod to me, but there was, of course, no reason why he should remember me. He had given visas to thousands of people. I had just stood before him. I knew all about him, but he had no reason to remember me. So I looked his name up in the State Department directory, and, sure enough, he happened to be stationed in Washington at the time. I was a deputy assistant secretary and was much more senior than he, since I had been jumped in as a political appointee.

I called him on the phone and I said, "You don't know me; I've just been appointed to this job."

And he said, "Well, I've read your name. Yes, sir, what can I do for you?"

I said, "Well, I'd like to have lunch with you."

"Do I know you?"

"Well, I'll explain all about this when I see you. Meet me in the secretaries' dining room." You had to be at least a deputy assistant secretary to eat there. He wasn't even allowed to eat there, except as a guest.

So he said, "Okay, yeah." And we met there and we sat down and he said the equivalent of, "To what do I owe this honor?" He couldn't understand what I would be talking about with him.

I said, "Well, let's order our meal and I'll explain it to you."

After the waitress had taken our order, I pulled that frayed, tattered piece of paper out of my pocket and I handed it to him. He looked at it and he turned it over and he saw the stamp and saw his signature, and he looked at me. And he looked at it again and he was truly speechless for a moment, and then he said, "Well, I'll be damned."

That was probably one of the proudest moments of my life; as proud or prouder a moment than the day I was sworn into this job [as secretary of the treasury]. Fourteen years ago I had been a stateless refugee and this guy had put his stamp and his signature on a piece of paper, and now I was inviting him to lunch in the secretaries' dining room. It was a great moment for me—and maybe for him. [*Laughs.*]

I worked with the State Department for two years, and then there was a big trade negotiation going on, called the "Kennedy Round," that required sending a man to Geneva to be U.S. representative. The people in the White House kind of thought I was the right candidate, so I was appointed ambassador, a U.S. ambassador, at age thirty-seven. Only sixteen years after I came to this country, I went to Europe as a U.S. ambassador.

I was in Geneva for four years, representing the United States, doing this negotiation. And in 1967, the negotiation was concluded successfully. A lot of people heard and read about me, and the Bendix Corporation offered me a job as president of Bendix International. Four years later, I was appointed chairman of the board of the Bendix Corporation.

In 1976, after the election, I was asked to come and consult with President-elect Carter, because I was a Democrat. I hadn't supported him; actually, I had supported another Democrat. But he wanted me to talk about international economy, and I talked with him on two occasions. On the second meeting, he said, "Would you help me? Would you come to work in Washington?"

I said, "Well, I have a big job at Bendix, but I've always thought I'd like to come back for one more tour of duty. This country has been very good to me. It has allowed me to develop my talents to the fullest. I would be honored to serve in a job where I feel I could do something."

Carter said, "I'll call you." And in a few days, two or three days later, he called me and said what he really had in mind was a senior cabinet job, possibly the treasury. And I said I would take that because of the opportunity and the honor and the privilege. So that's how I got to be here.

Later I went to Berlin. Obviously, to be arriving in an airplane with the United States of America seal on the outside, and an honor guard, and the red carpet rolled out, and all the bigwigs waiting for me—well, it was a source of some satisfaction to me—a kind of poetic justice. One of the principal Berlin newspapers had a big, fat headline that read: "A Berliner Becomes America's Minister of Finance." I cut that out and framed it. I thought it was kind of coming full circle—that the people who had kicked me out now would put my picture on the front page and call me proudly a "Berliner."

# PART III

# IMMIGRATION
## A Continuing Process

*You know when I first found out that I was getting to be patriotic, if you could call me in any way patriotic? I used to watch these games, like the Olympics, and I found myself jumping with excitement for the Americans to win. [Laughs.] And I said, "What am I doing?" I'm always so objective; I'm not nationalistic. And yet, I'd get so excited, I suddenly found that I'm rooting like crazy for the Americans, and I said, "I guess I've really become an American."*

### Sean McGonagle
FROM IRELAND, 1966

# Laszlo Natalny

·····················FROM HUNGARY, 1956·····················

*A successful businessman who sold over two million dollars' worth of insurance last year, he has a genial, relaxed manner. He is married to an American woman, whose ancestry goes "way, way back before the Revolution," from around Philadelphia.*

Things really had been hectic and in fantastic turmoil ever since the beginning of the Second World War. It was a sick scene. Essentially the country was taken over around the fall of 1944 by a rabid Hungarian Nazi follower of Hitler [Döme Sztojay]. This happened in '44, and actually Hungary was a nominal ally of Germany. The governor of the country, Admiral Horthy, wanted to pull out of the war and make a separate peace, but he was overthrown and the country was occupied by the Germans. It was a great upheaval.

I remember it clearly. We were in Budapest. I was about ten years old, and there was a siege of the city of Budapest from Christmas of 1944 until late February of 1945, during which time the entire civilian population lived in cellars. We lived in the cellar of a good-sized apartment house. It's the kind of thing a ten-year-old remembers. It's a very interesting experience in many ways. We got used to dead people and we got used to bombing and shelling daily—these were daily events. I distinctly remember sirens and running into the cellar when the bombs would come, which started to come with regularity toward the end of '44.

Budapest did suffer terribly. There was fighting for Budapest, and the Russians surrounded the city by mid-December of '44. It was defended by about two hundred thousand German and about an equal number of

Hungarian troops, and there was vicious and heavy fighting for several months, and much of the city was demolished. It suffered terribly. Actually, a great many people died from the shelling and the bombing, and probably a larger number of people died of hunger. Because, of course, everything closed up and only those with enough foresight and enough money to lay in supplies made it. People died of hunger by the tens of thousands.

And then at the end of February of '45, the Russians took the city. I think most people were happy that it was over and there was some kind of peace. A great deal of the family's valuables were lost during this war, and so the immediate change was in the standard of living. My grandfather was a wealthy—well, a *farmer* is not really the word—he owned a large farm, and a great deal of the valuables were in the form of farm implements and livestock. The result was an immediate decline in the standard of living. There was from that point on really never enough money. We owned a condominium apartment, which was bought before the war, and therefore it was large and comfortable. But almost immediately it became necessary to rent out some of those rooms to raise money. So we were cramped, because a couple of rooms of our apartment were always rented out to people.

My father had difficulty finding work. He was basically a farm manager—a university-trained farm manager—and he did find work eventually but it was never in keeping with what he should have been doing. So ever since that time, it was one continuous long fight to make ends meet, really. And my mother worked pretty much, too, so this was again a big change. It's like your life really has changed from one extreme to the other extreme, almost. I don't want you in any way to construe that my family liked the Germans and the Nazis any more than the Russians. They were equally as anti-Nazi as they were anti-Russian.

My family background is sort of upper middle class—well-educated people that have done well in the prior regime. I'm going all the way back to the early 1900s. The opportunities for people like that were completely denied [under the Russians]. I, for example, had always felt that I had the brains to go on to professions and wanted to study further, but I couldn't because of my family background. I was not allowed to. The entire higher-educational structure was controlled by the government, and they wanted people in the professions—people to be doctors and lawyers and architects and so on—who they felt would be loyal to the government. And these are people with either poor peasant background—poor farmers—or poor workers who they felt would be safe for the government. They did not want anybody of intellectual or middle-class background. What they wanted was to wipe out this class completely. I could look forward to really very little good in any society where opportunities are denied. I had been ambitious, but it was of no use, because I knew I couldn't do anything with myself.

Not only were opportunities denied, but there was a big wave of deportation of these people from the capital to the countryside— forcibly. They were told to move, and they had to move very fast. Now in Hungary, Budapest is really the only city of any basis, and anybody that lived in Budapest cannot even imagine life being any other way. The countryside is like two hundred years back. So this was a very, very serious thing—to make people who lived all their lives in the city to move. And this was all done with that purpose—it was essentially to turn the society upside down.

The direct cause of my leaving Hungary and coming to this country was the Hungarian Revolution in 1956. I was in the middle of my two-year compulsory army service and I couldn't wait to jump into it, really. I deserted from the army upon hearing that there was an uprising in the capital.

I took this truck into the capital, found a revolutionary committee, and asked what I could do in the cause. And they said, "Well, what the city needs is a great deal of food." So I worked with this committee— they were, for the most part, college students—and made three or four trips in the countryside, collecting food. We'd pull into small towns, two or three of us, and announce that food is desperately needed and we will take anything. We had very little difficulty; they were very nice. The countryside was heavily anti-Communist because of the nationalization of the land and collectivization drive. In an hour we would load up a big truck with potatoes and flour, and we would deliver it.

So, on the morning of, I believe, the third of November, when the Russian tanks came, the radio announced it in the early morning and asked everybody to report. At this point the radio was in the revolutionary government's hands, as the whole country was for a period of about two weeks. And we were requested to report to the central area, and from there we were sent out in groups of about forty or forty-five each, to hold buildings.

Essentially, we were to hold key buildings along the roads that were coming into the main areas of the city. What we did was to stay in these well-built key buildings, and when the tanks came we attempted to stop them with whatever was available. We had guns. I myself had a Russian-made submachine gun. That was the weapon I used. This was something that we'd gotten from army arsenals. We also had hand grenades and a few special handheld antitank guns, but very few, really.

We tried with hand grenades, and those large T-54 tanks are pretty well armored, so what happened was that when the tanks started to demolish these buildings, we ended up in the basement of the building. We saw that this was pretty useless, and we pulled out and then dispersed. Their strength was just too great, and it would have been foolhardy and useless for any resistance. We gave up hope.

Immediately I started to make plans to leave the country. It probably would not have been too difficult if I had done it immediately. But I talked to some personal friends of mine, and it was the twenty-ninth of November when we finally organized ourselves to leave the country. And by then it was really almost too late. I forged army documents for us, and in army uniforms we started driving toward the border. The border-guard uniforms were the same as the army uniforms, so I had forged documents that said that we were border guards. And using the truck we still had, I would say that we were stopped at least fifteen times between Budapest and the border by various people. At first we were pretty shaky. We wondered whether our documents would pass. But by the third or fourth time we got so cocky, I think that toward the end we started to believe ourselves that we were border guards. We were really cocky and we felt, well, nobody can stop us.

And then we got to within about twenty-five miles of the border. There we abandoned the truck—ran it into a ditch—and we decided we were going to walk the rest of the way. That was a long walk. [Laughs.] That had taken from about five in the evening until about three in the morning, the next day. I know that my feet were swollen and bloody, and I really was incapacitated for about ten days afterwards, until my feet recovered.

This got very hairy. We ran into some Russian troops who were guarding the border. This is why it was too late by then. The border was in the process of being resealed. During this time, martial law was declared and anybody that was armed could have been summarily executed at this point. We had handguns on us and, I think, a hand grenade. We were stopped by the Russians, and they surprised us to the point that you really had no choice but to go along with them. And we went over to this tent that they had set up. This is maybe a mile and a half from the border. And we just stood in the middle of this circle, and everywhere I looked I saw these submachine guns trained at us, with little black holes.

Finally they woke up the captain, and this captain came out—rather a young captain, with a long, droopy mustache—and he was rubbing his eyes, because he had been sleeping. He said, in Russian, "Where are you going?" and I said, "We are border guards and we are going back to our posts." And I showed him our papers. He said to his sergeant, "Which way were they going?" And the sergeant said, "They were going west, due west." So he said, "Where is your post?" and I told him. He said, "That's south of here, but you are going west." And I said, "Well, we got lost. We lost our way."

He just shook his head. I don't think he believed us. So he said, "Are you armed?" and I said, "No," and he just nodded his head to that. And so he said, "Do you have any other documents on you?" And I handed him my driver's license, which had my picture on it. I don't think he could read these things, see, because of the difference in alphabet. He looked at it like he could, but I really don't think he could. And that thing had my picture in it; and that convinced him, that picture, somehow, that that was for real. So that was the last thing. He just shook his head and said, "I don't want to catch you again going west. Just go back to your way and go south." And that was the end of it.

We just started walking south, and we walked as far as we could, and when we didn't see them anymore, then we went west again. The crossing over itself was interesting. You see, the border was extremely well protected, and so between the actual borders we had to cross a large strip that was sand—maybe ten or twelve feet of sand—very carefully combed so that you couldn't see any tracks on it. There was no actual barbed wire, and there were basically no trees there. There were some guard towers, and we didn't know whether they were manned or not. It turned out they weren't. I think the Russians just didn't have enough troops; they still weren't organized.

We made it about two in the morning. We knew that the border was not a straight border, but rather it was quite uneven, so our chief worry was—right after we crossed into Austria—that we may stumble back again. When we walked into Austria, we walked about a mile and we saw a light at a house, and we are still worried about stumbling back into Hungary, so we sort of crawled up to it and there was a light in a window. We crawled up and listened, and we could hear quite a number of people, but they were speaking Hungarian, which upset us no end. And then from the conversation we figured out that they were Hungarian refugees that have crossed the border and stopped there.

This station was set up by the Austrian government for the refugees, and that's why they put lights in it. So we walked in, still in our army uniforms. There was, oh, maybe twenty or twenty-five people, mostly young men and some families, some older people, some children. There was just straw on the floor, and everybody was lying down on the straw and being very happy and singing, and somebody passed around some liquor and we were just greatly relieved that we were there. It was immense relief. We were put in internment camps, and we were very well taken care of. Food was provided and we were given clothing, mostly new clothing. I think the Red Cross helped, and the American government.

Different countries had made commitments to allow so many

Hungarian refugees. They all wanted single young men more than any other kind of refugee. So a great many countries actually came into this camp and suggested, you know, they would welcome our coming there—Australia, New Zealand, Canada, Switzerland, Sweden, I believe Spain—they were actually advertising. They were recruiting. And, of course, the United States as well as any other country.

We could choose. And we really could have gone anyplace. I never had any doubt whatsoever what I wanted to do. I was just totally convinced the U.S. is the place where I wanted to come to—the excitement that is in this country, the high standard of living, the opportunities that are unlimited, the way you could move around, the way you really could pick and choose your lifestyle.

We signed up, and it was really no problem at all. We signed up, and we came through American military transport. We arrived in a typical December day. It rained and we couldn't see much, other than the barracks of Camp Kilmer and a little bit of the highway. Again, I remember a sense of optimism, that things would work out. I just thought that, you know, this is the land of opportunity and, somehow, my opportunity is going to be there. We were again well housed, well fed—by American army at Camp Kilmer. We were there about two weeks, something like that. People were coming and going every day. Anybody that was sponsored and anybody that had any relatives at all, they would come and get them. I didn't have anybody here, so I just sort of went along with the tide, and eventually what they did was put us on a bus, gave everybody five dollars in cash and some meal tickets, and we were driven to the YMCA in Manhattan.

It was exciting. I don't remember being frightened at any point. Not once do I remember waking up and thinking, "Oh, my God, what's going to happen now?" I ran into some other friends at Camp Kilmer, and this is what led me to the next phase of my life, which is that I got involved with an organization of Hungarians. Remember, this is not your typical refugee group that is sort of country bumpkin types. We're all about twenty, twenty-one years old, highly intelligent, by and large well-educated people. Actually, I was one of six people that founded an organization of Hungarian students in the United States. Our aim was to obtain scholarships in American universities for Hungarian students in large numbers, to publicize that there were thousands and maybe tens of thousands of Hungarians that wanted to continue their education in this country, but, of course, they needed help. This was called the American-Hungarian Students Association.

We publicized the need, and a lot of colleges in New England and New York and Ohio and out West had made available scholarships for Hungarian students. We had these offers pouring in, actually. We made an effort through all the Hungarian organizations to let the Hungarian students know that this was available and that they should register with us, and then we sort of attempted to put them in touch with the colleges.

This was not enough; we still had to earn a living. So we went to Cambridge with the help of a student association, and they found rooms for us in various places. I was living with a college professor in a nice old section of Cambridge, in a private room and a bathroom. But we still had to have jobs, because what little help we were getting wouldn't pay for it. So all of us had gotten some sort of menial job. My first job in this country actually was making paper bales in the outskirts of Cambridge. The job was to push the paper and to clean the pits and to sweep. It's unskilled work, basically. It was $1.00 an hour, and $1.25 if you had overtime. All of our spare time was taken up by the work in this Hungarian student association. It was a great feeling.

That went on until September 1957, and then one of the scholarships that came in was from a small college in Worcester, Massachusetts, and I requested that scholarship. I was interviewed by the dean of admissions and was accepted. I was at this point twenty-one as opposed to eighteen. I guess I was really almost four years older than the other students. It was really a great situation. Of course, the Hungarian Revolution was very much a novelty for them. They wanted to know about it. They were helpful, immensely helpful. I would say everybody through this whole period has been extremely nice.

I majored in history, and I did it in three years. I graduated fourteenth in my class. I went to work for an insurance company. I didn't think I could sell anything, and I certainly knew nothing about insurance. I really didn't start doing well until about '66, and then I was the top man in my agency. I've been very happy. I have a very pleasant office in Springfield; I now have a secretary; I enjoy my work. I can set my own hours. I can stay here and talk to you in the morning and go back and work in the evening. I can go to the office at midnight if I want to do paperwork. I am completely free to set my own hours. . . .

Nobody is ever completely satisfied. I had entertained thoughts of being a journalist and a writer. I had been very fond of the Hungarian language and Hungarian poetry especially, and I think I would have ended up doing something with that, had I stayed in Hungary.

I begin to look at that language with some nostalgia now, and I'd like not to forget it. Sometimes I pick up a Hungarian book, especially poetry, and I indulge myself for a couple of hours. I like to read things I've already read—the classics. To this day, I cannot get the same enjoyment out of English poetry that I get out of Hungarian poetry. I think I miss knowing that I have the command and mastery of the language.

# Heinz Eckhardt
···················· FROM GERMANY, 1958 ····················

In the beginning, the girls didn't speak any English at all. There was a friendly dog that visited us and he would come into the apartment, and the girls were so excited about him and they talked to him in German. And all of a sudden, I said, "Sit!" And the dog sat. And then we went out, and Zizi, she was then four years old, she said, "Do the birds sing English, too?"

# Sandor Vesely
···················· FROM HUNGARY, 1956 ····················

*Soft-voiced and mild-mannered, he is an engineer in a small electronics company in Baltimore.*

When the Revolution broke out, most of the students got armed. I stayed out of it. The schools weren't going, and I decided to go home, wait it out, and just see what's going to happen.

I was home perhaps a week when one of my friends came. He said that next day he is going to leave with his fiancée: "Why don't you come with me?" I thought about it and I decided to leave the country. . . .

First I set my mind on Australia, because it's so rough-and-tough and so short of people. Australia is so undeveloped and there's lots of opportunity for people who are willing to work, who are willing to take a chance on something. And I felt that that would be the country which provides most of the opportunity for someone who starts with absolutely nothing. But my friends didn't want to go to Australia. They said, "No, no way we would go to Australia. If you want to go, you go. We go to the United States." Again, you have to face the choice that do you want to go to a foreign country, again, all by your lonesome, or go someplace where the two friends want to go.

Well, this is the funny part. You know, the reason you want to come here is because you have your friends, and it so happens that your friends go on the day before because their papers came through sooner than mine, and you never see them again.

While I was going to the university here, it was very rough. Each book I opened—on every page I found about a hundred words that I didn't know. Now you can start to talk a little bit, but you can't color whatever you are saying. You can say, "I am hungry," or you can perhaps even say, "I am very hungry," but you couldn't say, "I am so hungry that I could eat a horse."

Plus, I didn't have anybody I could relate to, with the same problems—nobody who went through the same high school as you did, whom you could perhaps talk old times with and relive some of the experiences what you had. Most of the time you had the feeling that you are one man in an island, although there is million people all around you; but they really not around you. You are separated so much.

I was so homesick that I was ready to go home after about a year. I did talk to my sponsor, and I did tell him that I just can't take it any longer and I don't care what happens when I go home, especially because I left the country in the illegal way; but I'm going home and I am ready to take the consequences, but I just can't stand one more day. . . . But I stayed and I'm glad the way things turned out. . . .

# Betty Chu
............................ FROM CHINA, 1969 ·······················

*She is a secretary in a San Francisco hospital, and her husband works in a bank. She grumbles about doing the dishes, and he grumbles that she is too Americanized. They never go to Chinatown, because they find it "depressing."*

My grandfather was the head of the family. He was a very wealthy man. He was a shipowner, and he owned all these silk stores. My father was some kind of bank officer, but it wasn't really the source of income. I remember my early childhood as living in a huge mansion in Shanghai, with lots of servants, gardeners, chauffeurs, you name it. And all the old-fashioned cars: DeSoto, Nash, Packard.

It was the fashionable thing when I was born for the upper-class people to have Westernized atmosphere. My grandfather had a Westernized reception room, with a huge chandelier, where he would receive his foreign friends. And we had tennis courts in our backyard and a lot of Westernized things.

During my childhood and all those years that I lived in such luxury, I did see a lot of things that are very unfair, even to a child—the extreme difference between the rich and the poor. The servants that we had, they had to learn their manners in order to work in such a mansion, and they have to dress properly. But they all came from very poor rural families. They are allowed to go back to their home to visit maybe once a year, and they bring home any kind of garbage you throw out, because to them it was precious. One thing that stood out so vividly—in those days when girls had their period they used sterilized cotton. My sister used those. I was to the point of vomiting when I discovered one of the servants picking out her soiled cotton. I just couldn't understand anybody wanting to touch soiled things. I said, "What are you doing?" She said she was saving the cotton to bring home to make her children some cotton-padded jackets. They couldn't afford wool, and they used cotton. She was picking those out and throwing out the soiled part and saving the white cotton. She said, "Oh, it's such a waste to throw out good white cotton."

During my adolescent years the big change took place [the success of the Communist revolution in China]. My grandfather passed away by then, and everybody was saying how really fortunate he was that he didn't have to live to see all these things—to see what he created. . . . We were all terrified, because we understood the people who were going to take over the whole country is going to be—well, the way we put it—like our enemies. This was in 1949.

For myself I was more frightened then about the unknown than what it was really all about. After the Communists took over, the first few years, they were very lenient—meaning they tolerated a lot of things that we thought are going to be normal. I remember very clearly. I was in my early teens, so I really cared more about Frank Sinatra records than the real political scene. I guess to me it was a very important thing, and also boyfriends and parties and so forth. And they tolerated all those.

I guess people got bigheaded. They thought, "Oh, so it's going to be fine. It was all unnecessary that we were so much frightened." So we just relaxed. But my father resigned from his bank job, because he knew it's not going to be like this forever, and he started to make trips to Hong Kong, which was considered the free world, because he was thinking about moving the whole family there. It was tradition, I guess; the parents just don't bother to discuss any serious matters with their youngsters. Whether my older sisters and brothers knew anything, I don't know, but I just lived in my own secret world of my records—Frank Sinatra and Doris Day.

Well, things began to change and we felt ropes tightening up around our necks. It was about the Korean War time. A lot of really big things were going on, such as the reforms of the businessmen. But to a teen-age person, as long as they didn't directly affect the family, I didn't pay too much attention. It was kind of remote, just like the Japanese occupation.

Then the government started banning anything that's American, and they started what we would call brainwashing. They started all this propaganda about the worst enemy of the Chinese people were the United States of America and the people. Everything pertaining to the U.S. is just crime, sin, bad, stinks. So we just thought that for the sake of survival we'd just better go along with them and destroy or hide all our things that's American. I had to get rid of my records. It was heartbreaking.

Also, some of our friends started to change, change their political views. They thought it's about time young people wake up to face reality, instead of living in our silly world. And what happened to myself, personally, was that I gradually began to give it some serious thought, and I started reading those books. I have to tell you the truth: I was impressed with the theory. Gradually, I even accepted the idea of communism, and I thought, "Well, that is not bad after all. What if people should go through some hardships and suffer some loss? In any kind of revolution, people will have to sacrifice their own personal things and their dear ones." I really liked the idea. My family still didn't like it.

It got to the point, my whole family turned against me. They wrote to other people, my sisters and relatives, even out of the country, to be very careful, because I'm turning Communist. I don't blame them; I would have done the same thing. At that time I thought myself righteous, and I thought I was doing the right thing. I was willing to cut all the bonds with my family. I thought I was waking up.

After I got married—my husband used to work for a bank at that time—we had to think about our financial aspects as a family. So I thought maybe I'd better start looking for a job. Now, people don't just look for jobs. In order to get work, I had to go through this training. That was really something. They needed teachers very much, and they were telling the whole world that they are going to educate the people. It sounded good, really. So I went through this short training program, and I was a high-school teacher, assigned arithmetic, geometry, algebra, and the rest is political study.

Well, I got very much discouraged and disillusioned after I got to work. At first, with my trust in them, they gave me a certain amount of trust. They assigned me to a lot of work and a lot of extra jobs—not with extra pay, of course. I didn't mind that at all. I was a high-school teacher in a showcase school. I felt I also got to see a little bit more on the inside. And then, after a while, I just gradually realized how the whole thing is just like a showcase. You have one side to show the outside world, and the outside is only going to see this side. But now the whole other side—that's the real life.

I used to be the chosen one to teach a class when the important personnel come. They usually instructed me how to say, how to shake my hand, how to impress, and so forth. That was the one time that I was allowed to wear any woolen things and leather shoes. Although I did possess them, I didn't want to wear them. People were looking such looks that you would be so uncomfortable. So those were the days when they would say, "Well, if you happen to have some better clothing. . . ." knowing all the time that I have them. So I'd put on my woolen things, and that particular day nobody dare criticize me.

They wanted me to join certain meetings that are not really open to the whole staff. I began to realize that the nearer to the core that you get, I discovered it really wasn't that great at all. I witness all these people—like they are being used, including myself. We are all being used to the fullest, and then the minute they want you out of the scene, all they had to do is [snaps fingers], just like that and you're out.

There were all these movements. They always had a different topic, such as cultural revolution and anti-Confucius and so on. Then we witnessed what they called "the struggling"—meaning one individual in the middle of a room full of maybe two hundred people, and you struggle him. You're not supposed to physically struggle him, but after a while people's emotions got out of hand.

We were in a group discussion. We would listen to a speech from somebody up there, and then we divided into groups to discuss, and then everybody will have to express their opinions. You cannot get away without speaking anything. And no matter how careful you are, you have to say something. Otherwise, they will just sit and stare at you until you speak up. We tried to repeat whatever was said, but you know how people can interpret. Tomorrow at the discussion, we would say, "Now yesterday comrade so-and-so said such-and-such a thing. Now he better stand up and explain it." They're not supposed to physically attack the person. They can just ask him all kinds of questions. Ask questions—that's not putting it really correctly. They would say, "You're not telling enough. Come on and tell us. Otherwise you're going to. . . ." And they'd make all kinds of threats. That's how people got to live in fear.

The way I felt, it was all fixed. If the group wants to get so-and-so into trouble, then he's got it. People got frightened, because nobody likes to be the object. The final result, after months of harassment—you either got sent to some remote provinces, or anyway it was nothing good, nothing pleasant.

Due to the fact that I was a teacher in a showcase school, my boy was fortunate enough to be one out of millions to be allowed into that showcase nursery school. They were teaching the youngsters propaganda about American people. "America and American people are the worst enemies of our country" went on and on until the Soviet Union was number-one enemy on the list.

When my son brought home all this educational information, he was so frightened. He'd come home only on weekends, you see—that gives us people a chance to devote our whole self to work for the people. So he came home one weekend, and the poor little thing—he was just shivering and he had tears in his eyes, and he told me, "I know how the American people look like." I discovered later on, when I paid that nursery school a visit, it was a poster of a green-faced, very ugly-looking Uncle Sam, with his tall hat and his long, monsterlike fingernails. You know what the nursery-school teacher actually told the kids at that nursery-school age? She told them, "You know what the American people's favorite food is?" And the little kids were already trembling like leaves, and she said, "Little children's hearts." I thought that was very, very wrong.

That and some similar events led me to the secret—of course it had to be a very secret—decision that we have to leave. My husband and I secretly discussed it in the middle of the night; we felt safe between the two of us in the middle of the night. We finally decided maybe we can't take a big chance by letting my husband apply for the permit for us, because there is no such thing as the whole family applying. People don't have the courage to apply, because that exposes your intention, which means you are putting yourself on the opposite side of the people. You're an enemy right away. They never would admit that you could not leave the country, but the thing is you just cannot.

By then, part of my family were all out of the country. My brother was still living in the same house, different apartments. We used the same stairway. We don't talk to each other to avoid trouble and just so the neighbors can be a witness. We deliberately show the neighbors that we are not on speaking terms. Just in case something should come up with either one of us, the other is spared by saying, "Well, we haven't talked to each other for years because of our differences in opinion." We just nod at each other when we think nobody's watching. I think that was their policy—to isolate each other.

We were on food rationing all the time. People like us—it's the old Chinese habit to save jewelry. I still have a little ring, a little brooch, and I can still go to the government jewelry store—because those are the only jewelry stores allowed—and sell whatever valuables, gold or diamonds or anything, to the government. If I was really that good, I should donate all my personal belongings. But I didn't, you see. Whatever little piece I sold, I can then go to what they call the high-class restaurant. Now that is entirely different. That means you can eat a lot of whatever good food, without rationing tickets. So, we are still really secretly privileged. That's the way I look at it.

We just couldn't stay there and live with a pack of lies. I guess it was about 1960. It just so happened that it was the year of the big food shortage, so they are encouraging government workers to resign—like early retirement. Now that is something really very difficult, because most people are living on their salaries, small as they are. If you have an early retirement or resign from your job, how are you going to live? They encourage you to go to the rural area. They might assign you to a certain commune, and maybe you can work and get your share of food. Because the city is a showcase, and they cannot allow this to happen and show the outside world that you actually have hungry people.

So they were talking to my husband about early resignation. He was only thirty years old. So he thought he'll just get up all his courage and make one step and see if it will lead the whole family to disaster. He told his superior that he would like to visit his brother in Hong Kong, who would like to meet with him and discuss—he vaguely hinted that he might even talk his brother into coming back and work for the people. I don't know which was the main factor, the shortage of food or the fact that they need some examples. Like, "See, so-and-so is resigning before he gets to be thirty years old." He was granted a permit, much to the surprise of even us. Of course, I had mixed feelings, because I might never see him again.

So he left, just to Hong Kong. He only asked for a month, but everybody knew that it was just a laugh. He was trying to work and wait for us to get out. My superior knew about my husband's movement, and of course right away my whole status changed. Not that I still want to be in their favor anymore. But after that their attitude toward me . . . [sighs] . . . especially my little boy. He was going to nursery school at that time. The words get around in the neighborhood, so people knew his father was in Hong Kong. That put him in a bad spot, the poor kid. He came home, not really bruised but red-eyed, and he kept telling me secretly, without letting anybody else hear him, that people are just hitting him—little kids hitting him, pushing him around, and calling him "son of a Hong Kong spy." He asks, "Is my father a Hong Kong spy?" So then things went from bad to worse. It was very uncomfortable.

I had to make a big decision. I decided I'd better resign from my job, because while I was still a schoolteacher, I could never apply for a permit. Well, I went through all kinds of harassment just to resign from my teaching post. They said, "We need you. You should really come back to the people." Finally, they did let me resign because I was having some ill health. You could call it a depression. I was really depressed and I was looking like a ghost—so pale and yellow.

My son was still having all kinds of trouble at school with people, and he kept coming home and asking me all kinds of questions. I really didn't want to lie to him, but I couldn't tell him the truth. In order to give him an answer, I had to lie. It was too much—for a mother to lie to her own son in order to survive. So I made up my mind: This has got to end.

My husband and I managed to communicate with each other through letters. We had agreed on a code, so when he wrote me, why don't you live in the south and have a change of environment, I got the clue. I took my son to Canton. That's the farthest—nobody was allowed to go further down south. My husband could send money there; foreign currency was always welcomed. We were able to stay in one of the best hotels.

The people there, the waiters and the workers, they knew what I had in mind. The police kept visiting me night and day, and they made no secret of it. They just went in and out of my room. There was no such thing as a locked door. Have you ever heard of such a thing? A young woman with a young child in a hotel room and no locks? If the policeman wants to pay you a visit, he can come at ten at night— which was considered the middle of the night by their standards—and walk right in and say, "I want to talk to you about something." And he didn't have to show me anything—no badges, no nothing. He just walked in. So we lived there for six months.

People kept asking us, "What are you waiting for? Why are you still living in the hotel?" They are keeping their eyes on us constantly. I had to tell them that I am waiting for my husband to come and visit, and that I would try to convince him to come back to China to stay.

Finally he came for a brief visit of seven days. It was a big dangerous thing for him to do. He was well dressed, like a businessman or somebody of importance, and he brought a lot of money to spend. One day we went to the biggest park that I know of. In the middle of a meadow, where I was pretty sure there was no bugging, we talked for a few brief minutes. It was the only time of that seven days that we could really talk to one another.

I wanted to be smuggled out with my son. But we didn't succeed. Someone did come to contact us, but he indicated that the child was too young, and was I willing, if necessary, to sacrifice that child for the safety of the group. Of course not!

Plans were not for us to make. We didn't have our own fate in our hands. My husband went back to Hong Kong and I had to go back to Shanghai to see if we had any other chances. Since we had all this foreign currency, and I kept selling my gold, we could manage to live for a while.

When my son was seven, he started school. The first day of school, those first-graders had to stand there for two hours and listen to this political speech. I doubt very much if one out of those many first-graders understood a word of it. It was just unbelievable—things like that. That was the first day of school, and those little people stood there patiently—squirming, sweating, moving a little bit and shooing away flies, but they stood there under the sun. So I thought, "I cannot see my good, intelligent son being educated to become one of them. It's just too unthinkable. We'll just have to try to get away."

So I applied for a permit to visit my husband. You have to go through all kinds of humiliation. They laugh at you, scorn you, verbally abuse. In order to get what I wanted, the permit, I didn't mind what they said to me, what they did to me. I gave them all kinds of reasons—anything, everything. Six times I was rejected. [*Laughs softly.*] I can laugh now, but think of the tears I shed. By then my boy was a student, and pretty soon he would be wearing one of those red scarves to be a member of the Pioneer, and after that the next step is a member of the Youth Group, and after that the next step is a member of the Party—because otherwise you never make any good. You won't get a chance to go even to junior high school. . . . I just didn't want that kind of fate for my son. So I tried and I tried and I tried.

Then I was really frantic, because when the boy gets to be a certain age, he cannot be included in my permit anymore. And there was things that I heard about—like a mother and a child applied for a permit and they will give one a permit and none to the other. What are you going to do? Leave the child back? Finally, I got to pray a lot—all in secret, never in the open. I left the whole thing to the Lord. I just let the Lord decide whether I should leave the country and join my husband or not. I got hold of a dusty old Bible, and I said, "I don't remember my English anymore, but I'll read the Bible." So I prayed. And after the sixth rejection, the seventh time I was granted a permit.

I only applied for a month. They told me casually to mail back my permit. "And be sure to leave your rationing cards behind for rice and so forth. And what are you going to do with your apartment, now that you are going?" I said, "Oh, I have to keep it for when I come back." "Oh, when you come back, we'll get you someplace to live," knowing all the time that everybody's lying to each other. I said, "Well, whatever the government thinks I should do." The government would think you should give the apartment back, so they can give it to someone else.

I didn't dare take anything more than the shirts on our backs and a few souvenir items, just a very few. It was against the law to take any valuables out of the country. The only valuable you're allowed is a 0.3-ounce ring in gold. And who has that kind of a small ring? I had to take one of my gold bars and go to the bank and have them make those rings. I left my bedroom furniture, which was custom-made, to my husband's brother, because he was considering getting married. So whatever is in the drawers should be in their possession. At that time I didn't want anything else but my freedom. But now I think, "I wonder what happened to my jade? I wonder what happened to my diamond?"

Once I got the permit, we left on the third day. Just had barely time to get the train ticket and to get the shots and then get on your way. It was 1965, in the end of October.

We went to Hong Kong to join my husband. He was doing pretty good. He started from the very bottom, of course, and he was working his way up. It was a very big adjustment for both myself and my son. We had to adjust to everything else outside, and we also had to adjust to my husband, to living with him.

We stayed in Hong Kong a little over three years. I guess three years changed a lot of our attitudes for us. It took only a few Western movies to change my son's whole attitude toward the American people.

Things began to happen. They started to have bomb threats, and a lot of stores were changing their flags. The Communists took over Macao, and we thought Hong Kong was threatened. So that made us make up our mind, just like that. We said, "If it took us all that trouble to get out of the country to go to Hong Kong, *if* there is the remotest chance of their taking over Hong Kong, we're going to leave." My husband had worked nearly to the top of his organization, but he was willing to give up all of that. He was making a very good salary, high position, we had servants, but. . . . We had our little girl by then, and thinking of the future of the children, we don't want anything like what we experienced ever to happen to them. That's why we were really willing to give up all that. And my husband's brother here in this country was saying, "If you want to come over to this country, we'll sponsor." He came as a student, twenty years ago. We came as immigrants in 1969.

The FBI came to visit me after we arrived. It was a friendly visit. I was a little disappointed, because the man was very nice and friendly. He was sitting there just like a friend. First, he showed you the badges, like they do in the movies. Now, in China, they have authority to walk in, and nobody dare asks anybody to show anything. You better tell them everything or you're in trouble. But here, the man was very courteous. I guess at first I was a little bit tense, but he put me to ease and he was chatting like an old friend. He even said in case there is any trouble of any kind, I can call him. I had the phone number and the name of an FBI agent. I was very proud.

He did ask me some things, like, did I hear from my brother in China lately, and am I writing letters to him. I thought, "You would know before me anyway," so I told the truth: "No, I wasn't communicating with them." And I think he asked me if there's anyone that I know who came out of the country recently. I told him all the truth that I knew, and it apparently wasn't that interesting. [*Laughs.*]

My son is in high school now. With him it was one big adjustment right after the other. He had to learn the different dialect in Hong Kong, and then he had to learn American here. I don't know how the guy went through it, but he never stopped behind in his class. I don't know how he did it. I just don't know how he did it. He's always been a quiet boy. He just doesn't have that many friends. It does still worry me. [*Sighs.*]

One of my son's biggest disappointments is that my daughter doesn't speak Chinese. Well, she was a year and a half when she came over, and she thought she was American all along. Now she wants to grow up to be an Italian.

Last year, December, we became citizens. The doctor at the hospital where I work invited us over for a party. He surprised us by standing up and announcing it. He said, "Something very wonderful happened last week," and told everybody that we were citizens now. He gave us an American flag as a present, and everybody drank to us. It was very heartwarming.

# Labring Sakya

···················· FROM TIBET, 1960 ·······················

*In the late 1930s millions of readers and filmgoers were enthralled by* Lost Horizon, *the fictional story of a modern Westerner who traveled to a remote monastery in the mountains of Asia. Labring Sakya made the reverse journey in 1960 when the Chinese Communists took over the government of Tibet.*

I was nine years old when I went into the monastery in Lhasa. I could visit my family and go in and out, but all the boys in the monastery are expected to become monks in the monastery.

In Tibet the monks don't have to do anything, just study and pray. All the food is given by the government, and so much land for the monastery. The land was worked by some laymen, people who lived in the village around. Over here some people say they're like slaves. They weren't like that, actually. We had to pay and we had to give them some land or, if not land, had to give them something. But all we did in the monastery was pray and study.

From the time I was nine, that was the only life I knew, except when

I would go sometimes to visit my parents in the town. That was my life. . . .

Then, when I was thirty-four, the Chinese Communists began to take over Tibet. We couldn't stay, you know, couldn't stay there because we were afraid they would kill us. They sent to the monastery and said they wanted our leader, the Dalai Lama, you know. They wanted him to come to their headquarters. They would keep him there, and we didn't want to lose our leader, so we all just came away quickly. We walked from Lhasa to a monastery in the east, about eight days from Lhasa. We got there before the Communists got there. It was rough, rough, country and we had to cross a mountain. We had some food, a little food with us, but that was all. We stayed one month in the monastery in the mountains. Then one night the Chinese Communists came there. They were shooting guns, machine guns, you know. So we were all scared. There were eight hundred of us in that monastery—it was a small monastery for Tibet. Only six of us made it away. The others—I don't know if they killed them or captured them. They did capture them at the time, but most are killed now, I'm sure.

The six of us that got away, we had to run right away in the night, fast, you know—fast. [*Snaps fingers.*] There wasn't a road; it was just the jungle, so we came through the jungle. It was very difficult. It took us thirty-six days to come maybe fifty, sixty miles. We had to climb down and up mountains and cross rivers. It took us thirty-six days. Across the rivers there were these bridges; you know, they have those two bamboo lengths going from here to over there. You hold onto one and you walk on the other, and if the river is long the bamboo bends down. Sometimes you're up to your knees in the water, and it's fast water in those mountain streams and rivers. I was frightened. We had only a little food with us. We passed the local villagers, but they're almost, you know, like animals. They were very primitive. They don't speak Tibetan. They're sort of like half Indian, half Tibetan. They wouldn't look at us. They didn't offer us food. They stayed away from us. I think they were frightened.

When we got near the Indian border, the Indians knew about what had happened. They sent planes, and the planes dropped food to us. Other people were fleeing, too, by then. And when we got to the border, the Indians took us to a refugee camp. I was only in that camp for ten days when a professor came from the University of Washington. He had a grant from the government and from some foundation to work on a Tibetan grammar. He wanted somebody to work on the book with him. And he said to me, "Would you like to come?" And I said, "I'd like to." So I came here. He got the visas very quick—in about fifteen or twenty days. And we flew to Seattle. It was very fast—from the monastery in the mountains to the United States, altogether, in less than three months.

I had a picture in my mind of the United States before I came. I'd heard of such things as washing machines and dishwashers and electric stoves and everything to do the cooking. And I thought to myself when I lived in Tibet, "Well, it must be just like how humans do something." In my mind I thought the machine would come and take your clothes and go somewhere and wash them and dry them for you and fold them and bring them back to you, just like humans doing it. That was my picture in my mind. And I had thought there were lots of houses, very big, very big. And, actually, here the family houses are small! Many of them are smaller than in Tibet. Here I live in a little house on a little street. Of course, the monastery I lived in was very big.

There are monasteries here, too. I went over to a Catholic monastery here—it's almost the same as in Tibet. They're living the same there. There are the restrictions, the religion, and the study.

All the time I'm working in the university doing that research on the book, so it's not so very different, except that I go to the little house at night. They brought my niece over here and she stays with me and keeps house for me. I keep up my Tibetan culture and I eat Tibetan style—my niece cooks it. Things aren't so different here. People have to eat, they sleep, they do some work. Over here there is perhaps more tension, yes, more tension. But on the whole, life is not so different.

# Boris Koltsov

···················· FROM THE USSR, 1973 ····················

*Over the years, America has provided refuge for many separatist religious groups: the Plymouth Brethren, the Amish, the Hutterites, the Quakers. Among the most recent pilgrims are the Old Believers, who broke away from the Russian Orthodox church in 1666. Their doctrinal differences may seem minor to us today—how many fingers to cross oneself with, and whether to walk around the altar clockwise or counterclockwise—but they were passionately defended and suffered for. Many of the Old Believers lost their lives at the stake in the seventeenth and eighteenth centuries. In the last years of czarist Russia, they managed to survive by living in isolated areas, farming infertile land, and keeping a low profile. But when the Communists came in, such separatism was not possible. To maintain their religious heritage, they began a trek that took them, in stages, halfway around the world—to Siberia, Mongolia, China, Hong Kong, New Zealand,*

*Brazil, and, finally, the United States. Now they are settled in a remote farming area of Oregon, where they live in a little cluster of wooden houses, surrounded by fruit trees. The women still wear colorful Russian peasant dresses and embroidered caps. They make their tea in samovars, bake their own dark brown bread, and swaddle their babies. The men are bearded and booted and wear the traditional Russian smock. Boris Koltsov, who tells their story, is the patriarch of the group. With his long gray beard, calloused hands, and deep-set eyes, he looks like a character out of Tolstoy.*

In 1666, we Old Believers broke away from the main church of the Russian Orthodox religion. There was a lot of persecution, and many of us were persecuted because we didn't go along with Archbishop Nikon when he decided to modernize the church. We felt that what the church was in the past was right. Many people were killed, but we managed to keep our beliefs.

In czarist Russia, we lived away from the cities in a desert area and in small villages. Our parents taught us about religion, but we didn't have any troubles there with the authorities. Maybe we were too far away. I don't know. But when the Russian Revolutionists came in, they started putting our people in jail and harassing them in every way. They were against all religious groups, but we were the ones with the strongest beliefs, so they attacked us and destroyed our churches.

We had to get away. We traveled from city to city on the way toward the eastern border of Russia. We'd live for a little while and get settled and then move on to another city. We would hitch up our horses, load our things, and travel by night. We moved all the way to Siberia and we kept moving across Siberia. It was a dangerous trip. A lot of people lost their lives on the way. At the border there were soldiers with dogs and they would hunt you down. We finally got to China. We dug underground houses and managed to live there that way. It was a fertile valley near a river, and we did quite well. Altogether, about fifty families were there with us.

But then the Communists came into China, and we had to get away. We stayed until it got really bad. You know, people don't want to move when they love something, until it really gets bad and unbearable. But we understood that the Communists would be against religion, and we decided to get out. They let us go. They wanted the Russians out of China then. So we went to Hong Kong.

From Hong Kong, we wanted to go to the United States, but at first we weren't successful. So we went to New Zealand, and later to Brazil; but you know, Russian people don't like the hot countries, and we didn't like it down there. Finally we got permission to come to the United States.

Our people started in this area with nothing. We had no money to buy land with, but we earned it here—started out working for farmers, with the lowest jobs, and worked our way up. All we have was gotten in this country, we earned here.

Now we're having problems with the schools, and I don't know if it's ever going to be settled. The schools here teach a lot of things that are against God, like Darwin's theories. And some of the teachers believe that there's no right or wrong—whatever you think makes it right. If you feel that this is the thing you should do, it's up to you. That's the attitude about drugs and everything else. Some of the teachers themselves use drugs.

We Old Believers want to take our kids out of the schools after the sixth grade. We feel it's in the seventh grade that they're beginning to teach the things we don't like. The judge says we have to send our kids to school. He says, "If you don't send the kids to school, the parents are going to spend a day in jail for every day that their kids don't go."

This trouble with the schools is a real problem and I don't know how it can be settled. Maybe we'll have to move to Alaska or Canada or some other remote area to get away from it.

We've had a lot of struggles over the centuries, but we've managed to keep our beliefs and we don't want it to end now. We've moved before, and if we have to, we'll move again.

# Roberto Ortiz

·······················FROM CUBA, 1962·······················

*He is a large man, with dark eyes, curly hair, and a mustache. He speaks with enthusiasm. He has many friends and is well known around town. A special policeman in New Jersey, he goes to the community college two evenings a week, as he has been doing for the past five years, training for business administration. Recently, he expanded his business in Central America. He says, "I feel American. I am happy. The only thing bother me is the weather. This weather is for the birds."*

We were hard-working people, and we had a business in the wholesale market in Havana. It was the stomach of Havana, about two square blocks, a well-made building, made in the 1930s or something like that. All the food, vegetables, grains, food, fish—everything used to come there wholesale, and the small stores, the grocery stores and fruit stores, they used to come and buy wholesale in the market. This is like the ones in Newark and New York. They work all night long and they go home about noon. It was a real busy place. From eleven at night they started getting busy—by noon was dead again, all afternoon. It was real busy, and a lot of people used to make a living there.

My father and my uncle and my aunt were wholesale people all their life. Yeah, my grandfather came from Canary Island, and he married a Cuban girl in the eighties—I don't know, in 1880 or so—and they lived upstairs. Was an old Spanish building, and upstairs they got living quarters and they born upstairs. Is no longer in existence. In the 1930s they built this new building, and they went into there. We used to sell apples, pears, and grapes. Our store was about two yards wide and about five yards long, and that was a very expensive place. If we were to sell it, it would be at least ten thousand dollars. So we used to make a living there, and we were average people.

With Batista, the economic situation in the fifties, they were booming in Cuba. There were all kind of business down there. They got George Raft, the movie actor—he got a couple of big businesses down there—gambling casinos. The sugar business was great. Besides the sugar, we had tobacco, coffee beans, minerals; the tourist industry was big down there, too. Economically, Cuba was great in the fifties with Batista.

Then Batista got a reputation for killing a lot of people and giving a lot of castor oil to people. He was famous because of castor oil—for giving castor oil to his opponents so they get the runs for two or three days, you know—ugghh! Batista started getting a bad reputation. He started killing people. He killed twenty thousand Cubans—twenty thousand! He was insane.

Like one time, I remember, I was going to the commercial high school—they close the school after that. I remember I get off the bus right in front of the school, and they are running in front of me—the policemans, the intelligence force of Batista. They were running behind some students, and they don't care who they were. They were just running behind them with a piece of wood, like a stick, but a special wood—it's like a root—and they cover it with electric tape and it's very hard. And I get off the bus and in front of me a few students were running this way, and they got the policemen running behind them with the sticks, hitting them. I was lucky. If I got off one minute before that, I probably would be running, too.

If you got caught during Batista, you're not lucky. You got trouble. This is what made Batista so bad. I know a man—he was in a good position, and his son got involved in a political trouble with Batista. So the father went to the police precinct and talked to the captain there and offered him five thousand pesos. And the captain slammed the door and said, "Jesus Christ! That's too bad, because we just killed the son-of-a-b last night. I just lost five thousand pesos." He told the father just like that.

I remember in a little town, right after Castro took over, they took us to see some torture chambers right off Santiago. We took a climb up a couple of hills, and the torture chambers were made of tin—all tin. In the daytime, with the sun hitting it, it really got hot inside, and this is where they used to keep them. You could see blood all over the place and nails pulled out and things like that. "See what the Batista regime did?" they said. Of course, he was really bad.

So Batista was getting worse and worse, and people liked him less and less. In the meantime, Castro was raising his money and he was planning. He started getting bigger and bigger in the mountains, and things started boiling up in the cities. Castro's underground was putting bombs all over the place. I think back now and I feel lucky, because you pass a place and ten minutes later a bomb goes off and kill a couple of people. Then the last year of Batista, all the high-education centers, like the high schools and the universities, they were closed.

And then on January 1 of '59, Batista gave up and Castro came down from Oriente Province after the sixth. It took him about a week to come down from the mountains. He came driving all the way through the country. At that time I was for him. Everybody was, even the Americans. He was a big hero. I went to see him coming. I'll never forget it when he came. I saw him passing by on the top—you see those pictures on TV once in a while, when he first started, and he came with a victory face and the pigeons on his shoulders and all that. So everybody was for him, and everybody was talking about how rich the country was going to be, with no corruption, and so on. He was a liberator. He won the revolution. . . .

In 1960 things started getting rough. Castro took over the market. He confiscated and took over the market for the benefit of the people. He took over the market one night—just like that, overnight, with the militia. And the following month—it was a surprise move—he got the army in there, and all the owners got sent home. At that time my uncle was the owner, because my father passed away a couple years before. He was sent home and the employees took over. My uncle got hired back again, but it was on a salary—it was a salary job.

I went to work upstairs, since I was in accountant school, in the accounting office. They never told me how much I was going to make. I was working there two weeks and they gave me twenty-five pesos the first week. I was working twelve hours a day and I wasn't happy with it. That was in 1960. I was a kid, I was twenty.

People started getting disappointed—leaving. My cousin was the first one out. Then my sister came four months before I came. I came in '62. It was getting rougher and rougher to leave. It took five years for my mother to get out. Things started getting rougher and rougher, and as time went on, the more places you got to check with, more people you got to clear with. They just wanted to bother you and make it rough for you.

People didn't know what was going to happen. When you left the country after '60, you could not leave anything to anybody. You are supposed to turn everything to the government. The moment you submit the papers, you're not supposed to get anything out of the house. On every block they had a watching committee, watching everything you do. These people will watch you twenty-four hours a day, all your movements. When you leave, everything that you left inside—a watching committee would come and make an inventory and seal the house. They'd put paper in there with glue on the door and lock them up. And that was the end of it. You lose everything. Whatever was inside, it's the government property.

So a lot of people sneak things out of the house, and my house was like a clearinghouse. Everybody was bringing stuff in there to keep, so we had stuff from three or four or more different families. All the furniture and record players—smaller things, all kinds of stuff—could be taken out of the house at night, so the watching committee don't see it. Was brought into my house, because we weren't leaving. We were just watching it for them, you see—in storage for them, that's all, in case Castro fails and they come back.

*At that time, did you really think Castro might not last?*

Yeah, well, there was some kind of counterrevolution talks and Bay of Pigs. Bay of Pigs embarrassment! I saw that in Cuba. I was in there. The Bay of Pigs was a flop, but they fought and they fought bravely, too. They got on land and they fought. It was a flop because Kennedy—I will never forgive Kennedy for that. He chickened out at the last minute, just plain chickened out. Because he sent the men down and then he don't give us support. The only thing they need was a little bit of air support and Castro wouldn't be in Cuba today. I never will forgive Kennedy for this.

By that time things started to get tough over there. You could not get food. Food is starting getting very scarce. Restaurants started closing and stores closing, and the black market started very bad. When you go and see a relative and they don't have food to put on the table, this is bad! When you walk in there, and you see they don't want to eat because you are in there, and they are waiting for you to leave, to eat. And when you got to do the same thing home—I couldn't live with it, and I decided to leave from a combination of all these things.

I saw the beginning of the ration book. They counted the people and they give you a ration book for each family. You could choose your store, your corner store, and go in there and register with your book. So they used to distribute the food or the goods or whatever was coming, to the grocery stores, and you get your share in that particular store. They had it well organized.

I saw the beginning of that and the beginning of lines for anything. Lines for oil, for today was coming the rice, tomorrow was coming the meat in the butcher store, and so on. So the lines started getting longer for everything. Anything related to living, you'd see long lines.

A combination of all these is what made me leave the country in 1962. It took me ninety days waiting to get out. I'll never forget when I went to get vaccinated. They put me in line with thirteen or fourteen people. And they got a piece of cloth with alcohol on it, and the first guy in line got lucky, because he got the clean cotton. But the second guy got a little bit of the other guy; and when that cotton reached the last guy in line, you got everybody's dirt in your arm.

I was allowed to bring one suit, three pair of everything—undershirts, underwear, socks—and one towel and toothpaste and a shaving kit, and that's it. Everything else is government property. They searching in the airport. I was very lucky when I left Cuba that I have in that flight some kind of delegation from Venezuela, and they were very nice with us when we left. Now you have cases in the airport—a guy I know was telling me his wife was searched in front of him in her personal parts. And that is very hard to see somebody touching your wife in her personal parts in front of you, just to make you jump. They make fun of you even with that. Still, a lot of people took money and hide it in the heel of shoes and stuff like that. And they so stupid, they tell you about it. They make a big joke out of it. "Look what I got in the heel of my shoe." And if they find out, they make it rougher on people.

I got in Miami in May. I didn't like Miami. I don't know why. I went to Union City, New Jersey, because Union City is the capital of the Cubans in this part of the country. Yeah, there was a lot of Cubans there. I worked in a factory, with the whistle and the ten-minute break and the half-hour break. I got myself a room, with an old lady. I never had any problem. I was making forty bucks a week. I had a comfortable living. I was alone.

I went to school at Dickinson High in Jersey City at night. It was a regular high school for adults. I went at night for a year or so, because I could not finish my high school in Cuba. I had six months left to finish up, and I was given credit for my credits in Cuba.

Then the army got me in '63. That was my first real taste of American ways. I think it was a wonderful experience. I learned a lot in the army. I went into the basic training for eight weeks in school for personnel, and I went to Korea as a clerk—with no talking, with no English. [*Laughs.*] That was funny.

How I passed the class was funny. I used to go to school in the daytime—march to the classroom and so on—and I used to take notes from the blackboard, whatever I could—what I could figure he was talking about. He might be talking about sergeants and he might be talking about girls in Atlantic City—I don't know. I catch maybe 10 percent. But at night I used to take the other guy's book and study, and I passed the course and wasn't the last one.

In Korea I met a Korean girl, and we decided to get married. A lot of these marriages, they break. We have been lucky. We have been married for ten years now.

I finished my tour in Korea and I came to Fort Ritchie. We lived in a trailer house. It was cold like hell. She told me afterwards that she used to spend all day in a bathtub full of hot water. [*Laughs.*]

I was in Supply, and I had a nice job—forty-four hours a week job, as supply clerk. I worked in the NCO club sometime—cooking, washing dishes, making a buck an hour. Then I got tired of that and I was looking for something to do, because I like to keep busy, and I bought a little machine to make nameplates. I took a whole pay—$150—to buy this machine, but I was never short of money after that.

I got out of the army and came here, because it was on the way to Union City and I had a couple of friends here. I got an apartment and I got a job—a factory job which lasted three days. I could not take it—that whistle.

I got me a job in a food plant. I worked in there as a quality control for two years. I was happy in there; I was my own boss. I was doing a little work with my little engraving machine, but I could not do much with it, because it was only small. So I have to decide whether I want to go into this or forget about it. The same thing I did a few years before in the army—I took the whole money of my pay and put it in the machine, the big one.

So this decision I make—this is business. I was in a three-room apartment, and I put the machine in the living room. I finished my job, I used to go out to hustle. I used to go to the jewelers. I had to convince them that I want to do the job. I didn't know how to do it. That was the worst part. I didn't know how to do it, and I was taking the work in. I was learning as I was doing it, and every time I made a mistake, I wanted to die. But I stayed at work and I got work. I started turning out work and making more money and buying more equipment, and so on.

And finally, in '68, I got ahold of a store and kept it three months without doing anything with it. Then I made up my mind. I said, "The heck with it, I'm going to try." I quit my job and I went in there—I try. Thanks to God I had my clientele already—I got a few jewelers. I got a few people to work for and things went okay. Today my business is worth over sixty thousand dollars, at least, if not more. So I see a bright future.

This is still the land of opportunity. Over here you can accomplish whatever you want to do. If you want to be an accountant, you will be an accountant. If you want to be a lawyer, you work hard and you are a lawyer. If you want to open a store, you open a store. You work hard, you make it go. I think it's a great country.

# Ramon Fernandez

······················· FROM CUBA, 1961 ·······················

*He holds a middle-level executive position in a nationally known corporation, drives a shiny new sports car, and owns his own home in Miami.*

Where I lived wasn't too far from the Sierra Maestra where Castro started. I remember standing in the front door, and far away you could see planes going by and dropping flares and you could hear the shots being fired. They were trying to draw the rebels out of the mountains. And at night I remember many times just trying to go to sleep when you could hear the machine-gun fire at a distance—sometimes so close that we had to get underneath the bed.

My father was in favor of the Castro regime in the beginning. I used to go to help him when I was a child of ten, at night to help him take inventory and fill out the stock in the store, and this guy used to come in at night—once every couple months he would knock at the back door and my father would give him some money to support the cause. It was dangerous then if he got caught, but that was common among the people. They would try and support him. My father used to have a picture of Castro's brother. He looked so good. And then, of course, I remember very distinctly when Castro first came in with his victory. Standing in the front door and I could see the parade down the middle of the street—guys with all the colored clothing—camouflage, you know—and the beards and the big guns walking down the middle of the street, and people cheering and the flags and everybody saying, "Yay! Now we're going to have it good," and all that kind of things. They were heroes to me then, definitely heroes.

And then, of course, when Castro took over, everything was different. They began taking over certain companies—big companies and socializing them. You could see the trend. And my father used to argue with some folks about the way communism worked when it came into a country and the first things they started doing. Right away he started smelling a rat. One day there was a big hassle in the Catholic school. The guys came in with guns and started threatening the nuns. Things like that. A couple of priests got beaten up. They were trying to stop all kinds of religion. So my father decided it was time to leave the country. . . .

We flew to Miami. Miami was full of Cubans then. And my father started working and we moved into this little house—a one-bedroom house; a bedroom—it was more like a big closet—like a beach house, where you don't want to live. It was pretty bad. The government gave us a hundred a month for a family and gave us food—Spam, lard, rice, beans, things like that, and a big piece of cheese. I said, "I get tired of eating the same things over and over again." Of course, we expected everything. The beginning was really rough.

My father started working at the Americana Hotel in Miami. His job was to *help* a busboy. He used to work mostly nights. My mother started working in a factory where they made purses and handbags. My father was very proud. He didn't want to go downtown to get the food that we were given. To him it was humiliating to have to go through that, after feeling that you were financially well-off and you didn't have to have anybody to help you. That's the way he's always been. My mother had the good luck to go downtown and get the food that we were given. But he wasn't too proud that he couldn't do this menial job just to get food on the table, which he did. He was willing to go around picking up dirty dishes, and taking them down to be washed, and having to sit down eating in the corner surrounded by dirty plates. Kind of a shock to have your own business for a while and then have to go back to something like that.

I started to go to school and there were maybe another ten Cubans in the whole school, so at first, of course, they didn't have anything planned. Those few months I was in school they didn't have any special classes. I was just thrown into a class with people I'd never seen before, who didn't speak my language. I couldn't understand them. They couldn't understand me. They had us Cubans do a lot of copywork from dictionaries and definitions and things like that. We were like a flock of lost sheep. We couldn't go to any other classes except gym because we didn't have to talk there. Personally, I feel I learned more English from watching TV than I learned in school. I spent all summer in front of the TV set, and by the time I got to eighth grade I didn't have any problems at all. It was different then. There was a lot of friction in the school between Cubans and, shall we say, Americans—I don't know what other word to use. There was a leader of one gang and the leader of the other gang, and the two fighting. Big crowds around, but only the two throwing punches until the cops would come in and settle everything. It was mild compared to what went on afterward with the blacks and things like that. Really, it wasn't much.

Of course, from my personal standpoint there's no difference in color. I never even heard of racism until I got to the United States. In Cuba, you know, a person is black and you have mulattoes and things like that, but you go to the same restaurant that they go to and you pray in the same church they pray in; you never even think about it. We came here in 1961 and there were separate drinking fountains and everything. The blacks had to go to the back of the bus and things like that. I had a couple of black friends and I think they were very nice. As a matter of fact, I liked them better than I liked the rest of the kids I was hanging around with, because they were—should I say *oppressed* then? They seemed more open and more friendly toward you, knowing that you were a foreigner. Maybe because they feel, "I was there."

I remember one day getting in a bus, a crowded bus, and I'm sitting there, about ten to twelve years old, and this black lady comes on the bus and of course I wasn't even aware she was taught to sit in the back. So she comes into the door and I see a couple of people standing. I don't see any empty seats, so I get up to offer her my seat, and she just—she doesn't look at me, she looked right through me and she went right back to the back of the bus. I couldn't figure out what happened; why she didn't want to take my seat. Then I started getting wise when I looked in the back of the bus and all the blacks are sitting in the back.

I started asking questions. Of course, not even my father could answer them, because he wasn't even adjusted to the situation. So I started asking at school, "How come all the blacks ride in the back?" No one seemed to know why. "That's just the way it happens," they said, "because they're black." "Why? What's wrong with that? They don't have leprosy; why should they be separated?" I didn't understand. Of course, now everything is reversed. You have one extreme or the other. Now everything is black-oriented. You have one extreme or you have the other. There's no happy medium.

It wasn't easy for my family. My father coming home all tired out after fourteen hours of work. Couldn't play with me or couldn't take me out someplace because he had to sleep sometime; and my mother coming home with her hands all full of glue and dirt all over the place. That's when reality came along and I started helping out and getting a job. It wasn't bad. I'm not going to say it's bad. It was an experience.

After I finished high school, I got a job with this big company, and I took some training in computering. I started as a stockboy, and then I went to the engineering department and then to the receiving department and then into the transportation department, and I was promoted to supervisor three years ago and everything's been coming out right since. I'm manager of the order-entry and, of course, my computer training came in handy, because last year we went to a computerized system. And the only guy that knows anything about computering in the area is me. I'm no expert, but I know more than anybody else, so I'm running the whole department now. I came in at the right time and I guess I was lucky. . . .

Sometimes I have dreams, and I see myself walking into my grandparents' house in Cuba and I see them sitting there. She's just sewing like she's always doing at night, and my grandfather's smoking a cigar and watching TV. It brings back a lot of memories. The States is home. I have no qualms about it, but I'm still attracted to that little island, no matter how small it is. It's home. It's your people. You feel, if it's ever possible again, you'd like to reconstruct what was there. You want to be a part of it.

When the Bay of Pigs happened I was just a little boy, but I heard other people talking about it and I knew some guys that were there and were jailed. You become kind of angry about that, but there's nothing you can do about it. But you think "If only they'd given air support," then things would have turned differently. I wouldn't be here talking to you now. I just hope another time it will happen, and I feel, myself, that if the time comes and they try to do something and they say to me, "Do you want to go?" I'd be very glad to go in there and try to recover it.

# Su-Chu Hadley

······················ FROM TAIWAN, 1964 ······················

*The closest we are likely to come in the real world to Cinderella and her prince are Su-Chu Hadley and her American husband, Tim. She is deceptively fragile in appearance, with long slender fingers and a fleeting smile. He is blond, bearded, gentle. They live on a small farm in northern California now, but their story begins in the harsh world of prewar Taiwan.*

My parents were very poor and my mother had, altogether, eleven children: nine girls and two boys. She gave up the nine girls so she could go as a wet nurse for wealthy women, to make some money and help support the family. That's why she put us all out for adoption. When I was forty days old, she gave me away to another family with one boy. My foster parents were poor, too. They had a small property, about eight acres—no water buffalo or anything like that. We all just worked by hand, weeding, pruning, carrying the food to the market. Even when I was a little kid, I had to work on the farm; and from the time I was nine years old, I had to do all the cooking. I wasn't exactly a slave, but I was there to work and to help them.

My foster brother and I never liked each other. I hated him and he hated me. We had to sleep in the same bed, as children, because we had a one-bedroom house—a little kitchen and one bedroom, like a little chickenhouse. We slept in the one bed, but he would sleep on one side and I would sleep on the other side. And if he touched me, I would kick; and if I touched him, he would kick.

We didn't like each other, but we were supposed to get married when we grew up. In those days, when the Chinese had a son they might adopt a girl, and when those two are old enough they are supposed to get married. On the night of New Year's they buy you two pillows and they force you to go to bed. And the next day you are married. You have no choice.

My cousin, she was forced. Her adopted mother pushed her into the bedroom. My cousin didn't want to go, but they pushed her in with their son, and the next morning she was married. Now they have two kids, and you never hear them talk to each other at all. No, they never speak to each other. [Sighs.]

My foster parents sent me to school for only two years, when the Japanese controlled Taiwan during World War II. Then the war was over and they wouldn't let me go back anymore. My foster mother said, "You'll get married and have children. You don't need to go to school." I only went to the second grade. I wish I'd been more to school. It's hard to learn when you're older.

In the summer, every morning about one or two I had to get up and start the stove. First you put some paper in, then you put wood, and then the coal. And you cook a big pot and then get everybody up to eat. After that I would go to the fields to work. I cried a lot when I worked in the fields, a lot of the time. I would keep on working and crying all day. But I didn't show them. I just went on working.

My clothes were just rags, and until I was twenty I never had a pair of shoes. There were many times when I didn't get enough to eat. Of course, they were poor, my foster parents and their son, but still they got better than I did. If they didn't feed me, I would go out into the fields and eat raw potatoes. You can get lots of raw potatoes in the field. That's why, when I was a little kid, I was always sort of sick. When you eat too much raw potatoes you have worms inside.

My foster father was very bad-tempered, and he would often scream at me. They could hear it all around, and people would say, "Uh, oh, they're punishing their daughter." He liked to punish me with a kind of bamboo stick that's small but has sort of rough things on it, like thorns. And he would tie a whole bunch and hit me with that. That way, only your skin is hurt, it doesn't hurt you inside. But my foster mother, when she beat me, she would get a big stick, like a coolie pole, and she would beat me with that. The stick was always hanging there, waiting for me. If I was bad or cried or didn't work enough, she would tell me to go and get the stick and give it to her. Then she would make a circle on the floor and tell me to kneel there, and then she would beat me. And every time she said "Kneel," I would start to cry.

If I cried too much, they punished me a different way. They would take a bamboo pole and cut it and put it in the fire until it lit, and then they would put the other end in my mouth to shut me up. When I saw the fire, I would go, "Oooh," and I would be quiet. Usually when I cried, I didn't want any people to see. I was a little kid, but I was kind of strong, too.

One time in the summer, we worked all morning in the fields very hard. And the weather was so hot that everybody else went to have a rest. My foster mother sent me to go pick some pigweed to feed the pigs. So I went. Oh, I was so hot. I had to make two, three trips back and forth to feed the pigs. Each time I had to go through another farmer's sugar-cane field. It's cool to suck the sugar cane when you're hot. And I was so thirsty, and I said to myself, "Oh, God, that sugar cane sure look good. Maybe I'll go get one." I look around and I was pretty sure nobody was around in the field, so I went and sneaked one sugar cane, maybe about two, three feet long, and I broke it in two and put it in my basket. The owner came up and caught me. He grabbed me. I begged him, but he won't let me go. He took my basket and my shovel, and then I didn't know what to do, I was so scared.

I came home and told my foster mother. She said, "Okay, let's go talk and apologize to him." We have in our town something like a mayor or a judge. If something is wrong, you go to him. So this guy and my mother take me to him. To keep her pride, my mother ask me to kneel down in front of the man who owned the sugar cane, and I did. My mother took a piece of bamboo stick, right in front of the judge she took it—it was about an inch round and two or three feet long—and she said, "Why? Why did you steal that?" And I told her I was thirsty. So she said, "I don't teach you to do that. I don't tell you to go steal," and she started to beat me, and she beat me and beat me. I said, "I'm sorry, I'm sorry. I'm dying! I'm dying!" She beat me and beat me so that the stick broke, and the judge never said anything—just watched. And then he said, "Okay," when the stick was broken, "Okay, you can take her home, now." And we came home. This sort of thing went on and on all the time.

My neighbor's wife many times suggested that I should run away, because I was punished so hard by my foster parents, but I was too afraid that if they ever found out they would beat me to death. So, I never thought it was possible. And besides, where would I go?

When I was thirteen, my foster parents started sending me to the market with the vegetables. They would give me about ninety pounds of vegetables. I would carry it on my shoulder with a bamboo pole, a coolie pole with two baskets on the end of it. The night before, I would wash all the vegetables—spinach, radishes, all those things—and tie them in neat bundles. In Taiwan you have to make the vegetables pretty to sell them. I would put them in the basket, ready for morning. And then in the morning I would take them to the market about ten miles away.

The road was all gravel and you could feel your feet get numb because you have no shoes, but still you go. When you carry something like that with a coolie pole, you run fast and then you don't feel it is heavy. I would get to the market early in the morning and sell my vegetables and then come back. And when I would get back, I would go into the field and work. And before I went to bed, I would get the vegetables ready again for the market the next day. I didn't do anything but work.

In the winter, when there wasn't so much farm work to do, my foster parents would send me to work for other people in their houses—cooking and cleaning. I'd get paid two dollars a month. My foster parents would keep that money. Sometimes people would give me a little extra and I would hide it. I wouldn't give it to them. When I was nineteen I had altogether seventy-five cents, and they found out that I had it. They wanted that seventy-five cents from me, and I wouldn't give it to them. They beat me and they beat me and they beat me to get that seventy-five cents. My foster mother came with the bamboo stick and she grabbed my hair and she hit me and hit me, and when she let loose a little bit, I crawled under the bed. She grabbed my feet and she kept hitting me. And I said to myself, "Oh, I don't think they want me to live at all."

I broke away and ran to a neighbor's house nearby, and the neighbor's wife said, "I think you'd better go home or you're going to have trouble." And I said, "I don't care. If I die today, I don't care." Then my foster father came. He took a bunch of sticks with those thorns on them and he hit me and hit me. I just cried and cried, with him hitting me. Then my foster mother came over and hit me some more. My neighbor's wife said, "Go home. Go home." And I said, "Okay, if I die, I die. I'll go home." And I went home and lay on the bed. I was hurting all over. My foster father brought the bamboo again and beat me till I was numb.

Finally, they went out for a little while, and while they were gone I decided to leave. I packed some of my clothes and I ran out of the house. If my foster parents found out I was running away—oh, God! I ran through the fields. I was afraid to go on the road, because I thought my foster parents would see me and run after me. All night I walked through the sugar-cane and rice fields. Early in the morning I got to Taipei, the capital. I was all muddy and I was covered with blood. I got a piece of stick off the street and I scrubbed off the mud and I walked to my sister's house—my fourth sister. She'd been adopted, too, but her family was kinder to her.

I hid in her attic five days, and then she got me a housekeeping job.

Where I worked, the man had two wives. The first wife lived on the third floor, and the second wife lived on the second floor. I had to clean, scrub all the bricks of the house, and do the marketing and all the cooking. The first wife was older, and she always wanted me to cook the food longer and softer; and the second wife always wanted me to cook the food quickly and make it crunchy on the outside. I had to please everyone. That's where I learned to cook different styles. And in the nighttime, when I was through cooking, I had to wash all the clothes. I was cooking for thirteen people and washing clothes for thirteen people, and they paid me five dollars a month.

Next door there was an American, and they had two housekeepers and a cook. The cook made thirty dollars a month. I saw that and I started to try to learn English. I wanted to work for an American and make that big money. Every night, when I finished my work—about ten—I would sneak next door and learn English from that cook and then come back at eleven-thirty at night. In the morning I would have to get up again at six and start the cooking and the marketing and the cleaning.

After I'd been there for about one year, one day my foster mother saw me in the market and she grabbed me to take me home. I didn't want to go, but she was dragging me. Hundreds of people were standing around and somebody asked, "What's the matter? What's the matter, missus?" My foster mother called out, "This is my daughter and I raised her. I adopted her since she was forty days old, and now look, she doesn't want to go home!" One young guy in the crowd said to my foster mother, "How old is she?" And she says, "Almost twenty-one." And he says, "Too bad! She's twenty-one now, she's free."

When I hear that guy say that, it made me strong. Then I talked to my foster mother and I said, "Okay. Right now I'm making five dollars a month. I will give you four dollars. You will have some money, and I will not go home." She let me go then. So I give them the four dollars a month, and I kept a dollar. Later, I got a raise to six dollars a month, and I got two dollars a month and they got four dollars a month. They were satisfied.

And then one day I became a housekeeper and cook to an American, and I made twenty dollars a month. My first twenty dollars I gave to my foster parents, and then I gave them more money every month. They treated me bad and they beat me, but that was the way things were then. I still think I was lucky that they didn't give me to a teahouse or something like that, because some foster parents, when the girl is old enough, they give her to a teahouse for so much a year. One of my other sisters they gave to a teahouse, and they beat her and beat her there, because she wouldn't do anything. They beat her till she would. Now she has something wrong with her head, because they beat her so much and made her do those things. So I think I was lucky, even though my foster parents punished me so much and beat me. I worked hard and now I'm strong. It was better than the teahouse.

While I was working for this American family as cook, I met my oldest son's father. [*Begins to whisper.*] He was an American and he told me that he wanted me to marry him, but he couldn't while he was in the army. I trusted him. He gave me twenty-five dollars a month to give to my parents, and he asked me if I would stay with him. He said we would get married when he left Taiwan. I lived with him for two years, and then one day I saw him and the next day I didn't. I was looking for him and looking for him. And, finally, I found his army buddy and he told me, "Oh, he went back to the United States. He has a wife and four children back in the States. You want his address?" And I said, "No. I don't want any address from him." At that time I was pregnant, three months pregnant. . . .

Then for a while I was very down—no money, no nothing. I had to go home to the farm with my foster parents until my son was born. That was bad. . . . Afterward, my foster mother took care of him and I went back to Taipei and worked and sent her money. My foster parents were kind of nice to my son, because I sent them money.

I got a job as a waitress in an American officers' club and I stayed there for three years. While I was working at the club I met Tim. He was a civilian, doing some engineering work for the government. He was very, very good to me. We were married there in Taiwan, and he was kind and he wanted me to learn. He taught me a great deal. He sent to the United States for third- and fourth-grade books of mathematics for me to study, and he taught me how to do division, multiplication, how to divide a pie; and he taught me good English—gentle English, because the way I had learned, I learned to talk rough. I didn't learn nice words and I talked very loud. He taught me to speak softly and to use the right words. Every day, when he would go to work, he would say, "Honey, this is your homework today. When I come home, I want to check it." He taught me all these things. He was very good to me.

We took my son to live with us and had two children of our own in

Taiwan. Then my husband said, "They should be educated in the United States." So when my oldest was ready for school, we came to the United States. When I came to this country, I heard about all the divorces and I was kind of scared. I wanted to save money in case my husband kicks me out, so I can go somewhere. So I went and scrubbed floors for people, and my husband never knew. He didn't know for four years. I would take my children with me and work for a few days for free to show people what a good worker I was. And then I would work for them from about ten in the morning and come home at three, with the children. And Tim never knew. I saved all that money in case he would kick me out.

Then one day I heard about interest, and so I put my money in a bank. The next month the bank sent me a statement. And that day my husband got the mail. He came in and his face was kind of white. He was so hurt. He said, "Honey, why do you have to do that? Why do you have to sneak money in somewhere? Don't you trust me?" And I say, "I was just trying to save money in a corner, in case you kick me out, so I can have a plane ticket to go home." And he said, "You don't have to do that. In the law here, you can take half. If you're mad at me, just take a vacation. Just take the money, take a vacation one week and then come home." He said that to me; he didn't say "Go back. Go back to Taiwan." We were both crying. And I thought about it, and then I got the money out of the bank. It was $640 by then, and I let him have it to buy a truck for his work. I didn't sneak around anymore. After that I trusted him, and he trusted me again. . . .

I still send money to my foster parents. Every year I send them money because I understand that they are poor, and I feel, even though they were hard on me, they trained me well. Two years ago I went to visit them, and I felt I have to help them more because their son had drowned and they were alone. And I thought I would take them to the United States and help them. My husband said I can bring them to this country and take care of them if I want to. Then I found that they have kicked me out of their family. They had their little property, their eight acres, and these days property goes up in price. And they thought maybe I would go home to Taiwan and try to divide the property with them, so they went to court and took my name out of their family. When I wanted to bring them over I asked them to send me the household papers, and I find they had canceled my name out. So now I am no longer their child and I cannot bring them over. It's justice. But I still send them money, because I feel they trained me well.

[*At this point in the interview, Su-Chu's two daughters come into the room to say good-bye before going to the beach. They wear bikinis and carry a picnic basket and a transistor radio. After they leave, Su-Chu looks out the window for a moment. Then she speaks softly—*]

You can't know how it makes me feel to see them go off like this. They are ten and twelve, and when I was ten and twelve I was working in the fields all day. . . . Sometimes in the evening I cry, thinking of everything that has happened, and my children say, "Daddy, how come mommy cry?"

"She's remembering bad things from long ago," he tells them.

And then I look at him and at them and at my house here, and I say, "Well, at least I have a happy ending."

# César Le Clair

## FROM FRANCE, 1965

*Tall and ruggedly handsome, he is a waiter in a well-known New York restaurant, where he serves the patrons with European charm and élan. He is the proud father of two young children, is an active sportsman, and he likes to cook gourmet meals on his day off.*

I was born in France, on the border, Italy—Menton. I lived in that place, the French Riviera, the Italian Riviera. You got lots of tourists, the beautiful hotels, the restaurants.

In the Second War—1941, 1942—the Germans were all over. At this time, my brother was in the army. In France you go in the army at eighteen, nineteen years old. But the army became all German. [*Raspberry.*] So my brother was in the German army, under General Rommel, between El Alamein and Tobruk, and my brother was prisoner for the English people, the General Montgomery. So it became César's turn—eighteen years old. César says, "You got to be kidding. I no go there." So what happened? The Germans, they came one afternoon and they picked up my sister; because they said to my mother, "Where is your son?"

"My son no home."

"Well, where is he?"

"I don't know."

So, "Who's this girl?"

"That's my daughter."

"Okay, I pick her up until your son come back home. I take your daughter." She was sixteen years old. They take her in the prison till they get César.

So now I gave up, and the Germans, they take me. The train, it's supposed to go to Germany, because all the prisoner they take to Germany. But no regular train. This train take all the food and everything for the army and most fancy stuff from the museum—

everything on the train to go to Germany. They stopped a few days in north Italy, past Milano, at a prison.

In this prison not just the French or Italian people—German, too! Because when they came back from the Monte Casino, the German soldier refused! Not just the soldiers, but the captains, the lieutenants, yes. You sleep on the floor with special mattress—the food that you get for the horse?—straw, yeah, inside of the mattress. And so César very young and he knows the kitchen, so he has the chance to work in the kitchen with the German. The train leave and César stay here. Very lucky.

César stayed eleven months in this place. Then I came back home and supposed to go in the army. But I went to *force de la résistance*, the underground. The young people or the old soldier, they go in the mountain, for the resistance. I see these people with the long beard, with the machine gun around the neck, the pistol—everything robbed from the German soldier.

In the mountain they had a big *kaserne* [barracks] for the German soldiers. You leave in the nighttime and you come early in the morning on this road—all the German and French pass. You go in the nighttime, you go down the mountain and bring up everything you find there. Maybe a few you shoot, too—the German. You afraid, but what do you do? Because you're younger. You think now and—hah!—your skin, it come back chicken-skinny [goose bumps], but at that time you thought you were doing good.

One night we're coming down, three guys. We got the shotgun ready, automatic, everything, the German machine gun—it is beautiful. So the big chief, he said, "No shoot. Don't shoot, because you shoot, you in trouble." So at ten in the morning, the German came with a big motorcycle, one officer sit down in the sidecar. They came at the curve and they had to slow a little bit, and we jumped on the front—with no fire! You jump on the front and you stick with the machine gun, and they got to stop. Can you imagine you jump on the front? I don't know, maybe because you scared or maybe your pressure in your blood—I don't know—we started to shoot. The German officer right away dead. The other guy just hurt on the legs—because you don't know where you're shooting. I don't know if it's myself or the guy with me. But once you shoot, you got no time to stop. Now very exciting, because the German people, they got a beautiful pistol, they call P-38. So just pick up this pistol. And now for *four hour*, no stopping, on top of the mountain for four hour! Because right away was the big machine gun. The German people in the *kaserne*, they shoot, and you see the big bomb coming—*Bababoom, baboom!* And you go so fast, the same as the rabbit. The rabbit more slow than yourself. The rabbit is not comparison to myself. I have very bad experience and I'm scared.

A few more times like these, then . . . the liberation in 1945. . . .

After the war, I started work in the bar. You can't say *bar*, because the European bar—you got a big machine for the café espresso, you make the aperitif—no whiskey. No similarity in this country. The first season in Menton, the Hôtel Palace—you got the beach, you got the casino. They sent me to *l'Ecole de l'Hôtelerie* in Geneva. At the same time you go to school in Geneva, you work, too. You're working in Geneva, in the hotel, at the school, with the restaurant business. They teach you the restaurant business plus what you serve—what's the name, where it's from, how they make, every sauce, every meat. The school takes one year.

Most of these jobs you take in the season, summer or winter. It takes six months. Then maybe you find the director of a hotel. If he sees you, he like you, he think you work very well, you're a good waiter, so you get a chance. He say, "Would you like to come back to a job?" So when I finished in the summertime, I got a chance to come back in St. Moritz in the wintertime, in the Hotel Kulm. The season start December 15 and finish in April, when they finish the carnival.

They introduce you to everybody. They say, "This your waiter and this your busboy." The uniform with the tail, the shirt with the strong front, the special collar—the society collar, I don't know what you call it. So the number-one maître d' say, "You here for to work, for to make nice money, to make feel happy the customers. You here for the season. They no like to lose the waiter, because you no got replacement." Because everybody, they like to go and ski, but in the accident you break one leg, no replacement. So this is important question. I like the sport, you know. So in the nighttime, I go to rent the ski and the boots and all, and in the nighttime I go ski or sledding. *Mon Dieu!* Lucky—me lucky! No accident, I enjoy.

Plus in St. Moritz, too, you got the horse racing on the ice. Beautiful! In St. Moritz is French, Italian people, mostly English: Lord, Milord, Lady, Milady. The lady play curling. Some of the parking lot frozen, you see the curling. In the lunchtime they have a beautiful cold buffet—because they like to eat very fast and go play more. Plus, in the afternoon they serve tea. Most the young people, they like to take a basket lunch in the morning, and they come back for afternoon tea dancing. This a beautiful attraction. In the daytime, you no work with the tail. You work with the white jacket, but everything with the strong shirt and the special collar.

So when I finish St. Moritz, the maître d' tell me, "César, we like you come with me on Italian Riviera." I served for three season in Portofino, Hôtel Miramare. You find lots of German tourist, Swiss, Nordic; and I young and I like to enjoy. Many, many time I come back to sleep around three or four in the morning, because you finish your work, you like to enjoy. You got beautiful nightclub, or you go in the nighttime for swimming. This is beautiful. After midnight you go on the beach; not too many people. This is a tremendous time.

Between the seasons you get maybe one month or two months for vacation, so you come back home. I came back with no money. I had a little bit, just a little bit. On the Italian Riviera I bought a little Fiat in Genoa—two-color, beautiful. You see where it go, my money? This is in 1955. My mother very happy to see me, but most of the time they see me just in the morning, because all day long César no home.

Because you are close to Monte Carlo, you go gambling. And sometime you make maybe a hundred francs. And maybe you lose.

So you go sit on the beautiful beach and maybe you find a girl, a tourist, and you ask, "You go to Monte Carlo for play? Will you go?" So you take her. I got my little car and I pick her up and we go. We stop in beautiful restaurants—because I know everything—nice evening. Now maybe you got a chance to win. This girl maybe give you a hundred dollars—maybe you come back with three hundred dollars! So she say, "Okay, César, you keep this." And maybe César keep a hundred dollars.

Now I got the chance to go to San Remo, very close to home, in the Hôtel Royale. This a deluxe hotel, beautiful hotel. I stayed there for five or six years. I had my apartment, beautiful apartment, lots of friends, lots of everything—single. Because when you work in the hotel, in the restaurant, not possible marry; because your life too fast, too easy. You meet the very wealthy family, very intelligent people, very rich people, like Onassis. These people no tip, because they got the bodyguard man or the *secrétaire* or the lawyer. This Onassis, he pay no check—oh, no. Everything the *secrétaire* or the lawyer.

So in this hotel in the summertime, this big customer—purser in the ship. You see, in the Italian Riviera, in San Remo, you see most the time in the nighttime outside in the bay, you see this beautiful ship, and it has lights in the nighttime. They call it the "city on the ocean." Now, most of the people are rich and they are traveling, they take the Mediterranean cruise. So this purser, he ask me, "César, why you no like to work on the ship? It's a new ship, coming to the United States, the Italian Line, the *Michelangelo*. They stay for eleven months in the United States and they make the Caribbean cruise. I think you make more money than if you stay here. Plus you see New York."

My dream! I see America every day in the movie and the postcard. But in my mind it's a dream. So I got my day off and I talked with my mother, I talked with my father. I said, "Listen, I got a nice adventure." And my mother said, "Now maybe this adventure make your head on place." Because all the time she ask me, "When you get marry?"

So in three days, everything set up—passport, visa, everything. And I leave on this beautiful ship, October 1964. They stop in Gibraltar, they stop in Morocco, in Casablanca. It take eleven days.

So you meet new maître d', all new people, but friendly. No different from hotel—just hotel on the ground and this hotel on the water. Now this is a big ship, but your tummy got no habituation for this. Not used to it. Every day you sick, sick all the time—seasick. Friends say, "César, eat the apple. Eat the apple." So you eat the apple, and in the morning you come back to serve breakfast for the passengers—three hundred and fifty passengers coming to the United States. You force—you make yourself numb, you make more strong. You say, "No, I can't eat the apple." They say, "Eat one more. Apple or crackers." Eleven days!

So now, they stop one overnight in New York. Friends, to make me happy, they take me to Forty-second Street, to Times Square, Fifth Avenue. They show César all the big buildings. *Mon Dieu!* I don't believe it myself. You look and the buildings are so high—you know, the people, the traffic, all the different faces—the white and colored people. You see this, you forget you seasick, you forget everything. This is my dream coming true, my dream coming true.

And five in the afternoon, they pick up the other passengers for the first Caribbean cruise—ten day, I think, for four port. You believe it or not, the ship start and you forget you're seasick, see? I see now the new passenger, new faces, new American passenger. I had one table with six beautiful girls. One girl, very nice, very *sympathique*. I tried to talk a little bit, make a little joke. I make friendly with this girl. This girl is name Nellie O'Brien—Irish girl, American-Irish. The cruise finish, I say, "I'd like to see you more. Give me the number of the telephone and where you live."

The next cruise, I find mail. This girl, she sent card. César very happy. Imagine how exciting to come back in New York and to meet this girl! César all over the world, all over in Europe, and see many girl and many women. I don't know what it is with this girl. It's like lightning—love lightning. You see what I mean? Love light come— bingo!—you pick it up right away. This a romantic story.

So coming back to New York, this girl pick me up and take me home. They introduce the parents, everybody very happy with me, they make me comfortable. I no understand the English, but with love you speak every language. So I leave for the next cruise. Every port, César have one letter. I no understand English, so my friend, he told me what she say. César very happy. So every port, right away, jump to the post office, pick up the beautiful postcard in the Caribbean island, and send the postcard. My friend help me say, "I love you. César—kiss." He say in America you make the *croix* and it mean the kiss, *X*, *X*.

Every cruise I see nice tip, nice money, very happy. More weeks pass, more months pass—César in love with this girl. Now when you say love, you supposed to go in the bed with the girl, you understand? Now I tried, but she said, "Uh, uh." So, okay. I bought a nice ring in St. Thomas—one black and one white pearl. When I came back, I said, "I get this for you because you very nice with me. I think César in love with you." And her parents said, "César, that's nice, because Nellie, she more in love than you think." So everything go nice and smooth, and now César call this girl *fiancée*. So I belong to O'Brien family now.

Labor Day, every cruise finish. I talked with the captain about my situation. "I want to stop here in the United States, because I love with this girl, and I ready to marry this girl." He said, "You not supposed to stay here in the United States. When the ship leave, you supposed to leave, too. You got just a visa to stay in the United States because you work on the ship. But you very nice, we got no complaint for all year long. I make a recommendation for the immigration." And I got everything ready in one week—visa to stay in United States and marry.

I have a friend who work in New York in the restaurant Sardi, so I say, "René, why not prepare this nice buffet for the wedding?" He's the cook and César the waiter, and we make this beautiful, tremendous buffet. We worked very hard. Nellie's mother said, "César, César, go faster, faster, because three o'clock you supposed to go in the church."

We married with the tuxedo—beautiful, tremendous. I no see my wife with the white dress, because we supposed to remain apart and see nothing. For me everything new. So I go in the chapel with the best man, and they say, "César, now you're ready to go and meet your wife inside the altar." You don't believe the people inside! I see most the people, most the friend, and César by myself. Nobody of my family.

Now we leave the altar—walk out through the big door and the chapel. All the people now very happy; they take the hands, they make congratulations, very happy. César no can stand. There started a little tear in my eyes, but I said, "César, you make you strong. You not supposed to cry. This just come from my happiness." I got a picture with my tear, but you see my face, it's very happy. In my mind, this is my dream, my dream, this is my dream, this my dream!

You marry, you make love, and one day you got a beautiful surprise. My wife say, "César, I'm pregnant." Can you imagine how that make me feel happy? You were just in a room by yourself with this nice girl—now the family coming, now three people. You feel more happy. You leave in the morning with happy, and you come back home in the nighttime for more happy, to see all the family home.

Now is my second life here, my second home, my second everything. Starting all over, but more better and better and better. Because I'm married, I'm happy. I like my work. I love this girl. I love this country. This is my second life.

# Nikos Liadis

···················· FROM CYPRUS, 1950 ·····················

*A successful lawyer in a middle-class community, he came to the
United States from the island of Cyprus at the age of twenty-seven.*

I come from a very poor farming family. We had eight brothers and
sisters and two parents, was ten. And the farming and, generally
speaking, the peasant's life wasn't such an enviable one, especially on
the island of Cyprus, when you depend on rain; and we had very bad
drought at the time. There was no rain and no crops, and the animals
couldn't eat—there was no grass—and the peasant, the farmer, and the
shepherd were really having quite a few difficult times. In fact, most of
the people were lucky to get a piece of bread and olives and onion for
breakfast, and then skip lunch and try and get a pot of beans for the
evening.

Our village was at that time about five or six hundred people. When I
finished the elementary school in the village I was the first one in the
class, and that was out of curiosity, nothing more. I don't have any
brilliant mind or any faculties better than the next person, but I was
always first in my class, and when I graduated I remember the
schoolmaster told my father, "If you don't take this kid to high school,
you are going to do him an injustice." We needed two and a half
shillings to go and pay for the fee to be examined if you qualify to go to
high school. And as I said, in 1932 or '33, I think it was, my father
didn't have it.

We didn't have the two and a half shillings, and he was delaying and
postponing, and then, finally, one day I got angry and I said, "Dad,
September is coming. I haven't gone for the examination yet. The year
is going to start and I'm not going to be in high school."

So he says, "Well, tomorrow."

"No! This is it!" I lay down in front of the cows and I said to my
father, "If I can't go to high school, I don't want to live anymore. Go
over me with the plow."

I remember I saw tears in his eyes, and he says, "Okay."

He tied up the cows and went to the village. He borrowed—I'll never
forget this—he borrowed five shillings from the local grocer, who
happened to be a second cousin of ours, and he took me right to
Nicosia—it was about two or three miles—where I went for the
examination. We went either on a donkey or in a cart, I don't
remember.

When we got to the *gymnasium*—that's a high school, you know—a couple of the teachers saw me and asked, "What are you doing here?" I said, "I came here to take the examinations." They said the examinations were three months ago. I said, "Nobody told me." They said, "Too bad." And then I started crying. So a schoolmaster came in and he saw me. He says to me, "Why are you crying?" I said, "I came to take the examination. I want to go to high school." So—I'll never forget this man, he's still alive—he said, "Sit here. I'm going to arrange it." So he went out and he got to the mathematics teacher, who had pull, and he says, "This boy is crying and he wants to go to school. Why shouldn't we give him a chance?" So he called me over and he said, "Okay, we make an exception. We examine you." So that was the beginning of my high school, really. Even now when I think about it, I start crying. . . .

Then I began to wonder what is beyond the high-school education. Do the universities offer anything more, higher, finer, and better than what we were taught in high school? But that was more or less a dream. There is no university in Cyprus, and to go abroad and have to spend money for rent and books and tuition and what have you—it was out of the question at that time. But I had that inner desire, and I said, "If I don't go to university to learn something, I am being cheated."

But after high school the war broke out and we were limited to the island. Of course, it was a good thing to be there at that time. Because of security reasons we had the British navy. In fact, we never had any—other than a few sporadic attempts by the Italian air force to bomb the harbor of Famagusta—we didn't have anything else really. I was an interpreter in the army during the war—the English army. We had what we called the Cyprus regiment and the Cyprus volunteer force, and I was interpreting for the British instructors. It was quite an interesting experience. In fact, for a little while I was out in the field, which I enjoyed very much.

Then, after the war, I spent about a year in Cyprus doing odd jobs. Like I was helping on a farm. At one time I tried to raise chickens, but I wasn't too successful, thank God. So I decided that I have to try a little harder to get out of the island so I can go to the university, where I thought an education was necessary in order to satisfy my intellectual curiosity. I knew then that the United States was the country of opportunity, and since I was a child of a poor family, and I knew I had to more or less do it on my own, I felt this was the best place. And I had a brother here—he came in '29, I think. My brother became an American citizen, and after that he arranged for me to get my visa and come over to the United States.

My brother had a restaurant, and I started there, washing dishes. After a week or so I learned my way around; so I came out, I became a counterman for two or three weeks, and then I became a night assistant manager, and slowly, slowly, I became the manager and ran the place, for two or three years. And that was my first trade, so to speak.

My brother and I found out there was a diner here for sale, so we bought the diner and we started in the diner business in 1955. At that time my one nephew came over from high school. I enrolled him at D—— University. And six months or a year after that, my next nephew came in, his brother. And I said to myself, "I'm going to help these two boys through college," because really I was resigned to the idea that I'm not going to do it myself. I might as well help somebody in the family. Also, this was an old debt that I was paying back, because these boys' father helped me go through high school in Cyprus. So I figured, to pay back the old debt I'd see to it that his two sons get a college education.

Now when they got here—especially when the second one got here—I was traveling back and forth, going by D—— University. And I said to myself, "Isn't this a shame? I go by every day; why don't I stop in to see what it looks like from the inside? And besides, while I spend the time to help these boys with their schooling, I might do something for myself." So I considered the idea that—uh—let me try it. By this time I had a family, three children. Although an old man, what have I got to lose?

So I started with D—— University for two courses in a semester, as a special student. I took Greek drama and political science, and I got very much interested in the work. I said, "Well, I'm going to finish." So I continued the next semester. I took either nine or twelve credits, and I kept working in the diner all the time. I went to summer school, and I think I took four courses a semester, which gave me perhaps a year's work. I completed three-quarters of the bachelor's degree. That was the minimum required for getting into law school. So I applied to law school and I was accepted. I was a poor candidate, because my law aptitude was so low, but somehow I impressed them with my grades, and I—you know—cried that I never took examinations of this kind before, and it was some absolutely new thing to me, and that's why my record is so low. So I remember the dean of admissions says to me, "You impress me as a person and as a student, and I'm going to give you a chance. But you have to take the examination again." So I said, "Why not?" I took the examination the second time, but I was already admitted into the law school. At the time I got into law school I was thirty-eight or thirty-nine.

I worked through my college and through my law school. Well, in fact, when I was going to college I worked day and night; all night long, and I went to school half a day, that is, the morning. I started at eight and I finished at seven, and my brother used to put in the extra hour,

God bless his soul. The diner was open twenty-four hours a day, and he was working thirteen hours a day and I was working eleven, to make the twenty-four hours. And when I finished at seven, I went home, washed, changed my clothes, and ran down to D—— University. I sat there from eight to eleven the first semester, and then until one in the following years.

My wife, during the time that I was going to college and law school, was really a saint. She was working at night as a waitress when I was sleeping to get ready for law school the following day. She used to come in from six at night to one in the morning and, you know, we had a rough crowd there to feed. She was working there, and about one she woke me up to come to the diner and relieve her so she could go home, so she'd be ready in the morning to take care of the children to go to school.

Sometimes I couldn't keep awake in class. I told the fellow who was sitting next to me to give me the elbow once in a while. But I didn't have any problem really—I was so interested in what I was learning. But it was very difficult for me the first semester. I remember I just couldn't keep my eyes open—reading—and I remember I took American politics or American government. You know, where I come from there was no political life, as such, at the time. It was just that you're governed, and that's it. I didn't know what the structure of the American politics was. That was all new to me. . . .

We raised our children to know where they come from and what is their place in the American society. I believe to try to preserve the best we have in each nationality, and you don't preserve the best you have unless you are aware of your nationality, of your origin. For instance, I like to have my children know that Plato was a Greek, Aristotle was a Greek, *Oedipus Rex* was a Greek drama.

Of course, you cannot make the children understand that they are part of a minority. No, they feel they are full-blooded Americans, and there is no distinction, for instance, between an Irishman and a Greek, or a Jew and a German, or. . . . You know, it's very hard to make them understand that this is a country of different nationalities and perhaps discrimination in a subtle way. It's always around. They know that they've got to do better than the average child; otherwise I'm not satisfied. Because you cannot expect to survive unless you are better than average. Everything else is not equal. We are a minority. And I've got to be better than the next person, if I'm going to survive. And besides, who wants to be a mediocrity?

# Phillip Contos

*He works as a troubleshooter for an American shipping company with offices in New York and Greece, and he maintains a branch office out of his house in Mississippi.*

They say all the Greek people in Istanbul are left over from Constantinopolis, from 1453.* I say I'm Greek. I won't say I'm Turkish, because I just happen to be born there. I'm not Turkish. Till 1960 we had good years. And 1960, then everything begin. They was destroying the churches, houses, everything. We also have two cemeteries. One of the cemetery I visit the next day. I saw dead people. They pull them from the ground, open their cases, and put a knife in their heart.

And in 1964 they start repatriating people. They sent twelve thousand of Greeks back to Greece. They were Greek nationality, not Turkish. They took their houses, they took their stores, they took whatever they had. They sent them out of the border with broken bones, broken legs, and all kind things.

I was a Turkish citizen because I was born in Turkey. I was twenty. I was going to take a physical for the army next month—it would be three years. That's one reason I left. The Turks said that if the Greek population goes down to fourteen thousand, around there, Turkey takes over the churches. So the Turkish government wants us to leave. So I didn't have any trouble to leave. But when I left, they had me sign a piece of paper which says if I was going to be outside of Turkey more than thirty days, automatically I was going to lose my citizenship. But the Greek government doesn't want us to leave Turkey, because they want to keep the churches in the Greek community. And that's why Greece didn't allow me to stay there. They gave me a passport like a tourist, like reentry permit, not as a citizen, not even as a permanent resident. I don't have the right to work in Greece.

So I joined the merchant marine, because most of the ship doesn't have a Greek flag. They have Liberia or Panama, so no control. In the time I spent in the merchant marine, I went to forty-five countries. I had been in New York seven times during that time. I heard for this country, if you are without country you can stay. I find out all this, and

---

* In 1453 the Turks drove the Greeks out of Constantinople and changed its name to Istanbul.

since I been without any nationality, I made my decision to stay in this country.

I jumped the ship. That was the only way I could have come. I don't have plan to jump ship. I was asking the captain to release me in America, so I can go to the Immigration. But the captain refused to do it, because he was short-handed. So I just walked out of the ship. I left everything there. When I came here, I had no clothes, nothing. I jumped the ship, but I didn't jump like anybody else. I jumped the ship, and I was ready to give myself up and be here illegal. But I was trying to get some money, so I could pay the lawyer.

I went to employment office. They ask me if I jumped the ship, but they don't care. Wasn't state employment; was a private employment office in New York. Those people care about making money. They sent me here to diner. He don't care. Now is a law you cannot hire, but before was no law.

I don't speak not a single word. I had no relatives and no friends in this country. I was by myself. But my boss was Greek. He was nice for me. He help me to meet some other Greek people. And he talk to Liadis, Greek lawyer [see page 340]. He helped me a lot. I told him I want to give up myself. He called Immigration, and they give us appointment for about six weeks later. We went down there for the court. It took about five minutes. They gave me first thirty days extension, and then they been giving me every thirty days for four months.

And then one day they came to pick me up. You see, I had put the application in for extension and they did not give me.

I have to say, I never did expect to find this friendly people in Immigration. When they came to pick me up, I still was sleeping. So they wake me up; they ask me to get dressed and go with them. The first they did, they stopped in the first diner and offer me breakfast. I don't think in any other place you can find that. Other place they going to put the handcuffs and take you away. And they asked me if I had money to go back. They was willing to pay my bus ticket or help to come back home.

When we went to the Immigration, they open my file and they saw the application was there, and they gave me three months extension. Then they started giving me every six month. By that time, I was married and I had no more trouble, because my wife sign for me to stay here. She was permanent resident. I met her right here. They was a new family, Greek, and I was trying to help them like somebody else help me. We met and got married in nineteen days.

# Lee Chang

*He came to the United States three years ago on a visitor's visa and "disappeared." Like many other illegal Chinese immigrants, he lives in a dormitory over the restaurant where he works. He gets his meals in the kitchen, studies English and watches television with his fellow workers, and tries to keep one step ahead of the immigration authorities. He has managed to send over four thousand dollars to his parents in Hong Kong, enough to enable them to buy a modest house. Now he would like to use his earnings to start a take-out restaurant here. But. . . .*

One night about eight the Immigration people come to the restaurant and see me.

"Are you Chinese? You have paper?"

"Yes," I say. "Wait here. I go up to my room and get it."

They don't follow me upstairs. They just stand and wait for me. I go to sleeping room and open window and jump out. I don't know how far. I afraid, you know, but I just forget everything and jump. Even if there be river there, I jump. I hide in woods there all night.

The second time the Immigration people come, two stay at front door and one at back door. No way out.

"Immigration. You have paper?"

"Yes," I say. "I have paper."

This time they smile, they follow me. They look at paper.

"Your visa is past."

"But I working, I like it here."

"Okay," Immigration man say. "I give you four more months. Then you go."

I have to put up a thousand dollars bond. Take all my savings. If I go, I get it back; but I stay. Already one month over now.

I get lawyer, give him fifty dollars, and he tell me, "Best way is to get married. Get citizen girl, marry, you get paper very easy."

I like this way, too. Maybe some girl need money. Okay. I pay her two thousand, three thousand, four thousand. We don't live together, we just make the marriage paper and send to Immigration office, tell them we marry. Then maybe I get paper, then get divorced. But very difficult find this girl.

# Miguel Torres

*Miguel Torres is a slight, shy youth of twenty with a pale skin and El Greco features. He works in a mushroom plant in California. He has entered the United States illegally four times in the past year, and he has been caught three times. He told his story through a trusted interpreter.*

I was born in a small town in the state of Michoacán in Mexico. When I was fifteen, I went to Mexico City with my grandmother and my mother. I worked in a parking lot, a big car lot. People would come in and they'd say, "Well, park my car." And I'd give them a ticket and I'd park the car and I'd be there, you know, watching the cars. I got paid in tips.

But I wanted to come to the United States to work and to earn more money. My uncle was here, and I thought if I could come to him, I could live with him and work and he would help me.

It's not possible to get papers to come over now. So when I decided to come, I went to Tijuana in Mexico. There's a person there that will get in contact with you. They call him the Coyote. He walks around town, and if he sees someone wandering around alone, he says, "Hello, do you have relatives in the United States?" And if you say yes, he says, "Do you want to visit them?" And if you say yes, he says he can arrange it through a friend. It costs $250 or $300.

The Coyote rounded up me and five other guys, and then he got in contact with a guide to take us across the border. We had to go through the hills and the desert, and we had to swim through a river. I was a little scared. Then we come to a highway and a man was there with a van, pretending to fix his motor. Our guide said hello, and the man jumped into the car and we ran and jumped in, too. He began to drive down the highway fast and we knew we were safe in the United States. He took us to San Isidro that night, and the next day he took us all the way here to Watsonville. I had to pay him $250 and then, after I'd been here a month, he came back and I had to give him $50 more. He said I owed him that.

I was here for two months before I started working, and then my uncle got me a job, first in the celery fields picking celery, washing it, packing it, and later picking prunes. Then, all of a sudden, one day the Immigration showed up, and I ran and I hid in a river that was next to the orchard. The man saw me and he questioned me, and he saw I didn't have any papers. So they put me in a van and took me to Salinas, and there was some more illegals there and they put us in buses and took us all the way to Mexicali near the border. We were under guard; the driver and another one that sleeps while one drives. The seats are like hard boards. We'd get up from one side and rub, you know, that side a little bit and then sit on the other side for a while and then rub that side because it's so hard. It was a long trip.

When we arrived in Mexicali, they let us go. We caught a bus to Tijuana, and then at Tijuana, that night, we found the Coyote again and we paid him and we came back the next day. I had to pay $250 again, but this time he knew me and he let me pay $30 then and $30 each week. Because he knew me, you know. He trusted me.

We came through the mountains that time. We had to walk through a train tunnel. It all lasted maybe about three hours, through the tunnel. It was short; for me it was short. We're used to walking, you know. Over in Mexico we have to walk like ten miles to go to work or to go home or to go to school, so we're used to walking. To me it was a short distance to walk for three hours. And after we got out of the tunnel, we got into a car; and from there, from the tunnel, we came all the way into Los Angeles. That was the second time. We didn't see any border patrol either time.

The second time I was here for three months. My uncle managed to get me a job in the mushroom plant. I was working there when the Immigration came. There's this place where they blow air between the walls to make it cool and I hid there. And I was watching. The Immigration was looking around the plant everywhere. There was another illegal there, and he just kept on picking the mushrooms. He'd only been back a couple of days himself. The Immigration walked over there, and that kid turned around and looked at the Immigration and said, "What's the matter? What happened?" And the Immigration looked at him and said, "Oh, nothing," and the kid kept right on picking mushrooms. Yet he was an illegal! He knew how to act, play it cool. If you just sit tight they don't know you're illegal.

Well, the Immigration looked between the walls then and he caught me again. That was the second time. They put handcuffs on me with another guy and we were handcuffed together all the way from California to Mexicali.

Altogether I've been caught three times this year and made the trip over here four times. It's cost me one thousand dollars but it's still better than what I was making in Mexico City.

It's the money. When you come back here you get more money here than you do over there. Right now, the most, the most that I'd be getting in Mexico would be from 25 to 30 pesos a day, which is maybe

$2.00, $2.50. And here, with overtime, sometimes I make a $150 a week. Things are expensive here, but it's expensive over there, too. And I like the way people live here. All the—what do you call it—all the facilities that you have here, all the things you can get and everything.

The boss at the mushroom factory doesn't ask for papers. He doesn't say anything about it. The last time, he hired me back as soon as I got back here, without any questions.

I learned to hide my money when the Immigration catch me. You know, if you have a lot on you, they take you fifteen or twenty miles from the border in Mexico. But if you have just two dollars or so, they let you go right in Tijuana. Then it's easier to come back. You can just walk right down the street and find the Coyote or someone like him. A man I know was hitchhiking along the road near San Diego and someone picked him up and it was the Immigration man who had just brought him back to Mexico! The Immigration laughed and said, "You got back faster than I did." Of course, he took him back to Mexico again then. But that man is back in Watsonville now, working in the brussels sprouts. It takes a longer time for the Immigration to catch us than it does for us to come back. [Laughs.]

I'd like to be able to stay here, to live here and work; but the only way now is to find someone that'll say, "Well, I'll marry you, I'll fix your papers for you." There's a lot of them who do that. I'd be willing to if I could find someone that would do it for me. You pay them, you know. You don't sleep together or even live in the same house, but they marry you. A long time ago you could fix up papers for your nephew or brother, a friend, a cousin. It was real easy then. But now it has to be close relations: mother, father, wife, son, or daughter. My uncle can't do it for me. The only way I could do it would be if I could marry an American citizen.

I'd like to learn English because it would be easier for me. There is a night school here, but I don't like to go because after work I like to go out and mess around and goof off. [Laughs.] Maybe I'll go later. If I could just learn a tiny bit of English, you know, I could turn around and tell the Immigration, "What's the matter with you? What do you want?" and I wouldn't be recognized as an illegal.

# José Garcia

·················· FROM MEXICO, 1959······················

*He is forty years old, short, sturdy, swarthy, with a long black mustache and curly black hair. He and his wife and four children live in a rundown house on the Monterey peninsula of California, where much of the nation's fruits and vegetables are grown.*

I first came to the United States in 1959, and, in truth, the reason that I came was in order to make money. At that time, you know, you could earn from seven to ten pesos [a peso is worth about eight cents] a day in Mexico, whereas here you could earn from sixty to seventy dollars a week. And we were poor. Our whole family was poor. It was the money, that's why I came.

At that time they had a law about the *braceros* [Mexican field-workers]. You were allowed to cross the border with a permit, a work permit, for a certain length of time: sometimes sixty days, sometimes ninety days. As soon as we'd cross the border, we'd go to a place in Texas like a big hall, a dance hall, and the bosses would pick out maybe ten or twenty to go to this town, ten or twenty to go to another town. And then they would ship us out.

The first time, I came to a ranch on the other side of Santa Cruz. It was like a barracks, maybe ten or fifteen bunks or beds to each barrack. We went to a brussels-sprout ranch, and all day we picked the brussels sprouts. That's hard work. We worked between nine and ten hours for ninety days. I saved everything I made to take home with me, except what the boss took out for room and board. They would take out maybe between eighteen to twenty-two dollars a week for room and board.

The food was pretty poor. Really just rotten. They cooked everything mixed together. Carrots, turnips, corn, peas. And in order to find a piece of meat you needed a magnifying glass. The barracks were dirty, completely dirty. It was just awful. I feel kind of funny telling you, but the bathrooms—what you call them?—the outhouses were just awful. The board would be like maybe seven feet long, and in those seven feet they would have three holes; and the board would be covered, completely covered, with worms, white worms—those great giant white ones. That's why, to this day, I won't look at white rice. I won't eat no white rice because it looks exactly like those worms, you know. At that time a lot of us would not eat the white rice that they served us, because we said the cook used to go out to the toilet to get it.

That time I worked ninety days and saved my money and gave it all to my mother.

The next time I came over I had papers, and I worked in the fields for a while, but then I got this job in the mushroom plant. The main reason I like it is it's less heavy work and it's more steady. I've been here ten years now.

Of course, they favor the Anglos in the plant. They give them the easier jobs. They don't like the Mexicans to touch the machinery, you know. Where I work, if they had the custom of carrying things on a burro, they wouldn't let the Mexicans touch the burro. They would only let the Anglos touch the burro. They don't like us to touch things. They think we're all from the hills. The Anglos run the rollers to carry the straw and the compost, and just move the levers back and forth to make the machines work. But the Mexicans, the majority of the Mexicans pick mushrooms, plant them by hand—it's the Mexicans. That's the kind of work they think they're good for.

But, still. . . . I've been there a long time now. They let me drive the tractor. And the second boss in charge, he's really nice. Sometimes he says to me, "Take these mushrooms down to such-and-such a dock, or take them here or take them there." But I'm the only one of the Mexicans there that they'll let use the truck or the machinery.

They hurt you in words, too. The son of the main boss has a pickup, a green pickup, and it's fairly new. And sometimes the workers go over there and they lean against it when they're on their lunch or their break, and that kid will come up and say, "Hey, what's going on here? You guys having a meeting or something? Why are you leaning against my pickup?" He thinks his car is too good for us to lean against.

Still, things are getting better here. When I first came, there were some stores and restaurants that wouldn't even serve a Mexican. They'd say, "We're just closing," or "We don't have any more food," or sometimes just "Get out." They don't do that anymore.

I want to save money and buy a ranch here. There's one that's on San Juan Road, with ten acres of fields plus an orchard, an apple orchard, and a house with three bedrooms. That would be my dream. Yeah, my ambition, my dream, if I could have a ranch. I'd like raising animals there—chickens, pigs, cows, whatever is easier to sell, whatever there is a demand in. That's what I'd like to do if I could only get the money together.

# Orlando Galvez

············FROM COLOMBIA, 1973·····················

*He is a factory worker in Manhattan.*

In Colombia you hear about the United States; you can get anything in the United States. When Colombians come back home, they like to show off a bit. Like a visitor will come from here with a thousand dollars and spread it out, you know, whereas he probably may have borrowed the money up here to come down. He give the impression that if you want a dollar, okay, you sort of just go and pick it off a tree. When I came here I see what the situation is, I was so disappointed.

# Marta Ramirez

*She is a beautician in a small New Jersey community.*

My husband had a job as a government worker under Perón—not an important worker, just a clerk. When Perón was overthrown—zat!—he loses his job and can't get no other. He looked three months, and then we say, "The hell with it," and we sell the house—we didn't get much for it neither—and take the money to come to the U.S.

We arrive here in December. I go down to the town center to buy some things, and I see all the Christmas stuff and I say, "What is this Santa Claus?" and the lady in the store tell me, and I go home and I tell my daughter Angela, she was six then, "In this country Santa Claus brings you presents."

"Good," she says, and I take her to see Santa Claus in that little house they have in the shopping center.

On Christmas Eve she hangs up her stockings and we put some stuff in them and a nice doll besides—one of those dolls that says words. And the next day my daughter is very happy. We want to be Americans, that is why we do it that way.

Then on the Feast of the Epiphany, January 6, we go to church, and on the way home my daughter says, "Tonight the Three Kings will come."

"Angela," I say, "Santa Claus comes in the United States, the Three Kings don't come here."

"They come all over the world," she says, "you told me so yourself."

"No," I say, and my husband says "No, no," but she gets out her shoes anyway and puts them by the window. That is what we do in Argentina for the Three Kings.

I clean up the kitchen and wash the dishes and then I go in to cover up Angela, because it is cold. She is sleeping, so sweet, like a real angel, and the shoes are by the window. I call my husband and he looks at her and goes out and buys a—what you go on the snow with?—a sled.

In the morning Angela comes in to us and says, "You see, I told you the Three Kings come to New Jersey."

# Luisa Rojas

·················· FROM GUATEMALA, 1968 ····················

*She was raised by an aunt, went to work at the age of fifteen, and eventually saved enough money for a small business in the Guatemala City market, selling beans, corn, rice. Here, as a live-in domestic worker in New Jersey, she spent weekends in her apartment in Brooklyn, washing her husband's clothes and teaching him to cook. Now she moves from apartment to apartment, each one in better condition than the last, and commutes to daily housecleaning jobs.*

I want to say the truth. In my country is a business with the visas. Because everybody want to come and some people work with the consul—not with the American sponsor, because he is strict, but with the people that work in that consul. Some friends say, "Can you help me? I give some money to give visa to this person." And that happen. I went to the consul, but they don't give me visa. I have a friend, a lady, and she have another friend. And he is friend to someone in the consul. And he say to me, if I give some money to him I can have the visa. And I'm scared because I think maybe he's mean, you know, because sometimes they lie. I paid him before I have the visa, because they say you don't give money for start, they don't do. I think was a hundred dollars, and later this man have the visa for me for only one month, but I think I'm going to stay.

I went to New York. The next week I went—I walk around the place I live in Brooklyn. Is so many factories, and I find a job in a pen factory. On a Sunday I find. I made the whole pen. They show me how make it. I remember is a small machine, and I do with my foot. I put together. And when I went back to my apartment, I was so tired. Oh, my God, I remember I was so—my legs—I want to go to bed.

I got Social Security card from another person. My friend have that. She have it from a friend, and I got that Social Security. They never ask. Only I say that Social Security belongs to me, that's all. Every time when I see people coming into the factory with suit—a man with suit—I thinking it's Immigration. Every day thinking about Immigration, Immigration, Immigration. Always afraid.

If you go to Immigration, they give more time here. You pay only ten dollars. I went to the Immigration, and I remember they give me three months more, for ten dollars. And then when this finished, I went the second time, and they give me another three months for another ten dollars. You know, it's a business they do, too. I went three times and they give me three months each time. The thing is that when I came, I say in my mind, "I has to do my papers, because I don't want to be illegal here."

Some friends is looking for a job for me in a house, because my friend told me it's more easy to have a resident papers for a housekeeper. I stay two months in the pen factory, and then I came to a house. I work there for five months, a little more maybe. I was happy. The lady is nice lady. I'm afraid to talk to her about my papers, because the girls always scared when is a tourist, because you never know if the people good or not. Maybe the people mad and say to Immigration and cause trouble, and maybe Immigration come and take her away, you know. I always afraid. When I remember I feel bad, because she was so good with me, and when I talk about the papers, she told me she cannot help me because she helped another girl to make her papers. My feeling is always the same, and I thinking about how I has to leave the house and I has to leave her, you know, alone. And I think every day, "How can I say to this lady I'm leaving?" I had to leave because I need my papers.

My friend find another job in New Jersey and she say, "This is the time you make your papers, but you has to leave the house this weekend, for to start the next Monday in the other house." And I never feel to say to the lady, "I going away." I never said it to her. I went away and never said it to her. Very sad for me. And every time I'm thinking I was so bad with her, because I remember she was in bed and she never know I going away. Now I have experience and I say, "Why I never say to her I has to go away?" Anyway, I remember I started Monday my job I have now. My friend say, if they made my paper, I work for them, but if not, I not work. They knew from the start. Right away I told them I has to get started with the paper, and my boss bring me to the lawyer. It worked out. I was happy.

My husband was not so happy. He send me letters and say, "How's everything?" If I miss him. He don't want to come, because he work, and he don't want to leave his town. He was afraid I not come back, because he knew my family don't like my life with my husband. We not married. He's separated, you know. He have children, and he not stay with them. And my inside, maybe, say, "Leave this man." But I don't know, because I love him.

He had a job, but in that time they give layoff to him. He's a truck driver. Because his boss, he lost his business and they lay off him. And in that time he say, "Okay, here is the time I has to go." With the money they give—in my country they give some money to the people when they give layoff—he pay for the plane. Was not easy, and he so scared about not coming, because they say they don't give any visa to him, because is a bad time and the people has to have a lot of money and he has not too much money—only for the plane. You has to show the Immigration four hundred dollars when you come to the United States—four hundred dollars, yeah.

He had friend at the market, and she say she know someone can make his visa. He give some money to the man, and he never do nothing. It's his business to steal money from the people who need a visa. And later my husband give to another person, another forty dollars, and he steal the money, too. The third time, a friend—she have good relation with the consul, and they helped the visa for him. They don't give months anymore. They give only days—to my husband they give seventeen days.

He go into New York with my friend. In the same week he find a job in a factory. He stamp the little boxes of face powder. I bring him to the Social Security, and he got his own Social Security, because when he came the people can have Social Security. Now nobody can have it—only American people. I bring him to the Immigration and they give seventeen days and say good-bye. Then we are afraid the Immigration take him, and we went to the lawyer. You know, immigrant people always looking for a lawyer, because when they make legal papers—he's a special in that—only immigration business. He pay five hundred dollars—yes, five hundred dollars. He say he going to make his paper with—I can't explain—about the mechanic. Because they say this country need mechanic. He knew a few things, because he's a driver, you know. He never got his papers!

And then my papers worked. When I have one year and a half, they call me for make my papers. And I go to my country to make my resident paper. I stay only for two months. I stay with my family and come back here. And when I come here, I marry with him.

When we here, my husband and me together, we change our religion. We not really religious, but we are Catholic. But we study with Jehovah Witness in my country. My mother is Jehovah Witness. She told me everything about the religion, but I never accept because I don't feel to change. And we come here, we meet some people the same religion, and they started with the studies, you know. And the lady give the study to us, my husband and me. She say, "What is the step to be Jehovah Witness? One thing: has to be marry." And my husband send to the papers to Guatemala to divorce—because he was separated from his first wife for eight years. When we were married, we went to the lawyer again and we say to him, "We are married." And he change all his papers, because before he make for mechanic papers, but this time he marry with a resident woman. And he start with the papers again. I think he take a year and a half.

I work a few more months with the lady and I told her I can't stay with her anymore, because my husband need me in New York. I have a friend in New York, and she work daywork in house, and she find me a job. That's easy for me. A different house every day. I talk to my boss in New Jersey. I want to work two days for them. He was not so happy, because they like me to stay for the week. But later he say, "Okay, if you can come two day." I live in Brooklyn. From my home is two hours to New Jersey. I stay overnight.

I work only in house, and it's easy to do that when you are nice. But for my husband, because he can't find a job the same he have in my country—because he was a driver, a truck driver—he has to find job he don't know. Now he work in a foundry—metal. He don't like the job, but he has to have something, you know. Because it's very dangerous, hard job. He has to melt the metals and make again, you know? He say, he don't do it careful, if water spring in the dish they make the metal, this is explosion. And sometime he burn his arms, sometime his face. And I remember a long time ago, the metal burn his leg.

When we fix everything, you know, our lives, we thinking about his children. He say he wanted the children come, and I say okay, and we went to the lawyer to make another papers for the children. Because if we are resident, then they can come as resident. We give to them their residence. But when they came, the girls don't work, and it's very difficult.

My husband have a boy, and he's twenty-two years old, and they give a visa to him. I mean, we don't do anything for him. He told to us when he got his visa. It's a surprise, because I told you, at that time they don't give any visa. We don't know how he do, and he got a visa and he came. He have a tourist visa, and when he came here he say he want to start to study with the English class. And we went to Immigration with him to change his visa, because the lawyer say they can do this—for a student. But they don't do it, and we so upset about that, because they say he has to go back. They say he has to go back, and if he don't come to the Immigration with his paper, they coming to catch him. And he has to leave the house, because he don't want to make trouble. Now he live away from us. He's illegal now. He has a good job—a plastic factory—but last week they give him up, because they say Immigration is coming to the factory. Now my husband don't know what we going to do, because my husband is thinking about he going home. My husband worry too much, because he want to stay with his son. It's very difficult.

With all my problems, with my private life, I not so happy. Sometime I want to quit from here and I don't know where I want to go. But I think if I go away, I going home again. Because my husband, he think, too, if I stay here so long, he say maybe he's going to be more old and he's going to die here. And he want to die in his country. I think I never go home, because the life here is so different. I think it's better life here—to work here, to have the things you want, you know. But I love him and I don't want to leave him alone.

# Jaime Alvarez

*He comes from Peru and has a face like an Inca statue, with massive features and coarse black hair. Like many other newly arrived Latin Americans, he works on the cleaning staff of a large metropolitan hospital.*

At twenty-five years old, I got married and I went to work to the factory. They make the fish flour, uh, fish powder, for the dog's meal or cat's meal. And I working there for about four years.

Then we had one daughter, then two daughters, then three daughters—finally, four daughters. It was too hard to live in the city, so I built us a house on some land that the government rented to poor people on the outskirts of the city.

It was flat land. Not good for nothing. Not like a suburb—more of a flat shanty town. We had electricity, but no running water, no sewers. The streets were not paved. It took me a long time to get to work every day and to get home at night. We had a hard time having enough to feed the children on my job, and I could see that it would not get any better.

Finally I talked it over with my wife, and we decided that I would come to this country, where I could earn more money, and then the family would come over and be with me. I had heard about how much people make in this country. And, besides, I had a cousin in Connecticut. I wrote to him and he sent me some money, and I took my final pay from the fishmeal factory where I was then working, and I got on a plane and I came to Connecticut. My cousin took me in and helped me a little, and I learned a few words of English. But he really had no room for me, and I got a room of my own in another place soon.

Then I went to night school to learn English, and now I've been here five years and I am working on my high-school equivalency. . . .

I thought, at first, that my wife would come over in one year and then, maybe, the children—one by one in the years after. My parents could take care of them while my wife was with me here. First I thought, one year till they come, then two years, then three. Now I see it will take much longer. It's a very expensive trip from Peru—three hundred dollars for each person. And, besides, I have to have a place for them to live here.

Now I'm working in a hospital and I have room and board and my salary. I can't save money very fast because I have to send money every month to my family, for them to live on. And I just got a letter from my wife that she has to pay $250 in taxes for our house outside of Lima, or they cannot stay there. So I have to send some of my savings to her for that, and it will be longer till one of them can come over. And I don't know how long until they are all here. . . . Perhaps I will take a night, part-time job to earn more money, but then I won't be able to get to night school and get my high-school equivalency. . . .

People in this country are different. They are calmer. There, in Peru, we were so overwhelmed by money problems that it made us excitable. Every little disagreement led to a fight or a loud argument. Of course, there are differences in culture, too. But I think it is the money difficulties that are at the bottom of it. We were all so desperate there.

Here, in the hospital, if I have trouble with a co-worker, we talk it over, and if a supervisor gives an order, he doesn't do it in an insulting tone. And personal relations are pleasanter, too, if you aren't always worrying about money or arguing about how to spend what little you have. Of course, I am poor here, too, but I have my necessities and I can save a little and send some home.

And I am rising in my job. I am foreman of the cleaning staff for the whole floor here, now. And I have applied to be assistant to the director of maintenance. He says I have a good chance of getting the position, because I speak both English and Spanish and can talk with the employees who speak very little English. Almost all our new workers here at the hospital are from Latin countries, and they start out knowing nothing—not even the words for broom or soap. Everything must be translated. That's how it was for me, too, four years ago. But I went to school, and now, maybe, I will get a better job because of it. And then my family will come over and our dreams will be true. But I think that by that time my oldest daughter will be grown.

Well, I must have hope and I do have hope. I will see what the future brings.

# Rita Flores

···················FROM COLOMBIA, 1965·····················

*She lives with her husband and children in Miami, in a one-bedroom apartment littered with toys and decorated with kindergarten draw-*

*ings. She speaks earnestly and seriously but giggles at the antics of her
two children, who wander in and out of the room.*

A long time ago, when I was seventeen or eighteen, I studied
something about United States. I read that United States is beautiful
country. The people make money and live well. The people nice, the
people work, make a lot of money. That made these things interesting
for me to come over here. When I came over here—well, surprise for
me! Everything, everybody was strange. The people were different.
Hard to say how. But they were different. Everybody here live
independent. In our country, the people help more. They more
friendly. Something happen at the neighbor's and somebody else can
help you right away. . . .

In Colombia I be a nurse. It was pretty good. I worked and I got not
much money, but I could buy my things and give money to father and
mother. I worked for a lady—American lady. She had a heart attack in
Colombia, and I came to the United States with her to nurse her. Was
1965, I be twenty-five years old. I was in Miami, Florida. She was
seventy-five or eighty years old and she can't take me out. I had to learn
myself.

I remember, one Sunday I went to church and then I walked all night
[*laughs*], because I got lost. I was afraid to ask somebody where to take
the bus. I no find any telephone. I had money in my pocket but I was
afraid to take the taxi, because I didn't know how to tell the taxi where
I live. I was so hungry, but I was afraid to go to cafeteria to eat, because
I didn't know how to ask for meal or coffee or anything. I got home
around six-thirty in the morning.

I lived in the lady's house about six months. And then I made one
mistake one night. I broke a glass. [*Laughs.*] Was a delicate glass, and
it's easy to break, and I so tired. And she got nervous and she got mad
with me. I told her, "Well, if you no like my job and I not able to pay
you for glass I broke, I sorry."

Then I found job in the newspaper with Dr. Solomon. They really
nice, fine people, really good. I stayed there for a year and then I
quit—getting married! I met my husband in Colombia; but we never
saw each other again. I didn't know he was here. Well, one day I was
walking to buy pizza one Saturday night. And he drove the car and said,
"Hey, Rita!" He said he was looking for me. [*Laughs.*] He knew I was
here. And later on we got married.

We had tiny little room and we worked in hospital, in the laundry.
We were working both in there. Later on we had my son, Eduardo. And
we had little tiny room—only one room. We had a stove, refrigerator,
bed. It was difficult for us. I stopped working. My husband, he made
little money. He made a hundred dollars for fifteen days. We had to pay

thirty dollars a week for the room, and we paid the hospital and food and crib and stuff for the new baby, and diapers. We no had nothing.

Later on we decided to send my little boy to Colombia. We couldn't raise him with no money at all. I couldn't work; we didn't know anybody to take care of Eduardo. So I brought him back to Colombia. I have two single brothers and two single sisters and my father, and they lived with Eduardo there. All my sisters and brothers, they really good. And they love Eduardo very much.

My sister wrote me one time and said, "You have to come over here, because Eduardo very, very sick." The doctor told my sister he had homesick. He had fever, high fever, he vomited, he had headache. He stayed in the hospital for one week. They said he was so sick, because I came over here and left him there. But I couldn't go, because no money to go. He stayed for four years.

My husband and I worked day and night. My husband, he is young man but he is really good. He had little own business. He was doing floor wax. He had the places to go. He was working seven days in the week, day and night. I worked with him. We so busy, sometime we no had time to think of Eduardo. We tried to make some home and make and keep some money and have different life than we have before. Be able to have nice apartment.

Well, my sisters were really good. They told Eduardo, "Your mother's away. Your mother love you. Your mother write you. Your mother say hello to you. Your mother kiss with you." "Your mother"—always. Always my sisters reminded me to Eduardo. Then two years ago I went there to get my son. When I got there, it was seven in the morning, and he was just waking up, and he said, "Hello, Mamma," and he just looked at me. Because my sisters told him, "Your mother come tomorrow. When your mother come, tell your mother, 'Hello, *como esta!*'"

But he was scared. He cried a lot. I had hard time, very hard time. He cried a lot in the airport. He said, "You no my mother." And he cried a lot, and I cried a lot. And he was mean, but I know it's hard for him. Well, I said, take time, but very hard time, for him and for us. We bought a lot of toys, we took him out a lot, played outside a lot. I stopped working, because I expected the other baby. And then Eduardo was so happy, because later on he had sister. And he picked out the name—Victoria.

We had very hard time finding the apartment, because all the people say, "You have children?" "Well, I have one." "Oh, well, we no like children. They destroy. We no like children." But we found little apartment. My friend was living here and she moved, and we moved in. Now my husband found new job. He is supervisor at IBM. He take care of floors. I work sometime, baby-sitting.

Now we so happy; because we have nice apartment, and we can speak a little English. Well, I want many things. [*Laughs.*] I would like to speak perfect English and writing and reading. If I have time, I would like to go to the school and finish my high school. I would like to be a nurse. But at this time, I so happy. I have my children, my boy and my girl. We wanted a boy and girl, and we have it. And we so happy.

# Mario Lucci
·····················FROM ITALY, 1972·······················

*He is seventeen and star of his high-school soccer team in a Boston suburb.*

Our main sport was soccer, and I used to play soccer night and day, night and day. I started soccer when I was five years old, and I hope I play soccer till I die.

The church was in the center of town, and that's where we played soccer sometimes. The center—it's really beautiful at Christmas. They'd get all the logs around town—logs that are cut down and there's no use for them—they'd take them up there and just pile them up, and there's about fifteen to twenty feet of wood just standing up there near the church. It gets burned when Christmas Eve comes. Everybody comes out and it's beautiful.

Then, once a year, we had this holiday, where they used to take the body of Christ—well, they make believe it was the body of Christ—and walk around town, and everybody used to hang a long cloth down from their balcony and throw money or rice or whatever. I think it's in the summertime, I'm not sure. I'll ask my grandmother, my father's mother. She's eighty-five and she still goes to church every Sunday. She's so tight with the church. She's really religious. Every time I see anything about the pope, it reminds me of my grandmother.

My mother's father lived in Boston. He lived there for many years. I think it was in 1967—I was either five or six years old—my mother got a telegram saying that her father died. It was at night. I remember that scene. It was about ten at night, and the church bells ring. You know, when the bells ring everybody wants to go up and see what happened. So my mother went up there, and I went up with her. One lady had a telephone, and this lady told my mother that something drastic happened. She didn't want to tell us, but she wanted us to go to the church. The priest told us that my grandfather died. My mother was pretty upset, and she lit some candles.

Then one of the aunts—she lives in the United States—wrote and told my mother that she's got the citizenship from my grandfather. So my father got the wild idea, "Why don't we go check it out?" He decided to come here to the United States and see what it's like, because everybody said that the highways are paved with gold—that old story. Yeah, it's still going around.

My father says he'll move here first, then later he'll send us the papers and we'll come, too. That's how come me and my mother came after. First my father. Then my brothers Gino and Sal. Then, a couple years later, me and my mother and my grandmother.

We came by plane—Alitalia. I got on the plane, and then, when we were about two hours away from Rome, the engineer tells us there's something wrong with the plane. I got scared. We started going toward Rome again. As soon as we got down, I see my brother. He's still there. I guess he was just kind of sad to see us leave. When I saw him, I said, "Mom, let's go back home. I don't want to go to the United States." But we got on a different plane and we took off again.

We came in about two in the morning and we went through—you know, when they open the baggage. I think we brought some oregano and some laurel leaves. They took those. You couldn't bring those in. Then we saw my brother and got the baggage and went to his car. It was the biggest car I ever seen in my life—a Pontiac Catalina. I heard they had big cars in America, and I said "Wow!" I was interested to see all the people. In the early 1970s, you know, girls were still walking around in miniskirts. My mother was looking at them, and she put her hand over her eyes and said, "I don't want to see this." I saw people staying up in the street till three, four in the morning, just talking to each other and eating watermelons. I said, "That's weird." It was much different than the town I came from.

I came February 22, and March 1 started school. The shock! Well, in Italy people are really quiet in school, and they dress nice. But here—I think I was one of the politest kids in school! Everybody I saw I used to salute them, even though I didn't know them, because that's the way we were taught. The teacher's name was Miss Kiefer. It sounded like *schifo*. In Italian that means something of no value, bad. And in Italy the students are taught to say just *Signorina*—that means teacher. You can't call a teacher by their name, because to her it's like—I don't know how to say it here—like it's not nice. Every time she talked to me, I go, "Yes, teacher," because I don't want to get spanked. I finally straightened that out.

In Italy, if you start acting bad they smack you. I used to be one of those. I didn't take work serious. But when I did, I would really get down to it, and I wrote some nice poems. Well, in school they teach you to write little poems that rhyme, something sweet. I used to write it, and the teacher used to say I used to do pretty good work in poetry. Then, every time I went to school I used to go by a field, and I picked three or four flowers and take it to the teacher. They would like to have new flowers on the desk every day. It gave you the feeling of spring. Once I did it here. I was walking by this yard and I saw some nice flowers—tulips, I think it was. I went over there and I ripped them out. The teacher said, "Where'd you get these?" I didn't really understand what was wrong. Then Sal, my brother, told me. First he started laughing. I said, "What's the matter?" He goes, "You don't bring flowers in the United States." I said, "Why not?" He goes, "They're going to think you're a sissy."

The kids used to ask me to play sometimes—baseball. I never seen the sport, you know. When I saw the first baseball bat—you know the part you hit with? I grabbed it, so that the little part—you know, the handle—I thought it was like a golf club. I'd never seen one in my life before, so I thought it was like that. No, we never had baseball or basketball in Italy. We just played volleyball and soccer.

One of the boys on my street used to ask me to play baseball, and I used to make up excuses, because I didn't know how to play and I was scared to play with them. Plus, I couldn't speak, so I felt bad. I would stay inside. I was ten years old, and I used to play with this kid that was three years old. He was Italian, so I used to play with him. I didn't want to play with anybody else. He used to come over my house in the morning around seven—this was in the summertime—and we used to eat breakfast over my house. Then we used to watch TV from seven till five, and that's how I would spend my summer.

After a year, I started going to a special class, with Miss Gorelli. She used to teach me English. Then this other girl from Italy came. She was crying and I was trying to teach her, because I knew the way she felt. But *I* wasn't crying, because, you know, what are you going to cry for? You got to learn. You got to get accustomed to everything.

I really tried hard in school, and I tried to be good. I've been a good English student. The third year, I got a B-minus, and then I improved to an A. Yeah, I feel good in English. I can still read and write and speak Italian, but it's kind of blurry.

I was making friends and I started playing baseball, but I never learned how to play real good baseball, like hard hitting, fast pitching, and everything. After I found out that soccer was kind of dead in the United States, I started playing basketball, and after a couple of years I became a good basketball player.

When I went to junior high I used to go by bus. I stayed after one day, and when I walked out to get the bus, I still had some time, so I walked around the school. I wanted to see what it was like. I saw a bunch of guys kicking balls around. I said, "Are they playing soccer, or are they playing soccer?" So I got out there, and for the first time in the United States, I picked up a soccer ball. I still had a magic touch—after three years almost, yeah. That same season I played right wing. That was the best thing that could happen to me in the world, almost. I was happy.

My coach asked me if I wanted to teach some little kids. So after soccer practice I used to take these little guys—I actually teach them, from about six till seven—till it got dark.

By eighth grade, when the soccer season came, everybody came to watch me play, because—no bragging or nothing—I used to take the ball from everybody. I used to write the plays for my coach, and he used to send orders to the other guys to put in this kind of play. I was pretty good with that. Everybody knew me. I started feeling more—I was really Americanized almost. I figured those were my best years in the United States—in my life, really, so far.

I knew everybody by the time I went to high school. Probably the whole town knew me, because every time they mentioned soccer—"Hey, it's Mario!" My freshman year I played a couple of freshman soccer games. All of a sudden I got moved up to JV pretty soon. That's where I met new kids. I'm still meeting new kids.

I'm a sophomore in high school now, and I'm making a good, straight-B average. If I wasn't worried about soccer that much, I'd probably be better off. Yeah, when the soccer season comes, I go to class and I don't pay attention to what the teacher's saying. I just wonder about the game. I started getting involved in school things. I joined the Italian Club, and I've been wrestling. Now I know kids from all different nations. We got kids from Peru, we got kids from Iran. . . . I really like to meet new people. I like to be friendly with all new people, because in a way I know how they feel. And I like to help them out. If they're from a foreign nation and you ask them about soccer, they're going to say, "yeah," so I'll play with them. And even if they don't understand English, we can play. . . .

I was thinking about what I'd like to do. I wanted to be a doctor, and one disappointment was when my cousin told me, "As you get older, you probably won't like to be a doctor. There's too much work." I said, "Yeah, you might be right." So I stick to soccer. I really want to be a professional soccer player. My family don't like it—especially my brother Gino. He goes, "You ain't going to do nothing in soccer." I say, "Look at Pelé. He makes forty-four thousand dollars a game." And he goes, "I'll probably make more money in my whole career than you will in soccer." But if you're a good soccer player, you can make a couple of million dollars probably, before you retire—or even more. I hope I do!

# Salvatore Bianchi

························FROM ITALY, 1975·······················

*He came to Rhode Island from Sicily three years ago. Short and dark, with bright eyes and an eager manner, he talks rapidly, using gestures to help him with words still unfamiliar.*

My father was the owner of a construction company in Sicily. About fourteen years ago, start, in Italy, inflation. We lost everything. My father came here and he stayed here, because the family needed help, you know. Every week my father send money to us. And then my mother came after five years.

When my mother and sister left Italy, I was twenty-three years old. I didn't want to come. I know America is a good state and rich, but I didn't convince myself, you know. The thing is I have a girl. It's not really official, but my mother knows, all my relatives know about it. She comes from my town, and my mother knows her family. I asked my girl to come here, and she asked her parents, and they say, "I like Salvatore, but in America you can't go." I was depressed and unhappy. It was complicated to decide what to do. But my mother, all my family is in America, separated by miles. It disturbs me, because you know the family, the Italian family, especially in Sicily, patriarchal family, and I can't separate from them.

I was happy because I go to see my father and my mother, you know, but unhappy for other things. I explain to you. In my town in Sicily, after work, after five, six—especially in the summertime—we go outside. We go to the piazza. There are the cathedral, bars, everything. The people all go there to meet. Everybody does, especially on Sunday. It's a big *passeggiata* [promenade]—the band, everything. I go with my friends, we meet the girls—if somebody introduce us, we can talk—and we go together to the bar, we drink something, we sit, we discuss many things. I know a couple friends here, I know a couple girls here; but if you go outside, you got to spend money, a lot of money.

I know many, many girls here. I go to school, study English, and in the class, all people are from South America. Different, you know. I don't like that. I want Italian girl. American girl from Italian family, that's good. I like that. You know why? Because I know the Italian mentality. I find one girl—she's from Germany. She's divorced. Is not good. She like marriage, but for six, seven months, you know? I believe in marriage, permanent. I told you before, I like the family unity.

A year ago I went back to Italy, because I like to see my girl, my grandpa, my town, everything, you know. Nostalgia. Ooh, it was beautiful! I was sorry I came here. I know America is a good nation, but it don't look like my town, you know. I can't forget my—oh, what is it?—my past. I live in this country, but I still got nostalgia. I ask my girl again to come, but she say, "Salvatore, I can't." . . . I don't know, maybe if I find a good job and learn good English. . . . I want to try, but right now, it's a little difficult. I'm not sure, you know.

# Liv Jorgensen

···················· FROM NORWAY, 1969 ······················

*She is an elementary-school teacher in Westchester.*

I think one of the things that bothered me most when we came to this country was the way that my children wanted to live and what they may have wanted from me. They wanted me to become very, very American, in a sense. They probably wanted me to do more things that American mothers do and that I didn't want to do: driving them all over the place and being at their disposal at all time, which I was not. I avoided it by working, because I have been working just about since I came, and I felt that maybe they were deprived and maybe they were not. I don't think so. I think they have turned out to be reasonably competent and independent, and I know I would have spoiled them if I hadn't worked; because it is the way of least resistance, if you have time. I remember my daughter saying to me when she was about ten: "Sometimes I am sorry that you are not an American mother, because I have to walk to school when it is very cold." That was her definition of an American mother.

I think it is a bit of a myth, that women are freer in America than they are in Europe. There are certain things that American wives do. They take care of bills, they take care of budgeting. They take care of the money more often than I think happens in Europe. But whether this gives you freedom, I don't know. In Europe, for instance, I think there is a higher percentage of women in executive and professional positions than in America.

It seems to me that American suburban women—anyway, those that I can talk about—seem to be an awful lot at the beck and call of their—maybe not so much of their husband, but of their children. They just seem to apologize for wanting a life of their own, or they have to assert that, as if it were something unusual.

# Monica Dickens

·······················FROM ENGLAND, 1951·······················

*The first writer in the family since Charles Dickens, her great-grandfather, she has published over twenty-five books. She is an immensely popular author of novels, children's books, and memoirs in England, Australia, and New Zealand, less so in this country. She lives now on Cape Cod and still writes constantly.*

I was brought up in London, where I was expected to become a debutante and come out into society and find some young man, get married, and have children. That was the sort of established way of life in the late thirties. And I decided that this was not the kind of life that I wanted. I wanted to have a job, but I hadn't any training for a job at all. I thought that cooking would probably be something that you could learn as you went along, so I became a servant—mostly a cook, but a parlormaid, housemaid, charwoman, too.

My immediate family, my parents, didn't mind, because they were very enterprising and had a good sense of humor, and I think they were glad to see me doing a job. Some of the older members of the family thought it was pretty disgraceful and pretty weird, and they used to feel funny when I came to dinner at their house and they had, maybe, five or six servants, and they didn't want their servants to know that I also. . . . Because in those days a servant was a servant, and you wore a uniform and you were kept in your place.

I think it was a very lucky break that made me decide that I would go downstairs for two years. I was going to stay forever, but a young man from a publisher's office, who got interested in what I was doing, suggested that I should write a book about my experiences in the kitchen. As far as the family went, it wouldn't have been encouraged, because Charles Dickens was the author for all time, you know. There was a lot of family pride, and my grandfather, who was his son, used to give readings from Dickens's works, copying his father and that kind of thing. I was the first person in the family who did write professionally, after him.

The book [*One Pair of Hands*] was published in 1938 and was instantly successful. Almost immediately the war started, so I then became a nurse, started training in a hospital, and I wrote another book about my nursing training [*One Pair of Feet*]. By that time I was pretty much established as an author. So I went on writing books, and I wrote a book at least every two years. By the end of the war, I was working for a woman's weekly magazine, called *Woman's Own*. It was the first one that took women's magazines out of the small, domestic format, into a more colorful, more glamorous thing, which hooked in a whole lot of—um—your young mothers, young working girls. I had a weekly column, in which I could write anything I wanted. It was called, "The Way I See It." It was sometimes interviews with people, interesting people who were in town, it was investigating different kinds of jobs that women were doing, it was talking about problems, or sometimes it was what's known in the trade as "beastlies." You know, women with two handicapped children and a husband with only three legs or whatever. I could pretty much write about anything I wanted.

I bought myself a very nice cottage in the country, a four-hundred-year-old cottage, thatched roof and the whole thing. My sister's husband had left her, and she had four children, and they were always with me—weekends, holidays—so I was supplied with children and young people. And I had a lot of friends and I was successful. I'd turned down various people who had come along offering marriage, because they didn't want me to be a writer. They felt that that was something that I did just because I had nothing else to do. But since it was the most important thing in my life, I couldn't see marrying somebody who didn't want me to be a writer. [*Chuckles.*]

I was still interested in doing different jobs, not necessarily to get material, but because I wanted to do the jobs and have those adventures. During the war I worked in an aircraft factory, too—you know, things I never would have done otherwise. When I bought this cottage, I worked for the local newspaper—a small-town newspaper—as a reporter, for about six months, and wrote a book about that. I had a very good, happy, full life.

Into this sort of idyllic life appeared this American naval officer, whose wife had just died. He was in England working with the admiralty, working with the records of the defunct German navy, writing a report on some of their activities. We liked each other right away, and we decided rather quickly that we would be married. He was a very different type. He was not a sophisticated New York type. He comes from the Middle West and joined the navy at the age of fifteen, when he ran away from home, lied about his age, and worked his way up from being an ordinary sailor to being a commander. He was much more real and down-to-earth than people I'd met, and with a very different background from my own, which was fascinating. He was also the first person who ever said, "I'll do everything I can to further your career and help you, because I'm very proud of what you've done and I want you to do better."

Although I had been very happy and I had this wonderful life, there were obviously moments of panic when I'd wonder, "What will it be like when I'm fifty?" and "Do I want to live alone for the rest of my life?" So I was glad, really, to have my life switched around. I was thirty-five, too. I mean, I was a very elderly GI bride. [*Chuckles.*] I was ready to be a housewife and do all those conventional things.

Of course, it meant leaving England. Well, my family minded, I'm sure, but they were great about it. And as it turned out, it was a gain for them, because they've always all come over here in great droves for holidays on Cape Cod. And everybody liked Roy and everybody was pleased to get me off the shelf. [*Laughs.*]

I was in love and would have gone anywhere. It was so well worth it. Here was a new adventure! I'd been to New York a couple of times to visit and do publicity things for American publishers, but I'd never thought of living here. I'd never thought of it as a place where people actually lived. I mean, it was the place where you went to have fun. I found it very exciting. It represented excitement to me, because when I came I was somebody special, and everybody was interested in the name of Dickens, and so I was here as somebody with a "name," living in hotels and having parties given for me, which is very different from being somebody who lives here and buys the groceries and does the cooking.

Roy was not allowed to be married in Europe, because if you're on active duty you can't be married out of the country. So he came back here and he found a house in Washington and made all the arrangements—got a friend of his to give a wedding party for us, and that kind of thing. I had to sell everything I had—my house and my car, and find a home for my horses and all those things. I had to also get a visa as a permanent immigrant, which was a long and difficult process. It all represented adventure to me. The whole of the boat trip was part of the adventure, because I was fairly well known at that time, and I sat at the captain's table, and Vivien Leigh and Lawrence Olivier were there, and it was all parties, and "Oh, she's going to be married," and all. It was all part of the fantasy.

I was married the day after I arrived, which was sort of startling; and then we went to Washington, where he had bought a little house in Georgetown, a little tiny house. It was a nice way to start. Washington was pretty unreal, too. It was again a succession of parties, because people wanted to meet this new bride, and at first I thought, ' Vell, this is great." You know how one plays parts in life, and I think I was perhaps very much into playing a part. I was going to play the part of the good housewife, and I was determined to show that English women made better housewives than Americans. I wanted to wash and iron all

Roy's shirts and do them better than the laundry. I used to iron all afternoon and listen to all the soap operas, and it was a change from working. I wasn't doing any writing.

Housekeeping was much more convenient here. I'd never had a big refrigerator or a dishwasher or anything like that. Also, I went overboard with shopping, because we still had food rationing in England in 1951. To be able to go into stores and see all this stuff that I hadn't seen for years—I bought like crazy.

It wasn't too long before I became pretty miserable. Roy was gone all day and I had the car, and I'd drive everywhere and I'd travel all over Washington and go to museums and art galleries and things like that. That was exciting at first; but, you know, when the first excitement wore off, I began to realize that just being an ordinary housewife wasn't going to be enough for me. I started answering ads for dentist's receptionist and things like that. And my husband, who is the most unstuffy man in the world, came out with the startling news that officers' wives didn't go out to work anywhere.

I was a little intimidated by the average American navy wife, who was a very competent, sort of a station-wagon wife, you know, who could produce a three-course meal for ten people without disappearing to the kitchen all the time. I mean, I could do the cooking and all that, but I couldn't appear looking svelte and gracious in the living room, and I found that a little hard to cope with. And I didn't have the right type of small talk. If I had any sophistication, it wasn't in that style. So I felt a little lost and out of place. Well, I've never been very good at just sitting and chatting, doing what Americans call "visiting," doing things like going to the officers' wives club. I'd never been in great big groups of women like that, all wearing hats. I'd never been into that sort of artificial life. My manners were wrong, and I didn't know how to make small talk. I felt very out of place.

I thought, "My God, what have I lost? Who am I now?" I'd enjoyed popularity in England, and everybody knew me anywhere I went because I'd been on television and seen around quite a lot, and I liked that. Particularly through this magazine, all the readers used to write to me and I used to meet people in stores and they'd say, "Oh, you're Monica. How are you?" and all this stuff. I began to worry about sinking back into being a nobody. I remember going out once with some of Roy's friends—we were invited to the theater by somebody, and we went to a restaurant first. Some newspaper woman came up and was introduced to me, and "Monica Dickens" was just a total blank. In my conceited way, I felt very hurt.

The reason I had built up a name for myself was because I had that need, which I had known since a child, to be famous. I didn't know how I was going to do it, but I wanted people—everybody—to know my name. You get used to having that entrée into anywhere you want to go, anything you want to research. It's very handy if people know who you are. It began to hit me that nobody knew who I was.

So I began to write a book, about an English girl who marries a naval officer and comes to Washington. I made her marry somebody who was a very dislikable person. She'd married by mistake to get out of a bad situation, because I thought that if it was so difficult being married to someone you really liked, what a nightmare it would be if your marriage wasn't good. I was able to give her all the traumas, all the snubs and insults that I'd suffered. And then I was fine, because I could put it all into the book. I could give the woman all my problems.

I had not become pregnant, and since I was at this point about thirty-seven, I didn't want to wait too long and lose all chances, so we decided we would adopt a baby. This was impossible over here. I was a Catholic and he was not, and he was in the service, and the adoption agency said that service life was too unstable. I had a friend who was an adoption officer in England, so she got us a baby, sort of round the back door somewhere, from England. That was an adventure, too. The child was a year old, so here I was confronted with a year-old baby that I knew nothing about.

Then the book came out—it was called *The Nightingales Are Singing*—and the navy wives didn't like it very much. Roy was thinking of retiring anyway, because he'd been in the navy such a long time. And the baby gave us extra incentive to start living in the country.

He already had this house on Cape Cod, and he decided that he would retire and we would live on Cape Cod. That was very much what I liked, because we had a big garden. I mean there was a garden to *make*. It was just land, and I made it into an English garden with a lot of flowers and things. And then I began to have horses again, which has always been very much a part of my life.

My daughter went to the little nursery school, and after that I felt much more that I belonged here, because it gave me entrée, really, with the other women and mothers. I felt much more settled and became part of village life. And then we adopted another baby, also from England.

We were going to England at least once a year, and that was very helpful. Going back to England and finding it was still there, and people still knew me, and that all my friends still liked me and all that was very reassuring. I was able to come back here much more happily.

I have probably adapted myself. Yes, I've obviously taken on American ways and American customs, ways of thinking, ways of doing things. I am now an American citizen, which I held out against for a long time. [*Chuckles.*] I'm very glad to be an American citizen. I wouldn't want to live anywhere else but in this country now. I think it's the sanest country in the world. I like its ideals. I feel that Americans are still very idealistic, much more so than other countries. I think they make wonderful friendships. I like the warmth. I like the depth of feeling, that people are open to each other on a far deeper level than they are in England. And I like the fact that people here can get anywhere. You can be born with very little and come from a fairly poor family, and you really can make it if you're intelligent and hardworking. In England that is still difficult. . . .

I became a bit better known and got some good relationships with publishers here. I booked myself in with an agent. They just send you anywhere they can get bookings—women's clubs, college groups, anywhere. And I went out and did a speaking tour—about Charles Dickens mostly—for about three months. Went to about thirty states. That was fun. I've always liked being Charles Dickens's greatgranddaughter. You know, it's still fun to play Monica Dickens.

# Gujri Bazaz
··················FROM INDIA, 1974 ······················

*The living room and dining room walls of her Victorian house in Indianapolis are covered with her own paintings—forests of tall, slender trees and expressionistic landscapes. Indian batiks, baskets, and bells are everywhere. The furniture is modern and informal, as is the young woman herself, in her flowered wraparound skirt, T-shirt, and sandals.*

My mother was married when she was nine and father was fifteen. My mother says, "I didn't even know what it means. I used to hate your father. How dare he bring me from my home to his home?" They never slept together—they didn't know what it meant. She was more friendly with my uncle, my father's younger brother, because he would play with her. They had a three-story house, and all the storage of the kitchen was on the third floor, and the kitchen was on the first floor. So her mother-in-law would tell her, "Go and bring some red chilies," or whatever. And she would feel very scared, because there was no light.

My father was going to school. As a matter of fact, I remember my mother telling me, when your husband appeared for a high-school exam, the wife's parents would bring meat and a special kind of bread for the occasion. And when he passed his high school, they distributed the sweets and meat and bread to all the neighbors. My mother never went to school. My father wanted her to study, but those days, it was not right for a girl to get educated. So my father used to teach her at home. The family was good economically. By birth my father is a Hindu pandit—Hindu by religion and the uppermost caste in India.

My father had his own paper in Kashmir, and he was very active in politics. Because of his views, he was in jail for three years. All his profession went topsy-turvy because the publication of his paper stopped, and he didn't work anywhere, like a regular job. And then they sent him—externalized him from Kashmir—so we settled in Delhi.

I was about two and a half when I came to Delhi with my family. I had a very happy childhood. I never remember asking for something and not getting it. I had people around—grownups, relatives, cousins, brothers, and sisters, coming and going. Some people working, some going to school. All my family members are educated—like my eldest sister is a doctor. She is the head of the Department of Pathology there [India] in one of the hospitals. Three of my sisters are doctors, one is a musician, and I am an artist. My eldest brother is a pharmacist, and my other brother is working with a steel firm. Another brother is in an advertising agency, and another brother is a radio engineer.

My father wanted me to become an artist. Now I really think that it's good that I am one. I am an artist. At that time, I thought, okay, you know, either you become an artist or you become a doctor. It doesn't matter. Whatever your father says, you do.

I went to a very old university near Bombay, Baroda. This was a coed university. I was very friendly with boys. I would talk with them in the school. We'd go out maybe on Saturdays and Sundays for dinners—no more than that. I was taught not to be too much friendly with boys, not too intimate. You can discuss art as much as you wanted to, but—even kissing—that's not supposed to be good. You are not a good girl if you do that. If I did it, my father wouldn't say anything, but he wouldn't like it. Because I was taught that way, I never felt a kind of vacuum or whatever.

I met my husband about three years before we got married. We became very good friends because he was very much interested in art, and usually the majority of the population anywhere in the world are not interested in art [*laughs*], so I found him interesting. He was working. He's an engineer and he was working in Simla. We used to write to each other about different things of art, and we used to meet sometimes. He would come down to Delhi from Simla, which is in the north of India, to meet me. And we thought we should get married. I told my parents I wanted to get married to him, and they said fine. The majority of the people—80 percent—have arranged marriages, and they meet for the first time at the ritual. But this is a very unusual family, mine.

Before we got married, he wrote once and told me, "I'll go to America. I have got the visa and everything is ready. I just have to go. I'll get a job there, and I'll come back. We'll get married, and you can come with me." You see, my husband is a very inventive person. His mind is always working, working. He wants to find out about new things. But he was in a government office—Board of Electricity—and there wasn't much work to do. He just had to sit and drink coffee and read novels. He could go out and play billiards on his lunchtime—long lunch break. He said his mind was getting—. He thought, "If I continue working in this office, I'll reach up to this point and that's all, this is the end. But if I come here [U.S.A.], I'll learn new techniques. I can have more experience in a country which is so flourishing in technology and engineering."

I told him, "No, I'm not going to get married if you go, because my parents are here." I really wanted to get married, because we used to meet once in a year or so, and it didn't make any sense. I thought it will be just lovely. I had this very large family, and I thought living in a small family would be better. I would have the person I really love, and I would live with him in this beautiful, healthful hill station, Simla. . . . About ten days after I finished my master's degree, we got married.

Marriage according to the Vedic rites takes three days. My husband came from Simla to Delhi, and my parents arranged a hotel for his parents and relatives. And then they came to our home for dinner. After dinner we had the marriage ceremony. There is this fire burning in the middle, and there is this Brahmin, like a priest, who sits there and chants the mantras. The bride and groom sit near the fire. The fire is a god in front of you, who is witnessing your marriage. There are other relatives sitting there—whoever can be awake till the early morning hours. It goes on for four hours, five hours—you sit in front of the fire. The priest says, "Put this little rice in the fire." You put it there. Then, "Put this flour in the fire. Put these nuts. Then these dates."

I wore a gorgeous sari with a lot of goldwork on it. The typical color is red—red or bright, flaming orange—because it's purity of love, you know, symbolism. My husband wore the tight pajama, with a semibrocade coat with a mandarin neck.

I was dizzy with all these happenings around me, and I was wearing all this gold, and I was very tired. He stayed in my house, but the boy and the girl don't sleep together that night. Then in the morning, I went with my husband to his parents' hotel—all dressed up with a new sari and new jewelry. And there again I sat. All the relatives—these were the selected ones who had come to Delhi—they saw me. And they gave me their sari and their jewelry. Then we went back to Simla. It's about nine hours drive in the car. We reached Simla about two at night, and everyone's waiting in his house to have this nice time. They are playing music and they're singing and dinner was ready. They had such a lovely dinner, which I never ate. I was so tired.

You know, you're not supposed to sleep till late, because you are sleeping with your husband first time. I was real dead tired, and we slept like logs. I got up at nine and my husband got up at nine-thirty. Then I saw everybody sitting outside. It's funny to tell, but, you know, if you are twenty-two and you are being intimate sexually with somebody for the first time, it must be a very important event in your life. And when you get up, all the people are watching, especially the old ladies. They look at you—whether you had a nice. . . . They are worried, you know, if their son is normal, if he had anything wrong with him. As a matter of fact, one or two girls from his family were of my age, and they asked me, "Did you have a nice night?" I said, "Yes, I had a very comfortable night." [Laughs.] I was very stupid. My husband teases me sometimes.

This was an important occasion in the family, this marriage, and in the evening a holy man came—a saint, or whatever—they have great respect for him. I was supposed to kneel down in front of him. In India there is a tradition—you touch the feet of your elders and they give you blessing. My father never wanted us to touch anybody's feet. He was very political about girls. He wanted us to become very strong, because girls in that society, you know, are in a secondary position. I was supposed to touch this man's feet, and I never did. I think that was very rude, because everybody else was watching me. I was offended, really mad. Why should I? I am not at all religious, I am an atheist. And then they made me sit in one place which was made for me, a small mattress. I had to sit there with my head covered with the end of the sari for four or five hours. And that man was sitting on a higher table, and he was talking about the religious book we have.

Everybody came. All the ladies crowded in that room. They'd come to see how pretty I was. My husband's family is very beautiful—they are typical Kashmiris. His sister is a beauty, and they thought I will be a beauty, but I am very ordinary-looking person. Some of the women don't mind saying, "Oh, you know, we were expecting something better."

I hated it. Ten days back I was in the university, and now here I'm sitting like this. My husband was watching me from the door. He knew I hated it.

And then, the next day, we went for our honeymoon—ten days in Kashmir—and that was very, very nice. When we came back, everybody was gone.

I was so excited about the marriage, living with my husband. For about four or five months I thought this is the life—reading all day, going out for movies, for dinners with my husband. What luxury! I never knew I would get bored of it.

His mother is very young. She's not like my parents. She was busy. She's a very active person. She's a member of the Red Cross society, and she had very good religious friends, who would discuss religion with her. She would finish her housework and she'd go out; just say, "I'm going and I'll come back later," and I was left alone. It's like somebody coming now and living in my home. I wouldn't like it either, now I think about it.

I used to sit in my room and read books and write letters to my family and my friends. I always loved Simla, but I started hating it; because from the time the sun would come inside the window to the time it would go down, I was lonely. I didn't dislike it, but it was boring. Mentally, it's torture for me, because I was used to a big family coming and going. I didn't know Simla would be so bad, because we had all these so-called romantic get-togethers there, and I had very good memories of the place. But then suddenly I found it almost like a monastery, eating my life up. I realized that it's a very small place. No scholar would come there unless he wants to just shrug off civilization. That was very frustrating so soon after the busy university life. I thought I have to live here the whole of my life, and there is no one with whom I can talk art. There was one gallery, which was horrible. They had horrible paintings there.

I used to cry to my husband and tell him I want to go back to Delhi. I used to cry almost every evening. He was really understanding, but then he was fed up with these constant things. Every evening, my crying. And he really loves his mother, as everyone would—he didn't know where to go, whether to do this or that. He didn't want to go and live in a place like Delhi or Bombay, which is so crowded, because he's always lived in a place like Simla. No, his parents wouldn't like the idea of leaving them and going to another state to find a job. If he was in the same country, he would live at his parents'.

I didn't want to stay home, and I found a job in the school in Simla as an art teacher. My mother-in-law didn't mind my working, but we had to live in the hostel if I was to teach there. The school provided the apartment for their teachers. My husband said fine, and we lived there, but his parents didn't like it at all.

Oh, it was excellent. It was in some way in contrast with what was happening to me before that. But my husband says it was not at all good for him. Now he tells me he was always tense, thinking that in the same town are his parents, who don't like the idea at all of living separate. My mother-in-law never came to see us. Never. Only once, we invited the whole family to have lunch at our place. It was a very tense situation. I had worked so hard for the lunch, and nobody talked. It was very bad. Well, I don't think there's anybody to be blamed but the circumstances.

One fine morning I found I was pregnant. I worked till about seven days before my daughter was born and then I came home—so-called home. I had called my mother to come. I wanted her to be with me. The baby was born a little late, about four days after it was supposed to. My husband's parents were tense, because the baby was not being born. My father-in-law believed in astrology, and if the baby was born after that period, it was going to be very bad for the family. My father knows everything about religion; he knows this is the period, but he doesn't believe it. My father was really mad, but he couldn't say anything, because he thought it unnecessary to create a crisis there.

And then it was a girl! In India it's not a nice thing to have a daughter. A first daughter is okay, because she's like Lakshmi, a goddess who brings prosperity to you. The first one is okay, but not during that particular period. Their friends would come and tell me, "Don't worry, that's okay that it's a girl." I couldn't understand at first. I had no idea about all this background. I said, "I'm not worried, I'm happy."

After a week, my parents left, but I was glad with my daughter. That made some change. My mother-in-law didn't like how I was so clumsy. She didn't like the way I massaged her with the baby oil, or whatever. There was always something wrong. It was very irritating. I used to get irritated about many little things, just because I was fed up with everything then. And that was the time when my husband said, "Why don't we go to America?" His parents would accept his coming here. That's the first status symbol, if your son is doing very well in a foreign country like America or, for that matter, Germany.

About five months later, we came here. First my husband had trouble finding a job. Some of the firms have very bad impressions of Indians. They think that they don't work very well. I don't know why. Maybe they met the wrong people—some Gujaratis who are very business-minded and become engineers just because their parents have money. But my husband said he wants to show his work, and if they don't like it they can just throw him out. So one firm gave him a job, and they were highly impressed. He really improved the Indian image. In America, we thought whoever Indians we meet are all cream of the crop. They are not, not at all. There's some of them destroying the image, and we feel bad. We have some wonderful people, but here I see all these ladies and men who are not the best of Indians.

He resigned that job, because he got a better one. This is his third job, and he is earning double the amount he was earning back then, and it's only two years. Now he thinks he's getting what he's worth, and he's happy with his work. His employers are very happy with him, too. . . .

America is very much talked about in India. You dream of certain things. You think you just press the button here and everything is ready for you. Your breakfast comes in front of you, or whatever. You have this in mind, and then when you come, you see you have to do everything yourself—no servants, nothing.

Well, in Simla I could have a very peaceful life. My husband's family is well off, they have a servant. It was a very nice place, but I hated it. So I really liked coming here. I don't know how to tell you, but this was a great adventure. It was the beginning of a new life. It was really nice here, and I loved it, but I felt very lonely—again, but in a different sense. Sometimes you really want to go in the evening to meet your sister or your brother or your parents, but that is not possible. You have to sacrifice something.

# Karim and Aziza Mohammed

···················· FROM EGYPT, 1967 ······················

*After Dr. Mohammed received his M.D. in obstetrics, he joined the faculty of the university in Cairo. While he was still an assistant professor, he was appointed by the university to accompany an international medical team, vaccinating people in the Gaza Strip. One American doctor he met later invited him to come to the United States.*

KARIM: I did not come as an immigrant. I came as an exchange professor. I took a leave of absence to go to the university of Case Western Reserve. I had an open mind. I said, "I may stay, I may not."

I was a full professor in Cairo, and I had a private practice, too. I was very successful. In the university you have to work certain hours, from nine to two. Before that, before nine and after two, you are on your own, you have your own private patients. I used to start surgery at five in the morning. And I'd finish at eight or eight-thirty so that I'd be at the university on time. You leave the university, do your work, and by the time you reach home at six or seven, they call you for an emergency. And the system in Cairo is that you work six days a week. The weekend is only one day. You have only one day a week as holiday, and that is Friday. And even Friday morning we used to have surgery, because everyone is free. I was very busy and there was not much time for the family.

At first it was fun and a challenge, you know. You feel proud of it. And then it becomes a burden. And the only way out of it is to leave it all. When Dr. Edwards suggested to me that I come to the United States in 1967, I said, "This is not too hot, the life I've got. To make money, I don't have time for anything else." So I said to my wife, "Let's go. We have never been to the United States. Let's go there and take a chance of working there for some time." There was the challenge to grow. In Egypt, competition is limited. I had reached the top. I had nowhere else to go. I had achieved everything I wanted. I wanted to try to do something more.

My wife didn't like to leave Egypt because of her family. You know, our families are attached, and if one moves from Cleveland to Columbus, your family will think that's very bad and they cry and so on. She said, "Why should we leave? We have everything here. We reached what we wanted to reach. We have everything we wanted. What else do you want?" She couldn't understand why should we move.

AZIZA: I didn't want to come, because I didn't want to leave my family. Maybe if I was a working woman I would have been more occupied with my work. But it's the family that was the hardest thing, to leave the family.

I was very homesick—very, very homesick; because family life in Egypt is still very strong, you know. I wasn't working—I never worked in my life. But still, I wasn't one minute bored or lonely in Egypt. I'll tell you why. Besides regular visiting, we have the sporting clubs, like the country clubs. It isn't a place to go just to play sports. You can sit in the sun, you know. Every day I passed by my mother—oh, definitely, every day—and my in-laws. We had the alumnae of my school, the American College for Girls, in Cairo. And we met once a month. All of our family went there—my mother and my sisters and now my niece. We do the social work—volunteer housewives, mostly from educated, high-middle-class families, are the ones that do this work. That was the outlet for women to go out and to do some work but not paid work. That was acceptable. In my time everybody went to have the education, even master's. But we didn't work. We stayed home. We did the social work. Egypt has illiteracy, so one of the work was to teach, educate the poor in the villages, teaching reading and writing. We do that with the servants, too; by the way. It's not like servants here.

Servants usually come from villages, not educated at all. So we get them, we dress them, we feed them, we educate them, and we pay them. All my own servants I taught. . . .

You know, in Egypt we have the arranged marriage. It's safe, because you look at the background of each other. The family of the bride will know that that man has a good future. It is a safer way of marriage, because, you know, when you marry here, young and just love, you don't look to other things. It's not only love, you know. There's economical, financial, social. . . . So usually, even if you didn't have time for dating, usually it works, because it's the same background. You don't know exactly the other person, but it's more predictable—his manners and his conduct and so on.

People approached my father many times, but he wouldn't ask me all the time, because if he always told me someone was interested, maybe then I'd spend all my time thinking about this man or that man. So he match. So one day he came to me and he said, "How about it? Are you interested in getting married?" I said okay. Then they made an appointment, and the young man, Karim, came with his family to visit. We had a little party, especially so we can meet. He looks at me to see if he likes the way I look, if I'm pleasing to him. I look at him to see if I like his face, if he's not repulsive. In our case, we actually had seen each other before, because my cousin was a colleague of his, so it was not a new face. We talk, we try to know a little bit about each other. And the families talk. We were interested. Afterwards my father said to me, "Well, what do you think? Are you interested?" I said, "Yes, I like him. I think he will be all right." And his father asked him, "What did you think? Did you like the girl?" and he said to his father, "Yes, okay. Go ahead."

Once we both agreed, then we made an engagement party. An engagement party is different from what it is here. It's not a formal announcement. It's really a symbol that we can date, because in Egypt there's no dating. But now we can date. Oh, with chaperones! Who is the chaperone? Maybe my younger sister or his brother or my cousin. It can be anybody, but there has to be someone along.

Some engagements take three months, some take a year. It depends on how long it takes the father of the girl to get together the money for the household and to prepare all the furnishings. The system is that the bride always furnishes the house. The bridegroom pays a certain amount of money, and the bride supplies almost all the furniture. Not like here, not both start with nothing. In my case, we were engaged for three months, and when we married our house was all ready for us. . . .

When my husband decided to come here, we were married for ten years. He was one of the best doctors, and he was earning a lot. We just moved a few months before to a new house, and you get attached to certain things that you are used to. I think my husband was sure he was going to stay, but I was trying to tell myself that I wasn't staying. I kept my house and my furniture in Cairo. Everything was locked.

When we first got to Cleveland, somebody was meeting us—a doctor, Egyptian. He took us to a hotel and from there we looked for apartments, because in Egypt houses are very expensive. It's apartment living, like New York or something like that. We found one near the good school district, in Shaker Heights. It was a two-bedroom apartment, two rooms and a living room. It was too small. We couldn't bear it. The other thing—the sound from the rooms and the next-door apartment—that was something different. You hear the sound from room to room, because you build with wood. In Egypt it's all concrete, even small homes.

We bought furniture and so on, but we didn't settle. And that was a big emotional problem for me, because I didn't work, I was at home. And we weren't starting our life. At the beginning, especially for a person like myself, I couldn't find friends. I'm not an outgoing person.

Another difficult thing for me was housework. In Egypt I had a cook and I had a butler and I had a maid. I just supervised all that work at home. I just show that this room was to be cleaned, I tell the cook what to go and buy and what to cook. I didn't do the cooking, I didn't do the shopping, I didn't do the bathrooms. Oh, I was so tired the first three months here! It was so hard for me. My muscles just ached, and I'm not joking.

And the treatment of the elderly! When I first came, it really made me sometimes cry to see an elder person going in the freezing temperature, carrying shopping bags, to get food. You know, I stand up for an older woman or man. If someone's coming out of a store, I get out of the way and I open the door. That made me upset, when I saw other people not doing that for an older person.

KARIM: I was impressed by the hospitals—excellent! You know, the facilities, the equipment, everything you wanted to have to perform your job is available—not true in my part of the world. And then the facilities for teaching and education and development! The journals, we had in Egypt, but not every journal available here. And the audio-visual aids—this impressed me. If you want to do research, you have all the facilities—go ahead and do it.

As regards the climate, what impressed me is the green color—beautiful lawns and huge trees. This I liked so much. Egypt has green, but it doesn't rain, so the green is different. Here is as if you wash every leaf on the tree. And the maple trees are just gorgeous.

When the winter came, I realized how difficult it can be. The Cleveland is very rich in maple trees.

weather is very cold, very humid. My wife was not used to the ice, and she fell on the ice coming out of the house. She had a severe knee injury that required hospitalization. It was really a disruption of our life. I think it was an emotional trauma for the kids. They were young, they didn't know the language very well—because, you know, we came in July and she had the accident in January.

AZIZA: My mother came then to keep me company, because I was so homesick, so depressed. But my mother doesn't know how to do tea, even, so I had to have somebody to serve her, too, while I was in the cast. Then my mother-in-law came after three or four months. Each one came, stayed three months. My mother came three times; my mother-in-law came twice; and then we went back twice. When we first came, we thought it was too far away, we'd be cut off; but once you go and they come, you find it becomes easier.

KARIM: My father died while I was here. I didn't have a chance to see him. If my mother dies—I expect it to happen and I hope I will be there before she dies, but if she dies . . . I'll be sorry. I don't want to feel a sense of guilt all my life for this. As I said, I would feel sorry, but I don't want it to be a traumatic thing all my life—keeping myself guilty and trying to punish myself for not being there. Because I could be in Egypt and out on a trip and then she might die. My mother was here, visiting, and my father died when she was here, so it could happen. It could happen to anyone. I tell Aziza, too, the same thing. If her mother dies while she's here, it's bad, but this is God's will.

AZIZA: It will happen to me. It is going to happen. . . . I knew that my husband wanted to stay for good, but I was hoping for any reason he wouldn't like it, or the government wouldn't give us residency status in the United States, or something. That's why I insisted to have our house there closed, not rented. But after two years, once we had our residency, our green card, I said, "Okay, sell the house there."

My brothers take care of everything. When we became residents here, in order to go back to Egypt again we have to have the approval of our government—that they approve that we became immigrants to the United States. Bureaucracy—took six months, seven months, for my brother to run from one place to another. The papers, the papers, you know. That is something that you don't find in the United States. Nobody does for you anything except you yourself, but there—family.

So we moved to a house and we started to be settled. The first day, all the neighbors came and they said, "Welcome." A neighbor across the street—they were Jewish and they knew that we're Egyptians—they came, too, and they found people are people. It doesn't have anything to do with politics. Most of our friends now are Jewish. It seems that they are attracted to foreigners, or maybe it's because our customs are similar to theirs. Really, I think it's because of our feelings about the family. We notice that they, too—their families are very close, the children are still at home, and that's what we like about each other. But we don't talk about politics, because they are biased and we are biased. We found when we first started to talk about it, it's not good. So now we just have a rule: We don't talk about politics and we don't let it interfere with our friendship.

I am American in a way of simplicity. When I first came, I was too conscious of how I'm dressed. When I went out, even to the supermarket, I had to get dressed, with my shoes and my handbag dark blue if my dress is dark blue, and with my jewelry. Because I couldn't go out in Egypt without being completely dressed and perfectly matched, because I might see someone I know, and they'll say, "Oh, I saw so-and-so and she wasn't dressed quite right. Her shoes didn't match." But here I find that nobody knows me, nobody cares what I am—which is very good, the simplicity. That's something that I like here, because life is easier.

KARIM: You know, since I came, there is a challenge all the time, and that kept my mind busy—work. It's very hard for a foreigner. You work harder than the others and you want to excel. I definitely feel that there has been discrimination because I'm foreign born. Not because I'm Egyptian, but because I'm not Anglo-Saxon, not American born and not American graduated. For example, in Egypt I was a full professor, and here I'm an associate professor. I think it's definitely because I'm not American. I think ultimately I will become a full professor, but, of course, I will have to publish 150 percent more than an American doctor, and I'll have to prove myself more. But eventually I will reach my aim. I like what I'm doing here. The hospital is great. I do clinical care, teaching, and research. I like that very much. It's hard to do the three, but I like the three—like having three children, you like each one. I think I would be bored if I left one go. I wouldn't be happy.

And then, only lately, after I finished writing my second book, I had some time to think. And I was a little bit depressed and homesick. I wouldn't say I would be sorry that I made the change. You know, the older you get, the more you realize that there is no perfect place or perfect person. Each place has its advantage and disadvantage. I don't think I would have grown as much as I did if I stayed in Cairo or been known nationally or internationally if I stayed in Cairo. But I regret something—for the kids—because of their religion and their language. There are no facilities here, no church—we call it a *mosque*. But at the same time, they know they are Moslems. I wouldn't mind if my children married an American, but I hope my grandchildren will keep the Moslem religion. The religion is very important, definitely, to us and to them, too. They know.

AZIZA: Because I pray five times a day, and they see me praying. You don't have to go to a mosque to pray. You pray at home. There's a Moslem student association at the university. My children go to prayer and they take a religious class and Arabic class there. But when it's our holiday or our feast, they see we are the minority. It's not like being in the middle of everybody celebrating.

KARIM: But, you know, they have advantages here. The education is better, their future is better. There are better opportunities when they graduate, more opportunity in the job market. I think the future here in the United States. . . . You know what will happen, you can plan for fifty years. You can plan for the children. We don't know what the conditions in Egypt will be in two years. You can't plan.

   The children are Americans. There's nothing wrong with that. But I say: "Until I die, I cannot and will not give up three things: my religion, my Arabic name, and my family." I hope they realize this, too. The important thing is that we should not give up a culture for a culture. The equation would be zero. You have to take the good of both cultures, because every culture has something to offer. And this is what I expect my children to do. Egypt has had civilization for thousands of years, and I think one should be proud of this background and origin. If you can combine both cultures. . . .

AZIZA: If you ask me if I'm sorry we came, I still wish I could have stayed in Egypt. I wish I could have been there all this time. Yes, I do. I wish I could have been there with my family.

# Einat Ben-Ami

·················· FROM ISRAEL, 1960 ······················

*The two-story house in a Philadelphia suburb is full of greenery. Plants are everywhere—hanging from baskets, sitting on the wide window sills, even covering the floor under the windows. On the walls is a profusion of paintings and prints.*

The Israel that I remember really doesn't exist. I know it. When I grew up, there were a quarter of a million inhabitants in the whole country; a country where you left the doors open, where everybody was your friend. If anybody had trouble, the whole neighborhood knew about it and did something. The Tel Aviv that I remember doesn't exist. When I went back for a visit, I couldn't find my way! The center of the city is exactly where there was a huge swamp and we used to pick daffodils there. All these places that I knew as a child don't exist, really. There's very little of it that stays. It's only in my imagination, maybe in some of the books that people wrote. Here, like this picture—you don't see horse-drawn carriages in the street anymore, but you saw them when I was ten, eleven. I grew up seeing these things.

I lived in a small town near Tel Aviv. It was a tiny town. If someone sneezed on one side, you knew it on the other side, and you knew it well. You knew all the details, too. It was an area which grew oranges, citrus orchards. There were no roads at all. They built the roads when I was eleven. We walked in the sand, and sand tends to get into your shoes, so we walked barefoot most of the time, holding our shoes until we got to school.

We had a donkey and a little buggy, and we'd take it and go to the beach. Well, the beach was there. It was open. There were no lifeguards or anything like that. It was part of nature. I remember going to pick flowers, and we had a lot of beautiful white flowers. All the flowers you see here that are cultivated, all the tulips and the anemones and the cyclamen and poppies, all of them are wild flowers in Israel. They grow wild in the fields.

Every once in a while a group of British soldiers would come and camp. We were not allowed to talk to them. You don't talk to the enemy. This was the enemy, even though at that point they were fighting the war in Europe. We always felt sorry for them, because they were dressed so funny for the Israeli heat. They always were red and hot. They were the first drunks that I've seen. Nobody got drunk in Israel. During Christmas, Easter—that was the only time our doors were locked. Because these soldiers would get drunk, and you never knew what they'd do. Actually, we were more afraid of them than of the Arabs, because the Arabs were neighbors.

I would see the Arab women. As a child I was terrified of them. They wore black clothes, long robes, this whole body covered with black, and the forehead with all kinds of jewelry. They would come on market days to the village.

And I remember the underground. My father was very much involved. I have no idea what he did. All I knew is that he would disappear from the house if a boat came. We lived very close to the seashore, so when they brought the illegal immigrants at night, all the men in the village would disappear. There were nights in which there were only women and children in the village. It was in the morning I remember seeing them coming back, and you knew that a new boat arrived and everybody was safe. There were several times when they weren't, but you lived with this. It was terribly exciting, because you felt part of it.

There was once when the British soldiers found out about a boat coming. This is the most memorable occasion I remember. I was at school, and all of a sudden one of the teachers comes in and presses the alarm button, the siren for the whole village. It went on and on and on and on, and we were getting excited. All of a sudden, all the male teachers disappeared from the school. Only one, the old one, who was still pressing on the siren, was there. Meanwhile, we see a whole group of British soldiers, the whole unit, driving through the village. Several announcements came that certain kids go to certain other kids' homes because some mothers weren't home. My mother and our neighbor went from house to house to collect kids. They didn't know where there were parents and where there weren't. We had—I don't remember how many kids in our house.

There were two kibbutzim on the seashore. What they did, they got all the illegal immigrants into these kibbutzim, and they got all the Israelis who were helpers in there, too. All these people got into the kibbutzim, and then they got a lot of trucks which were supposed to be Red Cross. And now the British surrounded them, and there's nobody coming out or in, right? They surrounded this place for three days. For three days, there were no males in the whole village. Then all of a sudden, people got sick in the kibbutzim. You have to take them to the hospital. And that's how they got all the new immigrants in. The British gave up. They couldn't deal with that. . . .

Since the age of twelve, I grew up in Tel Aviv. My parents bought a bookstore there. The war [War of Independence] officially started '48, but '47 *we* started. The shooting started from Jaffa, right after the Declaration of Partition, before it came into effect. You could walk in Tel Aviv only up to a certain street. Beyond that street you were in danger, because the Arabs were shooting from the mosque tops. See, the mosques have these minarets, which go up on top and overlook the whole area, and they would put their machine guns on top of the minaret and shoot toward Tel Aviv.

The bombing started right after that. There was no radar, there was no warning system. It's funny, I'm thinking how stupid kids can be. We would hear an airplane and then start placing bets. Is it ours or not? Now, if the bomb dropped, it wasn't. And that's how we lived. Our parents must have been hysterical, but I thought it was terribly romantic.

One day a bomb dropped right in front of the bookstore, and I think my parents owe their lives to books, because the shells and all the particles of the shells got into the books. The windows in our house were several times shattered, but somehow you live with that. We were not afraid. For us, it was fun and games. In Israel, since it's sand, all the apartment houses are built on columns, and all this area was surrounded by sandbags. The parents made a shelter with sandbags, and for a year and a half that's where we kids slept. We thought it was terrific. We didn't sleep half the time. It was like going to summer camp.

We went to school regularly, though. They mobilized all the retired schoolteachers, all the women who'd stopped teaching, and school never stopped in Israel. Food was scarce and there were lots of things that you couldn't get, but life went on normally. There was a lot of friendship, a lot of closeness. You know, you felt you were building something. You had a cause, you had a purpose. You were creating something. . . .

I went to college in Tel Aviv and I met my husband in Tel Aviv. He was an economist, and I was writing children's stories and publishing them. We were married, and we had a baby, and my husband decided that he wants to go for graduate degree—to the United States, very simply because here they give scholarships. Actually, I didn't believe that he'd get a scholarship, which was probably why I didn't say anything when he started applying, because in Israel it's not a common thing to get full scholarship for this kind of thing. I said, "Oh, God, here he is with a child, with a wife. Who will give him a scholarship, anyway?" I said, "You want to apply? Go ahead," and I went on living as usual, without really thinking that it might materialize. It so happened that it did materialize.

I was very ambivalent, because at that point I had to give up my career. I was still not writing as well as I would like to write, and now I had to switch a language. Well, I knew I was giving up my career, but the agreement was that we are going just for a year so that my husband will get his master's degree. We owned a co-op condominium apartment in Tel Aviv, and we left it. We left everything. And when we came here, the scholarship, which looked to us quite a lot of money in Israeli terms, proved to be very little, quite meager. It was another, extra hardship.

We landed in New York and stayed with relatives for a week. The thing that impressed me most—I don't want to say *depressed*—it was gray. At that time—this was 1960—people didn't even dress in bright-colored clothes. Everything was gray, gray, gray, gray. Our ideas of how houses are, are taken from *House and Garden* and *House Beautiful*, all these ladies' magazines—mostly suburban, beautiful houses with grass, and sun always shining. And we came to the Bronx, which was gray and ugly and no trees at all and no grass. Yuchhhh! It was horrible. But this was a transition. We knew we were there only for a week and it really didn't matter.

Then in Philadelphia we rented a garden apartment near the nature reserve; only the nature reserve in Philadelphia is a swamp. [*Laughs.*] They reserve the mosquitoes. And, again, the gray. The sky here is gray most of the time, and I think this is the most depressing thing. Oh, I can overcome it. See, I create my own areas of green.

We met people, and that was one very nice thing. We met students from all over the world. The university had a foreign students' house, and they had activities for newcomers. Things that were as simple as where do you buy diapers and where do you buy an ironing board— every little thing became a problem, especially when you have a baby and you are not mobile. But they did everything they could to help us settle in. They were very thoughtful. They organized activities, and the wives had something to do once the man started studying. That was good, because the school year starts in September, and then it becomes winter and in winter nobody lives outside. I come from a country where you go outside constantly. Oh, I felt so isolated. I didn't think there were people living in our street. And we lived on one of the major streets of Philadelphia. I never saw my husband. He was studying. And one student organization was the only place where I met people for six months.

After his master's degree, he decided that's not enough. He wanted to go for a Ph.D., and he stayed two more years. How did I feel then? Well, I was already here, so I may as well stay another year or two and he could finish his Ph.D. Meanwhile, our daughter was born. This was still temporary. We were living out of suitcases for a long time. I was visiting, just visiting all the time.

By the time my husband graduated, we were suspecting some developmental problems with our daughter, which turned out to be justified. She had a lot of things that were wrong at that time, and she needed a lot of special care. When she was four, it was diagnosed with no reservation that there was brain damage—that there was retardation. We had to make the decision if we are going to stay. It became more and more obvious to me that probably we'll have to stay here, because in Israel there were no facilities for her care—special-ed classes, speech therapy, visual perception therapy. All these things were not available in Israel.

We filled out alien registration cards, but the whole thing was still temporary. We saw ourselves as Israelis. We did not see ourselves as American. We still didn't see ourselves as settling here. We were still talking about "when we get home," and when we said *home*, it was Israel. The one who finally alerted us to it was our oldest son. He was eight, and he said, "What are you talking about home? We live here, that's our home." Then we applied for citizenship papers.

You know, we have to overcome guilt feelings. We were raised in

Israel in a period when the country was established. Our parents were pioneers. They left everything to establish a country, and we were almost negating everything that they were doing by staying here. I still have to justify myself all the time.

We were teen-agers during the War of Independence. We belong to the generation who remembers the underground, who felt proud of the making of the country. There is a whole generation of young people who grew up after the State of Israel was established. For them, Israel is a normal, regular country, and that's their right to leave it. I don't think they have the guilt feeling that we do. For them it's much easier. For them it's choosing a different, easier lifestyle. For us there's a lot of sentiment, a lot of emotion. But I had no choice. I didn't stay here because I wanted to stay here. We decided to stay here because we felt that's the best place for our daughter.

My family understands it. I'll have problems later, when my parents get old and I'll have to worry about who takes care of them. They are realistic in the sense that they both studied English, so in case one of them has eventually to come here, when they cannot be alone, at least they'll be able to speak. This is something we have to be aware of. There are certain responsibilities that one has to experience.

I'm at home here now. I really don't know how it happened. Everything that has to do with Israeli culture is still dear to me and probably will be one of my main interests in life. I'm just looking around me—all the pictures here—it's all Israeli. I don't have a single thing that's not. I'm thinking about adjustment problems. When you are Israeli, I think maybe it's easier, because the Jewish community here identifies with Israel. You don't feel completely torn from your culture. We have a house and we replanted fruit trees, which are going to bear fruit this year. We turned clay soil into almost workable soil by composting it. We feel part of it. My next-door neighbor says, "Here she is, reclaiming the Philadelphia land." In a way, we created a little Israel here.

# Robert Vickers

· · · · · · · · · · · · · · · · · · · · FROM ENGLAND, 1964 · · · · · · · · · · · · · · · · · · ·

*In the period after World War II, many scientists came to the United States from all parts of the world because of greater opportunities here for research and professional advancement. Robert Vickers was part of this "brain drain." He wears rimless glasses and neatly tailored suits, but his drooping mustache and unruly hair give him a vaguely poetic air.*

The tradition in England for middle-class people, which is what I suppose we were, was to send their children, especially the boys, to boarding school. So about age ten, my twin brother and I were sent off to a boarding preparatory school. I was there until age fourteen, and then I won a scholarship to a public school, which is a private school in England, and I was then at boarding school in Canterbury. My brother wasn't quite so academically advanced as I was, and he went to the local grammar school. I always felt a little bit guilty about that.

I really flourished in the public school—did very well academically and spent a good part of my time in musical activity after school. The school, by the way, was the oldest public school in England, founded in 900 A.D., and it was actually situated right in the precincts of the cathedral, which is the seat of the Church of England. I was in the choir and madrigal groups and all that sort of thing, and we sang at services in the cathedral.

My interest in mathematics stemmed from about my first year in public school. We had a teacher-in-training, and he was a bit more imaginative than our regular teacher—very old spinster, with her hair tied back in a bun, long dresses. Anyway, he said anyone who wanted to know more about this particular thing—which was logarithms—could come back to his room afterwards and he would explain it further. So I went to his room, and I was the only one. He showed me a little more about these things, and I think it was from that time that I always had this interest in mathematics, and there was always great feedback from the various teachers that I've had, you know. So that was really nurtured.

Then I won a scholarship to Cambridge, in mathematics, of course. I would say that every one of these different school experiences was like the best experience of my life, and it just sort of got better and better in Cambridge. It was—to use the vernacular—a mind-blowing experience. It was living at its very best. I spent six years there, and I do feel it was a very exceptional opportunity to have partaken of that sort of life.

The typical, classical thing in England is for the student, once he's graduated from Oxford or Cambridge, he goes and spends a year touring the continent—Italy, Greece, and so forth. Visiting the States was my answer to that, I suppose—rounding out my education or something. I think there are very good mathematicians in England, but it was clear that there was a lot that would be good to be exposed to over here. People were more avant-garde, even in mathematics, in America. We would tend to be more traditional in England.

One thing that has always turned me on about America is the fact that people, because they're not so hidebound in their thinking as perhaps English people are, tend to be much more innovative. In mathematics that was certainly true. I was well aware of that before I came here. That's one of the reasons I wanted to come. There are all sorts of exciting things going on here. A lot of them are highly experimental, and some of them are completely up the wall, as in many things American. But the fact is that people are doing this experimenting, and I think that's a wonderful thing. It doesn't matter if they fail, because there's something to be learned from every sort of human endeavor and experience. In England, there are innovative things being done, but they're always done, funnily enough, in a much more traditional way. And when it's done, it's done very properly, and the thing is almost guaranteed to be successful from the start.

I came here in the fall of 1964 to take a job as lecturer at Stanford University in California. I must say that I really had no clear notion of what America was. I think it was largely fantastical, my feelings about the place. I suppose America must have seemed very glamorous.

The fact is that I think most Europeans, and certainly English, are secretly a little bit envious of all the things they hear about "America the Great." I'm pretty sure I had those feelings, too. Undoubtedly I wanted to expose myself to some of that richness. [*Laughs.*]

I'll never forget the day I arrived. I left London in—well, it was sort of a standard English fall day, 65 degrees or something—and landed at Los Angeles. Then the plane came up to San Francisco, and I was met by a colleague. He drove me on the Bay Shore Freeway to Palo Alto, where Stanford is. I don't know if you've seen the Stanford campus—it's Spanish architecture. And I remember this burning red sun going down on the horizon, and this extraordinary architecture, which was quite foreign to me, and this humid, dripping environment. The temperature, I think, was something like 110 degrees. The young girls there all seemed to be wearing either pink tops and white tennis shorts and sandals, or white tops and pink shorts and sandals. They all seemed made of a stamp, and they reminded me of—well, you see, in England when you buy a box of marshmallows, they're always arranged in rows of pink and white, and these girls just looked like a box of marshmallows.

I needed something to eat, so my colleague took me to a rather splendid charcoal-broil hamburger joint. It was the first time I had seen this type of operation. It was something very American. The hamburgers come stacked with bits of paper in between. I remember the cook tearing off the paper to take the first round of hamburger, and a little bit of the hamburger came off with the paper, so he just threw the whole thing away! This was absolutely shocking to me.

One of the images that really sticks very firmly in my mind is the El Camino Real, which is where you see all the hamburger stands and gas station after gas station and used car lots and all that sort of thing. That's the brash, hard side of America, and that really hit me.

Capitalism gone wild—these huge billboards along the roadside and all that. This was like civilization gone crazy somehow. I must say life in California in general—the feeling I had was, it was a bit like living in Disneyland. I don't think I really ever came quite down to earth after that first day there.

I had wonderful, wonderful times there at Stanford. It was a very free and easy sort of life, quite different from anything else I'd ever had. It was probably good, in a way, that I could have that opportunity finally just to really enjoy myself in a sort of liberated way. I didn't feel as I would in England, that I had to conform to this, that, and the other sort of thing. I was completely on my own in a completely alien culture, where the only thing in common was the language. Things were done on such a vast scale in America, too. Everybody had cars, and huge cars at that, and they'd think nothing of driving from San Francisco to Los Angeles. In England, a holiday with that much driving in it, you'd probably have to plan for five years, and everybody'd think you were daft for doing it. Why not get the train? Oh, it was definitely broadening. . . .

One of the things I had told myself regarding women: only two types of women I would never marry. One was a red-headed woman and the other was an American woman. I'd been very unimpressed by American women I'd met in England and things I'd seen probably on TV. They just seemed to be sort of loud and much too extrovert, overly dressed, all this heavy jewelry. In comparison with English women, they just seemed to be everything that a woman shouldn't be. I didn't really want anything to do with an American woman, and within two years of my being here, I had met and married a red-headed American. [Laughs.]

When I met my wife-to-be, Anne, which was at the end of my first year here, I'm not quite sure what I thought, but I did expect to return to England. As the end of that first year approached, I decided that I would like to spend another year, anyway, in America. It was during that time that I was trying to find something for the next year that I met Anne and got to know her. And then it became apparent as the year wore on that we wanted to get married. Anne certainly didn't have any particular desire to go to England, and I felt quite happy at the idea of staying in America.

The only way I could legally stay in the country was to take a job with a company that received money from the government, like defense contracts. And that is exactly what happened. At the end of the second year we got married.

I was now in a totally unplanned-for situation. The decision to stay and get married and take a job in industry was like a complete break with the past. What I'd known up until then was university life, and I suppose I'd always thought that ultimately I'd try to get some post in a university. But now, because of circumstance, I had a job in industry. The work was interesting and very close to my own interest. I learned an awful lot. I felt it was really worth it. It was nice to discover that one really could apply all this learning in this very industrial setting. In England, the opportunities for that are very, very much less. In fact, I think probably one of my reasons for staying must have been to some extent the fact that the only thing in England that I would be interested in would probably be some sort of junior post in a "red-brick" university somewhere [any university in England except Oxford and Cambridge]; and that wasn't really all that exciting to me. The idea of all this opportunity here for working and applying one's skills I think was an important part of my decision to stay.

# Ari Amichai (I)

···················FROM ISRAEL, 1964·······················

*He is a chemist in a large pharmaceutical company in Michigan.*

I had educated myself out of my country. Israel—and quite a few developing countries—doesn't have substantial industry to maintain research at high level. So if one wishes a high level of specialization in certain fields, you find that while it is very easy to obtain a job in an industrialized country like the States or Germany or England, you can't get the same job, say, in Israel or India or Taiwan; because the industry there is so small and is so dependent on important know-how, that there is no need to work there in research. And the number of research openings is exceedingly small.

Initially, I came to America to study in the university. That was in the second half of 1964. At that time, the places in the Technion were so tight that they suggested that either I wait a year or go abroad to study. I chose to go abroad, and since English is the first foreign language in school in Israel—they teach it for eight years—the choice was either the United States or England. So I came to America as a freshman.

Later on I saw that in America a filling-station attendant had a B.A. At that time the Los Angeles police was contemplating having the policemen on the beat have a B.A. I thought, if this happens now in America, it will take ten years and it will have been also in Israel. So there's no sense in returning with only a B.A.

I did my M.A. and I did my Ph.D. Then I made it a point to meet with

Israeli scientists in various international symposia around the world, and I spoke to them and nothing happened. Economically, they don't have the ability to support broadening of research or broadening of teaching in university. Introducing new fields, anything like this, they just can't.

So I resigned myself to stay in America, and I feel I am very happy. I have to admit it.

Economically, we have no complaints at all. America is definitely the place. If you want to improve yourself economically, this is the place.

[Additional comments by Ari Amichai appear on pages (411 and 434.]

# Lena Klassen

···················· FROM INDONESIA, 1958 ·····················

*She is a dusky blonde, with slanting green eyes and a voluptuous figure. Now forty-one, she looks much younger. Born in Indonesia of mixed native and Dutch stock, she was a member of the privileged class of colonial administrators before World War II.*

When the war started, the Japanese came with bayonets and took my father to a camp. My mother and sister and I had to go to a village, a little village, where we lived with her sisters and her brothers and their children. It was crowded, but for the children it was almost like camping. We didn't have to go to school, and it was almost fun.

The bombings were scary, and we saw a lot of murders when the Japanese came. There was a river nearby where we lived, and we'd see bodies floating past and just look at it and you get used to it. I think you become callous. You're not afraid of it. You know, you just look at it and you don't think. You say, "Yecch, another dead body," or "There's another one coming by." It may sound cruel, but that's how it was. We'd just stand by the side of the river and didn't care much for anything.

Personally, we were never harmed by the Japanese. My father was beaten a few times by them during his imprisonment, but to us they never did anything much. What could they do with a six-year-old girl? There was no medical care, of course, throughout the war; no dental care. There were women that were pregnant and it was hard for them.

After the war was over my father was freed, but the smaller villages where we were were not freed; and the Indonesians took over. The Dutch had the big city then, Jakarta. My dad located us through the

Red Cross and he sent a request for our release, and they did let us go in the most hazardous way. They picked us up from the camp, the Indonesians, and there was still shooting all around. The leftover Japanese were still resisting in the small villages, and there were all kinds of uprisings. And we were transported in a great big truck; we'd duck now and then from the shooting, traveling at night. And then we came to a larger city and the Red Cross had those little planes—they didn't even have a door in the plane—and they took us—and gave us gum for our nerves. They took us to some sort of big building, and we had to strip completely, women and men in one big room, and they cleaned us up, DDT for our lice, and examined us for diseases. It was very embarrassing. I suppose it was a health measure.

We went to Jakarta where my dad was. My mother went first to see him. She left us home with the nuns; we stayed in a convent. And my mother came back with him. It was pretty hard to adjust for all of us. My mother had kept him alive, you know, with pictures all those years, and we always talked about him, that he's coming back some day. So when I saw him I knew who he was, but I didn't really have the father-daughter relationship. You know, if they say it's my father, it's okay with me; but I didn't have the feeling. I think up to this day there's something missing in our lives—between my sister, myself, and my dad. We've lost those years, those important years. It was five years, you know. It was hard for my father, too, you know. After five years, you say, "Here are these two kids and they are yours and you have to live with them." It's like when you're cooking and there's just one ingredient missing and you feel there's something missing, but I don't know what it is. It doesn't taste right, but you can't really say what it is, and I think that's what my father and my sister and I have. We missed those years.

When the Indonesians took over it was harder for us, because for three hundred years the Dutch were there, and they didn't want any part of us. They looked on us as Dutch, even though we were half Indonesian. We had to go back and forth to school with a military escort. You couldn't ride on the trains. The maids didn't want to work for us anymore; not because they didn't want to, they were afraid to. The local people were against us and there were quite a bit of shootings. One time we were threatened. My father worked as a bank manager of a small Dutch bank, and one day we had a lynch mob on our front lawn. My father locked us up in a room and my mother was terrified. The house was next to my dad's office, and we had a Dutch flag on our front lawn during business office hours, and one day the mob came out with knives and machetes and they tore the flag down and trampled it. Like the riots nowadays here. [Chuckles.]

And so the people in the bank decided we should leave. It was too dangerous. It's not just my father, it was his family that was being threatened. So within three days we had to pack and leave; got on a boat and took us three weeks from Indonesia to Holland in 1951. A lot of people at that time had to choose between becoming Indonesians and staying, or going with the Dutch. There was never any question for my father. He loved the country, but he felt he was Dutch.

When we arrived in Amsterdam it was very exciting. I could go to school again—I hadn't gone for years—and my old friends were arriving and I could see them again. I had a terrific time. My sister had a little more trouble adjusting. She's darker skinned than I am, and there was a lot of prejudice against the people from Indonesia. They didn't consider us pure Dutch, which of course we're not. We have some native blood in us, but still . . . there were some bad times.

People are funny about lots of things there [Holland]. They're very narrow-minded. You have to ask permission for everything. If you live in a certain block, you cannot paint your house a different color. Everybody has to have the same color paint. My mother had a balcony with that wrought-iron railing, and she wanted to paint it white. Couldn't do it. You have to ask permission. They won't let you because everybody else's was black, so you have to leave that black. I don't like  that kind of conformity. That's what I don't like about life over there. It's too socialized, that part of life, I think. Just cannot plant anything in the front yard, either, because if it's too big or blocks the house number of something, they make you take it down. Now I think that is terrible—when people tell you what color you can paint your house or where you can put your tree.

I married a boy from the same Indonesian-Dutch background, and as soon as we could we left Holland. My husband's reasons were advancement. There were more possibilities in this country. Because Holland is very small and there isn't that much job opportunity. It's socialized everything. So if it's not your turn to be promoted, you're not going to be. Everything has to be done in order, no matter how good you are, whether it's a private company or a government office. He couldn't live with that. He said, "When I graduate, I'm not going to sit there and wait my turn."

So we registered with the Immigration as soon as he graduated, and we came directly out to California. An army captain he had met in Holland arranged for us to live with some friends of his. They were good people, took us in without question, didn't ask for money till my husband got his first pay.

My husband found a job right away. He was trained as an engineer, and that helped. I was, I think, in a state of shock. Suddenly you live with Americans in their home. I was terrified. It was too sudden. I cried all the time. For about a week I did not speak one word. It was too much in such a short time. I was completely bewildered. The couple worked all day, so I was home by myself. I was avoiding the neighbors. They would come over and I would just not answer the door. I thought I wanted to go home.

But we stuck it out, and eventually I decided "If I'm going to live here, I think I'd better start talking and doing a few things and, you know, coming to life." I made friends, learned to drive, had coffee with my neighbors. It just took time.

All my kids are dark like my husband, dark eyes, dark hair, dark skin; because my husband's grandmother on his mother's side is pure Indonesian. On my side, the mixture goes further back. Here I think people are not so narrow-minded. Of course, I'm talking about California, not other states; I don't know about them. But here you get your Italians, your Mexicans, Portuguese, Chinese, Japanese, whatever; and so you become, I think, more liberal about everything.

I've had no problem with the people or the country. The problem was really within myself. But, you know, my little girl [aged four] said a strange thing the other day. Maybe kids are smarter than they used to be. She said, "How come your skin is white and mine is not?"

I said, "God made some people with white skins, some with yellow skins, some with brown, some with black."

And she said, "But I like white better."

"Why do you like mine better? Yours is much prettier, nice and tan."

"Uh, uh, I like white better."

"Well, I can't help it. You're just like daddy. Daddy's brown and you're brown."

And then she said, "But why did God make my skin brown if he knew I liked white better?"

And I had no answer for that one.

We've never had any trouble with prejudice. Well, there was one neighbor; she called my children niggers, and that shows how much she knew. *That* they definitely are not. But that's the only time.

We've really had an easy time. The only trouble was within myself.

# Irina Aronoff

···················· FROM THE USSR, 1976 ·····················

In Russia we hear that in America you don't like black people, Negroes. That white people throw stones at the black people. That white people don't want their daughters, their sons, to study in schools with black people.

When I was a little girl in school, we gave money for the black people. The teacher told us that the black people, the Negroes, cannot study. She said to us, "Who has books at home? Who has notebooks? Pencils, pens, money? Whatever you can give, as much as you can give, give to the black people in America." Of course I gave!

I used to think that the Negroes had a bad situation. I thought that the Negroes were poor people, that they aren't allowed to study, to go to the university. Now I see the black people—doctors, teachers. It's not what I thought. I don't understand.

# Kitty McGonagle
·················· FROM IRELAND, 1966 ·····················

No matter how much you read, you get the wrong impressions sometimes. For instance, I thought everybody lived right with each other. I didn't know there was segregation in the North. I didn't know there were ghettos. I expected to see my neighbors black, you know. You see, you read the newspapers and you see in the funnies, you always had a group of kids and there was always a few black kids in there. And I assumed, well, that's normal in the United States. Everybody lives together. And this wasn't quite so.

# Claudine Renaud
·················· FROM MARTINIQUE, 1966·····················

I was undecided, because the same week on TV I saw a lot of riots in Newark, and that scared me because I am black. It was 1966, I think. I said, "Oh, my, I'm not going to come to this country. To see the people fighting like that, that will kill me." And I didn't answer. But I ask my cousin—I ask her advice if I can come, and she tell me I can come, because the colored people mix with the white people. I don't have to be afraid, and anyway I have to try.

# Imogene Hayes

·················· FROM JAMAICA, 1962 ······················

*A plump black woman in her twenties, she is an active member of Jehovah's Witnesses. She lives in Brooklyn with her husband and two young children.*

I had a job in the post office in the town I was from and I wanted to leave Jamaica because my mother had nine of us at home, and it was a customary thing for the bigger ones to start working and help with the smaller kids. Coming here was being in a position to help my smaller brothers and sisters. Coming here was much more a challenge to me than going to England, although it's much easier going to England.

When I came here I heard about an employment agency in New York that were getting sponsors for foreigners. So I went to the agency and they got me a sponsor. It was a small family in Westchester County. It was a sleep-in job. You know, it's easier for a woman, because she gets a live-in job; she has a place to sleep and she gets food and it's easier.

Of course, you know, back home in Jamaica you are used to having someone come into your house and do the housework and wash the dishes and make the beds. And all you have to do, you just have to get up and have your breakfast and go to work. And here, now, all of a sudden you're doing those jobs yourself; you're doing those things for someone else. But I knew I had to get a visa. I wanted to stay and I wanted a visa and that's why I was willing to do it, because that's the only way I could get a visa. If someone sponsors you.

They were very nice. I was not actually treated as a maid. In Jamaica, my mother and my father, we used to have this girl working. She would never have breakfast with us at the table. She used to have her breakfast afterwards. In other words, we would treat her more as a maid. But here I didn't think of myself as a maid. I did feel a bit out of place maybe, because I was black and they were white. But they tried their best to make me feel at home. I would have meals at the table, and they left the whole house to me after they found out I was reliable and not dishonest. I stayed with them for about nine months, and I would send my money home to my mother.

Then my mother came afterward. She came to stay. We both had separate jobs. She was in Long Island and I was in Westchester, and we would get together on our days off. It would be like a big thing. We'd go shopping and we'd buy everything we could think of. We'd make these parcels and barrels, and we'd ship home clothing and everything for my father and my brother and sisters.

My father never wanted to come. He had a very good job. But he would visit. Every year he would come on a vacation and go back. Eventually my mother convinced him. He left Jamaica in '70 or '71. He was never happy here. He would work, but he would never be happy with the job. He was never happy with the salary. My whole family is here now. My mother sponsored everybody. First we had to work to save a bank statement, because we had to have a certain amount in the bank before she could sponsor them.

My father's intention was to buy a home and put us in, because he didn't want us in the apartment we were in. It was too small and it was too many of us. We could never find a big apartment for eleven people. We had to buy a two-family house. The neighborhood at that time was a mixture. Our block was mostly Italians. They call it East New York.

We wanted a house, but we didn't actually know what was going on until we got in the house. One day my sister was looking out the door, and some white boys passed and told her they were going to burn us in the house. We were so scared, we didn't want to go to sleep at nights, and we were sort of afraid of even going outside.

Regardless of what happened, my mother didn't want to go back. She liked it here. For one thing, she had never worked when she was in Jamaica. She would have to listen to my father back home. And here, she started to work and she could speak up.

I left my sleep-in job after I met my husband. He convinced me. See, he was in Brooklyn. So I came to Brooklyn and I got a job in the First National City Bank.

Sometimes my husband talks of going back to Jamaica. I am maybe not 100 percent comfortable here, but it wouldn't be my wish to go. Because, see, I left such a long time now that I don't know what it's like over there as far as the kids are concerned.

One thing I know for sure: Here the teachers are afraid to discipline a child, because the parents will sue. Back home, nobody is running to sue you for anything. And the social environment here is not what I think I would want for my kids. They have drugs in school, and the kids being fresh, and so forth.

But I have to base my ideas and my opinions mainly on my religion. I think if my children grow up and go to church, and they know what's right and what's wrong, then, even though they're being discriminated against, it won't affect them. Because I know when Jesus Christ was on earth, he went through a lot of this.

# Hamilton Hayes

*One of his company's first black employees, he works as a draftsman and attends college at night, studying for a bachelor's degree. The company pays his full tuition. He is married to Imogene Hayes.*

When I used to go to school, Jamaica was still a colony, although it was self-government. But we didn't feel as second class, because mainly the government was run by blacks, by Jamaicans. The industries were controlled by England. It was basically English civilization. The high-school curriculum was set by Cambridge University. Very strict discipline—always some church service in the morning, kids have to wear a uniform.

I used to run around with my friends—you know, play cricket, shoot birds, and things like that.

All my friends who I went to high school with left. Some went to England, some came to the United States, and some went to the university in Jamaica. I didn't know if I wanted a bachelor's degree or what university, but I knew I wanted something more than I had at high school. What I wanted was to go to England—mainly because of things I've heard about United States. English school system is better. Here [in the United States] schooling is so easy, you can buy a degree. You don't have to do nothing at all to earn a degree, whereas in England you have to earn it.

Then I met a teacher who encouraged me to come to the United States. He gave me the name of a school, a vocational school located on Jamaica Avenue in Queens. So I wrote the school and they sent me the papers, and I went to the American embassy and I got the visa. . . .

I was disappointed in the school I went to. You know, they send you a brochure and it looked fantastic on paper. They took a picture of the library, and when I saw this picture I figure it's okay. You know, our high school was one whole building with books for a library, and our high school's not that tall, compared to that picture. And when I came, it was just a storefront. My bookshelves in this room have more books than what they had for that library! A one-year vocational school and it is a fraud. There are quite a few of them in this country that are frauds. They usually write especially to foreigners, and they give a big buildup in their brochures, and when you come, there is something different.

I was stuck, and I had to go through the whole year. I was paying

$1,185 for the whole year, and they promised to place you in a job. When I finished I couldn't get a job, because they said, "That school is no school at all for training." I couldn't go back to Jamaica, because what I've got there was nothing at all. I couldn't go back to that.

I ran around Queens, Brooklyn, looking for a job—I don't know how many places—putting in applications. There were times I had to beg people for money to get home. I didn't have the bus fare from the city. Well, what am I going to do? There's no way I can walk home. So I just had to have the courage, and somebody said okay, and I had a way to get home. I couldn't get a job, probably because I'm black.

I was so naïve about the whole thing. Of course, I didn't know any form of discrimination till I came here. And looking back, it was. Because I'll tell you, I went to White Tower restaurant for a job and there was a white guy there, filled out a form. The lady—she was white—gave me a form and she waited until she took all the forms. She looked them over and she said to me, "What kind of job you want?" I said, "Counter, something like that." She said, "Okay." Then she asked the white guy, "What do you want?" He said, "Counter," and she said, "Well, I have something better for you."

Oh, that was a most difficult time for me. I was depressed. How many times I cried I wanted to go back home. It was very rough, and I felt like going back home many times, but I said, "I come here to get something. I'm going to face it through." That's what kept me going.

I got odd jobs, factory jobs. There was one place, you have to operate the machine. The machine was operating you, really. And you have to keep up with it. Then one was in Queens. They were making plastic moldings for toys, and those things were hot coming out, and you have to wear gloves. You stand over the machine, and when I was ready to move, I couldn't. It was as if my whole knees were locked in the socket; I couldn't move them back.

I decided to apply to New York City Community College in Brooklyn, and I was accepted. On the notice board at the school were ads of firms looking for students, and I applied to one. They process motion picture films for TV and things like that. The person who was in charge of the film section was a Jamaican, and he called me that night. I was supposed to report to work the next day. It was very good. I was going to school at night, and I was working during the day. And the school was much better, too.

Most of my friends were Jamaicans. The Americans at school talked to us, but they grouped to themselves. We Jamaicans grouped to ourselves, also. People say that we are clannish—I think because of the environment, white and black.

Like I said, I was very, very naïve as far as this condition is concerned. If I ask a person, "Can I have a date with you?" and they said no, I didn't feel any way funny. In fact, there was one girl who told me, "You are not like them," meaning black Americans. "You are like us." I said, "No, I'm black just like them."

I'm very, very skeptical about people here, especially white Americans. I think they're probably the biggest frauds you can think of. For example, when I finished community college, I got a job as a draftsman. You meet quite a few people, and some of them are very nice. Some of them are the nicest people you can think of. But behind their backs, they talk about blacks. I'm basing my experience on this fellow—white—and he would go out of his way to do anything for you—for the job, really. You know, stop and stay, "Hi! How are you doing? How is everything?" I mention him to somebody, and he said, "You'd be surprised to know that person used to complain about blacks taking over, you know, should be shot, and everything like that." He's German descent and still wears his crew cut, and I guess if he had a swastika. . . .

A friend of mine is Jamaican, and the secretary in his area, she's white. She came in one morning, much earlier than usual, and she saw him and said, "Hi!" and he went over and kissed her on the cheek. And another woman said to her, "Why are you going around kissing niggers like that?" This one who said it, everywhere she sees me, she's always smiling: "Hi! How are you doing? How's everything?"

Black American—like I said, I identify with them—to a certain point; because there are still a few who don't like West Indians at all. Some black Americans feel that West Indians are very clannish. They say that Jamaicans think they are much better than Americans. One black American girl asked me a question: "Why is it that West Indians can come to this country and in a short time own a home? Is it they're miserly or something like that?" I said, "No. West Indians as a whole are thrifty, but their *backgrounds* are different. Back home the first thing you think of is owning your home, whereas up here in America, the first thing Americans start on is a Cadillac or something like that." She wouldn't accept that, but I think quite a few Americans feel that West Indians coming into this country try to get rich overnight.

No matter what the situation, as long as I'm in this country I'll feel like a second-class citizen. Sometimes I wonder if I made the right choice coming here in the first place. Because people I have known in Jamaica when I was there, they weren't doing as well as I was doing at that time, and they're very much advanced now. Based upon what I've seen there—I went back in '73 for Christmas—probably I would have been much better off there. I don't want to think about whether I'm sorry or not, because then you tend to get frustrated about the whole thing. I chalk up coming here as an experience in life.

# Tunde Ayobami

·················· FROM NIGERIA, 1969 ··················

*Dressed in a batik shirt of characteristic Nigerian pattern and color, he speaks in a soft, lilting English. His wife, a black American, says, "If people are showing a prejudiced attitude toward him, he just pretends he didn't know it." He says, "I became understanding. People are this way, they're not going to change; I'm going to change. I became tolerant—that's the word to use." Still, he sometimes talks about leaving his home in Illinois and going back to Nigeria if he can "be hired by an American company."*

When I was going to high school, my parents separated, and my mother couldn't take all the children. My twin sisters were about six months old, and one stayed with my father. I was taking care of her. You know, the custom is putting the babies in a pouch on the back and tying them. At first I was a little bit shy, being a boy, and it was something meant for a woman to do. It's not like staying in the house. I'm talking about going out, walking about a mile and back, and the baby on my back. You know, like going out on errands, going to market. And people just look at me when I go in the store, and they start laughing. A lot of the women give me praise, and then I start feeling good, so then I didn't worry about it.

So I was living with my father. He work for the government—shows films, educational films, to tourists. There's no way to describe the house. In fact, I would say it's a shack. Families living in one or two rooms, and everybody shares the same bathroom and the same kitchen.

My parents were Baptists, and I went to a Baptist missionary high school. English was the language in the school, and you have to learn the local language, too—Yoruba. It's my tribal language, and it's the third widely spoken language in the continent.

After I left school I got a job in a broadcasting house. I was involved with overseas transmission—news stories, propaganda, and all the rest of it—during the Nigerian-Biafra war. Not exactly a newscaster, but I had access to everything I want to find out. It was a good job, but it wasn't meant for me.

I wanted to come here for a long time, but everybody has an alternative—either coming to the U.S. or going to the USSR. They have a university—they call it Friendship University—in Moscow. And I had the opportunity to go to the USSR to study for free. Like I said before, the easiest one is always the one with no money. In other words, all you have to do is take a taxi to the airport and get into the—what's this Russian airline—Aeroflot. And it takes you to Moscow and they drive you into the college. That's all! But here you got to get all kinds of money and prepare documents and passports. But Africans, in general, they are not so crazy about communism. Africans, as far as I'm concerned, are capitalists. Well, I just didn't like the Russian ideas.

I knew about the U.S. while I was growing up, because I did have a lot of friends. I mean Americans who came to Nigeria to teach, mostly white. We met and we exchanged addresses, magazines, things like this. This was while I was in the high school. They tell me all the things about America, all good things. So I was keen to come in here.

My father, of course, he didn't want me to go anywhere. Because for one thing, I'm the number one in the family and I'm supposed to take care of everybody. He was thinking of when he dies; who is going to be the head of the family. But, by the same token, he always respect my individual decision. Well, I said I'm going to travel out to the U.S.

I have a friend—then he was about fifteen years old—I'm talking about white American family, from Bristol, Rhode Island. We got in touch through the ham radio operation. Then we started to write each other. And when I was coming here and I didn't have any money, he sent some money to me. It was 1969, and I was about twenty-one. I come with the idea of just going to school and going back; because, for one thing, I didn't know what to expect. I just knew what I was going to do: Go to school, get my degree, and go back.

Aviation was in my mind when I left, and I got an admission to an aviation training center in Florida. But once I went through the Atlantic, I changed my mind. [*Laughs.*] That was my first time in a plane. It was scary up there. When I got up there, I couldn't see any houses. I couldn't even see any water. All you see is white clouds. So I said there is no way I was going to do this—a pilot. I decided not to go to Florida.

I landed in JFK and I found my way to Rhode Island, to the family. Oh, they are wonderful. That's my American mother and father. She was a marvelous woman. That's why I call her mom, even up to now. I stayed with them for two months. Within this two months, I was introduced to all kind of people. Everybody want to see our picture together, everything like that. There was a big write-up in the *Bristol Journal*. And I met the reverend of the church, and everything.

The family has a small construction business, and I helped them out. And I was working as a gardener in Mrs. Marjory Carruthers's. She was really rich. I was mowing the lawn with the lawnmower, taking care of the flowers.

I was disappointed for the fact that the money wasn't easy to get. Judging from the Hollywood pictures and how people were smashing cars and everybody walk leisurely on the street, I thought I was going to a paradise; you don't have to earn money. [*Laughs.*]

After a couple of months I found a school, Bristol Community College. I was looking, because I didn't want to go to Florida, like I said. They took me and they give me a first-semester scholarship.

Then I didn't want to be driving from Bristol to the school, because I didn't have a car. The guy I went to talk to in school introduce me to Peter, and Pete told me, "Hey, if you are looking for a place to live, I have an apartment on so-and-so street." I said, "Okay, let's try it." I was so innocent.

It's one of those old houses—two-bedroom apartment with a living room. Yeah, my own bedroom! At first I liked it. It was really different, but it was part of the experience, I feel. During the week, maybe eight people—hippies—stay there. But on the weekend, maybe about twenty. You know, they bring their bags, and three in there and four in here. Oh, they were excellent people. I liked them. But you cannot study there, because they always play the music loud and smoke, and they can't open the windows and everything seeps into my bedroom. They didn't get involved with the drugs until later on; and when it was getting bad and they were disturbing the neighbors, the neighbors had to be calling the cops. I found out that just being present where they are using drugs make me one of them, you know. So that was when I decided to leave.

Meanwhile, a guy came—a black American—by the name of John. He was told about me in the school, and so he introduced himself and invited me for some drinks. Then we started talking and talking, and his intention was to come and get a partner for an apartment. So I move into his apartment. We were compatible, and we became very good friends.

I used to go to school eight to three. From three to eleven I go to work. First, I was working in a textile mill. I operate the dyeing machines—real dirty job. Then I went to a cookie place, a bakery, and I started off on the assembly line. Well, the belt was moving, and you got to pack them in the box, the container, with my apron on and my hat. We have to [*claps hands twice, sharply*] pack them in there and we have to do so many things, because everything was rushing. Oh, yeah, it was a tough job. You're standing, you can't go anywhere, everybody is keeping up production. See, you can't talk to machines. If you want to go to the men's room, you have to call the foreman to come and stand in for you. Then I was promoted to the bakery room. That is in the oven room; 120 degrees on a normal day.

I got involved in different things, and I got to meet different people. I was a Sunday School teacher. It was the Baptist church in Fall River, and I'd go there every Sunday. A wealthy lady, she bought a bike for me, and I went to church on my bike. I was teaching the tenth and twelfth graders. I had a lot of talks, you know—interviews and talk shows—I'd go to the Kiwanis, the deacon's lunch. I talked about Africa and business in Africa and how Americans can come to Africa, and all these kind of things.

I was the first Nigerian in the area. Before I came here, none of us had the idea of going to the suburbs. New York, Boston, Philadelphia—big cities. When I go to visit them, they say, "Where are you, anyway? I never heard of the place. We'll come to see you sometime." So they come and stay over the weekend; and we travel around, I show them places. Most of them didn't know any other place but New York City. But I tell them this place is really peaceful. And when they come to Rhode Island, I try to find jobs for them and find school at the same time. They pay less money for the school, which is an attraction. And I introduced a lot of Nigerians to the church. So everybody come, and most of them have been able to finish school and go to wherever they want to go.

When I finished Bristol Community College, I applied to four-year colleges. I got an admission to Southeastern Massachusetts University, and that was where I went. I finished my college program—medical technology. After I finished school, I got interviews from different companies, and this company hired me. I was in the lab, doing hematology. It was a good job. You know, the lab is always interesting. But the moment you are not given an opportunity to do anything—you know, like management changes and everybody has different ideas— and when the company say, "Well, this is the way we're going to stay," it became so boring staying in the lab, because we do the same thing every time. So I decided to leave the lab and get into sales, technical sales.

I went to the boss and I said, "I don't want to be in the lab. I want to get into sales somewhere." He said there was no position, but later I found out it was because he didn't think I would ever make a good salesman. Most people didn't think I would make it. First, because of my accent; they said I would never sell anybody.

So I was waiting for the best time to quit the company. But the management changed, and the new guy, the vice-president, thought it was a good idea to challenge everybody who wants to do something, so I got into the sales field. I'm one of the first black employees in sales in my company. In my division, I'm the first one. In another department there is another one—not African.

Now I'm a technical sales rep, and what I do—besides make money for the company—is to go to some customers. My territory includes

Pennsylvania, Illinois, Minnesota, Wisconsin, Indiana. Maybe an average of two days a week I'm not home. But it depends on planning. I like it. I like it very much. The territory was dying before I took it over, and now the sales has been going up, up, up, up, up, up. Since I've been on the road, my territory has been improved about 200 percent. The vice-president just wrote me a note, congratulating me. He said, "Keep it up."

Why? Well, number one is I work hard on the territory—more than most of the salesmen that are in there. Every day the average salesman makes about three calls and then comes home. I go five, six, seven. I leave home by six and I make many calls—which makes me coming home after everybody. All of them quit by three; I'm still on the road till four-thirty. I quit at five. On my own, because I'm on salary. It's not a commission, so it's no incentive. That's why a lot of them didn't do the job as it should be done. Some of the customers told me they had dropped the business because the salesman hadn't called on them in a year, two years. I check up, I follow up on samples, I try to develop the business.

Well, in sales, you see your contribution. It's not like in the lab where you come out with a product, and before you turn your head, the boss is taking over and saying, "Yeah, I made it. It's my idea." He gets the credit and you do the work. But now you see that when you work hard, the money comes in. This is the contribution. Every month I can say I made a hundred thousand dollars, or sometimes five hundred thousand dollars, for the company—from me! They know *I'm* the one getting the business. I hope for the future. I think I can get into management, which is one of the reasons that I took the job.

# Rennie Stennett

··················FROM PANAMA, 1969······················

*Holder of the record for the most hits in a single game—seven hits out of seven times at bat, in September 1975—he plays second base for the Pittsburgh Pirates.*

I used to dream a lot. I'd see myself pitching in the World Series and stuff like that. But I was mainly busy going to school. I played mostly every sport in school. The first thing I did was I was a swimmer. I never did like American football, but I played a lot of soccer. It was a lot of fun, especially playing in the mud and the rain. The ball—nobody can kick it, because you can't keep your foot on it. It was real exciting. And then I was a lot better basketball player than baseball player by far when I was in high school.

I'd be playing in a basketball league and a baseball league, and sometimes both play the same day. The basketball game would be at six and we would play the second game of the baseball game—second game start at nine. So when I finished playing basketball, I'd catch a bus and go up about fifteen minutes to the stadium and play baseball in the same night. Get home at two, get up to go to school in the morning, plus studies and all that stuff. And I used to do it. I had good stamina. I could play all day. I remember swimming all day in the river, and from there I'd go and play basketball. I was just going, going, going, going. They never gave letters like they do here, because I think I would have gotten them all. But I won "best athlete" in high school. My brother won it, and my sister won it, and another brother won it. It seemed like it was in the family.

My mother was always for me going out and play sports. But she never used to pay too much attention to me. She was really busy, because she was a hairdresser. Yeah, she was always busy. When I was in high school, a lot of people started talking and telling her about me, and my name started coming out in the papers. That's when she and my father would come and see me pitch.

My father, he works on the tugboat, like a seaman, on the Panama Canal. You know, when the ships come, they'll stop, and he would go out in this tug and tow it through the canals. That's what he does. We were a lower-income family.

I'm really proud of my father—the way he brought us up, without having anything like money and stuff like that. He's so religious, you know. Our school bus would leave at eight, and he used to have us getting up at five to say the rosary every morning. We had an altar in his room, a small altar, and we would say the rosary. I'm successful in my career, and I think that has a lot to do with it. I'm not saying I'm really religious or anything. I go to church and believe in God, but I still have a lot to learn about everything. . . .

It [sports] was mainly for fun then. The scouts been coming since I was in eighth grade, trying to get me to finish school in the United States. They always come down, looking for guys, good ballplayers. The club I was going to sign with at first was the Giants, because they used to come every year. The guy would come to my home and talk to my mother and father, take me all over Panama, and stuff like that. They wanted to bring me over here and I think they was going to pay my schooling, plus I play baseball for that team. Of course, I wanted to play, but my dad, he tell me he want me to at least finish high school.

I guess it was about the last four months in school when I started thinking professional. The Pirates came just before I got out of high school, and that was perfect time. And they offered me a little bit more than the other club. So I went with them.

It was really tough at first. First of all, where I grew up there was black and white lived there, and we go to same church and everything and no problems. We never had the kind of race problem they had here. I knew about it by the newspapers. So when I came here, I didn't even speak to a white person. I don't want them to think they're better than me, so they stay over there and I stay in mine. Sometimes I used to get hate mail. You know, people call me names and stuff like that.

My first year I didn't play league. I played in the minor leagues, Class A. I hate riding buses, but I know it was worth it. Well, in the minors you don't have the beautiful ball parks to play in; the lights are not good, you can't see that good. Most of the pitchers, they're young and strong, and they're throwing the ball hard—they don't know where it's going. You have those coaches trying to teach you, but you've got to make it on your own. It was tough. You is the one got to make that adjustment and groom yourself. And when they think you're ready, they'll bring you up to the big leagues.

Well, I'd played in the minor league that year, and just after the season—see, the minor league only play four months—I went back there [Panama]. I want to continue my education, to get credits meanwhile, and I went into a junior college. I was going into physical ed, something that I can be good in. And then I had a chance to work, so I decided to do that, too.

They were interviewing different people for a job on the Canal. I was going—you know, regular shirt and pants. My father said, "Well, you're going for a job, you shouldn't go like that. You should have on a tie." I didn't have much, but I put it on and it really worked, because most of the other guys got the jobs lifting up things, and since I was in a tie, they asked me if I ever did any kind of accounting or anything like that. I didn't, but I tell them I could do it. And that's why I got that job, as a checker on the dock. That's the person that check the items that come off the dock, like different foods and radios and different things. I had a list with what's supposed to be on the ships, and I was to check those. . . .

The second year I played with Class A again. The third year I jumped to Triple A. At the half of the season I came to the big leagues. Some guys take about seven and eight years to get to the big leagues, but I was lucky. I did it in two and a half. . . .

Of course, I read so many things about America. All I had the impression is just money. Whenever it come around to money, the American will be the smartest person in the world, and he will do anything, even kill. That's the impression I get by the movies. Every movie, it's the same—if it's a Western or whatever it is, you will see when it come round to getting that money, the American will be the smartest and toughest, even if it kills him to get the money. This is what it projected in Panama. And then it seems like when I come over, I think it's the same way. You know, you got to have money. Over here a lot of people say, "Hey, you're nothing unless you got money."

Nowadays most people like to meet me because of who I am. I make a lot of money. So I have to be a little on my guard all the time, to find out if the person likes me for me or just for what I am or what I have. That's very important to me.

# Ari Amichai (II)

In the first year you are stunned and you admire practically everything. Then you go into a transition, a shift, and you start comparing it with your own country, and the comparison is very negative, against America. We went from one extreme of a very negative approach. Then, gradually, the pendulum shifted, and it took you about five- to six-year's stay in America, until, I think, finally you reached a well-balanced understanding of what things are—*how* they are and how they came about—and you are not as critical anymore. You don't admire things blindly, but you are not as critical, because you understand what caused it. And this you didn't understand before.

It's only in the mirror of time that you can do it. A person that comes from Israel to America today will give you a completely different picture of the same thing that I will give you. Even if you will look at the same thing. So I think that was our, I would say, pilgrimage in America. Like, you are going through phases in your cognizance of what's going on, and gradually it percolates into a well-balanced understanding. I will give you an example—very interesting example. When we were in Israel—it was right after Kennedy was killed, by the way—I remember they started the Selma march and other civil-rights movements in the South—and we said how come the whites don't give them, etc., etc., etc.

It's extremely easy to pass judgment from afar. I came to America and I went to Wisconsin and I was in a little white community and they always said, "Freedom to the Negroes in Alabama." As long as they stay in Alabama, of course. Only when I came to Cleveland and I *saw* really what's going on—I started sort of reassessing my convictions. You know, how hard it is to keep freedom and at what cost do you give freedom? And what is the meaning of freedom? That's important. And it's easy to say *freedom*, but I believe freedom is the choice of responsibility. This is not my definition. That is Immanuel Kant's definition. It's the choice of responsibility! A free choice of responsibility is freedom. Not just irresponsibility. And in many instances, I saw that people want to take freedom in its most base meaning of complete anarchy. So even my opinion of freedom and what should be done about it was for quite a few years in a flux. And only now I think I understand. I *think* I can speak with some authority on what I believe is freedom and what should be done. As an outsider, it was everything very simple—black and white. There was no gray in between, just black and white.

# Lynn Redgrave

·················· FROM ENGLAND, 1974 ······················

*A member of a distinguished British acting family—father, Sir Michael Redgrave; mother, Rachel Kempson; sister, Vanessa—she first became known to American audiences for her starring role in* Georgy Girl. *She is married to producer John Clarke, and at the time of the interview was starring in his production of Shaw's* Saint Joan *on Broadway, and was also hostess of a popular women's television talk show, "Not for Women Only." She is tall and slender, wearing black slacks and sweater. Her face is animated and she gestures broadly as she talks. She takes time off from the interview to attend to a mother's duties when daughter Kelley, age seven, comes home from school; she gives her milk and cookies and helps her into a leotard for dancing lessons. Their conversation is as follows:*

*DAUGHTER: Mummy, how did you get teached to turn into an actress?*

*MOTHER: I went to a school, darling.*

*DAUGHTER: How old were you when you started?*

*MOTHER: Oh, I started when I was sixteen. I didn't start when I was a little girl.*

*DAUGHTER: Oh. Want to know how to count by twos?*

*MOTHER: Come on, love, because you'll be late for your class otherwise. And tell them when you get there that I'm coming and that I'll pay then, because daddy got some money from the bank. Okay? Quickly now, because I have to go and talk, dear.*

I never used to come when my dad would come and do Broadway shows. It was the great excitement: Dad was going to Broadway! One really did imagine it like the movies showed it, and the funny thing was that was what it was like when I got here. That was what was so wonderful about it. People now say, "If only you'd known New York in the thirties, or New York in the twenties," or whatever—a great era, you know, when it was fantastic. Well, to me, I still found it fantastic.

I came for a week in September of '66 to publicize *Georgy Girl*, and the film company brought me over, so I had one of those rarefied weeks in the Sherry Netherland. I was mad about it! Oh, God, I was hysterical for a week before I came. I was so excited. I was going to New York! It seemed to me the most exciting thing, and it lived up to my expectations when I got here. I thought it was absolutely thrilling. Of course, I saw things under a very nice light, because I was being taken around and treated nicely. I wasn't having to fight for anything, so I saw a very nice view of the whole thing.

Americans are extremely hospitable. If a new person arrives and you don't know anybody, at least ten people will make sure you get to meet some people. It was like that from the very minute I arrived, and I don't think it was just because I'm an actress.

That's how I met my husband. He was born British and he had been a child star, and a very famous one at the time. I always call him the Shirley Temple of England. He was that famous, as far as England was concerned. When he was seventeen, he'd gone past the cute child bit, and he felt very closed in by having been a child actor. So one day he went down to a shipping line and signed up for the merchant marine, came back and said to his parents, "I'm joining the merchant marine next Friday." They said, "How long for?" and he says, "I will go round the world and I'll be back in three years." That was called leaving home extremely.

He never went back to live, because when he had landed back there, he found the merchant marine didn't count as service, and they were waiting for him for two years in the army. Having just been around the world for three years, he said, "The hell with that," and went to Canada—went to Canada with the view of wanting to come here.

We met in London, when he was on a visit back to England. We were both in a TV play together, and then he came back here, which was where he was living. I barely knew him. I mean, I knew him, literally, as another actor I'd worked with. There was no romance going on. But he had given me his number and said, "If you do come to New York"—because I'd told him when I'd worked with him that I may come to New York. He said, "Take my number. I'd love to show you around."

I came over a couple of months later to do a play on Broadway, and I did, in fact, call him within a couple of days of arriving, since I knew nobody. He invited me out, and within a very short time it was onto a whole other basis [*laughs*], which was very nice.

We got married in April 1967. I wasn't thinking of getting married. I came to do a play. And within three or four months I was married, so that plan changed a little.

We went back to live in England, because I had a movie I was meant to go and do in England. But I also couldn't imagine living anywhere but England at that point. I just felt that I was tied into it. I'd never thought about living outside of the country I was born in.

My husband had lived here for some time. It was years and years since he'd lived in England. He thought he'd like to try it again. It seemed like a good time. So we tried it. We lived in London, but we kept a little, tiny apartment in this building, and every year we would be here.

People would say to me, "You really should stay over here. You could get a lot of work." And I would say, "I don't think I'd get enough to do." You see, I thought that I wouldn't. I didn't imagine myself being able to work on a full-time basis here. I thought I wouldn't fit in in some way. I don't know why, because ever since I've been here I've done more work than I ever did in my life.

I was happyish. At the point we married, I'd suddenly had a big burst of success, so that I was into a whole new thing and didn't really know how to handle it. John helped me a great deal with that, because it was suddenly a whole different world altogether. And then we had the two children.

After a few years, we began to be very disenchanted with London, generally, with English living. My husband got very frustrated with London again. He found everything cramped, small, the scale of everything very confining. He found the speed with which things happened, decisions were made, or business deals could be done . . . it's like a caterpillar moving, or a tortoise, compared to what he was used to. He definitely was not reenchanted by the place when he got back there. That may well have colored my attitude. Who knows how much that affects one? If the person you love is not enjoying themselves too much, you either hate him for it or maybe you begin to see a little through their eyes, which may well have been the case. I don't know, we got very unhappy with the whole situation there.

Around that time that we were getting more and more unhappy, we had gone on a holiday to Ireland, and on one of those idyllic Irish sunset views, we had seen a *For Sale* sign on a house. We said, "To hell with it! It's only fifty minutes on the plane, or overnight on the ferry, to England. Why not? Let's move in there. It'll be good for the children. We'll have a nice outdoorsy sort of life." And I always liked to ride horses. It was a gorgeous spot. We were twenty minutes from the airport, we didn't feel in back of nowhere. So then we tried the great idyllic dream of living on a cliff in Ireland. That was our pastoral period. [*Laughs.*]

At that point, because my children were sort of little, we would mess on the beach and play with the dog and do all the sort of family things, which were really lovely and I'm glad I did them. But I also did begin to get very restless. If the pace is slow in England, it's slower in Ireland. [*Chuckles.*] We thought we were going to live in Ireland and we could easily get to England to work. We could do a little bit of work in Ireland. We could get to America pretty easily. We thought we were going to have the best of both worlds. But, in fact, we just didn't find it possible.

It lasted two years. It might've lasted longer, had I not been offered another Broadway play, which brought us back here. We came back in 1974, February the fourteenth, St. Valentine's Day—so it sticks in my memory. The play I was doing was *My Fat Friend.*

To begin with, we didn't know if the show would run. And at one point it didn't look like it would, right early on. We thought we'd pack our bags and go back. But it ran all through the summer, and then in the fall it was going to run a little more, and then it was going to do a tour, and that would take us through till January. But then, when the end looked in sight, we had to ask ourselves the question, "Now what are we going to do? Are we going back?" And we decided that we didn't want to go back. That was a very natural decision from my husband's point of view, since he'd always wanted us to come back here. And for me—I had to come to terms with the fact that I like to work an awful lot more than I like to look at scenery. So it was around fall of that year, of '74, that we decided.

You see, you can do very good work in England, and you can work with very good people, and there are an awful lot of theaters, considering the size of the place, which is really small. At any one time, you will probably find more shows on the West End than on Broadway. But there are a lot of things. . . . I would never have done a talk show if I was in England. No actress would ever be asked to do a talk show in England, and, if you were, you would only be doing it because you literally couldn't get work elsewhere. It's a whole different way of thinking. There are many more areas in which you can work here.

You see, I don't just work in New York. I've worked in Chicago. In fact, I did *Saint Joan* in Chicago before we did it here. And the year before I was out in Lake Forest, and I did *Misalliance* out there. I toured in that. Two summers I've done summer tours here, where we'd go all over, like New England, and I love that. It's sort of a nice working holiday for the family. There is no such thing as summer stock there. It does not exist in England. There's much more you can do here, really. And it so happens that I've come here at a good time in my life, when there's an awful lot more for an actress in the thirties than there is when you're twenty. I don't fit into the ingénue mold, you know, and so there's just that much less for me to do. Now, I'm at a time which I guess for an actor are the best years—from thirty to forty; and then again after sixty. You definitely then cross a barrier into another whole range of interesting parts. I know my mother's done this. She's in her sixties and in the last ten years has had a whole renaissance of her career, because she suddenly was old enough. When you're in your fifties, you're just not quite right for the other woman, who tends to be forty to forty-five. It's the weirdest thing. And then suddenly you're into it again—quite old enough for those marvelous character parts. I've always felt you've got twenty bloody good years from thirty to fifty, when you can play all the strong, energetic things. . . .

There are things I like about London, but I don't think I could live in London again. Well, I et the apple in the Garden of Eden, you see, and I got special knowledge that people who never came to New York didn't have. The energy of New York, the pace of it, the enthusiasm of it—if you never knew those things, you don't miss them. But once you've tasted them, if that's the sort of thing you like, I don't think you can go back to something else. There's an energy here that I thrive on. There are people in England who say to me, "Well, my God, your children will grow up in America and what will happen?" Well, it would seem to me that if they grow up here and carry on as they're carrying on, I think they're ahead of the game, rather than behind it.

I think that for a child to grow up in New York is an astonishing, if somewhat abrasive, education. It depends what sort of world you've got to live in. For some people, it's not necessary that they be equipped to deal with New York. They live on a farm and they have a wonderful, idyllic life, and it simply doesn't matter. But our life is—you know, a certain way of life, and there's no getting away from it. And our children have adjusted to it now. We go on tour—the whole family—and they come to the theater and they are exposed to a great many things that children who live our sort of life need to be exposed to.

The children go on the public bus to school, and they're very aware of the hazards of city things. They do all the proper things—phoning if they can't come immediately—and they know all the little details that anybody that grows up in a city has to know. You can't have total innocents walking about. We just have to have them aware, and it's a shame, because, of course, children are very trusting. One hates to spoil that. But they accept it and it hasn't made them terrified of people or shy or reticent. I guess we've hammered into them certain rules of public travel—one of which is not shouting in a loud voice who I am and whose child they are. [*Laughs.*] You know, suddenly on a bus, "MY MOTHER'S IN A SHOW ON BROADWAY!" Now they say, "It's all right to tell so-and-so you're an actress, isn't it?"

I occasionally will get a nostalgic feeling for something English. I cry when Princess Anne has a baby, and I love all that. When we were in Chicago, Kelley and I went and stood outside the Museum of Science and Industry because Prince Charles was coming. We stood outside for twenty minutes, getting freezing cold, and I whispered, "That's Prince Charles." Well, I mean, that may be a little dumb, but I got quite a thrill out of it and I felt very proud, and I waved. I liked the fact that everybody around was going, "Isn't he cute?" and "Isn't he charming?" and I felt, "Hmph, there he is and very good for him."

But on the other hand, I don't see that there is nothing else. I think that one of the problems that a lot of English people have is this feeling that nothing exists outside England. The English way of doing some things is charming, lovely, wonderful, and I love it. I relish the fact that that's where I'm from, but, in fact, I enjoy my Englishness far more now I'm here than I ever did there.

Unlike any country in the world, you actually can be accepted here. I was so amazed at how quickly I was not "the English person," but the person who lives in New York. And now we've been here four years, people think of us as part of the place. We're not the people who might be leaving any minute. It's made a very nice difference. To begin with, we were the special visitors, but now we have a much more solid base, because people know we live here. An American can come and live in England, and he could live there fifty years, and he's still the Yankee who came to live down the road—a little bit of an oddity and a curiosity. You don't have those barriers here. I mean, people think of me as a New Yorker, of which I'm extremely proud. I feel very good about that. It's very nice and I find it very comforting that I get called by the mayor's office to appear at some function for New Yorkers and nobody mentions that I'm English. I'm a New Yorker. I like that.

# Premier Nguyen Cao Ky

·············· FROM SOUTH VIETNAM, 1975 ··················

*It's a common story after great political upheavals: a head of state becomes a grocery store clerk, a general becomes a dishwasher, a governor becomes a waiter. When he was premier of South Vietnam, Nguyen Cao Ky was a flamboyant figure in a black flightsuit with lavender scarf and pearl-handled pistols, forever pushing the Americans to expand the war to the North. Now he runs a small liquor store on the outskirts of Los Angeles and lives with his wife and six children in a nondescript home in a middle-class housing development. Still trim and dapper at forty-seven, he wears well-tailored beige slacks and a flower-print silk shirt.*

Even before I left, even five minutes before I left, I had no idea in my mind that I'm going to leave, because that day the Communist forces were advancing to the capital, Saigon. But, to the last second, I was still trying to direct, to gather the troops to fight and to hold, to fight back. It never came to mind that I am going to leave, because, as a professional soldier in a war situation, there is no alternative. Win the battle or die at the battle. That's the way that my grandfather and my father teach us. That's the way that we, in Asia, believe in, you know.

But then, all my efforts failed. Of course, I tried many months before the end of the war, not just the last days, to carry on; but both the American government and the Vietnamese government, at that time President Thieu, they didn't help me. I have the impression that both of them want me out, you know, so that they can do whatever they want. I think that, at that time, they already had the plan to evacuate, but they didn't tell us. No, they didn't tell anyone.

The situation in the last few weeks was that no one was in command. It was totally, as you know, a debacle. The chief of general staff resigned. He left the country without telling anyone that he left. [*Chuckles softly.*] So, I was by myself, and trying to do something. And finally, that morning, April 29, I found myself alone at the big headquarters of the general staff—big and empty, because all the officers, including the soldiers and the NCO's, all, all had left.

From there I tried to call the paratroopers, the air force, the navy, the marines. They all said, "Well, we are preparing to go, because the American officials gave us the green light to go." At noontime, all the American helicopters came in for the final, big evacuation. On the ground, you know, there were hundreds of thousands of Vietnamese, running—right, left, every way, to find a way to escape. After I saw that, I look around, I just look around. And there are ten people with me—my bodyguards, you know, they were with me for many years—and they said to me, "Well," they said, "General, it's time for us to go, too." Because there was nothing I could do. If I was responsible, then I would stay; but, as you know, for the last three or four years, they kept me out. I had nothing to do with the collapse. It's their fault.

So I took my own helicopter and flew out. But I didn't know where to go, because, you know, with a helicopter you have a very short range. You can't go far. Fortunately, on the emergency channel, I had contact with an American ship outside, so they directed my helicopter and we flew out to the sea. It took me, I think, about thirty-five minutes, and then I landed on the aircraft carrier *Midway*, and that was it.

You know, all the families of the high-ranking people in South Vietnam, they had left Saigon months before. But my wife, she wanted to stay with me, and she stayed. Finally, on the twenty-eighth, I sent my wife and my family out—one day before the Communists came in. I told them, "It's time for you to go. I don't want you around," I said to my wife and children. "I don't want you around when I have to fight the last battle." That's why she left the day before. The Americans sent a plane to evacuate them, along with thousands of others. I didn't know where they were, until I was moved from the aircraft carrier *Midway* to the flagship *Blue Ridge*, and I asked the officer to check about my family. A few hours later they told me that they were in Hawaii, and that's it.

I stayed on the *Blue Ridge* until the end of the evacuation operation. I think I was the only one from Vietnam that they really treated with distinction and kindness. The other officials, both military and government, they really were not treated very well, no. Even five-star generals, foreign ministers, they were treated, you know, just like simple soldiers. They had to group on deck and had no sleep and nothing to eat for a long time, almost as if they were prisoners of war. While for me, well, they gave me a cabin and they assigned a group of sailors, so anything I need, they provide to me. And then from the flagship, they flew me directly to the United States.

When I arrived here in California, I stayed in Camp Pendleton for eighteen days, and there I lived in a tent, a tent like the other refugees, because I don't want to have a special treatment. That camp was really well organized. We had everything we need, but that's all. You had nothing to do. Most of the refugees had nothing to do, except for me; I had too many visitors, too many reporters. I don't know why. All the journalists and the television, the press, they came to me every day. I had a press conference every day, every minute. At the end, I had to ask the camp commander to stop that kind of treatment, you know.

Then, after eighteen days, I went to Washington with my family. While I was there I met again with senators, congressmen, officials— what can I say to them if I meet them? Kissinger and Vance and others. So, when I see them again, you know, it's embarrassing for both of us; because I think they are responsible for what happened. Everything I told them, years and years ago, they didn't listen to me. When I said it, well, they could think that I was wrong and they were right; but now, after what happened, they realize that I am right and they were wrong.

Basically, the difference is between East and West. That's why the relation and the cooperation between Americans and Vietnamese failed after fifteen years. Not because of the war, not because of strategy and tactics, but because of the complete misunderstanding between Americans and Vietnamese. Those who were responsible in Washington, people like Kissinger, for example—he knew nothing about Asia. He has a little knowledge about Russia and the Middle East, but no, no, nothing, zero about the Vietnamese and Asians. Not only did he not know the Vietnamese, who were friends; he didn't know about the Vietnamese enemy, the Communists. They said, "If you give the people everything they need—house, refrigerator, radio—they will not go Communist." But, no, that is not true. That's what they thought.

I told them, "We need a good leader. A true leader. Someone that can oppose Ho Chi Minh in the North." Now Ho Chi Minh, I don't accept him, because he's a Communist—but I do have to admit that he's a good and true leader, because people believe and support him. So what we need in South Vietnam is the same thing, a Vietnamese leader. You cannot create that. You must let the Vietnamese, themselves, make the choice. But, no, the Americans want someone that they can trust. They want someone that will always say, "Yes. Yes sir, yes sir." That's why they don't like me. They don't want me in power, because I'm too independent, too nationalistic. They want me to be an American boy, but that's impossible.

I told President Johnson, the first time I met with him, "Everyone knows that, without the backing of America, our side could not sustain a long war. And without the backing of the Russians and the Chinese, the other side could not. We know that. Everyone knows that. But, on the other side, you never hear about Chinese generals or Russian generals." It was always the Vietnamese—Ho Chi Minh, his army. So, for the people, it was a Vietnamese war—the Vietnamese fighting for their own nationalistic cause. While, on our side, it seemed Ky was the American puppet, because every day, on the TV, on the radio, we see pictures and declarations—Johnson's here or McNamara's there, Westmoreland—it's like an American war. So at the end, the Communists are right, because they are fighting for a nationalist cause against the imperialist Americans. At the end, we, the true nationalist Vietnamese, lost our own identity.

After I stay in Washington with my family about a year and a half, I decide to move down here to Southern California because I hate politics, and business opportunities are better here, and, besides, down here you have the biggest concentration of Vietnamese in the United States.

The American press, and even people, are still talking about me as the leader of the Vietnamese in the United States. Maybe it's true, but, personally, I have no intention to be a leader. I don't want people to think that. And what can I do to help them in my position? But they do come to me when they need help. I never ask them, but if someone needs help and they come to me, well, my house is open for them, but that's all. And people come to me with small or big problems: red tape, money, there are all sorts of problems that refugees have.

But I don't have those problems. People know me, so they believe I am really very rich. There are all those stories of gold and smuggling opium and that I'm worth, you know, a million dollars. No one ever asks me for my credit. I don't have a bag of gold, but it's just the same as if I have a bag of gold. They never even ask me my credit. To buy a car, to buy a house, to start the business—"Okay. You're Marshall Ky," and that's it. They know I'm a leader.

I can even cosign for a car for a friend. A car dealer asked another Vietnamese, "Do you now have a job?" And he said, "Yes." And he said, "Who do you work for?" And he said, "I work for Marshall Ky," and the car dealer said, "Okay, if you work for that man, it's okay." [*Chuckles.*] He said, "The only thing that I want you to do is, when you come in the next day for the car, bring Marshall Ky so we can shake hands with him." So he came back and told me, and I said okay. And the next day I went down with him to the car dealer, and he got the car. You see, you don't have to have the bag of gold; people just have to think you have a bag of gold.

I really came with nothing, nothing. I wasn't like some of those others, who have money in Paris and Switzerland in a bank under another name. I'm living simply, because I should live simply, because I have to live simply; but that's all right with me. Because I was educated in foreign countries and traveled often around the world, from the outside, I look like a very modern man. But, inside, deep inside, basically, I am Vietnamese, Asian. My way of thinking, my way of life, are 100 percent Vietnamese. I'm not Buddhist, I'm not Catholic; I am Confucian. Confucianism is pure Asian. So, living here myself and for my family, we have many problems adjusting—not physically, but morally.

The relationship between teachers and American children, I don't like that way. Children have the right to treat the teachers as equals. For us, in ancient times, we are taught that first, the king, the emperor—in other words, the nation; and second, the teacher; and third, the parents. That is the order of respect. So, you see, teachers have a very high position in our society, because we think parents give you birth, but the teachers. . . . teachers give you knowledge: how to become a good man. But here, in this country, I found out the children have no respect for the teachers. That's not right.

And concerning the parents' respect and authority, the same thing happens. Teen-agers can go out and find a part-time job and earn four hundred, five hundred, six hundred dollars a month. Well, they become independent. And the society corrupts them, too, so they have less and less respect for their parents. It happened to my own son. Here, working at four dollars an hour, he has a sports car. Oh, yes, you see, they adjust very quick and it corrupts them. Yes, it does. I am very angry, but what can I do? If I beat them, you know, they will try me at the court. That's crazy. You are parents and you can't give a spanking to your own sons and daughters. I can't accept that. In my country, they will listen to me; and if not, well, we'll send them to the front line, and two years in the army and fighting the war will make them, you know, good boys. But here, what can I do? It's very frustrating. I know that Americans have the same problems, because many of them come to me and complain about their teen-agers.

*What would you say are the good things in America?*

[Long pause.] I don't know . . . maybe the climate . . . this is a beautiful place. It is beautiful country, but that's all. I don't like the way of life. Too much hurry, hurry, hurry, and not enough time for relaxation. That's why, you know, you have too many mental problems. You have all kinds of problems, physically and mentally. I think you are lucky, but you are not the happiest people in the world. No, I don't think so. Maybe I'm too lazy.

Frankly, I think Americans pay too much attention to materialistic things. You're working too hard to get more, more money, so you've lost, most of the time, the true goal of life, the ultimate goal of life. Materially, when you look at an American, a millionaire, with his big house, big boat, big car, everything, you think he's a happy man. But when you become friends with him, and watch him closely, the way he works every minute, every day, every month of his life, then you feel pity, because he's not happy. I know one American, very rich, and we became very friendly. He's a multimillionaire, but every day he's worrying about his money, you know, and how to make more. I told him, "If you make ten million dollars more, what's the difference? Just tell me. You can't eat five, six meals a day. Already your house is too big for just the two of you. What can you do with millions more, just tell me? Why don't you stop worrying about business and try to enjoy life? Enjoy yourself and use that money to help people."

The other day, a television interviewer, an NBC man—what's his name? Tom Snyder. He asked me, "You own a liquor store now? You stand behind the counter and sell liquor? How can you do that?" And I said, "I am doing an honest business. I am earning a small amount of money for my family. I'm proud of that."

The basic difference between East and West is this: We believe in destiny. I believe that everything that happens to me is destiny. American people believe that *you* can change all, you can change the shape of your life. I don't think so. Even your intelligence—you are born intelligent, you are born smart. No one can teach you to be smart; nothing you can do to increase or improve your intelligence. You talk about being born equal—oh, no. [*Laughs.*] No, you are not born equal. Why is someone born in a Rockefeller house and the other in a poor house? It's destiny. Some people say they can be successful because they work. Yes, but they are born hard workers, and intelligent, and that's why they make a success. It's all destiny. I've escaped death many times, very close, when the one next to me died, not me. Why? Well, Christians, Catholics, they talk about miracles, right? I think it's destiny.

I think I did the best job among the premiers in the last fifteen years in South Vietnam. That was my destiny. So, today, I'm selling liquor. I'm still happy, because I say, "Well, it's my destiny," and what will happen to me next, it will happen, too. I believe that my destiny is I will some day have to go back to Vietnam. You wait and see. The world is changing, changing from the beginning for millions of years, a continuous cycle of changing. There will be a change in power, and I will go back.

# Tuan Pham

···············FROM SOUTH VIETNAM, 1975···················

I was a doctor in Vietnam and I passed my medical examination here, but I still didn't pass the English examination. So I was working for a doctor in a private hospital and I take blood. And one day the doctor told me to come in at a certain time, I have to take blood from a patient. And I came in and the nurse was there, and the patient and his family were sitting in the back of the room, and the nurse told the family to leave and just leave the patient there. And I took the blood and I did whatever I had to, and then the patient left and then one of the family came in and said to me: "Do you know who I hate? First I hate blacks. Second, I hate yellow. I love animals more than you and blacks. Get out of here." Do you know what I did? I cried and I left my job right away. I quit that job and I said I'm not going to even try to be a doctor here. And now I'm working as a chef in a restaurant.

# Hoa Tran

*It is a run-down neighborhood in Columbus, Ohio—a sparsely furnished living room, stuffing coming out of the sofa, torn shades at the otherwise bare windows. Hoa Tran speaks in broken English, trying to find words to describe his former life as governor of a major province in Vietnam.*

I studied public administration. Six months after I graduated, I became deputy of a district. The first thing deputy have to do, they have to sign all the check for pay for village officer. And I have to sign all the receipt for tax. And I have to sign official document. I have to decide—for example, if a village in our district ask me money to build a dam of brick, I have to investigate.

During that time I was married to a teacher in Dalat. We knew each other before, when we were in high school, but she's a Buddhist and I'm a Catholic. Her family love me, but they're sorry that I'm Catholic.

I love her, and I waited until she believed in God and she talked to priest and converted to Catholic. The family didn't know anything about it. In the wedding day we did everything right with her family. They decided which day we marry in Saigon. But before that, we went to Dalat to marry in church. [*Chuckles.*] No family, but a lot of friends.

Then in Saigon we celebrated ancestor ceremony with the family—her family on a side, my family on another side, and we have to kneel before them. In her house we have to build altar, and we stand before that altar and we light the candle and we put on a big bowl with incense inside and we pray something for the ancestor . . . "we are going to be married, and please you come to accept our wedding." They say that the smoke rising can make the ancestor feel that they are present. They say that the ancestor is still there. They believe that his ghost is with us. I am educated, but I still do it. I do it because I want to pay respect to my ancestors. It is something special. And the two families put out the box with the rings and I put one on her finger and she put one on my finger. After that her family gave her some gifts, and my family gave us some gifts. And we had to take her from her house to my house. It's symbol. And we had party at nighttime in a restaurant. . . .

They transfer me often. In '69 I was promoted to deputy—that's the governor—of a big province and a very nice province, near to Saigon.

We had a very big house, air conditioning, furniture, servants, car, soldier to chauffeur, gardener, and, of course, guard. Government pays. In that province, I had to resolve every problem. I had to deal with the assembly. I had to contact with American advisers. We worked very closely with American advisers. I had to deal with delegations. For example, they celebrated school graduation, they organized a big sport event; I had to preside. Very nice, very interesting, and very responsible job. I was thirty-two, thirty-three. Ah, yes, was a nice time.

Almost every week we gave party. We invited American people, or delegation came from central government, military, prime minister's wife. Everybody wanted to come, because it is big province and the weather is very nice. I had to welcome them almost every day. We went to the airport and brought them; went with them to the pagoda, to the seashore. We had many public guests, but we didn't want to invite them in our house. If you have friends, that's okay, but not for official. When they came, we had to get money from my province to order food from restaurant, and they served everything. But my wife had to organize, had to order food. . . .

*Did you know you'd have to leave?*

I didn't know anything, really. I had a friend, American adviser, and I went to his house and I asked him what could be happening. It was Friday, I think. He said, "Tomorrow we have the big meeting. The general will come here and he will tell us what problems are going on between Vietnam and Communists." And Sunday afternoon—I remember March 30 was a Sunday—after mass, about five, we came back to see him, and his wife was packing. By that time his word came and he say that condition was very bad now. "Why you still here?" he asked me. "You look very peaceful." "Because," I said, "I didn't know anything. I just came here to ask you."

I drove my wife to airport, but around airport was the barbed wire. They didn't let anybody come in. I told guard I'm deputy; but he say, "No! Only military, not civilian." But then I met my friend, he's major, and he saved me. He said, "Okay, I'll let you go." They gave me four tickets for my wife and three children. I took her home, picked up some clothes—but only enough for vacation—and drove back to airport. I thought they will come back soon. I had to stay. I'm the deputy.

In that night I couldn't sleep. I couldn't figure out which way I can go to Saigon. In the morning the conditions become panic. Nobody going to work. Every face looked pale. At ten I received a message from Saigon that I have to move all the money from the treasury back to Saigon. They say they will send airplane to take me. I took a machine gun and a pistol. I drive myself to airport, but the condition was very bad, and they say I couldn't go. I met a friend—he's a pilot—and he told me, "Okay, leave the car there and keep your eyes straight ahead," because he afraid they shoot us. I gave him my car keys—my fingers on pistol. He send me to field officer, said, "He's deputy, my friend, please take him to Saigon."

In Saigon they asked me to organize office for the people who can come out of provinces. They had to come to my office and make the papers. I didn't think that Americans would leave Saigon. I thought that maybe they could keep Saigon for neutral. The day we left our country, I played tennis. I still didn't know we can't come back.

Sunday was April 30. The Saigon radio say that the condition was very bad. That's in code, but I know the code. You have to go someplace to take a chopper to go out of the country. At that time, I was wearing tennis clothes. I went to a friend and I asked him, "What are we to do now?" And he said, "Okay, come with us." His relative was captain of the navy boat. I couldn't believe it! Just chance! I asked myself, "What happen if I came there five minutes before? What happen if I go five minutes later?" This was the thirtieth, April 30. . . .

My wife have a sister and a brother-in-law who came here ten years ago. They sponsor us. Is lucky? Sometimes it feels not lucky. They sponsor us—we say, "Okay, easy." But they couldn't help us like American community. We don't have opportunity to contact American family. I went to the Catholic church, but they didn't have nothing. I came to see the father, the priest, and he didn't help nothing. I ask him to help me find odd jobs. He said now the jobs are very tight. "If you want, I can send you to agency."

I worked in a warehouse for six weeks. I had to work from eight in the evening to four-thirty in the morning, put together the order, put in the truck they deliver for the grocery, I think. It was hard to accept, but we had to—heavy work, nighttime. Then her brother-in-law read in newspaper that a Japanese restaurant need waiters, and I apply. I worked as waiter, but I wanted to improve my life, have some skill better than waiter.

So after that I decided to go to college. I'm studying accounting. Some Vietnamese friend told me it's very easy to find job if I graduate from this college. You get very good education. Top income will be after I graduate. I think that I will have a permanent job.

There are things I'm unhappy about, but I push them aside. I don't think about that. But that's my personal philosophy. I have friends who are very discouraged, very unhappy. They had high positions; now they're delivering milk, working in factory. When I told my friend I'm working as waiter, he said, "But what about your head? You're used to working with your head." I laughed.

We live very poor, we are short of everything. Like we don't have enough money to buy a lot extra, like a lot of new dresses and new coat, or buy new furniture or TV. You can look around, you can see this apartment. But we accept it. I accept everything that fate give to me.

# Thien Vinh

·················· FROM SOUTH VIETNAM, 1975 ····················

*When he was interviewed, he had been in the United States for only six months. He was living with his wife, six children, mother-in-law, cousin, and nephew in a duplex house, next to a used-car lot on a heavily trafficked street in a New Jersey suburb. An oversized refrigerator-freezer, an upright piano, a color television set, and a washing machine had been donated to the family by his employer and local citizens. His teen-age daughters were learning to drive, the younger ones were taking piano lessons, and the fifteen-year-old boy had earned enough from his newspaper route to buy a ten-speed bicycle.*

As a young boy, Vietnam was under the domination of France. We didn't like the French, because we don't like they say, "You can't have this or can't do this." When I was five years old, something like that, my father joined the liberation force. That's not the Communists, but purely nationalist. But then that force, later on, was abused by the Communists, and they turned that force into Communist. So my father was stuck with them, and he left us—my mother, four brother, sister—with my grandparents.

As soon as I graduated from high school I was drafted. At that time we was having war between the French and Vietnamese, and the battle in Dien Bien Phu was still going on. I was sent to the military academic school—they train officers. I was supposed to have quick training, then jump over Dien Bien Phu. At that time I didn't worry at all. Seems to me I enjoyed it! I liked to be a parachutist. I liked to jump in the sky, and I studied to jump to the battle in Dien Bien Phu. I wanted to be a hero. But luckily, by the time I graduated from military school there was the cease-fire—the Geneva agreement took place. Then five months later—in 1955—I was discharged from the army.

There was evacuation flights every day, and Americans sent two ships to Vietnam to help evacuate the people who want to go south. I had relatives in Saigon—very remote relatives, but they gave me lodging and boarding, and I stayed with them for about one year to improve my English.

When I felt confident enough I started applying for a job, and first I got a job as an interpreter for the U.S. Military Assistance Advisory Group. I was a civilian at that time, working for the U.S. Army. It was a good job. Thanks to that group, I learned quite a lot and I became very skillful in English. Then after one year, I started thinking of something else, because I hoped that some other company would pay a higher salary.

So I applied for a job in a contracting company. I had to go out with the supervisor to the field to make sure everything's okay. He was a general supervisor of the area. I worked for him as a personal interpreter. And I was well paid at that time—good job, good pay. I stayed with them until their contract expired, and I moved to another company, also an engineering company. Same kind of work, translator. All American companies.

Then I noticed an ad in a newspaper that a news agency wants an office manager, and I went just for a trial, and I was accepted out of fifty candidates. From then my whole life changed, because a news agency is really an interesting company, and there is a lot of interesting work. You know everybody. VIP, high-ranking officer in military or civilian. You know people outside the country, too. And besides, the most important—very good pay.

I was no longer interpreter-translator. I was actually the office manager. That's man who manage everything in the office. I had to take care of correspondence, visa, immigration problem. I took care of renting office space, private home for correspondents, reservation, airplane ticket, charter airplane for them to go here and there, because at that moment transportation very tight. I had to get appointment with the prime minister, the president, the director of the Vietnam press. Sometimes, because we were short-handed, I had to cover the press conference, something like that. And I came back to office to just write a report what happened in there and give it to reporters. They rewrote it. Then, besides, the most important thing, I had to learn how to operate the teletype machine.

Yes, I knew everything: what the prime minister said, the president said, what was for distribution in the interview. Whatever happened in the area, I knew.

I had a wife and family by then. I must say I led a very comfortable life in Vietnam. We had a car, a house, everything in the house: a piano, five or six ceiling fans, one air conditioner. What you have here, I could afford to have in Vietnam. We bought a piece of land, about thirty miles outside the city, and we grew fruit trees. This was for our future; and maybe five, ten years later, we could benefit from those fruit. And now is the time they bear fruit, but we didn't have chance to. . . .

We lived normally, but I knew everything in the news, and someday the Americans would withdraw from Vietnam—I knew that. After '68, the American attitude started changing. Through the news, I knew more aid was cut—American aid to Vietnam was cut—and there was a debate in the Congress. So I knew what was going to happen to Vietnam. I didn't know that this event would happen so quickly.

All the family were very reluctant to leave. I had spent most of my life for the house, for the property there. And everybody was reluctant to leave, because we didn't want to leave all the property behind. We didn't want to leave the relatives. But I was aware of the danger, and I had been working for the company for almost twenty years—for quite a long time. I was reluctant to go, but I had to go. I had been in the army, so I was considered the most dangerous element. No possibility of staying.

The news agency paid to charter a plane, but we couldn't make it to the airport because a lot of secret police agents around. That plane landed and was sitting at the airport for three days. The problem was how to get into the plane. This was all illegal, you know. The government at that time did not permit any single individual to leave the country. Then, also, the agency would be responsible for involving in a kind of illegal traffic. So all the means failed. We thought we could never leave Vietnam.

My wife and all my children almost gave up, and they decided to stay no matter what happened. And then everybody so nervous. For the last two weeks I couldn't work or anything. Agency told me to tell the children to quit the school, and all the children had to stay at home all the time. Just stay home—waiting, waiting—nervous, very nervous.

Then the agency told me, "It's the time now. So bring your family to the house of a correspondent"—two-story house, very spacious. It was close to the Independence Palace, and the first day I moved the children there, there was the strafing at the palace—very close, across the street. All the children lay under the bed, because bombing everywhere. My mother-in-law stayed there with us. She wanted to share the last minute, in case she could not make it. Well, they both cried and cried. My wife desperate—she didn't want to go, to separate from her mother. But I assured her that she could make it, because I already arranged in advance, with a charity organization. They had their own plane to transport the orphanage.

This time the plane also failed. Then I decided not to go anymore, because was utter confusion and too much problem. My wife was almost giving up. She said, "No. Go back home." She went to ask the fortune teller if we could make it, and the fortune teller said, "Yes, you could." We didn't believe.

Then all the news agencies signed a joint letter to President Ford, for order Ambassador Martin to give top priority to the news agencies. So the evacuation plan started on April 22. We had to organize among ourselves, because the plane had only certain seats. We had to draw straws—who was going first. . . .

I was the one who set up the new office in Vietnam. Then I started hiring—hiring other people: a new teletype operator, an accountant, office boy, driver—to help me. And I had, by the time I left, one reporter—Vietnamese reporter—and a photographer. I left the driver behind and office boy behind, because the agency couldn't afford to do that. The reporter—he didn't want to go. Only his wife and children now live in the U.S. He stayed. He said he wanted to be a witness of history, or something crazy like that.

Then, suddenly, one afternoon I received notice: "You leave this afternoon, four o'clock." Just one hour, two hours notice. Chief of the agency drove us to the airport to make sure that nothing's going to happen. We had the escort of the U.S. officer, and there was the Vietnamese and military police guarding the airport. And I was scared at that moment. Oh, I was extremely nervous.

We went to the U.S. terminal. There was a yellow bus waiting—like a school bus—to take us right to the plane. And we marched through the tailgate into the plane, with the two MP's guarding on both sides— Vietnamese MP's. The evacuation by that time was official.

Once I got aboard the plane and once the tailgate was closed, then I could relax. Then everything was over. We were jammed up—no seats, a military plane—only side seats for the paratroop to jump. Everyone sat on the floor.

We arrived in Guam at four in the morning. Everybody hungry and cold, and when we got into the hangar, there was a reception. Well, we felt *very* happy. Then they transported us to abandoned military camp where is our living quarters. Seven days there. We had to wait until the first batch of Immigration officials arrived from Washington.

When I arrived in Guam I called New York, and news agency sent a correspondent to meet me. He asked me what I want. I needed slippers, I needed a set of chess, I needed a jacket, this and that. And he went to PX to buy everything for us. He bought a flower for my wife— everything. So we felt happy then. We lived in a building, a three-story building. We had our breakfast, lunch, and supper, still had something to eat at night when we watched the movie. Everybody was very interested to know what the future is. I was very confident. I didn't worry at all.

The Immigration people arrived, and they started processing us. We got a kind of basic card, something like that, and we carried it to Los Angeles, to Camp Pendleton.

The news agency put us in the hotel, there in Los Angeles. And the next day, I went to the office and I asked the bureau chief there if I can stay there to work, because I like Los Angeles—my first impression. He said, "I want you to go back to New York. So why don't you stay here ten days to familiarize with the city and come to the office anytime you want." He rented a car for me. I drove my wife and children around—everywhere. Ten days—just for pleasure!

So in New York, put in hotel first, in Central Park West, and relaxed for one week. They asked me to come in the office, just for a talk, a business talk. They asked me where I wanted to live, what I wanted to do. I told them, "As you know, I am an office manager in Saigon. I don't ask too much here. If you can find any job for me—I know the situation very tight. The company has not hired anybody since quite a long time. So whatever job. . . . "

They said I know a lot in the wire room; so "Why don't you just go to wire room to work there. And if you don't like it, then I'll think of something else." Same teletype machine, but this is twenty times bigger. In New York, everything is up-to-date. Hundreds machine connecting, linking with the world outside—Paris, London, Rome, Beirut, Bangkok, New Delhi, Hong Kong, everywhere. Domestic—Boston, Chicago, Los Angeles, Detroit.

I compare it with my job in Saigon. It's not very satisfying, not very exciting, not interesting. But—no other choice. It's better than anything else. Yeah, still get all the news. I still talk with people around the world on the teletype. But I have less responsibility here. Later on, maybe—maybe one or two years later I will maybe get a promotion, change to another division. . . .

# Huong Vinh

················FROM SOUTH VIETNAM, 1975··················

*She is Thien Vinh's wife. She used to be a housewife in Saigon; now she is a housewife in a New Jersey suburb. Her husband drives her to New York's Chinatown once a month, to stock up on the foods her family is used to eating. She is thirty-eight, attractive, the mother of six children, aged five to nineteen.*

My husband work for American company in Saigon. We have six children, and we live in a comfortable house. We had everything we want, everything we need: We had a car, we had a piano, washing machine, one motorcycle, one air conditioner. We had six ceiling fans. I had to leave everything behind.

We had one week to prepare. It was arranged by the company, with the American Embassy. Only Thien know. He didn't tell much. We are very sad. We couldn't decide anything. We just took a few clothes. My daughter took one book of her friends, where they write the name. Mostly we wanted . . . we have three hundred tapes of Vietnamese song. We take one, we have one now. I wish it to remember my country.

In that week, I do nothing. Just go out and look at my friends, talk with my friends. I couldn't tell them. I had to pretend, because my husband said we had to keep the secret. I look around my house, I look at everything. I cry, my daughter cry, all of us cry.

We left in silence, in the morning, very early. The little children like it. They are happy. They thought we could come back. . . .

American life is very different from Vietnamese. I miss the way every morning I meet some of my friends and we go to the market together. I miss my cousin, my sister-in-law. . . .

I hope to be happy, but I'm not really satisfied. I need a more comfortable house for my children. I look around, I see this table, these six chairs, that sofa. It's not like our house in Vietnam. We had a whole set; all pieces match, everything nice. I remember everything I have in Vietnam. Here—this house—is not like I remember my life.


# Mai Vinh

·················FROM SOUTH VIETNAM, 1975··················

*She is the daughter of Thien and Huong Vinh. There was a bitter civil war going on in Vietnam while Mai was growing up, but her memories seem like those of a middle-class American teen-ager.*

Every month, once a month, my friends come to my house in Saigon. We sleep in my bed, some on the floor. In the morning we load all the things—food and blanket—on our motorcycles and we go to the beach. It take about three hours. On the way to the beach, the people sell the food on the farm—Vietnamese food—and we buy it. At the beach we climb the hill and take some pictures and we swim and we play. At three we go back to Saigon, and my friends go back to their house. At night is a party in my house. Everybody come back—ten girls and ten boys—and my sister and her friends, too. And we dance—American music, tango, waltz, cha-cha. We make food and we talk and we laugh. . . .

[*She begins to cry.*] My father said we had to leave Vietnam, because if we stay there he will be killed, because he works for American company. The company help us. They say we have to wait, and when the plane come, we go. I went to school, but my friends didn't know I would leave. I couldn't tell them. I had to pretend, because my father said we have to keep the secret. We have time, but we didn't know anything to prepare. I didn't know anything to take with me. Some clothes is all, my traditional dress, two dictionaries. We left everything in Vietnam. I knew I will leave, but I don't prepare anything.

I'm sad. I was sad about leaving my friends, my relatives. My grandmother lives with us, but the company permit only parents and children, not grandmother, so we have to leave our grandmother. [*Cries.*] We are very sad. I have a lot of relatives stay there. I was sad about everything.

Then my father's friend comes, in the morning, early in the morning when we wake up, and said, "The airplane will come today." We left Saigon early, before everyone—April 23, and the Communists occupy Saigon on April 29.

We went first to Guam and we stayed there half a month. All the refugees stayed there. We slept and ate. We didn't do anything. My mother worries about my grandmother. [*Cries.*] We always feel sad. When we heard about the Communists occupying Saigon, we cried.

The company take us to New York. We were there in the hotel two weeks. My father is happy; he go to work in his company. We stay in the hotel. We didn't go out. It's too noisy. We don't want to live there, in New York. My father's company find a house for us in New Jersey. We hope we can be happy here.

As for me personally, I'm very sad because I have no friend with the same age to talk to, to play with. I like swimming, singing, dancing, painting, although I paint very bad. In Saigon, when the holidays come, my friends and I have often so many parties, picnics. And we are very happy. Now I don't know how my friends are, alive or dead. [*Cries.*] I miss them. I hope that I will have many new friends as lovely as my old friends.

# Kurt Schaeffer

···················FROM GERMANY, 1967·····················

It's extremely difficult to have American friends. One has acquaintances, but I would not know of anybody in this country with American background that I could call my friend. Americans, in essence, inherit friends from the previous occupants of the house they move to or the apartment they move into that comes already made with the neighborhood and friends, and it's very cordial as long as one lives in the place and promptly forgets about everybody once one moves to another place.

Presumably, American friendships are formed during the high-school years, which I don't have here, or during university years. I have observed that. Otherwise, one's friends are the people one works with and one lives next to, and it takes a real effort to break out of this circle. Also, one cannot make demands on American friends. It is a loose relationship which is, in essence, the trading of invitations; but it is not a close personal relationship which would permit you to discuss intimate or personal matters or get some *real* good advice or ask favors of any significance. Unless one was *sure* one could repay them.

# Ari Amichai (III)

···················FROM ISRAEL, 1964······················

I would like to have more real friendships and less formal friendships. In Israel, if you belong to the right group you have a lot of friends, and the acquaintanceships are much less formal than here. I mean, you can just drop suddenly in. There is no such thing like, you know, informing you ahead of time, and what have you. Israelis, in many, many aspects are more open; they're more direct. Questions that I'm not asked among Americans are not only asked, but are fully answered among Israelis. Like, for example, "What is your salary?" You know, a question like this is not asked among Americans. Every Israeli knows the salary of all his friends, of course. And no one is ashamed or tries to hide it under the pretext that it is personal. Because this keeping things to yourself—personal *this* and personal *that*—actually causes this separation. I would like a little more openness, yes. Many Americans are very blank; it is difficult to penetrate.

Everybody lives here and you hardly know your neighbors, you know. Like my brother-in-law. They live in New York. They don't know who lives behind them and on the side. Everyone is to themselves, and this is a pity, because if you need something, you find yourself isolated.

# Galina Kamenetsky

········· FROM THE USSR, 1973 ·················

Of course we miss our Russian friends. A real friend to find, it is not easy. You know, American friends—we met a lot of people. Everybody smile to you and say, "See you later," and 99 percent of them never meet us again.

# Larissa Brazovsky

············· FROM THE USSR, 1976 ·················

*In the late 1960s, faced with growing discrimination in the Soviet Union, Russian Jews began to press for the right to emigrate, previously denied Soviet citizens. Beginning in 1972, the Soviet government has been allowing a certain number to leave each year. Many have gone to Israel, but more than seven thousand settled in the United States. Among the latter was the Brazovsky family. Larissa, sixteen years old, was brought to New York by her parents. She describes her feelings one month after her arrival.*

I didn't want to come to America. I said, "Why do we have to go? Why? Why should I want to go?" I love the Russian language, Russian music, Russian books, Russian people. I said, "I don't want to go."

I was an *Oktyabrenok** at eight years, and I had a pin—a red star with Lenin in the middle. Not all children get this—only children who study well. If you are an *Oktyabrenok* and you're a good student, at thirteen you can be a *Pioneer* and you get a red ribbon to wear. I was a *Pioneer!* As a *Pioneer* you make a promise to help everyone.

After *Pioneer* comes *Komsomol. Komsomol* is a very important, very high person. We help poor people, old people. Old men, old women, they're sick, they can't go to the store. I go to their house and ask them what they need, and I go to the store and shop for them. Oh, it's wonderful to be a *Komsomol!* A *Komsomol* can't do anything bad. I

*Oktyabrenok, Pioneer, and Komsomol are names for members of Russian Communist youth organizations.

was at the head of the *Komsomol* organization in my school, the top student. And when I went to college, I would be a Communist. You have to be a *Komsomol* to be a member of the Communist party.

When the Communist party heard that my father applied for a visa, they called me to their hall and they asked me, "Why are you going?" They said, "You're going to a capitalist country. Do you want to go? Why do you want to go?" They wanted to give me money. They said, "Let your mother, your father, your brother go." But I said, "My mother's going! I'm sixteen, I must go with my mother." They took my [*Komsomol*] card and they tore it up. Ooh! I cried. I felt so bad. I was so ashamed. . . .

I had many friends in Kiev—Russian friends, not Jewish friends. In Kiev I went out with my friends. Kiev is a very beautiful city—many movies, many colleges, dance clubs. And there were many boys and girls. We went walking, we went to movies, we sang. I was hardly ever home. Here in America there are beautiful things, food, money. I can't read money, I can't talk to it. These things are not friends. I miss my friends.

I met some girls here, but they're not my friends. A friend is someone that *understands* you. A friend is someone you speak your native language with; I can speak to her in the same language, Russian. In English I want to say something and you don't understand me. I want to say something and I can't. I can't say what I want to say. I talk, but people don't understand me.

I'd like to go back to Russia—not only because of my friends. You understand, it's uncomfortable when I go on the street and I don't understand what people are saying. I go crazy! I don't understand! I'm like a baby. I don't know what people want of me.

# Sofia Rabinovich

·················· ·FROM THE USSR, 1974· ··················

*In her native country she was a practicing physician, medical researcher, lecturer, and author of many professional books and articles. Now sixty-two, she spends her time studying English and translating her papers.*

I knew each minute of my life that I am Jewish. It was my mother— when I was a little child, she *benscht licht* [blessed the candles] on Sabbath evening, Friday evening before Sabbath. Then something changed. You know, it's difficult for a child to understand. I was too young to understand, but I know that everybody stop to go to church.

Christian people stop and Jewish people stop. With the Revolution, *nobody* was religious.

When I was in high school, before World War II, nobody had a problem if he was a Jew or if he was not a Jew, because everybody was equal. But with World War Second, started grow the customs against Jews. It was because of Nazis.

I was a student in medical school, and I was in the Leningrad blockade. They closed the door to Leningrad. You cannot go out, you cannot go in, and you always under the attack of bombs. And hunger, because you had not food. It was a terrible time. I cannot explain how it was. It was unusual cold in Leningrad that time, and there was no heating, no water, no food. How to stay alive? It is difficult to believe how it was. You had special cards for some little bread. It was a little piece of bread, but it was very important. In the middle of the room, you had a little stove. And what you burn? Your desk, chairs, everything what you had.

Some people died, students died, teachers died. Some people tried to stay in bed, maybe it will help, and these people died first. But life continued, because only when you do something. . . . You lose your weight, you are like a skeleton, but you live. It's a lucky chance. We stayed alive. But I think maybe people, when they believe in something, they believe that it will be better. I think it is typical Jewish. My mother always told me, "It will be good! Leningrad will be free, and we will stay alive. Don't worry."

I finished medical school in 1942 and I received a diploma. Then I served in the hospital. After the war, I began to work in the research institute as a radiologist. A scientist invited me, and he recommended me to a position in research. I was very lucky, because it was not difficult for me. It was very, very interesting. I worked very hard. I wrote a lot of interesting things. I was very active—tried to do some reports, the conferences, the meetings—and I always had what to say.

I grew from one position to another, and I received the highest that can be for a man—not a woman, for a man! For a woman, it was unusual to be chief of a special research department. It was a very high position. It didn't matter that I was Jewish. They are not so foolish. They know what is good and what is bad, and they need people who do something good. So if they need something, and you're Jewish, well. . . .

*How could you give all that up?*

For my son. Because for my son it was no future there. You know, he had the golden medal after school. See, it's special. It's not often it's given. For special persons who are not only smart, but they do very well. It is special for their results in their studying. And he received the golden medal.

He decided to be a doctor, and he finished medical school in 1972. He was an excellent student, and he finished very good. When a person finished very good, he could choose his place. If he is an excellent student and he finish with the highest position, highest honor, it's no question: He always choose and he do *what* he want. But my son could not. He said that he wanted to be in research, and they told him, "No! You will not go in research. You will go as a practitioner in a little town, in the country." Because he was a Jew. It was not another reason—everybody knows, everybody knows. It is enough to have a point in your passport that you are a Jew.

It is known that everybody in Russia has a passport and there is a point 5. Everything begin with point 5 and finish with point 5: nationality. If you work, you apply for something, always they raise the point about nationality.* And of course for a Jewish person, every step is difficulter than for another. And everybody knows it in Russia—everybody!

He was disappointed. But, then, a young man, he started to work, and he had some interest in this work, and. . . . But I understand it go from bad to worse, and he will never have a position in the hospital. It's impossible. We always thought about our son, and we wanted to do for him the best. I had a very good position, but I was disappointed. So we decided to go from Russia.

It was excellent time, 1974. The relation between Russia and United States, it was the best. They needed United States as a very strong country, and they needed some help. For example, wheat they needed. It was the best time. We were lucky. We applied for a visa. I left my job, and my husband left his job, and my son left his job. We waited maybe three or four months. They sent us a card, said, "You can come for visa." . . .

The first stop was Vienna. We stayed there maybe five days. Then Rome, six months. My son prepared for the medical exam. He started to study, and he passed his exam in Rome, and he came here as a doctor.

The Jewish organization HIAS, they care about us. It was never in history, this kind of help. I think no nation has this kind of way the Jewish people now have. It's wonderful. We had no problems, because the Jewish organization sent us a special worker that was so kind. It's difficult to understand that people can be so kindly to another people. She did everything. She met us at the airport, gave us a hotel, showed us where to shop, where to live. She explained us what the life is here.

*In the Soviet Union, *Evreski* ("Hebrew") is considered a nationality.

Each step they supported us. They sent us to school, they gave us money. They did for us absolutely everything what is necessary.

We came in February, and in May my son began to work. He found a position in a hospital. He's a internist, a resident, first year. He study and he work very hard. Of course, he receive not enough money, but it's enough for us, this life that we have. So we finished with the Jewish organization help.

I heard "Voice of America," and I read the special magazine *America*, published here and sent to Russia. But we met more than we expected, because when you see the real life. . . . First of all impressed me the religious ways.

We are not religious, because nobody in our life taught us this part of life. But maybe now we will learn how to be religious, because I believe in religion, that it teaches people something special. I think religion is absolutely necessary for people. I have not had this part of life, and my experience told me that people need something. It's not enough to have bread, to be lucky in your family, to have books and music and poetry. It cannot be a real life without religion.

I like the way that America has in religion. When I came, I was surprised that I saw little different churches: a Methodist church, Orthodox church, Catholic church, the temple. Everybody go and do what he want and choose his religious way. It makes America great. American people don't understand how lucky they are that they can do practically what they want. It's a real freedom.

We saw we can go to the temple. I can tell you that I *never* thought it can be so. The first time, when we were in East Orange, people invited us to the temple. We were surprised that the people can come and they are not afraid, and they pray, and everything is so beautiful. Until now, I never had the possibility to be glad that I am Jewish. It very impressed me, and I like it very much.

If young Jewish womans want to be together, they can have special organizations, and they are free to do what they want! Two womans came and took me to a big group—maybe a hundred or more people. It was a beautiful evening, because it was a lot of fun. I like this way here, that you have some prepared beautiful dishes, decorations, and flowers. And then a concert, and some of them gave a show. A person from Hadassah spoke to them and asked them to give some money to Hadassah. Then another woman, another problem. All problems they discussed, it was Jewish problems. For me it was a very good experience, very interesting, and I never understood that it could be so. . . .

People here are rich. They don't understand that they are rich. The houses, how they live, the comfort, the things that they have, a lot of clothes. . . . You know, it is not necessary to have absolutely everything like you have here. Of course, *we* had a lot in Russia, a little bit more money than somebody else. Our salary was higher than somebody else. For our family it was not so bad. What it is to be not poor in Russia, it is to be poor here. We had bread, clothes, a nice apartment. What is a nice apartment? Three little rooms—it is the best apartment that could be. We had not so many different foods as here. And everything only in season. You cannot have fresh fruits and vegetables all seasons like here. You could get milk in the morning—not every day, of course. And you can have maybe one or two kind of sausage and maybe one or two kind of cheese—not in each shop.

There's not enough food. My friend called me before I left Russia and said he's in line. It was evening, and he is in line for meat. In the morning, he will receive some meat. For us this was not a problem. I had many patients, and some were managers of food stores. These people liked me because I was their doctor, and when they knew some meat was coming into the store, or when they have some special food, something good, they called me to tell me to hurry to the store. So always when there was meat, we had meat. But it is long, hard job to shop for food in Russia. You have to go to many stores until maybe you can find what you want, what you need. And then you have to stand in line in all stores, long lines. It's a lot of time, a lot of work.

But people in Russia try to be happy, too. To always worry, to always feel that you are unhappy—it's a terrible way. You will die if you will be always worried. You try to find the best way for you. Some people like music. In Russia we have beautiful place for music, we have good museums. If you want to be happy, you can be happy in any place. Russia is a big country and I think a rich country, but it's another way of living there. The people is not worse than here in America, not worse than here. It's a lot of very nice people and a lot of educated people and very interesting people, but—another life, another life.

## Yuri Sinelnikov

*Short and wiry, balding, with bright staring eyes, he nervously chain-smokes as he talks with a staccato delivery. Moderately dissident in his native country, he came here for creative freedom but is now resentful because he hasn't yet had an opportunity to exercise it. While waiting for one of his scripts to be translated into English, he is looking for work as a teacher of Russian. Meanwhile, he stays at home in the Bronx, watching television, studying English, and speaking on*

*the phone to his many Russian and American friends, trying to
arrange deals, contacts, meetings, jobs in the film or television
industry.*

It was a terrible time when I was born—1937—because three months
after my birth was arrested my father, and he was murdered later in a
Stalin concentration camp. My father worked as engineer for ships. He
didn't have interest for politics, but at this time were murdered many
intellectual people. In our family were arrested, a little bit later, two
brothers of my father and my aunt's husband. Four people in our family
were arrested and murdered. But I knew this only when I was fifteen or
sixteen years old. It was secret and mother told us only later, because
in Stalin time it was so dangerous, so dangerous. Because people who
were arrested and murdered in Stalin concentration camp were enemy
of people.

When my father was arrested, my mother had three children: my
brother—we are twins—and my thirteen-year-old sister. And we lived
in one room—five of us, because there was also my grandmother—in
communal flat, in the center of Leningrad. We lived maybe twenty-
nine years in this same apartment. Only last seven or eight years I lived
in separate apartment.

Five families lived in communal flat, with one kitchen for all
families, one bathroom for all families. In this apartment lived so
different people, and interest of these people so very different. Of
course, if you live in this condition, absolutely impossible to have good
relations between people, because it is abnormal. If you must wait in
line in the bathroom and the kitchen, absolutely abnormal life. It was a
terrible life, but majority of Soviet people lived and live now in these
circumstances.

It was so long ago—maybe I was seven or eight or nine years old—I
felt that I am Jew. It's so difficult to explain, but you *feel*, you feel in
your skin every day, every hour. You feel if you work, you feel if you
study in institute, you feel if you live in communal flat, you feel if you
walk on the street. You feel this all the time.

It is very easy in Russia to know you are Jewish. All Russian people
have passport. This is special document, and in this document you
have a few lines. The first line is your last name, the second line is your
first name, third line is name of your father, fourth line is year you are
born, and fifth line is very famous line in Russian passport: your
nationality. If you would like to get job, if you would like to join an
institute, etc., you must show this document. Without this document,
absolutely impossible Russian life. All Russian people know absolutely well who is Jew and who is not Jew.

When I graduated from high school in 1955, I decided to go in university, in literature faculty. I studied in the evening, and I worked in movie studio as assistant of cameraman. A friend of my mother worked at this time in movie studio, and this friend helped me to get job. I graduated after six years and decided to work in movie studio all time of life. First I worked as assistant cameraman, and then I worked as assistant of film director, and last nine years I worked as film director and scriptwriter. I worked in two Leningrad studios. First studio was for educational movies, and second studio was for documentary movies. Very big studios.

First I didn't have trouble, but trouble I had little bit later, when I worked as film director and I made one movie about Solovetskiye Island. This island is on the north of Russia. It is a very interesting place in Russian history. This island—before the Revolution, it was fortress and monastery; but after Revolution, it was a concentration camp. If you read a book of Solzhenitsyn, *Gulag Archipelago*, many pages of this book are about this place, about this concentration camp.

Our movie must be, of course, not about Soviet concentration camp, but about geography and history of this place. But when we began this movie, I thought about my father, who was arrested and murdered in Soviet concentration camp. It is absolutely impossible to know where, because it's absolutely unknown. It's possible that my father was murdered in *this* concentration camp, in Solovetskiye, and I decided to tell maybe a little bit about this time when on this island was a Soviet concentration camp.

But absolutely impossible to do, to tell all truth in Russian movies, because to show movie in the movie theater, first must show many people in department of movies in Moscow. We showed this movie in Moscow, but we had trouble. I went to Moscow many times with this movie, and each time when I showed this movie in Moscow, I must change. Change, change, and change—many times. We had so many things, episodes, in this movie—interviews with people who were arrested in 1937, 1941, and in other years. And many episodes we must throw away—for example, first episode: many people who came to cemetery as reminiscence for these people from concentration camp. We film it—these people—with candid camera.

Finally, this movie was very changed, and the movie which will be possible for people to see on the screen was not what we thought about. When this movie was finished, it was absolutely another movie. In a short time, I lose my job.

I found a job in another movie studio, but I made only TV commercial. It was a new field for Russia, because Russian people don't have enough merchandise, foods, etc. But it was maybe prestige for Russian government, and so we made this TV commercial. It was very interesting job for me, because we studied experience of American and European TV commercials. There is in Moscow one organization who has relationship with foreign countries, and it is possible to show in this office different TV commercial—American and European and Japanese TV commercial. Different people, who went to foreign countries, brought to Russia different literature about TV commercials in America and European countries. And I also saw in this special office for filmmakers many American movies which were impossible for other people to see—for example, *Midnight Cowboy, Godfather, Easy Rider, The Graduate, Rosemary's Baby.*

Of course, absolutely impossible to visit foreign countries. It is privilege of a small group of Russian people. It is so difficult to get permission of the government to visit foreign countries as tourist because, if many Russian people will visit foreign countries, these people will see real life in these countries, and is so big difference between this life and life of Soviet Russia. So it is impossible for Russians to see another life.

Russian life like a life in jail. All Russian people have a special stamp in passport that you live in this street, in this building, in this apartment, in this room. It is forbidden to move in another street, in another apartment. You must get special permission of Russian police. And it is absolutely impossible to move from one city to another city. If you go to another city, then in this city in which you lived now must move the same number of family, of people. It's a life of slaves, of slaves. But people got accustomed to it during so many years, to be slaves—before the Revolution, and after Revolution much more. I think that majority of Russian people don't think about it.

Little by little, I began to hate this life, this system, this government. I felt the situation especially the last years when I worked in movie studio. Absolutely impossible to do in movie studio what you want. Majority—not majority, *all* Russian movies, all Russian plays, all Russian books—are propaganda, only propaganda. I hate the system; I don't like to live all my life in jail. We decided—I and my wife—to leave Russia.

There is a special office in Leningrad and different cities of USSR, for visa for foreign people and for Soviet people. And you must go to this office. For Russian government, we must say we go only in Israel. But I didn't want to go to Israel, because Israel don't have a big movie production and only America has a big movie production. And I consider that in America there is the most democracy in the whole world.

So you go to this special office, and you must have so many papers, so many documents—from work, from apartment where you live. I must get from my movie studio a special paper, my character. It's paradox, Russian paradox. If I leave Russia, why I need this character paper? Why I need? For whom? For American government? [*Chuckles.*] That's funny.

So in my movie studio, we have a big meeting—maybe two hours, maybe one hundred people in a big hall—and different people asked me different stupid questions. For example, "You will do in Israel movie against Soviet government?" "You are enemy of Soviet government?" "Are your wife Jewish, too?" "No." "Why did she decide to leave Russia?" I answer, "She is my wife." And one woman asked me, "If a man does stupid thing, does his wife do this same stupid thing?" I answer, "My wife decided that her husband does not do stupid thing." And this is the questions—very funny.

I lose my job that day. My wife didn't work now, too, because it was a little bit dangerous for her. She worked in Russian institute, in a special program with security; and if you have security, you must wait for visa for one, two, or three years. We could live, because my salary before was much higher than medium salary in Russia, and we had some money saved. Medium salary is maybe one hundred rubles in the month. My salary was three hundred rubles in a month.

Of course, we needed money for visa, because visa is so expensive—about one thousand rubles. We needed maybe three thousand rubles, because we must buy two visas, for me and for my wife, and tickets for airplane and for baggage. My brother left Russia first, and when he came in Italy, he went to—not HIAS, but international Jewish organization—I forget the name. And this organization sended to us two parcels—different things, clothes—which we can sell and have money for visa. Also, we had in Russia antiques, furniture, and different things. It was forbidden by Russian government to take out antiques and furniture, so we sold it.

We waited three months for visa. Many people, whom I considered as our friend, left us during this time. Afraid to lose job, afraid . . . afraid . . . .[*Sighs.*] Ninety-nine percent of Russian people are afraid. But several friends visited us very often—not afraid.

Then we got visa and left by plane for Vienna. It was a very good feeling. We flew from Leningrad and landed in Vienna. It was absolutely another feeling. It's very difficult to explain, but—maybe—a feeling of freedom. It was in the evening, and one man from Jewish office met us. We didn't have money, because it is forbidden by Russian government, but we knew—from radio, "Voice of America"—that Jewish organization HIAS will help us.

We lived in hotel in the center of Vienna for about two weeks, and then we went by train through mountains to Roma and lived there maybe about three months. People wait for visa in Roma—visa for America—during three months, four months. American government must give permission to enter in America, because we are refugees. We have special card. When we arrived in America, Jewish agency took us from Airport Kennedy directly to an apartment. In the next days came a social worker from Jewish agency, and she helped us during this time in all things. A very good woman.

When we arrived we decided my wife will work at first, and I will have time. I knew very well that with my profession will be very big problem, because for my profession it's necessary to know very well language and to meet with different people, to have good connections. I know connection and recommendation, it's very important here in America.

But I didn't think that it will be so difficult with profession of my wife. She is engineer, but she knows very well work of draftsman, too. It is very difficult to find job even as draftsman, because majority American people don't like immigrants from Russia. American people consider that Russian immigrants have bad experience, are bad engineers. They are afraid of Russian people. I don't know—maybe spies, maybe politics, I don't know exactly. It's very difficult to explain in speech what I feel in my soul, that these people afraid of us. But I know absolutely exactly that it's not problem for American people to find job. I know that many people who arrived in America from India find job. These people find job so easy. But for Russian people very difficult. And now my wife studies in school for beauty culture. . . .

I meet many people. Parents of these people arrived in America from Russia many years ago, from small Ukrainian towns, and didn't have professions, didn't have education. It was absolutely another thing; it was absolutely another time in America. And these people consider that we must—immigrants who arrive now from Russia—must begin with simple work.

Engineer works as washer of dishes, for example. Film director takes garbage, etc. It's not good. It will be necessary for Americans to help us to find better jobs, because now many people who arrive in America from Russia send letters in Russia. Russian people have information about life of immigrants from Russia. It is prestige matter for America.

I have so many ideas for movies, but it is so early to say. From time to time I watch TV and movies about Soviet life. But these movies are so funny, so naïve. These movies cannot tell the real Russian life, because the people who film these movies don't know real Russian life. I don't remember now exactly the name of these movies, but, for example, movie about a Soviet biological scientist, Lysenko. Another movie with famous actor Clark Gable, about love between Russian ballerina and—it's so funny, so stupid. So many movies about Russian spies. It will be for me much easier to tell American people real Russian life. It is impossible for American filmmakers to know simple Russian man, with medium Russian salary, in usual Russian apartment. This side of Russian life, it will be interesting, absolutely sure, for American people, because this side is absolutely unknown. . . .

I am absolutely happy that I left Russia, and I am sorry that many people who like to leave Russia cannot leave, because maybe parents, maybe they are afraid for new life, maybe. . . . The first reason why we leave Russia, it is because we would like to have freedom. But majority of Russian people don't understand what freedom is, because Russian people didn't know what freedom is. And these people, majority of immigrant people who arrive in America from Russia, don't need freedom. I spoke with many of these people: "Why you left Russia?" And these people don't know why. Many of them would like to see a new country, new cities, many would like to have a big salary, become rich people. But only reason to leave Russia is for freedom.

I have freedom here. I can see here not propaganda movies, not propaganda plays, not propaganda literature. I can talk with different people. If I want, I can move in another city, in another country. Maybe I don't go in another country, but I know absolutely exactly that is possible. Is feeling, feeling.

# Vo Thi Tam

···················· FROM VIETNAM, 1979 ····················

*In the summer of 1979, the world's press and television screens were filled with heartrending photographs of the Indochinese "boat people" who fled their Communist homelands in flimsy boats. An estimated 40 percent of them died before finding temporary shelter in a refugee camp.*

*Vo Thi Tam was one of the lucky ones who eventually made it to the United States. A few days after her arrival here, she told her story in the living room of a small house near Seattle where she was staying with her sister's family. Tears streamed down her cheeks as she spoke.*

My husband was a former officer in the South Vietnamese air force. After the fall of that government in 1975, he and all the other officers were sent to a concentration camp for reeducation. When they let him out of the camp, they forced all of us to go to one of the "new economic zones," that are really just jungle. There was no organization, there was no housing, no utilities, no doctor, nothing. They gave us tools and a little food, and that was it. We just had to dig up the land and cultivate it. And the land was very bad.

It was impossible for us to live there, so we got together with some other families and bought a big fishing boat, about thirty-five feet long.

Altogether, there were thirty-seven of us that were to leave—seven men, eight women, and the rest children. I was five months pregnant.

After we bought the boat we had to hide it, and this is how: We just anchored it in a harbor in the Mekong Delta. It's very crowded there and very many people make their living aboard the boats by going fishing, you know. So we had to make ourselves like them. We took turns living and sleeping on the boat. We would maneuver the boat around the harbor, as if we were fishing or selling stuff, you know, so the Communist authorities could not suspect anything.

Besides the big boat, we had to buy a smaller boat in order to carry supplies to it. We had to buy gasoline and other stuff on the black market—everywhere there is a black market—and carry these supplies, little by little, on the little boat to the big boat. To do this we sold jewelry and radios and other things that we had left from the old days.

On the day we left we took the big boat out very early in the morning—all the women and children were in that boat and some of the men. My husband and the one other man remained in the small boat, and they were to rendezvous with us outside the harbor. Because if the harbor officials see too many people aboard, they might think there was something suspicious. I think they were suspicious anyway. As we went out, they stopped us and made us pay them ten taels of gold—that's a Vietnamese unit, a little heavier than an ounce. That was nearly all we had.

Anyway, the big boat passed through the harbor and went ahead to the rendezvous point where we were to meet my husband and the other man in the small boat. But there was no one there. We waited for two hours, but we did not see any sign of them. After a while we could see a Vietnamese navy boat approaching, and there was a discussion on board our boat and the end of it was the people on our boat decided to leave without my husband and the other man. [*Long pause.*]

When we reached the high seas, we discovered, unfortunately, that the water container was leaking and only a little bit of the water was left. So we had to ration the water from then on. We had brought some rice and other food that we could cook, but it was so wavy that we could not cook anything at all. So all we had was raw rice and a few lemons and very little water. After seven days we ran out of water, so all we had to drink was the sea water, plus lemon juice.

Everyone was very sick and, at one point, my mother and my little boy, four years old, were in agony, about to die. And the other people on the boat said that if they were agonizing like that, it would be better to throw them overboard so as to save them pain.

During this time we had seen several boats on the sea and had waved to them to help us, but they never stopped. But that morning, while we were discussing throwing my mother and son overboard, we could see another ship coming and we were very happy, thinking maybe it was people coming to save us. When the two boats were close together, the people came on board from there—it happened to be a Thai boat—and they said all of us had to go on the bigger boat. They made us all go there and then they began to search us—cutting off our blouses, our bras, looking everywhere. One woman, she had some rings she hid in her bra, and they undressed her and took out everything. My mother had a statue of Our Lady, a very precious one, you know, that she had had all her life—she begged them just to leave the statue to her. But they didn't want to. They slapped her and grabbed the statue away.

Finally they pried up the planks of our boat, trying to see if there was any gold or jewelry hidden there. And when they had taken everything, they put us back on our boat and pushed us away.

They had taken all our maps and compasses, so we didn't even know which way to go. And because they had pried up the planks of our boat to look for jewelry, the water started getting in. We were very weak by then. But we had no pump, so we had to use empty cans to bail the water out, over and over again.

That same day we were boarded again by two other boats, and these, too, were pirates. They came aboard with hammers and knives and everything. But we could only beg them for mercy and try to explain by sign language that we'd been robbed before and we had nothing left. So those boats let us go and pointed the way to Malaysia for us.

That night at about 9:00 P.M. we arrived on the shore, and we were so happy finally to land somewhere that we knelt down on the beach and prayed, you know, to thank God.

While we were kneeling there, some people came out of the woods and began to throw rocks at us. They took a doctor who was with us and they beat him up and broke his glasses, so that from that time on he couldn't see anything at all. And they tied him up, his hands behind him like this [demonstrates], and they beat up the rest of the men, too. They searched us for anything precious that they could find, but there was nothing left except our few clothes and our documents. They took these and scattered them all over the beach.

Then five of the Malaysian men grabbed the doctor's wife, a young woman with three little children, and they took her back into the woods and raped her—all five of them. Later, they sent her back, completely naked, to the beach.

After this, the Malaysians forced us back into the boat and tried to push us out to sea. But the tide was out and the boat was so heavy with all of us on board that it just sank in the sand. So they left us for the night. . . .

In the morning, the Malaysian military police came to look over the area, and they dispersed the crowd and protected us from them. They let us pick up our clothes and our papers from the beach and took us in a big truck to some kind of a warehouse in a small town not far away. They gave us water, some bread, and some fish, and then they carried us out to Bidong Island. . . .

Perhaps in the beginning it was all right there, maybe for ten thousand people or so, but when we arrived there were already fifteen to seventeen thousand crowded onto thirty acres. There was no housing, no facilities, nothing. It was already full near the beach, so we had to go up the mountain and chop down trees to make room for ourselves and make some sort of a temporary shelter. There was an old well, but the water was very shallow. It was so scarce that all the refugees had to wait in a long line, day and night, to get our turn of the water. We would have a little can, like a small Coke can at the end of a long string, and fill that up. To fill about a gallon, it would take an hour, so we each had to just wait, taking our turn to get our Coke can of water. Sometimes one, two, or three in the morning we would get our water. I was pregnant, and my boys were only four and six, and my old mother with me was not well, but we all had to wait in line to get our water. That was just for cooking and drinking, of course. We had to do our washing in the sea.

The Malaysian authorities did what they could, but they left most of the administration of the camp to the refugees themselves, and most of us were sick. There were, of course, no sanitary installations, and many people had diarrhea. It was very hard to stop sickness under those conditions. My little boys were sick and my mother could hardly walk. And since there was no man in our family, we had no one to chop the wood for our cooking, and it was very hard for us just to survive. When the monsoons came, the floor of our shelter was all mud. We had one blanket and a board to lie on, and that was all. The water would come down the mountain through our shelter, so we all got wet.

After four months in the camp it was time for my baby to be born. Fortunately, we had many doctors among us, because many of them had tried to escape from Vietnam, so we had medical care but no equipment. There was no bed there, no hospital, no nothing, just a wooden plank to lie down on and let the baby be born, that was all. Each mother had to supply a portion of boiling water for the doctor to use and bring it with her to the medical hut when it was time. It was a very difficult delivery. The baby came legs first. But, fortunately, there were no complications. After the delivery I had to get up and go back to my shelter to make room for the next woman.

When we left Vietnam we were hoping to come to the United States, because my sister and her husband were here already. They came in 1975 when the United States evacuated so many people. We had to wait in the camp a month and a half to be interviewed, and then very much longer for the papers to be processed. Altogether we were in the camp seven months.

All this time I didn't know what had happened to my husband, although I hoped that he had been able to escape some other way and was, perhaps, in another camp, and that when I came to the United States I would find him.

We flew out here by way of Tokyo and arrived the first week in July. It was like waking up after a bad nightmare. Like coming out of hell into paradise. If only—. [*Breaks down, rushes from room.*]

*Shortly after she arrived in this country, Vo Thi Tam learned that her husband had been captured on the day of their escape and was back in a "reeducation" camp in Vietnam.*

# Johanna and Ali Patel

·················FROM SOUTH AFRICA, 1978··················

*Johanna Patel is a white woman, from an Afrikaans-speaking family. Her husband Ali is a native-born South African of Indian ancestry, officially "colored" by the laws of his country. It was a criminal offense for them to associate, love one another. To marry was out of the question. Yet they lived together in Johannesburg for two years in hiding, in fear, before their flight to this country. What makes it possible for some people to flout the laws and customs of their country, their families, their training?*

JOHANNA: It's unbelievable the way everybody thinks in South Africa. We learn from childhood, when you address a black man, he's not allowed to answer you back. Even if you're a kid and you're addressing a black, he's not allowed to answer back. As a little girl, I watched my father screaming at this black who worked for us. Instead of using nice words, he used the most disgusting language. They just weren't treated as human. Most people in South Africa just live from day to day and don't give a thought to "Why are these people bad? Who says they're bad? What proof have they got?" I couldn't figure it out.

Ever since I could think for myself, I thought, "If they're supposed to be so bad, the blacks, just because of the color of the skin, then why the hell are they here?" I didn't hear this from anybody, but I couldn't see the point of treating dogs and cats better than they treat blacks, and I thought to myself, "Why should I, as a white person, have the right to be superior of someone that's just got a different color skin than me?" Because a lot of them are as smart as a lot of the whites, and the ones that are not so smart, it's not their fault; it's just that they don't get the proper education. The government doesn't supply them with the proper books and schools and universities and things. You can't compare them with the whites, not at all.

*Did you ever express these thoughts to anyone?*

Yes, I did. And that's where the big break in my family came. My mother had died when I was seven, and my father when I was twelve, so I had only my sisters and my guardians, and I didn't get on with any of them. My sister used to call me *Kaffirbrudie. Kaffir* is what they call a nonwhite if they want to degrade him, and a *brudie* is Afrikaans and it means "brother." They tried to degrade me, but it didn't catch on. I just said, "Well, too bad." My family were rich and they thought they were better than other people, and they never could agree with my thoughts or with the friends that I brought home. My father had left me some money, so finally I left.

Then I was all alone, and I was lonely. . . . By the night that Ali and I met, I felt really lost, helpless. I had it in mind that I was going to commit suicide. I had actually gone out and bought a gas stove, one of those little Primus stoves. In fact, I was going to do it that very night. It was standing by my piano in the living room that night that he first came to my apartment with his friend. I didn't know he was Indian, because he was fair and I'd never really met an Indian before, a fair Indian. I thought Indians were black, you know. I invited them in for coffee, and immediately Ali and I, we took an interest in one another and we talked a lot.

While we were talking, he spotted the stove, and he said, "What do you need a gas stove for?" He immediately caught on. He burst into tears. I was taken by surprise, because it was the first time in my life that a person cried over me. I was stunned. I had my mouth wide open, and I just stared at him. I couldn't believe that someone was actually crying because I wanted to die, you know.

After we had coffee, he asked me whether I liked to go fishing, and I said yes, because I did. And he said, "Well, I usually go fishing at the Mahli Dam. Would you come with me?" So that same night we took off, just the two of us. By the time we got there it was about four in the morning, and we sat and watched the sun rise. What was beautiful was, while we were there, they opened up the gates of the dam and the water came splashing out. Oh, that was fantastic! We sat in the car and later we got out and had a little campfire. There's a lot of space there, where people can be really private.

*What did you think, Ali, that night when you first met Johanna?*

JOHANNA: What did you think, my darling? Tell me, I'm burning.

ALI: Well, I thought you were the girl I was going to end up with. [*Laughs with a soft, knowing laugh.*] I couldn't live without her after the first week. I'd had a lot of girlfriends in my life and I never really felt like this. What was happening to me? I couldn't eat, I couldn't sleep, I couldn't do anything until I was with her. When I was with her, I felt very much at ease. I'd reached a certain age and I'm older than her, but I just felt this was something new; it had never happened to me before, because I had never been in love before.

I had a friend there in South Africa, who was very close to me, and he talked to me every morning, and he'd look at me and he'd tell me, "Listen, I've known you all my life and we grew up together, but I've never known you like this." And I said, "Yes, I know. You've just got to leave me alone so I can find my bearings, because I don't seem to know how to communicate anymore." I couldn't tell him anything about her, because it was becoming so difficult because she was white. She was pretty, but that wasn't all. It was her personality and the way she treated me. I knew there were going to be lots of problems, and I knew we'd have trouble, but I made my mind up. She was the girl for me. I wanted her for myself and I wanted to marry her. After that, everything fell into place.

*Were you worried, Johanna, about the problems you might have?*

JOHANNA: No, because I had made a promise to God that the first man that came along and gave me his love, and who I fell in love with, no matter who he was, I would stick to him until death part us. And it turned out to be a nonwhite, and it didn't matter to me that he was a nonwhite. The fact that I had someone in love with me was enough for me, and I was prepared to even give up my life for that person.

We became engaged two weeks after we met. When Ali used to come to see me, he never took the elevator. He walked up the stairs, you know, eight stories. He used to come at ten at night, and he'd leave at four or four-thirty in the morning, not to be seen by anyone. One weekend, Ali decided he was going to spend the whole night with me in my flat, and, by chance, I got a telegram from my sister that she's coming to Johannesburg with her husband and she might spend the night with me. I wrote to her, "I'm sorry, I've been invited away. I won't be there for the whole week." And I kept my lights off that night.

Ali and I were talking in the bed, and the next thing I know, there's a knock at the door. I didn't answer it, because I knew that the lights were off and they might see I'm not there. But then I heard my sister's voice, and I heard her saying, "Look. The bathroom window's open. Let's climb through." I decided it's better to let them come in than to let them find me like this, hiding behind the door or in bed. And I figured I didn't see any reason why my sister should give me away. So I introduced them, and told them that Ali was an Arab. And Ali, he knew how to lie, so he told them a lot about Iran. He's never been there in his life, but he really convinced them for a while.

Later, when they found out he was Indian, I had a fight with my sister on the telephone. She wanted to break us up. My sister said, "What do you want to live with that guy for? He's a coolie."

I said to her, "What makes you so much better? Why is he no good?"

She said, again, "He's a coolie."

"All right, did God say because his skin is black that he's no good?"

She said, "Look. If you're going to drag the church into this, I'm not going to talk any further with you." And she slammed down the phone.

I didn't bother to keep contact after that.

They threatened me, and I said, "Carry on. I don't mind. If you want me in jail, go ahead; but remember, if I'm caught, the next morning you'll find your names in the paper, and I'll make sure that everyone else's name and address in the family is mentioned in the press, too." I knew that I was safe, because they wouldn't want something like that to happen. They sent my guardian to see me, and he tried to put me off from Ali, too, but I said, "I'm sorry. I am sure that I'm in love. I'm not going to leave him. Not for you, not for money, not for anyone, and least of all, not for color." We wanted to leave the country then, but they wouldn't give me permission to leave or sign for my passport. And I was only nineteen, so I couldn't get one on my own.

We decided to move in with his family in the Indian community. They had a house there, you see. I stopped working and I stayed in the house with them. I never left there, except at night. Imagine. For two years I just sat in the house; never went out, never saw the sun. No wonder I'm so white, you know. [*Chuckles.*] Sometimes I would go out in the car with Ali for a little ride after dark, but I would crouch down below the seat when we went through the white area. Otherwise, I stayed home. I would sketch or write a poem, do some housework. I never went outside in the daytime.

His family were wonderful to me. I haven't got words to explain how wonderful they were. In the beginning, when I met him, and when I thought about black and white, I thought to myself, I'm going to suffer. But his family treated me better than my own mother and father. My mother-in-law never spoke about me as a daughter-in-law; she said I was a daughter, and yet I wasn't even married to her son.

When we were living there with his parents, even in the night when we were in our room and the curtains were drawn, we would sleep sort of uneasy, as if we were expecting someone to jump in, you know. We couldn't be at ease. We'd simply keep the windows closed and the curtains drawn. After two years, not even the neighbors knew I was living there. It was a small house. It had only three bedrooms and a bathroom, a lounge and a dining room and kitchen. That's all. Only once, in those two years, I went out in the yard; that's when my mother-in-law wanted me to plant some seeds for her. I dressed like an Indian woman, and while I was gardening, the police were driving by. They were looking for a nonwhite that hadn't got a pass. You know, you have to carry a passbook in South Africa, and it gives you the right to be there. They can pull that book out and inspect it at any time. The police kept driving up and down, and I was just kneeling in the garden with my back to them, but they didn't notice me. There are Indians more fair than I am, and I had my hair tinted black; and with my Indian clothes on, they just didn't notice me. That was the only time I went out in those two years in the daytime.

I really realized what these people go through, suffering, when I actually stayed with them. You don't think further than the fact that they're not allowed to use the toilets. But if you have to live there, you think, "What about the kids?"

ALI: I had a nephew in Johannesburg, and one day I took him to the park. They have all these little amusement things—little horses that you put a dime in and ride, and that sort of thing. It's very appealing, a beautiful park. And my nephew wanted to go in there, and I said, "No. You can't." And he said, "Why? Why aren't we allowed to play there?" He saw the white children playing. He was about four years old. I found it very difficult to make him understand, but I thought it would be best to tell him the truth, so that he wouldn't get to know of this later on, when it would be more difficult for him. I told him, "Look, you are born a black man in this country, and therefore you're not supposed to play there." But he didn't give up. He said, "Even if I'm black . . ." and then he looked at his skin and he looked at mine, and he said, "But I'm not black, I'm brown." I didn't know what to do anymore, so I said, "Yes, but you're just a shade darker than the white man." He couldn't understand this. He thought a little more, and then he said, "But even if I am a little browner, what's the difference? Why can't I go play on the swing?" It took a child to see the illogic, the senseless idea behind the whole thing.

JOHANNA: As soon as I was twenty-one, I applied for a passport. We picked the United States to go to because it was the first country to start with equal rights. As far as we were concerned, it was the only country. Even though we knew that there were people that were prejudiced here we knew they couldn't say anything or do anything about us, because here we would have rights.

I had no trouble getting a passport, because I was white and there was nothing on record against me. But Ali had a little problem, because a person who was ever a political prisoner in South Africa has a symbol next to his name, and every symbol means something—good or bad or very bad—and when he went for a passport, they said there was a *G*, and the passport control man said, "Oh, you're one of those, h'mm?" My husband went for three months, every day, to the office, before he got his visa. The trouble was, when he was a boy of nineteen, someone paid him to distribute some antigovernment pamphlets. He was in jail for twenty-nine days, and that was still on his record.

ALI: I knew that at any given moment I could be rearrested again. There could always be trouble. At any occasion—if I felt happy or if I felt something for the future or if my business was going well, the thought would strike me that this was possible and that they could come to me and say, "We're taking you back to detention." That's why the Ninety Day law* is so inhuman, because they can literally arrest anyone in the street for anything they wish, you know, and put them away. Some of the people that I met in jail that time had been there for many terms of detention. They had sort of lost their sense of reasoning, you know. They didn't seem like humans anymore; because their hair was long, their bodies never had a bath, they hadn't been given proper food. One of the men in my cell couldn't even tell me his name, but his condition was the way it was because of the solitary confinement. It can lead to insanity. They give them electric shocks, anything they want. It's unbelievable.

JOHANNA: Finally, we got our visas and our plane tickets, and we left the country without being noticed. His parents drove us down to the airport. They dropped me off and waited for me to go in, and then he came in. He sat with his family. Everybody had come to see him off, and I was sitting there a little way from them, pretending not to know him. I didn't have anyone there. I didn't mind. We walked separately through customs, and nobody stopped us, and we got on the plane separately.

The moment they told us we can smoke and take our seat belts off, he got up and came over and sat next to me. It was a South African plane, with a South African crew, and it was a little tricky; but Ali

---

*Under South African law a person can be held in prison for ninety days with no formal charges against him, and this can be repeated indefinitely.

couldn't wait any longer. If they had wanted to, they could have turned the plane around and dropped us back. But, by that time, we were over the borders, over international ground.

We were on a direct flight to New York, but there was a blizzard and the plane was sent to Bermuda. We got there about six in the daytime, and they gave us rooms. Ali and I asked for one room, and the crew members heard of it. They gave us some dirty looks, you know, the South African Air Transport people. They knew something was going on, but by that time it was too late to turn back. Yes, they gave us very funny looks, but we were safe by then.

When we got to New York, there was still snow all around from the blizzard and the buses didn't come. We decided we'd take a taxi to a motel. We wanted to go to Great Neck, Long Island, because we'd heard there was a lawyer there who was good to immigrants, who would help us get asylum. He didn't know us, but we'd heard he was good. So we asked at the airport for a taxi, and the man said it would be fifty dollars to go from Kennedy to Great Neck. It was one of those gypsy cabs. He said, "Take it or leave it." And I said to Ali, "I don't care what it costs; just take me there." I really was tired. We had been forty-eight hours in the air. It took me a week to recover, to get back to myself, from the traveling and the tension.

When we first stayed at the motel here, we were walking out the door and I was busy locking it up when I saw a white man come down the aisle. We both got such a shock that we opened the door and started to go back in, and then I said, "What are we doing? We're in America today." We had thought to run in, and then, all of a sudden, we realized we're not in South Africa anymore. We're in America and we don't have to do that.

The lawyer was very good. We called him from the motel the next morning, and he took us into his home, his own home, and he arranged the legal things for us. We had only seven hundred dollars, because that was all we were able to take out of the country. But he helped us, and other people did legal work for us, too, without payment. We married two weeks after we came to the country. One of the judges who helped us performed the ceremony, and our lawyer was a witness. Later, we had a hearing with the Immigration Department, and the man said, "Listen. You have no problems. We're going to give you work permits, and you're free to live here. You've got asylum." It was the first time I was relaxed in two years.

ALI: Everything has happened so quickly for us in this country. It's unbelievable. We got the asylum in less than a month, which was something we never expected. Three months ago we were living in hiding, and today we're settling down. We're married. We have an apartment. I have a job. And we can stay here.

JOHANNA: When we came to this apartment, and I saw the white and black children playing together outside in the yard, I stayed there looking for about ten or fifteen minutes. I couldn't take my eyes off the scene. I couldn't believe it, you know. Even though I knew that in this country they do it, I couldn't believe I was watching it. I thought, "I wish I could have a picture of this to send to South Africa."

I still find myself looking around. I don't know what I'm looking for, but I'm looking. And then it will strike me that we're here, and I'll say, "Calm down. We're safe." One day last week I saw some cars following us, and I started to get down on the floor of the car, and then I realized we're in America now. We don't have to be afraid. It seems like a fairy tale now, that we can live together and not be afraid.